Feenin'
Copyright © 2025 Ann Modk

All rights reserved. No part of this book may be reproduced, stored in a retrieval system, or transmitted in any form or by any means—electronic, mechanical, photocopying, recording, or otherwise—without the prior written permission of the author, except in the case of brief quotations embodied in critical articles or reviews.

This is a work of fiction. Names, characters, businesses, places, events, and incidents are either the product of the author's imagination or used fictitiously. Any resemblance to actual persons, living or dead, or actual events is purely coincidental.

Published by Independently Published

Cover Design by This image was generated with the assistance of AI (DALL-E)

Printed in the United States of America

Feenin'
Copyright © 2025 Ann Modkins

All rights reserved. No part of this book may be reproduced, stored in a retrieval system, or transmitted in any form or by any means—electronic, mechanical, photocopying, recording, or otherwise—without the prior written permission of the author, except in the case of brief quotations embodied in critical articles or reviews.

This is a work of fiction. Names, characters, businesses, places, events, and incidents are either the product of the author's imagination or used fictitiously. Any resemblance to actual persons, living or dead, or actual events is purely coincidental.

Published by Independently Published

Cover Design by This image was generated with the assistance of AI (DALL-E)

Printed in the United States of America

FEENIN'
Love is the Ultimate Drug

Chapter 1

Dionne was sleeping peacefully, her breath steady as she sunk deeper into the soft, cream-colored sheets of the king-sized bed she shared with her fiancé, Malik. The tranquility of her sleep wrapped around her like a warm cocoon, a rare moment of calm in her otherwise busy life.

But the peace didn't last. The sharp ringing of her phone shattered the silence, jolting her awake. With a groan, Dionne turned over and silenced it, hoping to steal a few more minutes of rest before starting her day. Yet, just as she began to drift back into sleep, the phone rang again. She sighed heavily, reluctantly opening her eyes and reaching for the persistent device. The screen flashed a familiar name: her boss, Jean. Confused, since today was her day off, she hesitated for a moment before answering.

"Hello?" Dionne said, trying to mask the sleepiness in her voice.

"Sorry, Dionne. I didn't mean to interrupt your off day," Jean began, her tone apologetic but tinged with urgency. "But I was wondering if you could come in and show a house. The client is a big one, and he specifically requested the best."

Dionne rolled her eyes, her irritation bubbling beneath the surface. *So much for a day off.* Still, she understood the importance of pleasing high-profile clients, and Jean's insistence didn't leave her much room to decline.

"I'll be there in an hour," she said, her tone even despite her annoyance. Jean's relieved excitement came through the line before the call ended, leaving Dionne staring at her phone with a mix of frustration and resignation.

She tossed the covers aside and swung her legs over the edge of the bed, sitting up with a sigh. *So much for sleeping in.* Rising to her feet,

Feenin'

she mentally prepared herself for the day ahead. This wasn't how she'd planned to spend her day off, but if she was going to do it, she'd make sure she showed up as nothing less than the best.

Dionne was a luxury real estate agent working for Williams Luxe Realty, the premier real estate agency in Houston and one of the most prestigious in the country. She had been with the company since graduating college, climbing her way to the top through hard work and determination. Dionne specialized in selling multimillion-dollar homes, catering to top celebrities and influential clients. She didn't handle properties worth less than a million dollars—her reputation for excellence demanded no less.

Her sharp intellect, magnetic charm, and stunning looks often played a role in securing some of the company's most lucrative deals. Dionne's ability to blend professionalism with approachability made her a favorite among clients, and her track record spoke for itself. She was well on her way to becoming a partner at the firm, a fact acknowledged by everyone, including Jean Williams, the company's CEO, who recognized her as a rising star.

Dionne stepped into the shower, letting the warm water wash over her as she began her morning routine. After finishing her skincare regimen and moisturizing every inch of her smooth brown skin, she made her way into her expansive walk-in closet—a space as grand as a luxury boutique. The closet was meticulously organized, showcasing thousands of pieces from high-end designers. She scanned the racks before settling on her outfit for the day: a black Alexander McQueen pantsuit that hugged her toned, thick figure perfectly, exuding both power and elegance.

To complete the look, Dionne slipped into a pair of black Louboutin heels, their signature red soles adding a touch of boldness to her ensemble. Her long, natural hair, already straightened and styled into a middle part, framed her beautiful face effortlessly. With her glowing skin and commanding presence, Dionne embodied perfection to many—women admired her, and men couldn't help but notice her.

Standing at 5'4", Dionne's toned physique was the result of consistent dedication in the gym. Her sculpted abs, small waist, and curves turned heads wherever she went, but none of it mattered to her. Dionne was laser-focused on her career and goals. If something didn't contribute to her success or enrich her family's well-being, she had no time or energy for it. For her, beauty was secondary to ambition, and her drive was what truly set her apart.

Dionne added a touch of brilliance to her outfit with diamond jewelry, a perfect complement to her elegant yet commanding look. Grabbing her black Hermès bag and the keys to her matte black Lamborghini Urus, she left her house. The morning sun glinted off the shiny exterior of her car as she stepped into the driver's seat, her heels clicking softly against the pavement. The drive to the office was smooth, the city of Houston coming alive as Dionne navigated the streets.

Pulling into the reserved parking spot marked with her name, Dionne killed the engine and stepped out, her presence as polished and powerful as ever. Her heels echoed faintly as she approached the towering glass building that housed Williams Luxe Realty. The building stood tall in the bustling cityscape, a symbol of prestige and success.

Inside, the security guards at the front desk greeted her with warm smiles. "Good morning, gentlemen," Dionne said, her voice smooth yet commanding as she returned the gesture.

"Good morning, Ms. Smith," one of the guards replied. As she passed through the turnstiles using her ID card, another called after her, "Don't work too hard, Ms. Smith."

Dionne chuckled softly, glancing over her shoulder. "No promises, Jeff," she replied, her radiant smile lighting up the room as the elevator doors closed behind her.

When the elevator reached the main floor, Dionne stepped out into the heart of the action. The buzz of the office was immediate, filled with conversations, ringing phones, and the subtle hum of ambition. This was where Houston's top real estate agents worked—and Dionne was the best among them. Her colleagues greeted her warmly as she strode down the hallway toward her office, her confidence evident in every step.

Before heading to her own workspace, Dionne stopped by her boss's office. She knocked lightly before stepping inside. "Good morning, Boss," she greeted, her tone warm and respectful.

Jean Williams looked up from her desk and smiled. Jean was everything Dionne aspired to be—a powerful, black woman who had built a Fortune 500 real estate empire. In her mid fifties, Jean carried herself with grace and confidence, her smooth brown skin and long, luxurious hair giving her a timeless elegance.

"Good morning, Dionne," Jean said, motioning her in. "Come on in."

Dionne stepped into Jean's spacious glass office, noting the city skyline visible behind her boss. "Sorry to bring you in on your day off," Jean began, her voice apologetic but firm, "but we've got an important client looking to buy a house. This is a big one."

Jean handed Dionne a file, and she opened it to reveal a stunning mansion listed for $5 million. A small smile tugged at Dionne's lips. She

Feenin'

could sell this house in her sleep.

"The client should be here soon," Jean continued. "We need to seal this deal. He's very important for the company."

"I've got you, Ms. Jean," Dionne said confidently, her sharp eyes scanning the details of the property. She didn't miss.

Jean smiled, clearly reassured. "His name is Arris Black. He's a powerful businessman, and having him as a client would be a huge boost for the company," she said, emphasizing the importance of the meeting.

Dionne nodded, her mind already strategizing. "You can count on me. We'll seal the deal," she said, her confidence unwavering.

"With you on it, I know we will," Jean said, mirroring Dionne's assured tone. The two women exchanged a knowing smile—this wasn't just business; this was legacy. And Dionne was ready to deliver.

Dionne walked out of Jean's office, her heels clicking softly against the polished floors as she made her way to her own workspace. Her office sat in the corner of the building, offering a breathtaking view of the city skyline. The room itself was a reflection of her—elegant, sophisticated, and commanding. Decorated in pearly whites with subtle gold accents, it exuded vibrancy and power while maintaining a welcoming warmth.

Placing her black Hermès bag and file on the pristine desk, Dionne sank into her plush white office chair, swiveling slightly as her gaze drifted out the floor-to-ceiling windows. The city sprawled before her, alive with energy and promise. For a moment, she let herself breathe, taking in the view that never failed to inspire her. Yet, despite the beauty and the success it symbolized, she felt... stuck.

Dionne sighed, leaning back in her chair as a quiet restlessness settled over her. She had been working tirelessly in the business for four years, climbing to a position most could only dream of. Her career was thriving, her relationship steady, and her beauty undeniable. But even with everything she'd accomplished, a gnawing emptiness lingered. It wasn't *greed*—she wasn't chasing more for the sake of having it. It was a hunger, a drive, a *yearning* for something she couldn't quite name.

The buzz of her phone pulled her out of her thoughts. Glancing down, she saw Malik's name and photo flash on the screen.

"Hey Malik," she said dryly, her tone distant adding to the faint weariness in her eyes.

"Wassup," Malik replied, his voice steady but rushed. "Just letting you know I'll be home late from work tonight."

Dionne's sighed in frustration, and she instinctively rolled her eyes. This had become routine over the past two weeks—Malik working late at the hospital while she returned to an empty house night after night.

"Of course," she said, her tone polite but edged with irritation she couldn't fully hide.

"I'm sorry, babe," Malik added, his words automatic, as if he could sense her frustration.

"It's fine," Dionne replied, her voice clipped. She didn't want to argue, not now, not over the phone.

Malik was a lead doctor at the local hospital, his demanding schedule leaving little time for anything outside of work. With his good looks and charm, he could have had any woman he wanted, but he chose Dionne. They met during their junior year of college at a party, and what started as an instant connection quickly grew into a relationship. For six years, they had been together, but while their bond appeared perfect to the outside world, Dionne saw the cracks no one else did.

Their relationship had been full of spark and passion in the beginning. College life gave them time to explore each other, laugh together, and dream of a shared future. But as they matured and dived into their respective careers, that spark fizzled out. What remained was a shell of what they once had. For Dionne, the love she once felt had vanished long time ago. She didn't know if Malik felt the same, but deep down, she knew her feelings had shifted.

Things had become even more complicated a year ago when Malik's mother was diagnosed with stage 4 cancer. The prognosis wasn't improving, and Malik was consumed by fear of losing her. Determined to make her proud while he still had the chance, he worked tirelessly to fulfill her wishes—including the one that mattered most to her: seeing him married. But she didn't just want him to marry anyone—she wanted him to marry Dionne.

The weight of that expectation led Malik to force a proposal on Dionne. It wasn't romantic or heartfelt; it was an act of desperation to fulfill his mother's dying wish. Feeling obligated and overwhelmed by the situation, Dionne said yes, despite knowing in her heart that she no longer loved him. She couldn't bear to break the heart of a woman she loved like a second mother, especially in her final days.

Now, Dionne felt trapped in a relationship that suffocated her. She was tethered by guilt and obligation, knowing that to end things with Malik would devastate not only him but his mother. Yet, the thought of spending her life with someone she no longer loved was unbearable.

Dionne wrestled with the decision daily, the weight of her circumstances pulling her in different directions. She didn't know how much longer she could keep up the facade, but for now, she stayed— caught between her love for Malik's mother and her longing for freedom

Feenin'

from a relationship that no longer brought her happiness.

"Okay," Dionne said dryly, her tone flat as she stared out the window, not even pretending to mask her irritation. She didn't want to be on the phone anymore. Malik seemed to sense it, his voice softening in an attempt to smooth things over.

"Don't look like that, Dee. I promise—date night tomorrow at your favorite restaurant," he said, his tone hopeful.

And there it was—another bribe. Another hollow promise meant to distract her from his shortcomings as a fiancé. Dionne rolled her eyes, her patience worn thin. "I have to go," she replied, her voice cold and detached. She didn't care about his excuses or his attempts to make up for things with empty gestures. She was *tired*—tired of the cycle, tired of him, and tired of pretending.

Ending the call, she let out a loud, frustrated groan, burying her face in her hands. The weight of her thoughts was suffocating, and she couldn't seem to find a way out of the mess her life had become. But before she could spiral any further, a deep, commanding voice pulled her out of her haze.

"Sorry to interrupt, but I'm here to see a house. I was told to meet with Dionne Smith."

Startled, Dionne quickly straightened her posture, adjusting herself as she looked toward the source of the voice. Her eyes landed on the man standing in her office, and for a moment, she froze.

He was breathtaking. His smooth dark skin seemed to glow under the soft office lights, and his perfectly groomed 360 waves framed a strong, chiseled face. A full beard added to his allure, but it was his tall, imposing frame—easily 6'5"—and broad, muscular build that truly made him stand out. The tailored black Dior suit he wore hugged him perfectly, exuding wealth and refinement. He carried himself with the kind of confidence that turned heads without trying.

Dionne felt herself caught in a quick trance, her mind struggling to catch up. *Focus*, she reminded herself. But it was easier said than done. His presence was magnetic, and for a moment, she forgot where she was.

Finally, she cleared her throat and stood, offering a polite smile. "You've found her. I'm Dionne Smith. And you are?" she asked, her professional demeanor slipping back into place despite the way her heart raced.

The man returned her smile, his voice smooth and deep. "Arris Black. It's a pleasure to meet you."

Dionne felt the tension of her morning start to melt away as she composed herself. This showing was going to be interesting, to say the least.

Dionne smiled warmly, though butterflies stirred in her stomach under Arris's gaze. It wasn't inappropriate, but the way his eyes lingered told her he was definitely taking her in. His confidence was undeniable, and it made her feel momentarily unsteady, though she quickly reminded herself to stay professional.

"Well, Mr. Black," she began, her tone smooth and poised, "if you're ready, we can head to the property. If you're interested in purchasing the home, we'll return here to complete the paperwork and get your keys." Her words were accompanied by a polished smile, one she'd perfected over years of working with high-profile clients.

Arris mirrored her smile, the corners of his mouth lifting in a way that was both charming and confident. His demeanor was magnetic, and it radiated from him effortlessly. "Sounds good. Lead the way," he said, stepping aside to let her pass.

Dionne grabbed her keys and bag, maintaining her composure as she walked out of her office, her heels clicking against the polished floors. Arris followed closely behind, his presence impossible to ignore. As they exited the building, Dionne could feel his gaze on her as she walked. It was subtle but unmistakable, the kind of attention she had grown used to from male clients.

She smiled to herself, unbothered by it. As long as everything stayed professional, she didn't mind. Dionne had dealt with powerful men like Arris before—they all carried that same air of self-assuredness. But something about him felt different. She brushed the thought aside as they approached her car, ready to focus on what she did best: closing the deal.

Arris walked around to Dionne's car, pulling the door open with an effortless charm that left her momentarily stunned. "Thank you," she said softly, stepping into her Urus. He gave her a small nod, closing the door gently behind her. *Fine and a gentleman*, she thought, a smile creeping onto her lips despite herself.

Settling into the driver's seat, Dionne glanced at her rearview mirror, catching a glimpse of Arris as he climbed into his black Aston Martin. The shiny lines of the car and its unmistakable air of luxury screamed power and wealth—a subtle yet striking reflection of the man himself. She shook her head lightly, willing herself to focus, but the pull of his presence lingered.

As she drove, her phone lit up with a call from her best friend, London. She quickly declined the call, shooting a text to let London know she'd call her back once she was finished with the showing. Soon, they arrived at the property, a sprawling estate with a gated

Feenin'

entrance. Dionne entered the code, and the black gates slid open. The long driveway stretched before them, flanked by manicured lawns and towering trees. Arris followed closely as they approached the house.

Stepping out of her car, Dionne adjusted her bag and straightened her posture as her heels clicked against the driveway. Arris exited his car, matching her pace as they approached the towering black pivot doors. Inside, the grand entrance was illuminated by natural light pouring in from floor-to-ceiling windows.

"As you enter, you're greeted by these stunning pivot doors and an abundance of natural light from the massive windows," Dionne began, her voice smooth and professional. Arris looked around, his expression suggesting he was already impressed.

Dionne led him further into the house, stepping into the open-concept living, kitchen, and dining area. "The living room features a large fireplace, perfect for cozy winter nights, and a massive 85-inch LED TV—great for hosting the crew or indulging in a solo movie night," she said, adding a touch of charm that earned a chuckle from Arris.

"Off to the side, you'll find a sleek wet bar, complete with LED accents, mirrored shelving, and leather barstools," she continued, gesturing to the modern setup. She could feel Arris's gaze on her, a constant weight she was trying to ignore. She stayed focused, moving through the details of the house with precision.

"Now, the kitchen might be my favorite part," Dionne said with a smile, turning to see Arris mirroring her expression. "It's outfitted with high-end appliances, a massive quartz island with waterfall edges, and custom cabinetry with gold hardware. There's plenty of space for cooking or hosting."

Arris nodded approvingly, though his attention seemed split between the house and her.

Down the hall, Dionne gestured toward a private office. "This office features dark wood paneling, state-of-the-art technology, and inspiring views. Perfect for sealing deals or brainstorming your next big move."

Arris chuckled, his deep voice reverberating through the space. "You're very persuasive," he said, his tone low and smooth. His words, paired with the close space between them and his captivating smile, sent a ripple through Dionne that she quickly suppressed. *Damn, he's fine. But I have a man,* she reminded herself, pushing the thought aside.

"It's my job to be," she replied with confidence, flashing a professional smile. "And, I hope it's working."

Arris chuckled again, and they continued the tour. Dionne led him upstairs, detailing each part of the house. "This home features five bedrooms and two additional rooms: a spacious theater and a fully equipped game room," she explained, her voice steady and polished. "There are two half bathrooms downstairs, and every bedroom comes with its own private bathroom."

As they walked, she pointed out the fitness studio. "It also includes a private gym with all the latest workout equipment and a sauna for unwinding after an intense session."

They toured the bedrooms, game room, theater, and gym before finally arriving at the crown jewel of the house: the master bedroom. Dionne opened the door to reveal the expansive space, her tone as vibrant as ever. "And this is the master suite. It's the largest room in the house, complete with a sitting area, floor-to-ceiling windows, and a private balcony overlooking the backyard."

Arris took it all in, nodding as he surveyed the space. Dionne could still feel his eyes on her, but she refused to let it rattle her. She had a job to do—and she was determined to close the deal.

"A sprawling walk-in closet is tailor-made for ultimate organization, while the ensuite bathroom offers a spa-like experience with a rainfall shower, a soaking tub featuring LED-lit jets, and marble finishes throughout," Dionne added, her professional tone polished and persuasive.

Arris nodded again, the interest evident in his expression. Dionne could tell he was captivated by the home's features. As they left the master bedroom, she led him downstairs to the backyard.

"This outdoor oasis includes an infinity pool, an outdoor kitchen, a fire pit with a lounge area, and a rooftop deck," Dionne explained. Arris nodded once more, but his gaze lingered on her rather than the space. The way her brown skin glowed under the afternoon sun caught his attention, pulling him toward her in a way he hadn't expected. Still, he kept his thoughts to himself, maintaining his composure.

The tour wrapped up at the front of the house. Dionne turned to him, her tone as confident as ever. "This home comes with top-of-the-line lighting and security. You can control lighting, temperature, music, and security with a tap on your phone. It includes 24/7 surveillance cameras, biometric entry, and a panic room."

Arris admired the grandeur of the house as she finished speaking. "That's the end of the tour, so if you're—"

"I'll take it," Arris interrupted with a confident smile.

Dionne returned the smile proudly. "Great! Let's head back to my office to complete the paperwork, and I'll get your keys."

***

Feenin'

Back at her office, Dionne guided Arris through the final steps of the purchase. He signed the necessary documents with ease, cutting a check to pay for the home in full. Dionne handed over the keys and the folder with all the property details.

"Thank you, Arris, for choosing Williams Luxe as your agency, and thank you for trusting me as your agent," Dionne said with a warm smile.

"No thanks needed," Arris replied in his deep, smooth voice. "You're an amazing agent. Thanks for making this process so easy."

Dionne nodded graciously. "Congratulations on your new home. I hope you and your family enjoy it."

Arris chuckled softly, surprising her. "Thanks, but it's just me."

Dionne's brow lifted slightly. She hadn't expected a man like Arris—so confident, successful, and magnetic—to be living alone in such a grand home. "Oh, I'm sorry. I didn't mean to assume. It's just... you've purchased such a large home, and..." She trailed off, almost complimenting his looks but catching herself just in time.

Arris noticed her hesitation and smiled knowingly. "No need to apologize. I get it. But I needed a change of scenery, and this house feels like the perfect fit."

Dionne returned his smile. "I understand. Well, here's my business card. It has my phone number and email. If you have any questions about the property or know anyone looking to buy a home, feel free to reach out," she said, handing him her black business card.

Arris took the card, his smile widening. "Will do. Thank you again, Ms. Smith."

Dionne laughed softly. "Ms. Smith is my mother. You can call me Dionne. It was a pleasure being your agent."

They shook hands, but the moment lingered longer than expected. Arris's grip was firm yet gentle, and the softness of her hands did something to him he couldn't quite place. Reluctantly, he let go before the interaction became awkward.

With final goodbyes exchanged, Arris left the office, leaving Dionne with a strange mix of satisfaction and curiosity lingering in the air.

Dionne sighed, her thoughts lingering on the man who had just left her office. Arris's striking looks, smooth demeanor, and deep voice seemed to echo in her mind, refusing to be ignored. She shook her head, trying to push him out of her thoughts as she gathered her things. It had been a long morning, and she was determined to enjoy what remained of her day off.

She stopped by Ms. Jean's office on her way out, offering a polite goodbye. Ms. Jean gave her a knowing smile, clearly pleased with

Dionne's ability to close such a major deal. With a final wave, Dionne exited the building and slid into her Urus, setting her GPS for her best friend London's house.

The idea of returning to her empty home weighed heavily on her. Malik's demanding career had made lonely nights a constant, and the thought of spending another evening in silence made her chest tighten. But as much as she tried to focus on Malik's absence, her thoughts kept circling back to Arris—the confident way he spoke, the way his gaze seemed to see through her, and how effortlessly he carried himself.

"Get it together," Dionne muttered to herself, gripping the steering wheel tighter. Arris was just a client, and she was just a professional doing her job. Still, the memory of his presence lingered, a small distraction that she couldn't entirely shake as she drove toward the comfort of London's company.

***

Later that night:

Arris stood over the railing of his packed nightclub, *The Vault*, a satisfied smile creeping across his face as he watched the crowd below. The music was electric, the DJ spinning the hottest old-school classics and fresh new hits. People danced and laughed, losing themselves in the energy of the night. Arris adjusted the lapels of his black suit, his presence commanding even in a room filled with energy and chaos.

Arris Black was a man of ambition and mystery—the man every other man wanted to be and every woman wanted to know. As one of Houston's wealthiest and most influential figures, he owned multiple businesses scattered across the city. The Vault was his crown jewel: a dual-purpose establishment housing an elegant restaurant on the ground floor that transformed into an exclusive nightclub upstairs after hours. It was a haven for those seeking a taste of indulgence, and its reputation alone drew crowds eager to experience the thrill.

Arris's success story was the stuff of legends. A baseball prodigy in his youth, he was a household name in Houston sports before attending Jackson State, where he discovered his true passion: business. After returning home, he poured his efforts into investments, building an empire that extended far beyond the surface. Restaurants, youth centers, clubs, and other ventures bore his fingerprints, though the full extent of his holdings remained a mystery to most. Arris preferred it that way—moving in silence had always been his style.

His commanding presence made him unforgettable. Standing tall and confident, Arris was a magnetic force. His smooth dark skin, deep waves, and sharp, tailored suit projected a quiet power. But it was his

Feenin'

reserved nature that left people wanting more, drawn in by the enigma he cultivated so effortlessly.

The Vault was packed tonight, the air thick with laughter and the rhythmic pulse of the music. To most, he was just another patron in the crowd. Only a select few knew the truth—that Arris Black was the mastermind behind the city's hottest nightlife destination. And that was just the way he liked it.

He sipped his drink, surveying the scene with satisfaction. Business was thriving, and while the noise of the club swirled around him, Arris remained calm and centered, his mind already turning toward his next move. Always a step ahead, always in *control*. That's who Arris Black was.

Arris learned some of his most valuable lessons in his early years as a street hustler. Life had never been easy for him. Raised in a single-parent household, his father was in and out of prison, leaving Arris, his little sister, and his mother to navigate life on their own. Money was tight, and the struggle was constant. Determined to change his circumstances, Arris took matters into his own hands and turned to the streets.

For a while, he thrived there, finding a love for the game and the adrenaline it brought. At the same time, he dominated as a pitcher on the baseball field, earning respect for his skill and focus. But the streets came with risks, and when the game nearly cost him everything, Arris had to make a choice: school and baseball, or the streets. The decision came easily—he chose a path that would secure his future.

Still, the mindset he developed in the streets never left him. The same calculated strategies and sharp instincts he needed to survive back then became the foundation of the businessman he was today. His ability to read people, anticipate moves, and execute plans with precision made him unstoppable. Arris often credited his time in the streets for teaching him lessons no classroom ever could.

Love, however, was never a priority. He didn't have the emotional bandwidth for a woman in his life—not when his business was his only true companion. He entertained flings and fleeting connections, but they were purely for pleasure, never something deeper. To Arris, relationships were distractions, and if it wasn't about business or growth, he wasn't interested.

Arris lived by one rule: stay focused. And so far, it had served him well. The scars from his past didn't define him—they fueled him, driving his relentless pursuit of success.

"Aye, Arris!" a familiar voice called out over the booming music, cutting through the vibrant chaos of the club. Arris turned to see one of his best friends, True, approaching with his signature swagger. The two had been best friends since diapers, their bond unshakable despite the twists life had thrown their way.

True was a renowned tattoo artist and the owner of True Ink, one of the hottest tattoo shops in Houston. His work attracted top-tier celebrities and locals alike, making his shop a staple in the city. Arris dapped him up as they exchanged a grin.

"Wassup, True," Arris said once they pulled away.

"Man, it's lit as fuck in here!" True exclaimed, his eyes scanning the packed club. From the railing, they could see a sea of people—locals and celebrities alike—splashing cash, dancing, and soaking up the night's energy.

"Yeah," Arris replied, his tone calm and humble as usual, though the sight of the lively crowd brought a subtle smile to his face. Moments like these reminded him why he built The Vault—it was more than a business; it was a hub of energy, connection, and celebration.

"How did the house searching go earlier?" True asked, taking a sip of his cognac, his tattooed hand gripping the glass.

Arris's thoughts shifted back to that morning and the woman who had unexpectedly captivated him. Dionne. She wasn't just another real estate agent—there was something about her confidence, her energy, that lingered in his mind. Arris rarely thought about women outside of fleeting moments, but Dionne was different. She had a way of slipping into his thoughts even now, hours later.

"It went good," Arris finally said, masking his thoughts with a casual tone. "Found a solid spot right outside the city. Movers are already handling everything."

True nodded approvingly. "That's what's up. That house-hunting shit can be stressful as hell," he said, his voice carrying the weight of personal experience. He had recently moved into a new home himself and knew firsthand how draining the process could be.

Arris nodded in agreement, though his experience had been smoother than expected. Dionne and Williams Luxe had made the process seamless, and he couldn't ignore the way she'd handled everything with poise and professionalism.

"Yeah, but it wasn't bad," Arris said simply, keeping the rest of his thoughts to himself. Dionne's image flickered in his mind again, but he pushed it aside. There was no room for distractions—not now, not when he had so much to focus on.

Arris and True leaned back over the railing, watching the crowd

Feenin'

below revel in the music and energy of the night. "Nigga, you killing it!" True said, admiration evident in his tone.

Arris smiled, appreciating the acknowledgment. "I appreciate that," he replied. Glancing at his AP watch, he added, "But I'm about to head out of here."

"Leaving so soon? The night's just getting started, and there's some beautiful women in here," True said, his eyes already locked on a group of women dancing near the DJ booth. "Damn, she fine," he muttered, clearly distracted.

Arris laughed at his friend's antics, shaking his head. "Nah, man. I'll leave that to you. I need to be heading home," he said. Arris had come to the club to handle business, ensure everything was running smoothly, and check in with his team—nothing more.

True shot him a teasing grin. "You ain't taking a bad one home to keep you company in the new crib?"

Arris chuckled, unbothered. "Nah, rolling solo tonight," he said casually. His focus wasn't on the social aspects of the club; it never had been. Arris cared about the foundation—what kept the business running and thriving. The partying, drinking, and nightlife hype were for others to enjoy. For him, it was always about the bigger picture. If it didn't make sense or make money, it didn't hold his interest. He'd been that way his whole life.

People often told him he acted ahead of his 28 years, but to Arris, that was just who he was—a man with purpose, focus, and vision.

As they spoke, his assistant, China, approached him with her ever-efficient demeanor. Her iPad in hand, she rattled off updates. "Everything's good in the back. Alcohol is stocked, the menu for the investor event next week is finalized, and we're interviewing new chefs and staff tomorrow."

Arris nodded, satisfied with her report. "Aight, sounds good. I'll be back in the morning to check on things," he said.

China nodded and stepped back as Arris turned to True, offering a quick goodbye. The two dapped each other up. "Hold it down," Arris said with a grin before heading out. While others lived for the nightlife, Arris stayed focused on what mattered most—building and maintaining the empire he worked so hard to create.

Arris exited the club through the back entrance, avoiding the crowded front of the club. Sliding into his Aston Martin, he headed toward his newly purchased home. The drive was quiet, the hum of the engine and the city lights providing a moment of calm. When he arrived, he parked in the spacious driveway and entered the house, greeted by the sight of his belongings neatly arranged thanks to his movers.

He ascended the grand staircase, taking in the transformation of his new space. His bedroom, now decorated in tones of black and brown, reflected his personality—calm, sophisticated, and undeniably powerful. Arris stepped into the adjoining bathroom and began stripping out of the tailored suit he'd worn to the club. The steamy shower that followed was exactly what he needed to unwind. The hot water cascaded over his body, easing the tension in his muscles and washing away the day.

Once finished, he grabbed a towel and stood before the sink, brushing his teeth and moisturizing his skin with precision. As he reached for his cologne, his eyes fell on the black business card Dionne had given him earlier that day. Her name and number stood out against the elegant design, triggering thoughts of her.

He could still picture her—her confident smile, her poise, the way she seemed to command every room she entered. For a brief moment, he considered reaching out, an idea that felt both intriguing and unnecessary. Shaking his head, Arris dismissed the thought. She was just his real estate agent, nothing more. It was business, and now that it was complete, there was no reason for their paths to cross again.

Focus on the goal, not the distractions, he reminded himself. His life was already filled with enough chaos and ambition; he didn't have time to complicate it with a woman, no matter how captivating she might be. Women weren't his priority—money and success were.

With that resolve, Arris tucked her card into a drawer, ensuring it was out of sight. He slipped into a pair of shorts and climbed into his bed, the smooth silk sheets cool against his skin. As his head hit the pillow, his mind drifted to the empire he was building, pushing all other thoughts aside. Sleep overtook him quickly, bringing an end to another day in the relentless pursuit of his goals.

***

Morning came faster than Arris expected, and he found himself headed to the gym for an early workout before his busy day began. The gym, Next Level, was a hotspot for serious fitness enthusiasts and happened to be owned by his other best friend, Mario. Arris parked his car and stepped out with his gym bag in hand, the crisp morning air invigorating him as he made his way inside.

"Wassup, Erin," Arris greeted the receptionist, who also happened to be Mario's younger sister. She looked up and smiled, meeting him with a quick side hug.

"Hey, Arris," she said warmly.

"Yo ugly-ass brother here?" he asked with a smirk, earning a laugh

Feenin'

from Erin.

"Yeah, he's in his office," she replied, nodding toward the hallway.

Arris nodded in thanks and headed toward Mario's office, knocking lightly before stepping inside. Mario was behind his desk, phone pressed to his ear, an irritated expression etched across his face. "Man, I ain't giving ha ass no more child support," Mario barked into the phone, his frustration evident.

Arris chuckled softly, immediately understanding the situation. He knew Mario was talking about his baby mother, Briana—a constant source of stress in his life. Arris leaned against the doorframe, shaking his head as Mario talked aggressively on the phone.

This was one of the many reasons Arris avoided relationships. He had grown up watching his mother struggle alone, with his father absent in his life, and seeing the strain of love—if it could even be called that—left a permanent mark on him. To Arris, relationships seemed like a distraction at best and a liability at worst.

Now, even his best friend Mario, with all his success, was caught in a toxic cycle with Briana. The only reason she remained in Mario's life was their daughter, and even then, it was clear she cared more about the money than co-parenting. Arris didn't want that kind of drama, and his choices reflected it.

True was the same way—he indulged in flings and fleeting connections but never let anyone close enough to matter. For both Arris and True, love seemed like a gamble with too much risk and too little reward.

Mario looked up as Arris walked in, wrapping up his heated phone call. "Aight, give her ass the six thousand. I don't give a fuck anymore," Mario said angrily before hanging up.

Arris chuckled, leaning against the doorframe, but Mario wasn't in the mood for jokes. "Nigga, ain't shit funny," Mario snapped. "That bitch loves taking from me, yo. Like I don't see our daughter just as much as she does. And I know all that fucking money ain't for Mia—she spending the shit on herself."

Arris shook his head, his expression firm. "Stop calling her a bitch," he said sternly. He understood his friend's frustration but didn't tolerate disrespecting women, no matter the situation.

Mario sighed, throwing his hands up in mock surrender. "My bad, man, but she just pisses me off, yo. I swear I wanna send her back to court."

"Well, do it," Arris replied with a sly smirk. "I know a family lawyer—a good one."

Mario raised a brow, finally cracking a smile. "Nigga, how the fuck do you know a family lawyer? You ain't never been married or got kids."

Arris laughed, shrugging. "Don't worry about how I know her. Just know she can get you out of your situation. You want the number or not?"

Mario chuckled, shaking his head knowingly. "Yeah, send it to me."

"Hoe ass," Mario joked as he stood, the tension in the room dissipating.

Arris smirked. "Better than being a broke ass behind child support," he quipped, making Mario shoot him a sharp glare.

"Nigga, come on, so we can work out. True pulling up," Mario said as they walked out of the office.

Arris laughed, shaking his head. "You better stop talking shit before one of these women you fucking says you got them pregnant, and you'll be just like me," Mario teased, throwing a side glance at Arris.

Arris chuckled, waving him off. "I'm not you, brother," he said confidently.

Mario flipped him the middle finger. Arris was too calculated to slip up, too meticulous to let fun turn into a liability. While Mario and others saw his lifestyle as tempting fate, Arris saw it as control. He didn't gamble with his future, and he wasn't about to start.

Feenin'

Chapter 2

Dionne sat at her desk, scrolling through MLS listings, carefully curating the best homes for her clients. Despite her shortened day off the day before, she found solace in being back at the office. Her work brought her a deep sense of fulfillment and joy, and it was the perfect escape from the bubbling frustration she'd been feeling toward Malik.

The previous night had only added to her growing annoyance. Malik hadn't come home until two in the morning and left again at 5:30, giving her no time to see him, let alone talk. She hadn't laid eyes on him in two days, and the distance between them felt heavier with each passing moment. Dionne was exhausted from pretending their relationship was perfect. She wanted out but felt trapped by the circumstances surrounding them.

Her phone buzzed with a reminder of their dinner plans for that evening. Malik had made reservations at her favorite restaurant to make up for his absence. While the gesture felt hollow—a typical bribe to smooth things over—Dionne wasn't one to turn down a delicious meal, especially at her favorite spot. She resolved to go, if only to enjoy the food and perhaps clear her head.

Until then, work was her focus. The day ahead was packed: three house showings and two company meetings loomed on her schedule. It was busy, but Dionne didn't mind. Staying occupied kept her mind off the dissatisfaction creeping into her personal life. As long as she had work to ground her, she could keep everything else at bay, at least for now.

As Dionne immersed herself in her busy workday, her phone began to buzz, pulling her attention away from her computer. She glanced down and saw a group FaceTime call from her best friends, London and Karmen. A smile crept onto her face as she accepted the call, their vibrant energy immediately filling the screen.

She'd been best friends with London and Karmen since their freshman year at the illustrious Prairie View A&M University, right outside of Houston. London had been her roommate, while Karmen was her teammate on the soccer team. Together, they were her rock—her escape from the chaos of her demanding career and personal life.

"Hey, bitches!" London's voice rang out first, loud and full of bubbly energy, just as Dionne expected. London was the fiery one of the group, always down for anything spontaneous and a little crazy. She was the type of friend you could pull off a heist with one day and take to an elegant business gala the next. Her bold, no-nonsense energy carried over into her career as a hairstylist, where she worked on everyone from local clients to top-tier celebrities.

Dionne chuckled at her friend's typical enthusiasm. "Hey, y'all," she replied calmly, her tone balancing the hype London brought.

"I was just calling to see if y'all wanted to grab lunch today," Karmen chimed in with her soft, soothing voice. Karmen was the opposite of London—gentle, nurturing, and perpetually positive. Her sweet demeanor made her the "mom" of the group, always offering thoughtful advice or a comforting presence. Her job as a kindergarten teacher fit her personality perfectly, as she exuded patience and care.

"Girl, yes! I have one more client, but I'm free for lunch," London answered immediately, her excitement apparent. Her declaration earned a soft smile from Karmen, who then turned her attention back to Dionne.

"What about you, Dee?" Karmen asked, her voice hopeful.

Dionne, who always felt like a blend of the two—equal parts daring and nurturing—was grateful for the brief distraction from her work and personal frustrations. She looked at their eager faces on the screen, already feeling lighter just from their presence.

Dionne often found herself so buried in work that hanging out with her friends became a rare luxury. If she wasn't at the office selling million-dollar homes or closing deals, she was stuck pretending everything was perfect with Malik, especially in front of his mother. Her life felt like a constant balancing act, with no room for genuine joy. But today, the chance to escape her reality, even for a quick lunch with her best friends, was exactly what she needed.

"Yeah, just send me the time and address," Dionne said, her tone softening as Karmen's smile widened on the screen.

"Okay, I just sent all the info," Karmen replied, her excitement

Feenin'

evident.

The three friends continued chatting for a little while longer, their laughter and easy banter providing Dionne a brief respite from her hectic day. Eventually, Dionne excused herself, knowing she had a packed schedule. Lunch with her friends and dinner with Malik—it was going to be a long day, and there was still plenty of work to get through before she could even think about relaxing.

As the call ended, Dionne took a deep breath and refocused. She dove back into her tasks, working efficiently until it was time to leave for lunch. Despite the weight of everything on her plate, the thought of seeing London and Karmen gave her something to look forward to—a rare moment to just be herself.

***

Dinner with Malik came faster than Dionne expected. She walked into the elegant restaurant, her favorite—The Vault. Her long black dress hugged her curves perfectly, exuding both sophistication and allure. Her hair was styled in an elegant messy bun, with soft bangs framing her face, and her makeup was a subtle enhancement of her natural beauty. The red Louboutin open-toed heels on her feet clicked softly against the polished floor as she ascended the stairs, her hips swaying gracefully as she held the hem of her dress.

"Reservation for Harris," Dionne said softly to the hostess.

"Right this way, ma'am," the hostess replied with a polite smile, leading her through the bustling restaurant to a private table in the corner.

As they approached, Dionne spotted Malik sitting at the table, his smile brightening when he saw her. He stood immediately, his tall frame towering over her as he reached for her waist and pulled her into a gentle embrace.

"You look beautiful," Malik said, his voice low and warm.

Dionne felt a flicker of confusion at the unexpected gesture, but she played along, maintaining her composure. "Thank you," she replied, her tone polite but distant. She glanced him over briefly, adding, "Not too bad yourself."

She wasn't lying. Despite the emotional disconnect between them, Dionne couldn't deny that Malik was physically attractive. At 6'3, with smooth brown skin, deep waves in his neatly cut hair, and a full, groomed beard, he was undeniably striking. But it was his eyes that had captivated her when they first met—light hazel, they held a warmth and intensity that had once made her feel seen and adored.

Now, as they sat down, she found herself wondering if that spark she'd once felt for him could ever return, or if this dinner was just another performance in their strained relationship. For now, she decided to focus on the meal ahead and let the evening unfold.

They sat down at the table, each ordering a glass of wine. Malik's gaze lingered on Dionne as she perused the menu, trying to decide what to eat. His intense stare made her pause, and she glanced up with a confused expression.

"What?" she asked, her brow furrowing slightly.

"I love you," Malik said, his voice steady, his sharp hazel eyes fixed on her.

Dionne wasn't fazed. The words rolled off her like water on glass. She didn't feel the same, and no amount of declarations or gestures was going to change her mind. She set the menu down, her defenses rising. "What are we doing here?" she asked bluntly, her tone guarded.

Malik's smile faltered, replaced with a mix of confusion and irritation. "What you mean? It's a date, Dionne. You know, something couples do," he said, sarcasm laced in his tone.

Dionne rolled her eyes. His sarcasm was another trait she'd grown to dislike. "How was your day?" she asked, changing the subject. She wasn't in the mood to engage in one of Malik's defensive tirades. Arguing with him was like arguing with a black wall—pointless and draining.

"It was good," he replied, his voice cooling. Then, without missing a beat, he added, "But we need to talk about the wedding."

And there it was—the business-like tone, the shift to logistics. That's what their relationship had become: a transaction. Malik was fulfilling his mother's dying wish, while Dionne was stuck playing the role of the dutiful fiancée, despite knowing her heart wasn't in it. The physical chemistry wasn't there, and emotionally, they were worlds apart.

Dionne's jaw tightened as she rolled her eyes again, leaning back in her chair. "Can we talk about that later? Just focus on the present right now, and not... expectations," she said, her voice softening at the end. There was a hint of a plea in her tone, and to her surprise, Malik seemed to register it. His expression softened, and he nodded slightly.

For a brief moment, the tension between them dissipated. They stopped worrying about the future, about the lies they were living, and just existed in the present. It was rare, but for once, they acted like a real couple. They laughed over the wine, shared stories, and forgot about the weight of their crumbling relationship.

For Dionne, it was a fleeting glimpse of what could have been—but deep down, she knew it wouldn't last.

***

Feenin'

Arris walked into the restaurant with his usual purposeful stride, exuding confidence with every step. His presence naturally commanded attention, though he never sought it out. People greeted him warmly as he passed, and he returned their smiles effortlessly, his charm magnetic as always. Arris moved swiftly, navigating the space he knew so well, until his eyes landed on her.

There she was again—Dionne.

Seated in a booth, she looked as stunning as she had when he'd first met her. The sight of her brought an unintentional smile to his face, and before he could think twice, he found himself walking toward her. His steps were deliberate, his focus unwavering as he approached.

"Ms. Smith?" he said smoothly, his deep voice cutting through the ambient noise of the restaurant.

Dionne's gaze lifted to him, her eyes studying him briefly before recognition sparked. "Mr. Black, right?" she replied, a small smile gracing her lips.

Arris nodded, his smile widening just slightly. "It's good seeing you," he said, his tone carrying that same effortless charm.

"Same here," Dionne replied, her voice calm, though her smile hinted at a flicker of surprise.

Malik, seated across from her, cleared his throat loudly, breaking the moment. His displeasure was evident, but Arris barely acknowledged him. His gaze lingered on Dionne, as if Malik's presence was of no significance.

"I hope to see you again soon," Arris said, his words deliberate, as he subtly brushed his hand against her elbow as he turned to leave.

Dionne watched him go, her mind buzzing as Malik's irritation simmered across the table. Arris knew the effect he had left behind. As he walked away, he couldn't help but let a satisfied smirk play at the corner of his lips. Some moments spoke louder than words—and this was one of them.

***

Arris worked late into the night, ensuring everything at the restaurant was in order before heading out. As he stepped outside, the cool night air greeted him, but it wasn't the wind that caught his attention—it was her. Dionne stood near the curb, her elegant black dress swaying gently in the breeze, looking every bit like she had stepped out of a magazine. She was stunning, even with the hint of frustration etched across her face.

"What are you doing still here, alone?" Arris asked, walking toward her with his usual confident stride. He noticed the attitude radiating from her, but it didn't faze him in the slightest.

"Waiting on my Uber," Dionne replied, her tone clipped as her arms crossed over her chest.

Arris raised an eyebrow. "Where's your friend?" he asked, the subtle emphasis making her chuckle despite herself.

"He's my fi—" she started but faltered, catching herself. "He had to leave early."

Arris didn't miss the hesitation in her voice, and it piqued his curiosity. He stepped closer, his tall frame casting a shadow over her. "I can take you home if you want. It's late, and something tells me that Uber isn't coming," he offered, his deep voice laced with calm authority.

Dionne's breath caught as she glanced up at him, her usually steady composure faltering just slightly under his gaze. "That's fine, I can wait," she said softly, her voice unsure. Malik had left their dinner early, claiming he was needed at the hospital, leaving her alone late at night.

She didn't know Arris like that—not enough to feel comfortable getting into his car while he took her home. But the way he stood there, calm and assured, made her feel something she hadn't felt in a long time: safe.

I insist," Arris said, his smooth, confident tone washing over her like a warm wave. "It's getting late, and a beautiful woman like yourself shouldn't be out here alone."

Dionne glanced up at him, his presence towering over her in more ways than one. His tone was firm yet inviting, leaving no room for argument but somehow still making her feel at ease. She hesitated for a moment, her mind racing with all the reasons she should refuse. But the way he looked at her, with an intensity that seemed to strip away every barrier she built, made her decision for her.

"Okay," she finally whispered, her voice soft and almost timid. "You can take me home."

Without hesitation, Arris reached for her hand, his touch firm yet gentle as he led her toward his car. He opened the passenger door to his shiny Aston Martin and helped her in, his actions deliberate and smooth. Closing the door, he rounded the car and got in on the driver's side. The engine roared to life, and they pulled away from the restaurant.

As he drove, the air in the car felt charged, though neither spoke much. Arris stole a glance at her, his curiosity growing. There was something about her—something magnetic, something he couldn't quite place.

"Make a left," Dionne instructed, her voice as smooth and soft as silk, pulling him from his thoughts.

They drove through the quiet streets, the hum of the car filling the

Feenin'

comfortable silence between them. Arris's grip on the wheel was relaxed, but his sharp eyes didn't miss the way Dionne occasionally shifted in her seat, her mind seemingly elsewhere.

When they finally pulled into her driveway, Arris couldn't help but admire the beautiful home in front of him. The elegant, modern architecture spoke to her success, but the empty driveway told a different story. Her sigh, soft but heavy, as she stared at the house revealed more than her words ever could.

Arris glanced at her, his brows furrowing slightly as he picked up on the subtle shift in her energy. She looked tired—not physically, but emotionally—like someone carrying a weight no one else could see.

"Here you go, mama," Arris said, his deep voice resonating as he shifted the car into park. His gaze lingered on her for a moment, studying her with quiet intensity. There was something about the way she carried herself, poised and polished, yet tinged with an undercurrent of something unspoken.

"Thank you," Dionne replied softly, but her tone lacked the usual confidence. Arris picked up on the subtle crack in her facade, the emotions she was trying so hard to conceal.

As she reached for the door handle to step out, Arris's hand shot out, gently stopping her. His touch was firm yet respectful, his fingers just barely brushing against hers. She froze, her eyes darting back to him, startled.

"Never touch a door in my presence," he said, his deep voice carrying a commanding authority that sent a shiver through her. The intensity of his words made her instantly submit, her hand retreating as if compelled.

"Okay," she murmured softly, her tone barely audible as she removed her hand from the door handle.

Arris stepped out of the car and walked around to her side, opening the door for her with practiced ease. He extended his hand, and Dionne placed hers in it without hesitation. His grip was firm, steadying her as she stepped out. They walked together toward her front door, the night air filled with an unspoken tension that neither acknowledged.

Arris took in the grandeur of her home, a two-story mansion that spoke volumes about her success. "This all you?" he asked, his eyes sweeping over the property with quiet admiration.

"Yeah," Dionne replied, glancing up at the house she called home. The space was beautiful, but it often felt empty, echoing the loneliness she tried to ignore.

Arris turned back to her, his expression unreadable. "Well, you have a good night, Dionne Smith," he said, extending his hand.

Dionne placed her hand in his, their touch lingering longer than necessary. "You do the same, Arris Black. Thank you again," she replied, her voice steady, though something about the exchange felt more significant than it should have.

Arris's lips curved into a faint smile, his gaze lingering on hers just a moment longer than necessary. "Anytime, Ms. Smith," he said, his deep voice carrying a weight that made her pulse quicken. There was something in the way he said it, a subtle promise buried beneath the words that sent a shiver down her spine.

She stepped inside, the door clicking shut behind her, leaving Arris standing on the porch for a brief moment. He turned and walked back to his car, his thoughts lingering on the intriguing woman who had somehow captured his attention. As he slid into the driver's seat, a faint smirk tugged at the corner of his lips. Tonight had been unexpected—and for some reason, he didn't mind.

As Arris drove away, his mind was consumed by thoughts of her. *Dionne*. He didn't know what it was about her, but something pulled him in, like a force he couldn't resist. Her presence lingered in his mind, her voice, her gaze, the way she carried herself. He shook his head, frustrated with himself. Women were distractions, something he avoided at all costs. He didn't have time for that—not in his world, not with his ambitions. So why was she all he could think about?

The drive home felt longer than usual, each passing minute only intensifying his thoughts of her. Arris finally pulled into his driveway and walked into his house, the silence greeting him like an old friend. But tonight, it wasn't enough. He needed something—anything—to fill the void she had unknowingly left in him.

Without hesitation, he grabbed his phone and called one of his flings, someone who could offer him a fleeting escape from the thoughts gnawing at his mind. Arris wasn't one to indulge in emotional connections, but for now, he sought the physical release that could temporarily dull the ache of wanting what he couldn't have.

The rest of the night passed in a blur, his mind distracted by the blissful oblivion of the moment. Yet, even in the fleeting escape, her image remained at the edges of his thoughts. Dionne was unlike anyone else he had encountered, and that fact alone unnerved him.

By the time the night ended and he was left alone again, the thought of her still lingered, faint but persistent—a reminder that maybe, just maybe, she was something more than a passing distraction.

***

Feenin'

Dionne wandered through the house, her frustration simmering beneath the surface as Malik moved around on the phone, completely ignoring her presence. It was early morning, and she had decided not to go to work today, needing time to herself. Yet, even in the shared space of their home, it was as if she didn't exist. His casual dismissal, whether intentional or not, stung more than she cared to admit.

She sighed heavily, leaning against the kitchen counter, waiting for him to finish his call. When he finally hung up, he turned to her, acknowledging her for the first time all morning. "Don't forget we have dinner with my mother tonight," he said in his usual matter-of-fact tone.

Dionne nodded absentmindedly, her focus elsewhere, barely registering his words.

"Did you hear me?" Malik's voice turned sharp, his tone demanding her attention.

She shot him a cold glare, her frustration spilling over. "I heard you. I got it," she replied, her voice laced with attitude.

Malik's jaw tightened, but he let it slide, grabbing his things as he prepared to leave. "Don't wait up for me after. I have to report to the hospital," he added, his tone flat, as if it were just another part of his routine.

Dionne rolled her eyes, her patience nearing its end. "Of course you do," she said sarcastically, the bitterness in her voice cutting through the air.

He paused, his jaw clenching as he visibly held back a retort. "Just don't be late tonight," he said coolly before walking past her and out of the house.

The sound of the door closing behind him left Dionne standing alone in the silence. She exhaled deeply, her frustration bubbling over. The weight of their hollow relationship pressed heavily on her, and the idea of yet another dinner where she had to pretend everything was perfect felt suffocating. Tonight would be no different—a performance, a show for Malik's mother, while the cracks between them continued to grow.

Dionne sighed deeply, her frustration mounting. She was tired—tired of the charade, tired of pretending there was still something worth fighting for in her relationship. The love between her and Malik had withered away, leaving only an empty promise to fulfill for someone they both cared about deeply.

Deciding she needed an escape, Dionne headed upstairs to change. She slipped into a pair of comfortable "Gallery Dept" sweats, paired with a white crop top and a matching "Gallery Dept" hoodie. She completed the look with Nike Waffles on her feet and pulled her hair into a cute bun atop her head, leaning into the chill aesthetic. For a change, she wore her glasses instead of contacts, the frames giving her an effortlessly adorable look.

She grabbed her purse and headed out, determined to clear her mind at her best friend London's shop. Driving her Urus through the Houston streets, Dionne parked next to London's car upon arriving. She stepped inside and immediately felt the comforting warmth of familiarity as she spotted London working on Karmen's hair.

"Hey, boo," London greeted, pausing to hug Dionne.

"Hey, girl," Dionne replied with a small smile, returning the hug before turning to greet Karmen with another warm embrace.

"Girl! You've been MIA," London exclaimed, her tone a mix of teasing and concern.

"I know," Dionne admitted, rolling her eyes. "Between work and this wedding planning shit with Malik, I don't have time for anything else." Her voice carried the weight of her stress, the cracks in her composure threatening to show.

"Aww, I can't believe you and Malik are finally getting married. Took his ass long enough," London said with a laugh, her blunt humor shining through as Karmen nodded in agreement.

"You two are the perfect couple, though," Karmen added, her soft voice carrying an earnest sincerity that made Dionne shift uncomfortably.

Dionne forced a smile, but her heart wasn't in it. The praise felt like a cruel irony, considering the truth of her relationship. There was nothing perfect about her and Malik. It was a facade, a carefully constructed image hiding the emptiness beneath. She wanted to tell them, to unburden herself of the truth, but she couldn't bring herself to shatter their perception.

"What y'all been up to?" Dionne asked, eager to steer the conversation away from herself.

"Girl, working and planning to expand," London replied, her voice brimming with excitement. She paused, looking over at Dionne. "Speaking of, do you want to go to this investor party with me next weekend?"

Dionne perked up slightly. "Girl, I'm already going. I got invited through work," she said with a small smile.

"Good, cause I don't think I can play bougie by myself for too long," London joked, her laughter filling the room. Dionne chuckled softly, grateful for her friend's humor.

"How's Mama Glen doing?" Karmen asked gently, her tone filled with concern as she referred to Malik's mother.

Feenin'

Dionne's smile faded, her shoulders slumping slightly. "She's not getting better. It's just bad news after bad news," she said, her voice tinged with sadness. Despite everything happening between her and Malik, Mama Glen was still a central figure in Dionne's life—a second mother who offered her unconditional support and a safe space to vent without fear of judgment.

Both London and Karmen mirrored her sadness, knowing how deeply Dionne cared for Mama Glen. "I'm so sorry, Dee," Karmen said softly, reaching out to touch her arm.

"Malik wants to push the wedding up since she doesn't look like she's getting better," Dionne added, her tone heavy with resignation.

"Well, that's good. There's no point in waiting any longer anyway," Karmen said with a nod, her practicality shining through. Dionne nodded back, though her agreement was hollow. She didn't share London's sentiment, but she lacked the energy to argue.

"That man loves you!" London squealed, her excitement genuine. But Dionne shifted uncomfortably at the statement, unable to match her friend's enthusiasm.

If only they knew the truth, Dionne thought, forcing a smile that didn't quite reach her eyes. Malik's love—or what was left of it—felt more like an obligation than anything else. The weight of pretending was exhausting, and even in the company of her closest friends, the truth remained locked away, suffocating her from within.

Before Dionne could respond, the sound of the front door opening pulled all their attention. A man walked in, his presence commanding and magnetic. He stood tall at 6'3", caramel skin glowing under the shop's lights, with long, neatly kept locs and a full beard framing his perfectly chiseled face. Every woman in the shop turned to look at him, their conversations momentarily forgotten. By his side was a little girl, holding his hand. She was a mini version of him—thick, curly hair cascading down her back, caramel skin, and the same striking mocha eyes as her father.

Mario approached the group of women, noting that they were the only three left in the shop. "Umm... are you closed?" he asked, his deep, raspy voice carrying a hopeful tone.

London stepped forward with a smile, her usual confidence shining through. "Umm... no. What can I do for you?" she replied, her flirty tone unmistakable. Karmen and Dionne exchanged a knowing glance, muffling their chuckles at their friend's antics.

Mario looked at London, but when his gaze shifted slightly, it landed on someone else—Karmen. Her smooth brown skin seemed to glow under the light, her recently done boho knotless braids framing her delicate features. And then there was her smile—a quiet, genuine expression that could light up any room. Karmen shifted in her seat, feeling the weight of his gaze, her cheeks warming under his attention.

Dionne noticed the subtle pull between them and smiled knowingly. She could see it—the way Mario's attention lingered on Karmen and the way Karmen couldn't seem to look away.

Mario cleared his throat, forcing his attention back to London. "I was just trying to see if anyone here could do my baby girl's hair," he said, his smooth voice rolling through the shop like honey.

London crouched down to meet the little girl at eye level, her tone softening. "Hey, sweetie, what's your name?" she asked, her warmth immediately putting the child at ease.

"Mia," the little girl said softly, her shy smile drawing a collective coo from the women.

"Well, hi, Mia. I'm London—like the city in England," she said with a playful tone, her words bringing a bright smile to the little girl's face as if London had just told her something magical.

Mario watched the exchange with a quiet smile, his admiration clear. But even as he focused on Mia and London's interaction, his eyes occasionally flicked back to Karmen, and each time, hers seemed to meet his. Neither said a word, but the tension between them was unmistakable.

Dionne leaned back in her seat, her own amusement growing as she watched the silent sparks fly between Karmen and Mario. She exchanged a look with London, who smirked knowingly but kept her attention on Mia.

It seemed the day had just gotten a little more interesting.

Their eyes exchanged unspoken words, things their mouths couldn't say. The connection between Mario and Karmen was undeniable, even if neither of them acknowledged it outright.

"How do you want your hair, Mia?" London asked, crouching back down to meet the little girl's gaze. Mia's face scrunched up adorably as she appeared to think hard about her decision. Her curious expression drew chuckles from everyone in the room.

"Like hers," Mia finally said, pointing directly at Karmen.

All eyes shifted to Karmen, who smiled warmly.

Mario shook his head gently, his voice soft but firm as he spoke to his daughter. "That's a little too grown for you, Toot," he said with a hint of affection, his protective side shining through. Mia had long, beautiful curly hair, thanks to his genes, and he wasn't too fond of the idea of adding weave to her style.

Feenin'

London, catching on to his hesitation, quickly reassured him. "I can style her real hair to look just like that, without adding weave, if that's what you're worried about," she said confidently, reading his concerns as if they were written on his face.

Mario glanced at London and then back at Karmen, his gaze lingering for a moment longer. She really did look good with those braids—elegant and effortless. He could see why his daughter admired her.

"Okay, that's cool," Mario agreed with a nod. He reached into his pocket, pulling out a thick stack of cash. "How much?" he asked.

"Just $90," London replied casually.

Mario rolled out $250 and handed it to her without hesitation. "Don't ever undervalue your work," he said, his voice steady. But as he spoke, his eyes were locked on Karmen, making it clear the words carried more weight than just the exchange of money.

London noticed the way his gaze lingered on her friend and couldn't hide her smirk. Dionne caught it too, her own amusement growing. Karmen, meanwhile, blushed under the attention, her cheeks warming as she struggled to keep her composure.

Mario turned his focus back to his daughter, crouching down to speak to her softly. "Be good for Miss London, Toot," he said, kissing her on the forehead before standing. He gave the group a polite nod and smiled at Karmen one last time before heading for the door.

As the door closed behind him, the shop erupted into soft giggles and knowing smiles.

"Girl, he couldn't take his eyes off you," London teased, nudging Karmen playfully.

Karmen buried her face in her hands, her blush deepening. "Y'all stop," she mumbled, though a small smile peeked through her fingers.

"Uh-huh," Dionne chimed in with a smirk. "That man was focused."

Karmen laughed nervously, her heart racing. She didn't know what to make of the encounter, but one thing was certain—Mario had left an impression she wouldn't forget anytime soon.

"Girl! That man was fine, and he was definitely checking you out!" London exclaimed, her excitement infectious.

Karmen laughed nervously, trying to deflect. "You really gonna talk about her dad right in front of her?" she said, glancing at Mia, who was still engrossed in her iPad and fruit snacks. Karmen was doing her best to recover from the lingering effect Mario had on her, but it wasn't easy.

"Ouuu, you're right," London replied, her tone playful. "But we ain't forgetting about it."

Dionne laughed along, chiming in, "He was admiring you, sis. There's no denying it."

Karmen's cheeks flushed as she waved them off. "Stop! You know I don't need another man in my life after what happened with Trey," she said, her voice quieter now.

At the mention of his name, London and Dionne both rolled their eyes. Trey was a sore subject for all of them. Karmen had been in love with him since college, even giving him her virginity. They had stayed together after graduation, but everything changed when Trey's NFL career came to a screeching halt. He'd been a star receiver for the Texans until a devastating knee injury ended his career. The loss of his football dreams sent him into a spiral, and Karmen had become his outlet for anger and frustration.

Despite her love for him, Karmen had to walk away after Trey's abuse landed her in the hospital. It had taken all her strength to leave him and rebuild her life, but the scars—emotional and physical—remained.

London crossed her arms, her voice dripping with passion as she shot back. "Girl, don't let that bitch control your life anymore. If you want to date, or hell, just ride dick backwards for fun, you can! You're single and free. You're not tied to him anymore!"

Karmen's eyes widened in shock. "London! The baby!" she hissed, gesturing toward Mia.

London glanced at the little girl, who was still glued to her iPad. "Girl, she ain't listening to us. Dionne, tell your girl to stop holding herself back and get back out there."

At the mention of her name, Dionne looked up from her phone. "Yes, girl. Go out, date. Do something for yourself," she said encouragingly.

Karmen hesitated for a moment, considering their words. Then London's face lit up with an idea. "You know what? We should all three go out!" she declared, her excitement showing on her face.

Karmen and Dionne both snapped their heads toward her, eyes wide in surprise. "What?" Karmen said, blinking.

"Yes, like out, out. To the club. Clearly, we all need it," London continued, her tone serious despite the ridiculous grin on her face.

Karmen chuckled nervously. "I don't know about that, London."

"You're shutting that pussy down over a no-good-ass nigga, and Dionne's over here about to be out the game, and become a married woman," London said bluntly, pointing between the two of them.

"Damn, bitch," Dionne shot back, her words more defensive than playful as London's comment hit harder than intended.

"Let's just let loose for once. Enjoy a night of fun, like the old

Feenin'

college days," London pressed, her energy contagious. Both Dionne and Karmen exchanged glances, the idea sounding better the more they thought about it.

"You know what? I'm down," Karmen finally spoke up, her voice filled with a mix of apprehension and excitement.

"Me too, I guess," Dionne added, shaking her head at London's persistence.

London clapped her hands together, practically bouncing with excitement. "I knew y'all would come around! I know just the spot too!"

Dionne sighed, but the small smile on her face betrayed her. "This is going to be a night," she muttered, already bracing herself for London's wild plans.

Dionne had been looking forward to tonight all day—a night to let loose, forget her troubles, and revel in freedom and fun with her girls. She'd spent the afternoon chatting with her friends before stopping by her parents' house, a comforting detour that helped ease some of her tension. Now, as the time drew closer, she was back home, getting dressed for a night that promised to be everything her life currently wasn't.

She slipped into her outfit, each piece chosen to exude effortless confidence. The red sleeveless Dior shirt hugged her nice-sized boobs and showed off her toned arms, while the high-waisted jeans fit her perfectly, accentuating her figure. The red Maison Margiela split-toe boots added the perfect edge, completing the look with a hint of boldness. Her hair, styled in a silk ponytail London had installed earlier, flowed perfectly, framing her face as she sat down to do her makeup.

As Dionne focused on the final touches, the sound of the front door closing signaled Malik's arrival. He walked into the room in his black scrubs, looking her over with an appreciative gaze.

"Are those jeans for me or my mama?" he teased, his voice low and seductive.

Dionne groaned internally, realizing in an instant what she had forgotten. The dinner with his mother. The one thing she couldn't skip, no matter how much she wanted to. Her heart sank as the anticipation of her night out with her friends faded, replaced with the heavy weight of obligation.

But she was too practiced at masking her true feelings to let him notice. Turning with a smile she didn't feel, she replied smoothly, "They're only for you."

Malik grinned, stepping closer and grabbing her waist, pulling her against him. His touch was firm, familiar, yet it no longer stirred the emotions it once had. "I can't wait to make you my wife," he said, his voice soft but sincere as he held her close.

Sure, you can't.

As he held her, her mind raced with frustration. Tonight was supposed to be her escape, her chance to breathe, to let go of the charade she lived daily. But once again, she found herself trapped in the role of the supportive, devoted fiancée—a role she had no love left to play.

Before she could respond, Malik pressed his lips against hers with forceful passion. Dionne allowed his touch to linger, though her feelings were conflicted. Deep down, she missed being touched in this way, missed the intimacy they once shared. His lips trailed down her neck, hitting the sensitive spots that used to send shivers through her. For the first time in a long time, she caught a fleeting glimpse of the spark they used to have.

"Malik… you need to get ready for dinner," Dionne said softly, her hands lightly pressing against his chest in an attempt to create some distance. But Malik ignored her words, his lips trailing down her neck, leaving lingering kisses on her skin.

"No," he murmured, his voice low and almost pleading. "I need to feel you. I miss you, Dee."

Malik picked her up effortlessly, keeping his lips on hers, his movements swift and familiar. He carried her to the bed, laying her down as he continued to kiss his way down her body. A soft moan escaped her lips as he worked his way lower, removing her jeans and underwear with practiced hands.

In the next moment, Malik stripped out of his pants and entered her with a sudden, forceful thrust. Dionne's body jumped at the abruptness, a sharp pain breaking through the brief haze of pleasure. She bit her lip, trying to adjust, but the discomfort lingered.

This was another reason she struggled with Malik. He wasn't horrible in bed, but he wasn't great either. He was mechanical, focused only on what he wanted. His preference was always the same—rough, quick, and in one position: missionary.

Dionne, on the other hand, craved more. She liked her moments of roughness, but she also wanted to be desired in a way that made her feel craved, wanted, cherished. She wanted a lover who took his time, who explored her body, who made her feel alive. Malik was once that man, and it was becoming painfully clear that man was now gone, forever.

As he continued, Dionne's mind wandered, the spark she'd felt moments ago fading as quickly as it had appeared. She stared at the ceiling, wondering how much longer she could pretend to be satisfied—

Feenin'

not just in this moment, but in her relationship as a whole.

Malik's pace was quick, his groans filling the room as he thrust into her, completely lost in his own pleasure. Dionne lay beneath him, her body responding out of habit, but her mind far away. She wasn't enjoying it—she hadn't in a long time—but she was used to it now. The quick, non-passionate sex had become their normal.

"Fuck, Dee," Malik moaned, his voice strained as he climaxed, his body shuddering before he pulled out. He collapsed next to her on the bed, panting, a satisfied grin on his face.

Dionne stared at the ceiling, her mind blank, her emotions dulled. *This used to be different. We used to be different,* she thought bitterly. Their sex life had once been filled with passion, connection, and excitement. Now, it was rushed and mechanical—just another box to check.

Without a word, Dionne rose from the bed, gathering her clothes and slipping back into her jeans. She smoothed her hair, trying to reclaim some sense of herself as Malik got up and headed for the shower, humming to himself as if everything were perfect.

Dionne stood in front of the mirror, staring at her reflection. Her face told the truth she tried so hard to hide—she wasn't happy. Not in this relationship, not in this life she had built to please everyone but herself. The weight of pretending was etched into every line of her face.

Her phone buzzed on the dresser, a message from London about their plans for the night. Dionne sighed, her fingers hesitating before she texted back, canceling on her friends. The thought of a night out, of even a moment of freedom, felt like a lifeline she was letting slip away.

As she put the phone down, a deep ache settled in her chest. She needed something—something more than this hollow routine. She craved a thrill, an escape, a feeling of being alive again. The yearning for something free, untamed, and real burned inside her, more powerful now than ever. She didn't know what it was, but she knew she couldn't keep ignoring it for much longer.

Once Dionne and Malik were finished getting ready, they stepped out of the house and into his white Ferrari, the car gliding smoothly through the city streets as they made their way to his mother's home. The drive was quiet, filled with unspoken tension that Dionne tried to push to the back of her mind. She already knew what the night would entail—another performance, another exhausting charade.

As they arrived at Mama Glen's house, Dionne steeled herself, her mask of perfection slipping into place the moment they stepped inside. Mama Glen greeted them with a warm, radiant smile, her frail body moving toward them with arms outstretched. Dionne immediately leaned in for a hug, her affection for Malik's mother genuine despite the turmoil she felt inside.

"You two look wonderful together," Mama Glen said softly, her voice filled with pride as she glanced between them.

Dionne forced a smile, gripping Malik's hand for show, though the contact felt hollow. "Thank you, Mama Glen," she replied warmly, playing her part perfectly.

Throughout the evening, Dionne laughed at Malik's jokes, held his hand when Mama Glen commented on their love, and spoke excitedly about wedding plans. To anyone looking in, they were the perfect couple, deeply in love and ready to spend forever together.

But inside, it was breaking her. Every false smile, every scripted line, every act of devotion chipped away at the little bit of herself she still held onto.

She glanced at Mama Glen, her heart aching. The woman had been a second mother to her, a source of wisdom and comfort when she needed it most. Her happiness mattered, and if playing this role was the price of that happiness, Dionne would endure it—for now.

But as the evening wore on, Dionne couldn't ignore the growing hollowness in her chest. The life she was living felt like a prison, and with each passing moment, the walls seemed to close in tighter.

***

Arris moved confidently through his nightclub, wearing a perfectly tailored green Dolce & Gabbana suit that added to his magnetic allure. Heads turned as he passed, women unable to resist the combination of his commanding presence and undeniable style. He greeted a few familiar faces with casual nods and handshakes as he navigated the packed crowd, the electric energy of the night buzzing around him. Tonight was one of those nights where everything aligned—top celebrities, endless money flow, and an atmosphere that promised unforgettable memories.

As he made his way to the private section he reserved for his boys, Arris spotted Mario and True, already comfortable and in high spirits. "Y'all niggas straight over here?" Arris asked, dapping them up as he slid into their section.

"Hell yeah. Nigga, sit down, take a drink or somethin'. Always working," True teased, grinning as he handed Arris a drink.

Arris chuckled but obliged, taking a rare moment to unwind with his closest friends. "Man, it's some fine women in here tonight," Mario said, his eyes scanning the crowd with approval.

"No, for real, Arris. This shit is lit. You doing good, my nigga!" True

Feenin'

added, raising his glass to toast their success.

Arris smirked, clinking glasses with them before leaning back into the plush seats. For a brief moment, he allowed himself to relax, enjoying the camaraderie and buzz of the night. But duty always called, and it wasn't long before his assistant, China, appeared at his side.

"Top investor is here and waiting in VIP," she informed him, her tone professional as always.

Arris nodded, standing up and saying his goodbyes to Mario and True. "Aight, back to work," he said with a smirk, shaking his head as they hollered at him for being all business.

China led him through the club to the VIP section, where a poised woman in her mid fifties stood waiting. Her presence radiated power and elegance, and her youthful appearance belied her age. Arris recognized her immediately.

"Ms. Jean Williams?" Arris said smoothly, extending his hand. He never forgot a face, especially not one associated with business.

Jean turned at the sound of her name, her expression brightening as she recognized him. "Mr. Black. It's good to see you again," she said warmly, shaking his hand.

"Same here. I hear you're here on business," Arris said, his signature confidence carrying through his tone.

Jean smiled, a twinkle of nostalgia in her eyes. "Actually, I am—plus a little bit of fun. This place is incredible. It reminds me of my days when I was your age," she said with a light laugh.

"Well, let's talk business first, and then I'll make sure you get the full Vault experience," Arris replied, his charming grin making her chuckle.

"I like a man who prioritizes business," Jean said, her tone approving as they got down to it. "I heard you're looking to expand—building properties within the inner cities?"

"Exactly," Arris confirmed. "The focus is on building more housing for the homeless and people in need, as well as creating businesses that'll provide jobs. I'm looking for properties with potential, especially those with sizable land. Partnering with your agency would be the ideal move to make it happen."

"That sounds interesting," Jean said, her tone thoughtful but laced with intrigue. "I know someone who would be excited to work with you on that once we partner."

Arris's eyes lit up momentarily at the confirmation, though his calm, confident demeanor masked his excitement. He leaned in slightly, his voice steady. "So, are you saying that you're investing?" he asked, seeking the clarity he needed.

Jean smiled knowingly. "I'm saying stay by your phone. I'll have one of my most promising agents—and also my future partner—sit down with you to discuss the investment further."

Arris nodded, his gratitude evident despite his composed exterior. He extended his hand to hers, shaking it firmly. "Thank you so much, Ms. Williams. I won't disappoint."

Jean chuckled, impressed by his poise and charm. "I don't think you will."

"Now," she said, a playful glint in her eye, "about this Vault experience you promised me..."

Arris chuckled, his confidence unwavering. "Say no more. I'll make sure it's a night you'll never forget."

And he delivered. From the exclusive drinks to the personalized tour of the club, Arris made sure Jean saw firsthand why The Vault was the most talked-about venue in Houston. He introduced her to the celebrities in attendance, showcased the high-level service his staff provided, and ensured she experienced the perfect blend of sophistication and entertainment.

By the end of the night, Jean's laughter echoed through the VIP section as she sipped on a signature cocktail. She was thoroughly impressed, not just by the club but by the man who ran it all. Arris Black had proven to her that he wasn't just a businessman—he was the businessman she wanted to work with.

Chapter 3

One week later:

Dionne's green heels clicked rhythmically against the polished office floor, a sound that echoed her steady confidence. She had just finished showing a house and was preparing for an important business meeting that Ms. Jean had arranged. Some millionaire looking to partner, Dionne had been told—a potential game-changer for the company. With thirty minutes to spare, she returned to her office, taking a moment to unwind and scroll through her phone.

She chuckled softly at the barrage of messages from her friends, teasing her about bailing on their plans last week. Dionne had promised to make it up to them, but that hadn't stopped London and Karmen from flooding her with playful guilt trips. Her laughter lightened the weight of her busy day as the minutes ticked by.

When the time for the meeting finally approached, Dionne gathered her materials, straightened her blouse, and walked confidently toward the conference room. Her mind was focused, her stride purposeful. She thought she'd arrived early, but as she stepped into the room, the sight of someone already seated made her pause.

Her breath hitched.

Sitting there, calm and composed, was a man she hadn't expected to see again. Arris.

The man she had shown a house to weeks ago. The man who had taken her home and left her with a lingering memory she couldn't quite shake.

Arris looked up, his dark eyes locking with hers. That same confident, disarming smile spread across his face, and Dionne felt a

Ann

shiver trail down her spine despite herself. She swallowed hard, forcing herself to maintain her composure as she stepped further into the room.

Arris stood as Dionne entered, a gesture of respect that didn't go unnoticed. He extended his hand, his hypnotic smile firmly in place. "I didn't expect soon to come this fast," he said smoothly, his tone laced with charm.

Dionne smiled, shaking his hand, her professional facade masking the swirl of emotions inside. "Good to see you again, Mr. Black," she replied, her voice steady despite the nervous flutter in her chest.

"No need to be formal. Arris is fine," he said, his deep voice carrying a warmth that sent a subtle shiver through her. His eyes remained locked on hers, their intensity unsettling in a way that made her feel both vulnerable and intrigued.

"So," he said, his radiant pride evident, "you're the bright agent I'm supposed to negotiate this deal with?" His gaze flicked briefly down, subtly admiring how the green pantsuit accentuated her figure before returning to meet her eyes.

"In fact, I am," Dionne said confidently, refusing to let his demeanor shake her. "Are you ready to get down to business?"

"Lead the way," Arris replied with a slight smirk, clearly enjoying the energy she brought to the table.

Dionne took control, launching into the negotiation as they settled into the conference room. "Williams Luxe Realty is a powerhouse. My company, Blac could use that reputation to fast-track our developments. Let's partner—50-50 split," Arris began, wasting no time.

Dionne smirked, shaking her head slightly at his boldness. "50-50? Arris, Williams Luxe doesn't split evenly. We dominate. Here's the deal: you bring $15 million for acquisition and pre-development, and we take 70% control. You keep 30% equity and Blac's name on the project." Her tone was confident, unshaken, and she met his gaze head-on.

Arris leaned back slightly, intrigued, his smile growing wider. "So, I front the money, and you take the lion's share?" he asked, his smooth voice carrying an edge of challenge. As he licked his lips, his eyes scanned her, admiring the way her green pantsuit framed her body.

"You get the prestige without the headaches," Dionne replied without missing a beat, her attention on the files in front of her. She finally lifted her eyes to meet his, catching his gaze lingering on her. "Williams Luxe guarantees results, and your ROI will hit 25% annually, minimum."

Her commanding tone and sharp business mentality drew Arris in even further. She was unlike anyone he had met—a woman who exuded power without needing to prove it.

Feenin'

"You drive a hard bargain, Ms. Smith," Arris said, his confidence matching hers.

"I drive results," she countered smoothly, leaning forward slightly. "Blac needs Williams Luxe to dominate the skyline. Take the deal, Arris—you won't regret it."

Arris chuckled softly, shaking his head in admiration. "Bold. You've got a deal—can't wait to see where this partnership leads us."

Dionne's lips curved into a triumphant smile, catching his gaze once more, knowing exactly what game he was playing. "Good. Thanks for trusting Williams Luxe with your new investments," she said, standing to leave.

"How about we celebrate this deal over a nice dinner?" Arris asked, now standing, his eyes locked on hers with an intensity that was impossible to ignore.

Dionne smiled, intrigued despite herself, wondering how often he used this effortless charm—especially on women. But she couldn't deny that it was working in his favor. "Dinner?" she repeated, her tone laced with curiosity.

Arris chuckled softly, his confidence unwavering. "Yeah. I feel like food—delicious food—is the perfect way to kick off a great partnership," he said, flashing a confident smile that made Dionne chuckle despite herself. This man.

"You do this with all your new business partners?" she teased, her eyes narrowing slightly as she challenged him.

Arris leaned back casually, completely unbothered. "Only with the special ones… yes," he replied smoothly, his charm radiating.

Dionne shook her head in amusement but couldn't hide the faint smile tugging at her lips. "Okay, where?" she asked, deciding to indulge him.

"What's your favorite?" he countered without missing a beat.

"The Vault, downtown," she answered confidently, impressed by his quick comeback.

Arris's smile widened, his eyes lighting up. "The Vault it is. 7pm?"

"Sounds perfect," Dionne replied with equal confidence, feeling the weight of his gaze linger as he smiled back.

She gathered her files and walked out of the office without another word, her hips swaying subtly as she moved with grace and purpose. Arris didn't take his eyes off her, admiring every step she took as she disappeared down the hall. He sat back in his chair, a small smirk tugging at the corner of his lips.

She had won the negotiation, but it was her confidence, intellect, and beauty that left the biggest impression. For the first time in a long while, Arris found himself intrigued by more than just business.

This was going to be an interesting partnership.

Arris couldn't help himself. Dionne had an effect on him, and she knew it. Even though she didn't fully understand why, she could feel the shift in energy whenever they were in the same space. Walking back into her office, Dionne sat down in her chair, satisfied with sealing the deal with a top-tier client like Arris Black. Yet, no matter how much she tried to focus on the success of their meeting, her mind kept drifting back to him.

The way he looked at her—like she was the only person in the room—lingered in her thoughts. His gaze held something deeper than admiration, something that carried passion and curiosity, and it unsettled her in a way she couldn't shake. Dionne sighed, leaning back in her chair, her mind replaying every moment of their interaction.

The shrill ring of her phone jolted her from her thoughts. She glanced down, groaning in frustration when Malik's name lit up the screen. Reluctantly, she answered. "Hello," she said, her tone sharp and lacking any warmth.

"Don't wait up for me tonight. I'll be working late again," Malik said flatly, his voice void of any effort to make the situation better.

Dionne rolled her eyes, her patience long gone. She didn't even have the energy to argue anymore. "Okay," she replied curtly before hanging up without another word.

She tossed her phone onto the desk and let out a long breath. The numbness in her relationship with Malik was suffocating, and she needed an escape. Her mind raced, and then an idea struck. She opened the group chat with London and Karmen, firing off a quick message inviting them out to the club to make up for ditching them last time.

The response was almost immediate.

London: Finally, sis! Let's turn up!
Karmen: Say less. I'm in.

A small smile crept onto Dionne's lips. A night out—dancing, drinking, and forgetting about Malik—was exactly what she needed. For one night, she would let loose, leave the weight of her entanglement behind, and just feel free.

***

Arris had just left the Williams Luxe office, his thoughts consumed by the meeting with Dionne. The way her green pantsuit hugged her body in all the right places, the effortless confidence in her voice, and the radiant smile that lit up the room—everything about her replayed in his

Feenin'

mind as he drove. There was something about Dionne that drew him in, something she seemed completely unaware of, and that only intrigued him more.

He shook off the thought as he turned into the driveway of his mother's house. The large two-story brick home was a far cry from where they'd come from. Arris had worked hard to move his mother, Angel, out of the hood and into a better neighborhood. Even though her surroundings had changed, Angel was still the same cutthroat, fiercely honest woman who never minced her words.

Arris parked and stepped out of his car, letting out a loud, "Ma!" as his voice echoed through the house.

From the backyard, her sharp tone rang out, "Boy, you better stop yelling in my house! I'm in the backyard!"

Arris chuckled, following the sound of her voice. He stepped outside to see Angel bent over her garden, meticulously tending to her plants. Gardening was her passion—everything she cooked was grown from the ground, and she often bragged that it was the secret to her flawless appearance.

Angel rose when she heard him approach, her hazel eyes lighting up as she smiled. She was a stunning woman, with smooth brown skin and a pixie cut that framed her face perfectly. Despite being in her late forties, she looked far younger, her vibrancy shining through.

"Hey, son," she greeted warmly, pulling him into a hug.

"Hey, Ma," he said, holding her tightly before they moved to the lawn chairs in her backyard to sit and catch up.

"How you doing, sweetie?" she asked, her tone soft yet firm.

"I'm good, Ma. How are you doing?" he replied, smiling as she settled into her seat.

"Blessed," Angel said with a satisfied nod. "But I wish I could see my son more."

Arris sighed, guilt tugging at him. "I know. I promise I'll be by more often."

"And you better bring those stanky-ass friends of yours you call brothers. I miss them two, and my grandbaby Mia," Angel said with a pointed look, making Arris chuckle.

"Okay, Ma. I promise. I'll let Mario and True know," he said, shaking his head fondly.

Angel wasn't just Arris's mother; she had long considered True and Mario her sons as well. The countless times they showed up at her house, crashing on her couch or devouring her delicious home-cooked meals, gave her every right to claim them as her own. Over the years, they'd become like family, and Angel treated them no differently than she did Arris. Whether it was offering advice, patching them up after a rough night, or simply feeding them until they couldn't eat anymore, Angel had earned her place in their lives as more than just "Arris's mom." To her, they were her boys, and she loved them like her own.

Angel's expression softened as she asked, "Have you talked to your sister?"

At the mention of A'Lani, Arris's face lit up.

A'Lani was his 24-year-old little sister and currently in nursing school with dreams of becoming a pediatric nurse. She was the pride and joy of the family, but especially to Arris. Everyone joked that he treated her more like a daughter than a sister, but Angel adored their bond. The tight-knit relationship between them reminded her of the family foundation she'd always hoped to maintain.

"Yeah, I talked to her the other day. Said she's coming in town in a few days," Arris replied with a smile, the thought of seeing his sister brightening his mood.

"That's good," Angel said warmly. "The two of you back home, under one roof again." Her smile mirrored his, a rare expression Arris cherished. Growing up, seeing his mother smile had been a rarity, so being able to bring her even a moment of happiness now meant the world to him.

Arris leaned back in his chair, the comfort of the moment easing his usual tension. "You said you wanted to talk to me about something?" he asked, remembering the reason his mother had called him over. She'd texted earlier, saying it was urgent.

Angel's smile faded, replaced by a more serious expression. "I was trying to wait until your sister got home to tell you both," she started hesitantly, her voice tinged with worry, "but she already found out."

Arris's brows furrowed, the shift in her tone putting him on edge. "Ma, what is it?" he asked, his patience thinning as concern began to bubble up.

Angel hesitated, her fingers fidgeting slightly—a habit Arris rarely saw in her. "Your father reached out to both you and your sister."

The words hit Arris like a slap, his jaw tightening as a wave of anger rolled through him. Just the mention of his father made his blood simmer. Calvin Black was a man Arris had long given up on—a man who had consistently chosen the streets over his family. To Arris, his father had been dead to him for years.

"I didn't get shit from that nigga," Arris said, his voice calm but simmering with restrained fury.

Feenin'

Angel sighed, her tone soft yet firm. "He reached out to me to tell you. He knew if he sent you something directly, you wouldn't read it."

Arris clenched his fists, his jaw ticking as he tried to keep his rage in check. "What does he want, Ma?"

Angel's voice cracked, betraying her own conflicting emotions. "He wants to sit down and talk. He already reached out to Lani, and she agreed. She asked me to convince you, because she couldn't do it herself."

Arris stood abruptly, the revelation leaving him stunned. His sister—his baby sister—had agreed to meet with the man who had abandoned them. The man who had broken their family apart.

A'Lani was open to sitting down with the man who had abandoned them? Arris couldn't believe it. The idea churned in his chest, stoking the fire of the deep rage he held for Calvin Black. A rage so consuming that he'd sworn if he ever saw his father again, he wouldn't hesitate to make him pay for all the pain he'd caused. To hear that A'Lani—the one person he trusted implicitly—felt differently and was willing to extend empathy toward their father felt like a betrayal.

"I have nothing to say to that nigga," Arris said sharply, his voice trembling with barely contained fury. His fists clenched at his sides as he fought to control his emotions.

"You're not even going to hear him out with your sister? You're going to let her go alone?" Angel asked, her voice calm but laced with maternal concern. She knew exactly where to press—A'Lani was his Achilles' heel.

Arris's eyes narrowed as he turned to his mother, the challenge clear in his tone. "Don't you do that, Ma. Don't throw Lani in my face as some type of bribery or blackmail."

Angel held his gaze, but the fire in his eyes made her hesitate. She saw the unyielding rage and pain he tried so hard to bury, and she knew this was a battle she couldn't win right now. "Just think about it, sweetie, before making a final decision," she said softly, placing a gentle hand on his shoulder.

"Ain't nothing to think about, Ma," Arris snapped, his voice thick with anger. "That nigga's dead to me." His words cut through the air like a blade, the weight of his unresolved pain hanging heavy between them.

Angel sighed, watching her son's shoulders tense as he leaned in to place a kiss on her forehead. The gesture was tender, but Angel could feel the storm brewing behind it. His energy radiated hurt and fury, and it broke her heart knowing there was little she could do to ease it.

"I'll see you later, Ma," Arris said, his tone softer now, though the

Ann

tension in his voice was unmistakable.

Angel watched as he walked away, his stride purposeful but burdened. She stayed seated in the backyard, staring at the garden she'd been tending. She felt helpless, knowing that no words or reassurances could soothe the wound Calvin had left in her son's heart. Angel sighed again, whispering to herself, "Lord, help my babies heal."

Arris stepped out of his mother's house, his mind still simmering with the conversation he'd just had. His jaw tightened briefly as he exhaled, trying to shake off the lingering tension. Sliding into his car, he checked the time on his dashboard. He had a dinner meeting with Dionne in an hour to officially celebrate their new partnership.

The thought of seeing her again brought a small, involuntary smile to his face. She had been direct, professional, and sharp during their meeting earlier—a combination that intrigued him more than he cared to admit. When he'd told her to pick the dinner spot, he hadn't expected her to choose The Vault, his own restaurant. Her reason? She'd expressed that it was her favorite spot, unknowingly stroking his ego.

Arris chuckled to himself at the coincidence, keeping the fact that he owned the place under wraps for now. He was curious to see her reaction when he dropped the bombshell tonight. It wasn't often he indulged in surprises like this, but something about Dionne made him want to keep her on her toes.

With time to spare, Arris decided to head back to his place to freshen up. Tonight wasn't just about business—it was about leaving an impression. And he had no doubt that this dinner would be unforgettable, for both of them.

***

Dionne stood in front of her full-length mirror, giving her reflection one last look as she adjusted the pink corset that hugged her waist flawlessly, accentuating her curves, while her breasts sat perfectly, drawing attention to the elegance of her figure. Her outfit for tonight's business dinner with Arris was a flawless blend of elegance and ease, a balance she knew how to strike effortlessly. She had plans to meet her friends after, so she'd chosen something that worked for both occasions.

The pink corset hugged her small waist and emphasized her toned arms, while the Louis Vuitton carpenter wide-leg pants showcased her sculpted legs and perfectly rounded butt. Her pink Louboutin closed-toe heels added a touch of sophistication, elevating the entire look. Gold jewelry adorned her neck and wrists, complementing the outfit and accentuating her glowing brown skin.

Her long, straightened hair cascaded down her back in a neat middle

Feenin'

part, framing her beautiful face and enhancing her naturally striking features. Dionne took a step back, admiring her reflection. She looked good—better than good. She looked powerful, radiant, and ready to take on whatever the night had in store.

Her phone buzzed on the dresser, and she grabbed it, seeing a message from London in the group chat hyping her up about the picture she sent. Smiling at her friends' antics, Dionne took a deep breath. Tonight was about handling business first, enjoying a delicious meal at her favorite restaurant, and then letting loose with her girls. She was ready to own every moment.

As Dionne rummaged through her closet for her pink Louis Vuitton purse, Malik walked into the room, his footsteps slowing as his eyes landed on her. His gaze lingered, clearly admiring how stunning she looked in her outfit. "Where are you going, looking this beautiful?" he asked, his deep voice cutting through the silence and startling her.

"Ouu, you scared me, Malik," Dionne said, turning her head briefly before resuming her search. "I thought you had to work late tonight," she added, her tone indifferent, simmering with a hint of irritation as her hands sifted through the bags.

Malik's smile fell at the edge in her tone. "I left my lunch," he replied dryly, though his voice carried an undercurrent of annoyance now. He leaned against the doorway, his eyes narrowing as he watched her. Dionne, however, didn't care about his mood shift. She just wanted to find her purse and leave.

"Where are you going?" Malik asked again, his voice now sharp and demanding. Dionne froze for a split second before resuming her search for her purse, her movements brisk and deliberate. She was already late and didn't have the patience to engage in yet another confrontation.

"Business dinner," she replied, her tone flat, devoid of any interest in elaborating. She kept her focus on rifling through her things, avoiding the tension in the room.

Malik's jaw tightened, the veins in his neck subtly flexing as his eyes traveled over her. Admiration flickered momentarily, but it was quickly swallowed by suspicion. "Dressed like that?" he asked, his voice low but charged, a mixture of irritation and curiosity.

Dionne stopped, finally turning to face him. Her glare was fierce, cutting through the thin veil of control he was trying to maintain. "Yes," she said, her voice steady but simmering with restrained frustration. "There's nothing wrong with what I have on. And for your information, I'm meeting the girls afterward." Her words were clipped, but the way her hands clenched and unclenched at her sides betrayed the storm bubbling beneath her calm exterior.

Malik's gaze hardened, his teeth gritting as he processed her response. The way she brushed him off felt like a slap to his ego, and the tension between them thickened. "You didn't think to tell me?" he asked, his tone low but edged with accusation.

Dionne exhaled sharply, her frustration flaring. "Tell you? Malik, I'm not asking for permission to handle my business," she shot back, her voice rising slightly before she forced it back down, aware of how close she was to completely unraveling. She turned away from him, resuming her search with a renewed sense of urgency.

His gaze shifted to her left hand, and his brows furrowed. "Where's your ring?" he asked, his voice sharp.

Dionne froze, glancing down at her hand. She hadn't realized until now that she wasn't wearing it. She'd taken it off that morning before her run and had forgotten to put it back on. "I took it off when I went running this morning and forgot to put it back on," she said casually, her tone dismissive as she returned to her search.

"That's your excuse?" Malik's voice rose slightly, the defensiveness clear. "So you went all day not noticing you weren't wearing your engagement ring?"

Dionne sighed internally, already annoyed by his sudden need to make something out of nothing. She walked to her jewelry box, grabbed the diamond ring, and slid it onto her finger without looking at him. "Happy now?" she asked flatly, holding up her hand briefly before continuing to look for her bag.

Malik didn't respond immediately, his jaw tightening as he watched her dismissive movements. "Whoever you're meeting better be worth this kind of effort," he said bitterly, his tone laced with jealousy and accusation.

Dionne stopped for a moment, turning to face him with a look that could cut glass. "It's business, Malik. You know—the thing I do every day to keep myself sane while you're never around," she snapped, her voice calm but sharp. "And I don't need your commentary right now. I'm already late."

"You could at least pretend to act like you want me," he shot back, his voice laced with hurt and irritation.

Dionne turned sharply, her eyes narrowing as a bitter chuckle escaped her lips. "Pretend?" she repeated, her tone rising. "That's the problem, Malik. I have been pretending. Pretending to be happy, pretending everything is fine, pretending we're this perfect couple for the sake of your mother, when we both know we're far from that."

Feenin'

Her words hung in the air, cutting through the tension like a blade. "I'm tired of pretending," Dionne admitted, her voice cracking slightly, betraying the vulnerability she so rarely showed.

Malik's expression softened as he took in her words. The strain in her voice, the slight tremble as she spoke, made his chest tighten. Despite everything, Malik loved her deeply. He knew their relationship had lost its spark, but hearing the raw truth from Dionne hurt in a way he hadn't prepared for.

"I—" Malik began, stepping closer to her, but Dionne instinctively backed away, holding up a hand to stop him.

"No, Malik. Don't," she said firmly, her voice steady but trembling with restrained emotion. She knew what he was about to do—he'd try to use his charm, his touch, to deflect from the real issues. And she wasn't going to let him. "Stop trying to fix this with gestures and empty words. It doesn't work anymore."

"I love you, Dionne. I know this is hard for you, but it's hard for me too," Malik said, his voice soft but firm as he towered over her, his presence overwhelming yet comforting. Her back pressed against the wall, and she looked up at him, her eyes meeting his. For a moment, she saw the vulnerability and hurt etched in his gaze. Despite all the resentment and frustration she carried, deep down, Dionne couldn't deny that she still had love for him. Malik was her first love, the man who had once made her heart race, and she knew beneath all the pressure and pretending, he still loved her too.

"Don't give up on me. On us," Malik pleaded, his voice dropping to an almost whisper. "I promise I'm going to make this better."

His words hung in the air, and Dionne could see the desperation in his eyes, the raw truth behind them. She nodded silently, her voice failing her as she struggled to process the emotions flooding her chest. She wanted to believe him, wanted to hold onto the small glimmers of love that still lingered between them.

Malik's hand gently cupped her cheek, and she melted into his touch, her resolve softening as she tried to cling to the remnants of their once-strong bond. "Stay with me," he whispered, his voice filled with both love and longing, before leaning down to press his lips against hers.

Dionne embraced the kiss, her hands instinctively gripping his shoulders, letting herself feel the passion that still flickered between them. It was a kiss that reminded her of the good times, of what they used to be. But as the sound of her phone vibrating on the dresser filled the room, reality crept back in.

"I have to go," Dionne said softly against his lips, breaking the kiss as their foreheads rested against each other.

Malik nodded, stepping back reluctantly, his hands lingering at her waist before letting go. "You look beautiful," he said, his tone genuine as his eyes roamed over her one last time.

No matter how strained their relationship had become, Malik always looked at her like she was the most beautiful woman in the world. It was the one constant, even when everything else between them felt uncertain.

"Thank you," Dionne replied, her voice steady but distant as she grabbed her keys and purse. She took a deep breath, composing herself before heading for the door, leaving behind the weight of the moment and hoping the evening ahead would provide some clarity—or at least a temporary escape.

"I won't be home tonight. I'll be staying at London's," Dionne said, her tone casual as she adjusted her purse strap. Malik nodded, though the thought of her leaving the house looking this good gnawed at him. He hated the idea of her being out in public, dressed like that, without him by her side.

Dionne's beauty was undeniable—striking in a way that turned heads wherever she went—and the thought of other men approaching her stirred unease in his chest. He knew he hadn't been the best partner for her lately, hadn't been the man she needed in a long time, and that realization only heightened his frustration. The idea of Dionne finding someone who could treat her better, love her better, terrified him. The knot in his chest tightened at the thought of losing her, but he kept his expression calm.

As she walked out the door, Malik's eyes followed her, catching the glint of the engagement ring still on her finger. That sight brought him a small sense of relief. At least the ring might serve as a warning—a silent declaration that she was spoken for, unavailable.

Still, he couldn't shake the nagging fear. He knew their relationship wasn't what it used to be, and he wasn't blind to the cracks that had been growing between them. He clenched his jaw, silently vowing to do whatever it took to keep her from slipping away—if only he could figure out how to fix the mess they were both stuck in.

Dionne slipped into her car and as soon as she settled, she slipped off the engagement ring, placing it in the console without a second thought. Their love felt hollow, a performance she was no longer willing to put on for the world. Why wear a symbol of something that no longer felt real?

She headed to the restaurant where she was meeting Arris. This dinner was meant to be brief—a chance to outline their partnership plans, learn more about one another professionally, and toast to what

Feenin'

they hoped would be a prosperous collaboration. The air of business and anticipation mingled as she drove through the city lights, her mind focused yet curious.

Pulling up to valet, Dionne gracefully exited her car, handing her keys to the attendant with a polite "thank you" before ascending the short set of steps to the restaurant entrance. The building's elegant lighting reflected off her glowing skin, highlighting her poised and polished appearance. She nodded at the two doormen who greeted her warmly, their smiles mirroring her own as she stepped inside.

The ambiance hit her instantly—sophistication met with understated luxury. The soft hum of quiet conversation, clinking glasses, and subtle jazz notes created a serene backdrop. Her sharp eyes swept the room before a man approached her. His caramel-toned skin, precision-cut waves, and tailored blue suit exuded professionalism, his welcoming smile adding a touch of charm.

"Welcome, Ms. Smith," he greeted with confident ease.

Dionne returned his smile, nodding. "Thank you."

"My name is Martin, and I'm the head manager here," he introduced, his tone polished but friendly. "We've prepared a private booth for you and Mr. Black."

"Perfect," Dionne replied, appreciating his professionalism as he gestured for her to follow.

Martin led her through the restaurant, weaving between tables adorned with sparkling glassware and immaculate place settings. They arrived at a secluded booth tucked into the back of the restaurant. It offered an exquisite view of the city skyline through floor-to-ceiling windows, the twinkling lights casting a romantic glow over the table.

Arris sat at the table, his focus glued to his phone, oblivious to Dionne's approach. She took the opportunity to admire him, allowing her gaze to trace over his every detail. The restaurant's warm light reflected off his perfect waves, giving them an almost ethereal glow. His tailored brown suit hugged his muscular frame, with a crisp white button-down beneath it, two buttons undone to reveal a glimpse of his chest and the tattoos teasing beneath the fabric. The subtle shine of the two chains resting against his skin added to his effortless allure.

"Mr. Black, Ms. Smith has arrived," Martin announced smoothly, pulling Arris's attention from his phone.

Arris looked up, their eyes locking instantly. Dionne caught the slight hitch in his breath as he took in her appearance. His sharp gaze softened, approval clear in the way he looked at her. He rose swiftly, his movements smooth and respectful, an automatic reflex.

"Thank you, Martin," Arris said confidently, dismissing the manager with a nod. Martin left quietly, leaving them in the intimacy of their booth.

"Hey, Arris. Sorry I'm late," Dionne greeted, her voice soft yet steady as she approached.

"Your presence is always on time, Ms. Smith," Arris replied smoothly, his smile widening as his eyes openly admired her from head to toe. His unwavering gaze sent a shiver down her spine—not just because of the way he looked at her but because of the way his words rendered her speechless. Still, she maintained her confident posture, though her heart raced beneath the surface.

This man's words! He knows he's fine. She thought to herself, but she couldn't help the smile tugging at her lips as she noticed him subtly licking his own. With effortless charm, he motioned for her to take a seat across from him, his presence as magnetic as ever.

Dionne slid gracefully into the booth, her presence commanding yet relaxed. Arris called for their server and ordered a bottle of the restaurant's best wine before they turned their attention to business.

"I know you're a busy man, so I'll make this quick," Dionne started, diving into the matter at hand.

Arris chuckled lightly, his deep tone reverberating in the cozy space. "No need to rush, Dionne. My time is all yours, as long as you need it," he said confidently, his gaze never wavering from hers.

The brief pause in her composure was barely noticeable before she recovered, her professionalism intact. She handed him a folder thick with contracts. "Here are the agreements we discussed," she began as Arris opened the file and started scanning the documents. "This outlines everything: your $15 million upfront, our 70-30 equity split, and Williams Luxe taking full charge of project execution, from design to marketing."

As Dionne explained, her voice laced with conviction, Arris's focus shifted between the contracts and her. He scribbled his signature on each dotted line, his movements deliberate and assured. Something about her captivated him beyond the business aspect. It wasn't just her beauty—though undeniable—it was her confidence, her precision, the way she owned every moment in the room.

"I have to hand it to you, Dionne. You know how to make a man agree to things he wasn't planning on," Arris said, leaning back in his chair, exuding confidence as his eyes studied her intently.

Dionne set her glass down after taking a sip, a sly smile gracing her lips. "I don't just make people agree, Arris. I make them realize what

Feenin'

they've been missing. Blac needs Williams Luxe. You need me," she replied, her voice smooth, her confidence radiating.

Arris mirrored her smile, his thoughts drifting away from the business at hand to the woman sitting across from him. You have no clue, he thought, more intrigued by her with each passing moment. Something about Dionne pulled him in closer, an unspoken magnetism he couldn't ignore. As they continued to talk over food and wine, her wit, poise, and sharp intellect only heightened his fascination.

"You're dangerous, Dionne. I like that," Arris said, his voice dropping an octave as his gaze lingered, his tongue subtly running across his lips.

Dionne felt his words and the intensity of his gaze wash over her, sending a rush of warmth through her body. Still, she maintained her professional demeanor, sitting poised, her confidence unshaken. "I'm efficient," she said, tilting her head slightly. "And now, we're partners. Here's to building a legacy." She raised her glass, her smile unwavering.

Arris chuckled, his admiration for her growing with every word she spoke. "To a legacy," he echoed, raising his glass to meet hers. The clink of their glasses seemed to carry more weight than just a toast—it felt like the beginning of something significant.

"But we're more than just partners," Arris said with his usual confident smirk, his eyes locked on hers.

Dionne mirrored his smirk, resting her chin on her hands as she stared back at him, her charm on full display. "Oh really?" she asked, her tone light but laced with a playful challenge.

Arris chuckled, the sound deep and smooth, but he didn't let her throw him off. "We're friends," he declared, his confidence unwavering. The simplicity of his words struck Dionne, stirring butterflies she hadn't felt in a long time. She hadn't expected him to call her his friend—they'd just met, after all—but something about the title felt natural, even comforting.

"Well, cheers to friends," Dionne said, raising her glass with a warm smile.

Arris clinked his glass against hers, his eyes never leaving hers as he echoed her sentiment. "Friends."

They both sipped their wine, their eyes locking over the rims of their glasses, a shared smile breaking through as they set them down. For a brief moment, they laughed softly, the sound light and genuine, like two people discovering an unspoken connection amidst the professional façade.

Arris and Dionne shifted their conversation to lighter topics, letting business fade into the background, while they enjoy their delicious meals. "So, a baseball pitcher, huh?" Dionne asked, curiosity laced in her voice as she leaned forward slightly. She was intrigued by the glimpse he'd given her into his upbringing.

Arris smirked, leaning back in his chair, his gaze steady on her. "Yeah. Sound surprised?" he replied, his voice smooth and teasing.

"A little," Dionne admitted, her lips curving into a soft smile. "I would've pegged you as a basketball or football player."

Arris tilted his head, clearly intrigued. "And why's that?" he asked, lifting his wine glass to take a slow sip.

She hesitated for a moment, her cheeks warming. "Your physique, I guess," she said, her voice softer, a hint of shyness creeping in. She quickly dropped her gaze to her plate, but not before he caught her lingering glance.

"You're tall and... toned," she added, carefully choosing her words. She didn't dare let her thoughts slip into anything less than professional, though her heart betrayed her with its quickened pace.

Arris chuckled, his deep voice sending a ripple of warmth through her. "I played those sports too," he admitted, "but baseball was the one I loved the most."

Dionne nodded, her smile widening. "That makes sense. Baseball has this... strategy to it. It suits you."

"My brother also loved baseball," Dionne continued, her voice tinged with warmth as a small smile played on her lips. "Played a few years in the league too, and he thrives off strategy." She chuckled softly, the pride evident in her tone as memories of her older brother Demetrius flickered through her mind.

"Sounds like a smart man," Arris replied, his gaze fixed on her with genuine interest. He could see the way her expression softened, the pride and love for her brother shining through her words. It wasn't just her smile—it was the way her voice carried a certain lightness, as if Demetrius's success was her own personal triumph.

"Smart doesn't even begin to cover it," Dionne continued, her eyes briefly glazing over with nostalgia. "He's always had this way of reading people, knowing the next move before it even happens. Baseball was just another game of strategy for him." Her chuckle deepened as she added, "And he'll remind you of it every chance he gets."

Arris grinned at her playful tone. "Baseball has a way of doing that. It's more than just running bases and home runs."

Dionne tilted her head, her smile growing. "You sound just like him." Her laugh was light, and for a brief moment, she seemed to forget everything else weighing on her shoulders.

Feenin'

The conversation flowed effortlessly as she shared snippets of her own background, from her high school days on the track team to her love of soccer in college. Her passion was evident, and Arris found himself drawn to the way her eyes lit up as she spoke.

"So why'd you pick this spot tonight?" Arris asked, his tone casual, though curiosity flickered in his gaze. "I remember seeing you here last week... with someone." His voice trailed off slightly, and she caught the hesitation in his tone.

Dionne chuckled softly, immediately knowing he was referring to Malik. "This is my favorite place," she explained, her voice warm with genuine affection. "The food, the vibe, the music—it's all perfect here."

Arris smiled, leaning forward slightly. "What if I told you I owned this place?" he asked, his words carrying a subtle mix of pride and mystery.

Her eyes widened in genuine surprise. "You own this?" she asked, her tone incredulous.

He chuckled, nodding. "Yeah. When I moved back, I bought the building. It was run-down, abandoned—a place for drugs and trouble. I saw potential and decided to turn it into something... better."

Dionne's smile grew as she admired him, her voice filled with pride for his accomplishment. "You did good, Arris. Real good."

"Appreciate that," he said, his confidence shining through.

"I come here all the time," she added. "It's good to know it's owned by a black man. Makes me like it even more."

Arris's smile deepened, but the memory of seeing her with Malik the week before lingered in his mind. The question had been eating at him since then, and his curiosity got the better of him. "So," he began, his voice steady but direct, "you got a man?"

The bluntness of his question made Dionne choke slightly on her wine. She composed herself quickly, though, her mind briefly flashing to Malik. Technically, she wasn't single, but she didn't feel like she was in a relationship either. Her hand, bare of the engagement ring she only wore around him and his mother, caught her attention.

"That area of my life is... complicated," she said simply, her voice steady but guarded.

Arris picked up on the subtle shift in her tone and nodded, his expression softening. "My bad. Didn't mean to step into something personal," he said sincerely.

Dionne offered a small, masked smile. "No need to apologize," she replied lightly. "It's just... life, huh?" She let out a small, awkward laugh, though she could tell by the way Arris's gaze lingered that he wasn't entirely convinced by her attempt to brush it off.

He nodded slowly, his eyes locked on hers, as if trying to decipher what she wasn't saying. "Life has a way of getting complicated," he said softly.

And in that moment, despite the lighthearted nature of their earlier conversation, there was an unspoken understanding between them—something deeper simmering just below the surface.

The conversation shifted to a lighter tone, filled with laughter and easy exchanges. As Dionne's phone rang, she glanced at the screen and saw her friends calling. A flicker of guilt crossed her face as she realized she'd completely forgotten their plans. She had been so immersed in the moment with Arris that time slipped away from her.

"Oh no, I totally forgot—I was supposed to meet my friends tonight," she said, her tone slightly frantic as she typed out a quick text, apologizing and letting them know she was on her way.

Arris observed her with a calm intensity, his gaze unwavering. He could see the urgency in her movements, but deep down, he wasn't ready to let her leave just yet. Her presence was a rare kind of solace for him, one that made the weight of his responsibilities and personal struggles seem a little lighter. For a brief moment, Dionne made him forget about everything—the pressures of business, the unresolved tension with his father, and the endless expectations that came with being him.

"How about this," Arris said, leaning forward slightly, his voice low and steady. "Invite your friends here, and let me give you all the full Vault experience."

Dionne froze, his suggestion catching her off guard. The smoothness in his voice, combined with the intensity of his gaze, sent a flutter through her stomach. "Are you sure? I don't want us imposing on your evening," she said, her tone polite yet hesitant.

Arris chuckled softly, leaning back in his seat with an easy confidence. "Impose? Dionne, I own the place. My night is whatever I want it to be. And right now, I want to make sure you and your friends have a great time."

His words, spoken with such assuredness, left little room for argument. Dionne hesitated briefly before nodding, her lips curving into a small smile. "Alright. Let me text them and let them know."

As she messaged her friends, Arris couldn't help but admire her. The way she carried herself, the way her smile lit up the space between them—it all held him captive in ways he couldn't fully understand.

Arris stood, his tall frame commanding attention as he walked around the table, extending his hand toward Dionne. "Let me show you

Feenin'

a good time tonight," he said, his smooth voice laced with a confidence that made her pulse quicken. His gaze locked on hers, unwavering and intentional, as he waited patiently for her to take his hand.

Dionne hesitated for only a moment. Once the message was sent, she slipped her hand into his, and he guided her out of the booth. His grip was firm yet gentle, grounding her as he led her upstairs.

The scene changed dramatically as they stepped into the club's upper level. Security immediately parted for them upon recognizing Arris, their deference making it clear who he was. The once intimate, elegant ambiance of the restaurant downstairs gave way to a high-energy atmosphere. Music pulsed through the air, lights flickered rhythmically, and the room buzzed with people dancing and laughing, lost in the night's revelry.

Dionne's eyes widened as she took in the transformation. "I've been coming here for years," she said, her voice tinged with awe, "and I had no idea this was here."

Arris's hand tightened slightly around hers as they navigated the bustling crowd, ensuring she didn't get lost in the sea of people. Dionne couldn't help but notice his quiet protectiveness, an unexpected gesture that made her heart flutter. As they reached a spacious section overlooking the dance floor, a striking woman with a sleek bob approached them, her smile polished and professional.

"Hey boss. Everything's running smoothly," China greeted, her tone respectful and efficient.

"China," Arris began, his business demeanor taking over, "reserve this section for the night. No one comes in except me, her, and her friends."

China nodded, her sharp eyes flickering to Dionne for a brief moment before returning to Arris. "Got it. Full Vault experience, too?" she asked, a smirk tugging at her lips.

Arris glanced at Dionne, his own smirk mirroring China's as he answered. "Absolutely. Show her how it's done."

China nodded and walked off, her smirk lingering, leaving Dionne watching the interaction with a mix of curiosity and amusement. She turned to Arris, who now faced her fully, his smile as smooth as his words.

"You don't have to go through all this trouble," Dionne said, her voice soft but firm as she gestured toward the exclusive section he'd claimed for her.

Arris leaned in slightly, his presence magnetic. "Let me show you something different tonight," he replied, his voice low and inviting, his hand still securely holding hers. His confidence radiated, making it impossible to look away.

Dionne's resolve wavered under his gaze, but her own boldness flared. "You better not disappoint. We're not easy to impress," she teased, her tone daring.

Arris chuckled, leaning closer until their faces were mere inches apart. His eyes held a spark that mirrored her fire. "Just sit down mama and let me work," he said, his words deliberate and charged.

Mama? The nickname Arris used to call her sent an involuntary shiver down Dionne's spine. His smooth, deep voice carried both familiarity and an intensity that left her momentarily speechless.

The name rolled off his lips with a tone so smooth and sexy that Dionne couldn't bring herself to tell him to address her differently. Something about the way he said it made her feel a mix of power and surrender all at once. She didn't understand what it was about this man that made her yield so effortlessly, but every word he spoke, every move he made, had her stuck in his grasp every single time.

She remained silent, caught off guard by the way that single word seemed to tether her to him, reigniting emotions she thought she could control. Without realizing it, her body betrayed her, unconsciously submitting to the demand in his tone. Something about the way he said it made her feel seen, wanted, and entirely vulnerable all at once.

The air between them thickened with an intense tension. Dionne felt her pulse race, but she forced herself to remain grounded. He was captivating, no doubt, but she wasn't one to lose control. Not with a man like Arris Black.

The corner of his mouth lifted in a satisfied smirk as he straightened. For a fleeting moment, Dionne allowed herself to enjoy the feeling of his presence, but she quickly reminded herself who she was—and who she wasn't. Whatever magnetic pull Arris had over her, she was determined not to let it take her anywhere she couldn't return from.

Before Dionne could respond, the unmistakable sound of her friends approaching pulled her attention. "Hey, bitch!" London's vibrant energy practically matched the electrified atmosphere of the club as she strode over. Arris remained unmoved, his hand still firmly intertwined with Dionne's, even as her head turned toward her friends. Both London and Karmen immediately noticed the interaction, their curious looks quickly morphing into knowing smiles.

"Hey, y'all," Dionne greeted, her voice slightly shaky, still tethered to the charged moment she shared with Arris. Yet, she hesitated to pull her hand away. Karmen's eyes darted pointedly to their hands, her brows

Feenin'

raising in silent question. Catching her friend's look, Dionne finally released Arris's hand, breaking the connection. She discreetly rubbed her palm against her side, as if trying to calm the lingering buzz from his touch.

London's sharp gaze flicked between Dionne and Arris before her signature smirk appeared. "Are you going to introduce us to your... friend?" she teased, her tone dripping with playful insinuation. Dionne rolled her eyes at her friend's antics, but Arris only chuckled, his confidence unwavering.

"Arris, these are my two best friends," Dionne began, motioning toward Karmen first. "This is Karmen."

Karmen stepped forward, dressed in True Religion jeans paired with a matching cropped top that perfectly showcased her toned stomach. Her boho knotless braids were styled half-up, half-down, accentuating her natural beauty. She smiled warmly, extending her hand. "Nice to meet you, Arris," she said softly as they shook hands.

"And this," Dionne continued, gesturing toward her other friend, "is London."

London's commanding presence matched her backless brown dress, which hugged her figure perfectly. Gold heels adorned her feet, and her striking ginger wig added an extra flair to her already bold aura. She grinned at Arris, shaking his hand with a firm confidence. "Pleasure to meet you," London said, her voice smooth but edged with curiosity.

"This is Arris Black," Dionne said, her tone holding a hint of pride. "The owner of this place." She couldn't help the smile that crossed her lips as she introduced him.

Arris met her gaze, mirroring her smile with one of his own. The mutual respect between them was strong, but so was something more—a subtle energy neither of them could deny.

"Ah, so you're the man behind the magic," London said, her tone playful yet genuine. "This place is fire."

"Appreciate that," Arris replied smoothly, his eyes briefly flicking back to Dionne before addressing both women. "I hope you all enjoy the full experience tonight. Your girl here is special—I'm making sure you get the VIP treatment."

London shot a knowing glance at Karmen, who bit her lip to suppress a smile. "Special, huh?" London mused, her teasing nature fully on display.

Dionne groaned inwardly, shooting a warning look at her friend. "Don't start," she muttered under her breath, earning a laugh from Arris.

"It's nice meeting you, ladies. Enjoy the night. This entire section is reserved for you all. The bartenders will be around to get you anything you need," Arris said, his confidence evident as he addressed Dionne's friends with ease. Karmen and London exchanged a knowing look, both impressed by his charm and professionalism.

Then Arris turned his attention back to Dionne, leaning in closer. His hand lightly rested on the small of her back, sending an involuntary shiver down her spine. His voice dropped low as he whispered near her ear, "Enjoy your night, beautiful. I'll be back."

Dionne nodded, her breath hitching slightly, unable to form words. His lingering touch and the intimacy in his tone left her flustered, even as her friends stood silently observing the heated tension between them. Arris walked away confidently, leaving Dionne reeling from his presence.

London, ever the bold one, broke the silence. "Girl! Who was that man?! He is fine, and he is definitely into you," she exclaimed, her tone a mix of excitement and curiosity.

Dionne rolled her eyes, trying to shake off the lingering effect of Arris's touch. "He's just a business partner. Williams Luxe is working with his on a new project. That's the dinner I told y'all I had before coming out," she said, sitting down as the bartenders approached to taking their drink orders.

"Bitch, please!" London shot back. "You said dinner, not foreplay! Y'all looked like you were in love—or like you just finished fucking in the nearest office," she said, her words sending Dionne into a fit of laughter.

Karmen, usually the quieter one, chimed in, her voice soft but certain. "She's not wrong, Dee. He was looking at you like you were the only woman in the room."

Dionne waved them off, trying to downplay the moment, though her cheeks burned at their comments. "It's not like that," she protested, though even she wasn't convinced by her own words.

Despite her outward dismissal, Dionne couldn't ignore the way Arris's presence lingered. His touch, his voice, his gaze—they were imprinted in her mind, no matter how much she tried to push him out. She took a sip of her drink, determined to let loose and enjoy the night with her friends. Still, a part of her couldn't help but wonder what it would mean to indulge in the thrill that Arris seemed to promise, despite the chaos already present in her life.

"You two need to chill. Arris and I are just business partners. Nothing more. Did you two forget, I'm engaged!" Dionne said, her voice firm, though her true feelings bubbled beneath the surface.

Feenin'

"No, but clearly you did," London quipped back, a smirk tugging at her lips.

Dionne's brows furrowed. "What are you talking about?"

"You don't even have on your engagement ring," London pointed out, crossing her arms. "You haven't worn it for a while now."

Dionne instinctively glanced down at her bare ring finger, cursing London's sharp observation.

"You and Malik are good, right?" Karmen chimed in, her tone soft but laced with concern. She adored the idea of Dionne and Malik's love story, holding onto the version she'd known since their college days. What she didn't know was how drastically things had changed.

"Yes, girl. We're good," Dionne lied smoothly, forcing a reassuring smile. "It's just getting cleaned right now. I'll pick it up from the jeweler tomorrow."

"Oh, you had me worried for a second," Karmen said, visibly relaxing. "Everyone's rooting for you and Malik."

Everyone but me, Dionne thought bitterly, keeping her fake smile intact. The last thing she wanted was to delve into her crumbling relationship. This night was supposed to be her escape, not a reminder of her discontent.

"Can we stop talking about my love life for once?" Dionne said, grabbing her drink and raising it in the air. "Tonight is about taking shots and getting litty for the one time. Remember? College days revisited?"

"You right! Let's turn the fuck up!" London exclaimed, her energy instantly lifting the mood.

Dionne chuckled, relieved the conversation shifted. For the rest of the night, she let herself get lost in the music, the laughter, and the drinks. True to his word, Arris delivered on his promise, ensuring Dionne and her friends had an unforgettable night. He watched from a distance, subtly keeping an eye on her while giving her space to enjoy herself. For the first time in a long time, Dionne felt free, letting the night wash away her worries—even if only temporarily.

Dionne and Arris even shared a dance that night, a fleeting yet magnetic moment that neither would soon forget. The rhythm of the music seemed to guide them closer, the space between their bodies charged with an unspoken connection. While the alcohol coursing through their veins played a part, it couldn't take full credit for the chemistry that ignited between them. That brief moment on the dance floor became an unplanned escape, a reprieve from the weight of their worlds.

For the first time in what felt like forever, Dionne allowed herself to let go. The arrangement with Malik, the growing distance between them, and the demands of her career faded into the background. The music, her friends, the thrill of the club, and, most of all, Arris, pulled her into a moment of pure, unfiltered joy. It was a night of fun, freedom, and bliss—a reminder of the vibrant woman she still was beneath the facade she wore daily.

Arris felt it too. For the first time in years, his thoughts weren't consumed by business deals, tight schedules, or the resentment bubbling from his father's unexpected return. Tonight, all he saw, all he felt, was Dionne. Her smile, her laugh, the way she moved—it captivated him. It was rare for someone to shake his focus, but with Dionne, he wasn't just distracted—he was drawn in.

As the night wound down, and Dionne's laughter lingered in the air, Arris couldn't deny the pull he felt toward her. Tonight, he'd seen glimpses of the woman behind the professional poise, and now he craved more. More of her smile, her energy, her presence. She was a mystery he wasn't ready to walk away from, and the thought of getting to know her further was suddenly all he wanted.

Chapter 4

Dionne walked into the bakery with Malik's mother, Glen, walking beside her. Today was another day of playing her role—the doting fiancée, excited to marry the love of her life. But the weight of the charade sat heavy on her shoulders. This cake tasting, something that should have been a joyful milestone for a bride-to-be, felt like just another task in a long line of obligations. She was here not because she wanted to be, but because it meant everything to Glen, a woman she loved dearly despite the fractured state of her relationship with Malik.

"Dionne, sweetie, I think you should go with a red velvet cake," Glen said with a bright smile, her eyes lighting up as though she'd just solved an important puzzle.

Dionne forced a warm smile, masking her inner reluctance. Red velvet was one of her least favorite flavors, but it wasn't about her preferences today. "That's not a bad idea," she replied, her voice even and pleasant. "Let's see what options they have first, Mama Glen." Dionne's tone was as genuine as she could muster, and her smile mirrored Glen's affectionately, even though it didn't reach her eyes.

Glen beamed at her, her admiration for Dionne evident. "I can't wait for you and my son to be married," she said, her voice brimming with warmth and excitement.

Dionne nodded, her practiced smile firmly in place. She knew how much Glen adored her, how much she had admired her from the moment Malik brought Dionne home during their Thanksgiving break in college. Glen had often told her she knew instantly that Dionne was "the one" for her son. She loved Dionne's beauty, her intelligence, her relentless drive. To Glen, Dionne was the perfect woman to love, support, and challenge her son in all the right ways.

But what Glen didn't know—what Dionne was determined to keep hidden—was that the love she once felt for Malik had long since faded. She adored Glen as if she were her own mother, but the weight of the expectations placed on her, the pressure to fulfill a promise she no longer believed in, gnawed at her daily. Even now, as Glen chatted excitedly about cake flavors and wedding themes, Dionne's mind was elsewhere. It wasn't just the cake she was here to taste—it was the bitter reality of pretending to be something she no longer was.

Still, Dionne swallowed her discontent, masking her turmoil with the perfect façade Glen expected. As the bakery host approached to guide them through the tasting, Dionne braced herself for another performance.

"Welcome to *Sweeties Bakery*! You're here for the cake tasting, correct?" the hostess greeted warmly, her professional tone paired with a wide, inviting smile.

Dionne returned the smile, though hers was slightly smaller, more controlled. "Yes, it's for a wedding," she confirmed, her tone polite and composed.

The hostess's eyes lit up as she clasped her hands together. "Wonderful! Congratulations on the engagement. I just love seeing young love," she said warmly, her enthusiasm practically radiating off her.

Mama Glen mirrored the hostess's bright smile, her pride evident. Dionne, on the other hand, managed a polite smile, one that didn't quite reach her eyes but was enough to maintain the facade.

"Right this way," the hostess gestured, leading them to a cozy table adorned with an array of elegant cake samples. "I'll be back shortly with more options for you to try."

Dionne and Glen sat down, and soon the table was filled with a variety of beautifully crafted cakes. Each slice seemed like a work of art, but every time Dionne found something she liked, Glen had a reason to veto it.

"This one's far too sweet. Malik's not big on sweets," Glen said after tasting a fruity option.

"Chocolate? Oh, no, Malik isn't much of a chocolate person," she added with a shake of her head when Dionne suggested a rich chocolate truffle cake.

"Maybe a vanilla cake would be better. He's always liked vanilla," Glen concluded, her tone cheerful yet firm.

Dionne's frustration simmered beneath the surface as she forced herself to remain calm. Every comment Glen made revolved around Malik's preferences, leaving little room for Dionne's own input. Weddings were supposed to be a bride's dream day, but to Dionne, it felt

Feenin'

like this entire process was tailored to fulfill Malik's and Glen's desires.

As the hostess returned with another tray of options, Glen was mid-sentence, recounting a story about Malik as a child, further centering the conversation on him. Dionne leaned back slightly, her hands folded neatly in her lap, and forced herself to take a deep breath. She reminded herself why she was here—for Mama Glen, the woman who had shown her unconditional love, even if her son didn't anymore.

The next set of cakes arrived, and as Dionne picked up her fork to taste a new flavor, she silently prayed for patience. This wasn't about her, and deep down, she had always known that. But knowing didn't make it any easier to swallow.

"Malik tells me that you two haven't been active in the bedroom lately," Mama Glen said abruptly, catching Dionne completely off guard. She choked on the piece of cake she was eating, coughing as she struggled to regain her composure.

The unexpected remark about her and Malik's sex life floored her. Especially coming from his mother. "We've both just been a little busy with our careers," Dionne explained once she managed to settle herself, her tone calm despite the sudden heat in her cheeks.

"Yes, but you two still need to make time for each other," Mama Glen pressed, her tone laced with the maternal concern Dionne often found more overbearing than endearing. Dionne subtly rolled her eyes, masking her irritation with a sip of water. Here came the unsolicited advice she'd grown accustomed to.

"Malik mentioned you've been spending more time at the office than usual," Mama Glen added, her words causing Dionne to glance up sharply.

Of course, he did. She thought bitterly. Dionne felt blindsided, her irritation bubbling to the surface. So, he could confide in his mother about his feelings, but not her? The irony wasn't lost on her.

"Well, I suppose he forgot to mention his own long hours at the hospital," Dionne said, her calm voice edged with a simmering frustration. She kept her tone polite, but her words carried a clear undertone.

Mama Glen, ever the mediator for her son, pressed on. "He did mention the hospital's demands, but he also said he misses you, Dionne. He feels like you two aren't connected anymore, and that's a problem when you're so close to getting married."

The words stung. Not because they were untrue, but because Dionne had been feeling the exact same thing—only she didn't have the luxury of pretending their disconnection was temporary. *We're not connected* because there's no love left to connect us, she thought grimly but kept to herself.

"I wish he'd talk to me about how he feels instead of you," Dionne said, her irritation more apparent now. She met Mama Glen's gaze, hoping the message was clear: these conversations belonged between her and Malik.

"He's just worried, sweetie," Mama Glen replied, her voice softer now. "You know Malik doesn't always express himself the way he should."

Always making excuses for him, Dionne thought, clenching her jaw.

"He loves you, Dee," Mama Glen continued, placing a warm hand over Dionne's. "And I know you love him. Don't give up on him, baby. You two are going to have a beautiful marriage and give me some beautiful grandchildren."

She didn't know what she and Malik shared anymore, but it was far from the love they once had in college. Back then, they were young, free, and deeply in love. Now, the mere thought of having kids was something Dionne didn't even want to consider, let alone discuss. The weight of their forced engagement already felt suffocating, and the idea of bringing a child into this hollow relationship was out of the question. It would only complicate an already fragile situation.

Dionne managed a polite smile, though it didn't reflect how she truly felt. Her facade quickly shattered, however, when Mama Glen spoke again, her words cutting like a blade. "I want at least one grandchild before God calls me home. I already talked to Malik, and he said you two were working on having one."

The statement hit Dionne like a gut punch, her smile vanishing instantly. Her blood simmered beneath her calm exterior as she processed what she'd just heard. Malik had told his mother what? The lies he'd spun about starting a family enraged her. Malik knew exactly how she felt about children—she wasn't ready. Not now. Not in this strained and loveless arrangement they were both pretending was a real relationship.

She forced out a chuckle, shaking her head, though there was no amusement behind it. "Oh, really?" she asked, her voice dripping with sarcasm, her composure cracking. Mama Glen, either missing or ignoring Dionne's tone, continued, her excitement undeterred.

"Yes," Mama Glen said brightly, clasping her hands together. "You two need to put your careers on hold for a moment and give me a grandbaby."

Dionne's polite mask slipped further, though she managed a faint, strained smile to mask her frustration. Inside, she was fuming. Put

Feenin'

my career on hold? For this charade? she thought bitterly. The idea of sacrificing everything she'd built for herself just to satisfy a lie Malik had told was infuriating.

She nodded along, silently seething as Mama Glen rambled on about her hopes for their future family. But her thoughts were elsewhere, laser-focused on Malik. He knew better than to make such a monumental decision for both of them, let alone share it with his mother before even talking to her.

Dionne clenched her jaw, her mind already crafting the confrontation she'd have with Malik later. He needed to understand that this—all of this—was already more than she could handle. Adding a child to the equation wasn't just unreasonable; it was impossible. And she wasn't about to let him, or anyone else, force her into something so life-altering.

This wasn't love. This wasn't what she wanted. And no amount of pretending could change that.

"I'll talk to him about it," Dionne said, masking her inner frustration with a smile that didn't quite reach her eyes. She spent the rest of the cake tasting pretending to be engaged in the process, nodding along and offering polite commentary as Mama Glen continued her cheerful chatter. They finally settled on a cake—a compromise that satisfied Malik's supposed preferences, Mama Glen's excitement, and was just tolerable enough for Dionne to accept without further argument.

As the tasting wrapped up, Dionne felt a weight lift, knowing she'd soon escape the suffocating role she had to play as the doting fiancée. After ensuring Mama Glen got home safely and exchanging pleasantries she didn't feel, Dionne took a deep breath as she drove away, desperate for a reprieve.

Her mind was racing, her frustration simmering beneath the surface. She needed a moment of normalcy, a break from the wedding charade and Malik's endless demands. With that thought, she decided to visit Karmen at work. A little time with her best friend was exactly what she needed to clear her head and vent about everything weighing her down.

Gripping the wheel, Dionne felt a sense of relief wash over her as she steered toward Karmen's workplace. For once, she wouldn't have to pretend. She could just be herself.

As Dionne walked through the quiet halls of the elementary school, she finally reached Karmen's classroom. The day had finally drawn to a close, the hallways of the school now eerily quiet. Only a handful of teachers and staff lingered, their focus shifted to tying up loose ends and meticulously planning for the weeks ahead. It was the first week of the school year, and the weight of fresh beginnings hung in the air.

Peeking inside, Dionne saw Karmen seated at her desk, her head bent over a stack of papers. Across the room, a little girl sat quietly at a table, completely engrossed in her coloring book.

"Hey, boo," Dionne called softly, grabbing Karmen's attention. Karmen looked up, her face lighting up with a radiant smile when she spotted her best friend.

"Hey, girl!" Karmen responded warmly, standing to greet her with a hug.

"I thought you were done for the day," Dionne said, her brow furrowed as she glanced at the little girl. The child seemed vaguely familiar, but Dionne couldn't place where she had seen her before.

Karmen followed her friend's gaze and smiled. "Oh, I am. Just waiting on someone to come pick her up," she said casually, returning to her desk to resume grading papers.

Dionne's concern grew. "School ended almost an hour ago. Have you been able to reach anyone?" she asked, glancing back at the little girl.

"Yeah, I talked to her dad," Karmen replied, her tone as calm and unbothered as ever. "He's on his way now. Apparently, there was a mix-up—her mom was supposed to pick her up, but she never showed."

Dionne frowned slightly, her protective instincts kicking in as she glanced back at the little girl. "Poor thing," she murmured.

Karmen shrugged lightly, her warm smile never fading. "She's been good, though. Quiet, just coloring and keeping herself entertained."

Before Dionne could respond, the ringing of Karmen's classroom phone interrupted them. Karmen picked it up, listening for a moment before hanging up. She turned her attention to the little girl, her tone gentle and sweet. "Mia, sweetie, get your things. Your dad is here to pick you up."

Mia's face lit up at the mention of her father, her eyes sparkling with excitement. Karmen smiled warmly at the little girl's reaction, and Dionne couldn't help but mirror it. The bond between Mia and her father was evident, and it reminded Dionne of how hearing her own dad's name used to bring her joy.

Karmen walked Mia to the front office, Dionne trailing behind. As they approached, Dionne was surprised to see the same man who had walked into London's shop a few days earlier. Recognition hit instantly—the man who had been admiring Karmen then was now standing before them, waiting for his daughter.

"I'm sorry for coming so late. I hope it didn't interfere with the rest of your day," Mario said, his tone apologetic but warm.

Karmen chuckled, shaking her head lightly. "No need to apologize.

Feenin'

It just gave me and Mia here some time to get to know each other," she replied, smiling down at the little girl who was now clutching her father's hand tightly.

"Daddy, Ms. Moore gave me a sticker for getting all the questions right. And I got candy!" Mia said, her excitement bubbling over. Mario grinned at his daughter before glancing back at Karmen.

"I hope that was okay," Karmen said hesitantly. "I checked to make sure she didn't have any allergies before giving it to her."

Mario's smile widened, clearly appreciating her thoughtfulness. "Oh, no. That's fine. Thank you again," he replied, his tone sincere. He crouched down to lift Mia onto his neck, making her squeal with delight.

Karmen watched their interaction, her expression soft. Dionne, standing nearby, observed the scene with a small smile of her own. However, she couldn't miss the way Mario's gaze lingered on Karmen, filled with quiet admiration.

"Have a good rest of your day, Ms. Moore," Mario said, his voice smooth as he locked eyes with her.

"You too, Mr. Lovett," Karmen replied softly, her smile matching his.

"Bye, Ms. Moore! Bye, her pretty friend!" Mia chimed in, waving enthusiastically. Her innocent remark drew laughter from both women.

"Bye, Mia," Karmen said with a laugh, while Dionne waved.

Mario gave Karmen one last look, a flicker of something unreadable passing through his eyes, before acknowledging Dionne with a polite nod. Then, with Mia giggling on his neck, he turned and walked out of the school.

Karmen watched him leave, her gaze lingering for a moment longer than necessary. Dionne caught it but chose to say nothing—at least, not yet.

Karmen turned to see Dionne's wide grin as they walked back to her classroom to grab her belongings. "What?" Karmen asked, feigning ignorance.

"What? The way that man was looking at you," Dionne replied, her tone teasing.

Karmen playfully rolled her eyes, brushing it off. "Who, Mr. Lovett? He was just being polite and apologetic," she said, dismissing the lingering effect Mario had left on her.

"Girl, please. He was checking you out. I see something there," Dionne teased, her grin widening.

Karmen chuckled, shaking her head. "Looks like you need to get your eyes checked soon because there is nothing there. Mario is just Mia's father, and Mia is one of my students. That's a line I wouldn't cross, even if there was something there."

Dionne wasn't letting it go. "Mario? Oh, we're on a first-name basis now? No more Mr. Lovett," she teased as they exited the building.

"Now you're starting to sound like London's crazy ass," Karmen said, laughing. "There's nothing between me and Mario—Mr. Lovett, Mia's father, whoever you want to call him. Nothing. It's strictly teacher and parent."

"Got it," Dionne said, raising her hands in mock surrender, unable to hide her amusement.

Karmen laughed as they approached her car, but her expression shifted when she glanced at Dionne. "How did the cake tasting go with your future mother-in-law?" she asked.

"It was good," Dionne said nonchalantly, her tone steady, but Karmen's sharp instincts picked up on the subtle emotions beneath the surface.

"Doesn't seem good. Are you okay?" Karmen asked, her voice laced with concern.

Dionne held her composure, even though the weight of the truth lingered on her mind. She hated lying to her friends, but how could she begin to explain her situation? How could she tell them that the man they always saw her laughing with, the man who once filled her heart with joy, no longer made her happy? That the love story they celebrated wasn't a dream anymore—it was an unbearable trap she felt powerless to escape?

They had been ecstatic when Malik proposed. To them, it was the perfect fairy tale: college sweethearts turned husband and wife, building a family and a life together. It was the dream Dionne used to want too. But now, the dream had become suffocating, a facade she had to uphold for the sake of everyone but herself.

Dionne forced a small smile and offered a carefully crafted response. "Yeah, I'm okay. It's just... between wedding planning and trying to secure this partnership, it's exhausting. One of them needs to come through soon because I'm running on fumes. But everything is good between me and Malik," she said, her voice steady, punctuated by a reassuring smile.

Karmen's face softened, believing the sincerity in Dionne's words. She smiled back, satisfied that her best friend was handling everything, as she always seemed to do. "You'll figure it out, Dee. You always do," Karmen said warmly.

Dionne nodded, helping Karmen load the last of her things into her car. "Yeah, I always do," she echoed, though the weight in her chest told

Feenin'

her otherwise.

As Karmen drove off, Dionne lingered for a moment, letting the mask fall from her face. Her shoulders sagged as she let out a deep sigh, the smile fading completely. She got into her car, knowing she had to find some way to unwind before another long day at work tomorrow. The cracks in her perfect life were starting to show, but she was determined to keep them hidden—for now.

***

Arris was in his office, engrossed in contracts for his upcoming business ventures. The sound of a knock at his office door barely registered as he motioned for whoever it was to enter, his focus never leaving the stack of papers in front of him.

"I know I didn't travel all the way from Washington to see my brother, just for him to be too busy working to acknowledge his favorite sister," a familiar, teasing voice called out, breaking his concentration. Arris immediately recognized the voice and looked up, a grin spreading across his face.

"Lani?" he asked, his tone lighting up with excitement as he stood from his desk.

"Wassup, ugly!" A'Lani teased, her smile wide as he crossed the room in a few strides and pulled her into a hug. Lifting her slightly off the ground, he held her tightly, showing just how much he had missed her.

"I thought you weren't coming until the weekend," Arris said as he set her down, still surprised to see her.

"I was, but I decided to come see you and Ma early," she explained, her tone as casual as ever.

Arris stepped back to get a good look at his sister, pride shining in his eyes. A'Lani was only a few years younger than him, but their bond ran deeper than a typical sibling relationship. With no stable male figure in their lives growing up, Arris had taken on more than just the role of an older brother—he had become her protector, provider, and mentor. To A'Lani, Arris was more than her brother; he was her rock.

"You look good, Lani," Arris said, admiration in his voice. And she did. A'Lani was practically their mother's twin, with smooth dark brown skin, hazel eyes, long curly hair, and a toned, athletic build. Her smile lit up the room, but her laid-back, chill demeanor mirrored Arris.

"Thanks, big bro. You still looking like you don't get enough sleep," she quipped, making him chuckle as they walked over to the large couch in his office.

A'Lani's gaze wandered around Arris's office, her eyes lighting up

Ann

with admiration. A proud smile spread across her face as she looked at her brother. "You're really doing amazing, Arris. I'm so proud of you," she said warmly, her voice filled with sincerity.

Arris's lips curved into a small smile, her words hitting exactly where they mattered most. More than anything, he wanted to make his mother and little sister proud. "I appreciate that, Lani. It means a lot," he replied, his voice soft with affection. "But enough about me. How's school going?"

A'Lani's face brightened even more, her enthusiasm bubbling over. "I love it! We're finally stepping into clinicals and getting more hands-on experience. It's everything I hoped for," she said, her excitement evident. She had found her passion in nursing school, thriving at Howard University. She loved everything about her college experience—the academics, the freedom, even the parties. It was her time to grow into the woman she wanted to be.

Arris leaned back on the couch, watching her as she spoke, her happiness contagious. Even though he missed having her close, knowing she was thriving made the distance worth it. "That's great, Lani. I'm glad you're enjoying it," he said with genuine pride.

A'Lani's tone shifted slightly as she leaned forward, her expression turning more serious. "I know you're busy, Arris, but I wanted to stop by and say hi. There's also something I need to talk to you about," she admitted, her voice quieter now.

Arris's brow furrowed as he caught the change in her demeanor. Concern flickered in his eyes as he gave her his full attention. "What's going on?" he asked, his voice calm but laced with curiosity.

A'Lani hesitated for a moment before exhaling deeply. "Calvin reached out to me," she said, her words landing heavily in the room. The mention of their father—the man who had walked out of their lives—instantly darkened Arris's expression. He sighed sharply, leaning forward with his elbows on his knees, the tension in his jaw unmistakable.

"I heard," Arris replied curtly, his tone clipped as he tried to suppress the frustration bubbling beneath the surface. The name alone was enough to stir old wounds he had tried to bury.

"He wants to sit down and talk to us, and I think we should hear him out," A'Lani said, her tone steady, though her eyes searched Arris's face for a glimmer of understanding.

Arris leaned back, his expression hardening as he processed her words. "I don't have shit to say to that nigga, and I don't want to hear shit from him," he said calmly, but the sharp clench of his jaw betrayed the storm brewing inside him.

Feenin'

"Arris," A'Lani started gently, "don't you think finally hearing him out—or at least learning why he did what he did—might help with some of the anger you carry?" Her voice was soft but firm, a plea wrapped in reason. She understood Arris's resentment better than anyone, but she also believed that closure could offer them both some peace.

Arris's eyes darkened as he turned to face her, his jaw tightening even further. "Lani, you talking like he made a small mistake," he began, his voice still calm but vibrating with restrained fury. "That nigga abandoned us. All for some street shit."

A'Lani opened her mouth to speak, but Arris pressed on, his voice growing sharper. "He put drugs, money, and hoes before his own kids. I can't forgive a man like that. I won't. I went this long without him, so I can go a lifetime. I don't give a fuck what excuse he has to offer."

A'Lani let out a frustrated sigh, her shoulders slumping slightly. "But, Arris—" she began again, only to be cut off by her brother's unwavering resolve.

"If you want to hear him out, then by all means, do what you need to do to get your peace," Arris said, his tone softening slightly as he locked eyes with her. His gaze was no longer filled with anger, but with an almost tender protectiveness. "But me? I don't want anything to do with that nigga. He's dead to me."

A'Lani stared at him, stunned by his blunt declaration. For a moment, the room was heavy with silence, her disbelief hanging in the air like a cloud. She knew Arris's anger ran deep, but hearing him speak the words aloud felt heavier than she had anticipated.

A'Lani sat in silence, her emotions swirling as she watched her brother wrestle with his own. She didn't share Arris's bitterness. Yes, she was angry at their father for choosing the streets over them, but she was exhausted from carrying the weight of resentment. A sit-down with their father wasn't about him—it was about her own healing, her peace. She longed for Arris to find that same release, but she could see he wasn't ready. Pushing him further wouldn't help.

Before she could respond, the tension in the room was interrupted by the sudden sound of Arris's office door opening. China stepped in, her usual confidence faltering as she noticed A'Lani's presence.

"Oh, sorry to interrupt," China began, her tone professional. "Ms. Smith is here for your meeting. I can have her wait if—"

"I was just leaving," A'Lani interjected quickly, standing from the couch. The unspoken tension between her and Arris hung heavy in the air, but she didn't want to linger. Arris stood as well, his expression softening with guilt as he looked at his sister.

He hated the idea of them parting on uneasy terms, but the demands of work couldn't wait. Personal issues would have to take a backseat for now. Still, he couldn't let her leave without trying to ease the strain.

Arris pulled A'Lani into a hug, holding her tightly. "We'll talk later," he whispered, his voice low but filled with quiet resolve. He pressed a kiss to her forehead, a gesture of comfort and apology. A'Lani nodded, her expression softening, though the sadness in her eyes lingered.

"Bye, China," A'Lani said politely, offering a faint smile as she exited the office. China nodded in return, stepping aside to let her pass. Once the door closed behind her, China turned back to Arris, her professional demeanor resuming.

"Would you like me to bring Ms. Smith in now?" she asked.

Arris nodded, exhaling as he tried to refocus his mind on the meeting ahead. "Yeah, send her in," he replied, but his thoughts lingered on A'Lani. As much as he tried to compartmentalize, the unresolved conversation with his sister weighed heavily on his mind.

Minutes later, Dionne walked into the office, exuding effortless elegance in a sharp white Dior pantsuit. The asymmetrical blazer with black contrast lapels was tailored to perfection, highlighting her polished professionalism. Her white heels clicked softly against the floor, complementing her poised demeanor. Her hair flowed in its usual middle part down her back, a perfect frame for her striking features. Arris felt his breath hitch as she entered, her presence commanding the room effortlessly. She looked nothing short of perfection, as she always did in his eyes.

"Mr. Black," Dionne greeted, extending her hand with a polite smile.

Arris leaned back in his chair, a playful smirk tugging at his lips. "Oh, so we're back to being formal now? I thought we were past that. We're friends, aren't we?" he teased, his confident charm lacing every word.

Dionne chuckled softly, her smile growing warmer. "It's a habit, my apologies," she replied, her voice smooth as they shook hands.

Arris lingered for a moment, enjoying the subtle spark that seemed to pass between them, but he quickly composed himself. Since their night at The Vault, their relationship had shifted from strictly professional to a budding friendship, though the unspoken tension between them lingered beneath the surface.

"I found two new parcels of land outside the city. I know you've been looking for prime spots to build hotels, and I think these could be perfect," Dionne said, handing him a file with detailed layouts and all the necessary information. Arris took the file, flipping through the

Feenin'

pages and nodding in approval, though his focus was elsewhere. The earlier conversation with A'Lani about their father lingered in his mind, consuming his thoughts. Even as Dionne spoke, he found it difficult to shake the frustration and turmoil brewing within him.

Dionne picked up on the shift in his energy, the subtle tension in his jaw and the way his gaze lingered on the documents but didn't seem to register them. Choosing to stay professional, she focused on the task at hand. "So, what do you think?" she asked, breaking the silence and forcing his attention back to her.

"They look solid. How's the area overall?" Arris asked, looking up at her. His piercing gaze sent an involuntary shiver down her spine, but she maintained her composure like a pro.

"A lot of traffic flows through this area, with people traveling in and out of the city," Dionne explained confidently, her hands gesturing to key points on the file. "Building hotels there will capitalize on that movement and significantly boost your profits. The locations are accessible and have the potential to become landmarks."

She noticed the tight clench of his jaw and the rigid tension in his shoulders as she spoke, causing her to hesitate mid-sentence. Skepticism flickered across her face—he wasn't just distracted, he was somewhere else entirely. It was clear he wasn't in the right headspace to discuss business right now, and the weight of whatever was on his mind hung heavy in the room, tense and unspoken.

Dionne reached over, gently taking the files out of Arris's hands. He raised a brow, watching her with a mix of curiosity and surprise. "What are you doing?" he asked, his voice laced with intrigue as she closed the file and set it aside on his desk.

"Clearly, this isn't where your head is right now," Dionne said, her tone firm but calm, meeting his gaze directly. Arris blinked, taken aback by her boldness. He wasn't used to people reading him so easily, let alone calling him out on it.

"What's wrong?" she asked, her voice soft but probing.

Arris leaned back, chuckling lightly, trying to deflect. "What you mean? I'm good," he said, his charm slipping into his words like a shield.

Dionne didn't budge. "Your body's here, but your mind isn't," she said, her perceptive gaze cutting through his facade. She crossed her arms, tilting her head slightly. "We're friends, right?"

Arris smirked, amused by the directness of her question. "Yeah," he said, his voice dropping an octave as he tried to figure out where she was headed.

"Then talk to me," Dionne replied, her tone gentle but insistent.

"What's going on in that big head of yours?" She softened the moment with a teasing smile, hoping to make him feel at ease.

Arris chuckled, shaking his head. "You talking shit now?" he joked, leaning forward slightly. Despite his attempt to keep it light, there was a crack in his armor.

"Be serious for once," Dionne said softly but firmly. Her voice was steady, grounding, a stark contrast to the chaos he was feeling inside.

Arris studied her for a moment, the weight of her sincerity catching him off guard. He wasn't used to being asked how he felt—not like this. He'd always been the one holding others up, the one who bottled his emotions and carried on without leaning on anyone. Yet, in Dionne's presence, he felt something unfamiliar: safety.

"I'm good, Dionne. I promise," Arris said, his tone steady but lacking the conviction she sought. Deep down, he wanted nothing more than to let her soothe the storm raging within him, but old habits of self-reliance held him back.

Dionne offered a soft smile, deciding not to press him further even though she could see through his facade. "Alright," she replied, adjusting the lapel of her blazer as she stood. "I have a house to show in an hour, so I should get back to my office."

She gathered her things, but before leaving, she turned back to him. "Take a closer look at the files, and let me know if you want Williams Luxe to dig deeper into it for you." Her professionalism never wavered, but her voice carried a subtle warmth, showing she genuinely cared about more than just their business partnership.

As she turned to leave, Arris instinctively reached out, his hand brushing against hers. The touch stopped her in her tracks. She looked back at him, catching the turmoil flickering in his eyes. It was as if he was battling himself, caught between vulnerability and restraint.

For a moment, he said nothing, his hand retreating as quickly as it had reached out. Her touch grounded him in ways he didn't expect, leaving him exposed in a way he wasn't used to. "Thank you for this," he said finally, standing as he met her gaze. His voice was calm, but his eyes spoke of the unspoken weight he carried.

Dionne felt her heart skip, his sincerity and intensity stirring something within her. Butterflies fluttered in her stomach, but she maintained her composure. "Just doing my job," she replied with a faint smile. "Take care, Arris." With that, she walked out of his office, leaving behind a presence that lingered in the air long after she was gone.

Arris sat back down, staring at the door long after it closed behind her. Her presence, her voice, and even the brief touch of her hand felt

Feenin'

like a reprieve from everything he tried to keep bottled up. She was a comfort, a quiet escape from the chaos swirling in his mind, and yet she had no idea.

Arris couldn't understand how this woman, who had come into his life so unexpectedly, managed to leave an indelible mark every time she walked away. He found himself craving more—not just her presence, but the way she made him feel seen in a way no one else ever had. One day, he thought, he might be able to let her into the parts of himself he kept hidden. But for now, he'd keep his guard up, even as he yearned for the connection she offered without even trying.

***

Dionne entered her home, exhaustion clinging to her like a second skin after the long day at the office. Her thoughts, however, weren't on her work—they were on Arris. His demeanor earlier, the subtle weight in his voice, and the way his eyes seemed to carry untold burdens stuck with her. Something about him always drew her in, stirring a care and concern she hadn't anticipated. As she shrugged off her jacket and placed it on the hook, she shook her head, trying to push her thoughts aside.

But just as she stepped further into the house, a faint sound reached her ears, breaking through her reverie. Moans. Dionne froze, her body going rigid. For a moment, she questioned if her ears were deceiving her. No, it must be the TV, she thought, trying to rationalize it. After all, Malik had told her earlier he'd be working late tonight.

Her pulse quickened as the sounds grew louder, and her stomach churned with unease. Instinctively, she slipped off her heels, holding them in her hand to keep from making noise as she moved toward the staircase. Each step she took made the moans clearer, the unmistakable sounds twisting her stomach into knots. Please, God, let this be a mistake, she prayed silently.

Her breath caught as she reached the top of the stairs, and her gaze fell on her bedroom door, slightly ajar. The sounds from inside left no room for doubt. Against every instinct screaming for her to turn back, she stepped closer, her heart pounding in her chest.

Peering through the crack of the door, Dionne felt her world shatter. There, in the bed they shared, was Malik, entangled with a woman she didn't recognize. Her mind couldn't fully process what her eyes were seeing—their sheets, her space, their bed—and Malik desecrating it with someone else.

Rage surged through her, hot and overwhelming, but she refused to let it consume her. Not here, not now. With an unnatural calm that defied her emotions, Dionne quietly stepped back, her movements measured

Ann

and deliberate. She didn't scream, didn't barge in, didn't give them the satisfaction of her fury. Instead, she turned away and made her way to her sanctuary—her woman cave.

Dionne unlocked the safe, her trembling hands pulling out the cold metal of the gun. She walked into the living room, her steps heavy with rage, and sank onto the couch. The weapon rested between her shaking legs, her grip firm but unsteady as anger coursed through her veins. It wasn't just the sight of Malik with another woman that infuriated her—it was the audacity. The sheer gall of him to betray her, knowing she had stayed in this relationship, sacrificed her happiness, all to uphold the promise he made for his mother.

She'd been playing the role of the perfect fiancée, pretending to be in love, smiling for appearances, while inside she felt hollow. And yet, here he was, not just cheating, but defiling the bed they shared. Each thought added fuel to the fire, her rage simmering just below the surface. The woman's moans still echoed faintly in her ears, each one another dagger in her chest.

How could I have been so blind? The question played over and over in her mind, her anger rising with every passing second. Her legs shook uncontrollably, the tension in her body building as the sound of footsteps descending the stairs snapped her from her spiraling thoughts.

The steps halted abruptly.

Malik and the woman stood frozen at the bottom of the staircase, their wide eyes locking onto Dionne. The room fell silent except for the faint hum of the air conditioning. Dionne slowly lifted her head, her expression a storm of fury and heartbreak.

Malik's face twisted with guilt, his mouth opening as if to speak, but no words came. The woman beside him gasped softly, her eyes darting to the gun clenched tightly in Dionne's hand.

Dionne rose from the couch with a slow, deliberate movement, her gaze never leaving Malik. The weight of her anger filled the room, suffocating and heavy.

"Dionne?" Malik said, his voice breaking the heavy silence that filled the room. Dionne smiled, but there was nothing warm or inviting about it. Her smile was sharp, chilling, and sent a wave of dread coursing through him. The gun in her hand was steady, her grip firm, her knuckles slightly whitening as she held it. Malik knew at that moment he had crossed a line he couldn't come back from.

"Hi, Malik," Dionne said sweetly, her tone deceptively polite. Her gaze shifted to the woman standing beside him, who looked visibly shaken. "And who is this... white woman?"

Feenin'

Her voice carried a venomous undertone, and though the smile remained on her face, it only made the situation more unsettling. Malik opened his mouth to respond, but Dionne's eyes snapped back to him, silencing him before he could utter a word.

"White women?" Dionne continued, letting out a humorless laugh. "That's what you're into now?"

The woman, clearly uncomfortable, attempted to muster some courage. "Um... my name is Brittany," she said hesitantly, her voice trembling despite the slight edge of attitude she tried to add.

Dionne turned her full attention to Brittany, sizing her up with a cold, critical gaze before laughing again, this time with pure derision. "Brittany? Of course, it is," Dionne mocked, her voice dripping with sarcasm. "A typical white woman name for a typical white woman."

"I think... I should go," Brittany stammered, her fear now fully evident.

Dionne nodded, her expression unchanging. "Brittany is smart," she said coldly, her eyes narrowing slightly. "Yes, Brittany, you should definitely leave."

Brittany glanced at Malik for confirmation, her body frozen in place. Dionne noticed and tilted her head mockingly. "Oh, Malik, your puppy here is waiting for you to give her permission to go. How cute."

Malik flinched at her words, his hands twitching at his sides. "Go, Brittany," he said, his voice low and shaky, his eyes never leaving Dionne. "I'll see you at work."

Brittany sat frozen in shock, staring at Dionne for a moment longer before scrambling to her feet and leaving without another word. She didn't want to face the wrath that was brewing in Dionne, nor did she want to entangle herself further in their volatile relationship. The sound of the door closing behind her was like a drumbeat signaling the start of the real confrontation.

Dionne turned her full attention to Malik, her eyes blazing with disbelief and fury. "Really, Malik?" she said, her voice laced with incredulity as she stared him down. Malik shifted uncomfortably, the fear in his posture evident as his eyes darted to the gun still clutched in her hand.

"Dionne... just put the gun down and let me explain," he pleaded, his voice trembling.

Dionne let out a low, humorless chuckle, shaking her head. "No," she said firmly, her tone calm but deadly. "I'm keeping this gun in my hand while you explain. And if you say some dumb shit, Malik, that just gives me a reason to shoot your ass."

Malik swallowed hard, his throat bobbing as he struggled to find his words. He knew there was no escaping this. "It started..." he began, but Dionne cut him off, her voice rising.

"I don't give a fuck about when you started fucking your side bitch!" she snapped, her voice echoing in the room. "I want to know why! Here I am, pretending to love you in public for your mother's sake, and you're out here putting your dick in other women?"

Malik flinched, his hands raised slightly in a placating gesture. "I know, Dee. I messed up. I'm sorry," he said quickly, his words fumbling over one another. "It's just... you've been so distant lately."

Dionne stared at him in stunned silence before letting out a bitter laugh, shaking her head in disbelief. "Oh, so now it's my fault?" she said, her voice dripping with sarcasm. "Nigga, how the fuck would you even know how distant I've been? You're never here! You're always at that damn hospital—or at least, that's what you claim." She paused, her voice lowering as her anger simmered. "But now I know that shit was a lie too."

"You pushed me away, Dionne. Long before my mother got sick," Malik snapped, his voice tinged with anger. "You acted like you didn't love me anymore, throwing all your attention into your career."

Dionne stared at him, her frustration bubbling to the surface. "You love playing the victim, don't you?" she shot back. "I threw myself into work because home became stressful and draining!" Her voice cracked slightly under the weight of her emotions.

"And whose fault is that?" Malik countered sharply, his words cutting through the tension.

Dionne froze for a moment, disbelief flashing across her face. "Whose fault? How can you stand there and ask me that like our entire relationship hasn't revolved around what you wanted?" Her voice rose, trembling with anger. "I spent hours pretending to be the perfect, happily engaged woman for your mother—smiling, nodding, agreeing—all to make her and the man who used to love me happy." Her voice cracked, and she stepped closer, her eyes filled with fury. "Only to come home and find the man I'm pretending for—no, the man I used to love—fucking another woman in my bed."

Malik's voice dropped, a mix of desperation and disbelief. "You don't love me anymore?"

Dionne froze, her chest heaving as she stared at him in utter disbelief. "That's all you heard out of everything I just said?" She shook her head, her voice quieter but no less cutting. "I should've known better than to think you'd understand. You never listened before—why would

Feenin'

now be any different?"

Malik flinched at her words but quickly fired back. "And this is all my fault?" he demanded, his own anger igniting. "You really think I'm the only one to blame here?"

Dionne shook her head, her laugh bitter and hollow. "You're pathetic, Malik. Absolutely fucking pathetic. You can't see beyond your own selfishness." She threw her hands up, her voice rising with every word. "I gave everything to us—everything! And when I needed a partner, you checked out, and now you have the nerve to stand here and blame me?"

Malik stepped closer, his tone shifting to a pleading one. "I made a mistake, Dionne. I know I messed up, but my heart is with you. I love you."

She scoffed, folding her arms as her gaze hardened. "You don't love me, Malik. You love the idea of me. You love the convenience of me being here, pretending everything's fine, so you can keep up this perfect image for your mother." She stepped back, putting distance between them. "But I'm done. Done pretending, done playing your game, done sacrificing myself for people who don't deserve it."

Malik opened his mouth to speak, but Dionne raised her hand, silencing him. "You want to save this relationship? Save it for someone else, because I'm out." She turned and walked away, leaving Malik standing alone, the weight of her words echoing in the silence.

Malik took a step forward, hesitation etched across his face, but he froze when Dionne turned to look at him, the gun still clutched tightly by her side. His expression softened, shifting from fear to a desperate attempt to salvage what was left. "Out? What about us, our engagement, my mother?" he asked, his tone imploring as he reached for the one thing he knew might sway her: Mama Glen.

Dionne's eyes narrowed, the disbelief and anger in her gaze rose. "Really, Malik? You're using your mother as a guilt trip to keep me in this?" Her voice was sharp, cutting through the tense air between them.

"I understand your frustration with me, and I'm truly sorry," Malik continued, his tone now more subdued. "But don't disappoint my mother because of my mistakes." His plea hit a nerve, and Dionne's resolve faltered, her love for Mama Glen pulling at her even as her anger burned hotter. She wanted out—Malik's betrayal was her opportunity—but Mama Glen's unwavering support and love made her decision agonizingly complicated.

Dionne exhaled sharply, her grip tightening on her purse as she weighed her options. "I need a break from you, Malik. I need time to think," she said, her voice low but firm.

Malik nodded, sensing that pushing her further would only worsen the situation. "Take all the time you need," he said softly, though the panic in his eyes betrayed him.

"I'll be back to get my things when you're not here," Dionne added, her tone laced with finality. She reached into her purse, slipping the gun inside, the gesture not lost on Malik.

"Where are you going?" he asked cautiously, his concern evident.

Dionne turned to him, her expression cold and unyielding. "You don't have the room to ask me anything," she shot back. Her voice dropped, seething with controlled fury. "Burn those sheets upstairs… matter of fact burn the whole damn mattress, Malik. And if you're going to cheat, keep your strays out of my house. At least give me that much respect."

Without waiting for his response, Dionne turned and walked out, leaving Malik standing in the wake of her words, guilt and regret heavy in the air.

Dionne gripped the steering wheel tightly, her knuckles white as she tried to steady her breath. Her thoughts were a chaotic mess, each one a reminder of her sacrifice, her loyalty, and her unhappiness. She had given up so much of herself for Malik and Mama Glen, prioritizing their happiness over her own. Even after witnessing Malik's betrayal firsthand, she still felt tethered—bound by the love she had for Mama Glen and the promises she had made.

Her eyes stung with tears she refused to let fall, her jaw clenched as she willed herself to stay composed. No matter how much she wanted to scream, cry, or lash out, she knew it wouldn't change the reality she was stuck in. She took a deep breath, gripping the steering wheel even tighter as her foot pressed down on the gas, pulling out of the driveway and into the night.

London's house was her destination, her sanctuary. Her best friend had already agreed to let her come over, though Dionne hadn't shared why. She wasn't ready to relive what she'd just experienced by putting it into words. The thought of talking about Malik, about his betrayal, felt like reopening a wound that hadn't even begun to heal.

The drive to London's was quiet except for the low hum of the car's engine and her sporadic, deep breaths. By the time she pulled into London's driveway, her emotions had shifted from anger to exhaustion. She sat in the car for a moment, staring at the warmly lit house. London's home had always been a place of comfort, a space where she could let her guard down, but tonight, even that felt daunting.

Finally, Dionne got out of the car, grabbing her bag and heading

Feenin'

toward the front door. She didn't need to knock; London had already texted that the door was unlocked. As Dionne stepped inside, the familiar scent of vanilla candles greeted her, and London's voice called out from the living room.

"Dee, I'm in here!" she said cheerfully, though her tone quickly softened when she saw Dionne's face. "Oh no, girl, what happened?"

"I just want to sleep," Dionne said quietly, her voice heavy with exhaustion and pain. She didn't have the energy to dive into the storm of emotions swirling inside her, and the thought of recounting what had happened with Malik felt unbearable.

London studied her friend, seeing the weight Dionne carried in her slumped shoulders and the faint gloss of unshed tears in her eyes. She wanted to press, to help, but she knew Dionne well enough to recognize when to back off. "The room's ready upstairs," London said softly, her voice filled with warmth and understanding. "Get some rest, Dee. Whatever it is, we'll deal with it when you're ready."

"Thanks," Dionne murmured, her voice barely above a whisper. She started up the stairs, her steps slow, as if each one required more effort than the last.

Just as she reached the landing, London's concerned voice called out, halting her mid-step. "You sure you're okay?"

Dionne paused, gripping the railing for support as she turned back slightly. Her lips curved into a faint, tired smile, one that didn't reach her eyes. "I'll be fine," she said, her tone more for London's benefit than her own reassurance. Without waiting for a response, she turned and continued up the stairs, leaving her friend watching after her with worry etched across her face.

London sighed, running a hand through her hair as she sat back down. She didn't know what Dionne was going through, but she knew one thing for sure—when Dionne was ready, she'd be there to listen. For now, all she could do was give her friend the space she needed to heal, one step at a time.

Chapter 5

Arris stood at the center of the bustling activity in his restaurant, his calm demeanor unwavering as he oversaw the preparations for his annual investor event. It was a significant occasion, bringing together the most powerful and influential businesspeople for an evening of networking, fine dining, and entertainment. Everything had to be flawless—this event wasn't just a party; it was a testament to his meticulous standards and sharp business acumen.

China approached him first, clipboard in hand. "Decorations are almost done. The florists are putting the final touches on the centerpieces. DJ is set to do a sound check in an hour," she reported with precision.

Arris nodded, his focus shifting as Martin hurried toward him, his expression tight. "The chef is here, but we have a problem," Martin said, his tone careful but urgent.

Arris tilted his head slightly, his face calm but his eyes sharp. "What's the problem?"

"It seems the supplier delivered the wrong seafood order. It's fresh, but it's not what we requested for the menu," Martin explained.

Without missing a beat, Arris set down the glass he'd been inspecting and made his way to the kitchen. The hum of the restaurant staff grew louder as he entered, but his mere presence seemed to command immediate attention.

"What's the issue?" he asked the head chef, who was already pacing.

"The shrimp and scallops are fine, but they didn't include the lobster tails or the Chilean sea bass we planned for the main courses. They sent cod and king crab instead. It throws off the menu," the chef said, clearly frazzled.

Arris studied the order list and the substitutions, his mind racing with

Feenin'

solutions. "King crab can work for one of the appetizers—let's adjust the serving portions to make it elegant. As for the cod, create a second entrée option. Something simple but elevated. A wine-poached cod dish, maybe. We'll lean into it as a highlight for guests who prefer a lighter option."

The chef nodded, his confidence restored under Arris's decisive leadership. "I'll get on it."

Arris turned back to Martin. "Double-check with the supplier. I want the missing items here tomorrow morning at the latest. Offer a bonus for overnight delivery if needed."

"Yes, sir," Martin replied, already typing a message into his phone.

Arris stepped back into the main dining area, where decorators were perfecting the lighting and table settings. China caught up with him again, her sharp gaze assessing his every move. "Crisis averted?" she asked, arching an eyebrow.

"Handled," Arris replied smoothly, his confidence evident. "This event will be perfect. Make sure everyone knows that."

China smirked, reassured as she returned to her tasks. Arris scanned the room one last time before stepping back into his office to finalize the event schedule. Despite the hiccup, he knew one thing for certain: by the time the event rolled around, everything would be seamless. Perfection wasn't just his expectation—it was his standard.

As Arris finalized the last details for the event, China approached him with an uncertain look, her hesitation immediately catching his attention. "Um... Arris, you have a visitor," she said cautiously. Arris frowned, his focus interrupted. "Who is it?" he asked, irritation creeping into his tone. He didn't have time for distractions with everything that needed to be done.

"Um... it's your—" China began, but before she could finish, a deep, familiar voice cut through the room, making Arris's entire body tense.

"Arris!" The sound of his name spoken by that voice sent a jolt of rage through him. His head snapped up, and his blood instantly boiled at the sight of his father, Calvin, striding toward him. Despite their estranged relationship, the undeniable resemblance between them only fueled Arris's resentment. Growing up, he had hated when people said he looked just like his father, and even now, the thought made his jaw clench.

Calvin's smooth dark skin, salt-and-pepper waves, and full beard gave him an air of age and experience, but Arris saw nothing admirable in the man before him. Calvin had somehow retained a youthful appearance despite a life of street chaos, but to Arris, there was nothing youthful or redeeming about the man who had abandoned his family for the streets.

Calvin approached with a wide smile, completely unfazed by the icy glare Arris shot his way. "Son!" he said enthusiastically, as though years of absence and pain could be erased with a single word.

Arris's hand tightened around the clipboard he was holding, his knuckles whitening as his fury simmered beneath the surface. He had sworn the next time he saw Calvin, there would be no words—only fists. But he was in his restaurant, surrounded by his staff, and Arris prided himself on never letting anything or anyone jeopardize his business. Not even Calvin.

China, sensing the tension, discreetly stepped away to give them privacy, leaving father and son standing face-to-face in a silence thick with unspoken emotions. Arris's glare was sharp, his jaw set, while Calvin continued to smile as though nothing had ever gone wrong between them.

Arris's voice was low but laced with fury as he stepped closer to Calvin, his jaw tight and his eyes blazing. "The fuck you doing here? No, fuck that—how did you even find me?" he asked, his tone a quiet storm, each word dripping with restrained anger.

Calvin's demeanor shifted slightly, the enthusiasm he entered with dimming in the face of his son's rage. "Can we talk somewhere privately?" he asked, his voice softer, trying to reach the man who stood before him like a wall of cold steel.

"No," Arris snapped, his glare unwavering. "You can tell me why you're here, right fucking now." His tone was low, controlled, ensuring no one else in the restaurant could hear the heated exchange, though his body radiated tension.

Calvin hesitated, then said, "Your mother told me where to find you. I just want to talk."

At the mention of his mother, Arris's jaw clenched even tighter. A surge of frustration rose within him as he considered her role in allowing this confrontation. "I don't have shit to say to you," he growled, turning to walk away.

Calvin reached out, grabbing Arris by the arm to stop him. The moment his hand made contact, Arris froze. He looked down at Calvin's hand with a simmering rage that promised consequences, then slowly met his father's eyes with a glare devoid of emotion. "Get your fucking hands off me, my nigga," he warned, his voice eerily calm.

Calvin, sensing the thin line he was treading, released his grip and stepped back. "Come on, son—"

"I ain't your fucking son," Arris spat, cutting him off. His words

Feenin'

were sharp, like knives slicing through the air. "You made that decision when you chose to father the streets instead of your own fucking kids."

Calvin visibly recoiled as Arris's words landed with brutal precision, breaking him down piece by piece. Guilt etched itself deeply into his face, but Arris wasn't done. "If Ma or A'Lani want to hear your sorry ass out, that's on them," he continued, his voice still low but charged with venom. "But let me make one thing clear to you, my nigga: I fucking hate you. Whatever amends you're trying to make, let it go. You've been dead to me for a long time." Calvin stood there, his face a mixture of regret and sorrow, but Arris didn't waver. His words were final, a cemented line in the sand.

"Now you can leave the same way you came—on foot—or someone will carry your ass out if you touch me again," Arris said coldly, his piercing glare driving the point home. Without waiting for a response, he turned and walked away, leaving Calvin standing there, silenced and burdened by the weight of his mistakes.

Arris glanced back toward the door, watching Calvin leave the restaurant before exhaling the breath he hadn't realized he was holding. The anger inside him didn't dissipate—it simmered, a relentless storm brewing beneath the surface. A'Lani's words replayed in his mind, the truth of them gnawing at him. She wasn't wrong; he carried the weight of his father's betrayal like a festering wound, but he couldn't see any way to heal it. No apology, no conversation, and no attempt at reconciliation could undo the damage Calvin had caused.

What stung the most wasn't Calvin's presence—it was knowing his mother had told Calvin where to find him. The betrayal cut deeper than he cared to admit. She knew firsthand the depth of his resentment and pain, yet she had still forced him into a situation he didn't want to face. Being blindsided like this felt cruel, and it made the anger churn even hotter inside him.

"Boss, are you okay?" China's soft voice broke through his thoughts. She approached cautiously, her concern evident. China knew the history Arris had with his father—she'd seen the aftermath of his anger more times than she cared to remember. There had been moments when she had to talk him down from doing something reckless, her steady hand and calming presence often the only things grounding him.

Arris rubbed a hand down his face, trying to push the tension away, but it clung to him. "Yeah, hold it down here. I need to head out," he said, his tone clipped but steady. He knew he couldn't focus on work right now. Not with his emotions spiraling.

China nodded, her eyes scanning him with quiet understanding.

Ann

"Okay. Me and Martin got everything covered. Go home and get some rest," she said, placing a reassuring hand on his shoulder.

"Thanks. See everyone tomorrow," Arris said lowly, grabbing his keys and leaving the restaurant. Once inside his car, the walls of composure he had been holding up all day finally crumbled. His rage boiled over as he slammed his fists into the steering wheel repeatedly, each strike accompanied by the angry tears streaming down his face. The storm of emotions he had kept locked away for so long erupted, overwhelming him.

The hurt caused by his father filled every corner of his mind, suffocating him. Arris had once yearned for Calvin's love and approval. As a boy, he had idolized the idea of having a father who would show up for him. But all those memories of disappointment came rushing back now, sharper and more painful than ever. He remembered every missed baseball game, the empty bleachers where his father should have been cheering him on, absent because Calvin was too busy chasing the streets.

He recalled the prison visits, sitting behind a cold glass window, trying to find joy in the hollow conversations they shared. He saw his mother's tear-streaked face as she cried herself to sleep at night, heartbroken over the man who claimed to love her but kept shattering her heart. He relived the moments he had to step up for A'Lani, not just as a big brother but as a father figure, because Calvin had abandoned that responsibility.

The weight of those memories pressed down on him now, heavier than ever. For so long, Arris had carried the burden of being the backbone for his family, the one who couldn't falter. But right now, he felt crushed under the sheer enormity of it all. He needed relief—an escape from the pain that consumed him.

Taking a deep, shaky breath, Arris wiped his tears with the back of his hand. He needed to ground himself, to find some semblance of peace. And there was only one place where he could feel even a fraction of that: home. Turning the key in the ignition, he pulled out of the parking lot, his thoughts still churning as he drove, searching for solace.

Arris drove home, his mind racing as he tried to bury the anger boiling inside him. The moment he stepped inside, he made a beeline for his bathroom, desperate to find something—anything—that could cool the fire burning within. Turning on the shower, he let the hot water fill the room with steam, hoping it might help ease the tension in his chest.

As he opened the drawer to grab his durag, his eyes fell on the black card sitting neatly in the corner. Her name and number were embossed in elegant lettering. The sight of it made him pause, his hand hovering over

Feenin'

the card as a flood of emotions rushed through him.

He remembered the first time she'd handed it to him, her calm, collected demeanor paired with a subtle warmth that had intrigued him. She'd said he could call if he had any questions—business-related, of course. But tonight, his questions had nothing to do with contracts or investments. Tonight, he needed her presence, her voice, the inexplicable sense of peace she seemed to bring.

Before he could second-guess himself, Arris picked up the card and dialed the number. Each ring felt like an eternity, his heartbeat pounding louder than the sound of the water running in the background. Finally, after what felt like an eternity, she answered.

"What!" Dionne's voice, smooth yet intense, cut through the silence like a blade. The sharpness of her tone was a stark contrast to her usual composed demeanor, and yet, it held a strange power—one that chipped away at the storm brewing inside Arris. Her words weren't gentle, but to him, they were grounding, a tether to something stable.

Arris glanced down at the black card in his hand, his thumb brushing the edges with an absentminded precision. It wasn't like him to reach out to anyone, to admit even for a second that he might need someone. Vulnerability wasn't his language, yet here he was, letting her voice pull him out of his own chaos.

Hearing her again, even in her sharpness, felt like a strange kind of relief—like she could calm the fire raging inside him without even realizing it. He wasn't used to this, but somehow, with her, it felt... right.

***

Dionne strolled confidently through the sprawling backyard, gesturing toward its highlights as she spoke. "This space is perfect for entertaining," she said with a warm smile, addressing the family she was showing the property to. "A spacious patio for hosting gatherings, a large pool for relaxing during the summer, and even a basketball court for some fun family competition."

The house, listed at a staggering $10 million, was a masterpiece, and Dionne's pitch was seamless, her tone professional and engaging. Yet, despite her outward composure, her phone buzzed incessantly in her pocket, vibrating for the tenth time in under an hour. A quick glance confirmed it—Malik was calling again.

Dionne sighed internally, keeping her expression poised and focused on her clients. She had left the house after catching him cheating just days ago, and while she hadn't made a final decision about their future, his constant attempts to contact her were starting to wear thin. She knew his motives weren't rooted in love or remorse;

they were fueled by fear—fear that she would call off the wedding and shatter the image he was so desperate to maintain for his mother.

With a calm flick of her thumb, she declined the call again, sliding her phone back into her pocket. Malik's guilt wasn't about to interfere with her work. This sale was important, and Dionne was determined to keep her focus on her career, the one thing she still had control over. As she turned back to the family, her smile never wavered.

"Any questions so far?" she asked, smoothly steering the conversation back to the property. Whatever decision she had to make about Malik would have to wait—right now, her priority was sealing this deal.

"No, we want it," the family said in unison, their excitement evident. Dionne smiled warmly, a sense of pride swelling within her. "Great! Let's head back to my office and finalize everything," she said, maintaining her polished professionalism. The family nodded eagerly, and soon, they were driving back to her office to complete the transaction.

Inside her office, Dionne guided them through the paperwork, her expertise evident in the way she explained every detail. When everything was signed and finalized, she handed them the keys with a sincere smile. "Congratulations on your new home. Thank you for trusting me as your agent," she said warmly, shaking their hands. The family expressed their gratitude before leaving, their joy contagious.

As the door shut behind them, Dionne's phone buzzed again. She glanced at the screen and sighed—Malik. For the fifteenth time today. She groaned softly, hitting the silent button once more. His sudden need to contact her was grating. He hadn't shown this kind of attention when their relationship was on solid ground, and now his persistence only served as a reminder of his guilt.

A knock at the door drew her attention, pulling her out of her frustration. She looked up to see Ms. Jean standing in the doorway, her signature bright smile lighting up the room. "Hey, come in," Dionne said, standing to greet her mentor.

"Congratulations on another sale. That's your fifth one this month," Jean said proudly, stepping inside. Dionne couldn't help but beam with pride.

"Thank you, Ms. Jean. I'm just trying to be half as good as you," Dionne replied humbly, her smile widening.

Jean chuckled, shaking her head. "Girl, you're well on your way to being better than I ever was," she said sincerely, making Dionne's heart swell.

The compliment was everything Dionne needed to hear. Her ultimate

Feenin'

goal was to make partner at the company, and hearing Jean's pride in her progress felt like validation that her dream was within reach. For a moment, she forgot about the chaos in her personal life and focused on the sense of accomplishment she'd worked so hard to achieve.

"I just came to see if you were bringing your fiancé to the Black Investor party this weekend," Jean asked with a loving smile, her tone light and warm. Dionne's stomach tightened slightly at the mention of Malik. Outside of her friends, Jean was the only person who knew about the engagement. Another person she had to lie to, another stage where she had to act as if her relationship was perfect. The thought of Malik made her roll her eyes involuntarily, something Jean didn't miss.

"Well, I was planning on going alone," Dionne said, masking her frustration with a polite tone. "He might be busy working at the hospital this weekend."

Jean tilted her head slightly, her smile still present but with a hint of curiosity. "You should bring him! I still haven't met him, and I'd love to introduce him to some of my medical friends. Plus, you two could use a date night out," she added, her bubbly enthusiasm lighting up the room.

Dionne mirrored Jean's energy with a faint smile, though the annoyance brewing inside her was hard to contain. The idea of pretending to be the perfect couple in front of the most influential people in Atlanta was exhausting. The Black Investor party was a massive event, a hub for powerful and connected individuals. Dionne had been looking forward to networking and showcasing her professionalism, not playing house with a man she no longer felt anything for.

"I'll ask him," Dionne said, biting back her frustration and forcing a smile as Jean mirrored it warmly.

"Good. Now, I'm about to head out. Don't work too hard," Jean said with a playful smile as she stood, her departure a relief for Dionne, who was glad the conversation had come to an end.

"Have a good night, Ms. Jean," Dionne replied with a polite smile. As Jean exited her office, Dionne let out a small sigh, finally able to focus on her work. Her phone, however, had other plans, ringing incessantly. She ignored each call, knowing it was likely Malik trying to reach her. The day stretched on, but as night fell, it arrived quicker than Dionne expected.

Her heels clicked rhythmically against the pavement as she walked to her car, the cool night air brushing against her skin. She unlocked the car, slid inside, and prepared to drive home. Just as she was about to pull out of the parking lot, her phone vibrated once again. The familiar sound ignited her irritation. Without glancing at the screen, she snatched up the phone, assuming it was Malik.

"What?" she snapped, her frustration evident in her tone.

A deep, smooth voice responded, catching her completely off guard. "And here I thought we were friends, Ms. Smith," the voice teased, its warmth immediately recognizable.

Her heart stilled for a moment, her grip tightening on the phone. "Arris?" she said softly, her disbelief laced with nervousness.

"Yeah," he replied casually, though his tone carried a hint of caution. "Did I call at a bad time?"

Quickly recovering, Dionne shook her head, even though he couldn't see her. "No, not at all. I apologize. I thought you were... someone else," she said, her voice calmer as she hurried to explain.

Arris chuckled, the sound deep and rich through the speaker. "Sounds like you've had a long day," he said, his amusement barely concealed.

"You could say that," Dionne admitted, the tension in her shoulders easing slightly at the sound of his voice. There was something grounding about him, something that made her forget, even momentarily, the chaos of her personal life.

"What can I do for you, Arris?" Dionne asked, her confident, professional tone slipping back into place.

"I'm scared you're going to beat my ass if I tell you," Arris joked, referencing her earlier aggressive tone when answering the phone. Dionne couldn't help but chuckle, the sound like music to his ears.

"No, it's just been a long, stressful day," she admitted, her voice softening. She could sense Arris smiling, even though he didn't say anything right away.

"Well, I might have a way to make your stressful day end a little less stressful," he said smoothly, his confidence evident, making Dionne pause.

"Oh, really? Like what?" she asked, quickly recovering her composure, her curiosity piqued.

Arris chuckled deeply, the sound warm and inviting. "Come to this address, and you'll see for yourself," he said, his tone laced with intrigue. A moment later, her phone buzzed with a message containing the location.

Dionne glanced at the address on her screen, her brows furrowing slightly in curiosity. She wasn't sure what Arris had planned, but she could feel the weight of her day lifting slightly at the prospect of something different. Maybe this was the distraction she needed.

There was a brief silence on the line, prompting Arris to check in. "Still there?" he asked, his voice breaking through her thoughts.

Feenin'

"Yeah... umm, I'm on the way," Dionne replied, her tone a mix of nerves and anticipation.

"Good. Just call me when you get here," he said, and she could hear the smile in his voice, making her own lips curl into a small smile.

They ended the call, and Dionne adjusted her rearview mirror, a flutter of excitement rising in her chest. She didn't know what Arris had in store, but for the first time in a while, she felt a spark of curiosity and adventure. Taking a deep breath, she drove in the direction of the address he had sent, wondering what awaited her.

Dionne pulled up to the sprawling home, instantly recognizing it as the same property she'd sold to Arris. His house? she thought, her brows knitting in surprise. Before she could fully process the thought or step out of the car, her door was pulled open. Standing there was Arris, effortlessly handsome in a black tee that clung to his toned physique, shorts that revealed his inked legs, white socks, and slides. The black durag tied snugly on his head added to his charm, making him look more laid-back yet still undeniably confident. Dionne's eyes lingered for a moment, admiring how different yet captivating he looked outside of his usual polished suits.

Arris extended his hand to her, his intense gaze locking onto hers. Dionne smiled, taking his hand as he helped her out of the car.

"You know I can exit my car, and walk up a driveway on my own, right?" she teased, her voice light with amusement.

Arris chuckled, his deep laugh sending a flutter through her chest. "I told you, you'll never touch a door in my presence," he replied smoothly, his tone low as he subtly admired her.

Dionne glanced down at herself, suddenly aware of the contrast between them. She was still dressed in her professional attire—brown tailored dress pants, matching heels, and a crisp white blouse. Her hair was swept into a slick ponytail atop her head, a testament to her polished demeanor after a long day. Arris, on the other hand, exuded a casual confidence, completely at ease in his space.

Her smile softened as she caught the way his eyes traced her figure, and she couldn't help but notice the stark difference between Arris's attentiveness and Malik's distant demeanor. This small gesture—opening her door, holding her hand—was something she hadn't experienced in so long, and it stirred something unfamiliar yet comforting within her.

"You always this much of a gentleman, or are you just showing off?" she asked playfully, masking the vulnerability creeping up on her.

Arris smirked, his gaze never wavering. "It's not showing off when it's who you are," he replied, his voice calm but loaded with meaning.

Dionne's smile grew as she allowed herself to relax. She wasn't used to this—someone making her feel seen. And though she knew this was just a visit, nothing more, she couldn't help but appreciate the difference Arris brought into her world.

They stepped into Arris's home, and Dionne's eyes roamed the space with admiration. Even though she'd sold him the house, it looked entirely different—better—than when she had last seen it. The once-empty space had transformed into a home, with warm, inviting decor that reflected Arris's style. She smiled at the subtle yet intentional details, noting the contrast between the house she'd shown and the lived-in charm it now exuded.

Arris noticed her taking it all in and smirked. "I had to change some things up. You fuck with it?" he asked, his tone relaxed and natural, so different from the sharp businessman she usually dealt with.

Dionne turned to him, catching how at ease he seemed here, away from the pressures of work. He was laid-back and confident, but there was an edge to him that intrigued her. She nodded, her lips curling into a smile. "Yeah, you did good with the decor," she complimented, making him grin.

Still holding her hand, he led her deeper into the house, his touch lingering but never overstepping. Arris's subtle affection hadn't gone unnoticed, but it was never too much—always balanced, always leaving her curious.

When they entered the dining room, Dionne's eyes lit up at the sight before her. The table was set for two, with plates of food already prepared and glasses of wine waiting. The presentation was thoughtful, and her smile grew radiant.

"What's all this?" she asked softly, her voice tinged with surprise and delight.

Arris pulled her seat out for her, his movements deliberate and smooth. "Something to ease whatever stress your day caused," he replied, his tone calm but with an undercurrent of intention.

Dionne sat down, her gaze falling on the meal in front of her. Her favorite—lamb chops glazed with bourbon-infused peach sauce, mashed potatoes, and Collard greens. She looked up at him, her brow raised in pleasant disbelief. "You made this?" she asked.

Arris took the seat across from her, leaning back comfortably. "Yeah," he answered simply, watching her reaction as she took a bite.

The flavors hit her instantly, the lamb chops juicy and seasoned to perfection. Her eyes widened in surprise, and she let out a soft laugh. "This is really good," she complimented, making him chuckle.

Feenin'

"I heard from my chef that this was your favorite meal," Arris said, his eyes locking with hers. "Figured I'd see if I could top what we serve at my restaurant."

Dionne smiled, warmth spreading through her chest. "You did. I'm surprised," she admitted, taking another bite.

"Why's that?" he asked, his gaze unwavering, his interest evident.

She smirked, playful but honest. "You don't look like you can throw down in the kitchen like this," she teased.

Arris laughed, the sound deep and genuine. "Looks can be deceiving," he replied, leaning forward slightly. "There's a lot about me that might surprise you."

The confidence in his tone sent a ripple of intrigue through her. Dionne couldn't help but wonder what else there was to learn about the man sitting across from her—the man who, in such a short time, managed to turn her stress-filled evening into something unexpectedly comforting.

"Yea, like what?" Dionne challenged, her confidence shining as she sipped her wine. Arris chuckled, swallowing his food and preparing to respond, but before he could, his phone buzzed on the table. The name "Ma" lit up the screen, drawing Dionne's attention. She smiled warmly at the sight, but the look on Arris's face as he saw it was anything but cheerful.

"Sorry, I have to take this," he said, excusing himself from the table. The tension in his voice was clear, and Dionne couldn't help but notice the way his jaw tightened. Concern flickered across her face, but she decided to mind her business and returned her focus to the delicious meal in front of her.

Arris stepped into another room, his tone low but sharp as he answered the call. Meanwhile, Dionne's phone buzzed, breaking the quiet moment. She sighed, relieved to see it wasn't Malik this time, and answered with a warm tone. "Hey, Lon."

London's voice came through, loud and filled with attitude. "Don't 'hey Lon' me. Where the hell you at? It's getting late, and I know your ass ain't still at the office."

Dionne chuckled at her best friend's familiar scolding. She had been staying at London's place for the past few days, avoiding Malik while figuring out her next move, and it had slipped her mind to check in. "My bad, sis. I forgot to let you know. I'll be home soon," Dionne said, keeping her tone casual, not wanting to reveal where she was.

As she spoke, Arris emerged from the other room, his confident demeanor replaced with a simmering anger. The shift in his energy was unmistakable, and it made Dionne pause mid-conversation. Her concern shifted entirely to him, her eyes scanning his face for answers. London was still talking on the other end, but Dionne wasn't listening anymore.

"Okay, London. I have to talk to you later. See you when I get home," she said quickly, ending the call and setting her phone down.

Arris approached her, his expression hard and his shoulders tense. The warmth he'd shown earlier had vanished, leaving behind a stormy intensity that filled the room.

Arris hadn't spoken a word, but Dionne's instincts told her he was fighting a silent battle. She reached out, her fingers gently brushing his hand, pulling his attention back to her. "Everything okay?" she asked softly, her voice laced with genuine concern. He nodded, a half-hearted attempt to assure her, but his eyes betrayed him.

"You don't have to lie to me, Arris. Friends, right? Talk to me," Dionne urged gently, her voice calm and grounding. The tension in his shoulders seemed to ease, the weight of her touch and her soothing tone breaking through his defenses. He let out a long, shaky breath, leaning back in his chair as if releasing the invisible armor he carried.

"You ever feel like no matter how much you try to leave the past behind, it just… won't let you go?" Arris finally spoke, his voice low, tinged with frustration and exhaustion. The vulnerability in his words surprised even him, but Dionne didn't flinch. She leaned forward slightly, her gaze steady and understanding.

"All the time," she admitted, her tone reflective and warm. "But sometimes, the past sticks around because we haven't dealt with it yet."

Arris looked at her, her words striking a chord he wasn't prepared for. His jaw tightened, his thoughts racing as he absorbed the truth in what she'd said. There was something about Dionne's presence—her calmness, her ability to see right through him—that felt disarming. For the first time in what felt like forever, he didn't feel the need to shoulder the weight of his world alone.

The realization startled him. Here was a woman he barely knew, yet she seemed to understand the parts of him he worked so hard to conceal. She offered something he hadn't known he needed: reprieve. Dionne's touch, her voice, her unyielding patience—they all pulled him closer, and for once, he didn't resist.

"Running from your past?" Dionne asked gently, her hand still resting close to his, bridging a quiet connection between them. Arris looked up at her, his dark eyes holding the weight of emotions he rarely let anyone see. Yet, something about her presence softened the storm raging inside him.

Feenin'

"No, just trying to leave the past where it's at," he said, his tone calm but tinged with anger simmering just beneath the surface. Still, as he looked at her, his gaze softened, betraying a flicker of relief in her company. Dionne could sense the turmoil he was fighting to suppress.

"Want to express more of it?" she asked, her voice steady but inviting. "It looks like you're bottling up something that's been weighing on you."

Arris's lips curved into a brief smile—small, but real. For once, he felt seen, like someone had managed to peel back a layer he thought was impenetrable. "My little sister is back in town," he said, his smile lingering for a moment as he thought of A'Lani.

Dionne mirrored his smile, touched by the warmth in his voice when he mentioned his sister. "That sounds like a good thing," she said softly.

"It is," he admitted, but his expression darkened as he continued. "But she didn't just come to visit… she came because of Calvin."

The mention of the name made his jaw tighten, his smile vanishing as quickly as it appeared. Dionne's brows furrowed slightly, curiosity and concern mingling in her eyes. "Who's Calvin?" she asked gently, her tone urging him to open up without pressure.

Arris leaned back, the venom in his voice unmistakable as he replied, "He's the nigga that made me."

Dionne blinked, taken aback by the rawness in his words. It wasn't just anger she felt—it was hurt, betrayal, and a lifetime of unresolved pain that he carried in every syllable. "Your father?" she guessed, piecing it together.

Arris nodded, his expression hardening. "The man who was supposed to be, but he chose the streets over us. Over his family. And now he's trying to come back like nothing happened." His voice cracked slightly, but he recovered quickly, unwilling to let the vulnerability show too much.

Dionne's eyes softened, sadness evident as she took in the weight of his words. Arris couldn't believe he was opening up like this, especially to someone he barely knew. Yet, there was something about Dionne—a grounding presence that made him feel safe, even vulnerable.

Dionne didn't interrupt, but the gentle squeeze of her hand reassured him that she was listening.

"Now he wants to sit down with me and my sister to amend all the shit he caused us," Arris said, his anger simmering just beneath the surface.

"And I'm guessing your sister is open to it, while you're against it?" Dionne asked softly, her tone laced with understanding.

Arris nodded, his frustration clear in the way his jaw tightened. "I love my sister. I've always treated her more like my daughter than my sister. Because her own father didn't give a fuck about her, I had to step up." His voice cracked slightly, but he pressed on. "I don't want to break her heart by not giving her what she wants, but I can't face that nigga."

His words hung heavy in the air, the coldness in his tone masking the deeper hurt he carried. "I always said I'd kill that nigga if I ever saw him again," he admitted, his voice growing sharper, "but when he popped up at my place of business, I froze."

Arris clenched his fists, his confusion evident. "Everything in me wanted to harm his ass, but I couldn't." His eyes darted away, frustration etched into every line of his face. "At first, I told myself it was because I was at work, surrounded by my people. But that's not it."

Dionne didn't flinch at his admission, didn't show an ounce of judgment or fear. She just sat there, her quiet presence grounding him.

"You think... maybe it wasn't about him?" Dionne ventured carefully, her voice calm but probing. "Maybe it was about you. About not letting him take any more from you—not your peace, not your control, not your future."

Arris looked at her, the intensity in his gaze softening just slightly. For the first time, her words made him pause, forcing him to consider something he hadn't before. Maybe she was right. Maybe holding back wasn't weakness—it was strength. It was him reclaiming the power Calvin had stolen all those years ago.

"You've been carrying this weight for a long time," Dionne added gently. "Maybe it's time to let it go—not for him, but for you."

Her words lingered in the air, offering him a perspective he hadn't allowed himself to see.

Dionne looked at him with soft, sad eyes, her gaze filled with an understanding Arris hadn't felt from anyone else. The man who was always so confident and composed now seemed weighed down by pain, anger, and sadness. Something about seeing him like this made her chest tighten. She didn't understand why, but she wanted to take that pain away.

"I hate that nigga, man," Arris said, his voice rising slightly in frustration. Dionne didn't flinch at his tone. Instead, she stood, calmly picking up their plates and wine glasses before heading to the kitchen.

Arris sat silently, his eyes following her every move, his confusion growing. What was she doing? He watched as she washed the dishes with steady hands, the silence between them somehow comforting. When she returned, she extended her hand toward him.

Feenin'

Arris hesitated for a moment, unsure of her intentions, before taking her hand and standing. "Where we going, Dionne?" he asked softly, curiosity evident in his tone.

She smiled faintly, her voice gentle but resolute. "I need an escape from my stressful day, and you need peace with yours."

Guiding him to the couch, she urged him to sit, and before he could fully process what was happening, Dionne straddled his lap.

"Dionne... what are you doing?" Arris asked in a low, almost cautious tone. Her closeness was unexpected, but he didn't move to stop her. Instead, his hands instinctively settled on her waist, holding her in place as if afraid she might pull away. The warmth of her body against his grounded him in the moment, quieting the storm in his mind.

She looked directly into his eyes, her gaze unwavering. "Don't let your past define who you are today," she began, her voice soft but steady. He stayed silent, drawn in by her sincerity. "If talking to your father won't bring you the peace you need, then don't do it. I know how it feels to put someone else's happiness or healing above your own, and it kills you inside."

Her words hung heavily between them, but Arris could tell she wasn't just speaking for his benefit. There was a vulnerability in her tone, a quiet pain she was revealing without saying it outright. She was opening herself up in a way that mirrored what she was asking of him.

Arris studied her face, his grip on her waist tightening slightly. In her eyes, he saw a mix of fear, anger, and the same longing for escape that he felt. And in that moment, he realized something: Dionne wasn't just trying to help him; she was finding solace in helping him. He was her distraction, her reprieve from whatever she was battling.

"You're fighting your own war, aren't you?" Arris said quietly, his deep voice laced with understanding. Dionne's lips parted as if to respond, but she hesitated, her walls wavering. She nodded slightly, her vulnerability now fully exposed to him.

For the first time in years, Arris didn't feel alone in his pain.

"So tonight, let's just forget about everything," Dionne said softly, her voice steady but charged with unspoken emotions. "Our stressful day, our fucked-up past and future, and just live in the present." Her eyes locked onto his, drawing him deeper into her.

Arris studied her face, her words lingering in the air between them. "How do we do that?" he asked, his voice low and rough. His gaze trailed from her piercing eyes to the soft curves of her body pressed against his. The heat radiating between them was impossible to ignore, and it stirred something primal within him.

"Kiss me," Dionne whispered, her voice barely audible but laced with a magnetic pull that Arris couldn't resist.

A slow smile spread across his face, the kind of smile that revealed just how long he had wanted this moment. Without hesitation, he leaned in, his lips capturing hers. The kiss was gentle at first, exploratory, but it quickly deepened as Dionne's tongue teased his. It wasn't just a kiss—it was an unspoken surrender, a mutual escape from everything that had been weighing them down.

For a brief moment, the world outside of their connection disappeared. Dionne forgot about the mess that was her relationship with Malik and the expectations of his mother. Arris let go of the anger, the hurt, and the weight of his father's betrayal. In that moment, there was only them.

As Dionne let out a soft moan, it ignited something raw and hungry in Arris. His hands gripped her waist tighter, pulling her even closer as he rose from the couch with her still in his arms. Dionne instinctively wrapped her legs around his waist, her body fitting against his like they had always belonged there.

Arris carried her with purpose, his lips never leaving hers, as he made his way to his bedroom. The air between them was charged with anticipation, every touch, every breath, intensifying the unspoken connection they had been building from the moment they met.

He laid her down gently, his dark eyes drinking in every inch of her body still clad in the office attire she wore that day. Her presence, her beauty—it was like she was made to test every ounce of his control. He paused, his gaze meeting hers, his voice low and serious. "You're sure about this?"

Arris didn't want to cross a line she wasn't ready for, even though everything in him screamed to take her, to make this moment theirs. Dionne's lips curved into a small smile, her head nodding in affirmation. Her eyes said it all—she needed this as much as he did.

Arris's lips parted into a grin, full of restrained hunger, before he leaned down and captured her lips again. The kiss was deep, filled with unspoken desires. His lips trailed to her neck, where he licked and sucked at her skin like she was the most irresistible thing he'd ever tasted. He left marks—his marks—branding her in a way that said she was his, even if just for tonight.

Dionne moaned softly, her body melting under his touch. The sound drove him further, his hands finding the buttons of her blouse and undoing them swiftly but with care. He pushed the fabric open, revealing the black lace bra that clung to her flawless skin. Arris froze for

Feenin'

a moment, taking in the sight of her.

"Fuck," he muttered under his breath, a smirk forming as he let his hands brush over her bare shoulders. "You're perfect," he said, his voice laced with awe and hunger. To him, Dionne wasn't just a woman—she was an escape, an addiction he hadn't known he'd develop. She was everything he craved in this moment, and nothing else mattered.

Dionne's breathing quickened under his gaze, her need for release and distraction mirroring his. In this moment, they weren't business partners or friends. They were two broken souls finding solace in each other's arms, letting their shared intensity drown out the chaos of the world outside.

Arris didn't hesitate, his hunger for Dionne evident in every move he made. He captured her right breast in his mouth, licking and sucking like he was determined to taste every inch of her. "Shit..." Dionne moaned, her back arching as waves of pleasure rolled through her. The intensity of his actions overwhelmed her senses, leaving her craving more.

She felt desired in a way she hadn't in years. The way Arris looked at her—with an intensity that screamed possession, like she was his most cherished prize—made her heart swell. She hadn't seen that look from Malik in so long, and now, with Arris, it was all she could think about.

Arris continued his journey down her body, his hands skillfully removing her brown pants to reveal matching black lace panties. "You're so fucking beautiful," he murmured against her skin, his voice rough and low, sending chills down her spine.

Dionne barely had time to process his words before he hooked his teeth into the waistband of her panties, pulling them off with his mouth alone. Her breath hitched as he spread her legs wide, exposing her to his hungry gaze. Without hesitation, Arris dove in, his tongue finding her clit with precision that made her gasp.

"Fuck... right there," Dionne moaned, her back arching instinctively as her legs trembled uncontrollably. Arris grinned against her, the sound of her pleasure only fueling his determination. His tongue worked in fast, deliberate motions, hitting every spot she'd been longing for someone to find.

Her moans grew louder, her body completely surrendering to the sensations he was giving her. Arris gripped her thighs firmly, keeping her in place as he devoured her like a man starved. He wanted to memorize every sound, every shiver, every movement. He wanted to make her forget anyone else existed, to make her crave him as much as he craved her.

"Goddamn, Dionne. You taste so fucking good," he growled, his words vibrating against her sensitive skin, sending her closer to the edge. Her fingers tangled in his durag as she let herself drown in the pleasure only he could give.

Overwhelmed by the relentless sensation, Dionne instinctively started to scoot away, but Arris's firm grip on her legs kept her exactly where he wanted her. "Don't run, Mama. Feel that shit," he growled against her skin, his deep voice vibrating against her, sending a shockwave straight through her body. His mouth moved with purpose, devouring her insides like she was the last meal he'd ever taste.

Dionne's moans filled the room, raw and unrestrained, as the heat in her core built to an unbearable peak. Her orgasm loomed closer, a sensation she hadn't felt in almost a year. Arris could sense it, reading her body like it was made for him. He kept his pace steady, his tongue flicking her clit with precision, until she shattered beneath him, her climax ripping through her body.

"Ouu fuck," she cried out, her voice hoarse with pleasure as Arris stayed with her, riding out her orgasm with an intensity that left her breathless. He finally pulled back, his beard glistening with her wetness, and gave her a devious smile—a smile that screamed she'd just unleashed something in him she wasn't prepared for.

She barely had time to catch her breath before his fingers slid inside her, slow but deliberate. Dionne gasped, her body arching as he worked her with a rhythm that left her completely at his mercy. As his fingers moved inside her, Arris stripped out of his clothes, his toned body and tattoos now fully on display.

"Wait... wait, Arr—" she panted, trying to escape his relentless touch for a moment, but he wasn't having it. His grip tightened, his fingers curling in just the right spot, drawing a scream from her lips. He pulled her closer, his strength making resistance impossible.

"Nah, you wanted this... so take it," he said lowly, his voice dripping with dominance. Dionne's heart raced at his words, her chest rising and falling as her eyes locked with his. She loved a challenge, and there was no way she was about to let him think she couldn't handle him. Not with the way his gaze bore into her, daring her to give in completely.

Arris leaned in, his lips brushing against her ear. "I've been craving you since the first time I laid eyes on you," he murmured, his voice sending a fresh wave of arousal through her. Tonight, she was about to feel just how much he meant those words.

Arris finally stripped, revealing himself fully, and Dionne's eyes widened, a gasp escaping her lips as she took in the sight before her. She had never seen or imagined a man so endowed. Malik, in every sense,

Feenin'

couldn't compare. For the first time that night, a hint of nervousness flickered in her as the reality of Arris being inside her hit.

Arris, sensing her hesitation, leaned down and kissed her gently, his lips soft and reassuring against hers. "I got you," he murmured, his deep voice sending shivers down her spine. He slipped on a condom with ease, and positioned himself between her legs, guiding himself in slowly. The stretch was intense, her walls gripping him tightly as he entered her inch by inch, letting her adjust to his size.

"Shit," he groaned, his voice raw with restraint as he fought the urge to bury himself completely in her warmth. Dionne clutched the sheets, her back arching as she took deep breaths, trying to adjust to him. The initial discomfort began to fade, replaced by a growing pleasure that built with each slow thrust.

"Okay," she whispered, her voice shaky but filled with need, giving him the green light. Arris smirked, his pace quickening as he pulled out almost entirely before slamming back in, his strokes precise and powerful. Dionne's moans turned into cries of pleasure, her head falling back as her body surrendered to him.

"Fuck, Dee," Arris groaned, his voice strained as he gripped her hips, pulling her closer with every thrust. The sound of their bodies colliding echoed through the room, a rhythm of pure passion and connection. Dionne's nails clawed at his back, her legs locking around his waist, urging him deeper.

Her eyes rolled back as wave after wave of pleasure surged through her, her body responding to Arris in ways she didn't think were possible. This was supposed to be a quick distraction, an escape from the chaos of her life, but it was turning into something far more intoxicating.

Arris felt it too. Every moan, every gasp, every way her body reacted to his drove him closer to the edge. He'd been with women before, but none of them had made him feel this. This was deeper than just physical—it was consuming, raw, and impossible to ignore.

"You feel so fucking good," he growled, his lips finding hers in a heated kiss as he poured everything he had into her. For both of them, the world outside faded, leaving only the shared intensity of this moment.

His pace quickened, their bodies colliding with an intensity that echoed through the room. Arris gripped Dionne's hips tightly, flipping her over so her ass was perfectly positioned in his line of sight. The sight alone sent a wave of lust through him, making him feel like he was on the edge of heaven itself. Without hesitation, he slammed back into her, his thrusts deep and unrelenting.

"YES... Arris! Shit!" Dionne screamed, her voice raw with pleasure as he hit every spot that sent her spiraling. The sensations were so overwhelming she instinctively reached back, her hand pushing against his stomach in an attempt to catch her breath, but Arris wasn't about to let her retreat.

"Nah, you can take it, Mama," he growled, grabbing both of her hands and pinning them behind her back. The shift in control only heightened the intensity, her body arching as he drove into her even harder. He poured every ounce of his frustration, anger, and passion into each thrust, his grip on her firm but not harsh.

"This shit is so fucking wet," he groaned, his voice thick with arousal. The slick sounds of their connection only fueled him further as Dionne's screams turned into desperate moans that filled the room. He could feel her body clenching around him, signaling she was on the brink of release again.

Before she could fall over the edge, Arris pulled out, leaving her panting and trembling. Without giving her a moment to recover, he turned her over, his strength on full display as he lifted her effortlessly into the air. Dionne gasped, clutching his shoulders, her heart racing at the height and the vulnerability of the position. But Arris's hold on her was unwavering—physically and emotionally.

"Don't worry, I got you," he murmured, his voice a mix of reassurance and hunger. He positioned her just right, her legs over his shoulders as he dove into her with his mouth. His tongue moved with urgency, licking and sucking her clit like it was the only thing that mattered in the world.

"Yes... fuck, yes!" Dionne cried out, her body shaking uncontrollably as waves of pleasure crashed over her. Arris groaned against her, the vibrations sending shockwaves through her core. He was relentless, his face buried between her thighs, drinking her in like she was his lifeline.

Her moans grew louder, her nails digging into his shoulders as she surrendered completely to him. Arris wasn't just satisfying her physically—he was unraveling every barrier she had, claiming every inch of her, mind, body, and soul. And in that moment, nothing else mattered.

Dionne felt her orgasm approaching again, and so did Arris. Without missing a beat, he stopped, pulling her down until his dick was deep inside her once more. The fullness of him made her scream, her eyes rolling back as waves of pleasure overtook her. Arris had her feeling things she never knew she could, emotions and sensations that left her completely vulnerable but utterly alive.

Feenin'

He pressed her against the wall, thrusting into her with an intensity that left her breathless. Her body slid against the cool surface with every movement, her ponytail now a chaotic mess, strands sticking to her face. But to Arris, she was flawless—her disheveled beauty only making her more perfect in his eyes.

Her legs tightened around his waist, her moans rising in pitch. Arris looked up at her, captivated by the pleasure etched across her face. He could feel his own orgasm building, the way her walls clenched around him pushing him closer to the edge.

"Fuck, I'm about to—" Dionne started, but the words died in her throat as her body exploded. She squirted, her release so powerful it soaked Arris and the floor beneath them. Arris grunted, his own release following seconds later as he spilled into the condom. He held her steady, his breaths heavy, not caring about the mess they had made.

Dionne, on the other hand, felt her face heat up in embarrassment. She'd never squirted before, never even thought she was capable of it, and now she couldn't meet his eyes. Arris noticed, his own lips curling into a satisfied grin that contrasted her flustered state.

"Fuck, you're amazing," he said, his voice filled with awe as he carried her effortlessly into the bathroom. He sat her down on the toilet, gently holding her there to pee, as he moved around the room like he had done this a million times before. He turned on the faucet, preparing a hot bath for the two of them.

"Arris, I'm sorry about—" Dionne started, her voice small as she tried to apologize for the mess she made. But he quickly cut her off, crouching down in front of her so their eyes met. He cupped her face gently, his thumb brushing against her cheek before he leaned in to kiss her softly.

"Never apologize for creating a masterpiece," he said, his tone smooth and laced with sincerity. His words wrapped around her like a warm blanket, sending butterflies fluttering wildly in her stomach. She nodded, unable to find the words to respond, completely disarmed by the way he looked at her—as though she was the most extraordinary thing he'd ever encountered.

Arris stood, his confidence unshaken, and returned to preparing the bath, the steam from the water rising as the scent of lavender filled the air. Dionne watched him, her body still tingling from the way he'd just unraveled her, realizing that this night was unlike anything she'd ever experienced before.

Once he finished preparing the bath, Dionne slid into the steaming water, the heat instantly soothing the muscles Arris had thoroughly worked over. She let out a soft sigh of relief as the tension melted away. Arris climbed in behind her, the warmth of the water matching the heat of his body as he wrapped his strong arms around her.

"Thank you," he whispered in her ear, his deep voice sending a shiver down her spine despite the hot water. "I hope I was as much of an escape for you as you were peace for me." His words were sincere, laced with vulnerability that Dionne hadn't expected.

She smiled softly, leaning into his embrace. In truth, he had been her escape, just as much as she had been his. For the first time in what felt like forever, Malik, his mother, and the weight of her relationship hadn't crossed her mind. Even the incessant ringing of her phone, which had gone unnoticed during their time together, seemed like a distant memory.

"You were," she replied, her voice low but filled with honesty. She let herself sink further into his touch, savoring the rare feeling of peace.

They bathed in silence, the quiet between them comforting rather than awkward. It felt as though the world outside had ceased to exist. Afterward, they found themselves in Arris's bed, wrapped in soft sheets and tangled in one another. Dionne drifted off to sleep in his arms, her breathing soft and even against his chest.

But sleep eluded Arris. His eyes remained open, staring at the ceiling as his mind replayed the events of the night. He looked down at the woman nestled against him, her face relaxed in sleep, and felt something unfamiliar stirring in his chest. She hadn't just taken away his pain; she'd given him something to hold onto, even if only for a night.

Arris's thoughts spiraled, the lines between their temporary escape and something deeper beginning to blur. He craved more of her—her touch, her presence, her very essence. What had started as a fleeting moment to forget their troubles had turned into the beginning of something much more potent.

Lying there, he realized that Dionne wasn't just a distraction. She was quickly becoming his addiction.

Chapter 6

Dionne stirred in her sleep, the early morning sunlight spilling through Arris's expansive windows and gently waking her. As she opened her eyes, the first thing she noticed was the warmth of Arris's arm still securely wrapped around her. She shifted slightly, careful not to wake him, and glanced up at his face. He was still fast asleep, his features relaxed in a way that contrasted sharply with the intensity she'd seen in him the night before. One arm rested protectively around her, while the other was tucked casually behind his head.

Her gaze drifted to the intricate tattoos etched across his chest and arms, tracing the patterns with her eyes as she licked her lips unconsciously. Last night lingered vividly in her mind—a night that began with a thoughtful dinner he'd prepared, evolved into moments of raw vulnerability, and ended in passionate intimacy that still sent shivers down her spine. She felt the heat rise to her cheeks at the memory.

Dionne watched him for a moment longer, captivated by how peaceful he seemed. The anger and pain that had consumed him the night before were nowhere to be found now, replaced by a calmness that made her chest tighten in an unfamiliar way. Seeing him like this, free of the weight he carried, warmed her heart in a way she hadn't anticipated.

She didn't understand why she felt so drawn to him. They had only just met, and yet something about him made her care deeply, almost instinctively. It was as if she could sense the pain he carried beneath his confident exterior—a pain she wanted to ease, even if only for a moment.

Dionne sighed softly, lying back down and nestling closer to him, her head resting against his chest. His steady heartbeat was a comforting rhythm that made her forget, if only briefly, the chaos waiting for her outside these walls. She wasn't ready to leave this sanctuary yet—not just the comfort of his bed, but the safety she felt in his presence.

The sound of her phone ringing jolted Dionne out of her peaceful moment, and she moved quickly but carefully to silence it, trying not to wake Arris. Glancing at the screen, she groaned when she saw Malik's name flashing. Reluctantly, she answered, attempting to slip out of Arris's arms to speak privately, but his grip tightened instinctively. She froze, looking up at him. Even in his sleep, he held onto her with a protective strength that made her feel safe. A small smile formed on her lips despite the annoyance she felt for the call.

"Hello," Malik's voice came through the phone, snapping her back to reality. She whispered into the receiver, not wanting to disturb Arris, "What do you want?"

"Why haven't you been answering your phone? I've been calling you all night and this morning!" Malik's irritated tone grated on her nerves. She rolled her eyes, her frustration growing. "I was busy. What do you want, Malik?" she replied dryly.

There was a pause before Malik let out a heavy sigh, his frustration evident. "I was trying to tell you that my mother was rushed to the hospital yesterday," he said, his voice strained. Dionne's heart sank at the mention of Mama Glen. She sat up quickly, not caring if she disturbed Arris anymore. Her concern was entirely on the woman she adored.

"Is she okay?" Dionne asked, her voice soft and tinged with desperation.

"No, it's bad. You need to stop whatever has you so busy and come to the hospital," Malik snapped, his tone dripping with attitude. Before she could respond, the line went dead.

Dionne stared at the phone in disbelief, her emotions now a chaotic mix of worry for Mama Glen and annoyance at Malik's audacity. She took a deep breath, trying to gather her thoughts. The weight of the situation pressed down on her, and she knew she had to make a decision quickly.

Dionne pushed Malik's attitude aside, her concern fully fixated on Mama Glen. She shifted again, trying to move out of Arris's hold, but his grip instinctively tightened as his eyes fluttered open. He looked at her, his expression softening instantly at the sight of her worried face.

"Arris, I need to go," Dionne said, her voice cracking with the weight of her emotions. Arris sat up straighter, his concern evident. "Everything straight?" he asked, his hands still resting on her waist, grounding her.

Dionne hesitated, the urge to share her burden battling against her need to keep her personal life separate. She wanted Arris to remain her escape, not someone she had to add to the list of people to mask her

Feenin'

struggles around. "Yeah, I just have to go," she finally said, her voice quieter but firm.

Arris studied her for a long moment, his instincts telling him there was more to her sudden urgency, but he didn't push. Instead, he let her go, his hands lingering for just a second longer before he released her. Dionne quickly got up, realizing she was still wearing one of Arris's oversized shirts that hung loosely over her frame. She stripped out of it in a rush, exposing her naked body to him once again.

Arris leaned back, his gaze involuntarily sweeping over her. Despite the concern he felt for her, his desire remained, his tongue brushing over his lips as he admired her. He fought the urge to pull her back to him, to tell her she didn't need to leave and that whatever was troubling her, he'd fix it. But he held back, knowing it was too soon for those words, even if they burned in his chest.

Dionne dressed quickly, her movements hurried and purposeful, as if trying to outrun her own thoughts. Arris silently watched her, his craving for her deepening with every passing second. She was slipping away, and he hated it, but he respected her need for space.

Arris sat up, pulling Dionne by her waist, his hold tightened slightly, grounding her despite the chaos swirling in her mind. "Dionne, slow down. What's wrong?" he asked softly, his voice tinged with concern as he pulled her closer. He needed to feel her warmth, her presence anchoring him after the vulnerable night they'd shared.

Dionne's breath hitched at their closeness, her heart racing as her emotions waged war within her. "Nothing... I just need to leave. Now," she said, trying to keep her voice steady, though her composure was slipping. Arris could see through her words, the storm in her eyes betraying her calm facade.

"I'm not letting you leave like this," he said firmly, his hands gently rubbing her back, an instinctive effort to comfort her. Dionne's chest tightened at his touch, her conflicting emotions threatening to spill over. In a moment of impulsive need, she reached down, cupping his face in her hands before pressing her lips to his. Arris melted into the kiss, savoring the fleeting intimacy, but when she pulled away, her words sliced through the moment.

"Our night of escape is over. I have to go back to reality," she said, her voice laced with regret. Arris's heart clenched at her words, an ache settling deep in his chest. He didn't want their connection to end; he couldn't explain it, but he was already stuck on her. He needed her close, and the thought of her walking away left him reeling. Yet, he held back from saying what he truly felt, afraid it might push her further away.

At the end of the day, they were supposed to be business partners. Crossing that line too far could jeopardize everything, even if the lines between them had already blurred beyond recognition.

Dionne noticed the flicker of hurt in his eyes, though he quickly masked it behind a stoic expression. Her own heart ached at the sight, knowing she was leaving something unresolved. But her life was too complicated, too messy to bring another man into the chaos. Especially a man like Arris, who was already breaking down walls she didn't even realize were there.

"I'll walk you out," Arris said gently, his voice low as he stood, his towering frame effortlessly commanding the room. Dionne could hear the pain he tried to conceal, and it mirrored the turmoil she felt inside. She nodded, unable to find the right words to say, and followed him as he led her to the door.

Dionne slid her feet into the heels she'd worn the previous day, the sound of them clicking softly against the polished floor as she followed Arris downstairs. His hand, as always, was wrapped around hers, a small but comforting gesture that made her heart ache at the thought of leaving. When they reached her car, she instinctively knew not to touch the door. Arris opened it for her, his chivalry something she was quickly growing accustomed to—and something she knew she would miss.

Before she could step inside, Arris gently pulled her by the waist, turning her to face him. Their eyes locked, and the tension between them was evident. Dionne felt her breath hitch as the weight of his gaze settled on her. "Thank you... for everything," she said softly, her voice carrying a mix of gratitude and sadness. She knew neither of them wanted this moment to end, but reality was pulling her away again, stealing the happiness she'd found in his arms.

Arris cupped her face with his large hands, his thumbs softly brushing her cheeks. He stepped closer, backing her gently against the smooth surface of her Urus. The contrast of the cool car against her warm skin sent a shiver down her spine. "I'm here whenever you need another escape," he said, his voice low and laced with sincerity, his eyes never leaving hers.

"Me too," she replied, her voice just as soft, mirroring his words with a faint smile that didn't quite reach her eyes. Their connection was undeniable, even in the fleeting moments they shared.

Arris leaned in, pressing his lips to hers. Dionne didn't hesitate, deepening the kiss, their unspoken emotions pouring out through their embrace. It was a kiss filled with longing, unspoken truths, and the bittersweet promise of what could never be. When they pulled away,

Feenin'

Arris took a step back, his jaw tightening as he forced himself to give her the space she needed to leave.

"Be safe," he said quietly, his voice carrying a weight that made her chest tighten.

"You too," she replied, her tone soft as she slid into the driver's seat. Arris closed the door gently, stepping back as she started the engine. She glanced at him one last time, the image of him standing there etched in her mind as she drove away.

Dionne headed to London's house first, needing to change before going to the hospital. The last thing she needed was Malik questioning why she was still in her work clothes from the previous day. She sighed, the weight of her dual lives pressing down on her as she tried to compose herself. Reality was pulling her back, but the memory of Arris's touch lingered, a reminder of the escape she craved.

Dionne quietly entered London's house, her movements careful as she made her way to the room she had been staying in. She was grateful to find London still asleep, sparing her from having to dodge any probing questions about her late night—or the man responsible for the marks on her body. She slipped into the room and immediately began changing out of her work clothes.

She grabbed a pair of black Nike tights and a black graphic tee, pulling them on before catching her reflection in the mirror. Her eyes drifted to the faint marks Arris had left on her neck and collarbone, remnants of their passionate night together. A soft chuckle escaped her lips. Whew, that man... she thought, flashes of his touch and the way he made her feel rushing back.

Realizing she couldn't show up at the hospital looking like this, she zipped on a black Nike thermal that covered her neck, effectively hiding the evidence of her escapade. Her once bone-straight hair had been undone by the sweat and intensity of the night before, so she quickly tied it back, tucking it under a black Nike hat to mask her disheveled roots. A quick spritz of Chanel perfume later, she took one last look in the mirror, double-checking that all traces of Arris's presence were hidden from view.

Satisfied, she slipped out of the house quietly, not wanting to disturb London. As she drove to the hospital, her thoughts drifted back to Arris. She couldn't stop replaying the moments they shared, the way he made her feel seen, desired, and protected all at once. The memory of his touch brought an unbidden smile to her lips, but it quickly faded as reality crashed back in.

As Dionne drove, the realization hit her like a whisper in the back of her mind—she had cheated on Malik. Yet, what surprised her the most was how little she cared. The guilt that she thought would flood her veins never came. Instead, there was a quiet acceptance, a resolute justification that she couldn't shake.

Malik cheated first. He broke the trust long before she ever stepped outside their crumbling relationship. And if she was being honest, their love had died long ago, reduced to nothing more than a hollow arrangement built on appearances and the promises she made to his dying mother. It wasn't love; it was obligation.

This thought made her grip the steering wheel tighter, a small smirk playing on her lips as she drove to the hospital. Sleeping with Arris didn't feel wrong. If anything, it felt like she was reclaiming a part of herself that she had long suppressed. For the first time in a long time, Dionne felt alive—desired in a way that wasn't about fulfilling someone else's expectations.

Arris had been more than a distraction. He had been a momentary escape from her cage, a glimpse into the kind of passion and connection she had forgotten existed. And while she knew it couldn't last, the memory of his touch and the way he made her feel was enough to fuel her through the charade she had to keep up with Malik.

Dionne shook her head lightly, a bitter chuckle escaping her lips. "Guess we're even now," she muttered under her breath, the thought settling in her chest like a twisted sort of closure.

She was headed to face Malik and his mother, both of whom carried the weight of her obligations. Malik's infidelity had given her the perfect out, but Mama Glen's worsening condition complicated everything. She had made a promise to the woman she adored, and now she felt trapped between that commitment and her own desire for freedom.

Her frustration bubbled beneath the surface as she pulled into the hospital parking lot. No matter how much she tried to push it away, thoughts of Arris lingered. He was everything her life was missing—freedom, escape, and passion—but she knew she couldn't have him. Not while she was tethered to a marriage she didn't want and a promise she couldn't break. With a deep breath, she composed herself and walked into the hospital, bracing for the inevitable confrontation with Malik and the reality she couldn't seem to escape.

Dionne quietly entered the hospital room, her heart tightening at the sight of Mama Glen lying in the bed. Her complexion was pale, and the frailness in her hands as they trembled against the blanket broke Dionne's heart. Across the room, Malik sat slouched in a chair, his expression dark and heavy with an attitude that Dionne immediately

Feenin'

ignored. She wasn't here for him or his emotions—she was here for Mama Glen.

"Hey, Mama," Dionne greeted softly, her voice warm but tinged with concern. Mama Glen's face lit up slightly at the sight of her. "My baby," she said weakly, extending a trembling hand toward Dionne. Without hesitation, Dionne stepped closer and gently held her hand, squeezing it to offer comfort. "I'm here," she whispered, her own emotions threatening to bubble over.

"What happened?" Dionne asked, her voice cracking as she tried to keep her composure while looking at the woman who she loved wholeheartedly.

"I was feeling dizzy and collapsed," Mama Glen explained, her voice frail but steady. She glanced at Malik with a faint smile. "Good thing Malik was there."

Dionne turned her gaze to Malik, catching the way he glared at her. His eyes held suspicion and anger, but she wasn't about to let his mood faze her. She knew he had noticed the shift in her demeanor, the glow she carried that he couldn't take credit for. His scowl deepened, the idea of her slipping through his fingers, especially into the arms of someone else, clearly eating at him.

"What did the doctor say?" Dionne asked, turning her attention back to Mama Glen, her tone gentle but filled with worry.

"They're running more tests," Mama Glen replied, her voice growing softer. "But... the cancer is getting worse."

The words hit Dionne like a gut punch. She felt her throat tighten as tears pricked at her eyes. No matter how complicated things had become with Malik, Mama Glen had always been her rock, her confidante, her guide through some of the most challenging times in her life. The thought of losing her was unbearable.

Dionne nodded, swallowing the lump in her throat as she whispered, "I'm so sorry, Mama." She leaned in closer, squeezing Mama Glen's hand a little tighter, as if she could transfer some of her strength to the woman who meant so much to her.

After a while, Dionne settled on the couch on the opposite side of the room, putting distance between herself and Malik. She didn't miss the way his eyes followed her every movement, filled with suspicion and frustration. But Dionne refused to engage with him. Her focus remained solely on Mama Glen, the weight of the moment pressing heavily on her heart.

"Where were you?" Malik asked, breaking the tense silence. Dionne glanced up, her face instantly twisting into a glare, but she quickly softened her expression when she noticed Mama Glen watching her, curiosity evident in her tired eyes. Dionne hated that Malik was using his mother as a shield to pry into her business, but she composed herself, unwilling to create more stress for Mama Glen.

"I was working late at the office all night, and then stayed over at London's," Dionne explained, keeping her tone as even as possible. Every word felt like acid on her tongue, especially knowing Malik had no right to question her after his betrayal.

"I was calling you," Malik said, his voice calm, but Dionne could hear the restrained anger simmering beneath his tone. It was laughable, really—his attempt to control a situation he had no claim to anymore.

"My phone died," Dionne answered shortly, her irritation barely concealed. She refused to engage further, her focus on Mama Glen, but Malik's persistence was grating.

"Dionne, sweetie, where is your ring?" Mama Glen suddenly asked, her frail voice cutting through the tension. Her eyes dropped to Dionne's bare left hand, and Malik immediately perked up, his own suspicion rising.

Dionne paused for a moment, her mind scrambling for an excuse. "I went running this morning, so I took it off," she said softly, forcing a smile. "I never work out with my ring on, Ma."

She reached into her purse, pulling out the engagement ring she hadn't worn since leaving Malik's house, and slid it back onto her finger. "See? Back on," she said with a falsely sweet tone, directing her words more at Mama Glen than Malik. Her smile was forced, but Mama Glen's tired smile in return made Dionne's stomach churn with guilt.

Malik leaned back in his chair, a smug grin creeping across his face. There was nothing genuine about it—just satisfaction in knowing that as long as his mother was around, Dionne was tethered to him. He didn't care that their love was hollow, built on pretense and lies. For Malik, the facade was enough, and he'd use whatever leverage he had—including Mama Glen—to keep her in his grasp.

Dionne noticed the gleam in his eyes, and it only fueled her rage. He thought he had her cornered, but he didn't know how far she had already detached herself from him. Her hand tightened slightly around Mama Glen's, the only reason she hadn't walked away yet sitting in that hospital bed, fragile and unaware of the storm brewing between them.

Dionne caught the smile on Malik's face and rolled her eyes, her patience already wearing thin. Moments later, the doctor walked in, greeted everyone, and delivered devastating news. Mama Glen's cancer was spreading to other parts of her body. Although it wasn't progressing

Feenin'

rapidly, it was worsening her condition. The words hit like a gut punch, shattering the room's fragile hope. Dionne felt her chest tighten, unable to process the thought of losing Mama Glen.

The doctor expressed his condolences and gave instructions on managing her condition before leaving, leaving behind a suffocating silence in the room. Dionne sat quietly, her eyes fixed on Mama Glen, who had drifted into a medicated slumber. The weight of the news was still sinking in when Malik's voice cut through the silence.

"We need to push up the wedding," he said, his tone flat but insistent.

Dionne's head snapped toward him, disbelief etched across her face. "You're serious right now?" she asked, her voice laced with incredulity, unable to mask her irritation.

"What?" Malik replied, oblivious to the storm he had just unleashed.

Dionne leaned in closer, lowering her voice to avoid waking Mama Glen. "Your mother is lying in that bed, fighting for her life, and you're worried about a damn wedding?"

"She's dying, Dionne," Malik countered, his voice rising slightly before he caught himself. "And nothing's getting better. I need to fulfill her wish before she's gone."

Dionne sighed heavily, her frustration bubbling to the surface. "Do you even hear yourself? You're not marrying me because you love me. You're doing it to check a box on your mother's list. Do you know how insane that sounds?"

"I do love you," Malik said, his tone softening as he tried to bridge the growing gap between them. "I'm marrying you because I love you."

Dionne let out a bitter laugh, shaking her head. "If you love me, Malik, then explain why you cheated on me," she said, her voice cutting through the room like a blade.

Malik froze, his eyes darting to Mama Glen to ensure she was still asleep. His face flushed as he stumbled for words. "It was a mistake, Dionne. A stupid, selfish mistake. Please... forgive me," he said, his voice tinged with desperation.

Dionne shook her head, her disbelief noticeable. Malik stepped closer, his hands raised slightly as if to calm her. "Remember what we had, Dionne. I know things haven't been the same, but I promise I'll make it up to you. Just... give me another chance," he begged, his voice trembling.

Dionne stared at him, her emotions a whirlwind of anger, sadness, and confusion. She wanted to walk away, to finally free herself from the weight of their fractured relationship, but the thought of Mama Glen kept her rooted in place, her heart warring with her mind.

"You don't get it," she said finally, her voice barely above a whisper. "This isn't something you can just fix with words or promises. You broke us, Malik, and I don't know if I can piece us back together—if I even want to."

"Just let me prove it to you. Baby, please don't leave me—don't leave us. Think of my mother, baby," Malik pleaded, his voice trembling with desperation. Dionne felt a deep ache in her chest. Every fiber of her being screamed to walk away, to break free from the sham of a relationship that had become a suffocating prison. She no longer wanted to be with Malik, but the image of Mama Glen, frail and clinging to hope, was etched in her mind. With her cancer worsening, Mama Glen's time on earth was slipping away, and Dionne knew she couldn't bear the guilt of denying her one final wish.

"Okay," Dionne said softly, the word tasting bitter on her tongue. It wasn't a decision she made for Malik or for herself. It was for Mama Glen, and the weight of it crushed her.

Malik's face lit up with relief, his smile wide as he pulled her face gently into his hands. "Thank you," he whispered against her lips, pressing a kiss that she didn't return. The emptiness in her eyes was something Malik either couldn't see or chose to ignore.

As his lips lingered, Dionne's mind betrayed her, and the thought of Arris crept in. Memories of his touch, his voice, the way he made her feel seen and wanted. She had no business thinking about another man in that moment, but Arris had imprinted on her in a way she hadn't anticipated.

The sound of Mama Glen's soft voice broke through her thoughts, pulling them apart. "Aww, look at you two," she cooed, her voice weak but filled with warmth. Malik turned to his mother with a proud smile, holding Dionne's hand tightly as if to cement the image of their love.

But inside, Dionne was crumbling. The smile she gave Mama Glen was practiced, an expression she had worn countless times before. It masked the hurt, the betrayal, and the longing for a freedom she was too loyal to claim. Pretending to be in love with Malik was becoming harder with each passing moment, and yet, for Mama Glen, she would carry the burden. Even if it meant breaking herself in the process.

***

Arris walked into True's tattoo shop, his magnetic presence immediately drawing attention from everyone in the room. Unlike his usual sharp suits, today he was dressed casually in a red "Backwoods" graphic tee, gray "Essentials" shorts that showcased his toned, tattooed legs, white mid-socks, and red-and-white Nike Dunks. His Houston hat sat low, covering his waves, while his beard gleamed with precision

Feenin'

and care. He moved with confidence, exuding effortless cool as he approached the receptionist at the front desk.

"Wassup, Lori, True here?" Arris asked, flashing a polite smile as Lori looked up with a flirtatious grin. Arris wasn't oblivious to Lori's small crush, but he never entertained it—she was the same age as his little sister, and that was an immediate line he wouldn't cross.

"Yeah, he's in the back," Lori replied, her tone sweet as ever. Arris nodded in thanks before heading toward True's tattoo room. He knocked lightly before pushing the door open, spotting True lounging in his tattoo chair, a pencil in hand as he sketched for his next client.

"Wassup, Arris," True greeted, standing to dap him up.

"Chillin'. What's good with you?" Arris replied, taking a seat on the large couch in the corner of the room.

"Man, not much. Just been grinding, you know how it is," True said, his attention still partially on the sketch he was working on. True's love for art was evident in everything he did—whether it was tattooing, drawing, or painting, it was his passion and his escape.

"What about you? I swear, neither me nor Mario seen your ass in days," True added with a teasing smirk, glancing up at Arris. Arris chuckled, leaning back against the couch as he thought about his week. Despite everything he had going on, it was the night with Dionne that stuck with him the most.

He couldn't shake her from his mind—her touch, her smile, the way she carried herself with confidence and elegance. He craved to see her again, to feel her body against his, but even just her presence would have been enough.

"Just been handling shit," Arris replied vaguely, his voice calm, though his thoughts were anything but. True raised an eyebrow at him, sensing there was more to the story.

"Yeah? Handling shit or somebody?" True asked with a grin, pushing for details. Arris smirked, shaking his head.

"Nah, man. Ain't like that," he lied smoothly, though the memory of Dionne's soft skin against his still lingered vividly in his mind.

True laughed, leaning back in his chair. "Uh-huh, sure. You got that look, though."

"What look?" Arris asked, his smirk growing.

"That look like somebody got you *feenin'*. Don't even front." True said, giving him a knowing look. Arris chuckled but didn't deny it, keeping his cards close to his chest.

"Nigga, chill with that shit. This investing party been taking up most of my time," Arris said, quickly recovering from True's jab, even though he knew his boy was right—Dionne had been clouding every corner of his mind. "You and Mario still coming, right?" Arris asked, hoping to have his two best friends there to help ground him amid the chaos of hosting the event.

"Yeah, I'll be at your bougie-ass party," True joked, leaning back in his chair. "If Mario can get his head out this one girl's ass, he'll be there too."

"What girl?" Arris asked, his curiosity piqued. True chuckled like he was holding onto a secret.

"Mia's kindergarten teacher," True said, smirking. "I think her name's Karmen or some shit."

Arris tilted his head, the name sparking a faint memory. He'd definitely heard it before, but he couldn't place where. "She sounds familiar," Arris admitted, scratching his beard in thought.

True snapped his head toward him, his eyes narrowing. "Bruh, please tell me she's not somebody you already fucked."

Arris laughed, shaking his head. "Nah, bruh. I just heard her name somewhere, but I never fucked a girl named Karmen."

True sighed in relief, leaning back again. "Good, 'cause that nigga Mario is head over heels for her ass."

Arris's eyebrows raised in surprise. "Damn, it's that deep?" he asked, genuinely curious. Mario wasn't the type to catch feelings easily—at least not since his messy breakup with Mia's mother. He'd sworn off relationships, claiming he was all about taking his friends' advice and keeping shit casual.

"According to him, it is," True said with a laugh. "She's all that nigga ever talks about now. I guess both my niggas *feenin'* over women."

Arris chuckled but ignored True's slick comment about him. It was true Mario wasn't cut from the same cloth as him and True. Mario was a relationship guy at heart, no matter how much he tried to convince himself otherwise. Arris and True admired that about him—he wore his heart on his sleeve, even when it left him vulnerable.

"Guess he's finally over his baby mama," Arris mused, still wrapping his head around it. "Good for him, though."

"Yeah, we'll see," True said, shaking his head. "But just know I'm keeping my eye on both y'all fools at this party. Ain't no way I'm letting y'all act brand new with these women and ruin my fun."

Arris laughed, the weight of his thoughts momentarily lightened by True's banter. "Nigga, worry about yourself. Just be there on time."

Before True could respond, Mario walked in with Mia by his side. Mia's eyes immediately lit up when she saw Arris, and she ran to him,

Feenin'

her tiny arms reaching out. Arris scooped her up effortlessly, spinning her around as her laughter filled the room. She was his favorite niece, and it was no secret that Mia had Arris wrapped around her little finger. She was one of the few people in his life, besides his mother and A'Lani, who could get whatever she wanted from him without question. Arris had a soft spot for her, one that even his closest friends admired.

"Wassup, y'all," Mario greeted, dapping up True and Arris before plopping down on the couch.

"Damn, Mia, I can't get no love?" True teased, pretending to be hurt. Mia giggled, hopping off Arris's lap to give True a quick hug before scurrying back to Arris like she'd never left. They all laughed at her clinginess, shaking their heads in amusement.

"She really your shadow, bruh," Mario said, watching Mia settle back into Arris's lap with her iPad.

"Man, I don't even understand it," True added, smirking. "I'm the fun one."

"Whatever helps you sleep at night," Arris shot back, his arm securely around Mia as she focused on her game.

Despite not having children of his own, Arris's natural instincts with Mia and his sister, A'Lani, spoke volumes. Everyone who knew him could see that fatherhood was in his blood. Even though he'd grown up without a proper example of a father, he was determined not to repeat the mistakes of his own dad. When the time came for him to have kids, Arris was confident he'd be the best father he could possibly be.

"I hear you're in love, my boy," Arris teased, a smirk tugging at his lips as he leaned back, watching Mario's reaction. Mario's eyes immediately darted to True, who was grinning like he'd just shared a secret. Even though Mario shot him a hard glare, the slight smirk tugging at his lips gave him away.

"Nigga talk too fucking much," Mario muttered, though he couldn't keep the smile off his face.

"Tell me about her," Arris said, genuinely intrigued by his friend's newfound love interest.

Mario exhaled, leaning back on the couch, his expression softening as he thought about Karmen. "Man, she fine as hell. But it's more than her looks. Her aura, her vibe... it's just so soft. She makes you want to be soft with her, you know? Like, no games, no bullshit—just real."

Arris nodded, a smile creeping across his face as Mario spoke. He couldn't help but think about a certain someone himself. Dionne. Her presence had thrown him off balance, in the best way possible. The way she'd left him that morning, with the storm clearly brewing in her eyes, had stuck with him all day. He didn't know what she was running from, but he wanted to be the person she ran to. Shaking the thought away, he focused back on Mario.

"So, she the total opposite of Briana ass?" Arris asked, his tone laced with humor.

Mario and True both laughed, Mario shaking his head. "Hell yeah, the total opposite. Briana was a headache—still is. But Karmen? She's different. It's still early, but... it's good, man."

Arris smiled at his friend's honesty, happy to see him finding someone worth his time, but True, never one to miss an opportunity to clown, jumped in.

"Nigga in love and shit," True joked, his voice dripping with mockery.

The group erupted in laughter as Mario flipped True off, his grin making it clear he didn't care. "Fuck you, nigga," Mario shot back, but the warmth in his tone betrayed his happiness. The teasing, the banter, the brotherhood—it was moments like these that reminded them all of the importance of the bonds they shared.

"Speaking of, Arris, you mind watching Mia tonight?" Mario asked, his tone carrying a hint of frustration. "I got a date planned for Karmen, and her mama acting like she can't watch her own daughter for a couple of hours."

"Yeah, I got you," Arris said easily, adjusting Mia on his lap as she remained oblivious to their conversation, focused on her game. "A'Lani's here too, so you already know she's going to be hyped to see Mia."

"Appreciate that. I owe you," Mario said, clearly relieved.

"No need. I miss my niece anyway," Arris said with a smile, kissing Mia's cheek, which made her giggle, still glued to her iPad.

"Wait, A'Lani's in town?" True perked up, excitement lighting up his face.

Arris chuckled. "Yeah, she said she's coming by the house later."

"Bet. I miss my little nigga," True said protectively. "Gotta make sure them Washington niggas didn't change her."

Arris laughed at his friend's overprotective nature, shaking his head. "She's still the same. You'll see."

"So, you coming to the investor party this weekend?" Arris asked, shifting the conversation back to Mario, who was now grinning at his phone.

"Nigga, she got you smiling at your phone and shit," Arris teased, smirking as Mario snapped his phone shut.

"Man, shut up," Mario shot back, his voice tinged with playful

Feenin'

annoyance. "I can't wait until your hoe ass finally finds a woman and starts simping over her. I'm gonna talk big shit."

True burst out laughing. "Nigga, keep waiting. Arris don't even sit down long enough to settle for one woman."

Mario nodded in agreement, still grinning. "That shit gonna change. He's gonna meet his match and be dumb in love over her ass. Watch."

Arris shook his head, a playful smirk on his lips as he leaned back. "Y'all niggas don't know shit," he said, brushing them off, but the truth was, Mario's words hit closer to home than he wanted to admit.

After the night he'd spent with Dionne, the idea of having someone by his side—a real partner—had crept into his mind for the first time. But he didn't want just any woman. He wanted her. The thought of Dionne, with her sharp mind, undeniable beauty, and the way she made him feel at ease, stuck with him. He didn't know how it would play out, but one thing was clear: Dionne had already changed the game for him, whether he liked it or not.

Arris pushed thoughts of Dionne aside once again, focusing on the moment. "Nigga, are you coming to the event or not?" he asked, steering the conversation back to his earlier question.

Mario grinned, his excitement evident. "Yeah, I'll be there. But I might be bringing someone," he added, and they all knew exactly who he meant.

Arris chuckled, genuinely happy for his friend. It was refreshing to see Mario with someone he liked, someone clearly different from his baby mother. Glancing down at his watch, Arris realized he was running out of time to visit his mother.

"Aight, I'm about to head out. Come on, Mia—you're coming with me," he said, turning his attention to his niece.

"Yay!" Mia shouted, clapping her hands in excitement. Her joy warmed Arris's heart, and he couldn't help but smile.

He said his goodbyes to True and Mario before heading out with Mia perched on his shoulders. The women in the tattoo shop couldn't help but admire him as he walked out, assuming Mia was his daughter. The sight of Arris being so affectionate and attentive had them swooning.

Arris carefully secured Mia in the car, making sure she was comfortable before climbing into the driver's seat. They drove to his mother's house, the car filled with Mia's cheerful chatter. Despite the heaviness that lingered in the back of his mind, being with Mia always had a way of grounding him.

He gently set her down, ruffling her curls. "Go play, shorty. I need to talk to GG," he said with a warm smile. Mia beamed, running off to the room Angel had specially decorated for her visits.

Arris stepped outside, spotting Angel on the phone, her tone sharp and her body language tense. He stayed back, respecting her conversation, until she ended the call with a frustrated sigh. "Wassup, Ma," he greeted, his voice steady as he approached. Angel's face softened instantly, her smile replacing the frown from moments before.

"Hey, son," she said warmly, pulling him into a hug. They moved to the lawn chairs on the patio, the air heavy with unspoken words. Arris sat, his posture tense, knowing he couldn't avoid the topic any longer.

"Why did you tell that nigga where to find me?" Arris asked, his voice low but firm, anger simmering beneath his words. Angel's head snapped toward him, her eyes narrowing in warning.

"Boy, you better watch your tone and your mouth when you're talking to me," she said sharply. "I know you're mad about your father, but I am still your mother, and I'll beat your ass like you stole something if you come at me sideways again."

Arris exhaled, quickly recognizing he'd crossed a line. "My apologies," he muttered, his voice calmer but his frustration far from gone.

Angel's gaze softened slightly as she explained. "He asked about you and A'Lani. Wanted to know what you two were up to these days. I told him about the restaurant, but I didn't expect him to show up there."

Arris' jaw tightened, his fists clenching and unclenching as he processed her words. "Well, he did," he said, his voice low and filled with restrained anger. "And I almost did some damage to that man."

Angel sighed, leaning back in her chair. She studied her son for a moment before speaking. "Arris, I didn't tell him so he could cause trouble. I told him because, like it or not, he's your father. Maybe it's time you dealt with whatever's still festering inside you."

Arris shook his head, his fists tightening. "Ma, I don't need to deal with nun. That man abandoned us. He doesn't get to waltz back in like nothing happened."

Angel's eyes softened as she took in the hurt etched across her son's face. She never wanted this for him or for A'Lani. She had always wished she'd fallen in love with the right man—a man who could have been the father her children deserved. Instead, her choice had brought them nothing but pain, and now her children were carrying the weight of her mistakes.

"Your anger toward your father is understandable, sweetie," Angel said softly, placing a comforting hand on Arris's arm. She hoped her touch would ease some of the tension she saw simmering in him. "But

Feenin'

I really think it would be best for you—and for your sister—if you sat down and talked to him."

Arris stiffened under her hand, his jaw tightening as her words hit him. The very idea of facing Calvin made his blood boil. "Ma, what you and A'Lani don't understand," he said, his voice low but seething with emotion, "is that I have nothing to say to that man. If I can't bring the hurt and pain he caused us back on him without ending up in prison, then I'd rather stay far away from that nigga."

Angel shook her head, sadness filling her gaze. She knew her son's pain ran deep, and she wished she could find the right words to help him heal. But she also understood that his healing was a journey he'd have to navigate on his own. Forcing the issue would only push him further into his rage.

Before either of them could say more, the sound of Mia's small, cheerful voice broke through the tension. Angel's face lit up as Mia ran toward her, throwing her tiny arms around Angel in a big hug. The shift in atmosphere was immediate, and both Angel and Arris welcomed the distraction.

"Hey, my little princess," Angel said, her voice warm as she pulled Mia into her lap. The little girl giggled, her joy infectious.

Arris let out a breath he hadn't realized he was holding, thankful for the interruption. The longer he talked about Calvin, the angrier he felt, and he didn't know how much more he could take before that anger boiled over. He spent the rest of the afternoon bonding with Mia and his mother, letting the heavy topic of his father slip to the back of his mind.

But no matter how hard he tried, there was one thought he couldn't push away: Dionne. Her face, her voice, her presence—they lingered in his mind, a soothing balm for the fire raging inside him. He needed to see her again, to feel the calm she brought him. What was it about her? He didn't know, but the pull was undeniable. She was becoming his peace in a world full of chaos.

***

Dionne had just left the hospital and was now walking into London's house to gather her things. She couldn't believe she was actually doing it—going back to Malik to fulfill the promise she made to Mama Glen. The thought weighed heavily on her as she opened the door. The sound of her friends' voices carried through the house, making her groan inwardly. She knew the questions were coming the moment they saw her.

"Don't be trying to creep in here, missy!" London's voice called out, stopping Dionne in her tracks. She sighed, turning into the living room to face them.

"Hey girlies!" Dionne said, forcing a smile, her tone overly cheerful in an attempt to mask the turmoil swirling inside her.

"Don't be hey girling us! Where the hell you been?" London asked, her tone filled with motherly authority. Karmen chuckled at her delivery, but her eyes stayed on Dionne, reading her carefully.

"I was working late last night," Dionne said casually, lying through her teeth. She could see from their expressions that her friends weren't buying it for a second.

"So you slept at the office too?" London pressed, arching an eyebrow as Karmen leaned in, clearly curious.

Dionne hesitated, but she knew they weren't going to let this go. "No," she finally admitted. "I went back home to Malik."

The words felt bitter on her tongue, but she forced herself to say them. Her friends smiled at her revelation, blissfully unaware of her frustration.

"Oh, so you two made up? That's good!" London said brightly, her tone oblivious to Dionne's internal battle.

Karmen, however, wasn't so easily fooled. Her eyes narrowed slightly, picking up on the tension in Dionne's body language. "Made up? What did he do?" Karmen asked, her tone calm but pointed as she turned the spotlight on Dionne.

London's expression shifted as well, now mirroring Karmen's curiosity. Even though she'd let Dionne crash at her house for a few days, she hadn't pried into the reasons why. But now that Karmen had asked, she realized she wanted to know too.

Dionne sighed deeply as she sank into the couch, the weight of her situation pressing down on her. She loved her friends, trusted them with her life, but the idea of exposing her complicated reality—the loveless relationship she was maintaining solely out of obligation to Malik's dying mother—felt unbearable. It wasn't that she doubted their support, but she knew how unfiltered and honest they could be. She wasn't ready to face their opinions, not while her own emotions were so tangled. So, she opted for another lie.

"Malik's been working late hours at the hospital, and it's put a strain on our relationship. But we're good now," Dionne said, forcing a smile that didn't quite reach her eyes. London smiled warmly, seeming to buy the explanation, but Karmen's gaze lingered, her concern still evident.

Karmen didn't press further, though. She had known Dionne long enough to recognize when she wasn't ready to talk. Trusting that Dionne would open up in her own time, she let it go, though the unease in her chest remained.

Feenin'

"Well, that's good! You two made up," London said brightly, quickly pivoting to a new topic. "Now, about this wedding—when are we going to fit you for your dress?!" she asked, her excitement evident.

Dionne groaned internally at the reminder. Between work, Mama Glen's declining health, and her own emotional turmoil, she'd managed to avoid thinking about the wedding preparations. Until now, much of the planning had fallen on Mama Glen, but with her worsening condition, the responsibility was starting to shift to Dionne—a burden she neither wanted nor had the energy to carry.

"Umm... this weekend is the investor party," Dionne said, trying to muster some enthusiasm. "So, I guess we can go next week." Her voice faltered slightly, and though she tried to sound excited, her friends noticed the change in her tone.

"Next week it is!" London said with a grin, choosing to ignore the lack of excitement in Dionne's voice. Karmen, however, stayed quiet, watching her friend closely. She could sense that there was more going on beneath the surface.

"Dee, you sure you're ready to get married? You seem hesitant," Karmen finally asked, cutting through the surface of Dionne's facade. Her tone was calm, but her words hit the mark.

"Yes... yes, I am. It's just work coming down on me. Still trying to make partner," Dionne said, forcing another lie, though a sliver of it held truth. She was overwhelmed by work, but her hesitation about the wedding had nothing to do with her career. Her friends smiled at the mention of her long-time goal. They knew how hard she'd worked to become a partner at Williams Luxe Realty.

"It's coming, Dee. You've got this," Karmen said warmly, her words filled with genuine encouragement. Dionne returned her smile, but internally, she felt suffocated by the web of deceit she'd spun.

As the conversation shifted, Dionne suddenly felt a wave of heat, likely brought on by the stress. Without thinking, she unzipped her thermal jacket, momentarily forgetting about the marks Arris had left on her. The reaction was immediate.

"Damn, sis! You and Malik made up, made up! He was fucking the shit out of you with all those sex marks on your neck and chest," London exclaimed, her voice loud with excitement. Dionne's eyes widened in shock as they snapped down to her exposed skin, realizing her mistake.

She groaned internally, knowing there was no easy way out of this one. Her brown complexion wasn't light enough to make the marks overly visible, but it wasn't dark enough to completely hide them either.

"That's why her ass came in here with a limp earlier," Karmen teased, adding fuel to the fire. Dionne chuckled nervously, though her mind instantly drifted to Arris. The memory of his hands and lips on her skin sent a shiver down her spine.

"And now this bitch is having flashbacks!" London yelled, hyped up as ever, snapping Dionne back to the present.

"Malik maybe went a little too far with the biting and sucking," Dionne lied smoothly, zipping her jacket back up with forced nonchalance. But she couldn't stop the blush creeping up her face as memories of Arris flooded her mind. His touch, his voice, the way he made her feel—she craved it all over again.

Her friends teased her relentlessly, none the wiser that the marks they were admiring weren't from Malik at all, but from the man who had brought Dionne a kind of thrill she didn't know she needed.

"Girl, it looks like he was trying to eat you alive. I bet his ass won't be working late no more," London said with a sly grin, making them all chuckle.

"No, seriously, he was yearning for you, clearly," Karmen added, her tone playful. Dionne forced a smile, but her mind was nowhere near Malik. It was on Arris—the man whose hands and lips had worshipped her body like he couldn't get enough. The way he sucked and licked on her, like she was the only thing he craved, lingered in her thoughts.

"Okay, enough about me," Dionne quickly diverted, trying to shift the spotlight. "Karm, I see you glowing!" she teased, making Karmen blush as Mario's name immediately came to her mind.

"My girl is in love, and I love to see it. Both of my girls in love, and it's just my single ass over here," London chimed in, throwing her hands up dramatically. The group burst into laughter.

"Girl, that's by choice. A lot of men be coming after you, and you always diss their ass," Dionne argued, shaking her head. London nodded, fully owning up to it.

It was undeniable—London had the kind of looks that could stop a man in his tracks. Her caramel-toned skin seemed to glow effortlessly, a shade lighter than both Karmen and Dionne, and she stood at a petite 5'3". But it was her figure that truly turned heads—a body so perfectly proportioned it seemed almost unreal, though it was all natural. Her curves, especially her perfectly rounded butt, seemed to defy gravity, often compared to the size of a dump truck, a playful yet apt exaggeration by those who admired her.

Her tattoos told another story, stretching across her right arm like pieces of a daring puzzle, each one adding a layer to her bold and fearless personality. The ink was a testament to her unapologetic confidence,

Feenin'

her willingness to embrace her truth and own every part of who she was. London wasn't just beautiful—she was captivating, a walking contradiction of sweetness and fire, and she knew exactly how to use it to her advantage.

"They just don't be worth my time," London explained matter-of-factly, her voice cool and confident. Both Dionne and Karmen nodded in agreement, knowing London never settled for less than she deserved.

"Your man is coming," Karmen said, her always-positive nature shining through. Her words made London smile, her faith in the universe momentarily restored.

"I didn't forget... how are you and Mario doing?" Dionne asked, her curiosity piqued by Karmen's newfound glow.

"It's going good so far. It's still new, so I'm just taking it a day at a time," Karmen replied, her eyes lighting up as she spoke. Dionne and London exchanged smiles, happy to see their friend genuinely happy.

"And his daughter is so adorable," Karmen continued, her tone warm. "She's one of my brightest students." Her expression softened as she thought about Mia, the little girl who had clearly stolen her heart.

"Wait, you're talking to one of your student's parents?" London asked, her tone filled with disbelief. That was a rule Karmen had always sworn by. She'd said countless times she would never date or entertain one of her student's fathers. But Mario was different. She had tried to keep things professional and maintain her boundaries, but his persistence and genuine nature eventually wore her down.

"Yes, I am," Karmen admitted with a shy smile. "I didn't plan for it to happen, but he's... different."

"Well, I'm proud of you for opening your heart again, even if it's just the beginning," Dionne said warmly. "I can see that he makes you happy." Her words brought an even bigger smile to Karmen's face.

"Me too, sis," London added with her usual directness. "It was about time you moved on from Trey's bitch ass." Dionne nodded in agreement, and Karmen couldn't help but laugh softly at her friends' support.

They continued chatting for a while, the easy camaraderie among them lifting the mood. But Dionne's phone buzzed with yet another text from Malik, pulling her attention away. He'd decided to stay home from work, claiming he wanted to spend more time with her. Dionne knew it wasn't because of affection—it was suspicion. His relentless texts were a clear attempt to track her movements.

She had managed to escape for a bit under the guise of getting her things from London's house, but Malik's messages were becoming increasingly impatient. She sighed, feeling the tension creep back into her body.

"I should be heading home," Dionne said, standing up reluctantly.

"Alright, girl," London said, giving her a warm hug. Dionne said goodbye to Karmen, who hugged her tightly as well, her concern still evident but unspoken.

Dionne made her way to the guest room to gather her belongings. As she looked into the mirror, her eyes caught on the marks Arris had left on her skin. She sighed, trying to figure out how she was going to cover them up before Malik noticed. She knew she couldn't keep wearing the thermal jacket forever—it would only draw more attention.

The entire drive home, her thoughts were consumed by Arris. She missed him—his touch, his voice, the peace he'd given her for just one night. Part of her wanted to see him again, to feel that blissful escape. But she knew she couldn't. She had to play the role of the devoted fiancée for Malik's sake—and more importantly, for Mama Glen.

The night with Arris had to remain just that: a fleeting escape. A moment of indulgence she couldn't allow herself to repeat. But as she drove, the thought of him lingered, making her chest ache with longing she couldn't afford to feel.

Chapter 7

Dionne stepped out of the steamy shower, her skin glistening as she reached for her favorite lotion, carefully moisturizing every inch of her body. Tonight wasn't just another night; it was the Black Investor Party, and she intended to turn heads. She slipped into a black crocodile-skin tube dress that hugged her slim-thick figure like it was made just for her. The matching black open-toed heels accentuated her long legs, and the crocodile-skin Hermès purse she carried added the final touch of luxury.

Her hair, for once, wasn't in its natural state. She had opted for a bone-straight black wig, styled into a sharp middle part that cascaded down her back, adding a level of sophistication and drama to her already stunning look. She took one last look in the mirror, her hands smoothing over her curves as she admired the woman staring back at her. Dionne's bright smile reflected her confidence—she knew she was beautiful, inside and out, and she carried that assurance like armor wherever she went.

The chime of her doorbell pulled her from her thoughts. She grabbed her purse, already knowing who it was. Malik had told her he would meet her at the venue since he was finishing up at the hospital, but Karmen and London were her ride-or-die partners for the evening. Dionne opened the door, revealing her two best friends standing on her doorstep, both equally radiant.

"Hey, girls! Ouu, you two are beautiful!" Dionne exclaimed, stepping back to let them in. The trio exchanged warm hugs as they admired one another's outfits.

London wore a long red Versace gown that accentuated her curvaceous figure, paired with matching red open-toed heels. Her slicked-back ponytail added an edgy yet elegant vibe to her look.

Karmen, on the other hand, opted for a green Tom Ford dress that shimmered with every move, her gold open-toed heels tying the ensemble together. Her long, crimped hair flowed down her back like waves, giving her a soft, goddess-like appearance.

"Girl, us?! Look at you! That dress is hugging every curve—especially that ass!" London hyped, making Dionne laugh at her unfiltered antics.

"Malik is going to lose his mind when he sees you!" London added with a sly grin, but Dionne's smile barely wavered as she brushed off the comment.

"My driver's here, so we should get going," Dionne said, seamlessly redirecting the conversation as she grabbed her purse.

The trio walked out the door, the cool night air greeting them as they made their way to the shiny black car waiting in the driveway. Each of them radiated confidence, but Dionne couldn't shake the feeling of anticipation bubbling in her chest. Tonight wasn't just about business—it felt like a pivotal moment, one she couldn't quite put into words.

They arrived at The Vault, the air buzzing with sophistication as elegantly dressed men and women strolled toward the entrance of the upscale restaurant. The scene was a tapestry of wealth and influence, with luxury cars pulling up and valet attendants swiftly taking care of guests.

"Damn, this place screams wealthy!" London hyped, her excitement contagious as she looked around in awe. Dionne couldn't help but laugh at her friend's energy.

"I love seeing so many wealthy Black people here," Karmen added, her voice warm with pride as her eyes scanned the crowd. They all smiled and nodded, soaking in the rare sight of such affluence and elegance within their community.

Dionne's driver came around and opened the car door, the cool evening air brushing against her skin as she stepped out gracefully. Her friends followed, their heels clicking softly against the pavement.

"You two go ahead. I need to call Malik," Dionne said calmly, masking her growing frustration with a composed tone. London and Karmen exchanged a quick glance but nodded, heading toward the entrance, their dresses shimmering under the soft glow of the restaurant's lights.

Dionne pulled out her phone, dialing Malik's number as she leaned against the car. The call rang endlessly before going to voicemail. She groaned, already anticipating his excuse, and just as she was about to call again, her phone buzzed with a text.

Feenin'

Malik: Sorry babe. I won't make it tonight, we had an emergency at work. Love you.

Dionne stared at the message, her jaw tightening as the words burned into her mind. She let out a long sigh, frustration coursing through her veins. But what else did she expect? Malik always put his career first, leaving her to play the supporting role in his carefully curated life. Her feelings, her time—they were never his priority.

She took a deep breath, trying to steady the growing rage inside her. The last thing she wanted was to walk into the restaurant with her emotions on display. But as she looked down at the engagement ring on her finger, a bitter laugh escaped her lips.

One thing she wasn't doing tonight, now that Malik wasn't coming, was pretending. With a deliberate motion, she slipped the ring off her finger and tucked it into her purse, its weight replaced by a sense of liberation. For tonight, she would be Dionne—just herself, unapologetically.

She straightened her posture, fixed the strap of her purse, and began walking toward the entrance, her confidence glowing under the city lights. If Malik wasn't going to show up, she'd make sure she did.

Dionne stepped into the transformed restaurant and was immediately struck by the stunning elegance of the space. The once cozy, upscale eatery had been turned into a grand ballroom, its black and gold decor radiating power, sophistication, and wealth. The live orchestra in the corner filled the air with soft, melodic tones, adding to the room's enchanting ambiance. She let her eyes wander over the impeccably dressed crowd, scanning for her friends.

Just as she spotted London and Karmen across the room, Ms. Jean appeared out of nowhere, her usual vibrant energy shining through her warm smile.

"Dionne, hi!" Ms. Jean exclaimed, pulling her into a quick hug.

"Hi, Ms. Jean," Dionne replied, matching her enthusiasm with a smile.

"Wow! You look stunning," Ms. Jean said, stepping back to admire her. Dionne felt a slight blush creep up her cheeks at the compliment.

"Thank you, Ms. Jean. And so do you! That pantsuit is everything," Dionne replied sincerely, eyeing the effortless way Ms. Jean wore her tailored white suit.

Ms. Jean grinned at the compliment, but her expression quickly shifted to curiosity. "Where is your fiancé? I was hoping to finally meet him tonight."

The mention of Malik sent a bolt of frustration through Dionne, but she masked her emotions with the practiced ease of someone used to pretending everything was fine.

"He wanted to be here, but there was an emergency at the hospital," Dionne said with a smile that didn't quite reach her eyes. Her jaw tightened slightly with every word, the anger bubbling just below the surface.

The truth was, it wasn't Malik's absence that stung the most. It was the pattern. The broken promises. The feeling of being unsupported at moments that mattered to her. She had told him how important this event was—not just for her career but for her. He had promised to show up, and like so many times before, he had let her down.

What hurt more was the glaring contrast. Whenever Malik needed her—whether it was for a hospital gala, a work event, or even something as simple as picking out a tie—she was there, unwavering in her support. She played the role of the devoted fiancée flawlessly. But when it came to her dreams, her career, her passions, Malik seemed to falter, leaving her to stand alone.

"Oh man, I really wanted to meet him, but saving lives is more important," Ms. Jean said in her usual sweet tone, her words dripping with genuine understanding.

Dionne nodded, her fake smile plastered firmly on her face. "He told me he's really sorry he couldn't make it and that he's looking forward to meeting you soon."

Jean's face brightened, her smile mirroring Dionne's. "Tell him I'm looking forward to it as well. I'll let you mingle. I just wanted to say hi and see that beautiful face of yours."

"Thank you, Ms. Jean," Dionne replied warmly as they hugged one last time. She watched Jean walk off before turning to find her friends, spotting them a short distance away. As she approached, London's animated voice broke through the elegant hum of the party.

"This party is lit to be so bougie," London declared, clearly unbothered by the refined atmosphere.

Dionne and Karmen burst into laughter, shaking their heads at their friend's bluntness.

"You're not wrong," Dionne said, her laughter trailing off as she reached them.

"Dionne," Karmen said softly, her tone laced with intrigue, drawing Dionne's attention. "I think I found your 'friend.'"

Confused, Dionne tilted her head. "Friend? What friend?" she asked, scanning Karmen's face for clarity.

"You know," Karmen said with a small smirk, her gaze flickering

Feenin'

past Dionne. "Your friend from the club."

Dionne's brows furrowed as she tried to follow Karmen's gaze, but her poor eyesight made it impossible to see what—or who—her friend was talking about.

"Now you know I'm damn near blind," Dionne said matter-of-factly, her tone tinged with mock irritation. "These contacts are good, but they're not that good, Karm."

Her friends laughed, but London quickly sobered up and leaned in. "The man now approaching us with Karmen's man and another fine-as-hell man. Who is that?" London said, her tone shifting to playful flirtation as she nodded toward the trio.

Dionne squinted, turning her head again—and this time, her vision cleared.

Arris was walking toward them, his confident stride unmistakable, with Mario and True trailing behind him. The moment her eyes landed on him, a smile crept across her face, unbidden but impossible to suppress. Her heart fluttered, and those damn butterflies—the ones that had no business showing up—started swarming in her stomach the way they always did when she saw him.

Arris's dark eyes locked onto hers, a knowing smirk tugging at the corner of his lips, as if he already knew the effect he had on her.

"Well, damn," London whispered under her breath, clearly caught off guard by the trio of handsome men approaching. "Who is that?" she asked again, her tone more demanding now.

Dionne didn't answer, too focused on steadying the heat rushing to her cheeks as Arris closed the distance between them.

***

Arris walked around his restaurant, exuding confidence as the ballroom buzzed with people dressed in their most elegant, high-end attire. The space had transformed into a vision of luxury, its grandeur mirroring the success Arris had cultivated over the years. He moved through the crowd in his brown Dior plaid three-piece suit, his polished dress shoes clicking against the floor with each calculated step. His sharp gaze caught every detail, every face, and every moment that passed, but his mind was elsewhere. Specifically, on whether she had arrived yet.

As he made his rounds, greeting familiar faces and shaking hands with the city's elite, his heart picked up pace when he spotted Ms. Jean. He smiled warmly, politely exchanging pleasantries, but his thoughts lingered on Dionne. Was she here yet?

After a few more exchanges, Arris's eyes locked onto his two closest friends, Mario and True, standing casually near the bar with glasses of cognac in hand. Their effortless style made them stand out even in a room full of the city's wealthiest. Mario wore a green Italian Lomano Checks tweed suit paired with brown dress shoes, his freshly twisted locs framing his sharp jawline. True, on the other hand, donned a navy-blue Armani suit that contrasted beautifully against his rich brown skin. His fade was immaculate, showcasing his Eritrean heritage as the clean lines of his braids gleamed under the soft ballroom lighting.

Arris approached them, and they greeted each other with a quick dap and genuine smiles.

"Where's Karmen? I was ready to meet her," Arris teased, a playful smirk tugging at his lips as he leaned against the bar.

Mario chuckled, clearly amused by his friend's antics. "She's on her way. She decided to ride with her girls before I could even ask."

Arris nodded, his smirk widening. "Ah, she already ducking you, huh?" he quipped, earning a laugh from True and a sarcastic shake of the head from Mario.

Arris felt a sense of relief in this moment—away from the pressures of hosting, just laughing and talking with his boys like old times. But the lightheartedness was quickly interrupted when Mario's attention shifted, his expression softening into a smile.

"There go my baby right there," Mario said, his tone calm yet proud.

Both Arris and True turned their heads in unison, following Mario's gaze. Arris's breath hitched for a split second when his eyes landed on Dionne.

Although their eyes were all fixed in the same direction, each man was captivated by someone different. Mario couldn't take his gaze off Karmen, her green dress complementing her warm complexion, her crimped hair flowing like silk down her back. True's attention locked onto London, her red dress hugging her curves, her slick ponytail highlighting her striking features. And Arris—his focus was singular. Dionne, in that black dress that hugged her body perfectly, was all he could see.

"Damn," they all muttered at the same time, mesmerized by the trio of women as they walked into the ballroom.

"Man, who is that?" True asked, his eyes firmly glued to London. Mario turned his head toward True to see who had caught his attention, but Arris didn't even flinch. His gaze remained glued to Dionne, the way her presence commanded the room even when she wasn't trying.

From across the room, Dionne seemed preoccupied, her eyes glued to her phone, her expression unreadable but carrying a hint of frustration. She hadn't noticed his unwavering gaze, and it gave Arris a brief moment

Feenin'

to take her in without interruption.

"Arris!" Mario called out, finally snapping him out of his trance.

"Yea... wassup?" Arris responded quickly, turning his attention back to his friends, but it was too late. The damage was done.

Mario and True both exchanged knowing smirks.

"Nigga, you was staring at her like she hypnotized yo ass," True teased, his grin widening as Mario let out a loud laugh.

Arris smacked his lips in annoyance, trying to brush off the comment, but he knew there was no point denying it. True wasn't lying. There was something about Dionne that always put him in a trance. Her beauty was undeniable, but it wasn't just her looks. There was something deeper, something he couldn't quite name, that drew him to her like a moth to a flame.

"She's fine as hell, though. I'll give you that," True added, still smirking.

Arris didn't respond, just smirked back as he adjusted his blazer. He could feel his pulse quicken, his thoughts clouded with her presence. It wasn't just admiration or attraction—whatever it was, it ran deeper than he was willing to admit. And he wasn't sure if that excited him or scared the hell out of him.

"Well, you two niggas can stay over here and be weird. I'm going to be with my future wife," Mario said, a confident grin plastered across his face as he walked off toward Karmen. True and Arris exchanged amused glances before following behind him.

Arris spotted Dionne almost immediately, her eyes now locked on him. The small, knowing smile tugging at her lips paired with the glimmer of intrigue in her gaze was magnetic. Arris felt the familiar pull toward her, the one he tried to ignore but never could.

He approached her with his usual air of confidence, his steps measured and deliberate. Her eyes didn't waver from his, and the soft smile on her face told him she was just as affected by his presence as he was by hers.

"Mr. Black! Good seeing you," Dionne greeted, her tone professional and poised, catching him slightly off guard. But the glimmer in her eye betrayed her attempt to stay formal.

Arris chuckled inwardly, amused at the sudden shift in her demeanor. *Oh, she wanna be formal in front of her friends, huh? Like I didn't have her screaming my name the other night? Alright, I'll play along,* he thought with a smirk tugging at his lips.

"Same here. It's good seeing you too, Ms. Smith. Very good," he replied smoothly, his voice carrying that same low, velvety tone that always seemed to make her falter. As they shook hands, his fingers lingered just a little too long against hers, the faintest spark passing between them.

Dionne felt her pulse quicken, the intensity of his gaze melting through her composure. Her eyes flickered to his lips before darting away, and she realized with a jolt that her hand was still in his. Flustered, she quickly pulled it back and turned toward her friends to mask the heat rushing to her face.

"You remember my best friends, Karmen and London, right?" she asked, her voice steady as she attempted to reclaim her professionalism.

Arris's eyes lingered on her for a moment longer, tracing the curves of her body, noting the way the black dress hugged her perfectly, before finally shifting his attention to the women beside her. "Yes, of course. It's good seeing you ladies again," he said politely, his smooth tone making Karmen and London exchange a quick, knowing glance.

"Likewise," Karmen responded warmly, while London's curious smile widened. "Good seeing you too, Mr. Black."

Arris's polite smile returned, but his focus was already drifting back to Dionne. Even as he engaged with her friends, she was all he could think about. Something about the way she held herself tonight—confident yet guarded—only deepened his intrigue. And the fact that she kept glancing at him out of the corner of her eye didn't help either. She could try to stay composed all she wanted, but the connection between them was undeniable, and they both knew it.

Arris's eyes drifted back to Dionne, unable to stay away for too long. She was doing everything she could to avoid his gaze—her hands fidgeting with the strap of her purse, her eyes darting around the room—but he could see right through her. A knowing chuckle escaped his lips as he noticed the subtle flush rising on her cheeks. His presence was unraveling her composure, and he loved it.

Unable to resist, he placed a hand on the small of her back, the touch subtle yet deliberate. He felt her body tense for a moment before a slight shiver betrayed her reaction. Arris leaned closer, letting his fingertips linger just enough to send a message, but not enough to cross a line—at least, not yet. Dionne stiffened under his touch, but she didn't move away. In fact, he could tell she didn't want him to stop.

Clearing his throat, Arris kept the mood light. "Let me introduce you to my friends," he said, his voice smooth as always. "This is True. He owns a tattoo shop here called True22."

London's eyes lit up as she turned her attention to True. "Might need to add a few tattoos to my arm," she said with a sly smile, her tone

Feenin'

carrying a hint of seduction.

True caught on immediately, his response just as quick and sharp. "Come by the shop, love. I gotchu." His eyes lingered on her, taking her in with a boldness that matched hers.

Everyone chuckled, the playful flirtation between them impossible to ignore. Arris shook his head slightly, amused but unsurprised.

"And this is Mario," Arris continued, turning his attention to his other friend. "Though I'm sure you've heard about him already."

Dionne's gaze slid over to Karmen, who was blushing so hard it gave her away. Seizing the moment, Dionne smirked. "It's a pleasure to officially meet you, Mario. Heard a lot about you," she said, her tone laced with a playful edge.

Karmen rolled her eyes at Dionne's teasing, though her smile betrayed her amusement. "Good things, I hope," Mario replied, his attention fully on Karmen. His voice was calm, but the way his gaze softened as he looked at her spoke volumes.

"Oh, the best so far," Dionne said with faux sweetness before adding with a sharp edge, "Just don't fuck up, or we'll fuck you up."

"Big facts," London chimed in, her expression dead serious despite the laughter bubbling from the group.

Mario chuckled, but there was a sincerity in his voice as he replied, "You'll never have to worry about that." His eyes remained glued to Karmen, as if silently vowing to treat her right.

Karmen tried to hold back a smile but failed miserably, her embarrassment clear. She glanced at the floor for a moment, her cheeks flushed, before looking back up at Mario. The energy between them was unmistakable, and the unspoken connection hung in the air. Arris, however, couldn't help but focus on the woman beside him. His hand still rested lightly on Dionne's back, a grounding presence that tethered her to him.

"Well, I have to get back to hosting, but enjoy the party... and my friends," Arris said, his smooth voice laced with a playful tone that made everyone chuckle. The laughter didn't distract Dionne, though—not with his hand still firmly placed on the small of her back. As he leaned down, his lips grazed her ear, sending a spark through her body that made her inhale sharply.

"I'll be right back, mama," Arris murmured, his deep, low voice wrapping around her like velvet. His breath caressed her skin, igniting goosebumps along her neck. "In the meantime, enjoy your evening, but don't have too much fun without me." He gave her waist a firm squeeze before pulling away, leaving her rooted in place, her heart hammering in her chest.

Each word from him ignited something inside Dionne—desire, frustration, and curiosity all swirling together. She was annoyed at how easily he unraveled her, how effortlessly he had her feeling things she wasn't supposed to feel. As Arris walked away, his retreating form was the only thing she could focus on until he disappeared into the crowd.

Shaking off the haze he left her in, Dionne turned back to her friends, only to find them too engrossed in conversation with True and Mario to notice her internal turmoil. Taking the opportunity to refocus, she excused herself to mingle and network. This event was about business, and she was determined to leave her mark.

Switching gears, Dionne slipped seamlessly into her professional demeanor. She made her rounds, introducing herself to anyone worth knowing, pitching ideas, and ensuring that her name would be remembered long after the night ended. Her confidence radiated as she worked the room, leaving a lasting impression on every person she met.

Meanwhile, Arris was in his element as the host, ensuring the event ran flawlessly. He greeted guests, handled any hiccups with ease, and even secured new connections for himself and his restaurant. But no matter how busy he was, his eyes found Dionne over and over again. It didn't matter where she was or who she was talking to—his gaze always seemed to drift back to her.

And Dionne wasn't immune to his pull, either. Despite her focus on networking, she couldn't help but notice the way Arris moved through the room with such effortless charm and authority. Every now and then, their eyes would lock from across the room, a silent acknowledgment passing between them that sent a shiver down her spine.

At one point, Dionne was deep in conversation with a prominent real estate investor, discussing potential collaborations, when Arris walked by. His hand brushed lightly against her arm—a subtle yet deliberate touch that left her breathless. She glanced over her shoulder to find him smiling at her, his eyes glinting with mischief. The gesture was quick, fleeting, but it carried a message: I'm still watching you.

As the night went on, Arris continued to find ways to remind her of his presence. Whether it was a sly comment about how beautiful she looked or a lingering glance that sent heat rushing to her cheeks, he made sure she felt him even when they weren't standing together.

Dionne did her best to maintain her composure, but Arris had a way of making her feel seen in a way that no one else ever had. And as much as she wanted to resist, she couldn't deny the magnetic pull between them—one that seemed to grow stronger with every glance, every word,

Feenin'

and every touch.

Arris tried his best to focus on the responsibilities of the night, maintaining his polished professionalism as host. But no matter how hard he tried, his thoughts always strayed to her. In a room full of elegant people, each vying for attention or conversation, it was Dionne who captivated him most. His eyes seemed to find her effortlessly in the crowd, like she was a beacon pulling him in. Each stolen glance, each fleeting moment their eyes met, only deepened the pull he felt toward her.

It frustrated him, this inability to compartmentalize his feelings. They were supposed to be business partners tonight—nothing more. Yet, every time she smiled, laughed, or even shifted her gaze in his direction, it ignited something deeper within him. Something he wasn't entirely sure how to handle.

Dionne wasn't faring any better. Though her demeanor was polished and her presence commanding, her thoughts betrayed her. Every conversation she held, every glass she raised in a toast, and every polite laugh she shared with others, her mind wandered. She found herself scanning the room, searching for him in the sea of people. And when her eyes inevitably found Arris, her pulse quickened, and the faintest smile tugged at her lips.

To anyone watching, their dynamic seemed perfectly professional. Their subtle exchanges were undetectable to the crowd around them, but between them, it was undeniable. The tension, the unspoken understanding, the magnetic draw—it was all there, simmering just below the surface.

Even in the bustling elegance of the ballroom, amidst the chatter, laughter, and music, their connection stood out to them like a silent melody only they could hear. A glance that lingered too long. A brush of hands as he passed by. A fleeting smirk exchanged from across the room. Each moment, no matter how small, was a reminder of the unspoken yearning they both felt.

In the chaos of the night, their subtle affection for one another was hidden from the world but glaringly evident to the two of them. No matter how hard they tried to stay in their roles, the pull between them was impossible to ignore. And as the night continued, it became clear— neither one of them wanted to fight it.

***

The party was alive, its energy pulsing through the room like a heartbeat. Hours had passed, but the crowd, now loosened by champagne and cocktails, laughed louder and danced harder. The once-formal atmosphere had shifted entirely, with the DJ replacing the orchestra and transforming the elegant restaurant into a vibrant celebration.

Dionne sat alone at the bar, her manicured fingers tracing the rim of her empty glass. Her friends had abandoned her to dance with True and Mario, leaving her with a bittersweet longing she couldn't shake. This was the moment she wished Malik was here—if only their relationship was what it used to be. She envisioned them swaying together in the middle of the ballroom, his hands on her waist, her head resting against his shoulder. The image filled her with a wistful ache. But reality snapped her back—Malik wasn't here, and their love felt as hollow as the champagne flute in her hand.

"Get two shots—one for me, and one for the beautiful lady," a deep, raspy voice commanded behind her, interrupting her thoughts. She didn't need to turn around to know who it was.

Arris slid onto the stool beside her, his hand grazing her waist in a way that felt both casual and intimate.

"You just can't keep your hands to yourself, can you, Mr. Black?" Dionne teased, her voice light despite the tension building in her chest.

Arris chuckled, low and smooth. "Nah, not when you look this good. Gorgeous ass," he said, his tone leaving no room for debate as his eyes roamed over her.

Heat rose in her cheeks, but she held her composure, chuckling softly. "You need to stop before someone hears you—or worse, sees us," she said, glancing around the bustling room.

Arris leaned back in his seat, utterly unfazed. "I don't give a fuck if they see us or not."

Her heart skipped a beat at his boldness, but she masked it with a sharp retort. "We're business partners, Arris. That's a little unethical."

Arris laughed softly, a sound that sent a shiver down her spine. "There's nothing unethical about it. But if you want to keep this lowkey, then we can."

"And what exactly is this?" Dionne challenged, taking the shot of tequila the bartender placed before her. She threw it back, welcoming the burn as it warmed her chest. Arris followed suit, his gaze locked on her the entire time.

"Whatever you want it to be," he said, his confidence unwavering.

Dionne rolled her eyes, though a small smirk played at her lips. "Well first, I am not your mama, so you can stop calling me that," she said, her tone stern but playful. She hoped it sounded like a reprimand, but deep down, the nickname had burrowed its way into her heart.

"That's not gonna happen," Arris replied, his voice firm, his smirk

Feenin'

teasing.

Her brow arched. "And why is that?"

Arris leaned in close, his scent—a mix of expensive cologne and raw masculinity—wrapping around her like a blanket. His voice dropped to a near whisper, and the intensity in his gaze pinned her to the spot.

"Because I love knowing that pussy gets wet every time I say it," he murmured, his words deliberate and provocative.

A shiver coursed through her body, and Arris caught it, his smirk deepening. He leaned back, deliberately creating space between them just as she found herself wishing he'd close the gap.

Dionne swallowed hard, trying to regain her composure as heat pooled in places she didn't want to acknowledge.

"Anything else, mama?" Arris asked with that signature smirk, his tone teasing, but his eyes heavy with unspoken want. Dionne rolled her eyes, trying desperately to recover, but it wasn't working. His presence, his touch, the weight of his gaze—everything about him pulled her in like gravity. All she wanted to do was say, fuck this party, fuck everyone, and take him to some private corner to let the fire between them consume her. But she couldn't.

She took a steadying breath, her voice shaky as she forced out the words. "Umm... we need to stay just business partners. No more... escape."

The sentence felt like sandpaper against her throat, each word grating and painful. She didn't want to end whatever this was between them, but reality stood in the way, glaring and unforgiving. Not only were they tied professionally, but she was engaged. Love or not, Dionne had chosen Malik—accepted him back—and their wedding was approaching. Cheating didn't sit right with her, even if it was justified as payback for his own betrayal. She had to end this before it spiraled further out of control.

She saw the flicker of disappointment in Arris's eyes, his confident smirk faltering ever so slightly. He hadn't expected this. Maybe he hadn't even prepared for it. But as much as it stung, he nodded, masking the hurt with a calm exterior. "If that's what you want... then I have to respect that," he said, his voice steady, though the faint crack in his tone betrayed him.

Dionne nodded, unable to meet his gaze now. She knew she'd hurt him—hell, she'd hurt herself too. But before she could look away entirely, Arris leaned forward, his hand brushing against her cheek, his fingers gentle as they cupped her chin. Slowly, he tilted her face up, forcing her to meet his eyes.

"Friends?" he asked softly, the vulnerability in his tone disarming her completely.

Dionne hesitated for a moment before giving him a small, bittersweet smile. "Friends," she whispered, though the word felt foreign and wrong between them.

Their eyes locked, both searching for something in the other that words couldn't express. They smiled, but the ache beneath those smiles lingered, heavy and unrelenting.

The bartender interrupted the moment, placing another round of shots in front of them. Arris picked up his glass, raising it between them with a goofy smirk, a transparent attempt to ease the tension. "To just friends, then," he said, though the teasing lilt in his voice didn't quite reach his eyes.

Dionne chuckled softly, her heart twisting. "Just friends," she replied, lifting her glass to clink against his.

The sound of the glasses meeting felt like a finality neither of them wanted. They downed their shots together, the burn of the liquor doing little to dull the sting of what they'd just agreed to. And though they were sitting side by side, the space between them felt impossibly vast.

The conversation shifted effortlessly, blending with the lively ambiance of the room as music and laughter filled the air. Even with the crowd bustling around them, Arris and Dionne were in their own world at the bar, completely absorbed in each other. Their conversation was light, playful, and filled with unspoken intrigue as they unraveled more layers about one another.

"Let's play a game," Arris suggested, his deep voice smooth and confident as he sipped his cognac. His suggestion immediately earned a soft chuckle from Dionne, who tilted her head in amusement.

"Okay, what's the game?" she asked, her tone teasing as she took another sip of her strawberry lemon drop.

"We'll take turns asking each other simple questions about ourselves. If you get it right, I take a sip of my drink. If you get it wrong, you drink," Arris explained with a playful grin, his charm radiating in waves. Dionne chuckled again, shaking her head at his boyish enthusiasm. She found herself warming to the man beneath the business persona she'd come to know.

"Alright," she agreed, raising a brow as her lips curled into a smirk. "Ladies first?"

"Of course," Arris replied, leaning back in his seat and motioning for her to begin.

"Okay, Mr. Confident," Dionne started, her smile mischievous.

Feenin'

"What's my favorite color?"

Arris leaned back, a playful thinking expression crossing his face, though his confidence remained intact. He didn't answer immediately, instead letting his gaze travel over her thoughtfully, as though he were piecing her together.

"Well," he began, his voice steady, "your car is black. The necklace you always wear has a black diamond nestled inside the pendant. And while you look beautiful in anything, you seem most comfortable and at ease when you're wearing black."

Dionne's eyes widened slightly, her lips parting in surprise as he finished his deduction with a smirk.

"So, I'm going to say black," Arris concluded, his voice low and confident, the corners of his mouth lifting in a grin as he waited for her reaction.

Caught off guard by how precise his answer was, Dionne blinked and quickly took a sip of her drink, the action confirming he was right. A soft laugh escaped her lips as she shook her head.

"You really pay attention, don't you?" she asked, her voice light, but there was an edge of intrigue to her tone. She hadn't expected him to be so observant.

"Always," Arris replied, leaning forward slightly, his smirk never faltering. "You'll find I don't miss much."

"That was too easy," Dionne teased, deflecting her flustered state with humor. She couldn't deny the fluttering sensation building in her chest from his attentiveness, but she wouldn't let him see how much he was affecting her.

Arris chuckled, his rich laughter rolling over her like a soothing wave. "Alright, my turn. Let's see how well you know me."

"What was my baseball number in college?" Arris asked, leaning back with a smirk, watching Dionne's eyes widen slightly. She knew he'd played baseball in both high school and college, but he'd never mentioned his number. Still, she wasn't about to let him see her uncertainty.

Dionne tilted her head, her mind racing through the little details he'd shared with her. "Well," she began thoughtfully, "I remember you said Bob Gibson was your favorite player, even though you never got to see him play in person because he retired before you were born."

Arris smiled, his admiration for her attentiveness evident as he nodded.

"And you wanted to be as great a pitcher as he was, so I'll say... 45." Her voice carried a mix of confidence and curiosity as she locked eyes

Ann

with him.

Arris chuckled, a deep sound that sent a tingle down her spine, before lifting his glass and taking a sip. "You got it right," he confirmed, the subtle admiration in his tone making her smile widen.

"Attentive," he added, his voice softer, but full of appreciation.

Dionne blushed faintly under his gaze. She could tell her ability to listen and remember the details about him wasn't something he was used to, and that realization made her feel something she hadn't felt in a while—valued.

For Arris, this moment meant more than she knew. Always playing the alpha, always carrying the weight of others' expectations, he rarely felt truly seen. But Dionne was different. She listened in a way that made him feel understood, and he hadn't realized how much he craved that.

They continued their game, trading questions and answers, laughing and learning more about each other with every exchange. Minutes slipped by, and both of their drinks dwindled, showing how well they noticed one another—and the gaps where they didn't. By the end, Dionne's glass was empty first, a clear sign of just how much Arris paid attention to the small, intimate details of her life.

"Clearly, you won," she admitted with a playful roll of her eyes, making him laugh. "But I have one last question."

"Go ahead," Arris said, leaning forward with a grin, his confidence unwavering.

"Based on my personality, what do you think my ideal date is?" Her tone was softer now, the question carrying a deeper weight. It was no longer about a game—it was about seeing how much of her he truly understood.

Arris leaned back with a knowing smile, taking his time as he thought. "Hmm... you're very chill, but you've got that spontaneous side," he said, his voice confident as she nodded, silently urging him to continue. "I'd say dinner, but nothing too fancy. Something relaxed and intimate, where you can really connect."

He paused, his eyes locking with hers. "I remember you said Love Jones was your favorite movie, and you've got those framed poetry posters on your office wall." Dionne's breath caught in her throat at how much he'd noticed—the details her own fiancé never seemed to see.

"So, I'd say your ideal date is at a spot with a poetry night—laid-back, soulful, and full of good energy," Arris finished, his voice low and confident.

Dionne blinked, momentarily stunned. Malik—her fiancé—had never even asked her what her ideal date was, let alone pieced together

Feenin'

such an intimate answer. But here was Arris, a man she barely knew, reading her like a book she didn't even realize she'd opened to him.

"Damn," she said softly, her voice betraying the depth of her surprise and emotion.

Arris chuckled, his smile softening. "I notice everything about you, Dee," he said in a low, intimate tone that made her body shiver involuntarily.

For a moment, time seemed to stop as they held each other's gaze, the world around them melting into the background. In that instant, Dionne realized just how much Arris truly saw her—something she hadn't felt in a long time.

Dionne and Arris continued to laugh and talk, completely engrossed in their own world and forgetting about the event happening around them. Every now and then, a song would play that they both liked, and they'd get up to dance briefly, their chemistry undeniable, before returning to the bar to enjoy each other's company.

"So, you're not afraid of anything?!" Dionne asked in disbelief, her tone playful yet genuinely curious.

"Besides failure? Nah." Arris shrugged casually but paused, his expression softening. "Well, that… and being a bad father to my future kids." His voice carried a weight that caught Dionne's attention, and the seriousness in his tone stilled her.

She remembered him sharing bits and pieces about his strained relationship with his father. The fear of becoming like the man who had abandoned him wasn't surprising, but hearing it out loud made her heart ache. She could see the flicker of vulnerability he rarely showed, and it only deepened her admiration for him.

"You will be a great father, Arris. I know it," Dionne said softly, her voice steady yet filled with sincerity.

Arris smiled at her reassurance, her belief in him shining through. For a moment, he allowed himself to lean into her words, letting them anchor him. But before the conversation got too heavy, he shifted the focus back to her.

"And what about you, Ms. Smith? What are you afraid of?" Arris asked, his confident, charming demeanor returning in an instant.

Dionne chuckled, shaking her head in disbelief at how effortlessly he could switch between deep and playful. "You're going to laugh," she said, her eyes darting away briefly, embarrassment creeping in.

"I promise I won't," Arris said, leaning in closer, genuinely curious. "Tell me."

Dionne sighed, glancing at him before finally admitting, "Heights."

Arris's lips curled into a grin, a chuckle escaping before he could stop himself. "See! I knew you were going to laugh," she said, playfully rolling her eyes.

He leaned over, placing his hand on hers for reassurance. The warmth of his touch sent a jolt through her, but she didn't pull away. "No, I find it adorable," he said, his voice laced with amusement. "But now I'm wondering—how do you manage business trips without flying?"

Dionne laughed, her shoulders relaxing. "I drive. Or my drivers handle it for me," she explained. "I've never really had to go far enough to take a plane. Plus, road trips are better for sightseeing anyway."

Arris nodded, genuinely impressed by her reasoning. He admired the way she had her own way of doing things—her independence, her charm, everything about her was magnetic.

Their conversation flowed effortlessly until Mario and True approached, London and Karmen trailing behind them. True spoke first. "We're about to head out. It's getting late."

Arris glanced at his watch, surprised at how much time had passed. He hadn't even noticed, too wrapped up in Dionne's presence. "Yeah, us too, Dee," London added, her voice a little tired but with a playful glint in her eyes that hinted she wasn't going home alone.

"Together?" Dionne asked, raising an eyebrow and pointing between London and True.

"Mind your business," London replied with a smirk, confirming Dionne's suspicions.

Dionne couldn't hold back her laughter. "Well, have fun. It was nice meeting you, True. Take care of my sister," she said, winking.

True chuckled. "You don't have to worry about that," he said confidently, his gaze lingering on London with admiration. "It was nice meeting you too," he added before they left, hand in hand.

Mario and Karmen also said their goodbyes, Mario giving Arris a quick dap before leaving with Karmen, who was glowing with happiness. Dionne watched her friends leave, smiling softly. She was genuinely happy for them, but the reminder that she'd be going home to an empty house made her heart sink slightly.

"Damn, I didn't know how much time had passed," Arris said, looking around and noticing the ballroom beginning to empty. The once vibrant energy of the event was winding down, signaling the end of the night.

"Yeah, that's what happens when you're having a good time," Dionne quipped with a small smile, the warmth in her tone enough to keep his attention locked on her.

Feenin'

Arris tilted his head slightly, his signature smirk creeping onto his face. "You ready for the night to end?"

Her curious eyes met his, a soft smirk playing on her lips. "I'm having a good time, and I don't think I'm ready for it to end just yet," she said, the intrigue in her voice matching the spark in her eyes.

"Good," he said, standing from his seat, his towering presence commanding her full attention. "Let me go talk to my team and say my goodbyes. Then we can leave."

Dionne leaned back slightly, her smirk turning playful as her curiosity piqued. "Where are we going?"

Arris chuckled at her question, finding her mix of curiosity and nervousness endearing. "You like spontaneous, right?" he asked, his confident smirk deepening as he threw her own words back at her.

Dionne couldn't help but laugh, remembering their earlier conversation when she admitted she loved doing spontaneous things. "Yeah, I do," she said softly, her voice laced with anticipation, though a flicker of nervousness danced in her tone.

"Then trust me," he said smoothly, leaning just close enough for his presence to leave her feeling flustered. "I'll be right back, Mama."

Before she could respond, he walked away, leaving her sitting there with a mix of intrigue and longing. She watched him move with effortless confidence, his broad shoulders cutting through the room as he made his way to his team.

Dionne exhaled slowly, leaning back in her seat as her thoughts raced. There was something about Arris that made her feel alive, like she was stepping into a world she didn't want to leave. He was everything she had always craved—attentive, confident, and thrilling. But the guilt tugged at her heart. He was everything she wanted but knew she couldn't have.

To distract herself, Dionne pulled out her phone for the first time that evening. Her smile faltered as she stared at the blank screen. No calls. No messages. Nothing from Malik. Her heart sank. It was like she didn't exist to him anymore, and that weight was becoming harder to bear.

She sighed in frustration, her emotions threatening to spill over, but she pushed it down, shutting off her phone completely. Tonight wasn't about Malik, she told herself. Tonight, for the first time in a long time, was about her.

Dionne felt Arris's presence behind her, his energy wrapping around her like a warm blanket. She quickly slipped her phone into her purse, pushing thoughts of her empty relationship with Malik far out of her mind. Tonight wasn't about him—it was about this moment, this escape, and the man who made her feel things she hadn't in years.

"You're ready, beautiful?" Arris's deep, smooth voice whispered close to her ear, sending an involuntary shiver through her body. The effect he had on her was undeniable—his words, his touch, and his sheer presence all ignited something inside her that she couldn't quite explain or resist.

"Yes," she said softly, her voice almost a whisper. Arris extended his hand to her, helping her down from the barstool. She hesitated for a moment, her eyes darting around the room to ensure no one was paying attention.

"Arris, you can't do things like that here," she said nervously, a hint of tension in her tone. She glanced away, not wanting anyone to notice the spark between them.

Arris chuckled, his confidence unwavering. "No one's around, Mama. It's just my team, and they know how to keep a secret," he said, flashing her one of his playful, yet irresistible smirks. She sighed, her playful eye roll giving her away. As much as she wanted to resist, his charm was magnetic, leaving her weak in ways she didn't want to admit.

Before she could protest further, he grabbed her hand again, his grip firm but gentle, and led her toward the staircase. Her heart raced, and despite herself, she followed willingly. They climbed the steps that led to the club, which tonight was unrecognizably empty. Usually buzzing with people and music, the space now stood silent, the soft glow of lights casting an intimate ambiance. Dionne looked around, the sound of her heels echoing in the quiet.

"Where are we going, Arris?" Dionne asked, her voice tinged with both curiosity and growing anxiety as he guided her through the hallways to his office. The intensity of his presence beside her made her chest tighten in a way that both excited and unnerved her.

"Just trust me, Mama," Arris said smoothly, his tone sending a shiver down her spine. He opened the door to his office, gesturing for her to step inside. The room was massive, with walls painted in deep royal blue and accents of black. It exuded power and masculinity, every detail meticulously designed to match the man who occupied it.

Dionne admired the decor for a moment before her gaze shifted back to him, standing near the desk with something in his hand. "Put this over your eyes," he said, holding up a black Louis Vuitton scarf.

She looked at him incredulously, a chuckle escaping her lips. "I'm not putting that on."

Arris ignored her protest, stepping closer. The glint of amusement in his eyes did nothing to soften the commanding energy radiating from

Feenin'

him. "Come on, Mama."

"Arris, I'm not putting that on! You're going to mess up my lashes!" she exclaimed, backing away slightly, her voice playful but firm.

"You don't need that shit anyway," he said, his voice low and unwavering as his eyes roamed over her, unapologetically admiring every inch. Dionne bit her lip to hide the blush creeping up her cheeks.

"Come here," he said again, this time more firmly, his confidence threatening to crumble her resolve.

"No, Arris," she replied, crossing her arms in mock defiance. "What do you have planned that requires me to wear a blindfold?"

He smirked, taking another step toward her. "I can't tell you—that's the whole point of the blindfold, Dionne. Now come here, like I said."

Even though the tone of his voice sent a jolt of heat through her body, she refused to back down. "No, Arris," she said again, stepping to the side like a kid avoiding a scolding.

Arris threw his head back with a laugh, shaking it as if she were a stubborn child he couldn't help but find adorable. "Why are you running, Mama?" he asked, his voice laced with humor.

"Because I'm not putting that on!" Dionne shot back, her serious tone clashing with the playful grin tugging at her lips.

He chuckled again, closing the distance between them. "Yes, you are. I'm not telling you again, Mama. Bring yo ass here," he said, his voice dropping into a softer, yet firmer tone that made her knees weaken.

Dionne tried to dart away again, but Arris was quicker. His large hand gripped her wrist, pulling her toward him with ease. She giggled as he pinned her lightly against the wall, her laughter tinged with nervous energy. "You always want to play," he said, his deep laugh vibrating through her body.

"Arris, I'm not putting that on," Dionne said breathlessly. "Now I'm even more nervous about whatever you've got planned."

His laughter faded, and his expression softened, though his eyes burned with intensity. "You don't trust me?" he asked, his voice low and tinged with something deeper.

The question sent a wave of emotions crashing through her. Dionne felt herself wavering, every inch of her body wanting to give in, but her mind fighting to maintain control. "Yes, I do. I think," she said softly, her voice betraying the internal battle she was losing.

"Think?" Arris repeated, tilting his head slightly as his lips curved into a knowing smile. "I need you to know, Mama. Do you trust me?"

Dionne tried to look away, but Arris was quicker. He gently gripped her chin, turning her face back toward him, his touch both grounding and electrifying. "Do. You. Trust me?" he repeated, his voice steady, his eyes piercing into hers.

"Yes," she whispered, barely audible, her walls shattering under the weight of his gaze. "Yes, I trust you."

Arris's smirk softened into a warm smile. "Then let me put this on."

Dionne hesitated before slowly turning her back to him, her heart pounding as his proximity sent waves of heat down her spine. His strong hands brushed her shoulders lightly, and as he draped the scarf over her eyes, she felt the warmth of his body pressing against her back. Her breath hitched when she felt the undeniable imprint of his arousal through his slacks, but she didn't move. Instead, she surrendered.

She reached up, moving her long hair aside as Arris tied the scarf gently at the back of her head. Despite her earlier protests, she couldn't deny how much she craved this moment, how much she trusted him, even though she barely understood why. His fingers lingered for a moment as they finished the knot, his touch sending one final shiver through her before he leaned in close to her ear.

"Now, let me show you why you can trust me," he whispered, his voice like velvet against her skin.

He turned her around, adjusting the blindfold gently to ensure it was secure. "Can you see?" he asked, his voice soft but firm. Dionne shook her head, her lips twitching into a nervous smile.

"Good," Arris said, licking his lips as he took the opportunity to admire her. The crocodile skin dress clung to her curves in all the right ways, showing off her flawless figure. Every inch of her exuded elegance and power, yet all he could think about was how much he wanted to show her how deeply she affected him. It wasn't just desire—it was the pull she had on his mind, his emotions. But he remembered her boundaries, the way she'd drawn the line between them. He respected it, at least for now.

"Arris?" Dionne called out, holding out her hands in search of him, her voice breaking through his thoughts.

He chuckled, stepping closer and taking her hands in his. "I'm right here, Mama," he reassured her. "You ready?"

"No," she replied with a playful laugh, though her tone betrayed her nervousness.

"Relax," he said, his voice low and soothing. "I got you." He moved behind her, his hands on her waist as he guided her out of the office. The warmth of his touch made her body tingle, grounding her in the moment even as uncertainty prickled at the edges of her nerves.

They stepped into the club's private elevator, Arris pressing the

Feenin'

button to the rooftop. The ride was silent except for the sound of their breathing. When the doors opened, Dionne immediately felt the cool night breeze on her skin, the wind carrying the scent of the city and the promise of something extraordinary. She could tell they were high up, the wind whipping her hair back, though her style remained intact.

"Arris, where are we?" she asked, her voice laced with both curiosity and anxiety.

"The roof," he answered simply, his grin widening as he guided her forward.

Her steps faltered when she heard the unmistakable sound of helicopter blades. She froze in place, her breath hitching. "Arris…" she said slowly, her voice rising with nervous energy.

"Mr. Black! The ride you requested is here and ready for takeoff," a voice called out, belonging to a man who seemed to be approaching them. Dionne's body tensed at the word takeoff.

"Takeoff?" she repeated, her voice almost a whisper as panic set in.

Arris chuckled softly, his hands steady on her waist. "Thank you, Chuck. We're ready," he said casually as the pilot nodded and walked off.

Dionne immediately reached up to remove the blindfold, but Arris caught her wrist gently. "Whoa, not yet," he said, his tone calm but commanding.

"Arris," she said, her voice trembling slightly, "what are you doing? What's going on?" The sound of the wind and the distant hum of the helicopter blades made her anxiety spike.

"Trust me," he said, leaning closer so that his words brushed her ear. "You said you loved spontaneous. I'm just giving you what you asked for.

Dionne let out a shaky breath, trying to steady herself. "Spontaneous doesn't mean putting me on a damn helicopter, Arris!"

His laugh was deep and rich, carrying over the sound of the blades. "Come on, Mama. You said you trust me."

"I did," she muttered, her heart pounding, "but I didn't know you'd take it this far!"

"Relax," he said again, his hands never leaving her waist. "I promise this will be worth it. I just want to show you something."

"Can I take this off now?" Dionne asked, her patience wearing thin as she fidgeted slightly.

"No, not yet," Arris said calmly, his hand firm on hers to reassure her. He guided her carefully into the helicopter, the sound of the rotors growing louder and making her already thin patience wear even thinner.

He helped her inside, his hand lingering on her waist as he strapped her in. Dionne sat stiffly, her nerves and frustration evident in the way she gripped the edge of her seat.

"We're ready, Chuck," Arris said with an easy smile, completely unfazed by the tension radiating from Dionne.

Moments later, the helicopter lifted off the ground. The sudden motion made Dionne's stomach flip, and her body instinctively tensed. Her fear of heights surged, and she clenched her jaw, trying to keep calm. Arris, on the other hand, looked calm and collected, his excitement evident. He waited until they were high above the city before finally leaning over to untie her blindfold.

"There," he said softly, pulling the scarf away.

Dionne blinked a few times, letting her eyes adjust. For a moment, she sat still, unsure of what to expect. Then her gaze dropped to the window, and the breathtaking sight of the Houston skyline stretched out below her.

Her heart raced as her eyes widened in panic. "Arris!" she yelled, gripping the edge of her seat tightly, her chest rising and falling rapidly.

Chuck chuckled from the front seat, and Arris couldn't help but let out a small laugh at her reaction. "Relax, Mama," he said, his tone light and playful.

"Get me off this thing! Now!" she said, her voice shaky with fear as she avoided looking out the window.

"Mama, just calm down," he said, his hand finding her thigh in an effort to ground her. "I got you."

"No, Arris! For real, let me down. I told you I'm afraid of heights!" she yelled, her voice rising with every word. The helicopter shifted slightly as Chuck adjusted their position, and Dionne's hand immediately shot out to grip Arris's arm tightly.

"See! I knew I should've never let you talk me into putting that damn blindfold on me!" she said, her words tumbling out in a panicked rush.

Arris couldn't help but chuckle at her. Even in her fear, she was captivating. "Dionne," he said softly, his tone more serious now as he leaned closer, "just trust me. I'm not gonna let anything happen to you."

She glared at him, but the warmth of his voice and the steadiness of his hand on her thigh began to chip away at her panic. "Just relax," he said again, his fingers brushing over hers to coax her into letting go of the seat. "Now, look." He gestured toward the window, his voice calm and soothing.

Dionne hesitated, her breath still uneven. Slowly, she turned her head and peeked out the window. Her fear was quickly replaced by awe as she

Feenin'

took in the shimmering lights of the city below. Houston stretched out like a glittering map, its skyline illuminated against the dark night sky.

"It's... beautiful," she said softly, the fear melting away from her voice as wonder took its place.

"She is," Arris said, his gaze not on the city but on her. The way her eyes lit up and the faint smile tugged at her lips only deepened the ache in his chest. He wanted her—every part of her—but he knew he couldn't have her, at least not yet.

Dionne glanced at him, catching his stare. "You're not even looking at the city," she said, a slight smile forming on her lips despite herself.

"I'm looking at what's more beautiful," Arris replied simply, his voice low and sincere.

Her cheeks flushed, and for a brief moment, the chaos in her life faded. Up here, it was just them, suspended between the earth and sky, with nothing but the city lights and the hum of the helicopter surrounding them.

As the helicopter circled the city, Dionne's initial fear was replaced with warmth and excitement. Seeing Houston from this perspective was breathtaking, and she felt her connection with Arris deepening. "I grew up there," he said, pointing toward a small neighborhood nestled in the rougher part of the city.

From their height, it looked tiny, but Dionne could feel the weight of his words. She turned her attention to him, her curiosity piqued. "How was it?" she asked, her voice gentle but filled with genuine interest.

Arris gave her one of his signature smirks, shrugging casually. "It was what it was."

Dionne chuckled, shaking her head at his usual laid-back demeanor. "And that means what?" she pressed, her eyes catching the sight of their intertwined hands. She smiled internally at the realization that, no matter how much she insisted they were just friends, Arris couldn't seem to keep his hands off her.

"It was cool," he started, his tone steady but reflective. "Regular really. Times were hard, but I did what I had to do to help my mother and sister the best way I could. Being the man of the house and shit." He chuckled softly, but Dionne could see the tension creeping into his shoulders as he spoke about his past.

"And you did a wonderful job," she said sincerely, her voice firm yet soothing.

Arris turned to her, his smile faint but appreciative. "You carry a lot of weight on your shoulders," Dionne continued, her tone softening as she studied him. She could see the strength in him, but also the burden he carried from being forced to grow up too fast.

"I always had to," Arris admitted, his jaw tightening as he looked out at the city below. "Calvin wasn't there, so I had to step in his place at 8 years old." His voice was calm, but the pain lingered beneath the surface.

Dionne reached out, her hand gently brushing against his beard, her touch grounding him. "You don't have to anymore, Arris. You might think you do, but you don't." Her voice was steady but laced with a tenderness that only she could give him.

Her touch seemed to melt the tension in his shoulders. He leaned into her hand, his eyes closing for a brief moment as her warmth calmed the storm brewing inside him. She smiled softly, knowing that no words were needed. Their bodies spoke a language that was unspoken but understood, a silent promise that they were there for one another.

"My feet are starting to hurt," Dionne said suddenly, trying to lighten the mood. "These heels are definitely not made for an all-night adventure." She laughed, wiggling her toes slightly as a playful grin spread across her face.

Arris chuckled, the heaviness from their earlier conversation fading. Without hesitation, he reached down, gently pulling her feet into his lap. He slipped off her heels and started massaging them, his hands firm but soothing. Dionne let out a sigh of relief, leaning back in her seat as the ache in her feet eased.

"You're full of surprises tonight, Mr. Black," she teased, her eyes twinkling as she watched him work.

Arris smirked, not looking up from her feet. "Just making sure you're comfortable, Mama. Can't have you walking around in pain."

The words made her heart skip a beat, but she quickly composed herself, trying to ignore the warmth spreading through her chest. "I could get used to this," she joked lightly, but a part of her meant it.

Arris finally looked up, his gaze locking with hers. "You deserve this—and more," he said, his tone serious now, as if he were making a vow.

For a moment, they sat in silence, the city lights reflecting in their eyes as the helicopter continued its journey. Neither of them wanted this night to end, but both knew it was already something they'd never forget.

"Enough about me—who is Dionne Smith outside of the powerful real estate agent?" Arris asked, his voice soft yet curious. His hands continued to work their magic on her feet, the warmth and firmness of his touch coaxing a rare relaxation out of her. Dionne smiled at his question, but there was a flicker of sadness behind it. She wasn't ready to lay her entire story bare, not yet.

Feenin'

"It was cool," she said, her tone measured. "It had its good times and bad times. But college...college had to be the best part of my life." Her lips curved into a warm smile, genuine and unguarded.

"How was that?" Arris asked, his curiosity deepening. His smile mirrored hers as they soared above the glowing city, the night wrapping around them like a comforting cocoon. He wanted to know everything about her—the layers she kept hidden, the stories etched into her being.

"I met my forever sisters," Dionne said, her smile brightening as she thought of London and Karmen. "I only grew up with a brother, and he was hell growing up—so protective, always up in my business—but I love him. So, when I met London and Karmen, I found sisterhood." Her voice softened with affection, the bond she shared with her friends evident in every word.

"Plus," she continued, her expression glowing with nostalgia, "college was so much fun. The parties, the campus...I even fell in—" Dionne stopped mid-sentence, her face faltering as a shadow of emotion passed over her. Malik. His name loomed in her thoughts, but she quickly pulled herself back, masking the moment with a quick recovery. "I fell in love with soccer," she finished, her voice steady now, though Arris's sharp eyes caught the hesitation. He didn't press her on it, though it lingered in his mind.

"College seemed fun," he said simply, his smile kind as if coaxing her to continue but not pushing her boundaries.

"It was," Dionne said, her gaze soft as she revisited the memories. "Wish I could live it again like it was my first time." Her voice held a wistful note, the longing for simpler, freer days shining through.

Arris tilted his head, studying her for a moment before replying with a small, knowing smile. "You've got that look," he said, his tone teasing but gentle.

"What look?" Dionne asked, turning her attention back to him, her eyebrows slightly raised.

"That look that says you've got more to say but don't want to share it just yet." He shrugged as if it didn't matter, but his eyes told her that he cared deeply about whatever it was she was holding back.

Dionne smiled, a faint blush rising in her cheeks. "Maybe one day," she said softly, her words carrying more weight than she intended.

Arris nodded, his smile remaining steady, though his heart beat a little faster. "One day," he repeated, a quiet promise hanging in the air between them.

"I think you should talk to your father," Dionne said, breaking the brief but comforting silence between them. Arris's expression shifted immediately, his brows furrowing as he looked at her, a mix of confusion and resistance in his eyes.

"Just hear me out," she added quickly, sensing his hesitation. He nodded reluctantly, his eyes still fixed on her, waiting for an explanation.

"My mother is sick," she began, her voice cracking slightly, betraying the pain she worked so hard to mask. "And she's not getting better. I'm spending the last of her days giving her everything she's ever wanted before she goes." Her voice wavered, and Arris's features softened, his hands continuing their soothing motions on her feet as if to silently reassure her that he was there.

Dionne took a deep breath and met his gaze, the weight of her words filling the space between them. "I love my mother, while you resent your father, but that guilt—of never saying or doing all you wanted to before they're gone—will eat at you for the rest of your life." Her tone was soft, but the raw emotion behind her words struck something deep in Arris.

He stared at her, his jaw tight as her words sank in. The anger he carried for his father ran deep, rooted in years of abandonment and pain. Facing Calvin felt impossible, yet hearing Dionne's perspective and the love she poured into her mother's final days made him pause.

"You don't have to forgive him or let him back into your life," she continued, her voice steady but tender. "But unleash everything you've been holding inside—everything you've wanted to say to him since he left you and your sister. Not for his sake, but for your healing." Her gaze held his, a quiet strength in her eyes that made it clear she was speaking from experience.

Arris nodded slowly, his thoughts clouded but tinged with a new clarity. Her words were seeping into the cracks of his defenses. "I'll think about it, Mama," he said softly, the nickname slipping from his lips like second nature.

Dionne smiled faintly, though her heart ached at the thought of Mama Glen. She wanted to tell Arris the truth—that Mama Glen wasn't her biological mother but her mother-in-law, the woman she was holding onto for the sake of a loveless relationship. But something about this moment, about Arris's openness, made her hold back. She didn't want their fragile connection to end because of Malik or the promise she'd made to Mama Glen.

"I'm sorry to hear about your mother," Arris said, his voice low but sincere, his gaze locking onto hers. Dionne felt his words settle over her, warm and genuine. She smiled softly, her thoughts drifting to Mama Glen and all the love she had given her over the years.

"Thank you," Dionne replied, her voice gentle. "She's lived a

Feenin'

wonderful life, and I've been blessed to be a part of it." Her smile was genuine, though tinged with sadness, and Arris mirrored it, his admiration for her growing even more in that moment.

For a few beats, they sat in silence, their connection unspoken but profound. Dionne realized that even though she had told Arris they could only be friends, she didn't want to let go of whatever it was they had. And for the first time in a long time, Arris wondered if he could allow someone close enough to see all of him.

The helicopter ride came to an end as they landed softly on the rooftop of Arris's building. The wind from the propellers tousled Dionne's hair as Arris helped her step out, his hand firm and steady on hers. "Thank you, Chuck," Arris said, nodding at the pilot, who smiled before stepping away. Dionne couldn't help but reflect on the experience as they walked hand in hand back into the building.

"I can't believe I'm saying this, but that was fun," she admitted, her voice laced with a mix of warmth and disbelief.

Arris smirked, his confidence undeniable. "And you faced your fear of heights," he teased, the playful light in his eyes making her shake her head.

"That part wasn't fun, and you're an asshole for that," Dionne joked, her tone light as she bumped his arm.

He chuckled, leaning closer as they walked into his office. "So you didn't enjoy the ride?" he asked, his voice dropping slightly as his gaze locked onto hers. His proximity sent a familiar wave of heat through her, her body reacting before her mind could keep up.

She tried to play it cool, but the smirk tugging at his lips made it impossible. "Yes," she admitted softly, looking away to avoid the intensity of his stare. As usual, Arris wasn't having it. He gently tilted her chin back toward him, forcing her to meet his gaze.

"That's good," he said, his voice a low rumble that seemed to vibrate through her. Then, before she could even process it, he pressed his lips against hers.

The kiss wasn't rushed or frantic—it was deliberate, like he wanted her to feel every ounce of desire he had for her. Arris knew the "just friends" boundary she'd tried to set was nonexistent for him. He craved her too much to ever settle for less. And as much as Dionne told herself she should resist, she didn't. Instead, her arms wrapped around his neck as her body melted into his.

He easily lifted her, her dress riding up slightly as her legs instinctively wrapped around his waist. Their kiss deepened, tongues battling for dominance, and for a moment, all the guilt and hesitation vanished. It was just them—no titles, no boundaries, just raw emotion.

But reality hit hard, snapping Dionne out of the haze. "Arris... we can't," she whispered, her voice trembling as she tried to push him back gently. Her hands were on his chest, but her body betrayed her words, still clinging to him.

Arris ignored her protest, his lips moving to her neck, leaving trails of heat in their wake. "Mama, I fucking crave you," he murmured against her skin, his voice thick with need. Dionne's eyes fluttered shut as his words and touch sent her into a spiral of pleasure. She moaned softly, her resolve weakening with every passing second.

Her gaze flicked to the clock on the wall: 4:06 a.m. The realization of how much time had passed hit her like a cold splash of water. She'd spent the entire night with Arris, ignoring her phone and all the responsibilities waiting for her. The thought of Malik, her loveless reality, pulled her back to the surface.

"Arris, we need to stop. I have to go," she said, her voice barely above a whisper as she forced herself to regain control.

Arris paused, his breathing heavy as he pulled back just enough to look into her eyes. The desperation, lust, and something deeper—something unspoken—were all written across his face. He saw her hesitation, the conflict warring inside her, and for the first time, it wasn't anger or frustration he felt. It was understanding.

"Okay," he said finally, his voice low and reluctant. But before letting her go, he leaned in, capturing her lips in one last kiss. It was slow, deep, and so gentle it left her knees weak.

When he set her back on her feet, his hands lingered on hers, his fingers intertwining with hers as if to say he wasn't ready to let her go. "Let me take you home," he said softly, his tone leaving no room for argument.

Dionne nodded, unable to find the words to protest. As much as she wanted to keep her worlds separate, she knew there was no escaping Arris's presence. She just prayed Malik wasn't home when she arrived, because explaining why Arris Black was the one dropping her off at this hour would be a storm she wasn't ready to face.

Arris drove smoothly through the quiet streets, the soft hum of the engine the only sound between them. Dionne sat silently, replaying the events of the night over and over in her mind. When they pulled into her driveway, she noticed Malik's car was nowhere in sight, and she let out a quiet sigh of relief.

"Thank you for tonight. It was... terrifying, but fun," she admitted, a light laugh escaping her lips as she looked over at him.

Feenin'

Arris chuckled, his dimples showing as he turned to her. "Terrifying, huh? I thought I'd cured your fear of heights." His teasing tone had the same playful charm that had been her undoing all night.

"Maybe just a little," she admitted, chuckling softly. "But seriously, it was amazing. Thank you.

Arris smirked, his gaze lingering on her longer than it should have. "Just trying to give you everything you've been yearning for," he said confidently.

The words hit Dionne like a ton of bricks. She froze, her chest tightening as her mind spiraled. What did he mean by that? Did he know? Did he see right through the walls she'd built to hide how unsatisfied she was with her life, her relationship? She wanted to ask but couldn't find the courage to form the words.

Before she could overthink it, Arris leaned over, cupping her cheek gently as he pressed another kiss to her lips. It wasn't rushed or hungry this time—it was soft, lingering, and full of something deeper she didn't want to name. When he pulled back, his eyes scanned her from head to toe, a flicker of frustration in his gaze, as if he was silently battling with the fact that he couldn't have her the way he truly wanted.

"You're something else, Mama," he said, shaking his head as a small smile tugged at his lips. Dionne, feeling her resolve crumble under his touch and gaze, quickly looked away, trying to compose herself.

Arris didn't say another word as he got out of the car and walked around to her side. He opened her door and extended his hand, his gentlemanly demeanor as irresistible as ever. She hesitated, not wanting to leave the safety of his car or the intoxicating pull of his presence, but she eventually slid her hand into his, letting him help her out.

As she stepped onto the pavement, she tugged at her dress, smoothing it down, only for Arris to pull her closer. His grip on her waist was firm, his presence towering over her. "Can't wait to see your beautiful ass again," he said, his voice low and dripping with seduction.

Dionne tried to keep her wall up, to hold on to the boundaries she'd set, but the way he looked at her made it impossible. "Good night, Arris," she said softly, her voice betraying her as it wavered slightly.

Arris chuckled, seeing right through her. He stepped closer, his large hands slipping down to grip her ass firmly, pulling her flush against him. Her breath hitched, her body betraying her mind. "We can play this 'just friends' shit as long as you want," he murmured, his lips brushing against her ear, "but you're mine, and I won't stop showing you that."

His words sent a shiver down her spine, and her legs felt weak beneath her. Her hands instinctively gripped his broad shoulders for balance as her body leaned into him, craving his touch. "Do you hear me, Mama?" he asked, his voice dropping an octave as his grip on her tightened.

She nodded, unable to find her voice, but Arris wasn't letting her off that easy. "I need your words, beautiful," he demanded, his tone firm but seductive. A soft, involuntary moan escaped her lips, and he smirked, knowing exactly what he was doing to her.

"Yes, Arris. I hear you," she whispered, her voice barely audible, but it was enough for him.

Satisfied, he stepped back, forcing himself to let her go even though every fiber of his being wanted to keep her close. Dionne stood frozen, her body still buzzing from his touch and his words, craving more even as her mind screamed at her to walk away.

"Good night, Mama," Arris said with a confident smile, his voice carrying the promise of more.

"Good night," Dionne replied softly, her voice shaky as she tried to gather herself. She watched as he turned and walked back to his car, the sight of him making her knees weak all over again. She knew she should go inside, but her feet felt rooted to the ground, her heart pounding as she tried to process what had just happened.

Dionne stepped into the quiet house, closing the door behind her as Arris drove off into the night. She leaned against the door for a moment, her mind replaying the evening with him. The deep conversations at the bar, their playful dancing, the breathtaking helicopter ride, and the charged moment in his office—every memory brought a smile to her lips and a warmth she hadn't felt in years. Shaking her head to snap herself out of it, Dionne exhaled deeply, her heels clicking softly as she climbed the stairs.

The smile on her face faded instantly as she entered the bedroom and spotted Malik sitting on the edge of the bed, his arms crossed, and his face set in a hard glare. The tension in the room hit her like a wave.

"Shit! Malik, you scared the fuck outta me," Dionne said, clutching her chest as her heart raced.

"You wouldn't be so scared if you were already here," Malik retorted, his tone sharp and accusatory. Dionne rolled her eyes, her frustration bubbling to the surface. Here we go, she thought, already tired of the argument brewing. All she wanted was to shower and wash away the remnants of the night—not because of regret, but because of the lingering effect Arris had on her body and soul.

"You know where I was," Dionne snapped, her voice calm but laced with annoyance. "At the important work event that you canceled on last

Feenin'

minute because of your job."

Malik's jaw tightened. "That doesn't explain why you're walking in here at 4 a.m. or why you weren't answering any of my calls. And I said I had to work," he shot back defensively.

"Yeah, you've been doing a lot of that lately," Dionne replied coldly, crossing her arms and meeting his glare with one of her own.

"I said it was an emergency! My job was more important than your event!" Malik argued, his voice rising. The anger and hurt in Dionne's eyes at his words instantly made his stomach drop with regret.

"More important?" she repeated, her voice low but sharp, the weight of her emotions cutting through the room. Hurt mingled with simmering anger, making her tone sting even more.

"I didn't mean it like that, Dee," Malik said quickly, his voice softening as he tried to backtrack. But it was too late. The damage had already been done.

"No," she snapped, her voice trembling as she stepped closer, her emotions boiling to the surface. "You meant exactly what you said. Your job is more important than mine. Like everything else in your life. It's always more important than me!"

Her words hit Malik hard, but he couldn't stop his own frustrations from surfacing. His jaw clenched as he tried to control himself. "That's not what I meant," he said through gritted teeth, though he could feel her slipping further away with each passing second.

"It's always the same with you, Malik," Dionne said, her voice breaking as her anger turned into pain. "I have supported you through everything. Every long shift, every canceled date, every missed anniversary. And the one time I need you to show up for me—for us— you make it clear where I stand."

"Don't deflect, Dee," Malik said, his tone hardening.

"Deflect?" Dionne asked, her voice rising slightly in disbelief. "I'm stating facts. When it comes to your big events, I'm there. I show up, I support you like a fiancée should. But when it comes to what's important to me? 'Oh, I have to work,'" she said, mocking his excuse with venom in her voice.

Malik sighed heavily, his tone softening slightly. "I know, and I apologize—"

"There you go with those tired-ass apologies," Dionne interrupted, her voice cutting through the room like a blade. "Save it, Malik. I don't give a fuck about an apology anymore." She turned on her heel, heading toward her side of the room. "I'm about to get in the shower."

As she moved past him, Malik stood abruptly, grabbing her arm and pulling her back. The force of his grip startled her, and the sharpness of the motion made her gasp.

Dionne ripped her arm away, stepping back as her glare burned into him. "Don't you dare put your hands on me like that again," she said, her voice low but trembling with restrained anger.

Malik's posture deflated as the weight of his mistake hit him. He raised his hands slightly in a gesture of surrender, his face etched with regret. "Dee, I didn't mean—"

"Save it." Dionne's words were clipped and final.

"Where did you go after the party? I know it didn't last until four in the morning," Malik pressed, his tone sharp and unwavering.

Dionne let out a dry chuckle, shaking her head. "I went to Karmen's house after. It's better than coming home to an empty ass house I'm supposed to be sharing with my 'fiancé.'" Her fingers made air quotes as she spat the word "fiancé," her voice dripping with sarcasm.

Malik sighed heavily, running a frustrated hand down his face. "I had to work, Dionne!" he snapped, his voice raised, but Dionne wasn't fazed. She squared her shoulders, standing firm.

"I know!" she shot back, her voice rising to match his. "And while you're busy telling your mother we're disconnected because of my busy work schedule, why don't you tell the truth for once? Admit that your job is more demanding than mine. Hell, admit that you love that damn job more than you love me! Or maybe there's another bitch you're entertaining that I don't know about. I'm sure Brittany wasn't the only one."

Her laugh was bitter, laced with hurt and fury, her words slicing through him like a blade.

Malik's anger deflated as guilt washed over his face. "I do love you more, Dee. Brittany was a mistake. There's no one else—just you," he pleaded, his voice softer now, almost desperate.

Dionne shook her head, the walls she'd built around her heart growing thicker. "Yeah, that's what you say," she muttered, her tone dismissive and cold.

Malik stepped closer, reaching out as if to close the growing chasm between them. "Dee, you have to believe me—"

She held up a hand, silencing him. "It's late, Malik. I need to shower and go to sleep. You should do the same. No telling when work will come calling again." Her words were coated with venom, a final jab before she turned her back on him, walking into the bathroom and locking the door behind her.

Leaning against the door, Dionne took a deep breath, willing the

Feenin'

frustration and anger to leave her body. She stripped off her dress and heels, stepping into the hot, steamy shower. As the water cascaded over her, she hoped it would wash away the tension of the argument and the exhaustion weighing her down.

But no matter how much she scrubbed, no water or soap could cleanse the thoughts of Arris from her mind. His touch lingered on her skin, his words echoed in her ears, and the way he made her feel refused to leave her heart. With Malik sitting in the other room, her thoughts were consumed by another man—a man she had no business feening for, yet couldn't stop.

Dionne closed her eyes, leaning her head against the shower wall as the hot water continued to flow. She didn't understand how things had escalated so quickly, how Arris had become a craving she couldn't control. But one thing was clear: she was already in too deep.

Chapter 8

Dionne, London, and Karmen were mid-workout at the gym, a usual bonding ritual filled with sweat, laughter, and catching up on each other's lives. As they moved between sets, the conversation turned to the night before.

"So, how did you two's nights go?" Dionne asked with a teasing smirk, her curiosity evident.

London didn't hesitate. "Girl, that man turned me every which way but loose!" she hyped, her voice full of energy, making them all burst into laughter.

"I don't even know how my ass is in this gym right now," London added, shaking her head with a grin. Dionne smiled, genuinely happy to see her friend glowing with happiness.

"So, does that mean you'll see him again?" Dionne pressed, a hopeful lilt in her voice.

"Yes." London's voice softened, and she blushed—a rare sight. "Matter of fact, he wants to take me on a date tonight."

Both Dionne and Karmen gasped in delight, exchanging surprised looks. Seeing London, who was always the self-assured, no-nonsense one of the group, gush over a man was a shift they didn't expect.

"Aww, I'm so happy to hear that, Lon!" Dionne said, her excitement contagious.

"Me too, sis. You deserve it," Karmen chimed in warmly, her admiration clear.

London brushed off their praise with a playful wave of her hand. "Alright, alright, don't get used to me acting like this."

"Oh, don't think we're letting you off the hook that easy!" Dionne quipped, turning her attention to Karmen, whose face immediately

Feenin'

flushed with color. "Karmen, spill! How was your night?"

"Aww, she's blushing! My girl is hooked!" London hyped, clapping her hands as their laughter filled the gym.

Karmen, clearly flustered, finally answered. "Y'all, stop! Okay, listen—last night was... different. I told him I wasn't ready to have sex yet, and he completely understood. We just sat up all night, talking and learning about each other until the sun came up."

Her voice carried a mix of admiration and awe as her feelings for Mario shone through.

"Aww." Dionne's smile widened, knowing how meaningful that was for Karmen, who valued genuine connections deeply.

"He really is a great guy," Karmen said, her happiness clear as she gripped her water bottle tightly, as if steadying herself against the whirlwind of emotions.

"That's good, sis. I'm happy for you," London said with a sincere nod, her typical sass momentarily giving way to heartfelt support.

The three women exchanged smiles, basking in the joy of their shared sisterhood. For Dionne, seeing her friends so content was a bright spot, even as her own complicated feelings lingered in the background. But for now, she chose to focus on their happiness, letting it fill the space between them.

"You all in our business. What about you, missy?" London teased, turning the attention squarely onto Dionne.

The memories of her night with Arris surged forward—the helicopter ride, the way his touch lingered, the vulnerable moments they shared. A flood of emotions crossed her face, but she fought back the smile tugging at her lips, masking it with a playful roll of her eyes. "I went straight home and slept in my empty ass bed," Dionne said with a fake attitude, casually lying about how her night really unfolded.

Her friends, oblivious to the truth, took her words at face value. "Girl, I can't wait until I see Malik's ass. I swear, I want to beat him down for standing you up last night," London said, her frustration with Malik dripping from her tone.

"Yeah, he was wrong for that," Karmen added, her tone soft but pointed. Then her face shifted to a knowing smirk. "But it didn't seem like it bothered you too much, especially with how focused you were on Arris all night."

London chuckled at Karmen's sharp observation, while Dionne rolled her eyes, clearly over their scrutiny. "We're just business partners," she said curtly, shutting down their assumptions before they could spiral.

"Business partners?" London quipped, raising an eyebrow. "We didn't say y'all were anything else."

Karmen leaned in with a sly grin. "We're just saying, the chemistry was strong, girl. I've never seen you look that comfortable with anyone—not even Malik."

Dionne bit her lip, failing to suppress the smile that crept onto her face. Her friends weren't wrong. Arris had a way of breaking through her walls effortlessly, leaving her disarmed and vulnerable, something even Malik had never managed. She shook her head and tried to brush off their comments. "He's just a good person to be around. But it's nothing more than business," she said, her voice firm, even though her heart betrayed her with its quickening beat.

"Uh-huh," London said, the knowing grin on her face making it clear she wasn't convinced. "Sure, sis."

"How did Malik make up for standing you up?" Karmen asked, smoothly transitioning the conversation as they moved into their next workout.

"Nothing," Dionne said bluntly, her tone laced with irritation. Her feelings for Malik—or the lack thereof—were written all over her face.

"He needs to do better," Karmen said sympathetically, her voice tinged with concern.

Dionne sighed, wiping sweat from her brow as she grabbed a sip of water. She didn't want to talk about Malik or their crumbling relationship. This was her time to find peace with her girls, not to rehash frustrations. "He does, but I don't want to waste energy talking about him right now," Dionne said, her voice firm but light enough to steer the conversation away.

London and Karmen exchanged a look before nodding, letting the subject drop. They returned to their workout, the tension easing into shared laughter and sisterly banter. For now, Dionne focused on the moment, the weights in her hands, and the rhythm of the gym—anything but the confusion swirling in her heart.

After her workout, Dionne decided to head home, shower, and change into something comfortable before visiting her parents. It had been too long since she'd spent time with them, and with her busy schedule finally clearing up for the day, she couldn't think of a better way to spend her free time. The house was quiet since Malik was at his mother's house, so she took her time getting ready.

Dionne slipped into a blue cropped True Religion jacket, paired with matching jeans that hugged her curves perfectly, and white Maison Margiela slit-toe ankle boots. She decided to forgo the wig, letting her natural 3c-4a curls flow freely down her back, framing her radiant

Feenin'

chocolate-toned face. The simplicity of the look made her feel fresh and confident. After grabbing her purse, she headed out the door and into her car, the engine roaring softly as she set off for her parents' house an hour away.

Halfway through the drive, her phone buzzed with a FaceTime call. Her heart skipped when she saw the name on the screen—Arris. She hesitated briefly before pressing the green button, and his face filled the screen. He was focused on the road, but his easy smile made her pulse quicken.

"Hey, Mama," Arris greeted smoothly, glancing briefly at the camera before returning his attention to driving.

"Hey, Arris," she replied softly, unable to hide the smile that formed at the sound of his voice.

"Where you headed, beautiful?" he asked, his tone dripping with warmth, sending butterflies fluttering in her stomach.

Before she could respond, he shifted his attention momentarily. "Hold on, Mama. Mia, you want ice cream?" he asked, looking back at the little girl in the backseat.

"Yes Uncle Arris! Don't forget the sprinkles!" Mia called out, her voice full of excitement.

"I got you, baby girl. Don't worry," Arris replied, glancing back at her briefly before returning his attention to the road.

Dionne took the moment to admire him. His black T-shirt clung to his toned, tattooed muscles, a gold chain glinting against his skin. His fresh lineup accentuated the waves that looked like they could drown anyone who stared too long. She licked her lips unconsciously, captivated by how good he looked.

"What you staring at, gorgeous?" Arris asked, catching her off guard as his smirk widened.

Dionne giggled, shaking her head. She loved how effortlessly he always pulled her in. "You. You look good," she admitted boldly, surprising herself with her candor.

"Thank you. I love the new look too," he said, his voice lower, more deliberate. "You should wear your natural curls more often."

Dionne smiled at the unexpected compliment, her heart swelling. Before she could respond, Mia's curious face popped into the frame.

"That's Ms. Moore's friend, Uncle!" Mia exclaimed, her excitement evident.

Dionne smiled at the little girl and waved with one hand while keeping the other firmly on the wheel. "Hey, Mia!"

"I know—that's your new auntie," Arris said confidently, his smirk deepening as he glanced at the camera.

Dionne's head snapped toward her phone. "What?" she asked incredulously, while Mia looked equally confused, her little eyebrows knitting together.

"How?" Mia asked, echoing Dionne's disbelief.

"Yes, Uncle Arris. How?" Dionne chimed in with a playful smirk, genuinely curious to hear his answer.

Arris chuckled, clearly unfazed. "That's my woman, Mia," he declared confidently, nodding toward the phone. His boldness left both Mia and Dionne momentarily stunned.

Dionne laughed nervously, trying to play it off as a joke while hiding the blush that crept across her cheeks. "Don't lie to that baby," she said, shaking her head.

"Say hey, Aunt Dee," Arris instructed, ignoring her protest.

Mia's face lit up as she turned back to the camera. "Hey, Aunt Dee! I like your hair!" she said brightly, her enthusiasm contagious.

"Thank you, baby," Dionne replied warmly, her tone softening. She shot Arris a glare, but he simply smiled, completely unbothered.

Dionne leaned into the camera with an arched brow. "Aunt Dee, huh? You just out here claiming me like that?" she asked, a playful smirk tugging at her lips, but her eyes held a hint of curiosity.

Arris leaned back in his seat, his hand casually resting on the steering wheel as he chuckled. "Claiming? Nah, Mama. Just speaking facts," he replied smoothly, his voice laced with confidence. "You know I don't say nothing I don't mean."

Dionne's stomach flipped at his words, and she quickly tried to cover it up with an eye roll. "Boy, stop playing with me," she said with a laugh, even though she felt the heat creeping up her neck.

Arris smirked, his gaze never wavering from hers through the phone. "I'm dead serious, Dionne. You just don't want to admit you mine yet, but it's cool. I got time."

"Mia, go inside GG's house. I'll be there in a minute," Arris told her, handing her the ice cream she'd been waiting for. The little girl hopped out of the car, happily skipping toward Angel's house, leaving Dionne and Arris alone on the call.

Once Mia was out of the car, she took a deep breath and spoke up. "Why did you tell her that?" she asked, her voice holding a stern edge, though the smile tugging at her lips betrayed her true feelings.

"Because it's true," Arris replied confidently, flashing a smile that made her heart skip.

"It's not," Dionne protested with a chuckle, shaking her head. "Now

Feenin'

that baby thinks I'm her auntie for real."

"Well, you will be soon. Just getting her prepared," Arris shot back, his charm effortless. Dionne couldn't help but laugh at his boldness, though her mind was racing with conflicting emotions.

As she continued to drive, Arris stayed on the call, his presence filling the space even from miles away. "Where you headed? You've been driving for a while," he asked, now seated comfortably inside his mother's house.

"My parents' place. They live about an hour outside the city," she explained, glancing at him briefly on the screen as he nodded in understanding.

"What you doing tonight?" he asked casually, though the glimmer in his eyes hinted at something more.

"Nothing," she answered honestly, her eyes returning to the road. She missed the way his lips curved into a satisfied smile.

"Let me take you somewhere tonight," he offered, leaning closer to the camera. The suggestion made her glance at him, her curiosity piqued.

"Where?" she asked, a mix of excitement and nervousness bubbling inside her. She knew better than to trust that mischievous smirk. The last time he wore that expression, she ended up in a helicopter, facing her fear of heights.

"Somewhere fun," he replied, his voice laced with amusement.

Dionne chuckled. "I'm a little scared after last night, but okay," she teased, earning a deep laugh from him.

"I promise I won't make you face any fears this time. I just want to see you again. I miss yo ass bad," Arris admitted, his voice dropping an octave. The sincerity in his tone sent a shiver down her spine, even through the phone.

"I miss you too," she said softly, her heart speaking louder than her cautious mind.

As she pulled into her parents' large driveway, Dionne sighed, realizing she had to end the call. "I just made it to my parents' house," she said, parking her car.

"Okay, Mama. I'll come pick you up tonight at seven," he said, his words making her heart race.

He's picking me up from my house? What if Malik is back? she thought, panic creeping in. Her stomach knotted as she imagined the potential disaster.

"Mama?" Arris called, snapping her back to reality. In her flustered state, she'd dropped the phone. Picking it up quickly, she looked back into the camera, catching his gaze.

"You so fucking beautiful," he said, his voice low and full of admiration.

Dionne felt her cheeks heat up, a blush spreading across her face. "Thank you," she murmured shyly. "And I can just meet you there. I'll be at my parents' for a while," she added, trying to come up with an excuse.

Arris's smile faltered slightly, his brows furrowing in displeasure. "You're not meeting me anywhere," he stated firmly. "I'm taking you on a date. I don't care if I have to drive all the way to your parents' house to get you."

Dionne sighed, rolling her eyes playfully. "Arris, you don't have to drive an hour to my parents' house. I can just come to you," she argued, already knowing how stubborn he could be.

"Dionne, stop playing with me. I'm coming to get you from your parents' house. Send me the address," he said, his tone brooking no argument.

She sighed in defeat, knowing there was no point in pushing back. At least it was safer than him picking her up from her house and risking Malik seeing them. "Okay," she relented softly.

"Good. I'll see you later, beautiful," Arris said, his smile returning as he ended the call.

Dionne sat in her car for a moment, her mind racing. Her feelings for Arris were growing stronger, but so was the weight of her tangled reality. Taking a deep breath to steady herself, she stepped out of the car and headed into her parents' house, preparing to temporarily push her conflicting emotions aside.

Dionne stepped out of her car, her thoughts still entangled with Arris. The anticipation of their plans later filled her with a mix of excitement and nervous energy. She shook her head, trying to focus on the moment as she approached her parents' front door and rang the doorbell. Moments later, the door swung open, revealing her mother, Danita, whose face immediately lit up with excitement.

"My babygirl!" Danita exclaimed, pulling Dionne into a warm hug.

"Hey, Mommie!" Dionne responded, her smile as bright as her mother's.

Danita was more than just a mother to her; she was her first best friend. Shopping trips, self-care days, and luxurious escapades spent spending her father's money—they were always partners in crime.

Pulling back from the embrace, Danita gave her daughter a playful once-over. "Okay!! My baby is fine!" she hyped, making Dionne laugh.

"I get it from my mama!" Dionne shot back, joining in the playful banter.

Feenin'

And it was true—Dionne was the spitting image of her mother. They shared the same smooth, rich brown skin, long, curly hair, and hourglass figures. The only feature separating them was Danita's streaks of gray hair, which only added to her timeless beauty. At 50 years old, Danita looked as though she could still be in her late 30s, often mistaken for Dionne's sister when they were out in public.

Dionne followed her mother into the house, the savory aroma of cooking drawing her toward the kitchen. There, her father, Lamar, stood at the stove, shirtless except for a black apron and a pair of sweats.

"Who do you think you are?" Dionne teased, her voice carrying through the space.

Lamar turned around, a wide grin spreading across his face at the sight of his daughter. "Hey, Dooda! Yo daddy sexy, ain't he?" he quipped, calling her by the nickname he'd used since she was a child.

Dionne laughed, walking over to hug him. She couldn't help but admire how her father had defied time. Even at 50, Lamar looked years younger. His 6'4" frame was still muscular, his dark chocolate skin smooth and glowing, tattoos covering his arms and chest. His salt-and-pepper beard was perfectly groomed, and his bald head gleamed under the kitchen lights. But his most striking feature was his bluish-green eyes, a trait passed down to her brother, Demetrius.

"Hey, Daddy. And I don't know about all of that," she joked, flashing a grin.

"Always hating," Lamar teased, flipping whatever he was cooking in the pan. "Yo mama loves it."

Dionne followed his gaze to where Danita stood, clearly admiring her husband with eyes full of love.

Dionne groaned dramatically, pretending to gag. "Y'all are too much!" she joked, though she secretly adored how deeply in love her parents still were. Throughout her life, they had been the epitome of partnership—facing challenges together, supporting one another, and never letting the flame of their love dim.

"You just jealous," Danita teased, winking at her daughter. "Soon, you'll have this too."

Dionne's smile faltered for just a moment, the weight of her reality crashing into her. She was engaged to a man she no longer loved, trying to convince herself that their union made sense when her heart screamed otherwise. Looking at her parents, so deeply in love, she realized how far she was from having what they shared.

"Yeah, soon," Dionne muttered under her breath, quickly plastering on a smile to mask her thoughts.

Ann

Danita placed a hand on her daughter's shoulder, snapping her back to the present. "Come on, sit down! Let me get you something to drink," she said warmly, pulling her into the heart of the home where love, laughter, and delicious food always awaited.

"How you been, baby girl?" Lamar asked as Dionne settled onto one of the island chairs next to her mother. His deep voice carried warmth and concern as he continued flipping whatever he was cooking on the stove.

"Good. Just working as usual," Dionne replied with a shrug, brushing off the weight of everything else she had going on.

Danita chimed in, her voice laced with excitement. "And how about you and Malik? When's the wedding again?" She beamed, genuinely thrilled at the idea of her daughter marrying what she believed was the love of her life—her college sweetheart. Little did she know that the love Dionne once had for Malik was now a distant memory.

Dionne forced a smile, masking the sinking feeling in her chest. "We're good. Mama Glen wants a winter wonderland wedding, so it's set for December," she explained, her tone too flat to match the excitement she was trying to convey.

Danita's smile faltered, her motherly intuition picking up on the lack of enthusiasm. She leaned in slightly, her brow furrowed. "You don't seem excited about it. Are you two good?" she asked softly, her concern growing.

Lamar turned from the stove, his piercing eyes fixed on his daughter, his jaw tightening. The protective energy radiating from him was clear. If Malik wasn't treating Dionne right, Lamar was more than ready to step in.

"Yes, we're good," Dionne said quickly, trying to ease the tension. "It's just... between our busy work schedules, Mama Glen's sickness getting worse, and all the wedding planning, it's becoming a lot."

Danita's expression softened, a sad smile forming on her lips. "Poor Glen. The cancer's getting worse?" she asked gently.

Dionne nodded, her composure threatening to crack. "Yeah, the doctor said she only has about a year—if that."

Danita reached over, placing a comforting hand on Dionne's arm. "Oh, sweetie, I'm so sorry. But remember, God has the final say in how long she stays with us. We'll keep praying for her—and for you and Malik during this time. I know how much Mama Glen means to you, especially after everything she's done for you."

Dionne nodded silently, her throat tightening as she fought back tears. The thought of losing Mama Glen weighed heavily on her, not just

175

Feenin'

because of their bond but because of the promise she'd made to her—a promise that now felt like a noose tightening around her neck.

"Can we talk about something else?" she asked softly, her voice barely above a whisper, afraid that if she spoke any louder, her emotions would spill over.

Danita nodded quickly, understanding without hesitation. "Of course, baby. Whatever you need," she said reassuringly, giving Dionne's hand a gentle squeeze.

Lamar, always tuned in to his daughter's mood, glanced at her again before turning back to the stove. "You hungry, Dooda? Let me fix you a plate. Food solves everything," he said, his tone light and comforting, attempting to shift the mood in the room.

Dionne smiled faintly, grateful for her father's attempt to lift her spirits. "Yes, Daddy. That would be nice."

Lamar turned back to the stove, where the rich aroma of his cooking filled the air. He was preparing one of Dionne's favorite meals: smothered creamy onion gravy chicken, paired with buttery rice and a side of perfectly seasoned greens. The smell alone was enough to stir comfort in her heart, even as her emotions sat heavy.

"You know I don't play in the kitchen," Lamar said with a proud grin, stirring the chicken in its golden, creamy gravy. "Smothered chicken just like you like it—extra gravy, buttery rice, and them greens that make you wanna slap somebody." He winked as he tossed the greens in the skillet one last time.

Dionne chuckled softly, the smell pulling a genuine smile out of her. "You sure know how to spoil me, Daddy. That smells amazing," she admitted, letting her shoulders relax a little.

Danita smirked, leaning back in her chair with a playful glance at Lamar. "You're making me hungry, but don't forget this girl gets the first plate," she teased, earning a laugh from both of them.

"You already know," Lamar said, plating the food with care. He set the plate in front of Dionne, the steam rising from the perfectly cooked meal. "There you go, Dooda. Comfort food, just how you like it."

Dionne looked at the plate, her appetite coming alive at the sight of the tender chicken smothered in rich, creamy onion gravy, the rice glistening with butter, and the vibrant greens that smelled like pure heaven.

"Thank you, Daddy. This looks perfect," she said softly, taking a deep breath to soak in the moment of comfort her parents provided.

Lamar grinned, leaning on the counter to watch her take the first bite. "That's love on a plate right there, baby girl. You need anything else?"

Ann

Dionne shook her head, savoring the first bite of the chicken. The flavors exploded in her mouth, the gravy creamy and savory, the greens seasoned to perfection. It was everything she didn't know she needed at that moment. "This is perfect, Daddy. Thank you."

For a moment, everything felt just a little bit lighter.

"I talked to your brother earlier. He said he's coming into town soon," Lamar said, his tone carrying warmth as he glanced at Dionne. Her face lit up with excitement. She missed her older brother, Demetrius.

Demetrius lived in Dallas, where he worked as the general manager for the Dallas Stampede. At 32, he was four years older than Dionne, and despite the distance, they'd remained incredibly close. When Demetrius first moved for his career, Dionne had been upset, feeling like she was losing her best friend. But over time, she learned to admire his ambition and respected his drive to chase his dreams.

"Aww, is he bringing my nephew?" Dionne asked, her voice full of anticipation as she thought about Demetrius Jr., her five-year-old nephew who had the confidence and attitude of someone twice his age. DJ adored his Aunt Dionne, and he never missed a chance to declare her his favorite.

"I don't know," Lamar replied with a chuckle. "But you know Demetrius can't go nowhere without DJ running behind him."

Dionne laughed, nodding in agreement. "That's true. I miss them both so much. I can't wait to see them."

The conversation shifted to family, life updates, and reminiscing about old memories as they ate Lamar's delicious dinner. Dionne felt a sense of peace she hadn't experienced in a long time. Being surrounded by her parents, away from all the pressures of her life, reminded her of simpler times.

After dinner, she found herself sitting on the couch, snuggled under her dad's arm like she used to as a child. Her mother sat on the other side of Lamar, cozied up against him as they watched a movie. It was moments like this that Dionne cherished, moments that made her forget about her complicated relationship and everything else weighing on her shoulders.

As the movie played, her phone buzzed with back-to-back notifications. She glanced down and opened Malik's message first.

Malik: *Taking care of my mother tonight. Won't be coming home.*

She sighed, her fingers hovering over the screen before she simply liked the message and moved on. She didn't even feel disappointed anymore—she had grown used to it.

The next notification made an involuntary smile spread across her

Feenin'

face.

Arris: The address, Mama?

Her heart fluttered as she quickly typed back a response.

Dionne: You can pick me up from my house. I'm headed there now.

Danita immediately noticed the smile on her daughter's face, a smile that seemed to light up her whole demeanor. She raised an eyebrow, clearly intrigued. "Aww, Malik got you blushing at your phone," she teased, her excitement evident.

Dionne chuckled, trying her best to hide the truth. "Yeah, it's date night tonight. I should head home and get ready," she said, maintaining the lie with a bright smile. Of course, it wasn't Malik who was taking her out—it never was. It was Arris, the man who had her heart racing and her mind spinning with every thought of him.

Danita beamed, clearly thrilled at the thought of her daughter's blossoming relationship with Malik. "Okay, sweetie. You two have fun. Maybe give me a grandbaby tonight," she joked with a playful wink, causing Dionne to nearly choke on air.

"Daddy, get your wife. She's had too much wine," Dionne laughed, standing up as she prepared to leave. Lamar chuckled, shaking his head at the two women.

"What? I'm ready for some grandbabies," Danita said, pouting dramatically.

"You have one. DJ," Dionne reminded her, trying to bring her back to reality.

"Who lives in Dallas," Danita added wistfully, "and he's getting older. I'm ready for another one. One I can see every day."

Dionne laughed at her mother's persistence, shaking her head in amusement. "Daddy, please get your wife!" she joked, playfully rolling her eyes.

Lamar laughed heartily before walking over to his wife. "Come here, baby. She will give us a grandbaby when she's ready." His deep, raspy voice always had a way of calming and soothing Danita. Dionne watched in awe as her mother melted into his touch, nodding in agreement before they shared a soft kiss.

"Aww," Dionne said with a smile, feeling the warmth of her parents' love. She longed for that kind of connection in her own life, a relationship where the affection never waned and the love was constant.

After exchanging goodbyes and hugs with her parents, Dionne left their home, her thoughts already drifting back to Arris. It was time to get ready for their night together, and she couldn't help the excitement bubbling inside her as she drove home.

***

Arris lounged on the couch at his mother's house, scrolling through his phone as he waited for Mario to swing by and pick up Mia. Tonight, he had plans—plans he couldn't stop thinking about. Date night with Dionne was just hours away, and the anticipation was driving him crazy. Seeing her again, hearing her laugh, feeling her presence—it all brought him a peace he didn't know he needed. It was wild how quickly she had turned his life upside down in the best way.

Before Dionne, relationships weren't even on his radar. Women, to him, were distractions, and he never gave them more than a moment of his time. But Dionne? She made him crave more. Love, even. He caught himself smiling just thinking about her when the sound of A'Lani's footsteps broke his train of thought.

"Ou, I'm glad that girl finally went to sleep. She was running me wild," A'Lani huffed, collapsing onto the couch next to her brother. Arris chuckled at her out-of-breath state.

"Nobody told you to run around with her outside," he teased, his tone playful as he glanced back at his phone. Dionne had just sent him a picture—a picture he had asked for earlier because, as he'd told her, he wanted something to keep her close even when she wasn't around. The sight of it made his grin widen, and he couldn't help but admire the photo.

"Who got you smiling so hard?!" A'Lani asked, leaning over nosily. Arris quickly angled his phone away, but not before A'Lani caught a glimpse of Dionne's picture.

"Ouu, she's beautiful," A'Lani said with a sly grin. "Now I really want to know who she is."

"Yo nosy ass," Arris joked, shaking his head with a laugh. "Mind your business."

A'Lani leaned back, feigning offense but unable to hide her curiosity. "Damn, she has to be someone important if she got you grinning like that. You don't smile like that for no one. Is this your girl?"

"She's none of your business," Arris quipped, though his smile betrayed him.

A'Lani smirked knowingly. "My hoe-ass brother," she said, shaking her head. "When are you going to finally find a woman and settle with just one? You're not getting any younger, you know."

"When I'm ready," he replied coolly, but even as he said it, his mind wandered back to Dionne. If he were going to settle with anyone, it'd be her. No one else had ever held his attention like this.

A'Lani crossed her arms, her curiosity still burning. "Why do you do

Feenin'

the things you do, anyway?" she asked, turning to look at him.

"What you mean?" Arris asked, giving her a side-eye.

"I mean, you've never been in a real relationship. Ever. Why is that?"

Arris laughed softly at her persistence. "Relationships were never a priority for me. My money, making sure you and Ma were straight—that's all I ever cared about," he said, his tone more serious now.

A'Lani nodded, her expression softening. She knew how much weight Arris carried on his shoulders to make sure their family was good. "I get that. You always made sure we had everything, no matter what it took. But maybe it's time you do something for yourself, too."

Arris glanced back at the picture of Dionne on his phone, her smile staring back at him like it held all the answers. Maybe A'Lani was right. Maybe it was time.

A'Lani leaned back on the couch, her tone shifting to something softer, almost maternal. "We're good now, Arris. You got Ma in this big-ass house, living lavishly without a single worry for the rest of her life. My school is paid in full, because of you, and I'll be graduating soon and stepping into my career, making my own money. You don't have to carry us anymore."

Arris nodded, watching his sister closely, sensing she was leading to something deeper.

"Arris, you're set for life, money-wise. Your kids, their kids, and even their kids after that are set because of the work you've put in. It's time for you to enjoy the fruits of your labor—with someone who loves you and who you love back," she said, her words landing with a quiet power that hit him right in the chest.

Arris leaned back, processing her statement. She was right, and he knew it. He had worked tirelessly to ensure his family's stability, sacrificing his youth, his peace, and even parts of himself in the process. The weight of being the provider, protector, and backbone for his mother and sister had always been his burden to bear. But maybe—just maybe—he didn't have to carry it alone anymore.

"I hear you, Lani," he said after a beat, his voice low. His mind drifted to the life he'd always known—ever since Calvin walked out when he was eight years old and A'Lani was just four. Arris had stepped into a role no child should ever have to fill. He cleaned, cooked, did odd jobs—anything to help his mother. By the time he was 13, he had turned to the streets, risking his life to provide financially. It wasn't a life he wanted for himself, but it was the life he felt he had to live for his family.

He rubbed his hand over his jaw, the weight of A'Lani's words sitting heavy. "Hearing you say y'all don't need me anymore... it's a lot," he admitted, his voice cracking slightly.

A'Lani leaned forward, placing a hand on his knee. "Arris, we're always going to need you, just not like before. You've done your part—and more. Now it's time to put that energy into building your own family," she said, her voice warm with encouragement.

Arris nodded, though the thought of letting go of his protector role felt foreign and even uncomfortable. "Maybe one day," he murmured, his voice quiet but carrying the hint of consideration.

A'Lani smiled, seeing the shift in his demeanor. "Maybe one day, huh? Well, it might be with her," she said, gesturing toward his phone. "I've never seen a woman make your ass blush, let alone just by sending you a photo. Hell, I've never seen you blush at all." She grinned, her teasing cutting through the seriousness of the moment.

Arris laughed, shaking his head. "Man, she don't have me blushing."

"Nigga, please. She got you showing all 32, and I can't wait to meet her," A'Lani teased as she stood up. "I'm about to shower. Mia got me out here smelling like outside."

Arris chuckled as she walked away, but her words lingered, sinking in deeper than he was willing to admit. His mind drifted back to Dionne, and for the first time, he let himself entertain the idea that maybe she could be the one to finally change everything.

Arris glanced down at his Rolex, the gleaming timepiece telling him he was cutting it close to the time he had promised to pick Dionne up. Mario still hadn't arrived to pick up Mia, and the thought of being late didn't sit well with him. He knew Dionne would have a field day giving him grief if he didn't show up on time. She hadn't revealed that fiery side to him just yet, but he could sense it simmering beneath her polished exterior, and he didn't want to give her an opportunity to unleash it.

"Aye, A'Lani, can you bring Mia out when Mario gets here? He's supposed to pick her up, but he's running late, and I need to head out. Got something to do," Arris said, standing from the couch and grabbing his keys.

A'Lani nodded, but the curious smirk on her face told him she wasn't going to let this go without some playful prying. "Where you rushing off to? A date?" she asked, her grin growing wider.

Arris shook his head with a chuckle. "Yo ass too nosy," he said, trying to keep his tone light, but A'Lani wasn't buying his deflection.

"I see you didn't deny it," she teased, laughing at her brother's obvious attempt to dodge her question.

"Man, bye. Tell Ma I'll come by tomorrow, and give Mia a kiss for me," he said, heading toward the door.

Feenin'

"Oh, I really need to meet her. She got yo ass rushing out the door like a track star!" A'Lani called after him, her laughter trailing him as he walked outside. Arris didn't bother turning back; instead, he shot her the middle finger over his shoulder, making her laugh even harder.

Tonight, he was switching things up. Since he'd been driving Mia around earlier, he'd taken the black Jeep Rubicon out. The vehicle gleamed under the city lights as the sun dipped low, giving the street an almost ethereal glow. The blue neon accents on the Jeep's interior lights hummed faintly as he slid into the driver's seat, the anticipation of the night ahead buzzing in his chest.

Arris navigated through the city streets, his focus shifting between the road and thoughts of Dionne. Her smile, her laugh, the way her eyes held his without flinching—all of it lingered in his mind as he drove. He pulled into his driveway, parking the Jeep smoothly before stepping out. Time to get ready. The night with Dionne was just beginning, and he wasn't going to let anything or anyone delay him from seeing her.

Arris stepped out of the shower, his dark chocolate skin glowing under the warm bathroom lighting. He applied his favorite moisturizer, the rich cream enhancing the natural sheen of his skin. He brushed his waves with precision, ensuring they laid perfectly, then carefully groomed and moisturized his beard, the final touch to his polished look.

Arris walked into his expansive walk-in closet, his eyes scanning the rows of neatly organized clothing. He selected a pair of green cargo pants and paired them with a crisp white Chicago Bulls graphic T-shirt. To add a pop of boldness, he layered on a red-and-white varsity jacket. Completing his look, he laced up a pair of Chicago Jordan 1s, their red, white, and black tones tying the outfit together seamlessly.

Arris accessorized with gold jewelry that elevated his relaxed style: two gold chains gleamed against his chest, a gold Van Cleef bracelet adorned one wrist, while a gemstone Van Cleef bracelet added a subtle touch of color. His gold Cartier watch wrapped around his wrist, an effortless symbol of his taste. Finally, he sprayed himself with "Creed" cologne, the luxurious scent enveloping him and completing the transformation.

He admired himself in the mirror for a brief moment, nodding in approval before grabbing his Aston Martin keys and heading out. Settling into the driver's seat of the vehicle, he realized Dionne hadn't sent the address to her parents' house yet. Pulling out his phone, he sent her a text.

Arris: The address, Mama?

Her reply came quickly, and a smile tugged at his lips as he read it.

Mama: You can pick me up from my house. I'm headed there now.

Arris grinned, her words settling warmly in his chest. The thought of seeing her soon made his anticipation spike. He started the car, the low purr of the engine filling the quiet street as he pulled out of the driveway. Arris didn't know what it was about Dionne that drew him in so deeply, but he couldn't deny it—he *feened* for her in ways he couldn't explain. Just the thought of her smile, her voice, and her presence had him gripping the wheel a little tighter as he drove toward her house. Tonight couldn't come fast enough.

Arris made his way to Dionne's house but decided to make a quick stop at a nearby flower shop. He hadn't asked her what her favorite flowers were, so he picked the ones that caught his eye and felt as vibrant as her. After browsing, he settled on a bouquet of pink tulips, their soft yet striking beauty reminding him of Dionne. He tipped the florist generously before heading back to his car, flowers in hand, and continued on his way.

When Arris pulled up to her house, the timing couldn't have been better. Dionne was just stepping out, and he took a brief moment to admire her as she walked toward him. She had dressed exactly as he asked—comfortable but effortlessly beautiful. She wore a matching black jean set: a cropped jacket that showed off her toned abs and small waist, paired with black jeans that hugged her curves flawlessly. On her feet were black Travis Scott Jordan 1 lows, adding a laid-back edge to her look. Her natural curls were styled half-up, half-down, and her makeup-free face showcased her radiant skin, accentuated by lash extensions and her signature lip combo. Diamond jewelry sparkled under the soft glow of the streetlights.

Arris stepped out of the car, the bouquet of tulips in hand, as Dionne approached. He couldn't help the wide smile spreading across his face as she came closer. He opened her door, but before she could get in, he reached out, pulling her gently by the waist and closing the space between them. Dionne's breath hitched at the contact, her body instinctively melting into his touch. He leaned down, his lips just a whisper away from hers.

"Can I kiss you? Please say yes," he asked, his voice low and filled with yearning. His lips barely brushed hers, holding just enough distance to respect her boundaries, though his desire was evident. He could see the internal battle she was waging, her heart and mind at odds, but when she finally gave a small nod, it was all the confirmation he needed. Arris pressed his lips to hers, the kiss deep and filled with everything he'd been holding back. Dionne responded, wrapping her arms around his neck,

Feenin'

deepening the kiss as his hand stayed firmly on her waist.

When he finally pulled back, their breaths mingling in the cool night air, he kept her close in his arms. "These are for you," he said softly, holding out the bouquet. The way her face lit up made his heart swell.

"How did you know tulips were my favorite flowers?" she asked, her voice tinged with genuine surprise and delight.

Arris chuckled, shrugging with a playful grin. "Lucky guess."

Dionne shook her head, a smile tugging at her lips as she admired the bouquet. "Well, you're good at guessing," she said softly, her gaze lingering on him for a moment longer before they both climbed into the car. The night was off to the perfect start.

The entire drive to their destination, Arris held Dionne's hand in his, steering the car effortlessly with the other. The gesture was natural for him now, his need for her touch becoming second nature. Dionne smiled softly, warmth spreading through her at his constant affection. They talked the entire ride, their conversation flowing easily as they shared the details of their days, sprinkled with teasing banter and laughter.

After a while, Arris pulled into a parking lot, and Dionne's eyes lit up as she looked out the window. The neon lights of a skating rink greeted her, and a wide smile spread across her face. Skating was one of her favorite pastimes, a skill she'd mastered over the years. Memories of her and her brother spending Saturdays at the rink as kids and later impressing the crowd during Sunday adult skate nights flooded her mind. She turned to Arris, her eyes gleaming with excitement.

"What do you know about this place?" she asked with a smirk, teasing him.

Arris chuckled as he cut the engine. "I used to come here all the time with my boys. This was the spot back in the day."

"Back in the day?" she quipped with a raised brow. "It's still the spot. My brother and I practically lived here as kids."

Arris grinned, leaning back in his seat. "So, you know how to skate?"

"Do I?" Dionne replied, her confidence shining through. "I might have to teach you a thing or two."

Arris laughed, his deep voice filling the car. "Let's find out."

He stepped out and came around to her side, opening her door like he always did. Dionne climbed out as he reached into the backseat, pulling out a pair of black skates slung over his shoulder. She couldn't help but laugh at the sight.

"Oh, so you skate skate!" she teased, folding her arms.

"You funny," he said with a smirk. "I got you a pair too. Them rink skates are trash, and I don't want to hear no excuses when you bust your ass."

Dionne's laugh rang out as he handed her a box, revealing a pristine pair of Boost Riedell skates, nearly identical to his but in her size. She blinked in surprise, her jaw dropping slightly.

"How did you—wait, how do you even know my size?" she asked, inspecting the skates, clearly impressed.

Arris shrugged, his expression casual but his smirk smug. "I pay attention, Mama. You like 'em?"

"I love them," Dionne admitted, her voice soft with gratitude. She looked up at him, shaking her head in awe. "You're full of surprises, Arris."

"You ain't seen nothing yet," he said with a wink, grabbing her hand and leading her toward the entrance of the rink. Tonight was already shaping up to be unforgettable.

As they walked into the skating rink, the soothing sounds of slow jams filled the air, confirming that adult night was in full swing. The DJ booth glowed in the dimly lit space, the music setting a romantic and nostalgic vibe. Adults of all ages were gliding around the rink, some lost in their moves, others just enjoying the moment.

Arris paid for their entry and they headed into the lively atmosphere. They found a spot to sit and laced up their new skates, carefully locking up their shoes. Arris, ever the confident one, was the first to step onto the floor. He immediately started showing off, performing tricks and gliding effortlessly, his moves reminiscent of Sweetness from Roll Bounce. Dionne laughed, her amused giggles echoing as she watched him, but she wasn't about to let him outshine her.

With a smirk, Dionne stepped onto the floor and began to skate, showing off her own impressive skills. Arris stopped in his tracks, stunned by her grace and control. The way she glided effortlessly, her body moving in sync with the beat of Usher's song playing overhead, left him in awe. He couldn't take his eyes off her, watching her as though she were the only person in the room.

The vibe shifted as "Lay You Down" by K-Young began to play, its sensual beat slowing things down. Dionne was skating with ease, singing softly along to the lyrics, her movements smooth and relaxed. Arris, not missing the opportunity, skated up behind her and placed his hands on her waist. The warmth of his touch instantly grounded her, and he could feel the subtle shift in her body as she relaxed into his hold.

They moved together in perfect sync, gliding across the floor as if the music was guiding them. Arris leaned in, his lips close to her ear, softly singing along with the song. The low timbre of his voice sent a shiver

Feenin'

down her spine, but she didn't pull away. The crowded rink faded from their minds as they skated, their connection amplified by the music and the intimacy of the moment.

A woman, slightly older than them, skated by, her warm smile reflecting the sweetness of the moment. "You two are a beautiful couple," she complimented as she passed, her voice tinged with admiration.

"Thank you," Arris replied smoothly, pulling Dionne even closer to him. Dionne chuckled, her amusement at his boldness evident, but she didn't deny the assumption.

The beat dropped, and Dionne bent slightly, her movements deliberate as she pressed her butt against his. Arris inhaled sharply, his hands gripping her waist more firmly as her boldness caught him off guard. The way her body moved against him, her perfect form accentuated by her black jeans, left him dazed. His hold tightened instinctively, ensuring she stayed close.

They continued skating, moving effortlessly together as if they'd done it a thousand times before. Dionne's teasing sway against him, combined with the sultry music, made it hard for him to keep his composure. Arris, though usually in control, felt a heat rise within him that he struggled to suppress. For him, this wasn't just skating—it was foreplay, a dance of emotions and desires played out under the rink lights.

As the song neared its end, Dionne turned her head slightly, catching a glimpse of the effect she was having on him. She smirked, her confidence glowing as she whispered, "Try to keep up, Mr. Black." Arris chuckled lowly, his grip firm and his voice thick with intent. "Oh, I'm just getting started, Mama."

As the song faded and Dionne straightened up, Arris tugged her closer, his hand gliding to her neck with a gentle yet possessive touch. "Better chill before I fuck you up," he growled low in her ear, his voice laced with playful sensuality. Dionne couldn't help but chuckle, though the rush of his words sent a thrill coursing through her. The next song, a Trey Songz track, began to play, and they shifted back into a relaxed rhythm, skating side by side. Despite the casual pace, the effect of Arris' words lingered in Dionne's posture, her movements still charged with energy.

"Show me a trick," Dionne challenged, her teasing tone making him smile.

"Aight, watch this," Arris replied, a confident smirk crossing his face. He grabbed her hand and led her to the center of the rink, where fewer skaters roamed. Dionne stood still, arms crossed with an expectant grin, as Arris skated backward to create space. With precision and flair, he began spinning, each turn growing faster until he was a blur of movement.

Dionne stood mesmerized, her mouth slightly agape at how effortlessly skilled he was. However, as if fate had a sense of humor, a nearby skater lost her balance, her leg grazing Arris mid-spin. The unexpected contact sent him off course, and he wobbled dramatically. Dionne rushed forward, grabbing his hands just before he could fall.

"I got you," she said between laughs, steadying him with a grin that she couldn't suppress.

Arris, now balanced but mock-annoyed, smirked down at her. "I almost bust my ass, and you over here laughing?" he teased before launching a playful counterattack. His hands found her sides, tickling mercilessly.

Dionne burst into uncontrollable laughter, twisting and turning to escape his grasp. "Arris, stop!" she squealed, trying in vain to push him away, but his strength overpowered her. Her laughter became so intense that she lost her balance, teetering dangerously toward the floor. Arris, quick on his feet, caught her just in time.

"You good?" he asked with a smirk, his arms secure around her.

"Yes," she managed to say, catching her breath. Her cheeks flushed, not from exertion but from the way his eyes were locked on hers, dark and filled with an emotion she couldn't deny.

"You're so fucking beautiful," he said softly, his tone holding a depth that made her heart skip. Dionne's smile faltered, replaced by a bashful look as she blushed under his intense gaze.

As she stood upright, Arris kept her close, his hands never leaving her. With no hesitation, he leaned down and captured her lips in a heated kiss. Dionne responded instantly, her arms looping around his neck as their kiss deepened.

"It's a lot of love in the building tonight! Give it up for black love!" the DJ shouted over the mic, making the rink erupt in cheers and laughter. The sudden interruption broke the moment, and they both pulled back, laughing with their foreheads pressed together.

For the rest of the night, they skated hand in hand, laughing, making jokes, and stealing glances that carried unspoken words. They danced to the music, occasionally stopping for water breaks or to people-watch as others showed off their skills. The rink was alive with energy, but for Arris and Dionne, it felt like their own private world.

As the evening wore on and the crowd began to thin, they reluctantly decided to call it a night. Though the time had passed quickly, the

Feenin'

moments they shared felt infinite—filled with joy, laughter, and a connection that was undeniable.

They were back in the car, and Arris drove with one hand on the wheel, the other resting possessively on Dionne's thigh. His usual confident smirk played on his lips, but there was an unspoken urgency in his movements. Instead of heading to her house, he turned toward his, and Dionne didn't question it. She knew where this night was going.

As soon as they stepped inside his house, the front door barely closed before their lips crashed together, tongues tangling in a fiery kiss that left no room for hesitation. Arris easily scooped her up, her legs wrapping instinctively around his waist as he carried her upstairs to his bedroom. The way their kisses deepened and the hunger in each touch said everything—neither of them could wait another second.

Arris gently laid her down on the bed, his hands immediately going to the buttons of her jacket. Piece by piece, he stripped her, his dark, hooded eyes devouring every inch of her chocolate skin. "Fuck, baby. I missed you," he muttered, his voice deep and filled with desire as his eyes landed on the lace bra she wore. The way it hugged her body had his breathing heavy, and his arousal was painfully evident.

Dionne didn't respond with words. Instead, she pulled him back down to her, her nails grazing his neck as she kissed him with just as much hunger. Their tongues fought for dominance, but Dionne took control, rolling him over until she was on top. Straddling him, she looked down at him with a smirk, admiring the man beneath her. Arris was fine as fuck, his chiseled features and that cocky grin always making her weak.

She grabbed his shirt and pulled it off, revealing his tattooed chest and toned abs. Her lips found his again, but this time, she let her tongue trail down his neck, placing kisses and bites that left him groaning. Her lips continued their path down his chest, her tongue tracing every muscle as she moved lower, taking her time, savoring him.

Dionne reached the waistband of his jeans, her eyes locking with his as her fingers unbuckled his belt. Arris's breathing hitched, the intensity in his gaze never wavering. She slid his jeans and boxers down in one swift motion, and his hard length sprang free, thick and ready. Her lips curled into a smile as her hands wrapped around him, her warm touch making his body jerk slightly.

"Relax," she said softly, her voice dripping with seduction before her tongue flicked over his tip. Arris let out a deep groan, his head falling back at the sensation. Dionne didn't waste time; she took him into her mouth, slowly at first, her tongue swirling around the head before going lower.

The warmth and wetness of her mouth made Arris lose control. "Shit," he groaned, his hands gripping the sheets as she took him deeper. Inch by inch, she showed just how much she could handle, her throat relaxing as she took all nine inches of him, her movements deliberate and slow.

"Damn, Dionne," he muttered, his voice strained as her pace quickened. Her lips and tongue worked together in perfect rhythm, her hand stroking what her mouth couldn't reach. Arris's body tensed, his abs flexing as she continued her assault, his breathing uneven.

"Fuck," he groaned, his hand instinctively reaching to tangle in her curls. Dionne didn't stop, her eyes flicking up to meet his as she went even deeper, her throat taking every inch of him again. The sight of her, so focused and skilled, had Arris gripping the sheets tighter, his jaw clenched as he tried to hold himself together.

This wasn't just head—it was an experience, and Dionne was showing him no mercy.

"Shit, Mama," Arris groaned, his voice strained with pleasure as Dionne continued her relentless pace. The wet, sinful sound of her slurping filled the room, driving him closer to the edge. Her tongue glided up and down his thick length before she shifted her attention to his balls, licking and sucking on each one with precision.

"Fuck, you wilding," he hissed, his grip tightening in her hair as the sensations pushed him to his limit. Dionne smirked, unbothered by his comment, and went back to taking him fully into her mouth. She moved faster, her throat working to accommodate his size. She gagged slightly but didn't stop, her determination evident as her pace increased, leaving Arris on the brink of losing all control.

Her hands and mouth worked in perfect harmony, and Arris could feel his body tensing as the knot in his stomach tightened. "Shit, Dionne," he groaned, his deep voice dripping with need. Moments later, he erupted, his release filling her mouth. Without hesitation, Dionne swallowed every drop, her eyes locking with his in a way that made him weak.

Before she could move or say anything, Arris quickly grabbed her, pulling her up to his chest as he tried to catch his breath. "You're fucking unbelievable," he muttered, his voice hoarse and full of admiration.

Dionne chuckled, but her laughter was cut short as Arris flipped her onto the bed with ease, making her gasp. His hunger hadn't subsided, and he wasn't about to let her steal the show without giving her the same energy in return. He made quick work of her jeans and panties, tossing

Feenin'

them aside.

"Arris..." she started, her voice shaky as she tried to gather her thoughts, but before she could finish, his tongue was already on her clit. His lips and tongue worked fast, alternating between sucking and licking, sending waves of pleasure through her body.

"Fuck," she moaned, her voice breathless as she gripped the sheets. Arris didn't hold back, his hands gripping her thighs to keep her in place as his mouth devoured her. Dionne's body writhed under his touch, overwhelmed by the intensity of his actions. She gripped the sheets harder, her legs instinctively trying to close, but Arris wasn't having it.

"Nah, Mama," he growled, holding her legs open firmly as his tongue continued its assault. He slid two fingers inside her, curling them just right, hitting her spot with precision. Dionne let out a loud, uncontrollable moan as the pleasure consumed her.

Her body trembled, her breaths coming in sharp gasps as his tongue and fingers worked together in perfect rhythm. "Fuck, Arris," she whimpered, her voice shaky as she felt the rush building inside her. He didn't slow down, his movements becoming even more focused as he drove her closer to the edge.

Seconds later, Dionne cried out, her orgasm hitting her like a tidal wave as her release flooded into his mouth. Arris groaned, licking up every drop with satisfaction before looking up at her flushed, trembling body.

"You good, Mama?" he asked with a smirk, his lips glistening, but the fire in his eyes told her he wasn't done yet.

Arris didn't give Dionne a moment to recover from her orgasm before sliding inside her, their bodies connecting in a way that sent shockwaves through them both. His need for her had overtaken all logic, forgetting a condom entirely in his desperation to feel her. They both moaned in unison at the raw sensation, their breaths mingling as he filled her inch by inch.

"Damn... Mama," he groaned, his voice thick with desire as her warmth wrapped around him, gripping him perfectly. Dionne gasped, her moans blending with his as he stretched her, filling every inch of her deeply.

Arris wasted no time setting a rhythm, their bodies colliding with a wet, intoxicating sound. The room filled with their moans, the slapping of skin, and the overwhelming energy between them. He slowed his hips, pulling back to watch the way her wetness glistened and coated him, sending him into a frenzy.

"Arris..." Dionne started, her voice shaky, but her words got caught in her throat as the pleasure consumed her. He leaned down, kissing her neck and shoulders, his hips moving in a slow, deliberate grind that made her shudder.

"Yes, Mama?" he murmured, his tone low and seductive, his pace never faltering.

"I'm about to..." she managed to say between gasps, but before she could finish, Arris pulled out, leaving her trembling and panting from the edge of release.

"Ride your shit first, baby. I want you to cum on it," he commanded, his voice dripping with authority and lust. He laid back on the bed, his arms behind his head, watching her with hunger in his eyes.

Dionne didn't hesitate, climbing on top and aligning herself with him. She eased down slowly, taking him back inside her inch by inch. Her head fell back, her curls cascading down her shoulders as she let out a shaky moan. The fullness of him stretched her perfectly, sending a delicious ache through her.

Arris groaned, his hands instinctively reaching up to caress her breasts, kneading them gently as she set a slow, deliberate pace. "Fuck, you feel so good," he muttered, his voice thick with admiration.

She started moving faster, her hips grinding against him as their rhythm intensified. Her body moved with precision, her thighs working to ride him in a way that made him groan louder, his fingers digging into her waist.

"Just like that, baby. Keep going," he encouraged, his voice hoarse with pleasure.

Dionne lost herself in the moment, her moans growing louder with each movement. Arris admired her from below, the way her body moved, the way her head tilted back in ecstasy, and the way she gripped him like she never wanted to let go.

She was unlocking something inside him he didn't even know existed—a deep, undeniable craving for her that only grew stronger every time they were together. He knew she wanted to take things slow, but there was no slow when it came to her. Arris wanted all of her. Needed all of her.

And though she didn't realize it yet, Dionne was feeling the same. Whatever they had ignited in each other was growing into something neither of them could control—a *feen* for one another that burned through the chaos of their lives.

Dionne turned around, gripping his ankles for support as she started moving against him, her ass jiggling perfectly with every motion. Arris's control slipped as he watched her, mesmerized. "Shit," he muttered under

Feenin'

his breath, gripping her waist tightly as if to steady himself. But it wasn't enough. He stood, lifting her effortlessly, keeping her back flush against his chest. His need for her was written all over his face as he thrust into her, each motion deliberate, his hold firm.

Her soft moans quickly turned into screams, and he fucking loved every second of it. "You feel me now, Mama?" he growled into her ear, his breath hot against her skin. Dionne couldn't form words, only nodding as every thrust sent her closer to the edge.

She felt every inch of him, and it consumed her. Her mind screamed at her to pull back, to remember the life she was supposed to be living—but her body didn't give a damn. Her nails dug into his arms as her climax hit her like a wave, leaving her trembling in his arms. "Fuck!" she gasped, barely able to breathe as she came undone.

Arris didn't let her rest, though. "I'm not done with you yet," he said, his voice low and commanding. He laid her back down, his eyes dark with lust and something deeper. He flipped her over, her ass now perfectly positioned for him. He spread her cheeks apart, leaning down to press his tongue to her sensitive skin, licking her in a way that had her moaning his name.

"Arris—oh fuck—" Dionne moaned, her voice shaking as he devoured her. He didn't stop, his tongue and lips working her like he had something to prove. He shifted down to her soaked pussy, licking and sucking until her body bucked against him. She tried to close her legs, overwhelmed, but he pinned her cheeks open with his strong hands, his grip unyielding.

"Don't run from me," he growled, his lips brushing against her skin as he added two fingers inside her, curling them just right. Dionne gripped the sheets, her cries filling the room as he worked her relentlessly. "Fuck, Arris!" she screamed as another orgasm ripped through her, leaving her trembling and breathless.

Before she could recover, he slid inside her again, raw and hard. "Shit, Mama," he groaned, feeling her walls clench around him. The intensity made both their heads spin. "You feel so fucking good," he murmured, his voice filled with awe.

"Shit, Dionne. I'm about to—" he groaned, pulling out just in time, his release spilling over her skin.

Dionne didn't hesitate, taking him back into her mouth, licking and sucking him clean as if she couldn't get enough. Arris's head fell back, his legs shaking as she worked him over one last time, pulling every ounce of energy from him. "Fuck, Mama," he panted, his chest heaving as she finally pulled away, licking her lips with a satisfied smirk.

Arris chuckled, shaking his head. "I swear, I unlocked a crazy side of you."

Dionne grinned, wiping her mouth. "Looks like I did too," she said, her voice teasing but soft. He pulled her into his arms, her legs wrapping around him as he carried her to the bathroom.

"You're mine, Dionne," he said, his tone low and possessive. "And I'm not letting you go."

Her heart raced at his words, but she couldn't bring herself to argue. In that moment, she didn't want him to let go.

Chapter 9

One week later:

Dionne walked into her office, her heels clicking against the floor as she mentally prepared for her next meeting. She was in full work mode, determined to sell more houses and solidify her position as a partner. But the sight of a bouquet of roses on her desk brought her to an abrupt stop. Her brows furrowed in surprise as she glanced around, half expecting someone nearby to explain their sudden appearance.

She approached the arrangement slowly, her curiosity piqued, and plucked the small card tucked into the bouquet. A smile tugged at her lips—until she saw the name. Malik. Her mood soured instantly.

"I know I've been a bad fiancé, but I'll do better. Starting with these flowers and date night tonight," the note read. Dionne rolled her eyes and tossed the card onto her desk, letting it slide haphazardly among her papers. Another empty gesture, another bribe to cover his inability to show up for her in meaningful ways. She was tired of it. With a heavy sigh, she turned her attention back to preparing for her next meeting, determined to shake off the irritation.

As she shuffled through her paperwork, the sound of a deep, familiar voice filled the room, stopping her cold.

"Roses, huh?"

Her heart skipped a beat. She'd recognize that voice anywhere—the same voice that sent shivers down her spine and made her chest tighten with anticipation. Arris stepped further into her office, his presence dominating the space effortlessly. His gaze fell on the bouquet sitting on the edge of her desk, his jaw tightening ever so slightly before he masked his frustration with his usual confident smirk.

"Clearly, that nigga don't know you," he said, his tone laced with sarcasm and a hint of possessiveness. His smirk widened as he walked closer, his eyes scanning her face before landing back on the offending flowers.

Dionne froze, startled by his bluntness but unable to argue. He was right. Roses were her least favorite flower. Basic. Predictable. Something Malik should've known by now—but didn't. Yet somehow, Arris had figured it out without her ever telling him. It was just another example of how he noticed the details others didn't.

Dionne quickly slid the note under a stack of papers, not wanting him to see it.

Dionne covered her tracks with a confident smile, hoping it masked the small knot of guilt tightening in her chest. "For your information, a man didn't send me those. They're from a client—thanking me for being their agent." She straightened her posture, trying to make her words sound as believable as possible.

Arris's smirk widened, clearly buying her story, but the guilt she felt lingered. She hated lying to him, even in small ways, but her life was a tangled mess of complications, and the last thing she wanted was to risk losing him because of it.

He took a step closer, unable to resist her pull, and gently reached for her. His hands slid to her waist as his eyes roamed over her black pantsuit, the diamond embellishments on the shoulders catching the light. The blazer was slightly open, revealing just enough cleavage to be both professional and tantalizing. Her black Louboutin heels accentuated her figure, and her sleek bun added an air of polished sophistication.

"You're stunning," he murmured, pulling her closer, his tone deep and full of admiration.

Dionne's breath hitched at his touch, but she quickly pulled back, glancing around nervously to make sure no one saw them. "We're in the office, Arris. You can't do that," she said firmly, though the heat in her voice betrayed her.

Arris chuckled, raising his hands in mock surrender. "My bad. You're right," he said, though his smirk hinted at no real remorse. "It's just so damn hard looking at your beautiful ass and not touching you." His voice dropped an octave, the seductive edge making her cheeks flush.

"Well, you're going to have to try," she replied, trying to maintain her professional demeanor as she adjusted her blazer. "You're ready for the meeting?"

"Right behind you, Mama," Arris said with his usual charm. She turned, heading for the door with her usual poised stride. Arris followed, but not without letting his hand snap against her ass, the sound echoing

Feenin'

through the office.

"Ow! Fool, that hurt!" Dionne spun, swatting his arm with a glare that was only half-serious.

"I couldn't help it," he said, his tone unapologetic as his eyes drifted down. "It looks too damn good in those pants." His hand rubbed the spot he'd hit, soothing the sting as if that made it better.

Dionne glanced around, relieved that no one was nearby to witness their exchange. "Look, don't touch," she shot back, though the corners of her mouth betrayed a smile.

Arris chuckled, leaning closer. "I just told you how hard that is."

Dionne rolled her eyes, unable to hide the warmth spreading through her. "Let's go before we're late," she said, steering them both toward the conference room where Ms. Jean was undoubtedly waiting. She walked ahead, her heels clicking sharply against the floor, and Arris followed at a respectable distance—but not too far. He wouldn't miss the view.

The entire meeting revolved around the new land Arris was planning to purchase just outside the city—a prime location for hotels and stores catering to travelers coming in and out of the area. Dionne remained the epitome of professionalism, her sharp insights and poised demeanor commanding respect in the room. But no matter how focused she tried to appear, she couldn't ignore the weight of Arris's gaze.

His eyes lingered on her, intense and unyielding, every word he spoke directed at her even when addressing the entire room. The subtle way his deep voice wrapped around her name made her pulse quicken, and the way he watched her as though no one else existed left her flushed.

While most were oblivious to the electricity between them, Arris's assistant, China, wasn't. Every now and then, her eyes flicked between the two, a knowing smile tugging at her lips as she caught the subtle yet unmistakable spark in their exchanges.

Even the simplest gestures revealed their connection. When Arris shook Dionne's hand as the meeting ended, his touch lingered just a moment too long, his thumb grazing her knuckles. Dionne felt the tension between them as if it were tangible, and despite her attempt to pull away gracefully, Arris's hand resisted for a fraction of a second, his smirk making her heart race.

By the time Arris and his team had left, Dionne was barely holding onto her composure. The heat between them had left her feeling unsteady, her arousal simmering just beneath the surface. She closed the door to her office and made a beeline for her private bathroom, her breath quickening with each step.

Once inside, she locked the door and leaned against it, exhaling deeply. The dampness between her thighs was undeniable, a testament to the effect Arris had on her without even trying. Frustrated and overwhelmed, she peeled off her wet panties, tossing them aside before splashing her face with cool water in an attempt to steady herself.

"Get it together, Dionne," she whispered to herself, staring at her reflection. But even as she tried to compose herself, the thought of Arris—his voice, his touch, the way he looked at her like she was the only woman in the world—lingered in her mind, leaving her yearning for more.

Dionne walked back to her desk, attempting to settle back into work, but her thoughts betrayed her. Her eyes landed on the bouquet of roses sitting on the edge of her desk, a stark reminder of the man she was engaged to—a man she no longer loved. Yet her mind was consumed by Arris, the man who had effortlessly stolen her heart. The weight of her conflicting emotions pressed heavily on her chest.

Her heart yearned for Arris, but her loyalty to Malik and his mother kept her bound. She sighed deeply, running her fingers through her hair as she felt the suffocating pull of her situation. Torn between love and obligation, Dionne lowered her head to her desk and clasped her hands together, silently praying for guidance, clarity, and the strength to navigate the mess she found herself in.

Just as she whispered an "amen," a knock at the door pulled her from her thoughts. She looked up, her heavy emotions briefly replaced by surprise and excitement when she saw her older brother standing on the other side.

"Demetrius!" she exclaimed, jumping up from her seat and rushing to hug him. His tall 6'4" frame nearly engulfed her as he wrapped her in a bear hug. His rich dark skin glowed under the office lights, and his wide grin mirrored the joy on her face.

"Wassup, baby sis!" he greeted, his deep voice filled with warmth. When they pulled away, Dionne looked up at him with a mix of disbelief and happiness.

"What are you doing here?" she asked, her voice brimming with excitement.

Demetrius chuckled, his eyes crinkling at the corners. "I'm in town on business, but I had to stop by and see my favorite sister," he teased, his grin widening.

Dionne playfully rolled her eyes. "Nigga, I am your only sister," she retorted, unable to keep the smile off her face.

Demetrius laughed, throwing an arm around her shoulder as they

Feenin'

walked over to the couch. They sat down, ready to catch up, their sibling bond easing some of the tension weighing on her heart. For the first time that day, Dionne felt a sense of comfort.

"How's my nephew doing? Did you bring him?" Dionne asked, her excitement evident as she leaned forward, her eyes lighting up at the mention of her favorite little guy.

Demetrius laughed, his deep voice filling the room. "You know I can't go nowhere without DJ being my shadow," he replied, shaking his head.

"Aww, that's so cute," Dionne cooed, her smile widening.

"Yeah, he's good. He asked about you yesterday, said you're his favorite auntie. You know how he is," Demetrius said with a warm chuckle, making Dionne's heart melt.

"And how's Kierra?" Dionne asked, referring to Demetrius's wife.

"She's good. She was just asking about you the other day. Says she misses you and wants you to visit Dallas soon," Demetrius said, his tone softening.

Dionne smiled. "I miss her too. I'll visit soon, I promise. Once work lets up and... the wedding passes." Her words ended with a slight roll of her eyes, her tone flat.

Demetrius's smile faded as his expression hardened. "So you really marrying that nigga?" he asked, his disdain for Malik clear in his voice.

Dionne sighed, already anticipating where this conversation was heading. "Please don't start, Demetrius," she said, leaning back against the couch and crossing her arms.

"No, you shouldn't have started by staying with him. Why haven't you left that sorry-ass nigga yet?" Demetrius shot back, his frustration bubbling to the surface.

"It's not that simple," Dionne said softly, her voice barely above a whisper.

"It is that simple," Demetrius countered, leaning forward. "Leave his ass. How many times have you called me crying, Dee? Every time that nigga stood you up for work, forgot about important shit in your life, and worst of all—" His jaw clenched tightly as his voice dropped. "And I still owe him an ass whooping for cheating on you."

"Demetrius, please," Dionne cut him off, her voice trembling as her emotions threatened to spill over. "Just let it go."

Her brother noticed the crack in her voice and immediately backed off, his anger giving way to concern. "Okay," he said gently, his tone softening. "But listen to me, Dee. You deserve true love. You deserve more than what that nigga is giving you."

Dionne nodded slowly, her eyes fixed on the floor. She knew he was right. Deep down, she had always known. But the situation with Malik felt so tangled, so complicated, that she didn't know how to start unraveling it.

The siblings sat in silence for a moment, the weight of Demetrius's words lingering in the room. Finally, Dionne mustered a faint smile. "Thanks, Demetrius. You always have my back."

"Always," he said firmly, wrapping an arm around her shoulder and pulling her into a side hug. "You're my baby sister. Nobody gets to treat you like less than the queen you are."

"I have a meeting to head to. Just wanted to stop by first, let you know I was here, and see you," Demetrius said, pressing a soft kiss to Dionne's forehead. She melted into the gesture, the comfort and warmth of her big brother grounding her even for a moment.

"Come by Ma and Pops' house later," he added with a small smile. "DJ's going to be over the moon to see you."

Dionne returned his smile, but it was tinged with sadness. "I have date night with Malik," she said, her voice dropping slightly. "But I'll come by tomorrow."

She didn't miss the way Demetrius's jaw tightened at the mention of Malik's name. His frustration was clear. "That nigga better show up this time. On time," he muttered, unable to hold back his annoyance.

Dionne nodded quietly, knowing there was nothing she could say to ease Demetrius's disdain. With a final hug and goodbye, Demetrius left, leaving her alone in her office. She returned to her desk, attempting to compose herself, but the storm raging inside her refused to settle.

Demetrius's words echoed in her mind: You deserve true love. You deserve more than what that nigga is giving you.

She did deserve better, didn't she? But how could she chase it when she was bound by her promise? How could she free herself from the chains of a relationship that no longer served her? A tear slipped down her cheek, and then another, until she couldn't stop them. Her hands balled into fists, anger and heartbreak overtaking her.

With a sudden surge of rage, Dionne grabbed the vase of roses from her desk and hurled it into the trash. The sound of the glass clinking against the metal echoed in the silent office, but it wasn't enough to release the weight crushing her chest.

She couldn't focus on work anymore. She grabbed her purse and keys, standing abruptly. On her way out, she stopped by Ms. Jean's desk. "I'm heading out early. I'm not feeling well," she said, her voice barely above a whisper. Ms. Jean gave her a sympathetic nod, not asking any

Feenin'

questions.

Dionne drove home in silence, grateful for the empty house when she arrived. Malik was still at work, leaving her alone with her thoughts. She kicked off her heels, dropped her purse, and sank onto the couch, burying her face in her hands.

For the first time in a long while, she let herself feel every ounce of pain, anger, and longing she had been bottling up. Tears streamed down her face as she wrestled with the truth she had been trying to ignore: she was pretending to love a man she no longer wanted. Pretending to be happy. Pretending that Malik was the man of her dreams, when her heart screamed for something—and someone—else.

***

Arris sat in his office, leaning back in his chair as he tried to focus on the paperwork in front of him. But thoughts of Dionne and their earlier interaction kept creeping in, pulling him away from his work. Unable to shake the nagging feeling that something was off, he picked up his phone and dialed her number. The phone rang a few times before going to voicemail.

He frowned, his unease growing. *Why isn't she answering?* he thought as he dialed again, only to get the same result. Just as he was about to grab his keys and head out to check on her, a knock on his office door stopped him in his tracks.

"Come in," he called, his tone slightly clipped with frustration.

China stepped inside, holding her clipboard. "Arris, you have a visitor. He's not on the list of meetings, but he said he needs to talk to you about business."

Arris raised an eyebrow, the shift in his focus temporary. "Who is it?"

"A Demetrius Smith. He mentioned being an old baseball friend."

Arris's curiosity piqued, and a grin slowly spread across his face. "Send him in."

China nodded and left, and moments later, Demetrius walked in with the same wide grin Arris remembered from their younger days. Arris stood up, stepping around his desk as they greeted each other with a firm dap and a quick hug.

"Man, it's been a minute, D," Arris said, his voice light with genuine excitement.

"Since little league baseball," Demetrius replied with a chuckle as they pulled away.

Arris laughed, memories of their childhood games flashing through his mind. Though Demetrius was older, Arris's advanced skills had always landed him in higher-level games, giving them the chance to cross paths frequently. Even though they had never played on the same team, their shared love for baseball had forged a bond that lasted.

"You still hitting the field?" Arris asked, motioning for Demetrius to take a seat.

"Not as much as I'd like to. I manage the Dallas Stampede now," Demetrius said with pride as he settled into the chair across from Arris. "So I'm still around the game, just in a different way."

"Man, that's big. Congrats, for real," Arris said, leaning back in his chair with a smile.

"Appreciate it. And I see you doing your thing out here," Demetrius replied, motioning to the spacious office and the evidence of Arris's success surrounding them.

"Trying to keep the hustle alive," Arris said with a smirk, though his mind briefly wandered back to Dionne. He shook it off and refocused.

"So what brings you to Houston? Dallas ain't big enough for you anymore?" Arris teased, leaning back in his chair. Demetrius chuckled, shaking his head. "Nah, man. Just needed to get back home for a bit, see the family. Actually, I just came from visiting my little sister."

Arris raised an eyebrow, intrigued. "You got a sister? Why the hell I never met her?"

Demetrius laughed knowingly. "That was intentional, nigga. You've been a hoe since middle school, and there was no way I was about to let you anywhere near my sister."

Arris smirked, nodding. "Fair enough. You were probably right."

Both men laughed before Demetrius's expression turned more serious, his tone shifting. "But for real, I didn't just come to visit family. I wanted to talk business."

Arris leaned forward, intrigued now. "Alright, what's up?"

"You ever thought about stepping back on the field?" Demetrius asked casually, though his intent was clear.

Arris chuckled, shaking his head. "Man, nah. I still love baseball, but that part of my life is done. It's all about business for me now."

Demetrius grinned at his friend's answer. "Good, 'cause that's exactly why I'm here—with a business proposal for you."

Arris sat up straighter, the playful energy in the room shifting into something more focused. "Alright, I'm listening."

"So," Demetrius began, "I was offered the GM position for the Houston Comets. Five years, $60 million on the table."

Arris let out an impressed whistle, nodding. "That's a hell of a deal, bro. You taking it?"

"I want to," Demetrius admitted, his face darkening slightly, "but I

Feenin'

don't fuck with the current owner. Dude's a mess. He's been bankrupt three times just this year and has a string of sexual assault claims against him. The city hates him, and his legal team is finally convincing him to sell."

Arris's smile faded, his expression now serious. "Damn, that's rough. So what, you want me to buy the team?"

Demetrius nodded, hope glinting in his eyes. "Exactly. You've got the money, the business sense, and the respect of the city. People out here know you. You'd be the perfect face to rebuild the Comets and turn them into a powerhouse again."

"Demetrius, I've been done with that baseball life," Arris said, his voice laced with hesitation. "I don't know if I want to dive back into it." Baseball would always hold a special place in his heart—it was his first love—but that chapter had long closed. His plate was already full, and adding a baseball franchise felt like biting off more than he could chew.

Demetrius leaned forward, his voice calm but persuasive. "Alright, how about this? I pay half, you pay half. We split ownership contract-wise, but your name is the one on paper. Every profit we make, we split evenly, but I handle all the baseball business. You can focus on endorsements and the face of the franchise."

Arris thought about it for a moment. It wasn't a bad idea. "Send everything to my lawyer, and I'll look it over," he said after a beat. "I'll have a decision for you before the end of the season."

Demetrius nodded, a smile creeping onto his face. The season only had a few weeks left, so it gave Arris enough time to weigh the decision. "Deal."

Arris stood, extending his hand. "Welcome back home, D."

"Good to be back. Hopefully for good," Demetrius said, his tone hopeful as they dapped each other up.

Arris chuckled lightly. "We'll talk."

With that, Demetrius left Arris's office. Arris wasted no time packing up his things, eager to clear his mind. As he got into his car, Dionne's face crept back into his thoughts. He couldn't shake her from his mind. Reaching for his phone, he called her. After several rings, she finally picked up. The moment her face appeared on the screen, his chest tightened. She was lying in bed, her face partially hidden under the covers. The tear streaks on her cheeks were unmistakable.

"Mama, what's wrong?" he asked, his voice softening as concern flooded him. He immediately turned his car around, heading toward her house.

"Nothing," she replied quietly, but the crack in her voice betrayed her.

Arris's jaw clenched, his grip tightening on the steering wheel. "Then why you crying?" His tone was firmer now, a mix of worry and frustration at not knowing what had caused her pain. Earlier, she was vibrant and full of life, and now seeing her like this made his chest ache.

"I told you, I'm fine," Dionne said, quickly wiping at her cheeks, but her eyes couldn't lie.

"Why you crying, Dionne?" he pressed, his voice sterner this time. The background noise of his car speeding told her he was already on his way.

"I'm just emotional," she said, scrambling for an explanation. "I started my period." The lie slipped out effortlessly, and while it was partly true, it wasn't the real reason for her tears.

Arris didn't buy it. "Mama, don't play me. That ain't it." His tone was steady, but there was a protective edge to it that made her heart skip.

"Arris, seriously. I'm good," she insisted, her voice softer now.

Arris stopped by the store, grabbing her favorite snacks, a heating pad, and some over-the-counter medicine for cramps. The sound of rustling bags and shuffling came through the phone, catching Dionne's attention. "What are you doing?" she asked, her voice tinged with curiosity and exhaustion. He didn't answer, and simply hung up, getting back into his car and resuming his drive.

Minutes later, Arris pulled up to her house, spotting her car in the driveway. He grabbed the bag of items and stepped out, his heart heavy with concern. Picking up his phone, he called her again. "Open the door," he said firmly and hung up before she could protest.

Moments later, Dionne opened the door. Her hair was disheveled, tear tracks stained her cheeks, and she wore an oversized hoodie and baggy sweats. Despite her raw and vulnerable state, Arris still found her breathtaking. She looked up at him, surprised to see him standing there, but the soft smile on her lips gave away her relief.

"What are you doing here?" she asked, her voice low, though a hint of gratitude lingered in her tone.

Arris stepped inside without hesitation, closing the door behind him. He set the bag down before pulling her gently into his arms. "Are you okay?" he asked, his voice laced with tenderness as he wiped a stray tear from her cheek.

"I'm fine, Arris," Dionne replied softly, but her words didn't carry much conviction. "You didn't have to come all this way."

Ignoring her protest, Arris picked up the grocery bag and held it out to her. "I brought your favorite snacks, a heating pad, and some meds for

Feenin'

the cramps," he said, his lips curving into a small smile.

Dionne's chest tightened at his thoughtfulness. Tears welled in her eyes, and despite her best efforts, they spilled over again. "You're too sweet," she whispered, her voice cracking with emotion as she tried to hold herself together.

Arris frowned slightly, stepping closer and wrapping his arms around her again. "Mama, talk to me," he said, his voice soft but firm. "What's really wrong?"

Even as his embrace calmed her, guilt churned inside Dionne. Here stood a man who had shown her a level of care she hadn't felt in years, if ever. Yet, the truth of her situation felt like a weight suffocating her. She was another man's fiancée, yet her heart yearned for Arris—a man who had no idea of the tangled web she was caught in. Demetrius's words from earlier echoed in her mind: You deserve true love, Dee. You deserve more than what that nigga is giving you.

But did she? She wasn't sure anymore. In this moment, standing in the arms of the man her heart truly belonged to, she couldn't help but feel undeserving. Arris deserved true love too—love she wanted to give him but couldn't, not without unraveling the lie she'd been living.

Arris didn't need to hear Dionne's words to know the depth of her pain. Her cries told him everything. Without hesitation, he scooped her up in his arms, her legs instinctively wrapping around his waist, her arms clinging to his neck like he was her lifeline. He carried her to the couch and sat down, cradling her tightly. Her face pressed into his chest as she clung to him like he was the only thing holding her together.

"Please, talk to me, Mama," he pleaded softly, his voice laced with worry.

Dionne shook her head, her words trembling as they escaped her lips. "Just hold me. Don't let me go, please."

Her broken voice hit him like a punch to the gut, but Arris didn't hesitate. His arms tightened around her, one hand running up and down her back in soothing strokes. "I got you," he murmured into her hair, his tone low and reassuring. Every ounce of his energy was focused on grounding her, on giving her the peace she so desperately needed.

Slowly, the tension in her body began to ease, her breathing evening out as her tears subsided. She melted into him completely, her exhaustion taking over as she drifted into a peaceful slumber. Arris leaned back, careful not to jostle her, his gaze fixed on her face. The tear stains on her cheeks sent a wave of anger and helplessness through him. He hated seeing her like this, hated that he didn't know what was truly going on.

Time passed as he held her, unwilling to move or disturb her. But the sharp vibration of his phone pulled him from his thoughts. He glanced at the screen and saw True's name flashing. He sighed, debating whether to answer but knew True wouldn't stop calling until he did.

"Aye, nigga, where you at?!" True's loud voice came through the phone the second Arris answered.

"Yo, calm your voice down," Arris hissed, glancing down at Dionne to make sure she was still asleep. Her soft breathing brushed against his neck, reassuring him she hadn't stirred.

"What? You babysitting Mia again? Mario needs to hire a damn sitter," True joked, oblivious to the situation.

"Nah, I got caught up with something," Arris replied vaguely, trying to keep his voice steady.

True, as nosy as ever, pressed on. "You with a woman?"

Arris smirked but kept his response brief. "Nigga, mind yo business."

True laughed loudly, undeterred. "You got some pussy over there, huh? Nigga, leave it alone for a change and get here. The game is about to start."

Arris chuckled despite himself. "Aight, I'll be there in 30," he said before hanging up.

He looked down at Dionne again, his expression softening. She was still sound asleep, her face peaceful despite the dried tear stains that marked her earlier turmoil. A part of him didn't want to leave, but he also knew she needed rest. Carefully, he stood, carrying her up the stairs to her room. Her body remained limp in his arms, and she didn't stir as he laid her gently on the bed, tucking the covers around her.

Arris crouched down beside the bed, brushing a stray hair from her face. He leaned in, pressing a soft kiss to her forehead. "I'll be back, Mama," he whispered, his voice low and full of promise.

Forcing himself to leave, he made his way downstairs, each step heavier than the last. He checked the locks on the doors, ensuring her safety before finally stepping out into the night. The thought of her alone in her emotional state gnawed at him, but he promised himself he'd check on her the second she woke up.

Sliding into his car, he took a steadying breath, gripping the wheel as he headed to True's place. Even as the road stretched out in front of him, his thoughts remained firmly on Dionne.

***

Dionne stirred awake to soft kisses trailing from her forehead to her lips, a gentle gesture that made her smile. She thought it was Arris, his warmth and care still vivid in her mind. But as her eyes fluttered open, her smile faltered slightly when she saw Malik's face instead.

Feenin'

"Wake up, baby. You need to get ready," he said softly, his smile bright as he admired her. She rubbed the sleep from her eyes, disoriented for a moment as she realized she was back in her bed, not in Arris's arms where she last felt at peace.

"Where are we going?" Dionne asked, her voice groggy as she glanced around, trying to adjust to the light filtering into the room.

"It's a surprise. Just dress cute," Malik said cheerfully, flashing her a grin that left her wondering where this sudden burst of affection and enthusiasm came from. She decided not to question it, forcing herself to nod before sliding out of bed and making her way to the bathroom.

Once inside, Dionne stared at her reflection in the mirror. Her sleepy, red-rimmed eyes and slightly puffy cheeks revealed traces of the tears she'd shed earlier. She sighed, shaking her head at how little Malik noticed these things about her anymore. But then her thoughts shifted, replaying the care and comfort Arris had given her earlier. The memory of his arms around her, the way he held her like she was the most precious thing in his world, brought a small smile to her lips.

"Hurry, baby! I don't want to be late," Malik called from the other side of the door, snapping her out of her thoughts.

She rolled her eyes and quickly undressed, stepping into the shower. The hot water cascaded over her, soothing her muscles, but it did little to quiet her mind. Arris was still there, lingering in her thoughts like a drug she couldn't quit. She knew she shouldn't be thinking about him—especially not while preparing for a date with her fiancé—but she couldn't help it. The way he had shown up for her earlier, so selflessly, so genuinely, had touched something deep inside her. Something Malik hadn't reached in a long time.

But as much as she wanted to lose herself in thoughts of Arris, reality weighed heavy on her. She was engaged, and no matter how strained or empty her relationship with Malik had become, she had made a promise. A promise she couldn't easily break. With a resigned sigh, she let the water wash over her, silently willing her heart to fall in line with her obligations.

Dionne stepped out of the shower, her skin glowing as she applied her favorite moisturizer, the scent calming her slightly. She moved through her facial routine methodically, the rhythm helping to ground her. The makeup she applied was light yet effective, hiding the exhaustion etched into her features. At least outwardly, she looked put together, even if her heart felt like a chaotic mess.

After finishing, she walked into her spacious closet, staring at her wardrobe for inspiration. Malik hadn't provided any details about the evening other than "dress cute," so she decided to keep it simple but striking. She slipped into a black backless O-neck maxi dress, its long sleeves and snug fit accentuating her curves perfectly. She paired it with black YSL open-toed heels that added a touch of elegance and grabbed her matching YSL purse.

Moving to her vanity, Dionne straightened her natural hair until it gleamed, styling it into a silky middle part that cascaded down her back. As she worked, she made a mental note to book a hair appointment with London soon—she was ready for something fresh, something different. Once she was satisfied with her reflection, she took a deep breath, practicing a smile in the mirror before stepping out of the bathroom.

Malik was standing near the doorway, his eyes lighting up the moment he saw her. His gaze roamed over her figure, lingering on every curve as he licked his lips. "You look beautiful," he said, stepping closer, his voice low as he wrapped his hands around her waist.

Dionne caught his admiring look, but it did nothing for her internally. She smiled, but it was forced—another performance in this elaborate charade. "Thank you," she replied softly, her eyes moving over his appearance. Malik had dressed up for the occasion, wearing a black Dior collared shirt paired with black jeans and Dior low-top sneakers. His fresh lineup was crisp, and he did look good, but the spark she once felt was long gone.

To her surprise, Malik leaned in, pressing a kiss to her lips. Dionne didn't resist, but she didn't embrace it either. Her body remained still, her mind elsewhere, thinking of how different it felt when someone else's lips—Arris's—had been on hers. When Malik pulled away, she offered him another practiced smile, masking the emptiness she felt inside.

"You're ready?" Malik asked as he pulled away from her, his tone casual but detached. Dionne simply nodded, not feeling like talking much today. They left the house, Malik heading straight to the car without the courtesy of opening her door. She sighed softly, letting the disappointment roll off her shoulders as she climbed in herself. Once she was settled, Malik started driving, his attention more on his phone than on her.

The car ride was silent, save for the low hum of music playing on the radio. Dionne stared out of the window, her mind racing. No matter how hard she tried to focus on the evening ahead or anything else, her thoughts kept drifting back to Arris. His voice, his touch, his undeniable presence—it all lingered in her mind, refusing to leave.

As if he could sense her thoughts, her phone rang, and Arris's name lit up the screen. Her heart skipped a beat. She glanced at Malik, who

Feenin'

was busy texting while driving, barely noticing her. She declined the call, not wanting to draw any suspicion, but moments later, it rang again. This time, she hesitated, her finger hovering over the screen. She glanced at Malik, still engrossed in his phone. Annoyed by his disregard for their safety, she rolled her eyes and pressed the green button.

"Hello," Dionne answered softly, her voice steady and expressionless, masking the turmoil inside.

"Why didn't you answer the first time?" Arris's voice was low but firm, his tone sending an involuntary shiver down her spine.

"What can I do for you?" she asked, trying to maintain a professional tone, ignoring his question and the effect his voice had on her.

"Mama, stop that formal shit. For real. Where you at? You good?" His words came fast, his concern evident. Despite his serious tone, she couldn't help the small smile that crept onto her face, even though she knew she shouldn't be smiling at all.

Before she could respond, Malik glanced over at her, catching the faint smile. His brows furrowed in curiosity, his suspicion clearly piqued. "I can't talk right now. I'll call you later," Dionne said quickly, cutting the conversation short. She hung up before Arris could say anything else, her heart pounding. She knew she had probably pissed him off, and sure enough, her phone buzzed again almost immediately.

Not wanting to risk Malik's growing curiosity, Dionne turned off her phone entirely. The weight of guilt settled heavily in her chest as she leaned back into her seat, trying to calm the storm raging inside her. She hated lying to Arris, hated the situation she found herself in, but most of all, she hated the growing distance between what she wanted and what her reality demanded.

"Who was that?" Malik asked, his tone sharp with curiosity, his eyes narrowing slightly as he glanced at her.

"No one. Just a client," Dionne lied effortlessly, keeping her voice calm and steady. Malik's gaze lingered on her for a moment longer before he turned his attention back to the road. She breathed a silent sigh of relief, grateful he didn't press further, but she could still feel the weight of his occasional glances. Part of her didn't care, though; her mind was preoccupied with the guilt of hanging up on Arris and the lingering tension in her chest.

The car eventually pulled into valet parking, and Dionne looked out the window, noticing the rooftop setup. It was a movies-and-bar experience, combining two of her favorite things—food and films. For the first time that evening, a genuine smile broke across her face. Malik noticed and smiled as he got out of the car, hurrying to her side to open her door.

Oh, now you want to be a gentleman, she thought sarcastically, but she let it slide as she stepped out, adjusting her dress.

They walked into the restaurant hand in hand, looking every bit the perfect couple. "Reservation for Harris," Malik said to the hostess, who greeted them warmly.

"Yes! The rooftop has been reserved, and we have everything ready for you and Mrs. Harris," the hostess said with a bright smile, glancing at Dionne. Dionne returned the smile politely, her expression neutral as they were led upstairs to the rooftop.

The setup was undeniably romantic: a large, plush couch in front of a big white screen, perfect for the movie, and a table for two adorned with a candle flickering in the middle. Malik had certainly outdone himself in planning this. She couldn't deny that it was beautiful, even if her feelings for him no longer matched the effort he'd put in tonight.

Malik guided her to the table first, pulling out her chair with a small flourish. "We'll eat first, then settle in for the movie," he said, his tone soft and inviting. Dionne nodded, sitting down and smoothing out her dress. For a brief moment, she let herself relax, trying to focus on the present rather than the complicated feelings swirling inside her. Maybe tonight wouldn't be so bad after all—or so she hoped.

"This is nice, Malik," Dionne said, her gaze drifting around in awe. The city skyline shimmered in the distance, and the gentle breeze was just enough to soothe without a chill. For the first time in what felt like forever, the atmosphere between her and Malik was calm, almost perfect.

"I'm glad you like it," Malik replied softly, his eyes fixed on her. The rooftop lights cast a warm glow over her face, and for a moment, his expression seemed sincere, like the Malik she used to know. Then, his tone grew serious as he reached across the table, taking her hand in his. The unexpected gesture startled her, but she let herself relax, curious about what he wanted to say.

"I know I've been fucking up, Dee," he began, his voice carrying a weight that matched the emotions in his eyes. "But I promise, from now on, I'll give you the love you deserve."

His words hung in the air, and Dionne's heart tightened. She wanted to believe him. She wanted to trust that the man she once loved was still in there somewhere. But the damage he had done over the years felt insurmountable. Love had been replaced by resentment, and every moment now felt more like an obligation to Mama Glen than a relationship she was invested in emotionally.

"I don't know if I believe you," she said softly, her voice trembling

Feenin'

under the weight of her emotions. The Malik she had fallen in love with was gone, and she wasn't sure she could ever reconnect with this new version of him.

"I know it's not going to take one date or a few words to fix things," he admitted, his grip on her hand tightening slightly. "But please, just give me another chance. Not for my mother, but for us."

Dionne's mind raced as she sat in silence, processing his plea. His words sounded genuine, but hesitation clawed at her. The promise she had made to Mama Glen was a constant cloud over her decisions. It was the only tether holding her to Malik, the only reason she hadn't walked away already.

"Okay," she said finally, her voice low and devoid of the emotion she used to carry when she looked at him. The word felt hollow, but it was enough to make Malik smile, as if he had just won the biggest battle of his life. He lifted her hand to his lips, pressing a soft kiss against her skin.

"I promise you, Dee. I'm going to do better," he said firmly, his eyes locked onto hers, filled with a hope that she no longer shared.

Dionne nodded, unable to speak. Yet again, she was giving Malik another chance. Not because her heart called her to, but because her sense of duty to Mama Glen wouldn't let her walk away. Even as she sat across from him, she couldn't help but feel like she was betraying herself.

Dionne's smile strained and her heart heavy with the decision she knew she had to make. As much as she craved Arris—the way he made her feel seen, cherished, and alive—she couldn't keep playing both sides. She couldn't be the devoted fiancée to Malik while secretly giving her heart to someone else. The weight of it all was suffocating, and for the first time, she realized the depth of her emotions for Arris.

But in this moment, Dionne knew she had to let him go. As much as it broke her, she decided to end the emotional and romantic connection they had built. She would remain professional with Arris, keeping their relationship strictly business. The thought of severing ties with the one man who made her feel truly alive was excruciating, but her sense of duty to Mama Glen and her promise outweighed her own desires.

What she didn't know was that Malik's newfound affection wasn't entirely rooted in love. He had noticed the distance growing between them—the long hours at work, the constant phone calls, the faint glimmer of someone else's presence in her life. Though he had no proof of her infidelity, the mere thought of her slipping away terrified him. And Malik wasn't the type to let anything, or anyone, take what he believed was his. He would do whatever it took to keep her close, even if his methods weren't entirely pure.

The rest of the evening passed with an odd air of normalcy. They laughed over their meal, reminisced about better times, and watched Love Jones, her favorite movie. Malik seemed to be trying, really trying, to win her over again. For a moment, it almost felt like old times. The rooftop setting, the soft glow of the city lights, and his efforts to please her should have made her happy.

But they didn't.

No matter how perfect the night seemed on the surface, her thoughts never strayed far from Arris. The way he looked at her, touched her, and knew her without her having to say a word. His presence lingered in her mind like a melody she couldn't shake.

Her heart was breaking in ways she never anticipated. Yet once again, Dionne chose to put her happiness aside, binding herself to the promise she made to Mama Glen. The internal war raged on, but tonight, duty won over desire.

Feenin'

Chapter 10

Arris sat on the couch, his leg bouncing anxiously as he waited for A'Lani to finish getting ready. Today, they were meeting their father—a man Arris had no desire to speak to, let alone forgive. The only reason he even agreed to go was because A'Lani had begged him. She needed his support, and despite how he felt about Calvin, Arris couldn't say no to his little sister. With her heading back to school tomorrow, she wanted this conversation before Thanksgiving, and for her sake, Arris would endure it.

But his thoughts weren't fully on the impending confrontation. They were on Dionne.

For the past week, she had been avoiding him, dodging his calls and refusing to meet his gaze during their meetings. She always rushed out before he could get a word in, leaving him confused and frustrated. The distance she was creating between them was unlike her, and it gnawed at him. What changed? What had he done? Every call he made went unanswered, and every text was left on read.

Sighing, he pulled out his phone, dialing her number again despite knowing she wouldn't pick up. The line rang and rang before going to voicemail, the sound of her prerecorded message only fueling his irritation. He gritted his teeth, tempted to pull up to her house and demand answers, but he knew he couldn't. A'Lani needed him right now, and no matter how much he missed Dionne, he had to set those feelings aside.

A'Lani stepped into the room, radiating confidence in her red Fendi shirt tucked into high-waisted jeans that hugged her figure perfectly, paired with red suede heel boots. Her hair fell down her back in a flawless middle part, and Arris couldn't help but smile, pride evident in his expression.

"You look too beautiful for that nigga Calvin to see you," Arris said, his tone dead serious.

A'Lani chuckled, shaking her head. "That's the point. Let him see how good we're doing without him. We didn't need his ass to be great."

"Damn straight," Arris agreed, a grin tugging at his lips. "You ready?"

A'Lani nodded, and they headed to his Jeep. Ever the protective brother, Arris opened the door for her before climbing into his side. As he started the car and pulled onto the road, a heavy silence threatened to settle between them, so they filled the air with light conversation to distract from what awaited them at the restaurant.

"So, how are things with the mystery woman?" A'Lani asked slyly, a smirk dancing on her lips.

Arris chuckled, but the mention of Dionne made his jaw tighten slightly. His thoughts immediately drifted to her—her smile, her laugh, the way she avoided him lately like he was a stranger. He missed her more than he wanted to admit, but the wall she had put between them was starting to wear him down.

"You just can't stop being nosy," he joked, brushing off his real feelings.

A'Lani laughed, shaking her head at his deflection. "And you can't stop being secretive. I know you're feeling her, because the second I mentioned her, you smiled. No other woman does that to you, so she must be special."

Arris shook his head, impressed and slightly annoyed by how persistent and observant his sister was. "It's good, since you want to know so bad," he said with a smirk, his tone teasing but still holding a hint of restraint.

"Ouuu, my brother is in love!" A'Lani hyped, her excitement spilling into the car as she clapped her hands together.

Arris snapped his head toward her, a playful glare in his eyes. "Yo ass doing too much now. Ain't nobody in love."

A'Lani gave him a look like she didn't believe him for a second. "Nigga, please. She got your ass smiling, walking around glowing and shit. You can act like it's no big deal, but I know it's more than just her looks that got you hooked."

Arris kept his eyes on the road, avoiding her piercing gaze. Part of what she said was true, though he wasn't ready to admit it—not to A'Lani, not even to himself. Dionne had a pull on him he couldn't explain. She was all he thought about, the woman he craved in every

Feenin'

way. But now, with the distance she had put between them, all he felt was frustration and confusion. Why was she pulling away when they were just starting to build something real?

"I don't know what you're talking about," he said finally, his voice low, but even he didn't believe the words coming out of his mouth.

"Mm-hmm," A'Lani hummed knowingly, but she didn't push him further. Instead, she reached over and turned up the music, letting the smooth R&B fill the car as they drove toward what would undoubtedly be an emotional night.

Arris parked the car and cut the engine, glancing over at A'Lani. She sat frozen, her hands gripping the edges of her seat. "I'm scared, Arris," she admitted, her voice breaking as tears threatened to spill.

Without hesitation, Arris reached over, taking her hand in his. "I'm right here with you, every step of the way," he said firmly, his voice steady and reassuring.

A'Lani nodded but quickly glanced at him, her brows furrowing. "What if he says some dumb shit?" she asked, her fear giving way to frustration.

Arris didn't miss a beat. "Then I'll slap the fuck out of him," he said, his expression dead serious.

A'Lani gave him a blank stare, unimpressed by his response. "No, Arris. I don't need you going to jail behind him," she said sternly, knowing her brother's threats weren't just words—they were promises. "It's Calvin, so he's definitely going to say some dumb shit, but I need you calm. Please, for me."

Arris took a deep breath, the tension in his jaw easing as he nodded. He knew she was right, but his protective instincts made it hard to let go of the anger that always boiled just beneath the surface when it came to their father. "I got you, sis," he said, his tone softer now.

A'Lani gave him a small, grateful smile before they both stepped out of the car. Arris walked around to her side and opened the door for her, the gesture grounding them both as they prepared for the confrontation ahead.

They entered the small, modest restaurant Calvin had chosen. The smell of grilled meat and spices filled the air, but A'Lani barely noticed as her eyes darted around the room. Arris placed a steadying hand on the small of her back, guiding her forward.

"There," A'Lani said softly, nodding toward a booth in the corner where Calvin sat waiting. Arris and A'Lani exchanged a glance before walking toward him, each step feeling heavier than the last.

Calvin looked up, his face lighting up with surprise at the sight of

Ann

not just his daughter but also his son walking in with her. A smile crept across his face, though it was met with stone-cold expressions from the siblings. "Well, look at this. It's good to see you both. Man, I don't make ugly kids," he said, trying to lighten the mood with a chuckle.

Neither A'Lani nor Arris responded, their expressions unchanged as they approached the table. They sat down without a word, the tension thick enough to cut with a knife.

"How's business, Arris?" Calvin asked, his tone overly casual as if they were old friends catching up. Arris' jaw tightened, his eyes narrowing at the question. A'Lani subtly squeezed his hand under the table, her silent plea for him to stay calm evident in her touch.

"Nigga, I'm not here to play catch-up," Arris said, his tone icy and detached. "Lani has some things to say to you, and I'm just here for her support." His words landed with the weight of a gavel, leaving no room for misunderstanding.

Calvin turned his attention to A'Lani, the smile fading slightly as he took in the coldness in her eyes. She was battling the voice in her head telling her to leave, to not even give him this chance, but she took a deep breath, steadying herself.

"Babygirl, I'm listening," Calvin said, using the nickname he had called her since she was little. The endearment only fueled her anger.

"Don't 'babygirl' me," A'Lani snapped, her tone sharp enough to make Calvin flinch. "You don't get that privilege anymore."

Before Calvin could respond, the waiter approached to take their drink orders. A'Lani didn't even let him speak. "We're not ordering anything. We're not staying long," she said curtly, dismissing the waiter without looking away from her father. The waiter hesitated before glancing at Calvin, who nodded for him to leave.

A'Lani turned back to Calvin, her eyes brimming with years of hurt and anger. "Was I not good enough for you?" she asked, her voice trembling before she could stop it. She didn't wait for him to answer. "Was the streets that damn thrilling that you couldn't care for your own kids?"

Her voice grew louder, the emotions she had tried to keep bottled up now spilling over. Arris' hand tightened around hers under the table, grounding her before she could completely lose control. She turned to him briefly, his silent support giving her the strength to take a deep breath and compose herself.

"Lani—" Calvin began, but before he could even get the words out, Arris' sharp tone sliced through the air.

"She ain't done, nigga. You had your chance to care, and clearly, you

Feenin'

didn't give a fuck, so now you're gonna listen." Arris' voice was cold and lethal, his glare piercing Calvin. The weight of his presence made Calvin snap his mouth shut, his usual bravado shrinking as he waited for A'Lani to continue.

A'Lani's voice trembled, anger and pain mixing in every word. "I almost didn't come. I sat and thought about whether you even deserved to hear me out, because I knew whatever you had to say would be either a lie or just more bullshit."

"That's no way to talk to your fath—" Calvin tried again, but this time, Arris leaned forward, the sheer intensity of his movement enough to make Calvin backtrack. Before Arris could unleash the storm brewing inside him, A'Lani's voice stopped him cold.

"Don't you dare say 'father.' You are nothing more than a stranger to me. A surrogate, at best," A'Lani spat, her words hitting like venom.

Arris leaned back slightly, his jaw tight, his hand gripping hers under the table. He felt her leg bouncing with barely contained rage, and his squeeze on her hand tightened, silently telling her he was there, that she wasn't alone. His own blood was boiling, but for her sake, he held himself together.

Calvin slumped slightly in his chair, guilt flashing across his face as he closed his mouth and nodded, signaling that he would let her speak.

A'Lani's voice cracked as she continued, the pain raw in her tone. "I was a daddy's girl. I loved you," she said, her eyes glistening with unshed tears. Arris clenched his teeth, trying to keep his composure as he saw her heartbreak unfolding in front of him.

Her voice wavered, but she pressed on. "But you never loved me back. You loved drugs. You loved hoes. You loved the streets more than you ever loved me." Her tears began to fall, and she wiped them away quickly, as though trying to erase any evidence of her vulnerability.

Calvin's own eyes welled with tears, but he refused to let them spill. The guilt was etched into every line of his face, and his body language screamed regret, though he remained silent. Arris saw through the act, his own emotions barely contained as he looked at the man who had caused his sister so much pain.

A'Lani's grip on Arris' hand tightened, and he didn't flinch, letting her channel her pain through him. He wanted to protect her, shield her from this moment, but he knew this confrontation was one she needed for herself.

A'Lani's voice rose, raw and trembling with anger. "I am your daughter! The one woman in your life you were never supposed to leave for anything! I had to depend on my brother to be my father." Tears streamed down her face, but she wiped them away swiftly, her voice growing louder with every word.

"I just want to say fuck you, and fuck you for life! You left, so stay gone. I've done 20 years without you, and I have no problem going another lifetime." She finished, her tone sharp and final, no longer shaking with tears. Her eyes, now dry, burned with fury and heartbreak.

Arris stayed by her side, his steady presence grounding her, his protective instincts on high alert as he watched for any sign she might falter. Across the table, Calvin sat in silence, his shoulders slumped, his eyes heavy with regret and defeat.

"I'm sorry, babygir—" Calvin began, but A'Lani cut him off before he could finish.

"Arris, please get me out of here," she said, her voice calm yet resolute, standing up and gripping her brother's hand tightly. Without a word, Arris rose, his cold glare lingering on Calvin for a moment before he led A'Lani away from the table, leaving Calvin sitting there, alone and defeated.

The drive back to their mother's house was quiet. A'Lani sat in the passenger seat, staring out the window, her expression unreadable. Arris glanced at her occasionally, trying to gauge her mood, but her face gave nothing away.

When he tried to speak, she responded only with nods or brief non-verbal gestures, clearly not ready to talk about what had just happened. Arris understood her need for space, deciding to give her the silence she seemed to crave.

When they arrived at their mother's house, A'Lani got out of the car quietly. Arris watched her walk inside, his concern etched on his face. He wanted to comfort her, to make her laugh like he always did, but tonight he knew she needed time to process.

"I'll check on you tomorrow, Lani," he said softly as she disappeared into the house. With a sigh, he drove off, his thoughts heavy with everything they had just gone through.

Arris drove through the night, his thoughts spiraling as the events with Calvin replayed in his mind. The sight of A'Lani's tears and the tremble in her voice still echoed, fueling the anger that simmered beneath his calm exterior earlier. Now alone, his grip tightened on the steering wheel, his knuckles white as he tried to keep the rage at bay. He needed an escape, something—or someone—to take his mind off everything. Without hesitation, he reached for his phone, scrolling to her contact.

Her name and picture stared back at him, stirring something in his chest. He hesitated for a moment, wondering if she'd even answer.

Feenin'

She'd been distant for days, avoiding his calls and brushing past him in meetings, but he couldn't let it go. He needed to hear her voice, even if it was just for a moment. Finally, he pressed the FaceTime button, listening to the rings, his pulse quickening with each one. After a few rings, her face appeared on the screen.

Despite the frustration he carried, a smile broke through as he saw her. She was lounging on a couch, her curly hair swept into a messy bun, glasses perched on her face. The faint glow of her laptop reflected off her lenses, signaling she was still working. She looked effortlessly beautiful, and for a moment, his anger eased.

"Hello?" she said, her tone soft but guarded as she looked directly into the camera.

"Don't 'hello' me," he said, his voice firm but tinged with a smirk that softened his words. "Why you been avoiding me?"

"I am not avoiding you, Arris. I've just been busy," she replied, her voice gentle but not entirely convincing.

Arris chuckled, the sound deep and warm. "Busy, huh? Where you at? That ain't your couch."

Dionne couldn't help but laugh, shaking her head at how observant he was. "That's because it's not. I'm at Karmen's house, dog-sitting her puppy while she's on a date with Mario."

His smile widened at the mention of his friend's date but quickly shifted back to her. "So, you alone?" he asked, a subtle hope in his tone.

"Nope, I've got Jackson," she quipped, lifting a tiny black-and-white Shih Tzu into the frame.

Arris laughed, the sound rich and genuine. "So, you and Jackson holding it down tonight, huh?"

"Something like that," Dionne teased, rubbing the puppy's head affectionately.

For a moment, the tension of his day melted away, replaced by the comfort of her presence—even through a screen. "You're too cute with that dog," he said, his voice softer now.

"And you're too nosy," she shot back with a playful smirk.

Their banter was effortless, but Arris couldn't ignore the distance she'd been putting between them. His smile faded slightly as his gaze lingered on her face through the screen. "For real, though, Mama... You sure you're good? You been acting different."

Dionne's expression faltered for a split second before she quickly masked it with a light chuckle. "I'm fine, Arris. Really."

"Send me the address. I need to see you," Arris said, his voice laced with yearning. Dionne felt her heart flutter at his tone, but she quickly shook her head, pushing back the temptation. Even though she missed him, she had to maintain her distance now that she promised to give Malik a full chance. Besides, this wasn't her house, and giving out Karmen's address without permission wasn't right.

"No, Arris. This isn't my house," she said firmly, trying to stand her ground.

But Arris wasn't hearing it. "Either you give me the address, or I'll get it from Mario myself. Either way, I'm coming to see you," he said, his tone stern and leaving no room for argument.

Dionne rolled her eyes, annoyed at his persistence but knowing how serious he was. "Okay, Arris," she said curtly before hanging up, hoping it would be the end of it.

Arris stared at his phone, blinking in disbelief. She had hung up on him. He was ready to call her back and let her know how much that wasn't going to fly, but just as he was about to, a notification popped up on his screen. Dionne had sent the address.

A smirk spread across his face as he drove in the direction of Karmen's house. "That's what I thought," he muttered to himself. Whatever attitude she wanted to throw his way, he'd handle it in person. Tonight.

***

Dionne sat on Karmen's couch, focused on her laptop with Jackson snuggled under her, his soft snores barely audible. The sudden sound of the doorbell made her jump, snapping her out of her thoughts as Jackson perked up and barked at the noise. She sighed, already knowing who it was. Placing her laptop on the table, she walked to the door, and as soon as she opened it, Arris was there.

Before she could get a single word out, he stepped inside, gently but firmly gripping her neck as he guided her backward. The action sent a rush through her body, and the familiar arousal crept in. Jackson barked and jumped at Arris's legs, not in defense, but in pure excitement, his tiny tail wagging furiously.

Arris didn't pay the dog any mind as he backed Dionne into the wall, his eyes locked onto hers with a mix of intensity and frustration. In one swift move, he scooped her up, and her legs instinctively wrapped around his waist for support. His strength and dominance sent a shiver through her, and she found herself losing the resolve she tried so hard to keep.

"Why you been avoiding me?" he asked, his voice firm but calm, his grip on her steady.

"I'm not avoiding you, Arris," she said softly, trying to sound convincing, but the way her eyes shifted betrayed her.

Feenin'

"You seen me calling and texting, Mama," he pressed, his tone lowering but no less stern. "You been ducking me, and I want to know why."

"I've been busy with work," she lied, her voice wavering under his piercing gaze. She avoided the real answer, not ready to confront the storm of emotions swirling between them.

Arris studied her, his eyes narrowing slightly as if he could see through her words. He didn't push further, though. Instead, he leaned in, closing the distance between them, and pressed his lips to hers. The kiss was passionate and demanding, a reflection of the longing and frustration he felt.

Dionne melted into it, her arms around his neck. She missed him more than she cared to admit, and every ounce of that longing poured into their kiss. The tension in her body evaporated as his touch grounded her, his familiar scent surrounding her like a balm to her frayed nerves.

Arris kissed her like she was the only thing anchoring him to the world, his hands holding her firmly against him. Everything about her—the taste of her lips, the feel of her skin, the way her body fit perfectly against his—calmed the storm raging inside of him. For the first time since his meeting with Calvin, he felt a semblance of peace.

Their kiss deepened, both of them letting go of the outside world, lost in the moment they'd both been craving.

"Stop fucking avoiding me," Arris growled against her lips, his tone low, demanding, leaving no room for argument.

"I'm not—" Dionne started, trying to string together some excuse, anything that would justify the distance she had been putting between them. But before she could finish, a gasp escaped her lips as Arris' hand found its way back to her neck, firm yet careful, a possessive touch that sent a shiver down her spine.

His eyes burned into hers, raw, intense—every unspoken word, every ounce of frustration, longing, and love reflected in them. She froze, her breath catching as her legs remained locked around his waist, her back pressing against the wall.

"What did I say, Mama?" His voice softened just enough to send a different kind of heat coursing through her veins. "Don't do that shit no more."

Before she could respond, his mouth was on hers again, consuming her, claiming her. Dionne melted into the kiss, her body betraying her, surrendering to the pull she had been trying so hard to resist. Their tongues battled for dominance, but Arris was in control—his grip on her neck anchoring her to him, his arms keeping her exactly where he

Ann

wanted.

Arris finally pulled away, setting Dionne gently back onto the couch beside him. She adjusted herself, curling her legs under her as they settled into a comfortable position.

"I love to see you wear your glasses," he complimented, his tone soft yet full of admiration.

"I look like a nerd," she protested playfully, rolling her eyes as a small smile tugged at her lips.

"A pretty ass nerd," he countered smoothly, his voice dipping just enough to send a shiver down her spine.

"Arris, stop," she said softly, trying to keep her composure, though her voice betrayed her.

"What am I doing?" he asked, feigning innocence, though the glint in his eyes told a different story.

"You know what you're doing," she shot back, her voice laced with a mix of amusement and exasperation.

He chuckled, clearly pleased with himself. "And I don't see the problem with it either," he said confidently, leaning back into the couch as if he owned the moment.

Dionne shook her head, a quiet laugh escaping her lips. Of course you don't, she thought, stealing a glance at him.

"How was your day today? You seemed really tense," she asked after a moment, her tone shifting to genuine concern.

Arris gave her a faint smile, appreciating her attentiveness. "I went with my sister to talk to Calvin," he said, the smile fading as his jaw tightened at the mention of his father.

Dionne's eyes widened in surprise. She knew how deep his resentment for Calvin ran and how difficult it must've been for him to even consider being in the same room. "How did that go?" she asked softly, watching the tension rise in his shoulders.

"I didn't have shit to say to that nigga," Arris said, his voice cold and detached. "But A'Lani? She got everything off her chest."

Dionne nodded, her expression encouraging him to continue.

"Every tear that fell, every word she spoke—it made my blood boil," Arris admitted, his voice growing heavier. "Seeing her so angry, so hurt... I wanted to beat that nigga's ass so bad."

Dionne reached over, resting her hand on his forearm, her touch grounding him. "She was getting her healing, Arris. I know it hurt you to sit there and watch her go through that, but it was powerful for her— even through all those emotions," she said gently, her voice a balm to his rising anger.

Feenin'

Arris sighed, his shoulders relaxing slightly as he nodded. "You're right. She needed that," he admitted, his tone softer now. "I just hate seeing her like that. She deserved better."

"And so did you," Dionne said softly, her eyes locking with his. "But being there for her, supporting her—that's what mattered. You gave her the strength she needed to get through it."

Her words sank in, and for the first time all day, Arris felt a small weight lift from his chest. "Thank you, Mama," he said quietly, his hand finding hers, intertwining their fingers as he gave her a grateful squeeze.

The silence between them hung heavy, unspoken emotions filling the space until Dionne broke it softly. "When are you going to give yourself that same healing?" Her words were gentle but direct, slicing through the quiet like a whisper in the wind.

Arris furrowed his brows, confusion written across his face. "What do you mean?" he asked, his voice low and cautious.

Dionne tilted her head slightly, her gaze unwavering. "Arris, you carry a lot of anger because of your father. I know you want to move on without him, but he still has a hold on you, whether you admit it or not." Her voice was soothing, but her words carried weight. Arris's jaw tightened, his body stiffening at the truth she laid bare.

He wanted to argue, to brush off her observation, but the words stuck in his throat because she wasn't wrong. That familiar anger bubbled under his skin, a deep-seated hatred he couldn't shake. "You don't get it," he said defensively, his tone colder than he intended. He leaned back slightly, his walls rising.

But Dionne didn't flinch. She leaned forward instead, straddling his lap, her warmth and closeness breaking through his defenses. His hands instinctively rested on her waist, gripping her as though she was the only thing keeping him grounded. She gently lifted his chin with her finger, forcing him to meet her gaze.

"You're hurting," she whispered, her voice tender but firm. Arris's breathing slowed, her words chipping away at the armor he wore so tightly. He melted into her touch, his tension giving way to vulnerability.

"You've always had to be strong," she continued, her thumb lightly brushing his jaw. "You've carried the weight of your family on your shoulders, and that brought more anger and resentment toward your father. Now that he's trying to come back, all that pain you buried is bubbling to the surface."

Arris's grip on her waist tightened, his fingers digging into her as if trying to anchor himself to her calm. "That shit is so fucking hard to let go," he admitted, his voice raw and low. Vulnerability wasn't something

Arris offered easily, but with Dionne, it felt inevitable. She always found a way to crack his shell, to reach the parts of him he tried to keep hidden.

"I know," she said softly, her voice laced with understanding. "But holding onto it is only hurting you, baby. You deserve peace. You deserve to let it go."

Arris closed his eyes, her words piercing through the fog of his thoughts. He didn't respond, because deep down, he knew she was right. But he wasn't ready. Not yet. He wasn't like A'Lani; forgiveness wasn't something he could summon so easily. The pain ran too deep.

He leaned his forehead against hers, their breaths mingling as the tension between them shifted to something softer, something unspoken. Their breathing slowed in sync, and the world around them faded, leaving only the two of them tethered in this quiet moment.

"Don't leave me too," Arris murmured, his voice barely above a whisper. His words carried a weight that Dionne felt in every inch of her being. His grip on her tightened as though holding her any looser would allow her to slip away.

Dionne's eyes opened at his plea, her heart clenching at the vulnerability in his voice. The rawness of his words sent a shiver down her spine, and guilt immediately followed. This man, who had been abandoned and left to fend for himself in so many ways, was begging her to stay. But she wasn't his to keep—not fully. Her life, her choices, her obligations to Malik and Mama Glen—they all loomed like shadows over this moment.

And yet, none of that mattered right now.

"I won't," she promised softly, her voice steady as she met his gaze. She saw the relief flash in his eyes, the trust he placed in her words. His lips found hers in a deep, consuming kiss, a kiss that spoke of his need for her, his yearning, his unspoken fears.

Dionne surrendered to the kiss, letting his touch ground her, letting his presence silence the noise in her head. In this moment, it wasn't about Malik or promises or obligations. It was about the way Arris made her feel—alive, seen, and desired in a way she hadn't felt in years.

Her mind told her to stop, to end this before it went any further, but her heart had already decided. The way she *feened* for him was too strong to sever completely, no matter how much she told herself she needed to. For now, she gave in, letting the moment and her feelings consume her.

They spent the rest of the night wrapped in each other's presence, the weight of their separate worlds temporarily lifted. They laughed, shared stories, and indulged in the ease that came with being together. Dionne

Feenin'

felt the tug-of-war inside her intensify with each passing moment. On one side was the deep, undeniable connection she shared with Arris, and on the other, the promise she made to Mama Glen—a promise that kept her bound to a man she no longer loved.

She was torn, her emotions swirling like a storm, but tonight, she decided to focus on the now. She let herself enjoy the simplicity of being with Arris—the way he made her laugh until her sides ached, the way his presence felt like home, and the way he looked at her as if she were his entire world.

After their final movie ended, Arris stood, reluctantly preparing to leave. He wanted to stay, but he knew he couldn't linger. Karmen would return soon, and the last thing Dionne needed was questions she wasn't ready to answer.

"You sure you're okay?" he asked as they stood near the door. His hand cupped her cheek, his thumb gently brushing against her skin.

She nodded, offering him a small smile that didn't quite reach her eyes. "I'm fine, Arris. Thank you for tonight." Her voice was soft, almost fragile, but sincere.

He kissed her forehead, lingering for a moment before pulling away. "Call me if you need me. For anything."

"I will," she whispered, even though she knew she wouldn't. She had to distance herself, no matter how much it hurt.

Arris hesitated at the door, his eyes scanning her face as if trying to memorize every detail before finally leaving. The sound of the door closing behind him felt heavier than it should have.

Dionne cleaned up quickly, not wanting to leave a mess for Karmen. When her friend returned, Dionne gave her a quick update on Jackson and exchanged pleasantries before excusing herself to head home.

The drive back felt longer than usual, the weight of her choices pressing down on her chest. She thought about Arris, the way he made her feel alive, and then about Malik, the man she was returning to—a man she had once loved but now felt like a stranger to.

As she pulled into the driveway of the house she shared with Malik, a sinking feeling settled in her stomach. She turned off the engine and sat in the quiet, staring at the front door. Her body was here, but her heart... her heart was elsewhere, with a man she couldn't have.

Taking a deep breath, Dionne gathered herself and stepped out of the car, walking toward the house. She slipped inside, the familiar walls feeling suffocating. As she moved through the space, she knew that no matter how much she tried to ignore it, she was living a double life—torn between duty and desire, obligation and love.

***

One Week Later:

Dionne descended the staircase gracefully, her long red Tom Ford dress clinging to her curves and the high slit showcasing her toned leg with every step. The gold YSL heels clicked against the marble floors, the sound echoing softly through the house. Her long, slick ponytail swayed gently with each step, the elegant hairstyle perfectly complementing her light makeup that enhanced her natural beauty. Every detail of her look was meticulously put together to portray the image of a devoted fiancée, even though her heart felt far removed from the role she was playing.

As she reached the bottom of the stairs, Malik stood waiting for her, his red Dior suit tailored to perfection. The black tie and matching black Dior dress shoes completed his sharp look. His smile widened when he saw her, his eyes trailing over her form with admiration.

"You look stunning, Dionne," Malik said, his tone warm as he reached for her hand.

Dionne returned his gaze with a practiced smile, her heart not in the compliment. "Thank you," she replied softly, slipping her hand into his.

"Are you ready, beautiful?" he asked, holding onto her hand as though it were the most natural thing in the world.

She nodded, adjusting her gold YSL purse on her shoulder. "Yes, I'm ready."

Malik led her toward the door, his grip firm but gentle. As they stepped outside and into the night, Dionne took a deep breath, mentally preparing herself for another evening of playing the perfect fiancée. The Black-Tie Fundraiser was a prestigious event, and she knew the eyes of Houston's elite would be on them tonight. She was expected to smile, mingle, and support Malik as he basked in his accolades.

But as the driver opened the car door for them, and she slid into the luxurious interior, Dionne couldn't help but feel the weight of the facade pressing down on her. It wasn't the dress, the makeup, or the jewelry that made her feel heavy—it was the pretense. Once again, she found herself suppressing her true desires, her true feelings, and the lingering thoughts of a man who wasn't by her side tonight.

"Tonight's going to be amazing," Malik said, his tone excited as he settled into the seat next to her.

Dionne forced another smile, hoping it was convincing enough to mask the turmoil inside her. "I'm sure it will be," she said, looking out the window as the city lights blurred past, trying to focus on the night ahead instead of the thoughts that refused to leave her mind.

Feenin'

Malik's hand remained on top of Dionne's, a gesture that once would have warmed her heart, but now only added to the weight of her emotions.

Dionne gazed out of the window, her thoughts miles away. Pretending to be in a happy relationship was draining her more than she cared to admit. Sitting beside Malik, with the world believing they were the perfect couple, felt like a charade she could no longer sustain. But this was her reality—the price she had to pay to honor Mama Glen's wish.

"You look beautiful," Malik said, his voice soft as he kissed the back of her hand, his eyes full of admiration.

"Thank you," Dionne replied with a small, practiced smile. She glanced at him briefly before returning her gaze to the passing city lights. Malik had been noticeably more attentive and affectionate lately. From the gentle gestures to the romantic words, he seemed determined to rebuild what they had lost. But it was too late. Whatever part of her heart had once belonged to him was now in someone else's hands.

As Malik turned his attention to his phone, Dionne's thoughts drifted to Arris. She missed him terribly. Though she'd managed to keep their interactions limited to phone calls and texts, the pull she felt toward him was undeniable. He had been understanding of her excuses for not seeing him in person, but that didn't stop him from reminding her of how much he cared. The bouquets of tulips he sent to her office or doorstep made her smile more than she cared to admit. Each time she saw them, she was reminded of his attention to detail, his ability to know her so intimately without her having to say much at all.

Malik had questioned the flowers once or twice, but her explanation about them being from grateful clients always seemed to suffice. After all, she frequently received gifts from clients as a token of appreciation for her work. It wasn't a stretch of the imagination for Malik to believe her.

But as much as Dionne loved the moments she shared with Arris, she felt like she was living a double life. The weight of deceit was growing heavier with every passing day. She knew she couldn't keep up the facade forever, but for now, she didn't see another way. Until then, she'd continue walking the tightrope, caught between obligation and the love she wasn't sure she deserved.

They finally arrived at the venue, the grandeur of the evening reflected in every corner. The driver stepped out, opening the door for Malik and Dionne. Malik exited first, turning back to offer Dionne his hand as she gracefully stepped out of the car. The soft hum of

Ann

conversation and music greeted them as they entered the grand venue hand in hand. Under the glimmering chandeliers, Dionne's engagement ring caught the light, its brilliance impossible to ignore.

The large ballroom was a vision of sophistication, decorated elegantly in black and white, perfectly matching the theme of the fundraiser. Men were dressed sharply in tailored suits, each sporting a black tie as tradition dictated, while women dazzled in gowns of every cut and style, exuding grace and elegance. Whether attending as a supportive partner or a key figure in the event, every guest seemed to radiate an air of importance.

Malik led Dionne through the crowd with a confident stride, his hand never leaving hers. He greeted colleagues, hospital board members, and other influential figures with ease, his charming smile never faltering. He made it a point to introduce Dionne to everyone, proudly showcasing her as his fiancée.

"Isn't she stunning tonight?" Malik would say, beaming. "I can't wait for the wedding."

At first, Dionne smiled politely at his remarks, but as the night wore on, her irritation grew. The constant mentions of their wedding felt more performative than heartfelt. It was as if Malik cared more about how others perceived their relationship than the relationship itself. She nodded along, keeping her composure, but inside, she craved a moment of solitude—a break from the façade.

Malik was deep in conversation with one of his colleagues when Dionne seized her opportunity. Leaning in close, she whispered softly into his ear, "I'm going to get a drink, babe."

Malik glanced at her and smiled. "Okay, love," he said, returning his attention to his conversation. For the first time that evening, Dionne's hand was no longer in his, and she felt a brief but profound sense of relief.

She made her way to the bar, the clinking of glasses and soft hum of chatter around her providing a momentary distraction. She grabbed a glass of champagne, the cool flute grounding her as she took a sip. The bubbles fizzed on her tongue, offering a small reprieve from the tension of the evening. Standing alone by the bar, Dionne exhaled deeply, her polished exterior temporarily slipping.

This was the last place she wanted to be, but for now, she had a role to play. Even so, as she stood in the grand ballroom surrounded by strangers, her mind drifted to the man she wished was by her side—the one who made her feel alive in a way no one else could.

Dionne scanned the room, her eyes drifting over the crowd as she

Feenin'

sipped her champagne, savoring the brief moment of solitude. The lively hum of conversation and clinking glasses filled the air, but for once, she felt a small reprieve from the pressure of pretending. Her gaze lazily wandered to the entrance, and the champagne flute froze midway to her lips. Her heart plummeted as recognition hit her like a freight train.

Arris.

He strolled in confidently, a strikingly beautiful woman on his arm. The woman was older, poised, and undeniably elegant, her presence commanding as they glided through the crowd. Dionne's stomach twisted, but not with jealousy—this was panic. Her breath quickened as she instinctively leaned into the shadows, praying Arris wouldn't spot her. Not here. Not now. She glanced at the engagement ring on her finger, its sparkle mocking her turmoil.

Arris and the woman moved effortlessly through the room, exchanging pleasantries with familiar faces. Dionne's heart sank deeper when the woman stopped in front of Malik. The warm embrace and the animated smiles they shared confirmed they knew each other well. Dionne's chest tightened, but the real blow came moments later when the woman turned to introduce Arris.

No. This can't be happening.

Her mind raced as her stomach churned. She needed to get away, to disappear before the inevitable collision of her two worlds. Spying the restroom sign, she decided to make her escape, clutching her champagne flute as though it were a lifeline. She took a step, then another, but before she could make her retreat, Malik's voice stopped her in her tracks.

"Dionne!" he called, waving her over with a bright smile. Her heart stuttered, and for a moment, she considered pretending not to hear him. But the woman's warm, expectant smile and Arris's piercing gaze left her no choice.

Dionne turned slowly, her steps deliberate as she approached. Every fiber of her being screamed at her to run, but she forced a tight smile, masking the turmoil inside her. Arris's eyes never left her as she walked closer, his intense gaze drinking her in from head to toe. The admiration in his expression was unmistakable, but so was the flicker of confusion and something else—hurt.

Dionne swallowed hard, her nerves fraying as she tried to maintain her composure. She drained the rest of her champagne in one gulp, the bubbles doing little to calm the storm raging inside her. Her heels clicked rhythmically against the polished floor as she approached the group, but all she could hear was the thunderous pounding of her own heartbeat.

When she reached them, her eyes instinctively sought out Arris. His expression was unreadable, a mask of calm that only heightened her unease. Her gaze flickered to Malik, whose bright smile and enthusiasm were stark contrasts to the tension simmering between her and Arris.

"Dionne, I want you to meet someone," Malik said, his excitement oblivious to the electric undercurrent around them. Dionne forced a polite smile, though inside, she was trembling. She could feel Arris's eyes burning into her, dissecting her every move.

"This woman welcomed me with open arms when I first started at the hospital," Malik said proudly, his voice filled with admiration as he lightly rested his hand on Dionne's lower back. "Dionne, meet Nurse Angel. Nurse Angel, this is my fiancée, Dionne."

Dionne extended a polite smile, her gaze shifting to the older woman standing before her. "She was the RN when I first started, the sweetest nurse there," Malik added, his tone warm and appreciative.

Dionne's lips stretched into another artificial smile as she extended her hand toward Angel. She didn't miss the subtle tightening of Arris's jaw at Malik's use of the word fiancée, nor the flicker of anger in his eyes.

Angel, an elegant woman with a warm presence, beamed at her. "Oh my! You're so beautiful. It's such a pleasure to finally meet you, Dionne. This boy couldn't stop talking about you during our shifts together," Angel said with a soft laugh.

Dionne returned the smile, though her mind screamed at her to flee. "Thank you, Ms. Angel. It's a pleasure meeting you as well," she said, her voice steady despite the chaos within her. She shook Angel's hand, her eyes briefly darting to Arris, who stood silently, his gaze fixed on her with an intensity that made her knees feel weak.

Angel, ever observant, caught the subtle glance and gestured toward her son. "This is my son, Arris. He's just here as my plus one for the evening," she said warmly.

Dionne's stomach clenched as Arris stepped forward. His lips curved into a polite smile that didn't reach his eyes. "It's nice seeing you again, Dionne," he said, his tone smooth but tinged with a bite of sarcasm. "Like my mother said, you're a stunning woman. This man here is very lucky." His words were courteous, but the edge in his voice sent a chill down her spine.

He extended his hand, his piercing gaze locking onto hers. Dionne hesitated, the moment stretching longer than it should have, making the air around them thick with tension. Finally, she placed her hand in his, her touch tentative but firm.

Arris's hand closed around hers, holding it just a second too long.

Feenin'

His grip was warm, steady, and far more intimate than it should have been in front of Malik and Angel. His eyes never left hers, the unspoken questions swirling in their depths nearly breaking her resolve.

"It's a pleasure," Dionne murmured, her voice barely above a whisper.

"The pleasure's all mine," Arris replied, his voice low, smooth, and charged with meaning that only she could decipher.

Angel's curiosity peaked as she glanced between Arris and Dionne. "You two know each other?" she asked, her tone light but probing. Malik turned to Dionne, his brows slightly raised, clearly curious as well.

"Yes, Ma," Arris answered smoothly before Dionne could say a word. "Dionne works for Williams Luxe—the company I'm partnering with to build my real estate portfolio." His tone was calm, measured, but Dionne caught the tension simmering beneath it.

Malik nodded, his expression shifting to one of mild interest. "You didn't tell me you were partnering with investors," he said, trying to sound engaged in her work.

Dionne resisted the urge to roll her eyes, but her tone carried a subtle bite. "You never asked," she replied with a polite smile, one that masked her irritation. Arris, however, didn't miss the sharp edge in her words, even if Malik or Angel remained oblivious.

Arris tilted his head slightly, his gaze settling on Dionne with an admiration that was impossible to hide. "You have a powerful woman on your hands, Malik," he said, his voice smooth but taut, his jaw tightening with each word.

Dionne's heart pounded, the weight of the moment pressing down on her. She could feel Arris's frustration radiating off him, even as he maintained his calm demeanor. This was not the way she wanted him to learn the truth.

Malik, still clueless to the underlying tension, smiled confidently. "I know," he said, wrapping an arm around Dionne's waist and pressing a kiss to her cheek. Dionne stiffened slightly but forced herself to smile, though her heart wasn't in it. Arris's jaw flexed, his carefully controlled exterior beginning to crack as he watched the man who claimed to love her touch the woman he craved.

Angel beamed at the display, entirely unaware of the turmoil beneath the surface. "You two are just too cute," she said warmly, clasping her hands together.

Dionne's stomach churned, and she fought to maintain her composure. The situation was spiraling faster than she could control, and all she could think about was how wrong this felt.

"Well," Angel said, breaking the moment, "we're going to leave you two to mingle. I still have a few people to introduce Arris to. It was so good to see you again, Doctor. And Dionne, it was such a pleasure meeting you. I can't wait for the wedding!" Angel's excitement was genuine, her bright smile only adding to Dionne's guilt.

"Look out for your invitation in the mail," Malik said with a polite smile, as he gently placed his hand on Dionne's lower back, a gesture of reassurance and pride.

Angel returned the smile warmly. "I'll be sure to keep an eye out for it. You two make such a lovely couple," she said, glancing at Dionne and Malik before turning her attention to Arris.

"Good meeting you as well," Malik added, extending his hand to Arris with a firm grip. Arris clasped it briefly, his jaw tightening subtly as his unreadable expression gave nothing away.

"Likewise," Arris replied smoothly, his eyes flickering to Dionne for a fleeting moment, though his gaze carried an intensity she felt deep in her core.

Arris held Malik's gaze for a moment, his tone firm and deliberate. "Take good care of her," he said, the words heavy with unspoken meaning. His eyes flicked to Dionne, locking onto hers, and she saw the storm of emotions swirling within him.

Malik grinned, oblivious to the layers of the exchange. "Ain't gotta worry about that," he said confidently, pulling Dionne closer as if staking his claim.

Arris's eyes lingered on Dionne, searching for something—anything—that would tell him this wasn't what it seemed. "Good seeing you again, Dionne," he said finally, his voice soft yet charged, before turning to follow his mother.

As Arris walked away, Dionne's body felt like it might collapse under the weight of his absence. His presence had filled the air with electricity, and now that he was gone, it felt like the air had been sucked out of the room.

Malik looked down at her, his brow furrowing slightly. "You're good, Dee?" he asked, his tone laced with concern.

Dionne met his eyes and forced a smile she didn't feel. "Yeah, I'm good," she lied, her voice steady despite the chaos inside. Malik seemed satisfied with her response, but as he led her toward another group of colleagues, she knew the storm within her wasn't going to subside anytime soon.

Dionne went through the night dutifully by Malik's side. She smiled, she held his hand, and she played the role of the devoted fiancée, but her

Feenin'

eyes kept betraying her. No matter how much she tried to focus, they always found their way back to Arris, and every time, he was already looking at her. His piercing gaze ignited something deep within her—a mix of longing, guilt, and a thrill she couldn't ignore. Even from across the room, his presence was magnetic, and she felt herself unraveling under his watchful eyes.

Arris remained the epitome of composure, his poise unwavering as he moved through the event alongside his mother. But inside, he was a storm. Watching Dionne with Malik—seeing her hand in his, enduring the sight of Malik's touch—was testing his restraint. Yet, for his mother and the sake of appearances, he kept himself in check. Until he saw the opportunity.

Finally, Dionne was alone. She was standing near the bar, seemingly lost in thought as she sipped her champagne. Arris saw Malik deep in conversation with his mother and a group of colleagues, completely unaware of the moment slipping from his grasp. Arris didn't hesitate. He walked up behind Dionne, his hand sliding firmly yet gently to the small of her back. Her body instantly reacted to his touch, her breath catching as her spine straightened. He leaned down, his lips a whisper away from her ear.

"Come with me. Now." His voice was low and commanding, leaving no room for debate.

Before Dionne could respond, he was already walking away, expecting her to follow. She glanced over her shoulder, ensuring Malik was still distracted, before setting her glass down and walking in the direction Arris had gone. Her heart pounded with every step as she slipped into the private room where he was waiting. Arris closed the door behind her, the lock clicking softly into place, shutting out the world.

"Arris—" she started, her voice trembling, but he silenced her with his touch. His hands moved to her neck, firm but gentle, tilting her head up to meet his eyes. His emotions were laid bare—anger, frustration, hurt, and something deeper she couldn't quite name. Without a word, he lifted her effortlessly, setting her down on the edge of the empty table in the room. Her dress rode up slightly, and the intimacy of the moment was almost too much to bear.

"Engaged, huh?" Arris said finally, his tone deceptively calm, but the bitter edge in his chuckle betrayed him. His jaw tightened, and Dionne could see the war raging within him.

"I told you it was complicated," Dionne replied softly, her voice cracking under the weight of her guilt. She couldn't meet his eyes for long, the intensity of his stare making her chest tighten.

Arris reached for her chin, lifting her face so their eyes locked. "I don't know why I believed a woman like you was single," he said bitterly, his voice low but steady. His words cut deep, and yet the hurt in his eyes was louder than anything he said.

"I'm sorry, Arris. I didn't mean to—" she started, but before she could finish, he cut her off with his lips. The kiss was passionate, desperate, and filled with everything he couldn't put into words. Dionne froze for a moment, caught between guilt and desire, but the pull of Arris was undeniable. She gave in, her arms wrapping around his neck as she kissed him back.

Arris stepped closer, his body pressing against hers as his hands gripped her waist. The elegant slit of her dress revealed more of her toned leg as it rested against him. He didn't care that she was engaged. She was his addiction, and letting her go wasn't an option. Not now. Not ever.

Dionne's mind was racing. She had just told him she belonged to someone else, but here they were, tangled in each other, ignoring every boundary they'd drawn. She felt herself surrendering to him, knowing it would only make things harder, but unable to stop.

For Arris, there was no turning back. Dionne had become his weakness, and even if she wore another man's ring, he wasn't going to let her slip away. He didn't care how wrong it was. He needed her. And right now, he was going to make sure she knew it.

The kiss deepened, igniting a fire that neither of them could extinguish. Arris's hands moved beneath her dress, his lips trailing heated kisses along her neck, sucking gently, leaving marks on her skin. Each press of his lips sent shivers through Dionne as soft moans escaped her.

"Wait, Arris—" Dionne said softly, her hands pressing against his chest in an attempt to push him back slightly. She knew they needed to talk, to address the whirlwind of emotions about her engagement. But Arris wasn't letting up. His strength, both physical and emotional, anchored her in place, and the intensity of his need for her was too powerful to break away from, even for a moment.

"I love you, Mama," he murmured against her skin, his voice raw and vulnerable. The words made her freeze for a moment, her heart swelling with warmth even as guilt simmered beneath it.

"I know you feel it," he continued, his lips not relenting, his kisses making her body respond instinctively. His confession broke through every wall she'd built, leaving her defenseless. She did feel it—she loved him too. But how could she say those words aloud when she was still bound to another man? The truth stuck in her throat, unable to be voiced.

Feenin'

Arris didn't wait for her to respond; he didn't need to hear it. Her body told him everything he needed to know. The way she melted under his touch, the way her breath hitched with each kiss—she didn't have to say a word.

"Arris..." she breathed, her voice shaky as she tried to regain her composure, but it was slipping fast. His hands roamed higher, caressing her thighs with a tender yet possessive touch. When his fingers grazed the lace of her panties, she gasped, her body arching toward him as if to plead for more.

Without hesitation, he slid the delicate fabric to the side and pushed two fingers inside her. Dionne's legs parted instinctively, her body welcoming him. The wetness that coated his fingers was proof enough of her unspoken love.

"Oh my... fuck!" she moaned softly, her head falling back as she gave in to the pleasure.

Arris quickened his pace, his fingers skillfully exploring her while his other hand steadied her against him. Dionne gripped his shoulders for support, her nails digging into him as waves of pleasure threatened to consume her.

"Your body loves me. Your mind loves me. Every part of you, love me," he whispered confidently, his tone low and commanding. She couldn't argue. She couldn't speak. Her moans were the only response he needed.

Her body tensed, her walls tightening around his fingers as her orgasm washed over her. Dionne gasped loudly, her body trembling and collapsing against him as he continued to ride out her release.

As her breathing slowed, he leaned in and left a deliberate mark on her neck—a vivid reminder of him. "Make sure that nigga sees where your heart really is," he growled lowly, his voice rough with possessiveness. His words sent another shiver through her, leaving her breathless.

He slid his fingers out of her, licking them clean with a smirk that was both primal and triumphant. Without another word, Arris walked out of the room, leaving her alone, her body still trembling and her heart pounding in the quiet space.

Dionne touched the mark he left on her neck, not out of fear that Malik might see it, but because it was a tangible symbol of the feelings she couldn't deny. Her heart ached, torn between guilt and a deep, undeniable longing for the man who just left.

Dionne took a deep breath, steadying herself as she slipped into the restroom. Her reflection stared back at her, her cheeks flushed, her lips slightly swollen, and the vivid hickey on her neck screaming of her betrayal. Shaking her head, she walked into the stall quickly reached under her dress, sliding off her damp panties and stuffing them into her purse. She couldn't risk staying any longer, not with Malik nearby and Arris still prowling like a predator who had already claimed his prey.

Pulling out her phone, Dionne called the driver, her voice calm despite the storm raging within her. "Please pull around to the entrance. I need to leave early."

Exiting the restroom, she approached Malik, who was still engaged in a lively conversation with Angel and a few others. The guilt weighed heavily on her chest, but she pushed it aside, leaning close to him.

"Malik, I'm not feeling well. I'm going to head home," she said softly, her voice steady, though every fiber of her being screamed to run.

Malik looked at her with concern but didn't press further. "Okay, babe. Get some rest. I'll see you at home," he said, placing a quick kiss on her cheek.

Dionne forced a weak smile before turning away, her heels clicking against the marble floor as she made her exit. Arris stood in the distance, leaning casually against a pillar, his eyes following her every move. He didn't bother hiding his smirk, knowing full well he was the reason she was leaving. The sight of her walking away only fueled his determination.

Arris didn't care about Malik, her engagement, or the ring on her finger. He knew exactly why she was pulling away, but that only made his desire for her stronger. She could put up walls, make excuses, and even wear another man's name, but it wouldn't stop him.

The fire between them was too strong, and no ring or obligation could extinguish it. Arris wasn't letting go of Dionne—not now, not ever.

Chapter 11

Arris stepped out of his Jeep, the early morning sun highlighting his dark skin as he made his way into Mario's gym. He was meeting Mario and True for a workout, though by the looks of it, he was running late. Inside, the familiar scent of iron and sweat filled the air as he greeted Erin at the front desk with a quick nod before heading to the weights area. His friends were already there, mid-lift, throwing him questioning looks as he approached.

"Damn, nigga. Where you been lately?" Mario asked, setting down his dumbbells and eyeing Arris with curiosity.

Arris chuckled, grabbing his own set of weights. "Working," he replied casually, shrugging off the question.

True smirked, leaning against the bench press. "Nigga, please. Yo ass been doing more than working," he said, his tone dripping with amusement as he studied Arris' calm demeanor.

Arris shook his head, letting out a low laugh. "I don't know what you're talking about, bruh," he said, focusing on his set.

True wasn't letting it go. "I bet Ms. Dionne could refresh your memory," he quipped, the grin on his face widening.

Arris chuckled again, this time more to keep his composure. "Once again, I don't know what you're talking about," he replied, his tone smooth, but Mario wasn't about to let it slide.

"Wait a minute—Karmen's friend Dionne?" Mario asked, his brows lifting in surprise. "Nigga, you messing with her? Karmen told me she's engaged."

The mention of Dionne's engagement made Arris' jaw tighten, but he masked the reaction with ease, grabbing a heavier set of weights. "No, nigga, I'm not messing with her," he said evenly. "We just work together, and this nigga here,"—he gestured toward True—"is fishing for shit."

True crossed his arms, clearly not buying it. "Fishing? Nah. Engaged or not, I saw the way y'all couldn't leave each other's side at your investor party. Plus, yo ass been MIA ever since. Someone's got your time, and I'll bet $500 it's her."

Arris smirked, his expression giving nothing away. "You think you know everything, huh?" he said, setting his weights down with controlled force.

Mario shook his head, his curiosity still piqued. "For real though, if it is her, that's a dangerous game, bruh. Karmen said her fiancé's some top doctor. The type to sue you for just looking at her wrong."

Arris met his gaze, his expression turning cold. "I'm not worried about no doctor-ass nigga," he said, his voice steady. "And for the last time, we're just working together."

True's grin didn't falter. "Aight, bet. But if I catch you slipping, I'm running your pockets for that $500."

Arris didn't respond, his focus already back on his workout. His friends' teasing wasn't going to pull the truth out of him. Whatever was happening between him and Dionne was complicated—messy—but it wasn't something he was ready to share.

After the fundraiser, Dionne tried her best to keep her distance from him. Now that her engagement to Malik was out in the open, she felt the weight of guilt pressing down on her. The tension from that night lingered, and she thought keeping her distance was the only way to protect them both from further complications. But Arris wasn't having it.

Every time she tried to dodge his calls or avoid being in his presence, he found a way to remind her exactly where they stood in his eyes. He didn't care about Malik, their engagement, or any of the obstacles between them. Arris made it clear—Dionne belonged to him.

"You're mine," he'd told her, his voice low but filled with undeniable conviction during one of their last conversations. "I don't give a damn about that ring or that man. You feel it just as much as I do."

Dionne's resolve wavered every time she heard those words. The truth was, she did feel it. The fire between them, the magnetic pull she couldn't resist, the way her heart raced whenever he was near—it all told her that Arris wasn't someone she could simply walk away from. Yet, every time she looked at the diamond ring on her finger, she was reminded of the promises she'd made to Mama Glen, promises that were suffocating her.

But Arris? He wasn't bound by those promises. He wasn't willing to let her slip away because of obligations she didn't even believe in anymore. His actions, his words, and his relentless pursuit of her made

Feenin'

one thing abundantly clear: no matter how much distance Dionne tried to create, Arris was determined to close it.

Explaining those feelings to his friends wasn't an option. He knew they'd think he was crazy for pursuing a woman who was already engaged, no matter how strong his connection with Dionne was. They wouldn't understand that to him, it wasn't just lust or infatuation—it was deeper than that. She was his.

Instead of talking about it, he stayed silent, letting his frustration and emotions fuel him as he focused on his workout. The clanking of weights and the burn in his muscles were the only distractions he could count on to keep his mind off her, even if just for a little while.

But as much as he tried to stay focused, his mind wandered to Dionne. Her touch, her voice, her presence—it was all-consuming. He wasn't sure where things would go from here, but one thing was certain: she wasn't just another woman to him. And that thought alone made him grip the weights tighter.

"Well, then you can go ahead and send me that $500, because ain't shit going on with me and Dionne," Arris said, standing up after finishing his set, his tone dismissive yet calm. "Enough about me anyway. You two been deep in Karmen and London, so let's talk about that."

Both True and Mario laughed, knowing Arris had a point. "Man, I think I'm in love," Mario admitted with a sheepish smile, making Arris smirk.

"Here go his in-love-ass," True joked, shaking his head, which made them all laugh.

"Man, shut yo Nipsey Hussle-looking ass up," Mario shot back, cracking up as he did. The joke hit harder because True was practically a twin of Nipsey Hussle, a fact that had been an ongoing joke for years. True, however, always took it as a compliment since Nipsey was one of his favorite rappers.

"And I know you ain't talking," Mario continued, pointing at True. "Every time I call yo ass, you're over at London's place."

Arris turned his attention to True, his curiosity piqued. "Shi, that's my baby," True said confidently, catching Arris off guard.

"Okay," Arris said, raising his brows in disbelief. "I can understand Mario's simp ass falling in love, but London got you out the game too?!"

True laughed, nodding his head. "Shi, it's fucking wild, but yeah. London got my ass," he admitted, a grin spreading across his face.

Arris shook his head, surprised but genuinely happy for his friend. "That's good. You two deserve love," he said sincerely.

"Nigga, you do too," Mario said, his tone turning serious as he

Ann

looked at Arris. "I know we give you a hard time when it comes to women, but you deserve that shit the same as us, if not more."

True nodded in agreement, adding, "Facts. You're always the one holding it down for everybody else. It's time you got something real for yourself."

Arris paused for a moment, their words sinking in. His mind instantly drifted to Dionne, and before he could stop himself, a small smile spread across his face. "Shi, I think I already found my true love," he admitted, the words slipping out with ease.

True and Mario froze, their expressions a mix of shock and disbelief. Arris wasn't the type to talk about love, let alone confess something like that. "Wait, hold the fuck up," True said, pointing at him. "You serious right now?"

"Dead serious," Arris said, his tone calm but firm, his smile widening at the thought of Dionne.

Mario whistled, shaking his head. "Damn, nigga. Who would've thought? Arris in love."

Arris and love had never been in the same sentence. His focus had always been on his career, his family, and money. Love was the last thing on his list, so hearing him admit he'd found it was both shocking and exciting for Mario and True.

"Nigga, who?" Mario asked, his voice too loud, drawing a few curious glances from others in the gym.

"Why the fuck are you yelling?" Arris replied with a chuckle, shaking his head. "And I'm not saying who, because that ain't y'all fucking business."

Mario smacked his lips in frustration. "I'm telling you, Mario, it's that Dionne woman," True said confidently, ignoring Arris's warning. "Ever since she came into this nigga's life, he been distant, glowing, and shit."

Arris shot True a glare, masking his true feelings. "You didn't hear this nigga say she's engaged?" he replied, his fist unconsciously clenching at the words. He had to keep up the front. Telling his friends he was in love with a woman who was engaged to another man wasn't an option.

But deep down, Arris knew the truth. Dionne's love wasn't with Malik. He'd seen it at the fundraiser and felt it every time they were together. Her body, her touch, her eyes—they all told him where her heart truly belonged. Still, he knew his boys wouldn't understand the situation.

"Then who is it, if it ain't her?" True pressed, determined to get an

Feenin'

answer.

Arris smirked, trying to deflect. "Nigga, you worse than A'Lani's nosy ass. I'm not telling you, so let it go."

True smacked his lips in defeat, but the curiosity in his eyes didn't wane. They all got back to working out, but Dionne's face remained in Arris's mind. As he sat between sets, he pulled out his phone and sent her a quick text.

Arris: Just thinking about you. Hope your day's going good, Mama.

Satisfied, he tucked his phone away and focused back on his workout. Once they were finished, Arris dapped up his friends and left the gym. He climbed into his Jeep, the memory of Dionne lingering in his mind as he drove home.

When he got back to his place, he showered and dressed for work, his thoughts never straying far from the woman who had unexpectedly become his everything.

***

Dionne stepped out of her Urus, her heels clicking softly against the pavement as she approached Mama Glen's porch. It had been a while since her last visit, and with a rare day off, she decided to stop by. As she reached the door, she pulled out the key Mama Glen had given her and let herself in.

"Ma! It's Dionne," she called out, her voice carrying through the cozy house.

"In the living room, sweetie," Mama Glen's gentle voice responded.

Dionne followed the sound, entering the living room to find Mama Glen in her favorite reclining chair, a book resting in her lap. Dionne smiled at the sight of her. Today was one of the good days, and seeing Mama Glen looking brighter warmed her heart.

"Hey, Mama Glen," Dionne greeted, leaning down to hug her. Mama Glen's arms wrapped around her tightly, the embrace filled with love and familiarity.

"Hey, my baby," Mama Glen replied softly, her voice carrying a warmth that soothed Dionne's spirit. As she pulled away, Dionne sat on the couch nearby, taking in the peaceful atmosphere that always surrounded this home.

"How are you feeling, Mama?" Dionne asked, her smile gentle and sincere.

"Taking it one day at a time," Mama Glen said with a nod, her own smile steady. "But today's a good day. I feel better."

"That's good," Dionne said, her smile widening, happy to see her doing well.

"And how are you, sweetie?" Mama Glen asked, her tone curious. "I see Demetrius's in town. He came by the other day to visit me. That boy brought his son, and oh, DJ is just the cutest thing! So smart, too."

Dionne couldn't help but smile, the thought of her brother and nephew filling her with joy. "Yes, DJ's the best. I'm actually going to pick him up after I leave here. If things work out, Demetrius's planning to move to Houston for good."

Mama Glen's face lit up at the news. "That's wonderful! You and Demetrius have always been so close. Having him back here will be good for you."

"It really will," Dionne agreed, her heart full at the thought of family being closer. Moments like this reminded her how much she valued Mama Glen's wisdom and the comfort of being in her presence.

They continued chatting about everything under the sun, their laughter filling the cozy living room as they poked fun at the dramatic twists of the soap opera Mama Glen had been watching. The conversation drifted seamlessly, even touching on lighthearted memories of Dionne and Malik's earlier years together. But soon, the mood shifted as Mama Glen's eyes softened with concern, her focus fully on Dionne.

"Dionne, are you sure you're okay?" Mama Glen asked, her voice gentle but probing.

Dionne's gaze flickered from the TV to her, a curious look crossing her face. "I'm fine, Mama," she replied, slipping on the well-practiced smile she had mastered over the years. But Mama Glen's piercing gaze told her the façade wasn't working.

"I know you and Malik aren't happy," Mama Glen said plainly, her words hitting Dionne like a jolt.

Dionne froze, her body stiffening at the statement. "We're good, Mama Glen. I promise," she said quickly, trying her best to sound convincing. The last thing she wanted was to burden Mama Glen with the truth of her struggles. This was supposed to be a safe space, not a source of stress for the woman she loved.

"You don't have to lie to me, baby," Mama Glen said softly, her eyes filled with understanding. "Malik told me how distant you two have been lately."

Dionne's stomach churned, and before she could stop herself, her eyes rolled in frustration. Of course, Malik went to his mother about their problems instead of addressing them with her directly. He always did that, leaving her blindsided.

"We're working on it," Dionne said, her voice calmer this time as she

Feenin'

masked her irritation. She didn't want to add to Mama Glen's worries.

"I know he told me that too," Mama Glen admitted, her tone tinged with sadness. "But, baby, he's scared."

Dionne's brow furrowed in confusion. "Scared?" she repeated, the word sounding foreign in the context of Malik. What was there for him to be scared of?

Mama Glen sighed, leaning back in her chair as she gathered her thoughts. "He thinks he's losing you, Dionne. He knows he messed up, and he's trying to make it right, but he doesn't feel worthy of you anymore. He's afraid you'll leave him."

Dionne's heart twisted at Mama Glen's words, but not for the reasons she might have expected. Well, he's not wrong, she thought bitterly, though she kept the emotion hidden beneath a soft expression. Instead of voicing the truth, she leaned into the role she'd been playing for months.

"I can promise you, Mama Glen, me and Malik are good," Dionne said, her voice steady as she forced the words out. "Yes, things got a little rocky and distant, but we're both putting in the effort to get things back to how they used to be."

"That's good, baby. We also talked about premarital counseling," Mama Glen said, her tone casual, but the statement hit Dionne like a ton of bricks. She choked on air, her eyes widening in surprise.

"Premarital counseling?" Dionne repeated, needing clarification to make sure she heard correctly.

"Yes," Mama Glen confirmed with a warm smile. "I suggested that you two go to premarital counseling before getting married. That way, you can work out any issues and start your marriage on solid ground."

Dionne felt her blood boiling beneath the surface, but she kept her expression neutral. Premarital counseling? she thought. How's that supposed to fix a relationship where one person doesn't even want to be there?

Mama Glen continued, unaware of Dionne's internal storm. "The doctor says I have about another year or so," she said softly, her smile never fading. "So, I told Malik it might be best to push the wedding to the beginning of next year—or at least until you two are fully happy again after counseling."

Dionne's fists clenched in her lap as she tried to channel her frustration silently. The thought of sitting through counseling sessions with Malik, pretending to salvage a love she no longer felt, made her stomach churn. No amount of therapy could reignite what was already extinguished.

"Malik mentioned you two were already looking into it," Mama Glen added cheerfully. "He said your first session is coming up soon."

Dionne's jaw tightened. She hadn't even heard about counseling, let alone agreed to an appointment. This man has crossed the line, she thought. Pretending for Mama Glen's sake was one thing, but Malik setting up counseling sessions without her knowledge was another. She swallowed the growing lump in her throat and forced a smile.

"Did you not know about it?" Mama Glen asked gently, noticing the flicker of confusion on Dionne's face.

Dionne quickly shook her head, masking her frustration. "Oh, yes, I just forgot," she said smoothly, her voice steady. "We've been doing so well that I didn't think counseling was still necessary. But I guess we'll follow through and push back the wedding, as you suggested."

Mama Glen smiled, clearly relieved and pleased by Dionne's response. "It will still be a winter wedding," she added excitedly. "Since February 14th is still winter."

Dionne blinked, confused. "Valentine's Day?" she asked, her voice reflecting her surprise.

"Yes," Mama Glen replied, her eyes gleaming with enthusiasm. "Malik came up with the date. Isn't it perfect? The day of love!"

Dionne felt the anger bubbling up again, but she kept it buried beneath her practiced smile. She mirrored Mama Glen's joy as best as she could. "Yes, it's perfect," she said, her voice calm despite the storm raging inside her.

Perfect for who? she thought bitterly. Dionne made a mental note to have a very serious conversation with Malik later. He might think he was controlling the narrative, but she wasn't about to let him keep blindsiding her like this. The moment she saw him, she planned to set the record straight—and she had plenty to say.

Dionne left Mama Glen's house, her thoughts racing as frustration simmered beneath the surface. The premarital counseling, the rescheduled wedding date, the lies Malik fed to his mother—it all weighed heavily on her, her anger bubbling just below her calm exterior. As she drove to her parents' house to pick up DJ, her phone buzzed, snapping her out of her spiraling thoughts.

Glancing at the screen, a small smile crept onto her lips when she saw Arris's name lighting up the FaceTime notification. Without hesitation, she answered, and his image filled her screen. He sat in his office, his sharp suit perfectly tailored to his frame. The sight of him brought an instant calm, his presence like a balm for her frayed nerves.

"Hey, mama," he greeted, his deep, smooth voice sending a shiver down her spine and softening the edges of her frustration.

Feenin'

"Hey, Arris," she replied, her tone warm and tinged with a blush she couldn't hide. Her eyes flicked between the road and his face, the sight of him pulling her into a better mood.

"Where your fine ass headed?" he asked, leaning back in his chair, his smirk teasing and confident.

"To pick up my nephew. We're spending the day together," she answered, her smile growing as she saw him mirror it.

"You get the gift I sent you?" he asked, his tone laced with curiosity. Dionne's smile widened as she glanced down at her wrist, the diamond Cartier bracelet catching the sunlight. He'd sent it along with a bouquet of tulips the day before—a sweet gesture to show her how much he missed and loved her. She hadn't taken it off since.

"Yes, baby, and I love it," she said softly, holding up her wrist to show it off. "But you shouldn't have spent so much on me."

He chuckled, dismissing her scolding. "Shi, that ain't nothing. I wanted to buy you a car, but I didn't want that nigga questioning shit," he said, his jaw tightening slightly as his thoughts clearly turned to Malik.

Dionne felt the tension creep in and quickly changed the subject. "How's work going?" she asked, her tone light.

"It's good. Got a meeting in a few, but I wanted to check on you," he replied, going along with her shift in conversation.

They continued to chat, their conversation flowing effortlessly, until she pulled up to her parents' house. Arris's meeting was about to start, and they said their goodbyes, the connection lingering even after the call ended. Arris's voice echoing in her mind like a soothing melody. Despite the chaos of her life, his presence—even through a phone screen—always managed to calm her. She glanced down at the diamond Cartier bracelet on her wrist as she got out of the car, its sparkle catching the sunlight. The thought of him sending such a thoughtful gift filled her heart, though it also came with a twinge of guilt. As she stepped out of the car, ready to spend time with DJ, the thought of Arris stayed with her, his voice echoing in her mind and easing the storm Malik had stirred.

She walked up the driveway to her parent's house, the familiar sounds of laughter and conversation spilling through the open windows. Before she could knock, the door opened to reveal DJ, her five-year-old nephew, with a big grin on his face.

"Auntie Dionne!" he shouted, his excitement contagious as he launched himself into her arms.

"Hey, my little man!" she laughed, scooping him up and hugging him tightly. The warmth of his hug was exactly what she needed to distract her from her frustrations.

Her mother appeared in the doorway, smiling at the scene. "There she is. You're just in time—DJ has been bouncing off the walls waiting for you."

"Good thing I'm here to save the day then," Dionne teased, setting DJ down before greeting her mother with a hug.

"You staying for lunch?" Danita asked, motioning toward the kitchen where the smell of baked chicken and cornbread wafted through the air.

"I wish I could, but I'm taking DJ out for the day," Dionne said, glancing at her nephew, who was already grabbing his shoes and excitedly talking about their plans. "We're having an auntie-nephew day."

"Well, don't keep him out too late," her mother said, giving her a knowing look. "You know how he gets when he's overtired."

"Yes, ma'am," Dionne replied with a playful salute before taking DJ's hand and leading him to her car.

As they drove off, DJ chatted nonstop about everything he wanted to do, from getting ice cream to going to the park. Dionne smiled, his energy lifting her spirits. For the first time all day, her focus wasn't on Malik, Arris, or the complicated web of her life—it was on DJ and the pure joy he brought to her world.

***

Arris stepped out of his car, the silver moonlight casting an eerie glow across the driveway. His gaze fell on an unfamiliar car parked there, its shiny frame glinting under the night sky. A flicker of curiosity crossed his face, but he quickly dismissed it. Probably one of his mother's friends. She always had someone stopping by.

Gripping his keys, he unlocked the front door and stepped inside, the faint hum of the TV and the soft glow of lights giving the home a lived-in feel. "Ma?!" he called out, his voice sharp but controlled, knowing she hated him yelling in her house. He glanced around the quiet front room, unease prickling at the edges of his mind.

The house was still, too still. He stepped through the familiar space, his shoes barely making a sound against the hardwood floors. A glance out the back window showed her garden empty, the moonlight dancing on the dew-covered leaves. She wasn't there either—a strange absence in her cherished sanctuary.

Frowning, Arris turned back toward the house. Just as he opened his mouth to call her name again, movement caught his eye. His body tensed. A man, shirtless and wearing basketball shorts, stood casually in the kitchen like he belonged there. The sight made Arris's blood run cold.

Feenin'

"What the fuck?" he growled, his steps quick and purposeful as he closed the distance between them. Before the man could even register what was happening, Arris grabbed him by the shoulder and swung, his fist connecting hard with the stranger's jaw. The crack of bone meeting bone echoed through the house.

The man staggered back, clutching his face, but Arris didn't stop. He drew his fist back for another strike, rage blinding him, but a familiar voice cut through the haze.

"Arris! Stop!"

He froze mid-swing, his chest heaving. The man straightened, blood trickling from his split lip. It wasn't just anyone. It was Calvin—his father. His father, standing shirtless in his mother's kitchen.

"Calvin?" Arris blinked, his mind struggling to piece together the scene in front of him.

Calvin chuckled, the sound grating against Arris's nerves as he wiped the blood from his mouth. "Damn, son. You've got one hell of a left hook." His tone was light, amused, as if this was some kind of joke.

Before Arris could respond, the sound of hurried footsteps on the stairs made him turn. Angel appeared, her silk robe clinging to her frame, her long hair a wild mess that screamed of what had just taken place.

"What the hell is going on?" her voice cracked, slicing through the tension.

Arris's eyes darted between the two of them—his father's smug grin, his mother's guilt-ridden face. It all clicked at once. The air left his lungs in a sharp exhale, replaced by a fire that burned hot in his chest.

"You two... fucking?" he spat, the words tumbling out before he could stop them. His voice was raw, his confusion and fury spilling out unchecked. He didn't care where he was or who he was talking to. His mother and his father. Together. In her house.

Angel's face twisted in shame, but she didn't speak. Calvin leaned casually against the counter, as if this were normal, as if it shouldn't feel like the world had just tipped upside down.

Before they could respond, Arris spun on his heel, heading for the door. He needed air—space—anything to escape the suffocating weight of what he'd just seen. But Angel rushed after him, grabbing his arm before he could leave.

"Arris, wait!" Angel yelled, grabbing his arm, but he yanked away aggressively, his rage blinding him. His chest heaved as he turned back to face them, disbelief and fury swirling in his red-rimmed eyes.

"So this is why you wanted me and A'Lani to amend shit with his ass? So you two could fuck openly?" he spat, his voice cutting through the room like a blade.

Angel froze, guilt plastered across her face, her silence louder than any words. Calvin stepped forward, his tone trying to mimic authority. "You better watch your tone when you're speaking to your mother."

Arris's head snapped toward him, his body trembling with fury. "What the fuck did you just say to me?" His voice was low, dangerous, as he took a step closer.

Angel quickly moved between them, her hands pressing lightly against Arris's chest to hold him back. "Arris, please, just let me explain," she begged, her voice cracking under the weight of the moment. This wasn't how she had planned to tell him—any of this.

"There ain't shit to explain, Ma," he barked, his fists clenching at his sides, veins bulging against his dark skin. His eyes stayed locked on Calvin, burning with betrayal. "You fucking with this nigga again?"

Calvin stood there in his basketball shorts, unapologetically in their mother's kitchen as if he owned the place, and Angel let him. It wasn't just anger bubbling inside Arris—it was heartbreak. The man who had abandoned their family, who had left his sister sobbing from the damage he'd caused, was standing there without a hint of remorse.

Angel tried to reach for him again, her voice soft, desperate. "It's more complicated than that, sweetie—"

"Complicated?" Arris's voice rose, sharp and cutting. He backed away from her touch like it burned. "What's complicated is you being back with the man who left us, Ma. A'Lani just got done crying to this nigga's face about how bad he hurt her, and you turn around and fuck him?"

Angel's lips parted, but no words came out. Her guilt hung heavy in the air.

"You got one more time, son, disrespecting your mother," Calvin said, stepping closer now, his tone calm but firm.

Arris's head snapped to him, and he took a step forward, his rage boiling over. "Or what, nigga?" His voice was venomous, each word dripping with hatred. "I owe you an ass-whooping anyway."

Calvin squared his shoulders, and Arris mirrored him, their eyes locked, the tension in the room crackling like electricity. Only Angel stood between them now, her hands outstretched, pleading.

"Arris, stop! Please!" she cried, her voice frantic, but neither man looked at her.

The room was thick with the weight of years of abandonment, betrayal, and pain, and Arris could feel his control slipping. If he stayed, he knew this wouldn't end without blood.

Feenin'

"Arris... just go. Please." Angel's voice cracked, her words trembling with desperation.

Arris froze, his rage faltering for a moment as her plea sank in. "Go?" he asked, his voice shifting to a tone of hurt that cut deeper than his anger. "You kicking me out... for this nigga?" His eyes burned with betrayal, the fire in them refusing to dim even as his tone softened.

Angel stepped closer, her hands trembling as she reached for him. "You need to calm down, baby. You don't listen to anyone when you're like this," she said, her voice soft but firm, her hands lightly pushing him back, creating more space between him and Calvin.

But Calvin couldn't stay quiet. "You need to listen to your mother," he said, his voice laced with smugness, the slight smirk on his face enough to make Arris see red.

In an instant, Arris lunged at him, his body moving faster than his mind. "You think this shit is a game?!" he growled, his voice full of venom.

Angel grabbed him by his shirt with all her strength, her desperate pull causing the fabric to tear with a loud rip. "Stop it, Arris!" she cried, her voice strained, tears pooling in her eyes as she fought to hold him back.

"That busted-ass lip of yours ain't the only thing I'm gonna do damage to, my nigga!" Arris barked, his muscles taut, his eyes locked on Calvin like a predator ready to pounce.

But Calvin didn't flinch, his smirk still lingering, as if he enjoyed provoking the storm brewing in Arris.

"ARRIS, GO!" Angel screamed, her voice breaking as she continued to pull him back with every ounce of strength she had. "PLEASE!"

Arris finally stopped resisting, letting her pull him away, but not because he wanted to. He knew that if he stayed a second longer, he wouldn't just hurt Calvin—he'd kill him. His chest heaved, his fists clenched so tightly his knuckles turned white, but he let her guide him back.

"I can't believe this shit, bruh," Arris muttered, his voice filled with disbelief and raw pain. His burning gaze shifted to his mother, her tear-streaked face a mirror of guilt and regret.

"I'm sorry—" she started, her voice trembling.

"Save it, Ma," Arris cut her off, his tone sharp and cold. "Don't come calling me to save you when this nigga leaves and breaks your heart again."

He didn't wait for a response. He turned and stormed out of the house, slamming the door so hard the walls seemed to shake, leaving

Ann

behind the shattered pieces of his trust and the silence of his mother's tears.

Arris slammed the car door shut and tore down the street, the roar of his engine echoing through the quiet night. The speedometer climbed higher with every second, the rush of the wind doing nothing to cool the fire burning in his chest. His heart pounded in sync with his rage, his breaths ragged as tears stung his eyes. He blinked furiously, refusing to let them fall, but the weight of betrayal pressed down on him, suffocating and unrelenting.

His mind raced, consumed by the image of his mother standing there, tears in her eyes but still defending the man who had torn their family apart. Out of everyone in the world, she had chosen him. The thought churned in his gut, a mix of anger and heartbreak threatening to spill over. He clenched the wheel tighter, his knuckles whitening, desperate for something—anything—to release the storm building inside him.

He couldn't go home. He couldn't go anywhere familiar, not like this. The only person he needed right now was her.

Without thinking, he yanked the steering wheel, his tires screeching as he made a sharp U-turn and sped toward Dionne's house. It didn't matter that it was late, that the clock was creeping closer to midnight. He needed her. To see her. To touch her. To feel something other than the rage consuming him whole.

As he pulled up in front of her house, the sight of her car in the driveway sent a wave of relief through him. He cut the engine, pulling his phone out with trembling hands, and hit her number.

The line rang twice before her sleepy voice answered, soft and groggy. "Arris?"

"Mama..." His voice cracked, the weight of his emotions bleeding into the word. He took a shaky breath, trying to steady himself. "I need you. Come outside, please."

There was a pause, followed by the faint sound of shuffling. "Okay, baby. I'm coming," she said, her voice laced with concern despite her grogginess.

Minutes felt like hours as he sat there, the silence of the night pressing against him. Then the front door opened, and there she was. Dionne stepped outside, her figure illuminated by the soft glow of the porch light. She wore a large T-shirt and sweats, her bonnet still snug on her head, and yet the sight of her was like a balm to his frayed nerves.

Arris let out a breath he didn't realize he'd been holding, his fists unclenching as the tension in his body began to ease. She walked toward the car, her face etched with worry, and for the first time all night, the

Feenin'

raging storm inside him began to quiet.

Dionne hurried toward him, her heart pounding with urgency. The way he sounded on the phone had shaken her. She hadn't seen Arris in days, and she missed him more than she was willing to admit. But Malik was upstairs asleep, and she knew Arris couldn't stay.

"Arris, it's late. What are you doing here?" she asked, her voice tinged with worry and a hint of panic.

Arris's jaw tightened, his eyes narrowing as he took a step closer. "What? That nigga upstairs or something?" he snapped, his tone sharp and accusing. The anger radiating off him was thick, his body tense as if he were holding himself together by a thread.

Dionne stopped in her tracks, her eyes searching his face. Under the glow of the driveway lights, she saw the redness in his eyes, the tear in his shirt, the weight of something heavy pressing down on him.

"Baby, are you okay?" she asked softly, the concern in her voice cutting through the tension. She could see it—how hard he was trying to mask his emotions, to bury whatever was tearing him apart. But he wasn't okay. He was furious, and the way he was looking at her made her chest tighten.

He needed her. She could feel it. But she also knew what his presence here meant. Malik. Her engagement. The life she was supposed to be building with someone else.

Arris's fists clenched at his sides, and the thought of Malik upstairs only stoked the fire inside him. He had come here to find solace, but the reminder of what he couldn't have made his blood boil. If he didn't leave now, he wasn't sure he could stop himself from doing something reckless.

"I'm good," he said sternly, stepping back from her touch, his voice cold and distant.

"Arris…" Dionne called after him, her voice trembling. She didn't want him to leave like this. The worry in her chest was overwhelming, tugging at her resolve even with Malik asleep in her bed.

Arris shook his head, his eyes dark and filled with something she couldn't quite place. "Go back inside, Mama. Be with your fiancé." The word dripped with bitterness, the last syllable like a dagger to both their hearts.

Without waiting for her to respond, he turned and climbed back into his car. Dionne stared after him, her heart aching in a way she couldn't put into words. She wanted to run after him, to tell him she cared, to hold him and ease whatever storm he was battling. But she couldn't. She was bound to someone else, trapped in an obligation that felt more like a prison with every passing day.

Arris stayed parked, watching as Dionne stood in the driveway, her expression etched with confusion and worry. He waited, his eyes following her every movement, until she turned and disappeared back into the house like he told her to. Only when the door shut behind her did he pull off, the engine rumbling as he drove away into the quiet night.

Her presence had calmed him, if only for a fleeting moment. But the thought of her fiancé asleep upstairs, unaware of the moment they had just shared, twisted the knife deeper. His grip on the steering wheel tightened, and frustration boiled over. He slammed his palm against the wheel, the sharp sound cutting through the stillness of the car.

"Fuck!" he growled, his chest heaving as anger consumed him. His mother, Calvin, Dionne—all of it swirled together, a perfect storm of betrayal, hurt, and rage. He felt like he was drowning, with no one to reach for, no way to come up for air.

By the time he pulled into his driveway and stepped into the house, his emotions were a tangled mess. The quiet space offered no comfort, only amplifying the thoughts racing in his head. He sank onto the couch, his elbows on his knees, his hands dragging down his face.

The idea of calling one of his old flings flickered in his mind—a quick, meaningless distraction to burn off the fury coursing through him. But the thought barely formed before it was crushed under the weight of his guilt. Even though Dionne wasn't fully his, even though she was engaged to another man, the idea of betraying her, of sharing himself with someone else, felt wrong. She wasn't just another woman to him. She was the only one who could quiet the chaos inside of him, and no one else could ever come close.

With a heavy sigh, Arris pushed himself off the couch and headed for the bathroom. The icy spray of the shower hit his skin, shocking his senses and cooling the inferno raging inside him. He stayed under the water until his muscles relaxed, his fists unclenching at last.

Later, on his private balcony, he rolled a blunt with practiced ease, the rhythmic motion grounding him. The first drag hit his lungs like a wave of calm, the tension in his body slowly ebbing away as the smoke curled into the night sky. For the first time that night, the storm inside him began to settle.

But even in his haze, his thoughts drifted back to her. Dionne. The woman who held his heart in her hands, even if she didn't know it. The one person who could both calm him and drive him insane. The blunt dulled the edges of his anger, but it couldn't erase the image of her standing in that driveway, torn between him and the life she was bound

Feenin'

to.

As the ember of the blunt burned low, Arris leaned back in his chair, staring out into the dark, his thoughts heavy. No matter how much he tried to push her from his mind, she lingered there, a constant ache that refused to fade.

***

Dionne settled DJ into his car seat, tightening the straps before climbing into the driver's seat. She wasn't ready to send him back to his dad just yet. Today was going to be another auntie-nephew day, but this time, Karmen and Mia were tagging along. Karmen had offered to babysit Mia while Mario was at work, since he had no one else to watch her.

As she adjusted her seatbelt, Dionne's eyes drifted to her phone resting in the cupholder. The unanswered message she had sent to Arris stared back at her, a small weight pressing down on her chest. She'd reached out to check on him after last night when he showed up at her house, filled with rage and pain. Watching him leave, so torn and distraught, while she stood helpless because Malik was there, made guilt settle heavily in her chest. Once again, her loveless engagement had come between her and the love she truly felt for Arris.

Dionne sighed, locking her phone and shaking off the thoughts. She couldn't focus on that right now—not with DJ in the car, not with today planned for fun.

"Auntie, are we going bowling?" DJ's voice piped up from the backseat, snapping her out of her spiraling thoughts.

"Yes, sweetie. We're going to meet Aunt Karmen and Mia there," she said, masking her emotions with a warm smile as she glanced back at him in the rearview mirror.

"Who's Mia?" DJ asked, his tone curious.

Dionne chuckled softly. "You'll see once we get there."

"Okay," he said with a pause, his little voice turning playful and charming. "Is she cute?"

Dionne burst into laughter, her nephew's innocent charisma catching her off guard. "What do you know about a girl being cute?" she asked, amused by the five-year-old's question.

DJ grinned, his confidence shining through. "My daddy said I should always have a cute girl on my arm. Like you and Mommy."

Dionne's heart softened, a wide smile spreading across her face. "Your daddy's not wrong—you should. But she also has to be nice," she added with a wink through the mirror.

DJ nodded sagely, as if filing away her advice for the future. "She's gotta be nice. Got it."

Dionne couldn't help but laugh again, his sweetness and charm lifting her mood as they pulled out of the driveway. For a brief moment, the weight of her worries eased, replaced by the simple joy of her nephew's presence.

The drive to the bowling alley was filled with laughter, off-key singing, and exaggerated dance moves. Dionne couldn't help but smile at DJ's energy, his little voice belting out lyrics with unshakable confidence. Their impromptu karaoke session lifted her spirits for the moment, but her thoughts kept drifting back to Arris.

He still hadn't responded to her message, the silence gnawing at her. As they pulled into the bowling alley parking lot, she quickly typed out another text, her fingers hesitating for a moment before hitting send. Her worry deepened as she called his number, her heart sinking when it went to voicemail after a few rings. She groaned softly, her frustration creeping in.

"There go Aunt Karmen!" DJ yelled excitedly from the backseat, his small face pressed against the window.

Dionne looked up and spotted Karmen and Mia walking toward the bowling alley entrance, Mia holding Karmen's hand. "Ou, she is pretty, Aunt Dee," DJ said with excitement, his eyes locked on Mia.

Dionne chuckled, shaking her head at her charming nephew. "Boy, come on," she said, laughing as she got out of the car and helped him out of his seat.

They walked toward the entrance, meeting Karmen and Mia at the door.

"Hey, sis!" Dionne greeted warmly, pulling Karmen into a hug.

"Hey, boo," Karmen replied with a smile as they pulled apart.

"Hey, Aunt Dee!" Mia exclaimed excitedly, wrapping her arms around Dionne in a warm hug. Dionne laughed, shaking her head slightly at the fact that Arris had Mia calling her that.

"Hey, Mia," Dionne said back as they pulled away.

Karmen stood nearby, her brows furrowed in confusion. "Aunt Dee?" she asked, looking at Dionne with curiosity, clearly waiting for an explanation.

Before Dionne could scramble for a quick lie, DJ piped up, grinning from ear to ear. "Hey, Aunt Karmen!" he said, his timing impeccable as he saved Dionne from having to answer immediately.

"DJ!" Karmen exclaimed, crouching slightly as if to pick him up, but DJ quickly stepped back, holding his hands up defensively.

"Not in front of the pretty girl," he said, his eyes darting to Mia with

Feenin'

a small, knowing grin.

"Oh lord, this boy," Karmen said, shaking her head in amusement while Dionne burst out laughing.

"DJ, this is Mia. Mia, this is my nephew DJ," Dionne introduced, watching as DJ's charming demeanor took center stage.

DJ smiled brightly and extended his hand toward Mia. She hesitated for a moment, glancing nervously at Karmen, but eventually reached out and took his hand. To everyone's surprise, DJ leaned down and gently kissed the back of her hand.

"Hi, Mia," he said, his tone soft but confident, a grin lighting up his face.

Both Dionne and Karmen laughed in surprise and delight at his unexpected gesture, while Mia's face twisted in confusion before breaking into a shy smile.

"Lord, he's starting early," Karmen said, wiping a tear of laughter from her eye.

"Too early," Dionne agreed, still laughing as DJ stood there beaming at Mia, clearly proud of himself.

Mia tilted her head slightly, still unsure but clearly amused by DJ's bold introduction. She looked up at Karmen, who nodded encouragingly, and finally managed a small, "Hi, DJ."

As the two kids exchanged smiles, Dionne and Karmen exchanged knowing glances, both entertained and mildly concerned by DJ's precocious charm.

"Alright, Romeo, let's get inside before the lanes fill up," Dionne said, nudging DJ forward.

With laughter still lingering in the air, the group made their way into the bowling alley, the promise of a fun day ahead momentarily easing Dionne's worries.

They walked into the bowling alley, reserving a lane and gathering their bowling shoes. As the group settled in, Mia struggled with her shoes, her tiny hands fumbling with the laces. Before Karmen could help her, DJ rushed to her side, crouching down to assist.

Dionne and Karmen exchanged a glance, smiles spreading across their faces.

"Aww, they are too cute," Karmen cooed, watching DJ's gentlemanly gesture.

Dionne chuckled softly. "That boy is going to be a problem," she joked, shaking her head.

Karmen nodded in agreement, grinning. "The good kind of problem, though."

Mia's soft voice broke the moment. "Thank you, DJ," she said shyly, her cheeks slightly pink as she looked at him.

DJ flashed a big smile, clearly proud of himself. "You're welcome," he said, standing tall as if he'd just accomplished something great.

"Ms. Moore, can I go first?" Mia asked, her excitement evident.

Karmen smiled warmly at her. "Yes, sweetie, you can go first."

Mia's face lit up, and she clapped her hands. As Karmen set up the game on the screen, the order appeared: Mia, DJ, Karmen, and Dionne, who opted to go last.

The game began, and while Mia bowled—with DJ eagerly at her side, helping her with every little thing—Dionne and Karmen sat back, taking a moment to talk.

"So, what's going on, Dee? It's been a minute since we've seen each other," Karmen asked, her eyes flicking briefly toward the kids before landing back on Dionne.

Dionne offered a small smile, though it didn't quite reach her eyes. "Girl, same old. Just working and wedding planning," she replied, her tone light but detached. At the mention of the wedding, she gave a subtle eye roll, one Karmen didn't miss.

Karmen raised an eyebrow, leaning slightly closer. "Every time you talk about the wedding, you don't seem excited," she said, her voice tinged with curiosity and concern.

Dionne sighed, her fingers fiddling with the edge of her sleeve. "It's just... a lot. Mama Glen wants us to do premarital counseling before the wedding," she admitted, her tone weary.

Karmen's eyes widened in surprise. "Premarital counseling? You and Malik not happy?"

"No, it's not that," Dionne replied quickly, brushing off the suggestion. "She just thinks our careers are pulling us in different directions and wants us to work through any issues now, before we tie the knot."

Karmen nodded slowly, considering the explanation. "Honestly, that's not a bad idea. Mama Glen's right—premarital counseling might actually help you two get on the same page," she said, her tone supportive.

Dionne nodded, masking her true feelings with a neutral expression. She knew counseling wasn't the solution because the real problem wasn't career-related. Her heart had already drifted far from Malik. It belonged to someone else entirely—a man who was currently ignoring her, a fact that gnawed at her with every passing moment.

Her eyes flicked to her phone resting on the table beside her, hoping

Feenin'

for a notification from Arris. Nothing. The thought of him—his anger, his silence—was a weight she couldn't shake.

Karmen's voice pulled her back. "You sure you're good, Dee?"

Dionne forced another smile, ignoring the ache in her chest. "Yeah, I'm good," she lied, glancing at the kids as DJ handed Mia the bowling ball with exaggerated care, eliciting a small giggle from her.

For a moment, the laughter of the kids filled the air, and Dionne let herself get lost in it, if only to quiet the storm of emotions swirling inside her.

"Aunt Karmen, it's your turn!" DJ yelled excitedly, his little voice carrying across the lane. Karmen got up with a grin, leaving Dionne with a moment of quiet—just enough time to try calling Arris again.

For the fourth time that day, the call went to voicemail. Dionne's jaw tightened, and her fingers curled around the phone. He is testing me, she thought, a flicker of anger rising in her chest.

Just as she was about to sigh in frustration, Mia walked by, her small frame settling into the seat beside Dionne. She glanced up at her with wide, curious eyes.

"Aunt Dee, what is DJ's real name? He won't tell me when I asked," Mia said softly, her voice carrying a hint of curiosity that made Dionne chuckle.

"Demetrius Jr. That's why we call him DJ," she replied, her smile widening at the thought of her charming nephew.

Mia's face lit up with excitement. "Demetrius!" she yelled across the alley.

DJ snapped his head toward her so fast it was as if she'd said a forbidden word. His wide eyes darted to Dionne, full of mock betrayal. "Aunt Dee! You told her my real name. That was a secret!" he exclaimed, though his playful smile betrayed his irritation.

Mia giggled at his reaction. "I like your name," she said softly, her voice sincere.

Dionne couldn't help but notice the light blush dusting DJ's cheeks at her compliment. He stood there, momentarily flustered, before quickly recovering.

"Well, you can't call me that, though," he said, crossing his arms with mock seriousness.

Mia's expression shifted, her small face scrunching into a playful glare. "Why not?" she asked, crossing her own arms in defiance.

DJ grinned, clearly enjoying the back-and-forth. "Because all my friends call me DJ," he replied, his voice carrying a matter-of-fact tone.

"But we're not friends," Mia shot back with a tilt of her head, her confident retort catching him off guard.

Dionne smirked as she watched the exchange, her heart warming at how much these two acted like adults in miniature.

DJ chuckled, recovering quickly. "Not yet," he said, flashing a flirtatious smirk that seemed far too smooth for a five-year-old.

Mia rolled her eyes but couldn't hide her small smile.

Dionne laughed quietly, shaking her head as she observed them. They were too young to be this deep in conversation, but she couldn't deny how adorable their dynamic was. Both of them, so ahead of their years, carried a spark that hinted at the lively personalities they'd grow into.

"Alright, you two. How about we let Aunt Karmen bowl in peace?" Dionne teased, nudging DJ with a grin.

As the kids returned to their playful banter, Dionne's smile lingered. For a brief moment, she forgot her frustrations, the pure joy of their innocence washing away the weight of everything else—if only for a while.

"Dee, it's your turn. I almost had a strike," Karmen said, walking back to the seating area with a playful smirk.

Dionne glanced down at her phone again, her frustration flaring when she saw that Arris still hadn't returned her call or text. She let out a quiet, internal groan, her fingers tightening around the phone for a moment before she locked the screen and set it aside. Focus on today, she told herself. This time was for her friend and nephew, not her worries.

With a deep breath, Dionne stood, grabbing a bowling ball and stepping up to the lane. She lined up her shot, rolled the ball, and watched as it sped down the lane, knocking over every pin. Her face lit up as she jumped up and down, the excitement of getting a strike washing away a bit of her lingering frustration.

"You're cheating, Auntie!" DJ shouted playfully from his seat, grinning wide as Dionne turned to him and made a goofy face in return.

"Come on, Mia! We gotta get a strike now," DJ said, grabbing Mia's hand and pulling her toward the lane with a determined look.

Dionne laughed as she sat back down beside Karmen.

"We?" Karmen teased, raising an eyebrow at DJ as he turned to face her, confidence radiating from every inch of his little frame.

"Yeah! Mia told me she didn't know how to bowl, so I'm teaching her. We're on a team," he said matter-of-factly, flashing a proud smile.

Dionne shook her head, a warm smile spreading across her face as she watched her nephew. His generous spirit and natural charm were always on full display, and today was no exception.

Feenin'

As Mia and DJ took their turns at the lane, Karmen leaned back with a chuckle. "Mario's gonna get me. I babysit her one time, and she comes back with a boyfriend because DJ's not letting up off her," she joked.

Dionne burst into laughter, shaking her head. "Girl! You know he's too smooth for his own good," she replied, her tone filled with amusement.

"Look at them," Karmen said, nodding toward the two kids.

Dionne turned her attention to the lane, her heart melting at the sight. Mia stood with the ball in her hands, and DJ was right behind her, gently guiding her movements as they rolled it together.

"Aww, they're too cute," Dionne cooed, her voice soft with affection.

Karmen nodded, grinning. "They really are."

"Speaking of Mario, how are things between you two?" Dionne asked, steering the conversation away from her own struggles. She needed to shift her focus, to stop dwelling on Arris and the distance he'd created today. It wasn't like him—at all. They talked all day, every day, whether by phone or in person. Last night, when he'd shown up at her house filled with rage, the image had stayed with her, gnawing at her. She hadn't been able to sleep, her worry keeping her awake all night. Now, she was running on three hours of sleep and trying to push through her exhaustion.

Karmen's soft smile was at odds with the flicker of turmoil behind her eyes. "We're good, relationship-wise, but Mia's mother is... a piece of work," she admitted, her tone shifting.

Dionne's protectiveness flared instantly, her posture straightening. "She ain't fucking with you, is she?" Her voice held a sharper edge now.

Karmen chuckled at Dionne's quick defense. "No, not me. But she causes a lot of stress for Mario. He's a great father, and seeing him degraded by her every chance she gets—it makes me mad," she said, her tone soft but laced with frustration.

Dionne frowned, her concern for both Karmen and Mario growing. "Damn... I know that's gotta be a lot to deal with," she said, her voice filled with understanding.

Karmen sighed, her fingers fiddling with the edge of her sleeve. "It is. I try to be there for him as much as I can—taking Mia out so he can have a break—but I can see it's weighing on him. He's carrying so much, and she just keeps piling more on."

Dionne couldn't hide the smile tugging at her lips as she watched Karmen talk. "Aww, you like him," she teased, her voice dripping with playfulness.

Karmen rolled her eyes but couldn't stop the blush creeping up her cheeks. "It's more than that," she admitted quietly. "I love him, actually."

Dionne squealed in excitement, clapping her hands together. "Love?! Aww, sis, I'm so happy for you!"

Karmen's blush deepened, but her smile faltered slightly. "But... I don't know if I can keep being with him if his baby mother keeps doing crazy shit," she confessed, her voice cracking. "I dealt with that with Trey and his baby mother, and I can't go through that again."

The vulnerability in her voice made Dionne lean forward, placing a reassuring hand on Karmen's knee. "Karmen, listen to me. Mario is not Trey," Dionne said firmly, her tone gentle but full of conviction. "I've never seen you glowing like this before, or this happy behind a man. Mario loves you, Mia loves you, and you love them. Don't let his baby mother ruin what you two have built."

Karmen nodded, her eyes glossy as she absorbed Dionne's words. "You're right," she said softly, her voice wavering with emotion. "I just... I don't want to lose myself again, Dee. Not for anybody."

Dionne squeezed her knee gently. "And you won't. You've got us—me, London, and everyone else—right behind you, ready to fight for you if you need it. But don't let fear push you away from something real. You deserve this love, Karmen."

"Let Mario handle that," Dionne continued firmly, her tone taking on the older-sister authority Karmen had come to rely on. "And if he doesn't, that's when you step in and decide what you need to do. But don't compromise your happiness for anyone. Not him, not his baby mother, no one."

Karmen nodded, her lips curving into a small smile. "Thanks, sis. But it's the same for you," she said, her tone gentle but pointed.

Dionne's brows furrowed, her expression shifting to confusion. Before she could ask what Karmen meant, DJ called out her name excitedly, letting her know it was her turn to bowl.

"Bowl for me, DJ!" Karmen said, waving him off with a grin. DJ practically leaped out of his seat in excitement, grabbing a ball and heading to the lane.

Karmen's attention returned to Dionne, her gaze steady and serious. "I see you going through the motions with this wedding," she began, her tone soft but direct. "You don't look happy or excited about it. I could be wrong, but it feels more like you're doing it to make Ms. Glen happy than because it's the wedding of your dreams."

Dionne felt the words hit her chest like a weight. Karmen could always read her like a book, and today was no exception. But Dionne couldn't let her guard down—not now, not when she had perfected her

Feenin'

façade so well. She forced a smile, even as it stung to do so.

"That's not true, Karm," she replied, her voice calm and even. "I am happy about the wedding."

Karmen tilted her head, her eyes narrowing slightly. "You're sure?" she asked, her gaze piercing as she searched Dionne's face for any cracks in her armor.

"Yes, sis, I'm sure," Dionne said, her response short and clipped. She kept her tone light, though her hands fidgeted slightly in her lap.

Karmen studied her for another moment before nodding, seemingly convinced. "Alright. If you say so."

Dionne exhaled softly as the conversation shifted, grateful for the reprieve even though her chest ached from hiding the truth.

They returned their attention to the kids, watching as DJ helped Mia roll another ball, the two of them laughing and high-fiving afterward. Dionne leaned back in her chair, forcing herself to smile at the sight of their joy.

But no amount of laughter or distraction could quiet the constant buzzing in her mind. Every unanswered call, every ignored text to Arris gnawed at her, eating away at her composure piece by piece. She kept checking her phone between frames, hoping for a response that never came, her frustration and worry simmering beneath the surface.

Even as she laughed and played along with DJ and Mia, Dionne couldn't shake the feeling that everything in her life was unraveling—and the one person she needed most wasn't there to catch her.

After hours of bowling, eating, and playing at the park, Dionne was exhausted, her body aching but her mind racing. With a sleeping DJ buckled in the backseat, she drove to her parents' house, gently carrying him inside and tucking him into bed. Once she said her goodbyes, she headed home—or at least, that was the plan.

On the drive, her frustration boiled over, her finger hovering over the call button on her phone. For the hundredth time that day, she dialed Arris, her heart sinking as it went straight to voicemail yet again.

"Fuck this," she muttered, changing course. She wasn't about to let him ignore her all day without an explanation.

Dionne pressed harder on the gas as she sped toward Arris's house, her determination outweighing her exhaustion. Pulling up to his gated property, she punched in the gate code with practiced ease, driving up to his large home. His car was parked out front, and she wasted no time pulling in behind it.

Slamming her car door shut, Dionne marched up to his front door, her anger fueling every step. She rang the doorbell, following it with loud, insistent knocks. "Arris!" she called, her voice firm and demanding.

Minutes later, the door swung open, revealing him standing there shirtless, wearing grey shorts that hung low on his hips. His tattoos, dark and intricate, covered his chest, arms, and legs, drawing her eyes despite her anger. If she wasn't so mad, she might have lunged at him just to kiss the smirk off his face.

"Wassup, Mama," he said calmly, his deep voice low as he leaned casually against the doorframe, fighting back a smile.

"Don't 'Hey, Mama' me," Dionne snapped, brushing past him and stepping inside without waiting for an invitation. "Why the fuck have you been ignoring me all day?" Her tone was sharp, frustration dripping from every word.

Arris stood there, arms crossed, the hint of a smile tugging at his lips. Watching her worked up, her fire blazing, sent a thrill through him. He said nothing, just let her vent, his silence only fueling her rage.

"So, you're just gonna ignore me in person, too?!" Dionne demanded, her voice rising. Her eyes narrowed as a new thought crossed her mind. "You got a bitch in here or something?"

Arris raised a brow, amused, but before he could respond, she was off. Dionne stormed into the living room, then the kitchen, throwing open doors and checking corners as if she were conducting a full-scale investigation.

"Mama, what are you doing?" Arris asked, his voice calm but laced with amusement as he leaned against the wall, watching her with an entertained smirk.

Ignoring him completely, Dionne stomped through the house, checking every room on the first level. Her determination to find another woman was relentless, even as her frustration burned hotter with every empty room.

"You got me fucked up if you got a bitch in here!" Dionne yelled, spinning toward the stairs.

Before she could take another step, Arris grabbed her by the waist, pulling her back into him. His grip was firm, and the heat of his body pressed against hers made her struggle even harder.

"Arris, let me go!" she shouted, her voice trembling with anger, her eyes burning with tears. But it wasn't just rage fueling her—it was frustration. Frustration from him ignoring her all damn day.

"There's no woman in here," he said lowly, his voice calm and steady as he leaned close to her ear, trying to diffuse the fire inside her.

"I don't believe you. Move!" Dionne snapped, twisting in his arms and using all the strength she could muster to break free. But Arris was

Feenin'

too strong, and he held her firmly.

In one smooth motion, he pinned her against the wall, his hands gripping her wrists to keep her in place. "Calm down, Mama," he said, his voice still maddeningly calm, his eyes locking onto hers. He could see the tears threatening to spill over, a mix of fury and hurt she was trying to keep in check.

"Come down, hoe! I just want to talk!" Dionne yelled, her voice filled with rage as Arris kept her pinned to the wall, his strong arms locking her in place.

"Chill, Dionne. There's no woman in here," he said, his tone calm, almost amused, despite the storm brewing in her eyes.

"I'm about to punch the fuck outta you, Arris. Move!" she yelled, her hands shoving at his chest with all her strength. But, as always, his strength overpowered hers, and he barely budged.

Arris watched her, his calm demeanor unwavering as she struggled against him. He didn't know why, but seeing this fiery, untamed side of her made him... aroused. He had always known Dionne had a temper, but seeing it firsthand—directed at him—stirred something primal inside him. He'd been waiting to see this side of her, and now that he had, he was even more addicted.

"Calm down, mama," he said softly, his voice soothing but steady, his touch grazing her waist as if trying to ground her.

But Dionne wasn't calming down. The frustration and betrayal in her eyes were now mixed with unshed tears that glistened in the dim light. "Don't 'mama' me, Arris! I swear—" her voice cracked, and she quickly looked away, trying to keep her emotions from spilling over.

Arris's jaw tightened as he noticed the tears threatening to fall. He hated seeing her like this, even if her anger was a little misplaced. His hand cupped her cheek gently, forcing her to look at him.

"Talk to me," he said softly, his calmness unwavering even as her chest rose and fell with ragged breaths. "What's really going on, Dee? 'Cause it's not about some imaginary woman, or me not talking to you all day."

Dionne clenched her fists, her frustration pouring out as she glared up at him. "You just... you push me! You push me and act like you can control everything! Like you're just supposed to know me, and I'm supposed to—" Her words faltered, and she shook her head angrily. "I hate this! I hate that I can't even think straight when I'm around you!"

Arris's lips curved into a slight smirk, though his eyes softened. "So that's what this is about? You hate that I got you like this?" His voice was low and smooth, and despite her anger, the sound of it made her knees weaken.

"Arris, I swear to—" she started, but before she could finish, he leaned down, his forehead resting against hers.

"Stop fighting me, Dionne," he said, his voice a whisper now, carrying a weight that made her freeze. "Stop fighting what's already yours."

But even as his words held a truth that resonated with her, and she felt her anger waver slightly, the thought of his earlier behavior gnawed at her. He had ignored her calls all day, left her feeling abandoned, and now, the lingering possibility that a woman could still be upstairs clouded her mind once again.

"Arris, move," she said again, her voice shaky now.

But Arris just smiled, that infuriatingly cocky smirk that made her want to scream and kiss him all at once. Her fire, her crazy, all aimed at him—it aroused him, and he didn't even bother hiding it.

"No," he said softly, his tone teasing but firm. "'Cause ain't nobody here but me and you."

"Arris, don't play with me," Dionne said, her voice firmer, though quieter now. Her eyes searched his, still stormy with doubt. "You ignored me all damn day, and now you're acting like I'm crazy? For all I know, there is someone upstairs."

"Let me go," she demanded, her voice sharp.

Slowly, he loosened his grip, letting her step away from the wall. She turned to face him, her arms crossing tightly over her chest. "Why the fuck were you ignoring me all day?" she asked, her eyes narrowing.

He looked down at her, his calm demeanor unshaken despite her words. "Dionne," he started, his voice low and steady, "I wasn't ignoring you. I had business to handle, and I didn't want to rush through talking to you just to get back to it. You know you deserve all of me, not half-assed attention."

"And part of me didn't feel like talking," he continued, his voice calm yet teasing, watching as her smile instantly fell. The smirk on his lips widened, knowing exactly how much he was pushing her buttons.

"Arris..." Dionne said through gritted teeth, her voice dropping low, her hands clenching at her sides. "Stop playing with me, for real. I'm trying my hardest not to put my hands on you."

Arris's smirk grew. "I want you to put your hands on me," he replied, his voice dripping with amusement, his eyes glinting with mischief.

"You're crazy," Dionne said, shaking her head, though a small, begrudging chuckle slipped out.

"Don't look like I'm the only one," he shot back, stepping closer.

Feenin'

"You were about to tear my house up, thinking I had a woman in here. I love that shit."

His hands found her waist again, and just like that, the anger she'd been holding onto started to melt away. She tried to keep her glare, but his touch had a way of disarming her.

"I see your ass ain't stupid, though," Dionne muttered, her tone half-joking, half-serious.

Arris chuckled, leaning in closer. "Nah, Mama. I know better."

Before she could say anything else, he closed the distance between them, his lips capturing hers in a kiss that was both heated and unrelenting. Her hands instinctively moved to his chest, gripping him tightly as the kiss deepened, all the tension between them melting into something else entirely.

But just as the fire threatened to consume them, Dionne pulled back, her lips tingling, her chest heaving slightly.

"Seriously, are you okay? You showed up to my house last night angry. I was worried," Dionne asked, her voice softening her concern evident. Her gaze locked onto his, searching for the answer he hadn't yet shared.

Arris's eyes met hers, lingering with an intensity that made her heart race. He hesitated for a moment, the betrayal from last night still fresh, cutting deeper than he wanted to admit. But standing here with Dionne, the storm inside him began to settle. Her presence alone had a way of soothing him, grounding him in a way nothing else could.

Even though the betrayal from his mother and the anger simmered beneath the surface, Dionne's concern wrapped around him like a balm. He took in her expression, the way her brows furrowed with worry, and the love radiating in her eyes. The thought of Malik was quickly eclipsed by the connection they were sharing now, this moment belonging to them and no one else.

"Now I am," he replied, his voice low and steady. His words hung in the air, thick with meaning as his eyes swept over her, taking in every detail as if she were the only thing that mattered in his world.

The heat of his stare made a blush rise to her cheeks, and she tried to steady herself under the weight of his intensity. "Want to talk about it?" she asked gently, her hands moving up to caress his beard, her touch both comforting and familiar.

She wasn't sure how she'd gone from being ready to rip his head off to this—calm, soft, craving his presence—but that was just the effect Arris had on her. No other man could unravel her and put her back together like he did.

"No," he said simply, his voice deep and final. His gaze darkened, a new fire flickering in his eyes. "I just want you."

Before she could respond, his lips crashed against hers, silencing whatever words were forming on her tongue. The kiss was hungry, filled with everything he wasn't saying, and it sent a shiver down her spine.

"Even when I'm quiet, even when I'm distant, you're the one I'm thinking about," Arris murmured between soft, lingering kisses, his voice filled with reassurance. Each word felt like a promise, his hands steady on her waist as if anchoring her to him.

Dionne closed her eyes, letting his words and his touch wash over her, soothing the tension that had built from the uncertainty of the day. He kissed her forehead, then her lips again, his movements deliberate, filled with an intimacy that left no doubt about his sincerity.

"I don't mean to shut you out, Dee," Arris continued, his voice low but steady, the weight of his emotions clear. "But when I get that angry, I just need space. I never want to lash out on you because of my anger." His hands stayed firm on her waist, his touch grounding both of them in the moment.

Dionne's eyes softened as she searched his face, seeing the unspoken pain lingering behind his words. He wanted to tell her about what had happened last night—the heated confrontation with his mother and Calvin—but the mere thought of it stirred the same anger he was trying to suppress. She was his peace, the calm to his storm, and he didn't want to taint this moment or their connection by revisiting the chaos.

She could sense his inner battle even though he was trying to hide it. Concern flickered in her eyes, but she didn't press him. Dionne trusted that when he was ready, he'd tell her everything. For now, she focused on giving him what he needed—her presence, her understanding, and her love.

"Arris…" she whispered, her voice laced with reassurance. Her hands moved up to cup his face, her thumbs brushing against his jawline. "You don't have to explain everything right now. Just know I'm here, okay? Always."

Her words seemed to soothe him, her touch melting the tension in his shoulders. He leaned in, pressing a soft kiss to her lips, letting her warmth calm what his own words couldn't. Each kiss was a silent expression of his gratitude, his need, his craving for the solace only she could provide.

Dionne wrapped her arms around his neck, holding him close, feeling the weight of his emotions in the way he clung to her. They didn't need more words—this moment spoke for itself. She was his peace, and

Feenin'

he was hers, and together, they found a sense of calm neither could find on their own.

In one smooth motion, Arris scooped her up, his hands gripping her thighs as she instinctively wrapped her legs around his waist. Her fingers threaded through his durag as the kiss deepened, their emotions pouring into each other.

He carried her through the house, not breaking the connection between them until they reached his bedroom. The door shut behind them, and the world outside ceased to exist.

The rest of the night was spent tangled in each other, their bodies moving in rhythm, their unspoken emotions spilling over in ways words never could. They didn't need to talk—every kiss, every touch, every breath was enough to say what couldn't be spoken.

By the time they lay wrapped in each other's arms, the tension that had weighed them both down earlier had melted away, leaving only the unshakable connection they shared.

Chapter 12

Arris stepped into True's tattoo shop, the buzz of tattoo guns blending with the steady beat of rap music and the hum of casual chatter. The familiar atmosphere instantly put him at ease. He greeted Lori at the front desk with a quick nod and a grin before heading toward the back, where True's private tattoo room was.

Today, Arris had the rare luxury of a day off, and he'd decided to spend it getting some fresh ink.

Pushing the door open, he walked in to find True already at work. His smirk widened when he saw the person in the chair—London. She looked up from her arm, her expression lighting up as she caught sight of him.

"Hey, Arris," she said warmly, her voice carrying a friendly tone.

"Wassup, London. How you been?" he asked, leaning in to give her a side hug, careful to avoid the arm True was tattooing.

"Good, can't complain," she replied calmly, her smile easy as he nodded.

Over the past few months, Arris had built a small bond with both London and Karmen, thanks to their relationships with his boys. He'd quickly learned that London was the firecracker of the group—bold, outspoken, and unapologetic. Growing up with three brothers and no sisters explained why she clicked so effortlessly with him and Mario. Karmen, on the other hand, was softer, quieter—more reserved.

Arris respected both women for the way they complemented his friends. Seeing True and Mario happy made him happy, and it was a bonus that they happened to be close friends of Dionne.

"Yo," True said, looking up briefly from London's tattoo as Arris

Feenin'

walked over.

"Wassup, bro," Arris replied, dapping him up before heading to the couch. He dropped into the seat, getting comfortable as he watched True work.

"So, what you here for?" True asked without looking up, his attention still on London's arm.

"Figured I'd finally get that piece we talked about," Arris said, smirking.

True grinned, his focus never wavering. "'Bout time. I'll finish up with London, then you're next."

Arris nodded, leaning back on the couch. He let the music, the buzz of the tattoo gun, and the easy conversation between friends wash over him. It was the perfect way to spend a rare, stress-free day.

"I'm almost done, Arris," True said, his focus still locked on London's tattoo.

"You straight," Arris replied casually from the couch. He smirked, leaning forward. "London, you finally getting my nigga's name tatted?"

London's head snapped in his direction, her sharp glare meeting his teasing grin. "Nigga, please. If anything, he'd get my name tatted first before I do," she shot back confidently, making both Arris and True laugh.

"Am I wrong?" she added, raising a brow as she turned her attention to True.

True chuckled, shaking his head with a smirk, knowing better than to argue. London's satisfied smile widened as Arris laughed, shaking his head.

"That nigga hooked," Arris joked, his voice laced with amusement.

True smacked his lips in mock irritation, but London only laughed. "Alright now, lay off my man," she said, quick to defend him, her tone playful but firm.

Arris held his hands up in surrender, the smirk still on his face. "I don't want no problems, sis," he joked, his laughter blending with hers.

London's phone rang, cutting through the playful banter. True reached back without hesitation, grabbing it off the charger and handing it to her.

"Thank you, baby," she said with a sweet smile, her tone softer now as she took the phone and answered.

"Hey, bitch!" she yelled into the phone, her bold enthusiasm filling the room and drawing a laugh from both True and Arris.

"Hey, girl! What's the address again?" came the familiar voice on the other end, and Arris couldn't help the small smile that tugged at his lips.

Ann

He knew that voice anywhere.

"I'm about to send it to you," London replied, glancing at her screen. "True said when you come, just walk all the way to the back."

"Do she got my snacks?" True asked, his tone mischievous.

Before London could even respond, Dionne had already heard him. "Tell that nigga I got his high ass his snacks. He better have my money ready," she shot back, her tone sharp but playful.

True chuckled, shaking his head. "I got you, Dee," he called out, his laughter adding to the ease in the room.

Dionne wasn't just blending into his world; she was becoming part of it, seamlessly. His boys adored her, even though they had no idea about the two of them. True treated her like an annoying but adored little sister, constantly teasing and poking at her in a way that only made her more endearing to him. Mario, on the other hand, was the calm, protective type—always looking out for her without being overbearing.

Arris smirked to himself, his thoughts lingering on Dionne. She fit so well into his life it scared him sometimes. Even in the moments where their thing was supposed to be on the low, she managed to make her mark, and damn if he didn't love that about her.

Arris's heart fluttered the moment he heard Dionne's voice through the phone. He tried to play it cool, but he couldn't help leaning closer as London spoke. Thanks to her brightness being all the way up, he caught a glimpse of Dionne on the screen, her face filling the frame for a brief second.

They hadn't talked all day because Dionne had claimed she'd be too busy to be on her phone. He'd missed her like crazy. Still, as the hours passed and she stayed quiet, he couldn't help but wonder why she hadn't reached out, especially now that she seemed free. The thought lingered in his mind before he pushed it aside, not wanting to overthink it.

"Me and Karmen about to pull up," Dionne said through the phone, her voice effortlessly casual.

"Bet," London replied before they ended the call.

Minutes later, Dionne walked into True's tattoo room, Karmen following closely behind her. The energy in the room shifted immediately for Arris, his eyes drawn to her like a magnet.

Despite the pull to hug her or press his lips against hers, he held back, knowing they couldn't afford to show their connection in front of their friends. But it wasn't easy. Dionne looked different today—better, if that were possible—and it made his self-control damn near impossible to maintain.

She wore a Supreme hoodie that she'd stolen from his closet, a pair

Feenin'

of high-waisted jeans that hugged her curves just right, and a fresh pair of Jordan "Fire Red" 4s. But it wasn't the outfit that had him stuck—it was her hair.

The burgundy wig, styled in body wave curls and parted perfectly in the middle, framed her face so beautifully that it made his throat dry. His gaze lingered too long, taking her in until he felt the heat rise in his chest and the ache in his body intensify. Dionne had a way of doing that to him without even trying.

She greeted True and London first, giving them both hugs and handing True the bags with his snacks. Her voice was light and warm as she interacted with them, but when her eyes finally landed on Arris sitting in the corner, he caught the way her heart fluttered.

Her eyes lit up, softening when they met his, but she quickly masked it, playing it off like nothing was different.

"Hey, Arris," she said casually, leaning down to give him a side hug.

Arris chuckled softly, matching her energy, but he couldn't resist sliding his hand across her waist in a subtle gesture of affection. He held her there for a moment, long enough to let her feel his presence without making it obvious.

"I like your hair," he complimented, his tone low and smooth as his hand lingered.

Dionne's smile grew at his words, her body betraying her as it shivered under his touch. "Thank you," she replied, recovering quickly even though she knew he could feel her reaction.

She straightened and stepped aside as Karmen leaned in to give Arris a quick hug.

"Wassup, Karm," he greeted easily, though his attention was still locked on Dionne.

The two women sat down on the couch, Karmen sliding into the middle seat. Dionne chose to sit on the other side, purposefully putting space between her and Arris. She knew herself too well—if she sat too close, she wouldn't be able to stop herself from showing her affection, and the last thing she needed was for their friends to catch on.

Arris saw through her tactic immediately. She was running from him, keeping her distance to maintain their secret, but he allowed it—for now. The game she was playing only made him want her more, and the tension between them crackled like electricity.

For now, he leaned back on the couch, a sly smirk playing on his lips as he let her think she had the upper hand. But Dionne was his, and they both knew it.

"So, how did the dress fitting go?!" London perked up, her eyes bright with curiosity.

Dionne's heart dropped at the question, and her body stiffened. Across the room, Arris's jaw tightened, his carefree demeanor vanishing in an instant. He didn't need anyone to spell it out—he could piece together the reason Dionne had been too busy to talk today. It wasn't work or errands; she'd been planning her wedding.

The realization hit him like a punch to the gut. His jaw clenched, and his fists curled subtly at his sides as the conversation continued.

Dionne glanced at him, her eyes catching the storm of emotions he was trying to mask. The set of his jaw, the tension in his shoulders—she could see it all, and it made her heart thump painfully in her chest. She hated how much this hurt him, especially when she couldn't do anything to make it right.

"Um... it was good," Dionne said softly, her voice almost hesitant as she desperately hoped someone would jump in and change the subject.

"Girl, it was more than good," Karmen interjected, her proud smile lighting up her face. "That dress, especially the last one? It was perfect. Malik is going to want to remarry you the second he sees you in it."

London squealed in excitement, but Dionne barely heard her. Her eyes stayed locked on Arris, who hadn't moved from his spot on the couch. His anger was clear now, simmering just beneath the surface as he sat there in silence, listening to the conversation unfold like a bad dream.

"Damn, I wish I could've been there," London said, dramatically throwing her hands up. "I had way too many clients booked today."

"It's cool, sis. It wasn't that exciting," Dionne said quickly, her gaze flickering back to Arris as if willing him to look at her.

She wasn't lying. Trying on dress after dress for a wedding she didn't even want to happen had felt more like torture than anything else. The only relief had come when they'd finally found the dress, and the appointment was over.

Arris's fists unclenched slightly, but his posture remained tense. His expression was unreadable, but Dionne knew him too well to miss the storm brewing behind his calm façade.

For a moment, the chatter around her faded. Her friends were smiling, laughing, completely unaware of the tension in the room. But Dionne could feel it like a weight pressing down on her chest.

She forced a small smile, trying to keep up the act, but inside, guilt clawed at her. She wasn't excited about the wedding—she wasn't excited about Malik. And judging by the way Arris sat there, stone-faced and simmering, he wasn't about to let her forget it.

"I can't believe my girl is getting married to the man of her dreams!"

Feenin'

Karmen said, her voice filled with excitement and pride.

The words hit Arris like a dagger to the heart. Man of her dreams? The thought burned, his chest tightening as he stole a glance at Dionne. Her face told a different story—a guilty, almost annoyed expression that she couldn't quite hide.

He knew the truth. That title didn't belong to Malik; it belonged to him. It always had.

But then his eyes dropped to her hand, to the engagement ring that gleamed under the fluorescent lights, a cruel reminder of the lie they were all living. Her friends' excitement about her upcoming wedding only twisted the knife deeper. The very thought of her being engaged to another man was enough to shatter something inside him.

Dionne glanced at him, her chest tightening at the sight of his struggle. She saw the way his jaw tensed, the way his fists subtly clenched, his composure barely holding under the weight of this conversation. She didn't want this—none of it. Talking about the wedding in front of him, being engaged to Malik—it all felt wrong.

Because her heart wasn't in it. It was with Arris. It always had been.

The guilt gnawed at her, her mind racing as Karmen and London chatted excitedly about dresses, venues, and all the things she didn't care about. She could see the storm brewing behind Arris's calm façade, the anger he was forcing down to keep from losing it in front of their friends.

Arris felt like he was suffocating. Every word about the wedding felt like a blow, and the sight of that damn ring on her finger was a constant reminder that he was losing her—to him. To a man who didn't deserve her.

He couldn't lose Dionne. Not to another man, not to anyone. He refused to.

But he couldn't let his emotions slip, not here, not now. Not in front of her friends, who were blissfully unaware of the silent war raging inside him.

So he sat there, jaw tight, playing the role he had to. But deep down, the fire in his chest grew hotter, his determination hardening. She wasn't Malik's. She was his. And he'd be damned if he let her slip through his fingers.

Dionne's heart ached as she watched him, wishing she could say something, do something to ease the pain she could see in his eyes. But what could she say? She was living a lie, trapped in a situation she didn't know how to escape. And the man she truly wanted—the man she loved—was sitting right there, breaking silently because of her choices.

The room buzzed with lighthearted laughter and chatter, but between

Dionne and Arris, the tension was suffocating. Both of them trapped, both of them silently screaming, both of them unable to speak the truth that weighed so heavily on their hearts.

The conversation finally shifted, and Dionne felt a wave of relief wash over her. But just as she began to relax, True's next words sent her heart plummeting.

"Man, Arris, when are we going to meet this woman you say you're in love with?" True asked casually, wiping away the extra ink from London's arm.

The room fell silent as all the women's heads snapped toward Arris, their curiosity piqued. Arris's expression hardened, his eyes narrowing into a glare aimed directly at True. He didn't like being put on the spot—especially about his love life.

His gaze flickered to Dionne, catching the hurt in her eyes before she could hide it. She looked like her heart had just cracked in two, her expression one of disbelief and pain. The sight made him shake his head and chuckle softly. She knew damn well that the woman True was talking about was her, and yet here she was, looking like a sad, heartbroken puppy.

"You'll meet her soon, bro," Arris said, his tone light with amusement. His eyes lingered on Dionne, daring her to connect the dots. But the look of hurt remained etched on her face, and for some reason, it made him laugh. She really wasn't getting the hint.

"Arris, you're in love with someone?" London asked, her voice laced with genuine shock. "Like... a woman?"

Arris threw his head back with a laugh. "Why you sound so surprised?" he asked, the amusement clear in his tone.

London shrugged, her expression half-apologetic. "I'm just saying, True always talks about how much of a hoe you were and how you only cared about business," she said with a teasing grin, her words pulling a round of laughter from the room.

Arris's playful glare shifted to True, his lips twitching into a smirk. "Damn, so you out here gossiping about me now?" he asked, his voice sharp but softened by the smile on his face.

True shrugged, entirely unbothered. "Man, nah. We were talking about relationships. London asked why we were all single, so I explained," he said nonchalantly before smirking. "Don't play me like I'm some pillow-talking ass nigga."

The playful accusation earned another laugh from Arris, who shook his head. This was the dynamic of their friendship—constant shit-talking mixed with easy laughter, a rhythm that had been theirs for years.

Feenin'

The conversation drifted to other topics, the room returning to its lively buzz. But for Dionne, the words lingered. Her chest tightened as she replayed True's question and Arris's response in her mind. Every glance Arris threw her way only made it harder to hold herself together.

Across the room, Arris leaned back in his chair, his posture relaxed, but his mind was elsewhere. As the chatter carried on, it suddenly dawned on him—Mario wasn't here.

"Where's Mario?" Arris asked, his tone casual, though his eyes drifted quickly to Dionne. She was glued to her phone, her expression anything but amused. The subtle furrow in her brow made his concern spike, but he covered it, shifting his attention back to Karmen.

"He's on the way. He had to drop Mia off at Briana's house," Karmen explained, but her irritation was impossible to miss, her tone clipped.

"I want to beat that hoe so bad," London said suddenly, her voice sharp with anger.

Dionne's head snapped up at London's words, her protectiveness immediately kicking in. "What happened?"

True leaned forward, his brows furrowing. "Yeah, what's going on?" he asked, his voice steady but curious.

Karmen stayed quiet, the weight of the situation clear in the way she avoided everyone's gaze. But London wasn't one to hold back.

"That Briana hoe is playing with fire, fucking with my sis," London said, her anger building with every word. "If she wants to get on Mario's nerves, fine—that's on Mario. But dragging my sister into it? That's crossing a fucking line. Mario needs to put his hoe on a leash."

"Lon, just chill," Karmen said softly, her voice trembling. "That's still Mia's mother."

But now Dionne was fully locked in, her body tensing as her eyes zeroed in on Karmen. "What is she talking about?" Dionne asked, her voice steady but filled with a quiet fury.

Karmen sighed, reluctant to share more. London knowing about the situation was one thing, but Dionne had a different kind of anger—one that burned hotter and hit harder when it came to protecting the people she loved.

"Nothing. I don't want to talk about it," Karmen said, her voice cracking as she tried to deflect.

Dionne wasn't one to let things go, especially when it came to her friends. True and Arris were both silent but visibly attentive now, their protectiveness radiating in quiet waves as they waited for an explanation.

Karmen finally gave in, her shoulders slumping as she spoke. "I don't know how, but she found my address and pulled up while Mario and Mia were there. She acted a fool, tried to take Mia, and then started trying to fight me and Mario," she said, her voice trembling as she replayed the events in her mind.

"Mario got her to leave and made sure I was okay, but it was… a lot," Karmen admitted, her voice breaking slightly. "And now she's found me on social media, sending me all kinds of messages—talking about how Mario's still fucking with her on the low and how I need to stay away from her daughter."

The room fell silent, the weight of Karmen's words sinking in.

Dionne's blood boiled as she listened, her hands curling into fists at her sides. Her jaw clenched, and her eyes darkened with anger, ready to defend Karmen by any means necessary. Arris noticed immediately, the subtle shift in her energy unmistakable to him.

Before Dionne could say anything, Arris placed a reassuring hand on Karmen's shoulder, his voice calm and steady. "Don't let Briana get to you," he said firmly. "Mario loves you, Karm, and he's not going to let Briana's crazy ass come between what you two have. You've gotta trust that."

His words were meant to comfort, his presence solid and grounding, but his eyes flickered to Dionne briefly, a silent warning for her to keep her emotions in check.

Karmen smiled weakly at Arris's words, appreciating his effort to comfort her, but the damage was already done—for Dionne, at least. Rage coursed through her veins, the thought of Mario's baby mother messing with her best friend lighting a fire that couldn't be extinguished.

Karmen wasn't just her best friend; she was her sister in every way that mattered, younger by only three months. The bond they shared made the situation feel deeply personal, and the nagging texts from Malik blowing up her phone about their upcoming counseling session only added fuel to the fire. Now this? Briana threatening Karmen? It was too much.

Dionne's leg shook uncontrollably under the weight of her anger, her knee bouncing rapidly. Karmen noticed first, her protective instincts kicking in. "Dionne… calm down," Karmen said softly, her hand reaching out to steady Dionne's knee.

But the touch wasn't enough.

It couldn't compete with the storm of emotions brewing inside Dionne. Malik's texts were like an incessant itch, and Briana's audacity felt like a slap in the face.

"Fuck that shit," Dionne said, her tone eerily calm, her voice steady

Feenin'

in a way that made everyone in the room tense.

She stood abruptly, her movements sharp and deliberate. Karmen, panicked, quickly grabbed her arm, holding her back. "Dionne, no!" Karmen said, her voice trembling as she clung to her.

"Where does that bitch live?" Dionne spat, her tone fiery and cold all at once. "Because if she thinks she can just show up at your house, threaten you, and blow up your phone like she pays your damn bills or owns you, she's got another fucking thing coming."

The anger in Dionne's eyes was electric, and Arris stood from the couch, his protective instincts on high alert. He didn't speak immediately, watching the tension rise as he tried to gauge the best way to calm her.

"Dionne... please," Karmen pleaded, her voice cracking, tears threatening to spill. Her hands tightened around Dionne's arm, as if trying to physically anchor her.

But Dionne wasn't hearing it.

"Fuck yes, sis! Let's go!" London shouted, jumping up from the chair, her tattoo forgotten. Her fiery energy mirrored Dionne's, the two of them ready to ride for Karmen without hesitation.

True, however, was quicker. He grabbed London and pulled her into his arms, holding her tightly. "No the fuck you're not," he said firmly, his voice cutting through the chaos.

"True, let me go!" London yelled, struggling against him. "I'm about to fight with my sis, for my sis!"

True tightened his grip, his calm demeanor a stark contrast to her fury. "London, stop."

Meanwhile, Karmen clung to Dionne, her own fear and worry mounting. Tears welled up in her eyes, spilling over as she tried desperately to calm the situation.

The door opened suddenly, and Mario walked in, immediately feeling the thick tension in the room. His eyes scanned the scene: London struggling against True, Dionne on the verge of breaking free from Karmen's hold, and Karmen herself trembling, tears streaming down her face.

"What's going on?" Mario asked, his voice gentle but urgent as he moved to Karmen's side. He cupped her face, his concern written all over him. "Baby, why are you crying?"

Before Karmen could respond, Dionne's voice cut through the room like a whip. "Where the fuck does your baby mother live?" she demanded, her words dripping with anger as she glared at Mario.

Mario's brows furrowed, confusion flashing across his face. "Dionne, calm down," Arris said suddenly, his voice stern but low, his tone carrying a warning. He stood just a few feet away, trying to maintain the distance their situation required, but seeing Dionne this angry was unraveling his restraint.

Dionne's fists clenched at her sides, her body trembling as she stared down Mario. Arris stepped closer, his presence solid and grounding, but he didn't touch her—not yet.

"Dionne," Arris said again, his voice a little softer now but no less commanding. "This isn't the way."

Dionne turned her fiery gaze on him, her emotions blazing like an inferno. "Then what is the way, Arris?" she snapped. "Because sitting here, doing nothing while some bitch threatens my best friend, is not it."

The room fell silent, the tension crackling in the air like static electricity. True held London tightly, Mario's eyes stayed on Karmen, and Arris stood firm, his calm presence the only thing holding Dionne back from crossing the line.

But everyone knew the fire inside her wasn't extinguished—not yet.

"Wait, what?" Mario asked, his confusion clear as he looked around the tense room.

Dionne's eyes narrowed, her voice sharp and cold as ice. "Look, Mario, I fuck with you, but when your life starts to bring hurt or danger to my sister? That's when I step in."

Her tone cut through the air like a knife, sending chills through everyone in the room. Arris had seen Dionne mad before, but this? This was a whole new level.

"Me too! True, let me go!" London yelled, still struggling against True's grip. But he wasn't letting her go—not when Dionne was already on the verge of snapping. Adding London to the mix would be like tossing gasoline on an open flame.

Arris tried to make his way toward Dionne, but Karmen and Mario were in his path. His jaw clenched, his eyes never leaving hers, even though her fiery gaze stayed locked on Mario, demanding answers.

"Nobody is hurting Karmen," Mario said, his voice defensive as his eyes darted to Karmen, taking in her tear-streaked face.

"That's not what she said," Dionne shot back, her tone trembling with suppressed rage. "Your baby mother's showing up at her house and pulling bullshit like that."

She was trying to stay calm—this was True's shop, after all—but the fire inside her made it nearly impossible. Every word felt like it was about to explode out of her.

"I know, Dee. I handled that shit," Mario said firmly, his voice lowering as he tried to reassure her and Karmen at the same time. "She

Feenin'

knows not to come back to her place or even step near her again. I made that clear."

Dionne's arms crossed tightly, her fists clenching so hard her nails dug into her palms. "So, you know that bitch is reaching out to her through social media, degrading her, threatening her?"

Her words hit like a hammer, and Mario froze, his brows furrowing deeply. "What?" he asked, his voice low and disbelieving as he turned to Karmen. "She's doing what?"

Karmen flinched under his gaze, her fear evident as she shrank back slightly. She hadn't told him because she didn't want to add to his already heavy burden. Briana's comments and messages hadn't seemed worth the trouble—at least, that's what she'd told herself.

"So, you didn't know?" Arris asked, his tone sharp but his eyes still locked on Dionne, watching every flicker of emotion across her face.

Mario shook his head, his expression darkening. "Nah, bruh. I would've handled that shit immediately if I'd known." His voice softened as he turned back to Karmen, but his anger was clear in his eyes—anger at Briana for coming between him and the woman he loved. "Why didn't you tell me?"

"Because—" Karmen began, her voice trembling, but Dionne cut her off.

"It doesn't matter," Dionne snapped, her fury taking over. "Because I'm about to handle that shit myself. Mario, where does that bitch stay?"

Her words were laced with pure rage, her body trembling with the effort of holding herself back.

"Dee, please calm down," Karmen said through fresh tears, her voice breaking.

"Don't tell her, bro," Arris said to Mario, his voice low and steady, a clear warning.

Dionne turned on Arris, her eyes blazing. "It's cool. I'll just drive around this whole damn city until I find her bitch ass."

Before anyone could stop her, Dionne grabbed her keys and stormed out of the room, the sound of the door slamming echoing behind her.

"Someone, please go get her!" Karmen cried, her tears now flowing freely as she clung to Mario for support.

True was still too busy trying to hold London back as she continued to fight against him, her own rage bubbling over. "Let me go, True! I'm not letting Dionne fight this alone!"

Arris didn't waste a second. He brushed past everyone and followed Dionne out the door, his long strides quick and purposeful.

He knew better than anyone that if she got in that car, there'd be no stopping her—and the last thing he was going to let happen was Dionne getting herself into a situation she couldn't come back from.

Dionne stormed out, her fury propelling her forward so fast she barely registered her surroundings. Within seconds, she was at her car, yanking the door open.

Arris was right behind her, catching up just as she reached to get in. He grabbed her, spinning her around and pinning her against the car, his hands firm but careful, his presence towering over her.

"Arris, move!" she yelled through gritted teeth, her voice trembling with rage. "I am not playing with you right now."

His eyes narrowed, but his voice remained steady. "Calm down, Mama," he said firmly, though he could see his words weren't having the effect they usually did.

Her chest heaved as she glared at him, her emotions spiraling out of control. Her anger wasn't just aimed at Briana; it was an explosion of everything she'd been holding inside. The frustration with Malik and this counseling she didn't even want. The torment of playing the role of a fiancée for a man she didn't love. And the anguish of knowing that the man who truly held her heart was standing in front of her, keeping her from doing something reckless.

"Move, Arris," she snapped, her voice laced with venom. "That bitch needs her ass whooped!"

Arris stood firm, his dark eyes scanning her face, taking in every sign of the storm raging inside her. He'd seen Dionne angry before, but this was different— this was something deeper, something raw.

She'd been like this for days, even when she'd forced a smile or played it off. Ever since the night she'd shown up at his house, accusing him of cheating because he'd ignored her, he'd noticed it: the simmering rage, the way she carried herself like she was one push away from breaking.

"What's wrong, Mama?" he asked softly, his tone lowering in an attempt to break through her walls.

"Were you not in there? You know what's wrong with me!" she snapped, her voice shaking as the tears in her eyes threatened to fall.

Arris tilted his head slightly, studying her. Normally, his voice, his touch—he—could calm her, could anchor her. But this time, nothing seemed to work. Her anger wasn't just about Karmen or Briana. This was something deeper, something she wasn't saying.

"Talk to me, baby," Arris said gently, stepping closer.

Her tears finally spilled over, and her breaths became erratic. Her chest tightened painfully, and her hands flew to her chest as she gasped

Feenin'

for air. Her legs buckled, and Arris was there instantly, catching her before she could hit the ground.

"Mama! What's wrong?" he asked, his calm façade cracking as panic seeped into his voice.

Dionne clung to him, her vision blurring, her heart racing so fast it felt like it might burst. "Arris…" she panted, her voice laced with fear.

"I got you, baby. Breathe," he said, his voice steady as he tried to hold her together.

"I can't," she cried, panic overtaking her as she shook her head violently.

"Yes, you can," Arris said, his tone firm but gentle. He quickly placed her carefully in the seat. She bent forward, clutching her chest as if to keep it from breaking.

"Look at me, Mama. Deep breaths," he coached, crouching in front of her.

"What is happening to me?" she cried, her voice trembling with fear as her breaths came in sharp, shallow gasps.

Arris grabbed her hands tightly, grounding her as he knelt in front of her. "You're having a panic attack, baby. Listen to my voice," he said, his tone soothing but unwavering.

Dionne shook her head, her body trembling. "I can't…" she sobbed, her voice barely audible.

"Yes, you can," Arris insisted, his voice steady and sure. "Just follow me, okay? Breathe in through your nose for four seconds. Hold it for four. Then breathe out for six."

He demonstrated, inhaling deeply and exhaling slowly, his grip on her hands firm but reassuring. Dionne tried to follow, her breaths shaky and uneven at first, but she mimicked his movements, desperate to gain control.

Slowly, her breathing began to steady, though her chest still ached, the heaviness refusing to lift completely.

"You're doing good, Mama. Just keep going," Arris said softly, his eyes locked on hers. His voice was calm, his presence unwavering, but his heart ached seeing her like this.

"I can't…" Dionne whispered again, her tears falling freely.

"Yes, you can, baby. I've got you," he said, his voice filled with a quiet determination.

Bit by bit, her breaths slowed, the trembling in her body easing. But the ache in her chest—the weight of everything she'd been holding in—remained, pressing down on her like a boulder she couldn't shake.

Arris stayed with her, his hands still holding hers, his voice still guiding her. He wouldn't let her face this alone. Not now. Not ever.

Arris stepped closer, his movements slow and deliberate as he watched her panic ease slightly. Her breaths were still shaky, but she was trying. He needed to keep her grounded.

"Name five things you can see," he instructed softly, his voice steady and calm.

Dionne lifted her head, her eyes darting around as she searched for answers. "A red car... a dog... my nails... the pole light... and you," she said slowly, her voice trembling but steadying as she spoke.

Arris nodded, a small smile tugging at his lips. "Good, Mama. Now name four things you can touch."

Dionne took a deep breath, her hands roaming as she answered. "My steering wheel... my hair..." She paused, touching the seat beneath her. "The seat... and you," she said, her hand brushing against his as she spoke.

Arris's smile deepened. "Good, baby. Now name three things you can hear."

"The cars passing by... music... and your voice," she said, her words coming quicker this time. Her breathing was slowing, the panic receding.

Arris's chest swelled with relief, noticing how all her answers kept coming back to him. "Almost there, Mama. Name two things you can smell."

Dionne closed her eyes, taking another shaky breath as she focused. "My perfume... and your cologne," she said, her voice soft but clear.

Arris nodded, their hands still intertwined. "Last one, Mama. Name one thing you can taste."

Her eyes remained closed, her breaths finally evening out. Arris watched her intently, her lips parting as if she were about to speak. Instead, he leaned in, closing the space between them, and pressed his lips to hers.

The kiss was slow, deep, and full of everything neither of them could say in that moment. His tongue slid against hers, drawing a soft moan from Dionne as she melted into him.

When he pulled away, her eyes fluttered open, a calmness settling over her features. "You," she whispered, her voice steady now.

Arris smiled, his heart pounding as he pulled her into his arms, holding her tightly. She sank into his embrace, her head resting against his chest as his hand gently stroked her back.

"I always got you, baby," he murmured, his voice soft but resolute. "No matter what. Even when the world feels like it's closing in, I'll always be here."

Feenin'

Dionne exhaled deeply, her body relaxing fully against him. "What was that?" she asked, her voice quiet and a little startled. The weight of what she'd just experienced was still settling in.

"You had a panic attack, Mama," Arris said softly, his eyes searching hers with concern and tenderness.

Her brows furrowed, disbelief flickering across her face. "A panic attack?"

He nodded. "You've never had one before?"

She shook her head. "Never... I didn't even know..."

Arris cupped her face, his thumbs gently brushing her cheeks. "You'll never have another one as long as I'm around," he said firmly, his voice carrying a promise that sounded more like a vow.

Dionne stared at him, her eyes glossy with unspoken gratitude, a small smile breaking through the shock. She nodded, unable to find the right words, but knowing he felt her gratitude in her silence.

Arris pulled her close again, his arms wrapping around her as if shielding her from everything that had overwhelmed her moments before.

For the first time that day, Dionne felt safe—not just physically, but emotionally. She didn't know what was ahead, but she knew one thing: with Arris, she could breathe again.

"Let me get you home," Arris said, grabbing Dionne's hand and gently leading her out of the car.

Her steps were reluctant, her tone sharp despite the faint smile that tugged at her lips. "No, go be with the woman you're so-called in love with," she said, her words biting even as her eyes betrayed her true feelings.

Arris stopped and pulled her close, his dark eyes locking onto hers. "You're the only woman I'm in love with, Mama," he said, his voice steady and serious, leaving no room for doubt.

Before she could respond, he leaned down, capturing her lips in a soft, lingering kiss that melted away her defenses.

When they pulled back, Dionne exhaled shakily, trying to regain her composure. "I don't want to go home. I want to be with you," she admitted, her voice barely above a whisper.

Arris's lips curved into a small smile, his thumb brushing over the back of her hand. "Okay, baby," he said, his tone full of warmth.

He led her to the passenger side of her car, opening the door for her. "Wait," she said, pausing before getting in. "What about your car? I can drive."

Arris chuckled, shaking his head. "I'll have someone drop it off for me. I pay people for that. You just sit in this passenger seat and be pretty," he said, leaning in to kiss her again before helping her into the seat.

Sliding into the driver's side, Arris pulled out his phone and sent a quick text to his friends, letting them know everything was fine. He also messaged True, promising to come back for his tattoo another time.

Dionne did the same, texting her friends to let them know she was okay and heading home. She knew they'd call later, eager to dissect everything that happened at the tattoo shop. But for now, she tuned it all out, her focus entirely on the man beside her.

Arris drove with his usual ease, his hand resting instinctively between her thighs, his thumb idly stroking her leg like it belonged there. The gesture was small but grounding, a silent reminder of their connection.

Dionne smiled warmly, watching him navigate the road, his expression calm and focused. But beneath her exterior, emotions simmered—a mix of love, guilt, and longing.

She loved him, with every fiber of her being. Yet, in the quiet moments like this, when everything felt perfect, the weight of her reality pressed down on her. She couldn't give him everything he deserved, not while she was still tethered to a life she didn't want—a life with someone else.

Arris glanced at her briefly, catching her thoughtful expression. "You good, Mama?" he asked, his voice gentle but laced with concern.

Dionne nodded, forcing another smile. "Yeah," she said softly, though her heart ached with unspoken words.

Arris gave her thigh a reassuring squeeze, his touch grounding her once more. And for a moment, she let herself believe that this—them—was enough, even if it could never be everything they both needed it to be.

***

Dionne lay peacefully on Arris's chest as they lounged on the couch. They were supposed to be watching a movie, but somewhere in the middle, both had drifted off. Even in his sleep, Arris's hand rubbed gently over Dionne's bare butt, exposed since she'd taken off her jeans to be more comfortable. His touch was soothing, grounding her even in her dreams, as soft snores escaped her lips.

The quiet of the living room was interrupted by the sharp sound of Dionne's phone ringing. She didn't stir, her body too deeply relaxed in the comfort of Arris's arms.

The ringing stopped, only to start again seconds later. Arris shifted,

Feenin'

reaching over with one hand to grab the phone, while the other stayed where it was, absentmindedly caressing her. His jaw tightened when he saw the name on the screen: Malik.

He glanced down at Dionne, still fast asleep on his chest, her face serene and free of the burdens she carried while awake. The sight made him smile, a flicker of warmth cutting through his growing irritation. She was probably still drained from the emotional storm she'd weathered earlier, and he didn't want anything disturbing her peace—not even her fiancé.

When the phone rang again, Arris hit the decline button, sliding it facedown on the couch. He wrapped his arm more securely around Dionne, letting his own eyes drift closed. But the reprieve didn't last long; Malik's name flashed on the screen once more, the ringing cutting through the silence like a blade.

Dionne didn't stir, still lost in her peaceful slumber, her body molded perfectly against Arris's. But Arris's patience was wearing thin. His jaw clenched as he picked up the phone, staring at it for a moment before answering.

He didn't say a word, just held the phone to his ear, listening.

"Man, Dionne, where the fuck you at?" Malik's voice blared through the line, loud and laced with anger.

Arris's jaw tightened further, his free hand instinctively gripping Dionne a little tighter. The way Malik spoke to her, even when it wasn't actually her on the phone, made his blood boil.

Arris stayed silent, his own anger bubbling beneath the surface.

"Hello?" Malik barked again, the irritation in his tone growing.

Arris's thumb hovered over the mute button for a second before pressing it, cutting off Malik's voice. He leaned down, shaking Dionne gently. "Mama," he said softly, his tone coaxing but firm.

She stirred slightly, her body shifting against him, but instead of waking, she nestled deeper into his chest, sighing contentedly.

The sound of Malik's voice cut through the line again, muffled but still agitated. Arris's eyes darkened, the muscles in his jaw flexing as he resisted the urge to snap. *Damn, nigga, calm yo ass down*, he thought bitterly, his patience hanging by a thread.

He considered making his presence known to Malik, but a part of him held back, not wanting to escalate a situation that could put Dionne in a sticky spot later. But his restraint was thin, his irritation simmering with every ring, every sharp word Malik spat through the phone.

Arris took a deep breath, his hand still rubbing Dionne's back absentmindedly, grounding himself in her presence. She was the only thing keeping him from losing it entirely, the only reason he hadn't let his anger take over.

"Mama, get up," Arris said softly, pressing kisses to Dionne's lips until her eyes fluttered open.

"What, baby?" she murmured, her voice thick with sleep, her eyelids still heavy.

"This nigga wants to talk to you," Arris said, his tone shifting to something sharp and firm, laced with barely restrained irritation.

"Who?" she asked, her words slurred with exhaustion, not fully awake enough to care.

"Dionne!" Malik's voice blared through the phone, loud even though it was still on mute. The sound of his anger made Dionne's eyes snap open, the reality of the situation hitting her like a splash of cold water.

Arris's jaw tightened, his voice serious as he looked down at her. "Mama, get this phone before I cuss his ass out for talking to you like that."

Dionne sighed, sitting up quickly and snatching the phone from his hand. She took it off speaker and unmuted it, bringing it to her ear. She started to rise, intending to step into another room for privacy, but Arris wasn't having it.

He pulled her back against him, wrapping an arm securely around her waist while his other hand resumed its place on her bare skin. He continued his slow, deliberate movements, rubbing soothing circles on her butt, refusing to let her create distance.

Dionne smiled briefly at his possessiveness before finally addressing the voice on the phone. "What, Malik?" she said, her tone calm but laced with irritation.

"Where the fuck are you, and why haven't you answered any of my calls?" Malik demanded, his anger bleeding through the line.

Dionne barely registered his words because Arris chose that exact moment to lean in, his lips trailing along her neck. His kisses were slow and deliberate, his warm breath sending a shiver down her spine as he nipped lightly at her skin.

She bit her lip, fighting back a moan, her free hand weakly pushing at Arris's chest in protest. He didn't budge. Instead, his hold on her tightened, his movements slow and deliberate, his lips curving into a smirk against her neck.

"What do you want, Malik?" she asked, ignoring his questions as she squirmed against Arris's hold.

Arris knew exactly what he was doing, and he had no intention of stopping. He wanted Malik to hear—if not the moan she was struggling

Feenin'

to hold back, then the subtle change in her voice, the breathlessness that would betray her.

"You hit me up earlier saying we need to talk, and you're not here. I have to go to work," Malik snapped, his frustration mounting.

Dionne rolled her eyes, now remembering the conversation he initiated about premarital counseling with Mama Glen and how she'd completely forgotten about it.

"I said we'd talk. I didn't say when," she replied, her irritation seeping through her tone.

Arris, meanwhile, continued his slow assault on her senses. His lips trailed lower, his hand slipping beneath the waistband of her panties. Dionne's breath hitched sharply, her body betraying her as a soft whimper escaped. She quickly clamped her hand over her mouth, her heart racing as she fought for composure.

"So are we having this conversation or not?" Malik pressed, his patience wearing thin.

Before Dionne could answer, Arris's fingers slid inside her, his touch unrelenting and deliberate. A sharp, uncontrollable moan escaped her lips, and she quickly stifled it with her free hand, her body trembling against his.

"Dionne?" Malik asked sharply, his voice rising in suspicion.

Dionne tried to push Arris's hand away, but he was too strong, his grip unyielding. His smirk deepened as he watched her struggle, her body betraying her resolve.

"Hello! What are you doing, Dionne?" Malik's skeptical voice cut through the line.

"I'm..." Dionne stammered, struggling to form a coherent response. "Hold up, Malik," she said quickly before muting the call.

"Stop, Arris!" she begged in a breathless whisper as his fingers moved slowly, teasingly, inside her.

"No," Arris growled, his voice low and possessive. "That nigga needs to hear where you belong."

His fingers moved faster, his touch deliberate, drawing a loud, uncontrollable moan from her lips.

"Bruh, Dionne!" Malik's voice blared through the phone, snapping her back to reality.

Arris pressed his lips to her ear, his low whisper sending chills down her spine. "Hang up, Mama. He don't need you right now. I do."

Her hand trembled as she gripped the phone, her mind spinning as her body gave in to the sensations Arris was pulling from her.

"I'm... on... my way," she managed to get out, her voice trembling with the force of her emotions. She ended the call just as her orgasm crashed over her, her body shuddering as Arris kept his fingers moving, drawing every last ounce of pleasure from her.

When she finally came down, he pulled his fingers from her, licking them clean with a wicked smirk.

"You're wild," Dionne laughed breathlessly, the tension melting away for a brief moment.

"So, you leaving me for that nigga?" he asked, his tone teasing but his eyes sharp with unspoken emotion.

She rolled her eyes at his pettiness, though her heart ached at the truth behind his words. "I have to," she said softly, though every fiber of her being screamed to stay.

"You don't gotta do shit you don't want to," Arris countered, his voice steady and firm. "And your body's telling me you want to be here." He pulled her closer, his hands warm on her hips.

"I do, baby. But... everything is complicated right now," she admitted, her voice breaking as her hand caressed his beard.

He studied her for a moment, his jaw tightening before he nodded. "I'm gonna let you go to that nigga for now, but time's running out with him." His words were serious, carrying a weight she couldn't ignore.

She nodded, understanding the depth of his meaning. Their lips met again, the kiss filled with unspoken promises and longing.

"Leave these panties with me, though," he said, tugging at the waistband and letting it snap against her skin.

Dionne laughed, standing to remove them. She tossed the damp panties at him, and he caught them effortlessly, his grin mischievous.

She pulled her jeans back on, making sure her hoodie covered the mark Arris had left on her neck. As she slid her feet into her shoes, she sighed heavily, her reluctance to leave weighing on her.

Just as she reached for her keys, Arris grabbed her arm, pulling her back into him. His towering frame enveloped her as she laughed, her tension easing when she noticed her panties perched on his head like a makeshift hat.

"I love you, Mama," he said softly, his hand gently caressing her cheek as she melted into his touch.

Her eyes glistened with emotion. "I want to say it back so bad," she admitted, her voice trembling. "But it doesn't feel right when I'm about to go home to another man."

Arris nodded, understanding the conflict in her heart, but his need to hear it outweighed his pride. "I don't care, baby. I need to hear you say it. I need to know."

Feenin'

Her fingers traced his beard as she looked into his eyes. "I love you, Arris," she said softly, the truth spilling from her lips.

A bright smile broke across his face, his vulnerability shining through. In that moment, it didn't matter that she was going back to Malik—her heart was his, and that was all he needed to let her go for now.

He pulled her in for a deep kiss, the intensity of it leaving them both breathless. It was filled with love, longing, and a desperation to hold onto the moment for as long as they could.

When Dionne finally pulled away, she laughed, her forehead resting against his. "I can't take you seriously with my panties on your head like that," she teased.

Arris chuckled, pulling them off and playfully biting down on them, making her laugh harder.

He opened the door for her, their hands still intertwined as he walked her to her car. He helped her in, his hand lingering on hers.

"Be safe, Mama," he said, leaning in for one last kiss.

"I will. You too," she replied, her voice soft and filled with emotion.

As she drove away, Arris stood in his driveway, watching until her car disappeared from view. His chest tightened, but the smile remained on his face, knowing she loved him was enough for now.

Dionne sighed heavily as his presence faded into the distance. She missed him already, the ache in her chest deepening with each mile. The thought of going home to a man who no longer held her heart exhausted her.

She knew Arris was tired too—tired of watching her leave, tired of waiting for her to choose. The look on his face every time she walked away told her everything.

But it wasn't simple. Explaining her reasons for staying with Malik, for planning a wedding she didn't want, wasn't easy. It was a tangled mess of emotions and obligations that no one—not even Arris—could fully understand.

And yet, as her hands tightened on the steering wheel, one thing was painfully clear: her heart already belonged to Arris.

***

"Premarital counseling? Really, Malik?" Dionne said, her voice sharp as the argument erupted the moment she walked through the door. It started with him questioning where she'd been, why she'd sounded strange on the phone, and escalated to the core of her frustration: premarital counseling.

"Clearly, we fucking need it!" Malik shot back, his tone laced with anger and accusation. "You've been having these long-ass days at work, coming home late at night, taking secret phone calls and texts. Are you cheating on me, Dionne?"

His words cut through the room like a knife, but Dionne didn't flinch. She crossed her arms, her glare unwavering. "Don't you dare sit here and accuse me of cheating when you've been doing the same shit. Or have you forgotten that I actually caught your ass with a bitch in our bed?"

Malik's jaw tightened, guilt flashing across his face before he snapped back defensively. "How many times do I have to keep apologizing? How much longer do I have to pay for that mistake before you forgive me?"

Dionne's lips curled into a bitter smirk as she shook her head. "Forgive you?" she repeated, her voice dripping with disdain. "Nigga, if you think one fancy-ass date and some flowers at my job is enough to make up for that shit, then you don't know me at all."

Her blood boiled as she stared at him, anger radiating from her body. She'd just come from the sanctuary of Arris's arms, and the last thing she wanted was to stand here arguing with Malik about problems she no longer cared to fix.

Malik ran a hand over his face, his own frustration bubbling over. "You don't see I'm fucking trying? I signed us up for counseling to fix our issues!" he yelled, his voice rising to match hers.

"Yeah, counseling you didn't bother to discuss with me first!" Dionne shot back, stepping closer as her voice cracked with fury. "Instead, you ran to your mother like a little boy and blindsided me into agreeing to this bullshit. Again!"

"What the hell was I supposed to do, Dionne?" Malik yelled back, his eyes blazing. "You're never around for me to sit down and tell you shit anymore!"

Her chest heaved, her anger reaching a breaking point. "Now you know how the fuck I felt for the last few years of this relationship," she screamed, her voice trembling with raw emotion. "Now you know what it feels like to be degraded, abandoned, and left the fuck alone!"

The words hit Malik like a punch, his expression softening as her tears began to fall. But Dionne didn't care. She wasn't looking for his pity, and she wasn't interested in his excuses.

Their argument had become a screaming match—two people yelling to be heard, neither truly listening. But for Dionne, it didn't matter. Nothing Malik could say or do would change the way she felt.

She wasn't here for him. She wasn't staying for him.

Feenin'

She was here for one person and one person only: Mama Glen.

"I'm scared, Dionne!" Malik's voice cracked as he yelled, and Dionne froze in her tracks.

She'd heard Mama Glen say this before—that Malik was terrified of losing her—but hearing it come from his own mouth hit differently. It wasn't just a confession; it was a revelation, one that left her momentarily speechless.

Malik didn't stop, the floodgates opening as he continued. "You're a beautiful woman, inside and out. Any man would be lucky to have you on their arm, but you chose me, Dee! And I keep fucking up!" His voice broke, tears streaming down his face. "It feels like nothing I do nowadays can show you how much I love you."

Dionne stood still, her defenses wavering as she saw the pain etched across his face. She hadn't seen him cry like this before, not like this—raw, desperate, and exposed. For the first time in a long time, a pang of guilt tugged at her chest.

"Yes, I should have come to you first instead of my mother about counseling, or how I was feeling. But I was scared. Fuck, I'm still scared," he admitted, his voice trembling.

Her walls, which she'd fought so hard to keep intact, began to crumble under his words.

"I know you don't love me anymore," he said, his voice dropping to a whisper. "I see it in your eyes every time you look at me. And that shit fucks me up every fucking day." He wiped his face roughly, but the tears kept falling. "It's my fault. I put work above you. I cheated. I made you feel less than. But I want to make it right, Dionne. Please, let me make it right."

Dionne's eyes softened despite herself, his vulnerability striking a chord she didn't want to acknowledge. "Malik..." she started softly, but he stepped closer, grabbing her hands in his, his grip trembling.

"Please, baby. Don't leave me now. Not like this," he begged, his tone breaking her resolve piece by piece.

Her heart felt heavy, the weight of his plea suffocating her. She shook her head, trying to cling to her logic, her truth. "I can't—" she started to protest, but Malik cut her off, his voice trembling with urgency.

"Do it for my mother."

The words hit her like a punch to the gut. She froze, the air leaving her lungs as she stared at him.

"I already broke the heart of the woman of my dreams. Don't make me break my mother's heart too," he said, his voice cracking as tears slipped down his face.

Dionne felt herself falter, her body betraying her resolve. He was using Mama Glen to break through her defenses again, and like before, it was working. Her chest tightened painfully as she considered his words. Mama Glen didn't deserve to spend her last days watching her son's life fall apart.

Dionne closed her eyes, trying to drown out the emotions that threatened to overwhelm her. She hated that Malik knew exactly which strings to pull. And she hated even more that they worked.

"Please, Dionne," he begged, his voice barely above a whisper.

Tears slid silently down her cheeks, mirroring his. She hated this. Hated that she felt cornered. Hated that the right thing for Mama Glen was the wrong thing for her.

"Okay, Malik," she said finally, her voice trembling. "Fine. For Mama Glen."

Malik exhaled in relief, his tears slowing as a small, weary smile broke across his face. "When's the first session?" she asked, stepping out of his hold, needing space to breathe.

"In two days. At 11 a.m.," he answered quickly, his smile growing even though his eyes remained red and swollen.

"Alright. I'll be there," she said softly, her voice devoid of emotion. Every word felt like a dagger twisting in her own chest, the admission hurting far more than she wanted to admit.

"Thank you, Dionne," Malik said, his voice soft, full of hope.

She met his gaze, her tone cold and resolute. "I'm doing this for Mama Glen."

"I know," he said, nodding, but his voice was firm. "But I promise you, I'm going to fight for your love back. I still love you, Dionne."

He stepped closer, his eyes locking onto hers. Despite all the pain, all the mistakes, she could still see the love he carried for her. It was real, raw, and undeniable. But her heart didn't mirror his anymore.

Her love was reserved for one person now, and it wasn't Malik.

It was Mama Glen—and that was the only thing keeping her tethered to him.

Dionne stared down at her engagement ring, the diamond catching the light, mocking her with its brilliance. It felt like a shackle, a weight she could no longer bear. A single tear escaped, rolling down her cheek, but before she could wipe it away, Malik's thumb brushed it from her skin.

He leaned in, pressing a kiss to her cheek, a gesture meant to soothe. For him, it was an act of love, a silent promise that he was trying, that he still believed in them. But to her, it felt like a blade twisting deeper. A

Feenin'

betrayal. Not just to herself but to Arris, the man who owned the pieces of her heart that Malik would never touch.

She stood motionless, her breath shallow, the world tilting on its axis as she tried to steady herself against the weight of what she had just agreed to.

"I have to go to work," Malik said softly, his voice careful, almost hopeful, as though he didn't want to disturb the fragile silence between them.

All Dionne could do was nod. Words felt impossible, her throat too tight to form them.

Malik grabbed his things and walked out the door. The sound of it closing behind him echoed through the house, leaving her alone in the deafening silence. She remained where she stood, frozen, the walls of the room seeming to creep closer with every passing second.

She wanted to scream, to shatter the oppressive quiet. She wanted to throw something, anything, to release the storm clawing its way through her chest. But instead, she stayed rooted in place, her feet glued to the floor, her arms hanging limply at her sides.

The sharp trill of her phone cut through the air, pulling her momentarily from her spiraling thoughts. Her eyes flicked to it but didn't move to pick it up. It stopped ringing, the silence returning and feeling heavier than before.

Her vision blurred as the tears came, her chest heaving with suppressed sobs. Then, as if a dam inside her broke, the cries tore free, violent and unrelenting. She slid down the wall, her legs folding beneath her, her body collapsing under the weight of emotions she could no longer contain.

"Lord, please help me," she whispered, the words shaky and raw, her voice breaking under the force of her sobs.

But the prayer felt hollow, the words lost in the vast emptiness of her despair. The walls around her seemed to close in, her breath coming in short, sharp gasps as the panic clawed at her throat.

She tried desperately to remember what Arris had told her—five things you can see, four you can touch, three you can hear… But even thinking about him made it worse.

The thought of him walking away when he found out—when he realized she'd agreed to yet another obligation tethering her to Malik and Mama Glen—suffocated her. She could already see the pain in his eyes, the way he would turn his back on her, leaving her behind in a world she no longer wanted.

Her chest felt like it was caving in, the pressure unbearable as she gasped for air. Her trembling hands clutched at her chest, as though she could physically pull the pain out of herself.

The sobs turned to wails, her cries reverberating through the empty house. She cradled herself on the cold floor, rocking back and forth, tears soaking her cheeks. Her heart felt like it was breaking into pieces, each one heavier than the last.

The weight of her choices pressed down on her, suffocating her, burying her beneath guilt and regret. She hated herself for agreeing to this—for sacrificing her happiness for a woman she loved but for a life she didn't want. She hated Malik for using Mama Glen to manipulate her, hated herself even more for letting him.

But most of all, she hated the thought of losing Arris. The one person who made her feel free, who made her feel seen. And now, she was betraying him again.

Her body trembled as her sobs quieted to broken whimpers. Lying on the floor, Dionne felt like a hollow shell, her tears pooling beneath her.

She closed her eyes, whispering one last plea into the void. "Please, Lord… help me."

But the silence was her only answer.

Chapter 13

Arris sat behind his desk, flipping through the property listings Dionne had sent over for his new business ventures. Each listing was perfectly curated, another testament to how well she understood him. He couldn't wait to thank her in person when she stopped by his office, which he knew would be any minute. His focus was so locked on the papers in front of him that he didn't hear the soft knock at his office door.

China walked in, her usual bright smile lighting up the room. "You have a visitor," she said, her tone teasing as she already knew who it was.

Arris's lips tugged into a grin, his heart leaping at the thought of Dionne. And he was right—Dionne walked in moments later, her presence filling the room like a breath of fresh air. China stepped out quickly, closing the door to give them privacy.

Arris didn't waste a second. Rising from his chair, he strode over to her, his hands cupping her face as he pulled her into a deep kiss. His lips moved over hers with urgency, a silent expression of how much he'd missed her. Dionne responded instantly, parting her lips and deepening the kiss, her tongue sliding against his. The world outside his office faded, leaving just the two of them.

"Hey, baby," she said softly when they finally pulled apart, though Arris wasn't ready to let her go.

"Wassup, Mama? I miss you," he murmured against her skin, his lips trailing down her neck.

A soft moan escaped her lips as her head tilted back, giving him better access. "I miss you too," she breathed, her voice thick with need.

The brown Dior pantsuit she wore captivated him, the blazer slightly open, teasing him with a glimpse of her cleavage. He couldn't resist. Scooping her up effortlessly, he set her on his desk, standing between her legs as his kisses grew hungrier. His lips moved down her neck, leaving a trail of heat until he reached the curve of her breast.

"Baby, wait. We're in your office," she said cautiously, though her hands gripped his shoulders, her body betraying her words.

"I know," he growled, his voice thick with hunger. "And I'm about to fuck you on this desk."

Her eyes fluttered closed as his words sent a shiver through her, her body arching into him. Just as his fingers reached for the buttons on her blazer, a knock sounded at the door.

"Shit," Dionne whispered, quickly pushing him back and hopping off the desk. She straightened her blazer, smoothing her hair as she worked to compose herself. Arris smirked at her flustered movements, leaning back against the desk, unbothered.

"Come in," he called, his voice calm despite the heat simmering between them.

China stepped in with an apologetic smile. "Sorry to interrupt, but Arris, you have an unexpected guest."

Arris furrowed his brows, glancing at Dionne, who looked just as confused. But before either of them could ask, his mother, Angel, walked into the office.

"Hey, son," Angel said softly, a hesitant smile on her face.

Arris's chest tightened at the sight of her. He hadn't seen or spoken to her since the incident at her house a week ago, and the tension between them still lingered. He masked his frustration with a polite nod. "Wassup, Ma," he said dryly, standing straighter.

Angel's gaze shifted to Dionne, her smile faltering slightly. "Oh, I didn't know you were in a meeting. I can—"

"It's fine—we were just finishing up," Dionne interjected quickly, her tone polite but clipped as she fought to calm the lingering tension Arris had stirred in her moments ago.

"No, we weren't," Arris countered bluntly, his eyes locked on her.

"Yes, we were," Dionne shot back, glaring at him. "I have to go show a house." She grabbed her purse and keys, her movements quick and deliberate.

Arris's eyes followed her every move, his displeasure evident as he watched her prepare to leave.

"We'll talk soon, Arris. And it was nice seeing you again, Ms. Angel," Dionne said politely, flashing a warm smile at his mother.

"Nice seeing you too, Dionne. You're rocking that suit!" Angel said, her tone full of warmth and approval.

"Thank you! Well, I'll leave you two to talk," Dionne said, walking

Feenin'

out with her usual grace. She didn't miss the way Angel's face lit up as she watched her go.

Arris, on the other hand, stood rooted in place, his eyes glued to Dionne until she disappeared from view.

"She's such a beautiful woman," Angel said softly, a knowing smile on her face.

"She is," Arris replied without hesitation, his voice quieter, more thoughtful. His eyes lingered on the door, the ghost of Dionne's presence still palpable in the room.

Angel studied her son, her smile fading slightly as she connected the dots. The way his eyes had tracked Dionne's every movement, the way his voice softened when he spoke of her—it was clear that Dionne wasn't just a business partner.

But the knowledge confused her, given that Dionne was engaged to another man. Still, Angel said nothing, instead choosing to let the moment settle, her own thoughts swirling.

Arris remained silent, his mind far from the conversation waiting to happen with his mother. All he could think about was Dionne—and the pieces of himself he handed to her every time she walked into the room.

Once Dionne walked out, the air in the room shifted, growing heavy with unspoken tension. Angel stood there for a moment, watching her son, her guilt radiating like a spotlight between them.

"Can I have a hug?" she asked softly, noticing the stiffness in his shoulders and the way his jaw remained tight.

Arris hesitated, the weight of his emotions holding him back, but after a brief pause, he walked around his desk and pulled her into a hug. His arms were loose around her, his body tense, making it clear the gesture was out of obligation, not affection.

Angel felt the coldness, her heart aching as she released him. They sat on the couch, an unspoken understanding that this was about to be a difficult conversation.

"What you doing here, Ma?" Arris asked, his tone calm on the surface but laced with barely contained frustration.

Angel fidgeted with her hands, her usual confidence replaced by nervousness. "I came to talk to you… to apologize," she said, her voice trembling slightly.

"You ain't got to apologize," Arris replied flatly, leaning back against the couch. His jaw tightened as he stared straight ahead. "You grown. Who you fucking is none of my business."

The sharpness of his words hung in the air, cutting deep. Angel's expression hardened as she narrowed her eyes at him.

"I know you're mad at me, but you better watch your language when you're talking to me, Arris," she said sternly, her voice carrying the authority of a mother who wasn't afraid to call her son out.

Arris sighed, his tone still emotionless as he muttered, "I apologize."

Angel's eyes softened at the gesture, but the tension between them remained thick. She took a deep breath and decided to address the elephant in the room head-on.

"I know seeing me with your father—"

"That nigga ain't my father," Arris snapped, cutting her off with venom in his tone. His jaw clenched as his fists balled at his sides.

Angel flinched at the sharpness of his words, quickly correcting herself. "I'm sorry. Calvin," she corrected softly, her voice tinged with guilt. "I know it was hard for you to see me and Calvin together like that. But... we're trying to work through our problems."

Arris let out a bitter laugh, shaking his head as he looked away from her, his gaze fixed on the floor. The sound wasn't one of amusement but of disbelief and barely suppressed rage.

"Working through your problems?" he repeated, his tone low and dangerous. His eyes snapped back to hers, the fury in them impossible to miss. "Problems that destroyed me and Lani? Problems that tore this whole family apart?"

Angel's eyes filled with tears, but she didn't look away. "I know you've been carrying a lot of pain because of what happened," she said softly, her voice breaking. "And I know I can't erase what Calvin did, or how it hurt you and your sister. But people can change, Arris. He's trying to change."

Arris clenched his fists tighter, his nails digging into his palms as he worked to keep his temper in check. "Change?" he repeated, his voice dripping with sarcasm. "You think a few visits and some empty-ass apologies erase the shit he did? The shit we had to go through because of him?"

"Arris," Angel began, reaching out to place a hand on his arm, but he pulled away, the distance between them growing even wider.

"Do Lani know about you two?" he asked, his voice colder than ice.

Angel hesitated, guilt flickering across her face. "No... we wanted to tell you both at the right time."

Arris let out a humorless chuckle, shaking his head. "Right time?" he repeated bitterly. "There's never gonna be a 'right time,' Ma. Not for this. Not for him."

Angel's heart broke at the anger and pain etched into her son's face. She opened her mouth to respond, but the look in his eyes stopped

Feenin'

her. It wasn't just anger. It was betrayal, disappointment, and years of resentment all rolled into one.

"I don't care anymore," Arris said finally, his voice devoid of emotion. "I'm done with this conversation."

Angel's heart tightened at the coldness in his tone, but she pressed on. "Come on, Arris. Don't be like that. I think you should do the same with him—"

Arris's head snapped toward her, his expression darkening. "Don't be like what?" he interrupted, his voice rising slightly before he caught himself and took a deep breath, forcing his tone into icy calm.

"Look, Ma," he said, his jaw clenching, "if you want to work through whatever problems you two have, that's your business. But pushing those same expectations on me when it comes to him? That's crossing the line."

His voice was detached, cold, but the underlying fury vibrated in every word.

"I say this with the utmost respect, Ma," he continued, his fists clenching at his sides. "I don't fuck with Calvin. I want to kill that nigga with everything in me, but the simple fact that he's A'Lani's father, and you clearly still love him, stops me. So coming into my place of business to tell me that you're working shit out with that nigga and expecting me to do the same? You're wasting your time."

Angel's breath hitched at his words, but she refused to back down. "Sweetie, look at how angry you are," she said softly, trying to reach through the storm raging inside him. "It's all because of the pent-up anger toward your father."

"And that's why I need to stay far away from that nigga," Arris snapped, cutting her off before she could continue.

Angel took a shaky breath. "Please, Arris. Just hear him out. He really wants to make things right. Not just with me and A'Lani but with you too."

"Make things right?" Arris repeated, a dark chuckle rumbling from his chest. "Who made things right when you were crying because that nigga cheated on you?" he asked, his tone sharp and unforgiving.

"Arris, stop," Angel said sternly, her voice cracking under the weight of his words.

But Arris wasn't done. Years of pain, resentment, and anger poured out of him, unstoppable now. "No, Ma. Who made things right when that nigga got picked up by the cops, and we were left with no lights, no food, and no water to wash our asses?"

Tears streamed down Angel's face, but she couldn't find the words to stop him.

"Who made things right when A'Lani cried herself to sleep every night because of that nigga? Or when she had random panic attacks out of nowhere because she didn't feel safe in her own damn home?" Arris's voice grew louder, each word dripping with venom.

"Arris," Angel tried again, her voice breaking, but he ignored her.

"Who made things right when you got laid off for a month and we didn't have shit to eat at night? Huh?" His voice rose further, his rage boiling over, his eyes blazing with suppressed tears.

"Okay, you can stop now," Angel begged, but Arris pressed on.

"No, Ma. You came here, to my business, to talk about that nigga. So let's talk," he said, his tone now laced with biting sarcasm.

Angel shook her head, but Arris took a step closer, his presence towering over her. "Who made things right when I got shot because of that nigga? Who made things right when the job you were working stressed you out so bad you had to retire? Or when A'Lani wanted to follow her dreams, go to college, and have her tuition paid in full?"

Angel's sobs filled the room as Arris stood, his chest heaving with anger.

"ME, MA! ME!" he shouted, his voice cracking as he gestured to himself. "That nigga Calvin didn't do shit our entire lives. He didn't make shit right! All he ever did was fuck things up. And that's all he's ever gonna do because he's a fuck up!"

His words cut through the air like a blade, raw and brutal, each syllable filled with years of pent-up fury. He didn't care if the whole building heard him. He didn't care about anything but letting his mother know how deeply her choices had wounded him.

Angel's hands trembled as she tried to wipe her tears, her entire body shaking under the weight of his words.

Arris's voice lowered, but the venom in his tone was still clear. "So, yeah. You can take that nigga back if that's what you wanna do. Honestly, Ma, I don't give a fuck anymore. Because the one who's always gonna make shit right in this family is me."

Angel broke down, her sobs racking her body as she covered her face with her hands. She couldn't look at him, couldn't form the words to respond. Arris turned his back to her, his shoulders rising and falling as he fought to control his own emotions.

For a long moment, the only sound in the room was Angel's crying. Arris stayed standing, his fists still clenched, his body rigid with unspent anger.

Arris was exhausted—emotionally, mentally, and physically. Every

Feenin'

word exchanged with his mother felt like another stab to an old wound, a wound that never had the chance to fully heal. The longer they talked about his father, the closer he felt to breaking. He clenched his fists, trying to steady himself, but the storm inside him raged louder.

What he truly needed in this moment wasn't words or apologies. It was her. Dionne. The one person who could quiet the chaos and anchor him when everything felt like it was spinning out of control.

His mind was already racing, yearning for the calm she always brought him. Without hesitation, he sent a quick, discreet message to China, his lifeline for logistics, before turning his gaze back to Angel.

If he had known this conversation was coming, he would have told Dionne to stay. He wouldn't have let her leave.

"Arris... please," Angel said, her voice trembling as fresh tears spilled down her cheeks. She looked broken, desperate to reach him. "Just let me explain—"

Before he could respond, the door opened again, and China stepped in. Her timing couldn't have been better. Relief flooded him, giving him an excuse to end this conversation before it pushed him over the edge.

China took one look at the room—the fire in Arris's eyes, the tears streaming down Angel's face—and immediately understood the tension. She didn't ask questions, her professionalism intact.

"Brian—the investor—wanted me to let you know that he canceled the meeting for today and rescheduled for next week," she informed him, her tone calm and efficient. "Also, I've got the address for the property you just requested. I'll hurry; the showing ends in less than an hour."

Arris gave her a small nod, his voice soft but firm. "Thank you, China."

She offered him a reassuring smile before leaving the room, the door clicking shut behind her.

"I have to work, Ma," Arris said, his voice measured. Though calm on the surface, it carried the same undercurrent of anger and exhaustion that had been bubbling throughout their conversation.

Angel wiped at her face, her teary eyes locking onto his. "Okay," she whispered, her tone defeated. "But... can we talk later? I really want to explain everything."

Arris stared at her for a moment, his jaw tightening. As much as he hated this conversation—hated the topic and the man at the center of it—he couldn't deny his mother. No matter how mad she made him, no matter how much her choices hurt, she was still his mother. And he loved her.

"Yes," he said after a pause, his voice softening slightly. "I'll come by soon."

Angel exhaled a sigh of relief, her shoulders relaxing for the first time since she entered the room. Her lip quivered as she nodded, gratitude shining through her tear-streaked face.

Arris took a step closer and pulled her into a tight hug. Despite the anger simmering inside him, he held her as if to remind her that his love for her hadn't wavered. His lips pressed a lingering kiss to her forehead, a silent reassurance even as his heart burned with frustration.

"I love you, son," Angel whispered, her voice breaking under the weight of her emotions.

"I love you too, Ma," he replied, his tone low but sincere. "Drive safely."

Angel nodded, her trembling smile a bittersweet reflection of the moment. She left the office, casting one last look over her shoulder before disappearing into the hallway.

As soon as the door closed behind her, Arris let out a long, shaky breath, his hands gripping the edge of his desk for support. The air still felt thick, his chest heavy with everything unsaid. But one thought dominated his mind: I need Dionne.

Without wasting another second, he grabbed his keys and headed for the door. His focus shifted completely as he followed the directions to the address China had given him—the house Dionne was showing.

He didn't care what excuse he had to make up to see her. He didn't care if she was busy. All he knew was that he needed her—her voice, her touch, her presence—to calm the raging storm inside him. Because in this moment, she was the only thing that could save him from drowning.

***

"So this is the master bedroom," Dionne explained, her tone smooth and professional as she gestured toward the spacious room. "It comes with its own private bathroom—"

She was abruptly cut off by the man she was showing the house to. "Does it come with you too?" he said, his voice dripping with flirtation.

Dionne's polite smile stayed in place, but a flicker of irritation flashed in her eyes. She wasn't new to these types of comments, but they never failed to get under her skin. "No, it doesn't, Mr. Thomas," she replied evenly, keeping her voice professional and cool. "But I'm sure your wife will love this bathroom."

Her sharp response landed exactly where she intended, her gaze dropping pointedly to the wedding band on his finger.

Thomas chuckled, amused by her bluntness, clearly misreading her professionalism as coyness. "You're feisty," he said, his grin widening,

Feenin'

as if that made him more charming.

The entire showing had been like this—a series of flirtatious remarks, lingering glances, and comments that Dionne had to deflect while maintaining her composure. Though he was easy on the eyes—his thick beard, slightly tanned complexion, and sharp suit giving him an air of appeal—he wasn't her type. He wasn't even close. And even if he were, the bold ring on his finger was enough to extinguish any interest.

Dionne continued with the showing, her voice steady and unaffected as she led him back downstairs to the front of the house. She was counting down the minutes until this ordeal was over.

As they reached the foyer, she turned to face him, her practiced, professional smile firmly in place. "So, that's the end of the showing. Do you have any questions?"

She hoped her tone would signal that it was time for him to leave, but Thomas had other plans. His smirk grew, and he took a deliberate step toward her, closing the distance between them.

"Yeah, I have a question," he said, his voice dipping into what he probably thought was a seductive tone. "Can I take you on a date?"

Dionne's polite smile faltered slightly, irritation flashing in her eyes as she instinctively stepped back to create space between them.

"No," she said firmly, holding up her left hand to display the large diamond ring on her finger. "You're married, and I'm engaged."

The words came out smoothly, but the second they left her lips, her mind betrayed her. It wasn't Malik's face she pictured—it was Arris. The thought of him hit her so fast, so deep, that it made her heart flutter against her will.

Thomas smiled at her response, undeterred. The glint in his eyes showed he wasn't taking her answer seriously. "Neither my wife nor your fiancé has to know," he said, his smirk widening as his gaze shamelessly roamed over her. His tongue flicked out to wet his lips as he took another step closer.

Dionne's stomach turned at the audacity. Her expression tightened, the professional mask slipping for just a moment as she took another step back. She wasn't about to let him corner her—or disrespect her or her relationship further.

Before Dionne could respond, a familiar touch grazed the small of her back, sending a jolt through her body. She stiffened momentarily, her breath hitching, before her shoulders relaxed. She knew exactly who it was.

"Her fiancé knows everything," Arris said, his voice deep and cutting as he stepped forward, towering over Thomas with a protective intensity.

Thomas's confidence wavered as his eyes darted up to Arris, who looked at him with a stern, unflinching glare. The air shifted, heavy with tension, and Thomas instinctively took a step back, raising his hands in surrender.

"My bad bruh. Didn't mean no disrespect," Thomas said quickly, his tone defensive and suddenly meek.

"Ain't your bruh," Arris replied coldly, his smirk laced with danger. "And you meant exactly what you said. You just didn't expect her fiancé to show up."

The cocky grin on Arris's face made Dionne's heart swell, a warmth blooming in her chest as she stood frozen, watching the exchange. She could see Thomas squirm under Arris's gaze, his earlier bravado crumbling into discomfort.

Arris finally turned his attention to Dionne, and the look in his eyes made her feel like the only woman in the world. His expression softened instantly, love and longing replacing the hardness that had just been there.

"Hey, baby," he said, his voice low and tender as if the last few moments hadn't just happened. "I didn't mean to interrupt you at work. I just missed you so much... and I brought you these."

He revealed a bouquet of tulips from behind his back, and Dionne's breath caught. They weren't just any tulips—they were Semper Augustus Tulips, their red-and-white streaks shining like precious jewels.

Dionne's eyes widened as she took in the sight of the rare, impossibly expensive flowers. These tulips, known for their history as the most valuable in the world, had to be specially shipped from overseas and were meant to last a lifetime.

Her heart swelled, overwhelmed by his thoughtfulness. Before she could find the words to respond, Thomas broke the moment, his voice cutting through the tension.

"Man, those flowers are rare as hell!" he said, his tone filled with awe as his eyes lingered on the bouquet.

Arris's gaze hardened further, his lips curling into a dangerous smirk. "Take a picture," he said coldly, his voice like ice, each word deliberate and cutting.

Thomas blinked, confused, his discomfort growing by the second. "W-what?" he stammered, his confidence from earlier now completely shattered.

"Yeah, you heard me," Arris continued, stepping closer, his towering frame almost forcing Thomas to backpedal. His tone was laced with venom, dripping with disdain. "Take a picture and show your wife—so

Feenin'

she can see how much less of a man and husband yo' ass really is."

Dionne instinctively reached for his hand, her fingers curling around his to steady him, to remind him to stay calm. But the protective fire in his eyes told her he wasn't letting this slide, even if he wasn't saying everything on his mind.

The words landed like a slap, and Thomas's face flushed crimson, his bravado crumbling into pure fear. He tried to form a response, his mouth opening and closing uselessly as he shifted uncomfortably under Arris's glare.

Arris didn't flinch, his eyes boring into the man's soul, daring him to say something—anything—to defend himself. Thomas's hands trembled slightly, his gaze darting to Dionne as if looking for some kind of escape or lifeline.

Dionne didn't offer him any. She stood silent, her arms crossed, her expression neutral, though her heart swelled with admiration for Arris. The way he defended her, the way he held men like Thomas accountable, only deepened the love she felt for him.

"I—I didn't mean any disrespect," Thomas stammered, his voice faltering as he took another step back.

"Ain't no 'I didn't mean to,'" Arris snapped, his voice low but sharp enough to cut through the tension in the room like a blade. "You said exactly what you meant. Now, get the fuck outta here before I really show you what disrespect looks like."

Thomas shifted uncomfortably, clearly embarrassed now. "My bad," he muttered again, avoiding Arris's piercing gaze. He turned to Dionne, his tone laced with defeat. "I'll talk the deal over with my wife before making a decision, Ms. Smith."

Dionne gave him a curt nod, her professional demeanor intact despite the lingering tension in the air. Without another word, Thomas turned on his heel and hurried out, the embarrassment practically radiating off him.

As the door clicked shut behind him, the room seemed to exhale. Dionne turned back to Arris, her heart racing—not from fear but from the sheer force of his presence and the way he had just defended her without hesitation.

"You didn't have to embarrass him like that," Dionne said through soft laughter, shaking her head as she leaned into Arris.

Arris, however, didn't share her amusement. His expression remained serious, though a smirk tugged at the corner of his lips. "It's better than him being injured," he said, his voice low, the protectiveness in his tone unmistakable.

Dionne blushed under his intense gaze, the possessiveness in his eyes sending a shiver through her. "You're crazy," she said with a soft laugh, trying to play off the warmth rising in her chest.

Arris's smirk widened, his dimples deepening as he leaned in closer. "You love my crazy ass though," he replied, his voice dripping with confidence.

She shook her head with a grin, but she didn't deny it. She couldn't—because it was true.

In one swift motion, Arris scooped her up, her laugh echoing through the empty house as he carried her to the kitchen island. He set her down gently, his hands already working to unbutton her blazer.

"Arris, we can't fuck in here," Dionne protested, though her voice wavered, betraying how much she wanted him.

"Yes, we can," he said, undeterred as his lips trailed along her neck. His hands slipped the blazer off her shoulders with ease, his touch sending sparks across her skin. "I bought the place."

Dionne froze, pulling back slightly to look at him. "You what?" she asked, her voice filled with shock.

Arris's deep chuckle reverberated through his chest as he continued undressing her, unbothered by her surprise. "I called the owner and purchased it," he said casually, his tone laced with possessiveness. "I saw the way that nigga was looking at you, heard his little slick comments flirting with you and shit. Now, he can't have my woman—or this house."

His dark eyes glimmered with satisfaction, and Dionne stared at him, speechless. The sheer audacity of his actions should have startled her, but instead, it left her breathless—and undeniably aroused.

"Not I got you out here buying houses," she teased, her lips curving into a mischievous smile, trying to lighten the mood even as her heart raced.

Arris laughed, his deep, husky tone sending chills down her spine. "I *feen* for you so bad, Mama, I'd buy you a planet if I could," he said, his words filled with raw sincerity, though Dionne laughed softly, brushing it off.

She raised a brow, curiosity now piquing through the heat building between them. "So, what are you planning to do with this place, Mr. Big Spender?" she teased, her tone playful but edged with genuine intrigue.

Arris didn't bother answering with words. Instead, his lips crashed into hers, his kiss searing, needy, and full of conviction. His hands slid down her waist with purpose, tugging her blazer off completely as he deepened the kiss, pouring every ounce of his feelings into it.

"It's not mine to say," he murmured against her skin, his voice low

Feenin'

and filled with meaning. His lips trailed to her neck, his touch setting her nerves alight as her breath hitched.

"What?" she whispered, her voice shaky, a moan slipping past her lips as his hands gripped her hips firmly.

"It's yours, Mama," he said, his words sending a jolt straight to her heart.

Dionne froze, her mind racing to keep up with the weight of what he just said. "What do you mean, it's mine?" she asked, her voice barely audible over her thundering heartbeat.

"I put it in your name," he replied simply, his tone steady, yet filled with a raw possessiveness that made her body weak. His lips hovered near her ear, his warm breath sending shivers down her spine. "But right now, I'm going to show you exactly what it's used for."

His voice dripped with desire, dark and commanding, as his lips claimed hers once again. Dionne's mind reeled at his confession, but all thoughts of the house, its cost, or its significance melted away under his touch.

This wasn't just about the house. This was Arris, staking his claim, reminding her in every way that she was his—and no matter what stood between them, that wasn't going to change.

Dionne's breath hitched, her body already melting under his touch. Before she could form a coherent response, Arris's hands moved with precision, unclasping her bra and replacing the fabric with his mouth.

"Oh, shit," Dionne moaned, her head falling back as his lips found her breast, his tongue teasing her sensitive skin.

"You got me buying houses, Mama," Arris growled against her, his voice vibrating against her skin.

She couldn't help but laugh breathlessly through her pleasure, her fingers tangling in his hair as he continued his assault on her senses. "I can't believe you," she managed to whisper, though her body betrayed her words, arching into him.

"You'll believe me when I'm done showing you what this place is for," Arris muttered, his tone filled with promise as his hands gripped her thighs, spreading her legs.

Dionne bit her lip, heat flooding her as she gave in completely, her mind spinning from both his audacity and his touch.

Arris wasn't just a man; he was a storm—a relentless, possessive force that swept her up every time, leaving her powerless to resist. And, truthfully, she didn't want to.

Arris slid Dionne's pants down slowly, letting them pool at her ankles, her panties following soon after. Dionne's mind raced, unable to fully believe that he was about to fuck her right here on the kitchen counter of a house he bought—not because he needed it, but out of pure spite for Thomas daring to flirt with her.

Arris spread her legs, his hands firm on her thighs, and without hesitation, his tongue found her clit.

"Oh my fucking—" Dionne moaned loudly, her head falling back as waves of pleasure coursed through her body.

But Arris wasn't done. He pulled back just as quickly as he'd started, his need for her overwhelming every thought. He stripped out of his pants, his dick springing free, hard and ready for her.

He didn't waste a second, sliding into her in one deep stroke, eliciting a sharp gasp from Dionne. His movements were relentless, his thrusts powerful and unyielding as he pounded into her.

"Fuck!" Dionne cried out, her nails digging into his shoulders as she clung to him, her body arching to meet his.

Arris gripped her waist tightly, his fingers pressing into her skin as his hips moved with a steady rhythm, each thrust releasing the pent-up frustration and anger he'd been holding since his conversation with his mother.

Dionne's moans turned into screams, her voice echoing through the empty house as he hit every spot inside her with precision. His lips found her neck, kissing, biting, and claiming her with every move, his hands holding her as if he'd never let go.

Slowing his thrusts, Arris buried himself deeper, making Dionne feel every inch of him as her body trembled in his arms. He lifted his head, his dark, intense eyes locking onto hers as his grip shifted to her neck, firm but careful.

"Who did you think of when you said fiancé?" he asked, his voice low and commanding, his hips never stopping, his strokes slow and deliberate now, sending jolts of pleasure through her.

Dionne was overwhelmed, her mind clouded by the sensation of him filling her completely. She couldn't think, couldn't speak, couldn't focus on anything but him. A soft, broken moan escaped her lips, her answer lost in the haze of her pleasure.

Arris's hand on her neck tightened slightly, his lips brushing against hers, his tone firmer this time. "Who did you think of?" he repeated, his thrusts deep, his pace unrelenting as his eyes bore into hers, demanding her truth.

Dionne blinked up at him, her body shuddering as another moan slipped free. Her lips parted, and the words tumbled out before she could even think to stop them. "You... I thought of you."

Feenin'

Her voice was breathless, but her tone was laced with raw honesty. The truth of her confession hit Arris like a wave, and a smug, satisfied smile spread across his lips.

"I can't wait to make that shit true," Arris said, his voice dripping with conviction, his eyes locked on hers.

Dionne's body froze under him, her heart skipping a beat. He wanted to marry her? The thought sent her mind spiraling. She was already engaged to another man, yet here he was—bold, confident, and unapologetically claiming her as his own.

The look in her eyes as she said it spoke volumes—love, longing, and surrender all reflected in her gaze. There was no room for doubt. She wasn't lying. When she told Thomas she was engaged, it wasn't Malik she thought of. It was Arris. It had always been Arris.

Arris kissed her deeply, his lips moving against hers with the same intensity as his body. He poured every ounce of his emotion into the kiss—his love, his passion, his need to remind her that she was his, in every sense of the word.

"You're mine," he growled against her lips, his pace picking up again as Dionne moaned louder, her body trembling in his hold.

"Yes, baby," she breathed, her words broken by her cries of pleasure, her heart beating wildly as she clung to him.

In that moment, there was no house, no Angel, no Malik—only them. Their connection was raw, consuming, and undeniable. Dionne wasn't just thinking of him. She was his, body, heart, and soul. And nothing, not even the weight of her engagement ring, could take that away.

Her thoughts raced as his thrusts didn't falter, his pace relentless and matching the storm brewing in her mind. "Arris… please," she whimpered, her voice trembling, though not from pain. The overwhelming pleasure mixed with his words had her feeling things she wasn't ready to face.

"Please, what?" he asked, his tone low and teasing, his hands gripping her waist tightly as he pulled her to the edge of the counter. He didn't slow down—if anything, he moved harder, faster, pouring every ounce of his love, his anger, and his need into her.

"Arris!" she cried out, her nails digging into his shoulders, her body trembling as she teetered on the brink.

Her walls tightened around him, and Arris groaned, his head falling to her shoulder. "Fuck," he growled, his voice rough and filled with raw need. "I'll put a kid in you if you don't stop, Mama."

The seriousness in his tone sent a shiver through her, but the heat in her chest bubbled over, and she couldn't help the giggle that slipped from her lips. He was wild, completely unrestrained, and yet she loved him for it.

"I love yo' ass so much, Dionne," Arris murmured, his voice cracking slightly as if the weight of his emotions was too much to contain.

Dionne felt her orgasm building, a powerful wave that she couldn't hold back any longer. "I love you—" she tried to say, but her words were cut off by a scream as her release overtook her. Her body spasmed, and to her surprise, she squirted, soaking not only Arris but the kitchen floor.

"Shit," Arris muttered, his voice filled with awe as he slowed his movements, watching her body tremble beneath him. He pulled out just in time, releasing onto her thigh as his own body went limp.

Their heavy breaths mingled as Arris leaned down, pulling her into a deep, possessive kiss. Every ounce of passion, love, and devotion he felt for her poured into that kiss, and Dionne melted against him.

"You done working for the day?" Arris asked, his lips brushing against hers as his hands slid up her back. "I'm not ready to let your ass go yet."

Dionne blinked up at him, her body still trembling. "I have another show—"

Her sentence was cut off by a loud moan as Arris slid back inside her, slow and deliberate.

"Cancel it," he said firmly, his strokes deep and slow, making her eyes roll back.

Dionne opened her mouth to protest, but he didn't give her the chance. Grabbing her phone from the counter, he quickly unlocked it—already knowing her password—and went straight to her booking schedule. All the while, his hips continued to move against hers, drawing soft, breathless moans from her lips.

With one hand steadying her waist and the other canceling her final showing for the day, he sent a polite, professional rescheduling message, all without missing a beat. He put the phone down with a smirk, his dark eyes filled with satisfaction as Dionne gasped and clung to him.

Her protests were forgotten, her mind too clouded by the pleasure he was giving her. He lifted her off the counter, carrying her into the next room, and they continued, fucking in every room of the house. The tension, the need, the connection between them—it consumed them both, leaving no part of the house untouched by their passion.

Every corner of the house now bore Arris's mark, but it wasn't his—it was hers. The deed, the papers, every legal right to the property, all in her name. He paid for it in full, no questions asked, ensuring she had a

Feenin'

place to call her own—a sanctuary, an escape, somewhere she could go when the weight of the world pressed too hard.

The moment he caught Thomas's lustful gaze lingering on her, saw the audacity in the man's smirk as he flirted with what wasn't his, something inside Arris snapped. His possessiveness wasn't just a fleeting emotion—it was a visceral need, carved into his very being. He wasn't just claiming her in that moment; he was solidifying her place, her comfort, her freedom.

To Arris, that house wasn't just a piece of property anymore—it was a symbol. A declaration. Every brick, every wall, every polished surface shouted one undeniable truth: She belonged to him.

The idea of another man staking claim on anything, let alone someone as sacred to him as Dionne, was enough to make him act. He didn't just buy the house to get back at Thomas. No, this was about ensuring that everything she touched, everything she loved, belonged to her—and by extension, to them.

It wasn't rational. It wasn't practical. But Arris didn't care. His love for Dionne wasn't measured or restrained; it was raw, all-consuming, and, at times, overwhelming. He'd spend three million, thirty million, or his entire soul if it meant making her his in every way imaginable.

They would have stayed at the house all night, lost in each other, had it not been for the sound of Dionne's phone vibrating against the dresser.

"Who the fuck is that?" Arris growled, his lips still pressed to her neck.

Dionne reached for her phone with a shaky hand, her body still humming from their rounds. She glanced at the screen, her heart sinking slightly. "It's London. She's reminding me about girls' night."

Arris let out a low groan, annoyed that their time was being cut short. "You can't cancel on them?" he asked, his tone frustrated as he kissed her shoulder.

She sighed, running a hand through his hair. "No, I promised them I'd go out tonight."

Arris pulled back, his lips brushing hers in one last lingering kiss. "Alright, Mama. But I'm not done with you yet," he said with a smirk, his hands trailing down her body one last time.

It was supposed to be a quick goodbye. A kiss, maybe a lingering touch before she rushed off to get ready. But Arris had other plans.

"Sit on my face," he said with that signature smirk, his eyes dark with hunger.

"Arris!" Dionne gasped, swatting at his chest. "I have to get ready! The girls are going to kill me if I'm late."

"Just one last taste before you leave me," he murmured, leaning downward, his lips brushing against her neck, his hands gripping her thighs.

And just like always, she caved.

With a breathless sigh, she straddled him, hesitating for only a second before lowering herself above his face. She tried to keep her weight light, but Arris wasn't having that. His strong hands gripped her waist, yanking her down firmly against his mouth.

"Arris," she protested weakly, a breathy laugh escaping. "I don't want to suffocate you."

"You won't," he reassured her before diving in, gripping her legs tightly.

The moment his tongue made contact, Dionne's head tilted back, a sharp moan slipping from her lips. His movements were fast, precise, relentless. He devoured her like he had all the time in the world, sucking, licking, teasing until her legs shook around him.

"Mhmm, yesss," she whimpered, her hands pressed against the wall in front of her, her body rocking against his mouth.

The heat coiled in her stomach, the pleasure unbearable. And then it hit—her orgasm crashing through her like a tidal wave. She trembled above him, panting as he licked up every last drop, dragging out her pleasure until she was left breathless.

Finally, she lifted herself off him, her thighs still quivering. Arris grinned up at her, his beard glistening with her wetness, his tongue flicking out to taste it.

"You taste so fucking good," he murmured, licking his lips, his eyes locked onto hers like he wasn't nearly finished with her yet.

Dionne swallowed hard, her body still pulsing from his touch.

And now, she was definitely going to be late.

"Now you can leave," Arris said, his voice thick with satisfaction as he licked the last of her release from his lips.

Dionne stood there, still trying to catch her breath, her legs weak from what he just did to her. Her heart was racing, her body humming, and all thoughts of getting ready on time had completely slipped her mind.

She glared at him playfully, trying to regain some control. "You ain't shit."

Arris smirked, leaning back on his elbows, his eyes dragging over her body like he was already plotting the next round. "And yet, you keep coming back."

Dionne laughed softly—rolling her eyes, her cheeks flushing as she

Feenin'

gathered her clothes and began to get dressed. She could feel his eyes on her the entire time, his gaze filled with longing and desire.

After she was dressed and ready, Dionne turned to him, her heart aching slightly as she kissed him goodbye. "I'll see you later," she promised softly.

Arris pulled her close, his forehead resting gently against hers. "You better," he murmured, his voice low and intimate before finally releasing her. But just as she began to step away, he reached over, grabbing something from the counter.

"Don't forget these," he said, holding out the keys to her new home.

Dionne's eyes widened as she looked down at the set of gleaming keys in his hand. She shook her head in disbelief, a small, incredulous smile creeping onto her face. "I can't believe yo' ass really bought me a house," she said, her voice a mix of amazement and exasperation.

Arris smirked, pulling her back down to him. His lips captured hers in a lingering, passionate kiss, her soft moan betraying the emotions swirling inside of her.

"Ours is coming, baby," he said against her lips, his voice filled with quiet conviction. The weight of his promise settled over her, making her body shiver—not from cold, but from the overwhelming love she felt radiating from him.

But then the guilt crept in, sharp and unrelenting. Dionne felt her chest tighten as she pulled back, her fingers clenching the keys in her hand. Here this man was, loving her openly, planning their future together, while she was still tied to another man.

She knew the truth was closing in on her. The walls she'd carefully constructed to keep her life compartmentalized were crumbling. Time was running out, and she could feel the decisions she'd been avoiding pressing down on her shoulders.

Arris didn't notice the flicker of guilt in her eyes, or maybe he chose not to acknowledge it. He kissed her forehead gently, his hands brushing her sides as if to reassure her without words.

"Drive safe, Mama. I'll see you later," he said softly, his voice laced with love and a promise of more moments like this.

Dionne nodded, unable to form words, her throat tight as she turned to leave. The keys felt heavier in her hand with every step she took toward her car, the weight of their meaning sinking deeper into her heart.

As she pulled away from the house, her grip on the steering wheel tightened. She could still feel his lips on hers, hear the promise in his voice, and yet the engagement ring on her finger burned like a brand. How much longer could she keep pretending? she thought, the guilt clawing at her with every mile she drove.

***

The Next Day:

Dionne sat slumped at her desk, her head buried in her hands as the aftermath of her wild night hit her like a ton of bricks. Her head pounded from the drinks, her body was sore from Arris fucking her into oblivion the day before, and exhaustion weighed heavy from hours spent escaping her reality at the club with her girls. She couldn't even keep her eyes open as she stared at the mountain of paperwork in front of her, the letters on the page blurring into a jumbled mess.

Her head finally gave in, resting on her arm as her body begged for sleep. Within seconds, soft snores escaped her lips, but they didn't last long. A loud knock at the door made her jolt upright, her heart racing as she tried to play it off.

"Come in," she called out, quickly straightening her posture and wiping at her face to hide any trace of her sleepiness.

When the door opened and Arris walked in, her body relaxed, though her irritation still lingered.

"Oh, it's just you," she muttered sleepily, making him chuckle.

"Damn, that's how you greet your man?" he teased, his voice warm but laced with amusement as he took her in.

Dionne rolled her eyes, already annoyed but too damn tired to fight him. "Hey, Arris," she mumbled, her head starting to dip again as exhaustion pulled at her.

Arris walked over to her desk, his smirk softening into concern. "You need to take yo' ass home and get some sleep. You can't even keep your eyes open," he said, reaching out to lift her up, but Dionne waved him off.

"No, baby. Move," she said, her voice full of stubbornness despite her half-asleep state. "I've got too much work to do. Just let me finish."

Arris cocked his head, smirking. "Mama, you can barely hold your head up. If you think I'm about to let you sit here and kill yourself over some papers, you got me fucked up."

Before she could protest, Arris scooped her up like she weighed nothing, ignoring her weak struggles.

"Arris! Put me down!" she hissed, though her tone lacked bite as her body betrayed her and melted into his hold.

"Nope. You done," he said simply, carrying her across the room and sitting on the office couch with her in his lap.

"Arris, I'm serious," she grumbled, trying to wriggle free, but his arms held her firmly.

Feenin'

"Why you running from me?" Arris asked, his tone more stern now, his usual playfulness replaced with something heavier, something serious. His eyes locked on hers, refusing to let her escape, even if it was just with words.

"Because you—and those hoes I call friends—are the reasons why I'm so damn tired," she shot back, a yawn slipping out right after, betraying her frustration. Arris chuckled low, his deep laugh making her glare at him as she moved to sit on the other end of the couch, trying to keep some distance.

"How is that our fault?" he asked, his smirk both clueless and teasing.

Dionne rolled her eyes at him, her glare softening when she noticed the way he was staring at her—admiring her, like she was the only thing that existed in his world. "You're the reason my body is sore as hell, and they're the reason I've got this damn hangover," she said with a huff, though her lips curled into a small, reluctant smile.

Arris leaned back, his smirk growing wider, clearly unbothered by her complaints. "I can fix both of those things," he said, his voice low and smooth, like he was already planning her surrender. "A nice massage for that soreness, and some tea and a hot meal for the hangover. Problem solved." His tone was calm, but the gleam in his eyes told her he wasn't done. "We just have to head over to your new place for all that."

His words made her chuckle, but she quickly shook her head, determined to hold her ground. Her defenses were already crumbling under his gaze, under the magnetic pull that was Arris, but she couldn't give in—not today. "I can't, Arris," she said softly, standing up from the couch, exhaustion clear in every movement. "I've got too much work to do today. I don't have time for massages or tea, or whatever you've got in mind."

She started toward her desk, trying to remind herself of all the tasks waiting for her, but Arris wasn't about to let her go that easily.

"I know you came for the updated listings, so—" Her sentence was abruptly cut off when Arris grabbed her mid-step, pulling her effortlessly into his lap. The sudden movement made her gasp as her hands instinctively landed on his chest for balance, her legs straddling him in the process.

"Arris..." she started, her voice caught between a protest and surrender.

He didn't give her a chance to finish. His lips crashed into hers, searing and full of purpose. The kiss was all him—commanding, unapologetic, and impossible to resist. Her initial resistance melted away as his hands slid up her back, holding her in place, making it clear that running wasn't an option anymore.

"You're not going back to that desk," he murmured against her lips, his voice low and filled with the kind of certainty that made her body shiver.

Dionne tried to summon a response, tried to remind herself why she couldn't give in to him right now, but all she could feel was the way his hands gripped her waist, the way his lips moved against hers like he owned her. And in moments like this, it was hard to argue that he didn't.

Arris pulled away slightly, his eyes scanning her face with concern. The red in her tired eyes didn't go unnoticed. "Mama, you need to rest," he said, his tone more stern now, leaving no room for argument.

Dionne sighed heavily, leaning into his touch for just a moment. Sitting in his lap, his hands firm yet gentle on her waist, and the loving gaze he gave her—it was enough to make her defenses crumble completely. But she knew she couldn't give in. Not here. Not now.

Before she could respond, a sharp knock at the door made her jolt. Panic rushed through her as she scrambled out of Arris's lap, brushing down her clothes in a desperate attempt to look professional. Arris smirked, watching her flustered reaction with amusement.

"Act normal," she whispered softly, trying to steady her breathing.

Arris chuckled low, leaning back casually on the couch, his confidence unshaken. "I'm always normal," he said, the teasing laced with a hidden edge.

"Come in," Dionne said, her tone softer than she intended, as she moved behind her desk.

The door opened, and in walked Jean with a bright, welcoming smile. "Hey, Dionne," she greeted warmly before her eyes landed on Arris. "Oh, I apologize. I didn't realize you were in a meeting. How are you, Mr. Black?"

Arris stood, his professional demeanor slipping into place effortlessly. "I'm doing good, Ms. Jean. How about you?" he replied, his voice smooth and courteous.

"Well, thanks for asking," Jean said with a polite nod, clearly unaware of the tension lingering in the room.

Meanwhile, Dionne's heart raced as she glanced between the two. She hoped—prayed—that Jean couldn't sense the connection between her and Arris, or the tension that had been crackling like static moments before she walked in.

Jean's attention shifted back to Dionne, who pretended to focus on her computer screen to hide the nervous energy bubbling under the

Feenin'

surface. "I just came to tell you, you have a surprise visitor," Jean said, her smile widening.

Dionne's head snapped up, her heart sinking at the implication. A sense of dread washed over her before the door opened wider, and in walked Malik, holding a large bouquet of red roses and wearing a beaming smile.

"Hey, baby," Malik said brightly, his tone filled with affection. Jean mirrored his smile, clearly delighted by the gesture, but Dionne and Arris both wore entirely different expressions.

Dionne's fake smile didn't quite reach her eyes as she rose to her feet. "Hey, Malik," she said, her voice even, though internally, her nerves were shot.

"He showed up wanting to surprise you," Jean added, her tone brimming with excitement, oblivious to the tension she was standing in the middle of.

Dionne risked a glance at Arris. His jaw was tight, his frustration evident despite the calm mask he wore. His fists rested on his thighs, clenched tightly, as if daring himself not to react. He stayed quiet, his sharp gaze locked on Malik, waiting to see how Dionne would handle the situation.

Dionne stepped out from behind her desk, forcing herself to meet Malik halfway. Her body felt stiff, her mind racing with ways to diffuse the obvious storm brewing in the room.

"These are for you, beautiful," Malik said as he handed Dionne the bouquet of roses, leaning in to kiss her cheek. She forced a smile, masking the turmoil inside her. Every affectionate gesture Malik made felt like another dagger aimed straight at Arris, and the weight of that guilt was suffocating.

Arris chuckled low, the sound devoid of humor. His clenched jaw and burning eyes betrayed the storm simmering beneath his calm exterior. He wanted to say something, to claim the woman standing there playing the role of someone else's fiancée, but he held back. For her.

"Thank you, Malik," Dionne said with a sweetness she didn't feel, her tone steady even though her heart was racing. She had to keep up appearances—for Malik, for Ms. Jean, and most of all, for Arris. But the weight of every forced smile she sent Malik's way crushed her, knowing it chipped away at Arris's heart.

"I'll leave you two," Ms. Jean said, oblivious to the tension thickening the air. "It was nice to finally meet you, Malik. You're everything Dionne said you were." She beamed, her words hitting Arris like a slap across the face.

Ann

Malik's grin widened as he nodded toward Ms. Jean. "Nice meeting you too, Ms. Jean. I hope it was all good things." His attention turned back to Dionne, his gaze lingering as he admired her crisp white blouse and tailored purple slacks.

"Oh, nothing but wonderful things," Ms. Jean replied with a bright smile, her words unintentionally twisting the knife in Arris's chest. The more Malik fawned over Dionne, the tighter Arris clenched his fists. His nails bit into his palms, his silence a thin veil over the rage boiling inside him.

As Ms. Jean left, Malik turned back to Arris with a grin. "Oh, my bad. I was just so caught up in my woman's beauty. Good seeing you again, Arris," he said, holding out his hand.

Arris's eyes flicked to the extended hand, then to Dionne, who looked like she wanted to disappear into the floor. His jaw tightened, but he forced himself to play along. "Same here," Arris said flatly, gripping Malik's hand in a firm shake, his strength fueled by frustration.

"Malik, what are you doing here?" Dionne quickly interjected, desperate to defuse the tension thickening the room, though she knew nothing could lighten the weight pressing on all of them.

"I wanted to surprise you and take you to lunch," Malik said with his signature charming smile. Dionne mirrored it with a forced one, though her heart wasn't in it. She wanted to be anywhere but here. She wanted Arris.

Before she could respond, Arris's voice broke through, cold and sharp. "I should be leaving. Thanks again for the updates." He held up the folder he'd taken from her desk, his half-smile laced with bitterness.

Dionne's heart sank as he turned to leave, her voice trembling as she called after him. "Talk later?"

He stopped in his tracks, the tension in his body visible. He didn't turn around, but his voice carried a quiet hurt that made her chest ache. "Nah, you should enjoy your time with your fiancé. We can talk another time."

The words hit her like a punch to the gut. His tone was distant, his eyes devoid of the warmth that usually made her feel safe and loved. It was the look of a man guarding his heart, locking it away to keep himself from breaking.

Malik's obliviousness to the tension between them only fueled the simmering rage beneath Arris's composed exterior. Arris couldn't hold back any longer. "Aye, bruh," he said, his tone firm, cutting through the awkward silence like a blade.

Malik turned, his face full of confusion, clearly unaware of the

Feenin'

seething energy coming off Arris. "What's up?"

Arris stepped forward slightly, his dark eyes locked onto Malik with an unsettling calmness—one that carried more weight than any outburst ever could.

"Tulips are her favorite," he said, his voice smooth yet laced with something lethal. His lips curled into a slow, mocking smirk as he glanced at the bouquet in Malik's hand. "Roses?" A low chuckle rumbled from his chest, sharp with condescension. "Roses are too basic for a woman like her."

His words lingered in the air, cutting through the tension like a blade. Without sparing Dionne another glance, he turned and walked out, his presence leaving a void in the room that felt heavier than before.

Malik's brows furrowed, his confusion morphing into irritation. "What he say?" he asked, looking at Dionne for clarity. His tone carried disbelief, but there was a flicker of doubt in his eyes, the words clearly striking a nerve.

Dionne didn't hesitate. "Don't worry about it," she said quickly, brushing him off with a dismissive wave of her hand. Her tone was sharp, her patience with him thinning by the second.

Malik's mug only deepened as his attention shifted back to her. "Why you acting like that? I told you I was surprising you with lunch," he said, his voice tinged with frustration as his own attitude started bubbling to the surface.

Dionne rolled her eyes, her irritation evident now that Arris had left. The facade of playing the devoted fiancée was gone, and the effort of pretending had left her drained. "I have a lot of work to do, Malik," she snapped, her tone cutting as she made her way to grab her purse.

"You can't take a break for an hour to have lunch with your man?" he shot back, his voice now loaded with an attitude of his own. His frustration was a mirror of hers, though for entirely different reasons.

Dionne paused, her hand tightening on the strap of her purse as she considered him. She knew if she didn't give in, he wouldn't let it go. "Okay, Malik," she said finally, her voice drenched in sarcasm and laced with an edge that told him exactly how uninterested she was. She grabbed her keys, brushing past him without a glance.

But Malik wasn't done. His insecurity gnawed at him, spurred on by Arris's parting comment. "And how does that nigga know what your favorite flower is?" he asked, his tone low but biting.

Dionne froze mid-step, her head snapping back toward him. Her sharp glare burned into him, silencing him before she even opened her mouth. "The real question is why don't you? You're my man, right?" she shot back, her voice dripping with sarcasm as her words landed like a punch.

Malik's face fell, the sting of her question evident as guilt and anger battled for dominance. He wanted to argue, to defend himself, but the truth of her words weighed too heavily. His lips parted, but no response came, leaving an empty silence between them.

Dionne noted the way his mouth snapped shut, the defeat written across his face, but she didn't care. She was exhausted—physically, emotionally, and mentally. He didn't even notice the tiredness in her eyes or the strain in her voice. How could he claim to love her if he didn't even see her?

The silence between them was thick and suffocating as they walked out of the office. Malik trailed slightly behind her, his mind churning with insecurities. He couldn't shake the sinking feeling in his chest, the nagging suspicion that Arris knew Dionne in ways he never could.

When they reached her car, Dionne didn't wait for him to open the door for her. She climbed in and slammed it shut, the finality of the motion stinging more than her words had. Malik stood there for a moment, staring at her through the glass as if searching for a version of her he still recognized. But the woman in front of him wasn't the same. She wasn't his anymore, not really.

With a resigned sigh, Malik got into his car, following behind her as she drove to the restaurant. His grip on the steering wheel tightened with every mile, his thoughts circling back to Arris. The comments, the familiarity, the way Arris seemed to linger too close, to know too much—it all gnawed at him.

He didn't want to believe it. Couldn't. But deep down, Malik knew. If Dionne was cheating, if she had already checked out of their relationship, it wasn't just with anyone. It was with a man like Arris—a man who he couldn't compare to, no matter how much he had, no matter what he did. And that realization was the heaviest weight of all.

Feenin'

Chapter 14

Arris sat on the couch, tension radiating off him as his jaw flexed repeatedly. In one hand, he held a glass of whiskey that threatened to crack under the tight grip of his fingers, while the other hand clutched the TV remote like it was the only thing grounding him. But nothing was grounding him—not tonight. The source of his frustration burned hot in his chest: Dionne. Her smile, fake as it may have been, thrown at Malik earlier today. The cheap, unimaginative roses Malik had given her, as if she deserved anything less than perfection. And worst of all, the cold, undeniable truth that Dionne was spending time with Malik right now instead of him.

The thought alone was like a knife twisting in his chest. She was playing a role, one he knew she didn't want to play, but she was still with Malik, and he was stuck here—alone. His home, usually a sanctuary, felt suffocating tonight.

A sharp, intrusive sound shattered his spiraling thoughts: the doorbell. He groaned, leaning his head back against the couch. He wanted to ignore it, but what if it was her? That single hopeful thought propelled him to his feet, making him cross the room to answer. But when he opened the door and saw True and Mario standing there, he sighed heavily, frustration spilling over as he turned without a word and walked back to the couch.

"Damn, nigga, what's wrong with you?" True asked as they stepped inside.

"Why you sitting in the dark like some brooding ass villain?" Mario added, flipping on the lights.

Arris dropped onto the couch, his body heavy with tension. "Why y'all asking so many damn questions? Why are you two even here?" His tone was sharp, but the anger wasn't aimed at them—it was born from everything boiling inside him, especially Dionne.

True plopped down on the couch across from him, leaning forward. "Who the fuck pissed you off?"

Mario, ever the quiet observer, settled into the chair, his sharp eyes studying Arris's clenched fists and stiff posture. "It's definitely not nothing. You look ready to snap that glass in half."

Arris rolled his shoulders, leaning back into the couch, trying to feign calm, but the glass of whiskey trembled in his hand. "Man, it's nothing," he muttered, brushing them off.

True shook his head. "Nah, nigga. It's something. You're gripping that glass like it owes you money, and you ain't the type to sulk. What's up?"

Arris clenched his jaw, the muscles ticking as he stared at the untouched TV screen. He couldn't talk about Dionne—couldn't even let his friends know about her and the tangled web of emotions wrapped around her. So he pivoted, grabbing at the other thing that had been gnawing at him for weeks.

"Calvin is back, trying to make amends and shit," Arris said, his voice cold and sharp, every syllable dipped in venom. His jaw clenched so tight that the muscle twitched, a stark reminder of how much his father's name alone could set him off. But even as the rage simmered, there was more bubbling beneath the surface, emotions he wasn't ready to address.

True and Mario exchanged looks, their expressions softening with the weight of the conversation. They both knew what Calvin's absence had done to Arris, how deep the resentment ran. True broke the silence first. "Damn, why now?"

Arris shrugged, the movement rigid, like the frustration was coursing through his body and stiffening every joint. "That's what I wanna know. I caught him and my mama back fucking, so I think it's because of that," he admitted before tossing back another gulp of whiskey. The burn barely registered as the words left his mouth, each syllable heavier than the last.

True's eyes widened in shock. "Wait, Mama Angel is taking that nigga back?"

Arris didn't answer verbally, just nodded his head stiffly. Saying it out loud would make it too real, and the thought alone felt like swallowing glass. True's disbelief mirrored his own, but Arris wasn't surprised anymore—just angry.

"But I have a feeling it's something else," Arris finally said, letting out a breath that felt like it had been trapped in his chest for weeks. The words lingered in the air, heavy and unsettling, like a storm cloud

Feenin'

brewing on the horizon.

True and Mario stayed quiet, letting him work through the thoughts that had been haunting him. Calvin returning out of the blue, claiming to want to rebuild the family he'd shattered, didn't sit right with Arris. It was too sudden, too convenient. He knew his father too well, and the idea that guilt was motivating him was laughable. Calvin had never cared enough before, so why now?

"So what do you think it is?" Mario finally asked, his tone cautious, as if he were tiptoeing around a bomb he didn't want to detonate.

Arris shook his head, his frustration pouring out in a low growl. "Man, I don't know, and it's fucking me up," he admitted, his voice cracking slightly. The vulnerability was fleeting, quickly buried under the cold, detached look in his eyes.

True leaned forward, his elbows resting on his knees as he asked the question Arris knew was coming but didn't want to hear. "Well, have you talked to that nigga?"

Arris's head snapped toward him, his dark eyes burning with anger that made True shift uncomfortably. It wasn't directed at him, but the intensity was still enough to make anyone second-guess themselves.

"I don't have shit to say to that nigga," Arris bit out, his voice low and venomous. "If I see him again, I might kill his ass."

The room went silent, the weight of his words sinking in like stones. Mario and True exchanged glances, their concern evident. They'd always known how deeply Arris resented Calvin, but the rage they saw now wasn't something either of them could brush off. This was deeper than anger; this was years of hurt, betrayal, and abandonment manifesting into something dangerous.

They both remembered the Arris from back then—the quiet, reserved boy who seemed to shoulder the weight of the world on his small frame. When Calvin left, something inside Arris broke, and he wasn't the same after that. The abandonment didn't just hurt him—it changed him. It planted a seed of anger so deep that it became a part of who he was. Anything could trigger it, and when it did, there was no stopping it.

Arris always kept his distance, not because he didn't care, but because he cared too much. Once he got attached to someone, there was no pulling him away—he was loyal to a fault. But that same loyalty came with a dangerous edge. The moment he sensed even the slightest hint of abandonment, the anger he worked so hard to bury would rise to the surface, fierce and unrelenting. It was the worst when he was a kid. Back then, he kept his circle small—just his family and the friends who became brothers. Love? That was out of the question. He couldn't risk it. He knew that once he let someone into his heart, letting them go wouldn't be an option. Death would be the only thing that could separate them.

And then there was the rage. When Arris hit 100, there was no stopping him. No words, no reasoning, nothing could bring him back. It wasn't something he was proud of, but it was a part of him—a scar left by Calvin. Even as a grown man, Calvin was still his greatest trigger. Every wound, every ounce of rage, every crack in his foundation could be traced back to him.

"Look, bruh," Mario started carefully, "I get it. I really do. But carrying this shit is only gonna weigh you down. You already got enough on your plate, and that nigga don't deserve the energy you putting into hating him."

Arris let out a bitter laugh, the sound devoid of humor. "I don't put energy into hating him. That shit comes natural."

True sighed, running a hand over his face. "Still, bro, you can't let this eat at you. He don't deserve that much of you."

Arris didn't respond right away, his jaw working as he stared at the glass in his hand. He knew they were right, but that didn't make it any easier. The damage Calvin caused was permanent, and the idea of forgiving him—of even entertaining a conversation with him—felt like a betrayal to the version of himself that had to pick up the pieces Calvin left behind.

"I know you don't want to hear this shit, AB, but you gotta talk to that nigga, man," Mario said, breaking the heavy silence in the room. Arris's bloodshot eyes slowly shifted to Mario, and the weight of his gaze was enough to make anyone uncomfortable. It was a look that warned of the storm brewing inside him.

Mario didn't back down. "Hear me out, bro. That nigga Calvin hurt you—whether you want to admit it or not. He fucked you up, and you've been carrying that shit ever since."

Arris's jaw clenched, his knuckles white around the glass in his hand. Talking to Calvin wasn't just out of the question; it was a line he refused to cross. But Mario wasn't letting it go.

"Shi, even if you just beat that nigga's ass when you see him, at least you'd get it out of your system. But walking around mad as fuck all the time? Drinking your anger away because of him? That shit ain't cutting it no more. You're giving that sorry-ass nigga more power over you than he deserves," Mario said, his voice rising with a brotherly authority that couldn't be ignored.

Arris nodded slightly, the motion almost imperceptible. But the

Feenin'

anger in his eyes didn't dim. Dionne had told him something similar not too long ago, in her own way, and hearing it again now only made him angrier. Not at Mario, but at the truth he couldn't deny.

"I agree with Mario," True chimed in, his tone just as protective. "You're letting Calvin run your life, whether he's here or not. And he's gonna keep doing it until you handle that shit."

"I hear y'all," Arris said, his voice low and gravelly, the rage still simmering beneath the surface. His fists unclenched for a moment, only to tighten again as he thought about everything Calvin had done—or hadn't done.

Mario leaned forward, his gaze steady as he delivered the words Arris needed to hear. "Man, think about your future wife and kids."

At the mention of a wife, Arris's eyes softened despite himself. His mind immediately went to Dionne. Even though she wasn't his—not fully, not yet—she was the only woman he ever pictured standing beside him for the rest of his life. The thought of her calmed him slightly, but it also reminded him of why Mario's words mattered. Dionne deserved better than the man he was right now.

"They deserve a healed man, AB. Not one who's weighed down by ghosts. Your wife deserves a man who can give her his whole heart, not the broken pieces Calvin left behind. And your kids? They're gonna need a father who shows them what love looks like, not what anger feels like."

Arris leaned back on the couch, his expression softening slightly for the first time that night. The tension in his chest eased as his thoughts shifted to Dionne, the one person who seemed to anchor him in a way no one else could. He didn't care that she was engaged to another man. That ring didn't mean shit to him, because he knew her heart wasn't in it. Her heart belonged to him—he could see it in her eyes every time they locked with his, feel it in her touch when they were alone. One day, she would be his wife, and there wasn't a doubt in his mind about that.

True's chuckle pulled him out of his thoughts. "This nigga always on some simpy shit," True teased, a smirk tugging at his lips as he leaned back in his seat.

For the first time that night, Arris laughed, a genuine sound breaking through the heaviness. "That simp-ass nigga right, though," Arris said, nodding. "I gotta talk to that nigga—Calvin. But I ain't doing that shit for me." His voice carried conviction, the kind that left no room for questioning.

Mario tilted his head, his brow raised in curiosity. "Then who you doing it for?" he asked, leaning forward slightly, his intrigue clear.

Arris chuckled, shaking his head. "Man, y'all muthafuckas too nosy," he said, taking another sip of whiskey. "But I'll tell you this—I'm doing it for her."

True's smirk widened, his eyes darting to where Arris's gaze had fallen. "Who's her?" he asked, now fully invested in the conversation. His eyes landed on the rare tulips sitting in a vase nearby, the ones Arris had bought for Dionne. They'd talked about keeping them in her new house, but she insisted on leaving them with him for now, so they'd be there every time she came by.

Mario followed Arris's gaze to the flowers, his confusion etched clearly on his face. "Nigga, who?" Mario asked, his curiosity now fully piqued.

Arris smirked, his amusement only growing. "Damn, y'all too fucking nosy," he said with a shake of his head.

"Nah, nigga, you just too fucking secretive," True shot back with a laugh. "But I ain't tripping. We're gonna know soon enough. You? Once you hooked on somebody, you hooked. You'll bring her around soon."

Arris chuckled, not bothering to deny it. True wasn't wrong. His love was steadfast and unwavering. Once he gave his heart, it was all in, no second-guessing. That's just who he was. And Dionne? She held every part of it. Even with the complications of her engagement, even with the frustration simmering beneath his calm exterior, Arris wasn't going to let her go.

The conversation shifted after that, moving to lighter topics. Arris told them about the business proposal Demetrius had pitched him—an opportunity to co-own the Houston Comets. Both Mario and True were hyped, encouraging him to go for it, but Arris hesitated. He wanted to talk to Dionne first, to hear her thoughts. Her opinion mattered more than anyone else's.

For the rest of the night, Arris let go of the anger that had been eating at him—the frustration about Dionne's engagement, the bitterness toward his father, and the weight of his own emotions. He allowed himself to enjoy the moment, to appreciate the rare peace of just being with his boys. For now, that was enough.

***

Dionne stepped through the door, Malik close behind her, the effects of the wine she'd indulged in at dinner clouding her senses. Dinner had been his idea—a follow-up to their earlier lunch, as if he were trying to repair something that was already irreparably broken. She didn't want to be there with him, not at lunch, not at dinner, and certainly not now. But free food had always been her weakness, and wine... well, wine numbed the edges of everything she didn't want to feel.

Feenin'

Her body hummed, warm and loose, but her thoughts betrayed her. They weren't on Malik, not even for a second. They were consumed by Arris—his touch, his voice, the way he looked at her earlier in her office. That look, the raw mixture of anger and heartbreak etched across his face, played in her mind on a loop, making her chest tighten with guilt and longing. The wine only amplified her emotions, dulling her irritation with Malik while heightening her craving for the man who wasn't here. The man she wanted to be with.

Dionne headed straight for the bedroom, not bothering to acknowledge Malik's footsteps behind her. Her heels clicked against the floor with a purpose, her body swaying slightly as the wine took its toll. Malik trailed after her, his eyes locked on the curve of her hips in her fitted purple pants. The lust in his gaze was evident, and as she approached the bedroom door, he couldn't help himself. His hand shot out, gripping her butt cheek.

She froze mid-step, her back straightening as a wave of irritation rolled through her. Snapping around, she swatted his hand away with more force than she intended. Her glare was sharp, her eyes narrowed in warning.

"I can't touch you now?" Malik asked, his tone defensive as he crossed his arms, clearly taken aback by her reaction.

Dionne rolled her eyes, exhaling sharply as she turned away from him. "Not tonight, Malik," she said coldly, her voice laced with frustration. She didn't even glance back as she walked into the bedroom, the dismissal in her tone clear.

Dionne walked straight to the bathroom, her frustration simmering beneath the surface as she began peeling off her clothes. She was down to just her bra and those fitted purple pants when Malik followed her in, his presence immediately grating on her nerves. She turned sharply, her glare piercing.

"Damn, can I get any fucking privacy?" she snapped, her tone sharper than she intended but still full of meaning. She was exhausted—exhausted from his presence, his affection, his attempts to act like everything was fine. It was suffocating her.

Malik didn't take the hint, ignoring her tone as he stepped closer, his gaze burning into her. "I miss you," he murmured, his voice low and dripping with intent.

"Malik... move," Dionne said, her voice softer this time but laced with irritation. She tried to step away, but his hands caught her firmly, holding her in place.

"No. I want you," he said, leaning in to press his lips against hers.

Dionne's body tensed at the contact, and while the wine still buzzed through her veins and her body was alive with need, Malik wasn't who she wanted. It wasn't his touch or his lips she craved. It was Arris, and the thought of anyone else touching her felt like a betrayal.

She pushed against his chest, breaking the kiss and stepping back. "Stop," she said firmly, her voice calm but unyielding.

Malik frowned, his frustration now simmering just beneath the surface. "Why the fuck are you running from me? I just want to love on my woman," he said, his voice tinged with irritation and need.

"I'm not in the mood," Dionne said flatly, kicking off her pants and revealing her black lace panties. The sight of her half-dressed body seemed to wipe away Malik's frustration, replacing it with raw arousal. His eyes darkened as he stepped closer, his breath heavy.

Before she could react, his hand shot out, cupping her pussy through the lace, and she froze for a split second. Her body may have responded, her wetness betraying her, but it wasn't for him—it was for someone else. It was for Arris.

"Your body's saying you're in the mood," Malik said with a sly smirk, licking his fingers with a cocky arrogance that only fueled her irritation.

Dionne stepped back quickly, pushing him away with more force this time. "Stop touching me, Malik. For real," she said, her tone calm but the steel in her voice unmistakable.

Malik's smirk faltered, but he brushed it off, his drunken haze clouding his judgment. He moved toward her again, the alcohol amplifying his boldness and dulling his awareness of her anger. "Come on, baby," he murmured, his hands reaching for her again.

Dionne's patience snapped. "I said stop!" she barked, her voice louder now, cutting through the space like a blade. Her eyes blazed as she glared at him, her body stiff with frustration and resentment.

Malik froze, his hands falling to his sides as the weight of her tone finally hit him. For a moment, the room was silent, the tension thick between them. Dionne's chest rose and fell with shallow breaths as she held his gaze, her mind racing. She couldn't do this—not with him. Not when every fiber of her being was consumed by someone else.

Malik backed away slowly, his expression clouded with confusion and hurt, but Dionne didn't care.

"Are you cheating on me?" Malik's voice was low, frustration laced through it, but his eyes betrayed a softness—a glimmer of hope that her answer would soothe his insecurities.

Dionne exhaled deeply, her irritation climbing with every second

Feenin'

he stood there. "How many times do I have to tell you, Malik? I am not cheating on you," she said, her tone calm but carrying an unmistakable edge. He was ruining what little calm she had left.

"Then why don't you want to fuck me?" His voice cracked slightly, the vulnerability in his question making it hit harder than he intended. His eyes searched her face for any sign of emotion, but Dionne kept her features stoic, locked down, offering him nothing.

She shook her head and took a step back, putting distance between them. "I just said I'm not in the mood. I want to take a shower, get in bed, and get some sleep. I have work in the morning, Malik." Her voice was steady, eerily calm, but the irritation bubbling beneath it was unmistakable.

Malik took a step closer, ignoring her clear boundary. "We haven't had sex in weeks, Dionne. You don't kiss me anymore. You don't even look at me like you used to." His voice cracked again, the weight of his emotions clear, but Dionne didn't soften. She stepped back again, keeping the distance between them.

"Maybe that's because I don't trust you." Her voice was low but sharp, slicing through the heavy tension in the room. Her patience, already on its last thread, was beginning to snap.

Malik blinked, stunned into silence for a moment, but she didn't let the pause linger.

"I caught you fucking another bitch in our bed, Malik. The same bed I sleep in every night. And you think I want to kiss you? You think I want you to touch me after that shit?" Her voice rose slightly, her tone filled with disbelief as her words struck him like blows.

"I showed you my test results," Malik countered weakly, his voice defensive but tinged with guilt. "I'm clean, Dionne. I didn't bring nothing into this house."

Dionne laughed bitterly, her gaze burning into him. Whatever calmness had been there before was gone now. "And you think that's supposed to make it better? You think showing me a clean test makes up for the fact that you risked bringing a fucking disease into this house? Into me?" Her voice was sharp, filled with an anger that was simmering, threatening to boil over.

Malik's eyes dropped to the floor, guilt etched all over his face, but she wasn't done.

"You're lucky that shit came back clean, Malik, or you wouldn't even be standing here right now. Breathing. Healthy." Her tone was cold, venom dripping from each word, and the heat of the steam from the shower mirrored the storm brewing in the room.

Malik didn't respond, his guilt silencing him as her words continued to dig deeper into the wound.

"You still put your dick in someone else. You still brought that bitch into our home. You still fucked her in the bed I sleep in every night. And you think trust comes back just because you're clean?" She shook her head, her voice heavy with disgust. "You didn't just fuck up. You broke our already failing relationship. You broke my trust. And you broke whatever love I had left for you."

Her words hit him harder than any slap ever could. Malik's face crumbled, the weight of her truth sinking into his chest like a lead weight, but she didn't stop.

"So, no, Malik. I don't want to fuck you. I don't want your kisses, your apologies, or your affection right now. I just want to take my damn shower, go to bed, and show up to this bullshit counseling session you think is somehow going to fix all of this."

The steam from the running water began to fill the room, clouding the mirrors, the air thick with heat and tension. To Dionne, it felt like the perfect representation of what their relationship had become—choking, suffocating, filled with anger, betrayal, and resentment.

Malik stood there, his jaw tight, his eyes pleading for some form of forgiveness, but Dionne wouldn't give him that. Not tonight. Not after everything.

Realizing he had nothing left to say, Malik nodded silently and turned to leave, the weight of her words following him out the door.

Malik sat on the edge of their bed, his hands gripping his knees as his jaw tightened in determination. He replayed every word Dionne had thrown at him in the bathroom, each one slicing deeper than the last. He couldn't lose her—wouldn't lose her. This funk they were in, this distance, he told himself it was temporary. He could fix it, even if the cracks in their foundation seemed irreparable. He just needed more time, more effort, more something. Malik's mind raced as he planned his next move, vowing to do whatever it took to win her back.

Dionne, on the other hand, stepped into the shower, releasing a shaky breath she hadn't realized she was holding. The heat from the water cascaded over her, but it couldn't melt the tension in her muscles or extinguish the anger simmering inside her. She stood motionless under the spray, her head bowed, as the warmth did little to soothe her. Instead, her mind spiraled, replaying her life in vivid flashes—the little girl who had once craved love more than anything, who had believed in fairy tales and happy endings, now grown into a woman trapped in a life that felt like a cruel parody of everything she'd ever dreamed.

Feenin'

The reality of her situation crushed her. Here she was, tied to a man she no longer loved, playing the role of a devoted fiancée while her heart yearned for someone else. Someone who saw her, craved her, loved her in ways Malik never could. The weight of it all bore down on her, and before she could stop herself, hot tears mixed with the water streaming down her face.

Her thoughts drifted to Arris. The man who had somehow become her safe place, her escape. Her mind replayed the look of hurt in his eyes at the office earlier, the way his jaw had tightened when he saw her with Malik. He had walked away without a fight, but she could feel his unspoken words, his frustration, his disappointment. She had felt every bit of his pain because it mirrored her own.

"I'm sorry," she whispered to the empty shower, her voice cracking under the weight of her emotions. The apology wasn't for Malik. It was for Arris. For the love she was keeping just out of reach, the love she wanted so desperately to claim but couldn't because of the shackles she'd placed on herself.

Her chest heaved as she sobbed silently, her hands pressing against the tiled wall for support. The water, once scalding, now felt lukewarm against her skin, but she didn't move. She couldn't. She was paralyzed by the storm raging inside her.

She wanted Arris. **Feened** for him in ways that scared her. His touch, his voice, his presence—it all felt further away now, as if he were slipping from her grasp with every passing moment she spent tethered to a man who wasn't him. The thought of losing Arris broke her in ways she hadn't anticipated, and for the first time in a long time, Dionne allowed herself to feel the full weight of her choices.

As the water continued to run, she tilted her head back, letting it wash over her face as if it could cleanse her of the guilt, the longing, the pain. But it didn't. Nothing could.

***

The Next Day:

Arris sat stiffly at the table, his leg bouncing relentlessly beneath it as he stared at the empty chair across from him. The nerves clawed at him, but he kept his exterior composed—at least, as much as he could. The decision to meet his father wasn't one he'd taken lightly. After years of silence and resentment, he finally reached a point where he needed answers. Forgiveness wasn't even on the table; the anger he harbored ran too deep. But the gnawing questions—the why of it all—had driven him to take this step.

He glanced at his watch again, the minutes dragging like hours. The restaurant was eerily quiet, the faint clinking of silverware in the kitchen and the muffled sounds of Martin and his staff the only noise. Arris had cleared the place out, unwilling to risk a public scene. If this meeting went south—and he expected it would—he didn't want an audience.

The buzz of his phone jolted him out of his thoughts. He glanced down, his heart betraying him with a quick flutter when he saw Dionne's name on the screen. For a moment, he considered answering, the thought of hearing her voice soothing the tension in his chest. But then yesterday's events flashed through his mind—her with Malik, the fake smiles, the way she'd played the role of a devoted fiancée in front of him. His jaw tightened, and he declined the call, setting the phone facedown on the table.

He missed her, craved her, but right now, the weight of dealing with her and his father at the same time was too much. He needed space to think, to focus on this moment without her complicating his emotions. Setting his phone to Do Not Disturb, he exhaled deeply, trying to steady himself.

Just as he did, the sound of approaching footsteps pulled his attention. Arris straightened, his eyes locking onto Calvin as he made his way through the restaurant. The older man's presence filled the room effortlessly, his blue Puma tracksuit crisp, the matching sneakers spotless. His salt-and-pepper waves were freshly cut, the faint shine of pomade catching the light. Two subtle gold chains rested against his chest, gleaming under the warm glow of the overhead lights. There was a confidence in his stride, a commanding aura that seemed to shrink the room despite its emptiness.

Arris's jaw clenched involuntarily as Calvin reached the table. He hated it—despised it—but he couldn't deny what he saw in front of him. He was staring at a reflection of himself, or at least parts of himself. The effortless cool, the undeniable presence, the way Calvin could take over a space without uttering a word—all of it was there, staring Arris in the face like a cruel reminder of the man he'd spent his life trying not to become.

Calvin approached the table with a cautious stride, taking a seat across from Arris. "Wassup, son," he greeted, his voice laced with forced calm. Arris didn't return the sentiment, his jaw tightening as he clenched his fist under the table. The tension in the air was suffocating, thick with years of resentment and unanswered questions.

A waiter approached, placing two glasses of water on the table before turning to leave, but Calvin raised a hand to stop him. "Aye, man, you got something stronger than this?" he asked, his tone casual, as if this were a

Feenin'

friendly catch-up instead of a confrontation years in the making.

Before the waiter could respond, Arris cut in sharply, his tone ice-cold. "He good with water." The command in his voice left no room for argument, and the waiter quickly nodded before walking away. Calvin raised an eyebrow but said nothing, taking a reluctant sip of the water he didn't want.

"I'm happy you finally wanted to talk," Calvin said, breaking the silence. His voice was calm, almost too calm, as if he were tiptoeing around a landmine.

Arris didn't bite. His eyes burned with restrained fury as he leaned forward slightly. "Yeah? Then explain," he said, his voice low but razor-sharp, cutting through the feigned warmth in Calvin's tone.

Calvin exhaled deeply, leaning back in his chair. "What you wanna know?" he asked, hesitantly meeting Arris's gaze.

Arris looked away for a moment, his jaw clenching so tightly the muscles were visibly taut. He was biting back every venomous word he wanted to spit, forcing himself to stay in control. Finally, he spoke, his voice steady but loaded with anger. "Why'd you turn to the streets?"

He picked up his glass, sipping the water—not because he was thirsty, but to give himself a moment to calm the fire burning inside him. Calvin sighed, rubbing the back of his neck. "That's all I've ever known," he admitted, his voice carrying an edge of indifference. "I grew up around it my whole life, and the thrill of it just stuck with me."

Arris's grip on the glass tightened as Calvin spoke. The nonchalance in his father's voice was like pouring gasoline on a fire. "The thrill," Arris repeated, his tone dripping with disdain. "So the thrill was more important than your family?"

Calvin leaned back, trying to steady himself under the weight of his son's glare. "During that time, yeah," he said quietly, as if that would soften the blow. But there was no remorse in his tone, and that only made Arris's anger boil hotter.

"During that time?" Arris echoed, his voice rising slightly, his leg bouncing under the table with barely restrained rage. "Nigga, you abandoned us. For good."

Calvin shifted uncomfortably in his seat, his confident demeanor starting to crack under Arris's piercing gaze. "Man, Arris, it's a lot of shit you just don't know," Calvin said, his tone softening, as if that would excuse everything.

Arris leaned forward now, his voice colder than ever. "That's why we here, nigga. Explain the shit I don't know, because what I do know is you broke my mother's heart and left your two kids to grow up without their fucking father."

The venom in his words hit Calvin like a punch, and he squirmed in his seat, struggling to hold his composure. For the first time, he seemed unsure of what to say. The weight of Arris's pain and rage was suffocating, and Calvin had no choice but to sit in it, to feel it in every sharp word his son threw at him.

The silence stretched between them, thick and heavy, as Calvin tried to find the words to justify the unjustifiable. But no matter what he said next, it would never erase the years of pain he'd caused or the trust he'd shattered. Arris's dark eyes bore into him, waiting for answers he wasn't sure Calvin could give.

Calvin leaned forward, his elbows resting on the table as he ran a hand over his face. His voice cracked as he began to speak. "I'm a fucking street nigga, Arris. That's all I've ever been. Yeah, I loved your mother—hell, I still do—and I damn sure love the fuck out of you and A'Lani. But I loved the thrill of the streets more. I wasn't fit to be the man your mother deserved, or the father you two needed, so I left."

For the first time, there was a crack in Calvin's voice that carried the weight of regret. Arris heard it, but it wasn't enough to dull the fire roaring in his chest. His fists clenched under the table as he leaned closer, his voice sharp, cutting through Calvin's words like a blade.

"And you see where that shit got you," Arris snapped, his tone low but laced with venom. "You put fucking drugs, hoes, and street shit over your fucking family. And now, the same family you threw away, you're sitting here begging to take you back because the streets finally stop loving you back."

Calvin opened his mouth to respond, but Arris wasn't done. The anger that simmered for years erupted like a volcano, his voice rising as he let every buried emotion spill out.

"I had to step up and be the man my mama needed and the father A'Lani deserved because you couldn't get your shit together!" Arris's voice cracked with the weight of his words, his eyes burning with unshed tears. "I had to lose my fucking childhood, my innocence, to take on responsibilities that were supposed to be yours. Because you wanted to fuck bitches, sell and do drugs, and rack up charges. Fucking inmates and crackheads saw more of your ass than your own kids ever did!"

His voice was shaking now, no longer able to suppress the tremor of emotion in his tone. His hands gripped the edge of the table so tightly his knuckles turned white, and the tears that he'd fought so hard to hold back began to pool in his eyes, threatening to fall.

Calvin sat frozen, his bravado crumbling under the weight of Arris's

Feenin'

words. He opened his mouth to speak, but the sight of his son—his only son—breaking before him rendered him speechless. For the first time, Calvin could see the full depth of the pain he'd caused, the years of anger and heartbreak he had buried in his son's chest.

Arris's voice cracked again, and this time he didn't bother hiding the emotion that poured out. "You didn't just abandon us, nigga—you destroyed us. You destroyed me. You left us to fend for ourselves while you ran to the streets like a fucking coward. And now you're sitting here, looking me in the face, acting like that shit was just... some fucking phase."

Calvin's eyes glistened now, matching the raw pain reflected in his son's gaze. For all the mistakes he had made, for all the regrets he'd carried, seeing the depth of Arris's hurt was more than he had prepared for. He had expected anger, sure, but not this—a raw, unfiltered outpour of years of resentment and heartbreak.

Calvin stood abruptly, the scrape of his chair echoing in the empty restaurant as Arris rose too, his body tense, ready for whatever was about to unfold. Arris's eyes burned with rage as he stepped forward, his voice exploding in a way that shook the room.

"What, nigga? You can't hear the truth? The truth hurts, don't it, Calvin?" Arris spat, his tone venomous. His chest heaved with each word as the years of pent-up anger and pain poured out of him. "Your own daughter had fucking panic attacks because of your ass! You think that shit just disappeared? It broke her, Calvin!" His words sliced through the air, each one like a dagger plunging into Calvin's chest.

Arris's fists clenched tightly at his sides as his voice cracked with raw emotion. "And me? I have fucking anger and abandonment issues because of you! You left me fucked up! I had to get tested for shit, put on medication, go through counseling. But none of that shit worked! You know why? Because the problem wasn't me—it was YOU! It's always been you!"

Arris stepped closer, his presence looming over Calvin like a storm, his voice thunderous. Calvin, overwhelmed by the weight of his son's words and the truth he could no longer deny, tried to turn and walk away. The guilt and shame were too much to bear, and the sight of the hurt in Arris's eyes was like a mirror reflecting everything he despised about himself.

But Arris wasn't letting him go—not again. "Don't you fucking dare try to walk away again, my nigga!" Arris growled, grabbing Calvin's arm and spinning him around. Their eyes locked, pain and fury meeting regret and guilt. Calvin's jaw tightened, his tears flowing freely now as he tried to hold his composure.

"Hit me!" Calvin roared suddenly, his voice cracking with the weight of his own pain. "Hit me, Arris! Get it all out! I deserve it! Do it!"

Arris didn't hesitate. With everything in him, he threw a hard left hook, his fist connecting with Calvin's jaw with a sickening crack that echoed through the room. Calvin stumbled back, his head snapping to the side, but he didn't flinch, didn't block, didn't fight back. He stood there, absorbing every blow Arris threw, his blood staining the pristine restaurant floor.

"I FUCKING HATE YOU!" Arris bellowed, his voice breaking as tears streamed down his face. His fists moved on autopilot, each punch carrying years of hurt, anger, and betrayal. Calvin's nose bled profusely, his lip split open, but he didn't raise a hand to defend himself. He just took it.

Martin rushed in from the back, his eyes wide with panic as he grabbed Arris from behind, trying to pull him away. "Arris, stop! Stop, man!" Martin yelled, struggling to restrain him as Arris thrashed in his arms.

"LET ME GO!" Arris screamed, his voice raw and guttural, his tears falling unchecked. He wasn't the powerful, confident man everyone knew him to be anymore. He was the little boy who had been abandoned, the child who had to grow up too fast and carry burdens no child should ever bear. In that moment, he was nothing but the broken boy who had spent his life trying to piece himself back together.

Calvin wiped the blood from his face with the back of his hand, his chest heaving as he stared at his son. Through his swollen, bleeding lips, he spoke, his voice trembling. "Let him go," he said, his tone low but firm.

Martin hesitated, holding Arris tightly as he struggled in his grip. "Let him go," Calvin repeated, his voice rising with authority. "LET HIS ASS GO!"

Martin reluctantly released Arris, and the moment he did, Arris lunged forward, his fists swinging with renewed fury. Calvin braced himself, taking the hits without flinching, his body swaying but his resolve unbroken.

The once powerful punches began to slow, Arris's chest heaving with exhaustion as the rage and adrenaline seeped out of him. His fists fell to his sides, and before he realized it, his legs gave out beneath him. His head dropped against his father's chest, and for the first time in decades, Calvin wrapped his arms around his son tightly.

"I hate you, bruh," Arris said, his voice cracking as the words came out through broken sobs.

"I know, son. I know. And I'm so sorry," Calvin said softly, his own voice trembling with emotion as he held Arris close. "I'm gonna make this shit right. I swear I will."

The weight of his father's arms around him made Arris crumble completely. He leaned into the embrace, his defenses shattered, the walls he had carefully built over the years lying in ruins. He wanted to believe his father. He needed to believe him. But deep down, a small part of him knew that if Calvin abandoned him again, there would be no coming back. No recovery.

"I know you don't believe me, but I love you," Calvin said, his voice thick with regret as he kept his arms locked around his son. "I'm sorry, son. I'm sorry you had to do all this shit because I couldn't be the man I should've been."

Arris sobbed silently against his father's chest. Words failed him. He wanted to forgive Calvin, wanted to let go of the anger that had eaten away at him for so long. But the pain ran too deep, and forgiveness, he knew, would take time. He wasn't ready to give that yet—not fully.

Finally, Arris pulled away, gaining his composure as he stood upright. His chest still rose and fell rapidly, his breaths shaky, and his eyes were bloodshot from the tears and rage. For the first time in years, though, he felt lighter. It was as if the burden of all those years of resentment had been cracked open, just slightly, enough to let some air through.

Calvin looked at him, his face swollen and bloodied, but his eyes filled with regret and something Arris couldn't quite place—maybe hope. "I love you, son," Calvin said again, his tone softer, more sincere. Arris stared at him for a long moment, his lips parting slightly as if to respond, but the words never came. He wasn't ready to say it back. Not yet.

Calvin nodded, seeming to understand the silence. He reached into his pocket, pulling out a handkerchief to dab at the blood on his face. "I'm heading out," he said carefully, watching his son's reaction. "Your mother invited me to Thanksgiving. But I won't come if you or A'Lani don't want me there."

Arris released a shaky breath, his body still trembling faintly with the remnants of his earlier rage. He hesitated for a moment, his mind racing, before he finally spoke. "It's cool," he said, his voice quiet but steady. "I'll talk to A'Lani."

Calvin nodded, his face a mixture of relief and sadness. "Thank you," he said softly before turning to leave. His shoulders were slouched slightly, but there was something resolute in the way he carried himself.

Ann

He knew he had a long way to go if he ever hoped to repair the damage he had caused.

Arris stood frozen in place, staring at the door long after Calvin had left. The restaurant was silent except for the faint hum of the lights overhead. He couldn't believe what had just happened—that he had taken the first steps toward forgiving the man who had shattered his world. It wasn't an easy step, and it sure as hell didn't erase the years of pain. But it was a start.

For the first time in a long time, Arris felt like he could breathe. It wasn't peace—not yet—but it was the first crack in the armor he had worn for so many years.

"Are you good, boss?" Martin's voice sliced through Arris's thoughts, pulling him back to the present.

"Yeah, Martin. I'm good. Thanks, and sorry about all of this," Arris said, reaching for the broom to sweep up the broken glass that had shattered in the heat of his rage.

"No need to apologize. I got it. You head home and get some rest," Martin said firmly, taking the broom from Arris's grip.

Arris hesitated but eventually nodded, grabbing his keys from the counter. "Thanks, Martin," he said, his tone grateful yet heavy. He knew rest wasn't going to come easy tonight—hell, probably not at all—but there was someone whose presence he craved. Someone who could soothe the storm raging inside of him without even trying.

After saying his goodbyes to Martin, Arris stepped outside, the crisp night air hitting his face as he took his phone off DND. A flood of missed calls and messages popped up on the screen, most of them from Dionne. Ten missed calls from her alone made him chuckle under his breath, even though a small part of him still held onto the frustration from seeing her with Malik yesterday.

He hesitated for a second before calling her back, knowing she'd probably be mad as hell at him for ignoring her. The phone rang and rang, but she didn't answer, making him groan in annoyance as he gripped the steering wheel tighter. "Man, come on," he muttered, shaking his head.

He sent her a quick message:

Call me back when you can, Mama. I'm sorry.

Still feeling restless, he decided to take a detour. Driving straight home wasn't an option; his mind was too wired, too full of the confrontation with his father and the emotions he hadn't fully processed yet. Instead, he turned his car toward Mario's place hoping Mia was there. If anyone could help him decompress and take his mind off the

Feenin'

chaos, it was his niece.

As he drove through the quiet streets, the memory of Dionne's missed calls stayed at the forefront of his mind, nagging at him. He hoped she wasn't mad enough to ignore him for the rest of the night, because right now, she was the one thing he truly needed.

***

Dionne sat stiffly on the couch, her body tense as Malik spoke beside her with an air of confidence. She glanced at him briefly, but her eyes returned to the blank spot on the floor she'd been staring at for the past ten minutes. She felt trapped, suffocated by his words and the situation she promised Mama Glen she'd endure. This counseling session wasn't for her; it was for appearances, for keeping a promise. And yet here she was, sitting in a space meant for healing, feeling more distant than ever.

"So, how did this love story start?" Marie, their counselor, asked with a warm smile. Her presence exuded calm authority, a sharp and beautiful black woman who carried herself with an undeniable grace. Dionne had insisted on someone like her, someone who would understand the complexities of black love. But even Marie's calming energy wasn't enough to chip away at the wall Dionne had built up inside.

"College," Malik answered with enthusiasm, his voice carrying the warmth of nostalgia. He shot Dionne a quick smile before turning back to Marie, the brightness in his tone a stark contrast to the void in Dionne's expression. Marie's eyes flicked to her, clearly noting the dissonance, but she didn't push. Yet.

"She was amazing," Malik continued, leaning forward slightly as he spoke. "Majored in business, played soccer, and ran track. I was buried in medical books at the time, but one night I decided to take a break and hit a party on campus." He chuckled, as if reliving the memory brought him joy, though Dionne remained unmoved.

"That's where I saw her—this beautiful girl with smooth chocolate skin, a banging body, and long curly hair." Malik's tone softened, filled with admiration. "She was laughing with her friends in the corner, and I swear, it was like everything else faded out. I couldn't leave the party without her number. She looked perfect. Still perfect in my eyes."

Marie smiled warmly at his words, scribbling something in her notebook as her gaze flicked to Dionne, who sat silent and detached. Her stoic expression gave nothing away, but the tightening of her jaw told a different story.

"I was nervous when I walked up to her," Malik admitted with a small laugh. "But she gave me her number, and I felt like the luckiest man alive. And the rest is history. Now I'm engaged to the woman of my dreams." He turned to Dionne, his eyes shining with the kind of love and hope that used to make her feel special. Now, it made her feel cornered.

Dionne forced a smile, but it didn't reach her eyes. She knew Malik was trying, that he was fighting to keep something alive that had died a long time ago. But pretending to love someone who no longer held her heart drained her more than she cared to admit. Marie's gaze lingered on her, sharp and knowing, waiting to see if she would engage or stay behind the protective walls she'd built.

"Dionne, I want to hear your perspective. When Malik approached you, what was the first thought that came to your mind?" Marie asked, her voice soft but deliberate, drawing Dionne's attention. Dionne shifted in her seat, her eyes falling briefly to her hands before she spoke.

"My first thought was, 'he's cute'," she said with a small chuckle, the first genuine moment she had shared all session. Her tone softened as she allowed herself to go back to a time when their love felt pure and untainted. "Then the admiration grew when we had an hour-long conversation in the middle of a party, connecting like it was just the two of us in the room. We didn't care about anything happening around us." Dionne's lips curled into a faint smile, but the weight in her tone didn't go unnoticed.

"I really did look at Malik as my best friend," she admitted, her voice tinged with sadness that Marie immediately picked up on. Malik smiled at her words, but Marie's focus remained on Dionne.

"So, what changed?" Marie asked gently, her gaze moving between them. Both looked momentarily caught off guard by the question. The silence that followed was thick, broken only by the sound of Marie's pen tapping lightly against her notebook.

"Well," Marie began when neither of them answered, her eyes now steady on them, "I understand premarital counseling isn't always about fixing problems—it can also be about gaining clarity. But in your case, I sense there's a hole in the relationship. A disconnect. What caused that hole in a love that was once so strong?" Her voice was calm but unwavering, probing them with intention.

Dionne remained silent, her lips pressing together in defiance, while Malik spoke up quickly, almost defensively. "Our careers got in the way," he said, shrugging like it was a simple truth.

Dionne snapped her head toward him, her frown immediate. She couldn't hide her irritation at his response. It wasn't the full story—it wasn't even close. Yet again, Malik was skirting around the truth, avoiding the real reason their relationship had fallen apart.

Feenin'

Marie raised an eyebrow but kept her tone neutral. "How did your careers come in between your relationship?" she asked, shifting her attention deliberately to Dionne. She could see the tension in Dionne's posture and sensed there was more beneath the surface that needed to be said.

Before Dionne could answer, Malik jumped in. "Dionne started at a major real estate firm, and it required her to spend a lot of hours at work," he said quickly, as if to preemptively explain the situation.

Dionne rolled her eyes, her patience fraying. "I think she was asking me," she said, her calm voice carrying an undeniable sharpness that cut through the room.

Marie smiled softly, diffusing the tension. "I care to hear both sides," she reassured. Her attention remained on Dionne, silently encouraging her to speak her truth.

"Malik is a doctor," Dionne began, her voice steady but laced with irritation. "So, the long hours at the hospital and the constant calls during the day made it hard for us to prioritize our relationship." Her words were measured, but the subtle edge in her tone betrayed her frustration.

Marie nodded thoughtfully, watching the way Malik's body tensed at Dionne's tone and the way Dionne's fingers fidgeted against her lap. "I see. But it sounds like there's something more than just busy schedules. Dionne, is there something you want to say to Malik, but you always held back?" she asked, her eyes locking on Dionne's, refusing to let her retreat into silence again.

Before Dionne could respond, Malik's phone rang, cutting through the tense air. She rolled her eyes in irritation, her patience already thin. Malik glanced down at his phone before standing up to excuse himself.

"Really, Malik?" Dionne snapped, her tone sharp with frustration.

"I have to take this, Dee," he defended, not meeting her eyes, as he stepped out of the room.

Dionne scoffed and waved her hand dismissively. "Prime example," she muttered under her breath, already fed up. She leaned back into the couch, shaking her head, her annoyance clear.

Minutes later, Malik returned, his face wearing an apologetic expression. "Sorry, baby, but that was the hospital," he began, but Dionne immediately cut him off, already anticipating his excuse.

"Let me guess, you have to go," she said dryly, her tone laced with bitterness.

Malik nodded, looking guilty. "It's an emergency," he said, trying to reason with her, but Dionne was done.

"It always is," she said sharply, her eyes narrowing as she looked at him.

Malik turned to Marie. "I apologize, Marie, but can we reschedule?" he asked, his tone polite but hurried.

Marie offered him a kind smile, though her gaze flicked to Dionne's clenched fists. "Yes, of course. But, Malik, if you want this to work, you'll need to make as much time for Dionne and your relationship as you do for work," she said firmly.

"I promise this won't happen again," Malik said, his tone sincere, but Dionne wasn't buying it.

"Another broken promise," she said bitterly, her soft chuckle filled with frustration as she crossed her arms. Malik hesitated, glancing at her one last time, but ultimately left the room without another word.

As the door closed behind him, the silence hung heavily in the room. Dionne exhaled deeply, leaning forward to gather her things. "I apologize, Marie, for wasting your time. I knew this was a bad idea," she said, shaking her head.

But Marie held up a hand, stopping her. "You didn't waste my time, Dionne. You two paid for another hour, and I think we should talk," she said, her voice calm and welcoming.

Dionne looked at her, confused. "Just me? I thought this was premarital counseling. I need to be doing this with Malik," she said, her brow furrowing.

Marie chuckled lightly, her demeanor warm. "Yes, it is. But I also provide individual counseling within couples' sessions. It helps me better understand each of you on a personal level, and it gives you space to open up without your partner being present," she explained gently.

Dionne hesitated, the idea of talking about her feelings uncomfortable and foreign to her. She wasn't used to opening up, especially not to a stranger. But as the weight of her life pressed on her shoulders, she realized she was close to breaking. The constant pretending, the juggling of emotions—it was exhausting. She needed a release, and maybe, just maybe, this could help.

Marie must have sensed her hesitation. "You're carrying a heavy load, Dionne," she said softly. "If you don't release some of it, it's going to hurt you even more. Sometimes talking is the first step to healing."

Dionne looked at her for a moment, then nodded slowly. "Okay," she said finally, her voice quiet but resolute. "Let's talk."

Dionne sat down, taking a deep breath as she prepared herself for what was about to come. Vulnerability wasn't her strong suit, but if she didn't start letting it out, she felt the weight of everything might crush her. The lies, the pretending, the heavy facade—it was all becoming too

Feenin'

much.

Marie's warm gaze settled on her. "So, I couldn't help but notice the disconnect between you and Malik. How did that start?" she asked gently, her voice a mixture of curiosity and encouragement.

Dionne fidgeted with her hands, her nerves evident as she hesitated. Finally, she began. "At the start of our relationship, everything was... perfect. We were college kids, living our youth to the fullest, in love, and just happy." Her tone softened as a nostalgic smile flickered across her face, though it didn't last long.

Marie stayed quiet, her pen moving across the notepad, letting Dionne continue at her own pace.

"I admired everything about Malik," Dionne continued. "He was handsome, funny, driven in every sense of the word. That drive was what I loved most about him, but it's also what drove us apart." Her voice cracked slightly as she admitted this, her pain leaking through her words.

Marie furrowed her brow. "How so?" she asked, leaning in just enough to show she was fully invested.

Dionne exhaled deeply, her eyes shifting to the floor as she revisited a part of her past she had buried deeply. "Malik has always been the type of man who chases after goals. He's ambitious, always planning, always striving. It's one of the things that drew me to him... but also what made me resent him," she said, her voice quivering slightly.

"Why is that?" Marie asked, her tone careful, urging Dionne to keep going.

"Because I wasn't his partner in life—I was a goal," Dionne admitted, her voice carrying the weight of years of bottled-up pain. "He didn't see me as someone he loved. I was something he could check off his list: the woman who looked good on his arm, the woman who made him look like the perfect man on the outside. He didn't ask for my number at that party because he was interested in me. He didn't introduce me to his mom because he liked me. And he damn sure didn't propose because he loved me."

Her words came out sharper now, edged with bitterness and the sting of realization.

Marie leaned forward slightly, her brows furrowed as she tried to process Dionne's perspective. "Have you ever discussed this with Malik? Have you told him how you feel?"

Dionne rolled her eyes and shook her head. "No."

"Then how can you know this for sure?" Marie asked, tilting her head slightly.

Dionne sighed heavily, her fingers twisting the tissue in her hands as her gaze dropped. The truth was teetering on the edge of her tongue, weighing down her every breath. Finally, she spoke, her voice soft but filled with emotion. "Because the one thing Malik lusted after—the thing he admired most—was gone in an instant."

Marie leaned in further, her expression one of quiet encouragement. "And what was that?" she asked.

Dionne's throat tightened, and for a moment, she hesitated. "My beauty," she said, her voice breaking slightly. "I had a blood disorder—aplastic anemia. I've had it my whole life, but it got worse in college. My senior year, it was so bad I had to stop playing soccer. I spent more time in the hospital than anywhere else, but I didn't tell anyone—not even Malik."

Tears started to form in Dionne's eyes, and Marie handed her another tissue without a word, letting her gather herself.

"I was always tired, and I started looking... different. Pale. Drained. Like a shell of the person I used to be. Malik noticed, but he never asked. And honestly, I didn't care if he did. I was too tired to explain. I thought I was dying, so why stop him from enjoying his life?" Her voice was steady, but the sadness in her tone was unmistakable.

Marie nodded, her pen still. "What happened then?"

Dionne wiped her tears and took a shaky breath. "One day, I called him over to tell him what was going on. I wanted to explain why I'd been so distant, why I wasn't the same person he fell for. But I collapsed in his arms before I could get the words out. He rushed me to the hospital, and that's when the doctors told him everything." Her voice cracked as she relived the memory.

"He stayed by my side every day after that, making sure I had everything I needed. But the love... the love in his eyes? It was gone. He didn't look at me like I was his woman anymore. He looked at me like I was his patient."

Tears streamed down Dionne's face now, unchecked and free. "That's when I knew. Malik didn't love me. He lusted after me. And when that lust was taken away, so was the foundation of our relationship."

Marie leaned forward slightly, her face a blend of curiosity and gentle encouragement as Dionne opened up. "The way his eyes lit up when he spoke about you, the happiness in his tone—" Marie began, but Dionne quickly cut her off.

"All lust," Dionne said firmly, shaking her head. "You saw how he described me at the party: 'beautiful chocolate skin,' 'banging body.' That was all about my looks. Not once did he mention our deep conversation

Feenin'

that night or how we connected intellectually. It's always been about my appearance, and that's all it is now. I'm healthy and beautiful again, so he's back to looking at me like that."

Marie nodded, taking notes, but her brows furrowed slightly. "But he called you the woman of his dreams. I know learning about your sickness must have been difficult for both of you, but why do you think a man who says things like that doesn't love you?" she asked, her tone gentle, seeking understanding rather than judgment.

Dionne let out a heavy sigh, her voice soft but tinged with sadness. "I don't want to be 'the woman of my man's dreams.' I've been that for a lot of men—men who take one look at me or get lucky enough to hold a conversation. I want to be the love of his life. The woman he can't live without. The woman he feens for." Her voice cracked with emotion as her words tumbled out, raw and honest.

Marie's smile was warm, her nod encouraging as she saw Dionne's walls start to crumble. "That's a powerful distinction," she said softly.

Dionne continued, her voice trembling but steadying with each word. "This ring isn't about love. It's about making sure 'the woman of his dreams' doesn't fall into the hands of another man. So, like I said, Marie, Malik lusts me. He doesn't love me."

Marie's eyes twinkled with curiosity, and her next question carried a subtle, knowing edge. "But you've met the man who does, haven't you?"

Dionne's body went rigid, her eyes widening as Arris's face instantly filled her mind. The way he looked at her, touched her, and made her feel seen in ways Malik never had. She didn't answer, but the truth was written all over her face.

"You don't have to say yes," Marie said with a playful smirk. "But I see it—the glow in your skin, the shift in your energy. There's love in your eyes whenever I bring it up. You thought of him just now, didn't you?" She chuckled softly as Dionne fought hard to suppress her smile.

"Tell me about him," Marie urged gently.

Dionne blinked, momentarily confused. "I thought this was supposed to be about helping me and Malik fix our relationship, not me talking about another man," she said, her tone defensive but light.

Marie chuckled again, unbothered by the deflection. "It is about you and Malik. But to be the kind of wife who's fully connected to her husband on an intimate level, you first have to dive into yourself. That includes exploring all your feelings, desires, and truths—even if those truths involve... other people." She paused with a teasing smile. "Side pieces included."

Dionne glared playfully at that last part. "Arris is not a side piece," she said defensively, her tone sharper than intended.

Marie laughed, her eyes sparkling with understanding. "I know. He's clearly much more than that. What makes him more?"

Dionne sighed, chuckling lightly. "I see what you're doing here. Smart. Reverse psychology." Her tone held a note of respect, but she knew Marie was working her magic.

Marie tilted her head, giving a knowing smile. "So?"

Dionne took a moment, her defenses softening as her thoughts drifted to Arris. A bright smile stretched across her face as she finally spoke. "He reminds me of my father."

Marie's brows lifted slightly. "In what way?" she asked, her smile now mirroring Dionne's.

"Growing up, I adored my parents' relationship," Dionne began, her voice warm with nostalgia. "They had their arguments, sure, but the way my father still cared for my mother even when he was upset... it showed me what real love looked like. My dad loves my mom wholeheartedly. He's never gone against her. He provides, protects, and cherishes her."

Marie's smile grew as she listened, her pen hovering over her notepad but unmoving.

"I've always said I wanted a man to love me the way my father loves my mother. And Arris... Arris does that. He sees me. Not just the surface—but me," Dionne said, her voice soft but brimming with emotion. Her smile widened as she spoke, her eyes lighting up with the same love she felt in her heart.

"So, how do you know Arris loves you?" Marie asked, her voice soft but probing, curious to peel back the layers of Dionne's heart.

Dionne hesitated, her gaze dropping to her lap before she whispered, "Isn't love a drug?"

Marie tilted her head, intrigued by the question. "Yes—in fact— *love is the ultimate drug*," she said with a small smile. "Science has proven that love can create the same changes in our brains as certain drugs do— intense, euphoric, even addictive."

Dionne nodded slowly, her voice trembling as she replied, "Arris is the first man to ever *feen* me."

Marie's smile widened knowingly, her pen pausing over her notepad. "Do you *feen* for him?" she asked cautiously.

Dionne's breath hitched, her hands tightening in her lap. "Yes. Wholeheartedly," she admitted, her voice cracking under the weight of her truth. "And that's what scares me."

Marie leaned forward, sensing the raw emotion spilling out of Dionne. "Do you *feen* Arris more than you love Malik?" she asked

Feenin'

carefully.

Dionne froze, her hesitation clear as her mind wrestled with the truth she already knew deep down. After a moment, she lifted her chin, her voice steady and confident. "Yes."

Marie's expression softened, though her next words carried a firm weight. "Then you're in the wrong place. You need to tell your fiancé the truth before you're stuck in a prison masquerading as a marriage. Before you become an inmate instead of a bride. A slave instead of a wife."

Dionne's head shook instinctively, her fear bubbling to the surface. "I can't," she whispered, her voice thick with unspoken emotions.

"Why not, Dionne? It's just honesty," Marie pressed, her brows furrowed as she tried to understand the invisible chains binding Dionne in place.

Dionne's jaw tightened, her walls snapping back into place. "It's nothing," she muttered, rising from the couch and gathering her things. "I don't want to be here anymore."

Marie stood too, her voice calm but insistent. "Dionne, wait. You can't keep running from this. Whatever it is, you have to face it head-on."

"I need to get back to work," Dionne said briskly, her tone cold, avoiding Marie's gaze. "Take the last 30 minutes as a tip or something."

Marie didn't back down. "If you won't be honest for yourself, then do it for Arris," she said firmly, the weight of her words stopping Dionne in her tracks.

Dionne froze, her head snapping toward Marie, her eyes flashing with a mix of anger and pain.

"That man loves you," Marie continued, her tone softening but still pointed. "And I can see it in your eyes and body that you love him just as much. By staying in this relationship with Malik, you're not only hurting yourself—you're hurting the man who loves you more than anything."

Dionne's throat tightened, her chest aching with the truth of Marie's words. She shook her head, her voice low but resolute. "I can't. It's more complicated than you think."

Marie's heart sank, but she tried to encourage her one last time. "I'll see you at the next session. We'll work through this together."

"No, I'm done with this," Dionne said, her voice hollow as she turned toward the door. "Counseling can't fix what's broken between me and Malik—or within me. I'm sorry for wasting your time."

Before Marie could respond, Dionne walked out, the door closing behind her with a finality that echoed through the room.

Marie watched Dionne leave, her heart heavy with the weight of unspoken truths lingering in the room. She sat back in her chair, her pen resting idly against her notebook. She couldn't help but replay Dionne's words in her mind, the vulnerability in her tone, the crack in her voice when she spoke about Arris. There was so much love there—raw, unfiltered, and undeniable. Yet, it was buried under fear, obligation, and the weight of her circumstances.

Marie sighed, sinking back into her chair, her pen tapping lightly against her notepad. She knew Dionne was holding something back, something heavy, something she wasn't ready to face. Marie just hoped that Dionne would stop running and pretending before it was too late.

***

Arris stepped off the elevator onto Dionne's floor, his jaw tight and his eyes blazing with frustration. Each stride he took was filled with purpose, his entire demeanor radiating controlled fury. His phone had gone unanswered, his texts ignored, and every attempt to reach Dionne had been met with silence. After the emotional storm of his meeting with his father, Dionne was the only person he craved, the only presence that could ground him. Her avoidance was like salt on an open wound, and he couldn't take it anymore.

As he passed through the office, heads turned. The sharp lines of his face, the clenched fists at his sides, and the unrelenting pace of his steps left the staff curious and uneasy. But Arris didn't care. His focus was singular—Dionne.

When he reached her office, more secluded than the others, he didn't bother knocking. The door burst open with a force that startled Dionne, who was hunched over files on her desk. Her head snapped up, her expression shifting from annoyance at the interruption to confusion at the sight of him.

"Arris?" she said, adjusting her glasses as if to make sure she wasn't imagining him. The unexpected intensity in his gaze made her heart skip a beat.

Arris didn't respond. Instead, he shut the door behind him, and turned to her with the weight of his anger simmering in his movements.

"What are you doing here?" Dionne asked, standing up cautiously. She was confused, maybe even a little startled by his sudden presence, but deep down, she was relieved to see him. She had missed him more than she wanted to admit.

Arris strode toward her, closing the distance between them with an intensity that made her step back until she felt the cool glass of the window press against her. His hands landed on her waist—not roughly, but firm enough to keep her from moving. His dark eyes locked onto

Feenin'

hers, filled with a mix of anger and longing.

"Why have you been ignoring me?" he demanded, his voice low but filled with a controlled edge.

"Huh?" Dionne's voice cracked, caught off guard by his proximity and the heat radiating off him. She had never seen him this angry before, and it both unnerved and captivated her.

"You heard me," he said, his grip tightening slightly, though never enough to hurt. "You've seen me calling, texting. Why the hell are you ignoring me?"

She blinked, her heart pounding as she tried to gather her thoughts. "Oh... my phone was on Do Not Disturb," she explained, her words tumbling out quickly. "I forgot to take it off after my counseling session."

The confusion in Arris's eyes deepened, his brow furrowing as he tilted his head slightly. "Counseling session?" he repeated, his tone sharp with curiosity and suspicion.

"Shit, I didn't mean to say that out loud," Dionne muttered to herself, cursing her slip-up.

"But you did," Arris shot back, stepping back just enough to look her in the eye. His hands dropped from her waist, leaving her feeling unmoored and already missing his touch. "So what counseling session?"

"It's nothing," she tried to deflect, her tone dismissive as she folded her arms across her chest, trying to put up a wall he couldn't breach.

"Dionne, stop playing with me," Arris growled, his tone sharper now, cutting through her defenses. "What counseling session?"

She hesitated, her teeth catching her bottom lip as she debated whether or not to tell him. Finally, with a roll of her eyes, she relented. "Malik put us in premarital counseling," she said flatly, her irritation clear.

Arris froze for a moment, the tension in his jaw visible as his hands clenched at his sides. "So you're working it out with that nigga?" he asked, his voice low but deadly. He took a step closer, and she instinctively backed away, her body brushing the glass behind her. "Is that why you're ignoring me now?"

The rage in his eyes was a storm she had never seen before, and for the first time, she felt a flicker of fear.

"No, it's not like that—" Dionne started, her voice trembling, but Arris cut her off sharply.

"It's not like what?" he snapped, his tone calm but simmering with anger. "Because from where I'm standing, it looks like you're still fighting for whatever love is left between you two."

The weight of his words hung heavy in the air. His voice, while steady, carried an unmistakable edge of pain. Dionne's heart clenched as she stared at him. Behind the anger in his eyes, she saw something deeper—hurt, longing, and love. The idea of her still trying to salvage her relationship with Malik was tearing him apart, and she could see it.

"Baby... no," Dionne whispered, stepping toward him, her hands reaching out. But Arris took a step back, his jaw tightening.

"His mother thought it would help us be happy again," Dionne explained quickly, desperation lacing her words. "But it didn't work. I don't love him, Arris. I love you." Her voice cracked on the last word, her eyes searching his for a sign that he believed her.

Arris stood frozen for a moment, his hands clenched at his sides. Before he could respond, the sound of her office door opening shattered the tension between them. Dionne cursed under her breath, suddenly remembering the lunch date she had promised to London and Karmen.

Both women walked in, London smiling brightly, completely oblivious to the charged emotions in the room. "Oh, are we interrupting something?" London asked, her tone playful as her eyes flickered between Dionne and Arris.

Karmen, however, immediately picked up on the tension, her sharp eyes narrowing as they landed on Dionne. She was about to say something when Arris straightened his suit jacket, his movements deliberate.

"I need some air," Arris said curtly, his voice calm but clipped. Without another glance at anyone in the room, he turned and walked out, leaving an eerie silence in his wake.

Dionne's stomach churned as guilt and regret crashed over her like a wave. She didn't want things to end like this. She had to fix it. But before she could make a move, Karmen broke the silence.

"What's his problem?" Karmen asked, her tone filled with curiosity and concern.

"He probably just needs to clear his head," Dionne said quickly, her voice rushed as she tried to mask the chaos inside her. She grabbed her phone and purse, excusing herself before they could press further. "I'll check on him."

Without waiting for a response, she followed Arris out of the office, her heart pounding with every step. She didn't know how to make things right, but she couldn't let him walk away—not like this.

Arris was already gripping the handle of his car door when he heard her voice, soft yet trembling, calling after him. "Arris, please don't do this." The crack in her tone made his chest tighten, but he refused to look back. He couldn't. Not when every emotion inside him was at war—

Feenin'

anger, love, hurt, and the suffocating weight of feeling like he was losing her.

He wanted nothing more than to pull her into his arms, bury his face in her neck, and let her warmth soothe the storm inside him. But every time he closed his eyes, the image of her sitting in counseling with Malik replayed in his mind, tearing him apart. His abandonment issues flared, louder and more violent than ever, convincing him that Dionne was slipping through his fingers and back into the arms of a man who didn't deserve her.

"Arris," she called again, her voice softer, more desperate. Still, he didn't turn.

"You planning to tell me you're leaving me for that nigga?" His voice was cold, every word cutting like a blade. "Because if so, save it unless you want me to hurt that nigga."

Her breath caught at the iciness in his tone. His words hit her like a punch, but she knew she deserved it. "It's not like that," she whispered, her voice shaky as she took another hesitant step toward him.

Finally, he turned to face her, his jaw clenched, his eyes dark and filled with restrained rage and hurt. "Then what the fuck is it like, Dionne? Because every time I think we're on the same page, every time I let myself believe you're mine, I'm reminded you're still planning a future with him."

She stepped closer, her hand reaching out to touch his arm, but he flinched, stepping back like her touch burned him. "Arris, I don't love him," she said quickly, her voice breaking. "I told you—it's complicated."

"Complicated?" He laughed bitterly, the sound cold and humorless. "There's nothing complicated about you sitting on a couch, talking to a counselor about fixing your relationship with a man you're supposed to leave."

Her chest tightened, the weight of his words crushing her. She blinked back tears, her vision blurring. "I didn't choose this."

"You're choosing it," he fired back, his voice rising slightly, the rawness of his emotions slipping through. "Every single day you stay, every time you put that man's ring on your finger, you're choosing him. And every fucking day, it feels like I'm losing you to someone who doesn't deserve you."

Her throat tightened, her mind racing for the right words, but none came. The truth was messy, tangled in lies, fear, and obligations she couldn't explain. She took a shaky step closer, this time placing her hands firmly on his chest. Her touch was grounding, a silent plea for him to hear her out.

"You're not losing me," she whispered, her voice trembling. "I don't belong to him, Arris. I never have."

He closed his eyes at her words, the tension in his shoulders easing slightly as he exhaled a sharp, shaky breath. But the pain didn't leave his face. He opened his eyes again, his gaze meeting hers, raw and vulnerable.

"Then prove it," he said softly, his voice barely above a whisper, but the weight of his words felt like a shout. "Because I can't keep doing this, Dionne. I can't keep loving a woman who's walking down the aisle for someone else."

Her heart shattered at his plea, the desperation in his voice breaking through the walls she had built around her emotions. For the first time, the gravity of what she was doing—living two lives, pretending she could have it both ways—hit her full force. She saw the cracks she had caused in the man she loved and realized how much this was tearing them both apart.

"Arris..." Dionne's voice cracked as she whispered his name, a soft plea that carried the weight of her guilt and heartbreak. He didn't look at her. He couldn't. His hand gripped the car door, his knuckles white, as he swallowed the anger threatening to spill over.

"See you later, Dionne," he said, his voice low, controlled, but the bitterness in his tone was unmistakable.

The sound of her name instead of Mama cut deeper than she expected, like a sharp reminder of the distance she was creating between them. Her feet froze as he got into his car. She wanted to reach for him, to stop him, to explain—anything to ease the pain in his eyes. But she didn't. She couldn't. The truth was too tangled, too messy to unravel in this moment. And deep down, she knew he wouldn't understand.

As Arris pulled off, his tires rolling away from her and everything she was too afraid to say, Dionne stood rooted to the spot. Her chest felt heavy, her breath short. The look in his eyes, the hurt laced with anger, haunted her even as his car disappeared into the distance. She wanted to scream, to cry, to run after him, but all she could do was turn away.

Walking back into the building felt like an uphill battle. Each step was heavier than the last, her heart pounding with the weight of her choices. She pushed open the door to her office and found London and Karmen waiting, their chatter cutting off the moment they saw her face.

"Everything okay?" London asked, concern etched on her face as she noticed the distant look in Dionne's eyes.

"Yes, just business not going how we planned," Dionne said, forcing

Feenin'

a smile and masking the storm raging inside her. Another lie. Another deflection. She felt herself sinking deeper into the web of complications she'd created, but she couldn't stop. Not now.

"You two ready for lunch?" Dionne asked, her voice cheerful but hollow. London and Karmen exchanged a brief glance, both clearly sensing that something wasn't right but choosing not to press her further. They nodded, following Dionne as she grabbed her purse and keys. She led the way out of the office, her facade firmly in place, even as guilt clawed at her insides.

The drive to the restaurant was agonizing. Arris crowded her thoughts, the image of his hurt, angered eyes burning into her mind. She wanted to call him, to hear his voice, to tell him the truth—but she couldn't. Not now. Not yet. The weight of her promise to Mama Glen still loomed over her, shackling her to a life she no longer wanted.

As she followed behind her friends' car, the pressure became too much. Her grip on the steering wheel tightened, her chest heaving with suppressed emotion until it all erupted. Dionne slammed her fist into the steering wheel over and over, her screams ripping through the air, drowning out the blaring music. Tears streamed down her face, hot and relentless, as the pain she'd buried so deeply finally bubbled to the surface.

"Why can't I just fucking let go?" she cried to no one but herself, her voice cracking under the weight of her anguish. The walls of her car felt like they were closing in, suffocating her with the mess she'd made of her life.

By the time she pulled into the restaurant parking lot, Dionne forced herself to regain control. She reached into her bag for a tissue, wiping away the evidence of her breakdown. Her hands shook as she reapplied her makeup, dabbing concealer under her red, swollen eyes. She slid on her glasses for an extra layer of disguise, taking a deep breath to steady herself.

She glanced at her reflection in the mirror, her face a perfect mask of composure. No one would guess that moments ago, she'd been screaming into the void, drowning in guilt and pain. She plastered on a practiced smile and stepped out of the car, walking toward the restaurant where her friends waited.

Once again, Dionne was pretending. Even in front of the people she loved and trusted, she wore the mask. It was all she knew how to do anymore.

On the other side of town, Arris sped toward his house, gripping the steering wheel so tightly his knuckles turned white. The anger bubbling inside him was unlike anything he'd ever felt. Each passing mile only fueled the fire. The thought of losing Dionne—the one person he loved beyond reason—made his blood boil. Hearing that she was still fighting for her relationship with Malik sent him over the edge.

Once again, he felt abandoned. Betrayed. Someone he had given everything to was slipping away, and he didn't know how to stop it. But this wasn't just about his abandonment issues. This wasn't just old wounds reopening. Dionne wasn't just another woman. She wasn't someone he could replace or forget. She was his lifeline, his missing rib, the piece of him he never knew was missing until she came into his life.

She wasn't just love. She was survival.

She was his drug. More potent than any high he'd ever felt, she consumed him—mind, body, emotions, soul. Her absence left him hollow, her presence filled him in ways he didn't even know were possible. Without her, his world was gray. But today, hearing her talk about counseling with another man, watching her fight for another man's love, and seeing her hesitate when it came to their love—he felt that world crumbling.

As he pulled into his driveway, his chest ached. His breaths were shallow, his vision blurry from the unrelenting storm of emotions that refused to let him go. Arris slammed his car door and stormed inside, his body heavy with exhaustion, anger, and pain. As soon as he made it to his living room, his legs gave out. He collapsed onto the couch, staring blankly at the shelf where the rare tulips sat—the ones he bought for Dionne, the ones that symbolized her.

She was like those tulips: rare, irreplaceable, and breathtakingly beautiful. But unlike the tulips, she wasn't his to keep. Not really. She felt further out of reach now than ever before, and that realization gutted him.

Arris closed his eyes, his chest heaving as he tried to calm the storm inside him. But nothing worked. The anger was too raw, the hurt too fresh, and the love—God, the love—was too overpowering.

Every word she spoke to him earlier played on a loop in his mind, but none of it could drown out the truth his heart feared most: he was losing her.

And without her, he didn't know how to survive.

Chapter 15

Arris stepped out of his car, the polished black paint gleaming under the late afternoon sun. He adjusted the collar of his Balmain shirt, the fine fabric fitting perfectly over his broad shoulders. Black jeans and matching Balmain sneakers completed his look, the casual yet expensive outfit a testament to his style. His freshly cut waves gleamed under the light, and his sharp beard and edge-up showed off the precision of the barber's hand earlier that day. He was here for business, but the thought of catching up with an old friend added a small bit of ease to his otherwise tense day.

Arris approached the large home Demetrius had sent him the address to. The property was a little outside the city, surrounded by sprawling green space and privacy, fitting for the man he was about to meet. He rang the doorbell and waited, the sound of footsteps nearing on the other side. Moments later, the door swung open, revealing Demetrius holding his son, who was practically his clone.

"Wassgood, AB," Demetrius greeted, extending a hand.

"Wassup, D," Arris replied, dapping him up with a firm handshake and a shoulder bump. His eyes immediately shifted to the little boy balanced on Demetrius's arm. "Wassup, lil man. Damn, man, he looks just like you," Arris said with a smile.

Demetrius grinned, adjusting his hold on his son. "DJ, say wassup. This is your Uncle Arris," he said, pride evident in his voice.

DJ looked at Arris with big, curious green eyes, tilting his head slightly before offering a shy, "Wassup, Unc." His tone was soft, but he tried to mimic his father's confidence.

Arris chuckled and leaned in, extending his hand for a dap. "Aye, what's up, lil man," he said, bumping fists with the boy. "He got that same energy as you already," Arris added with a laugh, watching as DJ

Ann

grinned back at him.

Demetrius set DJ down, giving his shoulder a playful nudge. "Boy, go get dressed before your Auntie comes to pick you up," he said, shaking his head at his son's antics.

DJ ran off, his little feet pattering down the hall as Demetrius and Arris chuckled. "That little boy a fool," Demetrius joked, leading Arris toward his office.

Arris laughed, his deep voice echoing through the spacious house. "Man, he gone have all the ladies, especially with them green eyes you passed down to him."

Demetrius groaned, rolling his eyes as they entered his office. "Bruh, he already talking about some little girl he met. I had my sister babysit him one time, and he comes back talking about a girl he likes."

Arris leaned back in the chair across from Demetrius's desk, smirking. "Aye, be prepared for many more," he said, clasping his hands in front of him.

"As long as he don't turn out like your ass, we good," Demetrius joked, a wide grin on his face.

Arris laughed, the tension in his chest momentarily easing. "Nigga, whatever. You know he gonna be smooth as hell, regardless."

They settled into their usual rhythm of banter before Demetrius's tone shifted, more serious now as he pulled out a set of documents. "Aight, let's get down to it," he said, sliding a folder across the desk. Arris leaned forward, the weight of the meeting finally setting in. The camaraderie between them was comforting, but both men knew business always came first.

"So, you consider the offer yet?" Demetrius asked, flipping open the file that detailed the Comets facility and the franchise's proposal for ownership. The glossy pages showcased blueprints, revenue charts, and a breakdown of what the deal could mean for them.

Arris leaned back in his chair, his sharp eyes scanning the file briefly before he responded. "Shi, everything looks solid so far. But I gotta run it by my woman first," he said, his voice calm yet tinged with the weight of unspoken emotions.

It had been two weeks since he last spoke to her. Two weeks of unanswered calls and texts that he ignored, his pride and hurt standing in the way of reconciliation. Despite his silence, she was still the first thought in his mind, the person he instinctively wanted to consult about a decision this big. Arris missed her more than he wanted to admit, the ache of her absence gnawing at him daily.

Even now, he was still reeling from the discovery that she'd been

Feenin'

attending marriage counseling with Malik. The idea of her fighting for a man he believed didn't deserve her left a bitter taste in his mouth. How could she fight for Malik, when he was ready to love her openly and fully, no conditions attached? The thought stung deeper than he was willing to show.

Demetrius blinked in disbelief, leaning back in his chair as his grin widened. "Wait, hoe ass Arris has a woman?" he asked, his voice dripping with shock and amusement.

Arris shook his head, a chuckle rumbling from his chest. "Man, I'm not the Arris you used to know. I grew up," he said with a faint smirk.

"Damn," Demetrius said, shaking his head in wonder. "I have to meet the woman who locked you down. She must be something else."

Before Arris could respond, a knock interrupted their conversation. The office door opened, and both men turned to see who it was. Arris's heart immediately thudded against his chest at the sight of her. Standing in the doorway was Dionne, her face unreadable, though Arris could see the flicker of emotions behind her cool expression—longing, anger, and something else he couldn't place.

"Wassup, sis!" Demetrius said, standing to hug her.

Sis? Arris thought, the realization hitting him like a freight train. He pieced it together quickly, the connection clicking into place.

"Hey, D. I didn't mean to interrupt..." Dionne said, her voice steady, but her eyes briefly darted to Arris. She didn't miss the way his gaze locked onto her, but she masked her feelings quickly. Arris, on the other hand, caught the slight tension in her stance, the faint trace of anger—likely from him avoiding her for the past two weeks.

Demetrius, oblivious to the thick tension filling the room, gestured toward them. "Oh, Dionne, this is my homeboy Arris. He's my old baseball friend, but hopefully my future business partner." He grinned before turning to Arris. "And Arris, this is my little sister and Houston's badass realtor, Dionne."

Arris stood, his eyes glued to hers, and she didn't break the connection. For a moment, they communicated without words—her longing, his frustration, and the unspoken emotions crackling between them. It was a silent conversation no one else in the room could hear.

"It's nice to meet you, Dionne," Arris said finally, his tone neutral, betraying nothing of their history.

Dionne's expression didn't falter, but he caught the subtle mug she gave him before her face smoothed into polite professionalism. "Same here, Arris," she replied, her voice equally flat.

As they shook hands, Arris felt the heat in her touch, but she quickly pulled her hand away, the action speaking volumes. He knew she was upset with his cold demeanor, but he couldn't help himself. Protecting his heart was his priority, especially when hers still seemed to belong to someone else. The diamond engagement ring that gleamed on her finger was a painful reminder of the reality they were both trying to navigate.

"I didn't mean to interrupt your meeting," Dionne said, turning her full attention to Demetrius, her tone calm but her body language stiff as she clearly tried to ignore Arris's presence. She could feel his gaze on her, subtle but heavy, and it only fueled her irritation. "I just came to say that I have DJ. We'll be back later."

Demetrius grinned as he leaned back in his chair. "Don't be having my son around any more girls. He can't stop talking about the last one—I think her name is Mia."

Arris's eyebrows furrowed at the mention of Mia's name. His niece? This world really was too small.

Dionne laughed, her deep, warm laugh filling the room and, unintentionally, wrapping around Arris's heart. It was a sound he hadn't realized he'd been starving for until now. He missed her voice, her smile, and especially that laugh that always managed to melt every part of him.

"Aww, DJ has a crush," Dionne teased, her tone light and playful.

Demetrius rolled his eyes dramatically. "Man, his mama is gonna whoop my ass."

Dionne shook her head with a smile. "No, she won't. Mia's the sweetest little girl, and they're just friends," she said, her voice softening slightly.

Arris smiled faintly, his chest tightening as he listened to her talk about his niece with such warmth. Seeing her with the people he loved had always been something he treasured, but it only made the distance between them sting more.

"Good. Speaking of Kierra, she said she's coming into town the week before Thanksgiving and staying until we all go back," Demetrius said casually, leaning forward to glance at some paperwork on his desk.

Dionne's playful mug appeared immediately. "That bitch didn't tell me anything! I'm about to give her an earful," she said, though her tone carried her usual mix of humor and sincerity. Kierra was like the older sister she'd always wanted, and just hearing about her made Dionne's heart swell with excitement.

Demetrius chuckled, shrugging unapologetically. "Oh damn, I think it was supposed to be a surprise. Just act surprised then," he joked.

"Yo ass can't ever hold water," Dionne quipped, laughing softly.

Demetrius shrugged again, unbothered, while Arris stood silently,

Feenin'

observing the moment. Watching Dionne laugh, seeing her ease around Demetrius, only reminded him of how far away she felt from him now.

"Well, I should let you get back to business," Dionne said, shifting her tone to something more professional, more distant. "It was nice meeting you, Arris." Her words were polite, but her tone lacked warmth, carrying a sting that Arris felt deep in his chest.

Arris nodded, his response equally dry. "Same here."

As she walked out of the office, Arris's eyes followed her, unable to stop himself even as the ache in his chest deepened. He hated how things had played out between them, hated the cold distance she was putting up, but he also couldn't shake his own hurt and anger.

Demetrius glanced at him, clearly oblivious to the undercurrent of tension. "Man, you good? You've been quiet as hell since she walked in."

Arris forced a nod, swallowing the emotions clawing at his throat. "Yeah, just got a lot on my mind," he muttered, brushing it off.

But even as Demetrius went on about the Comets deal, Arris's thoughts were consumed by Dionne—the sound of her laugh, the look in her eyes, and the way she'd said his name like it didn't mean a thing when he knew, deep down, it meant everything.

"So that was your sister?" Arris asked, unable to hide the grin spreading across his face. Seeing Dionne again after two weeks felt like a breath of fresh air, even though his chest ached with all the unresolved feelings between them. Her presence still had the same effect—it stole his breath like it always did.

Demetrius shot him a look, immediately catching the shift in his tone. "Nigga, don't smile like that while saying it. This is why I kept her hidden from your hoe ass." Demetrius joked, but his tone carried a protective edge.

Arris chuckled, holding his hands up in surrender. "Relax, bruh. It ain't even like that. I was just surprised y'all were related. She fine as hell—no disrespect—and you, on the other hand..." Arris teased, letting the joke hang.

"Man, fuck you," Demetrius laughed, shaking his head. Arris laughed with him, the banter falling into the natural rhythm of their long-standing friendship.

"You in a relationship, remember? And she's engaged, so don't even think about it," Demetrius warned, his tone half-joking but firm.

The word engaged hit Arris like a punch to the gut, but he hid the sting behind a composed expression. "Nah, not on that," he said, his tone serious even though the truth was buried beneath the surface.

"Shit, honestly, I'd rather it be your hoe ass than the nigga she's marrying," Demetrius said, his voice dropping into a more serious tone.

Arris raised a brow at his friend's bluntness, catching the tension in his voice. It wasn't every day Demetrius spoke like this, and it immediately piqued Arris's interest. "Damn, you sound like you hate the nigga," Arris joked lightly, but his curiosity was evident.

"Shit, I damn near do," Demetrius admitted, his jaw tightening. "The only reason I haven't beat that nigga's ass is because Dionne loves him—or so she says."

Arris's jaw clenched instinctively, but he masked his growing frustration behind a calm demeanor. "What'd he do to make you hate the nigga?" Arris asked, keeping his tone casual even though every part of him was on edge. He wasn't one to gossip about another man, but if Malik was a threat to Dionne's happiness or safety, Arris needed to know.

"That nigga's done a lot of fucked-up shit, but recently he cheated on her with some bitch at his job," Demetrius said, his jaw flexing as his voice dripped with venom.

Arris mirrored the same rage, though he stayed composed to avoid raising suspicion. The thought of Malik hurting Dionne made his blood boil, but he kept his emotions in check.

"I can't wait to see that nigga again," Demetrius continued, his tone hard and unwavering. "I want to whoop his ass so bad."

You and me both, Arris thought bitterly, clenching his fists under the table.

"Damn, that's fucked up," Arris said softly, the genuine anger in his voice clear. "She doesn't even seem like the type of woman who deserves that shit."

"She doesn't," Demetrius agreed firmly. "My sister is the most genuine, sweet, kind-hearted person I know. She's been through some deep, life-changing shit and still came out on top. She deserves a man who loves every part of her, not some nigga who only sees her as a trophy to show off."

Arris nodded, swallowing hard. Demetrius didn't know the man he was describing was sitting right in front of him. Arris loved Dionne in ways that couldn't be put into words—every flaw, every smile, every moment she let him see the real her. She was more than a trophy to him; she was his entire heart.

But as much as he wanted to tell Demetrius that, the engagement ring she wore—and the complications it represented—kept him silent. Instead, he tucked away every word, every ounce of anger and love, and let the conversation shift, though his mind remained consumed by Dionne.

Feenin'

The room grew silent, the weight of their conversation lingering in the air before Demetrius finally broke it. "My bad, man. I didn't mean to sit here and gossip about my sister. That shit's just hard to watch and not do anything," he admitted, his voice heavy with frustration and protectiveness.

Arris nodded, his expression understanding. "No need to apologize. If A'Lani was with a man who wasn't deserving of her, I'd feel the same way. I just pray your sister knows there's a man out there who loves her more than anything else in this world. Who cherishes the ground she walks on. Who'll never make her question his love. Ever." His voice was steady but filled with conviction, every word coming from the depths of his heart. He was speaking about himself, but he kept that truth hidden from Demetrius.

Demetrius studied him for a moment, then nodded. "Damn, nigga, your woman got you poetic and shit. You must really love her ass," he said with a chuckle, trying to lighten the mood.

Arris laughed briefly, but his tone turned serious. "I *feen* for her, man. It's deeper than love. I just can't wait for the day she understands that," he said, standing and adjusting the chains on his neck.

Demetrius nodded, taking in his words. "She will. Bet she already knows deep down," he said, giving Arris the affirmation he didn't even realize he needed in the moment.

"I'll talk this over with her and hit you up before the season ends," Arris said, referring to the business proposal.

"Sounds good," Demetrius replied as they dapped each other up. "Take care, man."

"You too, D," Arris said before heading out.

As Arris climbed into his car, his thoughts were consumed by Dionne. Her face, her laugh, the way she spoke about his niece earlier—it all played on a loop in his mind. But the rage simmered just beneath the surface. The revelation that Malik had cheated on her made his blood boil. Sure, Dionne had strayed too, but deep down, Arris knew Malik had been the first to betray her, and that knowledge infuriated him.

The man who had everything—the woman Arris loved, a life of privilege—had disrespected her in the worst way. And for that, Malik was going to pay. Arris's jaw tightened as he gripped the steering wheel, his mind already racing with thoughts of how Malik would feel the weight of the pain he'd caused.

As he pulled out of Demetrius's driveway, his mind was a storm of anger and longing. He didn't know how yet, but one thing was certain—Malik wasn't going to get away with it.

***

The Next Morning:

Dionne stepped out of her car, the rhythmic click of her heels against the pavement echoing with every confident step she took. Today was business, no matter how personal the past few weeks had felt. She was here to show Arris a plot of land for the business venture he was considering, but the thought of being around him again made her nerves coil. She was relieved Ms. Jean and China were present, their presence acting as a buffer between her and Arris—a necessary shield to keep the tension at bay.

For two weeks, she had tried reaching out to him, desperate to explain herself, to apologize for the pain she'd caused, but every call, every text, every gesture had been met with silence. And then, seeing him at her brother's house, acting as if he didn't know her, as if they hadn't shared the moments that were still burned into her soul—it had been the final blow. She was slowly coming to terms with the reality that whatever they had was over. It was her fault, and she couldn't deny it. Arris had offered her the kind of love she'd always wanted, but she let it slip through her fingers, tangled in a web of obligations and promises she couldn't break.

Pushing her emotions to the side, Dionne straightened her shoulders and walked toward the group already gathered near the edge of the property. Arris stood with Ms. Jean and China, his tall frame exuding that same quiet confidence she still craves. The moment her heels hit the gravel, all three heads turned in her direction. Her eyes briefly met Arris's, his gaze unreadable, but she quickly shifted her focus, greeting Ms. Jean and China with a bright, professional smile.

Arris noticed her calculated avoidance, and a faint chuckle escaped his lips, though he kept his expression composed. Dionne didn't acknowledge it, staying laser-focused on the task at hand. She dove straight into discussing the details of the land, her tone steady and confident. Still, she couldn't ignore the weight of Arris's gaze on her. He wasn't making it subtle, either; his eyes remained locked on her every movement, every word, as if searching for something unsaid.

Throughout the entire land showing, Dionne maintained her professionalism, even as she noticed Arris's cold, detached demeanor. When she presented details about the property, he would only nod, his responses curt and dry. But when Ms. Jean offered her input, his tone would shift, becoming more engaged and thoughtful. The dynamic grated on Dionne's nerves, but she knew deep down that his behavior stemmed from the pain she'd caused him. He was hurt, and it was her fault. No

Feenin'

matter how much she wanted to make things right, nothing she said or did could convince him that her love for him outweighed anything she felt for Malik. The thought broke her heart.

"This location is perfect for a high-end hotel or mixed-use development," Dionne said, her tone steady, trying to keep her emotions in check. "The proximity to downtown, the airport, and major highways guarantees heavy traffic and visibility." Her eyes met his, searching for any flicker of recognition in his expression.

"Hm," Arris replied flatly, his response devoid of emotion, making her jaw clench in irritation. His aloofness was pushing her buttons, but she refused to let it show. She couldn't tell if he was acting like this to get under her skin or if he genuinely felt indifferent, but either way, it was wearing her patience thin.

She pressed on, determined to finish the presentation. "The zoning here is flexible, which means retail, luxury apartments, and even a rooftop restaurant are all viable options. It's a goldmine," she added, her tone unwavering.

"Maybe," he responded dryly again, a faint smirk tugging at his lips as he noticed her subtle irritation. He hated treating her like this—Dionne in that red dress was breathtaking, and every fiber of him wanted to pull her close. But that diamond ring on her finger, the constant reminder of her connection to Malik, made his blood boil. He couldn't hide the hurt, so he buried it beneath this cold façade.

Ms. Jean, sensing the tension but unaware of its true source, stepped in, her voice calm and measured. "Arris, she's not wrong. The traffic projections alone justify the investment. A hotel here could anchor this entire area."

Arris shifted his gaze to Ms. Jean, his tone softening ever so slightly. "You think it's worth it?" he asked, his voice now laced with genuine intrigue.

Dionne bit the inside of her cheek, trying to keep her frustration in check. She couldn't help but notice how quickly his demeanor changed when he was speaking to Ms. Jean. Normally, her opinion was the one he cared about the most, and now he was dismissing her like she was an outsider. It stung, but she swallowed her feelings and kept her composure.

China, standing nearby, caught the slight tension in Dionne's body language. She didn't understand the dynamic between Dionne and Arris, but she could tell there was something deeper going on. The subtle shift in the room's energy didn't go unnoticed by her, though she wisely chose to stay quiet, letting the scene play out.

Dionne kept her professional mask intact, even as the storm of emotions churned inside her. The way Arris was shutting her out, treating her opinions as if they held no weight, was unlike anything she'd ever experienced from him. It felt personal, and it hurt. But she reminded herself—she had no one to blame but herself.

"Absolutely. The infrastructure is already in place, and with the airport expansion and business district growth, it's a no-brainer. This isn't just about profits—it's about positioning Blac as a leader in urban development," Ms. Jean explained with a confident smile, her enthusiasm evident. Arris mirrored her smile before his gaze shifted back to Dionne, who met him with a hard, unwavering glare.

"Positioning matters," Arris said, his tone pointed as his eyes remained locked on hers. Dionne rolled her eyes in response, the tension between them thick.

"Exactly," Ms. Jean continued, oblivious to the silent exchange. "This isn't just land; it's a statement piece. The kind of project that puts Blac on the map for high-level investors."

"And with Williams Luxe handling everything from design to execution, you'd have a seamless process," Dionne interjected, her tone sharp but professional. "This is the deal that solidifies your brand." She held his gaze, and though she could see the flicker of love in his eyes, it was overshadowed by his distant demeanor.

"Noted," Arris replied flatly, his voice void of the warmth she once cherished. His coldness cut deep, and Dionne rolled her eyes again, her patience wearing thin. She was ready for this showing to be over, wanting nothing more than to escape his presence if he was going to continue acting like this.

"If you trust my judgment, Arris," Ms. Jean chimed in with a reassuring smile, "this is a project worth pursuing. It's time to stop hesitating and start building."

Arris nodded, a decision made. "Alright, let's do it."

Ms. Jean's face lit up with satisfaction. "Great! You can come back to the office, and Dionne will have all the paperwork ready for you to sign, or we can email everything to you electronically for you and your lawyer."

"Electronically is fine," Arris said, his tone calm but cutting as he glanced back at Dionne. "Not trying to cause Ms. Smith any more trouble." His pettiness wasn't lost on Dionne, and her lips tightened in frustration.

Oblivious to the underlying tension, Ms. Jean nodded and smiled, shaking Arris's hand to seal the deal. Dionne, despite her irritation,

Feenin'

extended her hand as well, forcing herself to remain professional. The brief handshake was cold and detached, mirroring the emotions swirling between them.

As soon as the showing ended, Dionne headed straight to her car, eager to get away from the man who could simultaneously ignite her passion and tear her apart. Once inside, she spotted Arris talking with China by his car. Her grip tightened on the steering wheel as she stared at him from a distance, the mix of anger and longing boiling inside her.

I should hit his ass, she thought darkly before shaking her head and starting her engine. Without another glance in his direction, she pulled away, driving in the opposite direction, ready to leave his presence and the emotional storm he always seemed to bring.

***

The weekend had rolled around faster than Dionne had anticipated, and though she welcomed the break from work, her thoughts were far from at ease. It had been days since she last saw Arris, and his continued distance was weighing heavily on her. Despite her repeated efforts to reach out, he remained unresponsive. Resigned, she had finally given up trying, but that didn't stop the aching void he left behind. Lying in her bed, she scrolled through her phone, her thumb hesitating over photos of her and Arris, moments frozen in time when things felt less complicated. The longing hit her like a wave—she missed him in ways she couldn't explain, the withdrawals from his absence leaving her restless.

The sharp sound of her doorbell broke her trance. Frowning, she glanced at the clock and wondered who could possibly be visiting. Malik was at work, and she wasn't expecting anyone. The bell chimed again, insistent this time, and she groaned, tossing her phone to the side as she slid out of bed. Tightening the sash on her silk robe, she slipped into her brown house slippers and made her way downstairs.

Still rubbing the stress from her eyes, she reached the door and opened it without bothering to check who it was.

"SURPRISE, BITCH!" Kierra's familiar voice rang out as she practically bounced into Dionne's arms.

Dionne squealed in shock and excitement, instantly wrapping her arms around her sister-in-law. "Oh my God, Kierra!" she laughed, jumping into her embrace. Kierra stumbled slightly but managed to steady herself with a dramatic grunt.

"Look, girl, your ass ain't light. That ass a cool 30 pounds all on its own!" Kierra teased, giving Dionne's butt a playful slap, causing it to jiggle.

Dionne laughed as she stepped back, holding the door open wider.

"Oh my gosh, sis, I miss you!" she beamed, her smile as bright as the Texas sun.

"I miss you too!" Kierra said, stepping inside with a wide grin. "I couldn't take another damn day in Dallas. I had to come see you."

"Bitch, please. You missed your man and your son. Let's be real," Dionne teased, earning a hearty laugh from Kierra.

"Two things can be true," Kierra smirked, her wit sharp as always.

Dionne couldn't hold back her laughter, shaking her head at her sister-in-law's energy. "I missed you so much, Kierra," she admitted with a warm smile.

"I missed you too, girl. You've been hiding out on me, and I wasn't about to let another weekend go by without seeing my baby sis."

Kierra's energy was infectious. Her boldness and no-filter personality reminded Dionne so much of London, but Kierra had her own unique charm. At 32 years old, Kierra's beauty was undeniable—her flawless chocolate skin, her long, natural hair, and her striking features made her a perfect fit for her career as a model. Standing at 5'7", her presence commanded any room she entered, and her unapologetic personality only added to her allure.

Kierra's words were like a breath of fresh air, and for the first time all week, Dionne felt herself relax, her burdens momentarily forgotten. She didn't know what the night had in store, but with Kierra around, it was bound to be an adventure.

Dionne laughed, her spirits already lifting just from Kierra's presence. "It's Friday night, and I know your ass isn't sitting in this house, in a robe, instead of being outside throwing that ass in a circle!" Kierra hyped, her tone dripping with playful judgment.

"Girl, I am tired. I worked all week, so I'm using this weekend to relax," Dionne protested, plopping onto the couch as Kierra shook her head with a knowing smirk.

"Not while I'm here. We about to turn the fuck up, so get your ass up and put some clothes on. London and Karmen are already waiting on us," Kierra announced, her tone leaving no room for negotiation.

Dionne raised an eyebrow, laughing despite herself. "You hoes planned this, didn't you?"

Kierra shrugged, completely unbothered. "Of course we did. You've been cooped up in this house for too long, and now that I'm in Houston, I'm about to show you a good time. No excuses, sis."

Dionne sighed, realizing resistance was futile. "Alright, fine. Where are we going? I need to know so I can figure out what to wear."

Kierra grinned, pleased with her small victory. "We're going to a

Feenin'

club London swears is the best spot in the city. So, dress... naked."

That made Dionne burst into laughter. "Girl, I am not about to walk into no damn club naked. Be serious."

Kierra laughed along with her, tossing her straightened hair over her shoulder. "Okay, okay. Just dress sexy, then. But wear brown or black."

Dionne tilted her head, eyeing her sister-in-law with suspicion. "Why brown or black?"

Kierra rolled her eyes dramatically, clearly not in the mood to explain. "You ask too many damn questions, Dionne. Just do as I say."

Dionne finally took a good look at Kierra's outfit—black leather pants hugged her curves, a see-through brown Fendi long-sleeve showcased her toned body, and brown open-toed heels completed the look. Her hair, styled in a middle part, fell down her back like silk. The ensemble screamed confidence and perfection, exactly how Kierra always carried herself.

"Okay, Miss Fendi. I see you," Dionne teased, standing up with a playful shake of her head. "You're already looking good, and here I am in a damn robe."

Kierra smirked, placing her hand on her hip. "That's why you need to hurry the hell up. London and Karmen are already there, waiting on us. We don't have time for you to take forever."

Dionne chuckled, feeling her sister's fiery energy seep into her. "Alright, alright, I'm going. But you're lucky I missed you, Kierra. That's the only reason I'm putting up with your bossy ass."

Kierra grinned, nudging Dionne toward the stairs. "Damn right you missed me. Now go! And don't come down looking like a damn librarian."

Dionne laughed as she headed upstairs, feeling a sense of calm wash over her despite the chaos of her life. Kierra's feistiness was exactly what she needed to take her mind off everything—even if just for one night.

Dionne rushed upstairs and hopped into the shower, letting the hot water wash away the stress of her week. She didn't know exactly what her friends had planned, but she was determined to let loose and enjoy the night. She needed this escape, and with Kierra's energy already lifting her spirits, she felt ready to embrace it.

After moisturizing her smooth, glowing skin, Dionne walked into her closet only to find Kierra already there, holding up an outfit like a stylist on a mission. Dionne raised an eyebrow, laughing at how orchestrated everything felt. "This is way too planned," she teased, narrowing her eyes at Kierra.

Kierra grinned mischievously, holding up a stunning brown

REVOLVE lace dress. "Girl, of course it's planned. I don't play when it comes to you. Now, put this on and thank me later."

The dress was sheer, hugging every curve and stopping just above her ankles. It left little to the imagination, but it was tasteful and elegant—sexy, without trying too hard. Dionne slipped it on, adjusting the straps and smoothing it over her body. When she looked in the mirror, even she had to admit she looked good.

"Bitch, you is fine!" Kierra hyped, her voice ringing with excitement. "That body is bodying! Whew!"

Dionne burst into laughter, shaking her head as she turned to admire herself in the mirror. Kierra wasn't lying—she looked like a walking masterpiece. Her curves were accentuated perfectly, and the rich brown lace complemented her brown skin flawlessly.

Kierra handed her a pair of matching brown Tom Ford heels and some subtle gold jewelry to complete the look. Dionne slipped on the heels, the added height elongating her frame and giving her even more confidence. She paired it with a ginger wig that flowed down her back in soft body wave curls, styled in a middle part. Dionne remembered how London insisted she try the bold color yesterday, and now it was clear why. The wig, the dress, the heels—it all came together beautifully.

Dionne sat at her vanity to apply her makeup. She went for a sultry, warm-toned look to match her dress, adding bold lashes and a glossy nude lip. When she was finished, she gave herself one last glance in the mirror, and her reflection stunned her. She looked radiant, glowing, and utterly sexy.

"Can't nobody tell me my sis ain't bad!" Kierra hyped again, her eyes lit up with pride as she looked Dionne up and down. "Girl, you about to have these people in the club pressed and stressed!"

Dionne laughed, her confidence soaring as she turned to face Kierra. "Okay, you did your thing with this one. I look good as hell!"

"Duh," Kierra said, flipping her hair dramatically. "Now let's go show the world what a bad bitch looks like."

Dionne grabbed her clutch, her smile wide as she followed Kierra downstairs, feeling like the weight of the week had lifted. Tonight was about freedom, fun, and forgetting everything—even if just for a few hours.

The black Escalade pulled up outside, and Dionne's eyes widened in shock, taking in the VIP treatment her friends had clearly orchestrated. She had always known Kierra, London, and Karmen were wild, but this? This was next-level, and now she was officially nervous about what they had planned for the night.

Feenin'

As the car rolled to a stop at a red light, Kierra reached into her bag and handed Dionne a blindfold. "Okay, you gotta put this on first," she said, her tone filled with mischief.

Dionne frowned, narrowing her eyes at Kierra. "Why do I need to put this on? What are y'all up to?" she asked, her voice laced with suspicion. The blindfold instantly reminded her of Arris—the night he surprised her with a helicopter ride. The memory sent a wave of longing through her, making her heart ache. She missed him more than she wanted to admit, and thinking about him only made it worse.

"Girl, just put the damn blindfold on," Kierra said with an impatient laugh, leaving no room for argument.

Dionne rolled her eyes, laughing despite her nerves. "Lord, why did you give me crazy bitches as friends?" she muttered, looking up as if seeking divine intervention, even though her eyes were now covered. Kierra snorted, clearly enjoying every moment of Dionne's discomfort.

Kierra gently draped something across Dionne's shoulders, adjusting it to make sure it stayed in place. The texture felt soft but unfamiliar, adding to the mystery. Meanwhile, the driver continued navigating through the city until they pulled up in front of The Vault, one of the most exclusive clubs in town. The bass from the music inside thumped through the walls, and the line of people waiting to get in wrapped around the block.

But none of that mattered. Tonight, Dionne wasn't just another guest—she was the guest.

Kierra stepped out of the car first, smoothing her outfit before glancing back at Dionne, who was still sitting in the Escalade, blindfolded and clueless. With the help of the driver, Kierra carefully guided Dionne out of the vehicle, making sure she didn't stumble in her heels.

Dionne clutched Kierra's arm, her nerves skyrocketing as she heard the muffled music grow louder. "What is going on?" she asked, a mix of curiosity and apprehension in her voice.

"Relax, sis. I got you," Kierra reassured her, placing a steady hand on Dionne's back as they walked.

The two ascended the stairs leading into the club, bypassing the long line and slipping inside through a VIP entrance. Dionne could feel the vibrations of the music through her body, the pounding bass becoming louder as they moved deeper into the club. The air was electric, and she could hear people cheering and laughing all around her.

"Kierra?" Dionne called out, her voice tinged with nervousness as her grip tightened slightly.

"I'm right here," Kierra said softly, giving her hand a reassuring squeeze. "Just trust me."

Dionne nodded, even though her heart was racing. Whatever they had planned, she knew there was no turning back now.

Minutes later, Kierra removed the blindfold, and the club erupted into cheers and applause, startling Dionne slightly. She blinked as her eyes adjusted to the flashing lights and the crowd of people celebrating her. "What! What is going on?" Dionne asked, her voice filled with surprise as she glanced around the packed club.

London and Karmen approached her, both wearing brown and black outfits, their smiles wide with excitement. "Bitch, this is your surprise bachelorette party!" London shouted over the music, her tone brimming with enthusiasm. Dionne's mouth dropped open in shock as she glanced down at the black and gold sash draped across her body, reading Bride to Be.

"Bitch, you getting married!" Kierra chimed in with a laugh, her bold energy matching the vibe of the night. Dionne forced a chuckle, grateful for her friends' thoughtfulness but unable to ignore the tight knot forming in her chest. This wasn't a celebration she truly felt connected to.

"You look stunning! And that ass is banging in this dress!" Karmen slurred slightly, clearly tipsy, as she admired Dionne. Her comment earned a genuine laugh from Dionne, though her heart wasn't in it.

Dionne's eyes scanned the room, taking in the extravagant setup. The club's elegant design and the packed crowd screamed luxury. They were at The Vault, and her mind immediately drifted to Arris. "How did you guys pull this off?" Dionne asked, her voice an odd mix of excitement and nervous curiosity.

London smirked, tossing her hair over her shoulder. "Arris came through for us. He set up most of this—he's the real MVP. We just brought the people and the strippers, of course," she said with a wink.

At the mention of Arris, Dionne's chest tightened, her emotions swirling. The idea of him helping to plan her bachelorette party—a celebration for her marriage to someone else—felt like a cruel twist of fate. If there was ever a sign that what they had was truly over, this was it.

"Strippers?" Dionne asked, arching an eyebrow as she tried to mask her inner turmoil.

"Hell yeah! Bring out the strippers!" Kierra yelled, her voice cutting through the crowd like a rallying cry. A group of tall, muscular men strode out, half-naked, their confidence undeniable as their perfectly chiseled bodies caught the light. Their tight pants left little to the

Feenin'

imagination, and Dionne's eyes widened slightly as her friends guided her toward a massive queen's chair in the middle of the club.

"Y'all crazy," Dionne muttered with a laugh, though she decided to let herself enjoy the moment. If this was her reality, she was going to make the most of it for the night. She drank, danced, smoked, and even let the strippers give her lap dances. For a few hours, she escaped the weight of Malik, Mama Glen, and her promises. She even tried to push thoughts of Arris away, though he was never far from her mind.

What Dionne didn't know was that she was being watched.

Upstairs standing over the railing, hidden in the shadows, Arris stood silently, his eyes locked on her every move. His commanding presence exuded power even from afar, and his gaze softened as he watched the woman he loved laughing and enjoying herself. She looked breathtaking in her lace dress, every curve accentuated, her hair flowing like a crown.

His emotions warred within him—love, jealousy, longing, and a deep ache. He hated seeing her celebrate a future with another man, but at the same time, he couldn't look away. Tonight, she was carefree, and seeing her happy—really happy—was something he cherished, even from a distance.

It took every ounce of restraint he had not to descend the stairs, pull her into his arms, and remind her exactly who she belonged to. The sight of her, so close yet untouchable, made his blood boil and his heart ache. He clenched his fists, grounding himself. This wasn't the time. Not here. Not now.

For the rest of the night, Arris stayed rooted in the shadows, his eyes never leaving Dionne. He didn't care about the strippers or the crowd. His only focus was her—protecting her, admiring her, and silently claiming her as his, even if she didn't realize it.

***

The bachelorette party ended with the girls piled back into the Escalade, laughter and chaos filling the air as Dionne's drunken energy dominated the mood. She was beyond tipsy, swaying between hyperactive and emotional. One moment, she was twerking in the seat to the music blasting on the radio, her dress riding up as she sang at the top of her lungs. The next moment, she was angrily tapping on her phone, her frustration evident.

"Girl, Malik is at work! He can't answer you right now!" London said, laughing, assuming Dionne was trying to call her fiancé.

But Dionne's mind wasn't on Malik. Her thumb repeatedly hit redial as Arris's name glared back at her from the screen. Each ignored call and unread emotional message she sent made her simmer with anger and hurt. She wanted him. She needed him. But his silence spoke volumes.

"Ugh!" Dionne groaned, throwing her phone onto the seat beside her in frustration. Her lips pouted, and her brows furrowed as the emotions she'd been suppressing bubbled to the surface.

"Bitch, your ass is drunk and horny. Here, drink some damn water," Kierra said, shaking her head with an amused smile as she handed Dionne a cold bottle of water.

Dionne took a few sips but waved the bottle away like it was irrelevant to her plight. "It's not helping," she mumbled, slumping back into her seat.

"I know what will help! Let's go get tattoos!" London yelled excitedly, her bright idea cutting through the tension in the car.

Dionne perked up immediately, her face lighting up with excitement. "Bet! I'm down!" she said, clapping her hands and sitting upright like a kid on Christmas morning.

"You crazy as hell!" Kierra laughed, shaking her head. "But fuck it, I'm down too."

"True is at the shop right now, and he said he got us. For the free too," London added with a wink, clearly implying how she planned to repay True later. The car filled with laughter.

"Wait, wait," Karmen chimed in from the backseat, her own drunken excitement bubbling over. "We all getting one, right? Like matching ones or something?"

"Hell yeah! Something small, classy, and sexy!" London said, already texting True to let him know they were on their way.

The driver turned the Escalade in the direction of True's shop, and the car was buzzing with the energy of spontaneous drunken decisions. Dionne felt a small thrill at the idea, temporarily pushing away her lingering thoughts of Arris. But even in the chaos of her drunken excitement, the ache for him remained, simmering beneath the surface.

The girls stumbled into True's shop, their drunken laughter filling the smoky space. The air was thick with the scent of weed, and True, clearly high out of his mind, was sitting in a chair with a blunt in hand. His bloodshot eyes widened slightly at the sight of the four women, their intoxicated energy filling the room.

"You niggas are fucked up," True joked, his gaze landing on Dionne, who looked the most wasted out of the group.

"We had to do it big for our girl!" Kierra chimed in, her voice loud and proud as the other girls nodded in agreement.

"Babe, this is Kierra, our oldest sister. Kierra, this is my man, True—owner of this shop and the love of my life," London said with a smirk,

Feenin'

introducing them. Kierra smiled warmly, shaking True's hand.

"Nice to meet you," Kierra said, eyeing him approvingly.

True returned the smile, though his attention was mostly on London, his gaze lingering as he licked his lips at the outfit she had on. "So, what can I do for y'all tonight?" he asked, his voice laced with amusement as he scanned the group.

"My girl here wants a tattoo to end off her bachelorette party," London announced, nodding toward Dionne, who was slouched on the couch sipping water, trying to steady herself.

True chuckled, his gaze now shifting to Dionne. "You good, sis? You look like you're on the brink," he teased, shaking his head at her state.

"Man, you got some weed or something? I need to feel something else besides drunk," Dionne groaned, surprising him with her bold request.

True laughed, handing her a freshly rolled blunt. "Here, hit this. You're about to be crossfaded as fuck though," he said, still amused by her behavior.

Dionne accepted it without hesitation, lighting it like she'd done it a million times before, which caught True off guard. "Damn, you don't play, huh?" he said, impressed. She just smiled as the first puff already began to soothe her frayed nerves.

"So, what you trying to get?" he asked as she pulled out her phone and showed him the design she had in mind. It was a detailed picture of a man's hand, strong and prominent.

"A hand?" True asked, confused but intrigued.

"Yeah, but I want a wedding band on his finger," Dionne said, her tone steady despite the intoxication. The girls, assuming it was Malik's hand, exchanged amused glances.

"So, you just said fuck our matching tattoos, huh?" Karmen joked, her words slurred but full of humor.

Dionne laughed, brushing it off. "We can get that next time," she said quickly, her focus laser-sharp on the mission at hand.

True squinted at the hand on the screen. Something about it seemed familiar, but in his hazy, high state, he couldn't quite place it. "Where you want it?" he asked, still trying to figure out why this hand seemed so recognizable.

"On my left breast," Dionne said boldly, shocking everyone in the room.

"Bitch, you're getting Malik's hand tatted on your boob?" Karmen asked, her eyes wide with shock as the alcohol and weed exaggerated her reaction.

Dionne nodded, though what no one else knew was that it wasn't Malik's hand—it was a picture of Arris's hand she'd saved. Her private little rebellion against her obligations.

"Can you do it?" she asked, turning her attention back to True.

"Yeah, I got you," he said, still slightly perplexed but shrugging it off.

Dionne laid down on the tattoo table, ready to commit to her secret. London stood by, covering her nipples with a towel to give her privacy while True prepped his tools.

As the buzzing of the tattoo machine began, Dionne exhaled, focusing on the sting of the needle and the meaning behind what she was doing. This wasn't just a tattoo—it was her way of holding on to Arris, even if no one else knew.

The tattoo session felt like a fever dream as Dionne laid on the table, letting True work. The room was filled with laughter, smoke, and lighthearted jokes that masked the significance of what was really happening. Every time the needle touched her skin, the sting reminded her of Arris—his touch, his voice, his love that she felt slipping away. This tattoo was more than ink on her body; it was a declaration she didn't even care to hide anymore. If the dozens of unanswered calls and emotional texts didn't make it clear, this tattoo would.

True focused on perfecting the details of the hand, oblivious to its true significance. The rough texture of the palm, the veins running through the back, the slight bend in the fingers—it was all Arris. He had no idea whose hand he was immortalizing on her skin, but Dionne felt every line and curve connect her closer to the man she craved. The pain of the needle was nothing compared to the ache in her chest every time she thought about him.

"Damn... you really getting that man's hand tatted on your boob?" Kierra said, her tone dripping with shock as she shook her head.

Dionne chuckled, her lips curving into a sly smile as she took another puff of the blunt, the weed easing her nerves. "Yep," she replied casually, as if she were getting a flower or a butterfly instead of a permanent mark that symbolized her deepest, most conflicted feelings.

"You must really love this nigga," True said, shaking his head in disbelief as he wiped excess ink from her skin.

"More than anything," Dionne said without hesitation. The room buzzed with murmurs of approval, her friends thinking she was talking about Malik, but every fiber of her being screamed Arris. The truth sat heavy in her heart, unspoken but undeniable.

True glanced at London with a grin. "Yo, Lon, would you get my

Feenin'

hand tatted on your boob?"

London gave him the kind of look that could kill. "Don't push it, nigga. I might get your name tatted. That right there—" she said, pointing at Dionne's breast, "—is some addictive type shit."

The room erupted into laughter, Dionne included, though her mind was far away. Her euphoric state dulled the physical pain of the tattoo, but it couldn't numb the ache of missing Arris. She glanced down at the design as True finished and began cleaning the area, carefully applying after care ointment over the fresh ink.

"All done," True said, snapping a few pictures of his work. Dionne stood and walked to the mirror, lifting her dress slightly to admire it. Her breath caught at the sight—Arris's hand, so perfectly detailed, etched right over her heart.

The tattoo was bold, intimate, and undeniably his. Arris' hand was inked across her entire left breast, perfectly detailed with the same veins, creases, and the tattoo he had on his own hand. It was positioned as if he was gripping her, holding her possessively, permanently claiming a part of her. The way the shading blended with her skin made it look real, as if his touch was forever imprinted on her body.

It was more than just ink. It was a statement. A silent confession of who really held her heart.

"She did that shit," Kierra hyped, her voice breaking through Dionne's thoughts.

"You better not wake up tomorrow regretting that shit either," London teased, smirking as she leaned against the wall.

Dionne smiled softly, tracing the edges of the saran wrap. "I won't," she said firmly, her tone leaving no room for doubt. The alcohol might've fueled the decision, but it didn't cloud the meaning behind it. Arris was the man who held her heart, and now that truth was permanently displayed on her body.

Pulling her dress back down, Dionne grabbed her phone and took a picture of the tattoo, sending it to Arris without a caption. She didn't need to explain it; the image spoke volumes. Whether he responded or not, she had made her statement. This wasn't about Malik. It was about the man she *feened* for and the hope that, somehow, he would still find his way back to her.

***

Dionne and the girls had ended their wild night at London's house, collapsing into bed together in a pile of exhaustion. The room was silent except for the sound of soft breathing, but Dionne was startled awake by the ringing of her phone. She groaned, her head pounding from the lingering effects of alcohol and weed, and squinted at the screen. The clock read 3:30 a.m., but it wasn't the time that shocked her—it was the name flashing across the screen: Arris.

Her heart skipped a beat as she scrambled to answer, careful not to wake the others. She whispered a soft "Hello?" into the phone, her voice still groggy but laced with nerves.

"Bring yo ass outside. Now," Arris said, his tone calm but firm, the seriousness in his voice unmistakable. Her breath hitched, her chest tightening at the sound of his voice. Before she could respond, the line went dead.

She stared at the screen, mugging the phone for a second before throwing off the covers. Looking over at her friends sprawled across London's king-sized bed, she tiptoed around the room, not wanting to disturb them. She glanced down at herself, realizing she was only in an oversized shirt. Quickly, she grabbed a pair of London's sweatpants, slipping them on before shoving her feet into a pair of nearby slippers.

As she quietly made her way out the room, her mind swirled with confusion and anticipation. How did he even know where she was? Why was he here after weeks of silence? But despite the questions flooding her thoughts, one thing was certain—she wanted to see him. She needed to see him.

Dionne grabbed her phone and made her way downstairs, stepping out into the cool night air. Her breath caught in her throat as her eyes landed on Arris leaning against his shiny Aston Martin. The passenger door was already open, as if he was silently commanding her to get in. He looked effortless, dressed in a white muscle tee that clung to his chiseled frame, gray sweatpants, and crisp white Air Forces. His durag was still tied neatly, adding a rugged edge to his look. The sight of him made her heart race, but she couldn't ignore the tension radiating from him.

Her steps slowed as she approached him, uncertainty weighing heavy after their last heated conversation. When she got close enough, Arris reached out, gripping her waist and pulling her closer. The sudden action made her gasp softly.

"Arris—" she started, her voice barely above a whisper.

"Get in the car, Mama," he said, his voice calm but firm, leaving no room for negotiation.

Dionne hesitated, glancing back at London's house, knowing her friends were still inside. But as always, her will bent under his presence. Without a word, she moved toward the open passenger door, and Arris followed, shutting the door behind her. He slid into the driver's seat, and

Feenin'

the car roared to life as he sped off into the night.

"Arris, my friends are inside," Dionne said cautiously, her eyes flicking to his stoic profile. He didn't even glance at her, his hands gripping the steering wheel, his focus locked on the road ahead.

"I don't give a fuck, Dionne," he said lowly, his tone sharp and cutting. The words sent a shiver down her spine—part fear, part arousal. His energy was dark, intense, and undeniably magnetic.

"They're going to be worried about me," she tried again, unsure if she was trying to reason with him or herself.

"Dionne," he said, his voice firmer this time. "Be quiet. Please." His jaw clenched, his muscles flexing as he gripped the wheel tighter, his frustration evident.

Recognizing his mood, Dionne finally sat back in her seat, her lips pressed into a tight line. The tension in the car was thick, her body simultaneously on edge and buzzing from being near him. She tried to focus on anything but the way his muscles moved, or how the veins in his forearms seemed to pulse as he drove with controlled aggression.

Wherever they were going, Dionne knew this wasn't just about the drive—it was about them. And with Arris, there was no way to predict what was coming next.

Arris pulled into his driveway, parking the car with an abrupt stop. Before he could even get around to her side, Dionne stepped out of the car, acting on instinct rather than thought. Arris was on her in seconds, pinning her back against the cool surface of the car. His body towered over hers, and his fiery gaze made her shiver.

"You've been around that nigga too fucking long," Arris growled, his voice low and simmering with restrained fury. He leaned closer, his breath brushing against her ear, sending a ripple of anticipation through her. "Get back in the car, Dionne."

Without hesitation, she obeyed, climbing back into the passenger seat as he swung the door shut. Moments later, Arris opened it again, pulling her out with a firm but gentle grip. His hand wrapped around hers as he guided her into his house, his presence overpowering as he shut the door behind them. Dionne was still trying to piece together what was happening, confusion and excitement swirling within her.

"Arris—" she began, but her words were cut short as he turned and pinned her back against the door. The intensity in his eyes made her breath hitch.

"Take this off," he demanded, his voice a low growl as he tugged at the oversized shirt she was wearing. His tone left no room for argument. Dionne, feeling vulnerable yet strangely exhilarated, did as she was told, peeling off the shirt to reveal her bare chest. Her heart raced as she stood exposed before him, her breath caught in her throat.

Arris's gaze dropped to her left breast, his lips curving into a slow, wicked smile when his eyes landed on the tattoo—his hand, perfectly etched into her skin. He stepped closer, his fingers lightly grazing the edge of the saran wrap covering it, before peeling it off carefully, his movements slow and deliberate.

"Yo ass is really crazy about me," he murmured, his voice dark and filled with something deeper than amusement. His smile widened, but his eyes burned with a mix of pride, need, and raw love. Dionne's pulse raced under the weight of his gaze, her vulnerability magnified by the way he was taking her in, as if seeing her for the first time.

Arris couldn't tear his eyes away from the tattoo. The veins, the curve of the fingers, the inked design on the hand—it was unmistakably his. She had taken a picture of the tattoo, sent it to him in a message he had ignored, and now seeing with own eyes she had permanently marked herself of him. Seeing it in person, the reality of it, left him in awe.

"You really tatted me on you," he said softly, his voice tinged with disbelief and admiration. His fingertips ghosted over the tattoo, sending a spark through Dionne's skin. "You're really mine like that?"

Dionne nodded, her voice caught in her throat as her body trembled under his touch. She felt exposed, not just physically, but emotionally. This wasn't just about the tattoo—it was a declaration of the love she couldn't keep buried anymore.

"Damn, Mama," Arris murmured, stepping closer, his voice thick with raw emotion and need. Dionne stood frozen in her spot, her breath caught in her chest. He didn't waste another second before wrapping his arms around her and lifting her effortlessly, drawing a gasp from her lips as her legs instinctively wrapped around his waist. She melted into him, the warmth of his touch reigniting everything she had been longing for.

Arris's mouth descended onto her breast—the one marked with his hand—his lips claiming it as his. Dionne hissed softly, the sting of the fresh tattoo sending jolts of pain and pleasure through her body. She moaned, her head tilting back, surrendering to the sensation as his tongue teased her skin, uncaring of her protests. The way his mouth worshipped her told her everything she needed to know—this wasn't just about lust, it was about possession.

"Baby...ow," Dionne hissed, her words mixing with moans as the duality of pain and pleasure overwhelmed her senses. Arris finally pulled back, his eyes locking with hers, filled with unfiltered desire and frustration. He didn't speak. Instead, he captured her lips in a deep,

Feenin'

searing kiss, pouring every ounce of his longing into it. She responded without hesitation, her arms wrapping around his neck, pulling him closer, needing him just as much as he needed her.

He carried her upstairs with purpose, his strides firm as he didn't break their connection. Once inside the bedroom, he set her down only to strip her bare in one swift motion, his hands rough but loving. Her breath hitched, her heart pounding as he pushed her back onto the bed, his body hovering over hers. Without warning, he slid inside her, his pace slow and deliberate, drawing a loud moan from her lips.

"Shit...baby," Dionne moaned, her nails digging into his shoulders as her body welcomed him.

"I love you," Arris growled, his pace quickening, his hands gripping her hips as his eyes flickered between her face and the tattoo. That tattoo—his hand inked over her heart—drove him wild. It was a physical manifestation of what he already knew: she was his.

"I... fuck! I love you too," Dionne cried out, her body trembling beneath him as he picked her up mid-thrust and pinned her against the wall. His pace grew harder, more urgent, fueled by the emotions he'd been bottling up for weeks. Each thrust was a mixture of anger, longing, and the overwhelming need to reclaim what was his.

"You chose that nigga," Arris spat, his voice sharp and laced with frustration as he buried himself deeper inside her. His movements never slowed, each thrust making her body arch against him.

"No... no, baby," Dionne sobbed, shaking her head as tears streamed down her face. She clawed at his back, her nails digging into his skin, her words breaking with every powerful stroke. "I didn't... I swear."

Arris's jaw clenched, his anger evident in the way his hands tightened on her thighs, holding her in place. He wanted to believe her, but the pain of feeling like second choice burned inside him. The sight of her tears, the raw emotion in her voice, made his chest tighten despite his anger. He kept going, pouring his frustration and love into each movement, unable to stop himself.

"Look at me, Mama," Arris demanded, his voice low but commanding as he didn't stop his deliberate movements. Dionne shook her head, her face turning away, unable to face the anger she knew she'd see in his eyes. She felt consumed by guilt, her tears falling faster. Sensing her hesitation, Arris slowed his pace, making her feel every inch of him. The pleasure was overwhelming, and a loud scream escaped her lips as her body trembled.

"You have to believe me," Dionne pleaded, her voice breaking with emotion as her tears streamed down her face. Arris wiped them away gently, his touch soft despite the tension between them. His pace continued, unrelenting but filled with purpose. "Look at me, Mama," he said again, this time softer, his tone coaxing her as though trying to soothe the storm within her.

Reluctantly, she opened her eyes, her red, teary gaze meeting his. The anger she expected wasn't there. Instead, she saw a deep, pained love staring back at her, and it made her heart ache even more.

"This tattoo," he began, his voice firm as his fingers traced the outline of his inked hand on her breast, "don't show me that you want me as bad as you say you do." His touch against her skin made her nipples harden, the arousal mixing with her raw emotions. His pace didn't falter as he stared into her eyes.

She nodded frantically, her words caught in her throat as the pleasure and pain of the moment became unbearable. Her tears flowed like a waterfall now, her body trembling against his. "Choosing me with your heart, Mama... that's what makes me believe you want me wholeheartedly," he said, his voice both a plea and a demand.

The weight of his words crushed her, adding to the already heavy burden she carried. Dionne nodded again, unable to form coherent words as her body gave in, her orgasm crashing over her like a tidal wave. She screamed out his name, her entire being trembling as the release tore through her.

Arris groaned, his gaze never leaving her as he leaned in, taking her tattooed breast into his mouth again. His tongue and lips worshipped her, his own pleasure building as his thrusts became erratic. He tried to pull out, but Dionne gripped him tighter with her legs, keeping him locked inside her.

"Fuck, Mama," he groaned, his voice breaking as his climax hit him hard. He released inside of her, filling her with everything he had. She took it all, her head falling back against the wall as her body quivered from the intensity of their connection.

"I love you, Mama," Arris said breathlessly, his lips finding hers in a deep, passionate kiss.

"I love you too," she whispered softly, her voice filled with honesty and raw emotion. He held her against the wall, their breathing still heavy as the heat between them simmered.

"Prove it," he said, his voice thick with both need and demand. Dionne nodded, unable to find the words to respond. He set her down gently, her legs shaking beneath her as she steadied herself.

She disappeared into the bathroom, needing to clean up and collect herself. When she came back out, she saw Arris standing by the door, his

Feenin'

shoes on and his car keys in hand. Her heart sank at the sight.

"I have to take you back to your friends," he said with a small grin, knowing full well that she didn't want to leave him. The look in her eyes told him she wanted to stay, to be with him longer, but they both knew the risk was too great.

Dionne nodded, swallowing the lump in her throat as she slipped back into her oversized shirt, sweats, and shoes. Arris watched her, his gaze softer now, but the tension in the air remained. They both knew this wasn't over, but for now, they had to part ways.

They got back into the car as the first rays of morning light began to spill over the horizon. The silence between them was heavy but not uncomfortable, filled with unspoken words and emotions neither was ready to say aloud. Arris pulled up outside London's house and parked the car, cutting the engine. He got out first, moving quickly to help Dionne out of the passenger side.

As she stepped out, he pulled her close by the waist, pressing his lips against hers in a kiss that felt like both a promise and a goodbye. She melted into his embrace, her arms wrapping around his neck, holding onto him as if letting go was the last thing she wanted. The kiss lingered, filled with everything they couldn't put into words, and when they finally pulled away, her eyes were glossy with emotion.

"I love you, Mama. I'll see you later," Arris said softly, his voice deep and steady, but his grip on her waist told her he didn't want to let her go.

Dionne's voice was just above a whisper. "I love you too, Arris." Her words carried the weight of everything she felt—longing, guilt, and the overwhelming pull to stay with him. Her gaze held his, the heaviness in her eyes betraying the storm she was trying to hide.

Arris stepped back slightly, giving her the space to walk inside, but she didn't move. Her feet felt rooted to the spot, her body torn between going back into the house and running back into his arms. He noticed, and a soft chuckle escaped him despite the ache in his chest.

"Go inside, Mama," he said gently, though his voice was laced with reluctance. "I'll call you later."

She sighed deeply, her shoulders falling slightly as she nodded. "Okay," she replied softly, her steps slow and heavy as she turned to walk away.

But before she could take more than a couple of steps, Arris reached out and grabbed her hand, pulling her back into his arms. He lifted her effortlessly, her legs wrapping around his waist as she buried her face in his neck, her tears threatening to spill again.

"I'm not going anywhere, Mama," he murmured into her ear,

his voice firm yet comforting. He held her tightly, his grip telling her everything his words couldn't. "But everything is up to you now."

She nodded against his neck, her heart breaking at the truth in his words. She knew the decision she had to make, and the weight of it felt heavier than ever. Arris slowly put her back on her feet, his hands lingering on her waist for a moment before letting her go.

Dionne nodded wordlessly, taking a shaky breath as she finally turned and walked toward the house. Her steps felt like they were sinking into quicksand, each one harder than the last. Arris stayed rooted to the spot, watching her until she disappeared inside the house.

He stood there for a moment longer, the rising sun casting a soft glow over him as he took a deep breath. He looked up at the sky, his voice low but full of conviction as he whispered, "God, that's my wife. I know it is. Please, just bring her to me."

With that, he climbed back into his car and drove off, heading home with a silent prayer on his lips and the hope that somehow, Dionne would choose him.

Feenin'

Chapter 16

Arris stepped out of his Jeep, walking up the long driveway to Mario's house. Today was all about Mia, and he was looking forward to it. Spending time with his niece was the only thing that truly gave him a break from the chaos in his life. Between his emotions over Dionne, his lingering anger, and the uneasy relationship he was trying to build with his father, his mind had been on overdrive. Mia was the only thing that could bring him back down to earth.

Just as he was about to ring the doorbell, the door swung open, and Briana stormed out. Her face was twisted in anger, and she brushed past him, bumping his arm on purpose.

"Damn, watch that shit," Arris said, his voice calm but edged with coldness as he turned to look at her.

"Shut the fuck up, Arris," Briana snapped, fire burning in her eyes. "Tell that bitch you call a brother to keep my daughter away from that hoe he calls a girlfriend."

Arris let out a dry chuckle, shaking his head. "Didn't you just leave his ass? You ain't tell him that on your way out?" He scoffed. "And watch your fucking mouth. Mia can still hear you, so take your bitter ass on."

He wasn't about to let her disrespect both Mario and Karmen. Arris had never liked Briana—he tolerated her for Mario's sake, but he always knew she wasn't the woman his boy needed. She was money-hungry, immature, and full of drama. Mario had been in love, though, so Arris stayed out of it, letting him learn the hard way. Karmen, on the other hand, was everything Briana wasn't. She was solid, loving, and most importantly, good for both Mario and Mia.

Briana scoffed, rolling her eyes. "Shut up, Arris. You just mad nobody want your hoe ass."

Before Arris could respond, Mario appeared in the doorway, his face tight with irritation. "Man, get the fuck off my property, yo. You got your money, now bounce."

Briana's voice grew louder as she ignored him. "I don't give a fuck about that little thousand dollars you gave me. Yo ass better listen to what the fuck I said. If I see that bitch around my daughter again, I swear—"

Mario cut her off, stepping closer, his voice dripping in venom. "Yo hoe ass ain't gone do shit. You just mad that she's a better mother to Mia than you ever were or could be."

The words hit like a gunshot. Arris saw the flicker of pain in Briana's eyes, but he didn't feel bad for her. She deserved every word.

"The truth hurt, don't it?" Mario pressed, his anger burning through his voice. "Now get the fuck out of here before my words ain't the only thing that hit yo ass."

Tears welled up in Briana's eyes, but she didn't say another word. She knew she had no comeback. Instead, she turned on her heel, walked to her car, and pulled off, tires screeching against the pavement.

Arris let out a low whistle, shaking his head. "Damn, bro. You ain't have to do her like that."

Mario exhaled, rubbing a hand over his face. "Man, I been holding that shit in for too damn long."

Arris followed Mario into the house, watching as his friend dropped onto the couch with a frustrated sigh.

"That woman gonna be the death of me. You should've let Dionne go beat her ass that day," Mario muttered, rubbing his face in exhaustion, his voice laced with pure frustration.

Arris chuckled at his seriousness, knowing damn well Mario meant every word. "Nah, that was for the best. Dionne seems sweet, but she got a temper. She would've killed that girl." He smirked, shaking his head as he thought about Dionne's fiery protectiveness. The memory alone sent a rush of heat through him, but he masked it in front of Mario.

Mario let out a tired chuckle, nodding. "You right. I saw that shit firsthand at the tattoo shop," he admitted, recalling how Dionne had no hesitation when it came to throwing hands to protect Karmen. "But still—Briana a piece of work, bruh." His frustration was evident, and Arris understood it all too well.

Arris dropped down onto the couch next to him, but his sharp eyes were already scanning the house. "I thought you was taking her ass back to court?" he asked, splitting his attention between Mario and his quiet

Feenin'

search for Mia.

"I didn't think I needed to once she started calming down, but ever since I got with Karmen, she been acting crazy and shit. But I am now, because Karmen almost left me because of her ass," Mario admitted, his frustration seeping through every word.

Arris' eyes widened slightly. "Wait, why?"

Mario exhaled heavily, shaking his head. "She was blowing up my phone, showing up at my house while Karmen here, acting fucking crazy. And she still reaching out to Karmen through social media, threatening her and shit."

Arris' jaw tightened at the thought of Briana harassing Karmen. That kind of toxic behavior was something he never fucked with.

"That shit gets exhausting," Mario continued. "Karmen was fed up. She told me about all the shit she had to deal with from her ex and his baby mama, and she don't wanna go through that again. The only difference between me and that nigga is I ain't putting my hands on her."

Arris stilled, his entire body tensing at those words. "Wait… her ex put hands on her?" His voice was low, tight with restrained anger.

Mario nodded. "Yeah, bro. It's some shit she ain't talk about a lot, but I know enough. When she told me we needed a break until I got this shit together, my heart broke in two. I never felt pain like that until I thought I was losing her." His voice cracked slightly, showing the weight of it all.

Arris understood that feeling more than anyone. No, he wasn't losing Dionne over baby mama drama, but every day that passed with her playing fiancée to another man, every moment she wasn't in his arms, he felt himself losing her. And that shit hurt. But he masked his emotions, swallowing the frustration, to be present for his friend.

"How are y'all now?" Arris asked, leaning back.

Mario ran a hand over his head. "We straight… but she pulling back. I once had all of her before this drama started, and now I feel like I'm slowly losing her 'cause of my shit."

Arris nodded, placing a reassuring hand on Mario's shoulder. "Look, bro. You and Karmen meant to be. I know that for a fact, 'cause I ain't never seen you glow like this over a woman. She loves you too, 'cause if she didn't, she wouldn't be giving you space to figure your shit out—she would've just left. If Karmen worth fighting for, then do whatever the fuck you gotta do to keep her."

Mario took in his words, nodding slowly before a smirk tugged at his lips, followed by a low chuckle.

Arris frowned. "What?"

Mario shook his head, still laughing. "Nigga, whoever got you hooked, got your ass good!"

Arris narrowed his eyes, confused. "The fuck you talking about?"

Mario leaned back, stretching his arms over the back of the couch. "The Arris I grew up with woulda said 'fuck both of them' and just did me. But now you over here talking about love like it's the most valuable shit in the world."

Arris chuckled, shaking his head. His mind immediately went to Dionne.

Mario pointed at him. "Whoever this woman is, she changed you, bro. And I fuck with it."

Arris smirked but kept his thoughts to himself. "I had to grow up one day," he said casually, though his tone softened. "She just… helped with that a lot."

Mario caught the shift in his voice, but he didn't press. Instead, he just nodded, knowing damn well Arris was holding onto a secret he wasn't ready to share yet.

"So you really not gonna tell me who she is?" Mario pressed, his brows raised in curiosity. His teasing tone was light, but there was genuine interest laced underneath.

Arris smirked, shaking his head. "Nah, bruh. I told you and True—y'all will meet her soon. Be patient, damn."

Mario scoffed, laughing as he leaned back into the couch. "Man, whatever. Keep your little secret."

Arris's smirk faded slightly as his thoughts drifted. His chest tightened, the weight of the unknown pressing against him. Was Dionne really his? Or was he just setting himself up for heartbreak? The idea of losing her to another man—losing her to a life she didn't even want—made his stomach knot. He forced the thought away. He couldn't think like that. Not now. Not when he still had a chance to show her she belonged with him.

"Where's my niece?" Arris asked, shaking himself out of his thoughts.

Mario stood up, stretching his arms. "She's upstairs taking a nap."

"Well, go wake her up. I got plans with my girl today," Arris said, nodding toward the stairs. His tone was light, but there was a deeper emotion behind it—a need for something stable, something untouched by the chaos in his life.

Mario chuckled, shaking his head. "Nigga, you need to hurry up and have kids so you can stop stealing mine."

Arris smirked, but this time, it held more weight. His mind

Feenin'

immediately went to Dionne—the way she looked at him, the way she felt in his arms, the way she carried the weight of the world on her shoulders, pretending she was fine when she was anything but. His fingers instinctively tapped against his thigh, his heart heavy with the thoughts of a future he wanted so badly with her.

"Soon, bro. Sooner than you think." His voice was low, full of conviction, but laced with the fear of uncertainty.

Mario stopped mid-step, turning to look at him. "Wait... You deadass?"

Arris didn't respond immediately. He just smirked, but his eyes gave him away.

Mario whistled, shaking his head as he disappeared up the stairs. "This shit is crazy," he muttered in disbelief.

Without another word, he headed upstairs to wake Mia, leaving Arris alone in the quiet living room.

Arris sighed, sinking into the couch and pulling out his phone. His fingers hovered over Dionne's contact, his eyes landing on the picture of her smiling back at him. Damn, he missed her.

He wanted to call. Just to see her face. Just to hear her voice. But he was trying to keep his distance.

Even after that night, after having her the way he needed to, after seeing his mark permanently etched on her skin, he knew it still wasn't enough. She had to choose him.

And until she did, he had to protect his heart.

That didn't stop him from checking in, though. The quick texts. The short calls. Just enough to keep her close, but not enough to let her slip back into his life without certainty. He had given her space to make a decision, but every day that passed without an answer felt like a slow death.

He exhaled sharply, thumb hovering over the call button. Fuck it.

Before he could press it, a tiny, excited voice rang through the house. "Uncle Arris!"

Arris snapped his head up just in time to see Mia running full speed toward him. The weight of Dionne in his chest eased just a little as he shoved his phone back into his pocket and scooped his niece up, spinning her in the air.

Mia giggled, holding onto his neck tightly. "You took forever!"

Arris chuckled, holding her close. "My bad, Niecy. I had to make sure your daddy was done being nosy first."

Mario walked in behind them, shaking his head with a smirk. "Nigga, whatever."

"Where we going, Uncle Arris?" Mia asked, resting her tiny hands on his shoulders.

"Wherever you wanna go, baby. You runnin' the show today," he told her.

Mia gasped dramatically, eyes lighting up. "We going shopping! I wanna get matching Ugg boots with Ms. Karmen!"

Arris and Mario exchanged a look, both of them smiling at the bond Mia and Karmen had built.

"Of course. Anything you want. But first, Uncle hungry," Arris said, rubbing his stomach.

Mia giggled, shaking her head. "Uncle, you always hungry. You gonna get fat!"

Arris smirked. "I still won't be ugly like your daddy, though."

Mia gasped, giggling. "My daddy is not ugly!"

Mario shook his head, chuckling as he kissed his daughter's cheek. "Aight, man. Get out my house before you corrupt my child any more than you already have."

Arris just grinned, adjusting Mia on his hip as he headed toward the door.

But even as he left, even as he let himself enjoy the lightness of the moment, Dionne was still on his mind.

***

Dionne strolled through the mall, DJ's tiny hand gripping hers as Kierra walked beside them. The holiday season was creeping up, and with Thanksgiving around the corner, she was savoring these last moments with her sister-in-law and nephew before they headed back to Dallas.

Spending time with them brought her a rare sense of peace, a reprieve from the prison she called her life with Malik and the relentless war raging in her mind. Arris. His name lived in her every thought, his absence suffocating. Even though they were back speaking, things weren't the same.

What used to be effortless, all-consuming conversations that stretched from morning to midnight were now clipped and distant. The texts, once filled with longing and desire, had turned into the bare minimum—"You good?" / "Yeah, you?" / "Stay safe."

She knew Arris was guarding his heart. She hadn't made a decision yet, and he wasn't going to let himself fall deeper while she stayed tethered to another man. But what he didn't know—what she couldn't bring herself to say—was that she craved him like air. She was starving for him in ways that made her stomach turn.

Feenin'

She could have him—all she had to do was make a choice.

But that choice was harder than it seemed.

It wasn't Malik that held her back. It never was. Their love had faded into an obligation long before Arris ever came into the picture. She wasn't in love with him, hadn't been in years.

But Mama Glen.

The promise. The duty. The sacrifice she had sworn to uphold.

Mama Glen's sickness was worsening by the day, despite what the doctors were saying. They claimed she was stable, that she had at least another year left, but Mama Glen knew better. She could feel the end creeping closer. And Dionne and Malik knew it too.

Dionne watched Malik sink further into his grief, his mother's inevitable loss weighing heavier on him than he let on. He was distant, barely speaking, moving through life like a ghost of himself. And though she no longer saw him as the man she wanted to spend forever with, she still cared.

So she stayed. She played her role for Mama Glen.

She let Malik believe he was getting his fiancée back, that she was still the woman he had once loved. She let him lean on her when he needed to, let him hold her at night even though she no longer melted into him the way she once did. She wore the ring on her finger like a shackle.

Every day she did this, every moment she pretended, the guilt sank its claws deeper into her skin. Because she knew where her heart truly was.

She knew who she belonged to. And it sure as hell wasn't Malik. It was the man she *feened* for. The one whose touch still burned on her skin. The man who had marked her, claimed her, in ways no one ever had.

Arris.

"These shoes are cute!" Kierra's voice broke through Dionne's thoughts, pulling her back to the present. She held up a pair of brown Balmain Skye ankle-high knit boots, examining them with a gleam in her eyes.

Dionne smiled, nodding in approval. "Ouu, sis, those are perfect for your Thanksgiving outfit."

Kierra grinned but hesitated. "I don't know if I want to drop $900 on some damn shoes, knowing I'll probably wear them once."

Dionne scoffed. "Girl, put that shit on my brother's card. He gave it to you for a reason."

Kierra smirked, slipping the boots onto her feet. "You right! The perks of having a rich husband," she teased, doing a little dance in her seat.

Dionne laughed, watching as Kierra admired herself in the mirror. "They look beautiful on you."

"Mommy, I like those," DJ chimed in, making both women laugh.

"You do?" Kierra asked, feigning excitement as she bent down to his level. DJ chuckled, nodding.

Dionne smiled, warmth spreading in her chest as she watched their interaction. The bond between Kierra and DJ was effortless, filled with love and admiration. It was the kind of love Dionne dreamed of—the kind of life she longed for. A husband who adored her. A child who looked at her the way DJ looked at Kierra. A future that felt full and real.

But right now, her life was anything but.

The weight of her reality pressed on her, but she pushed it away. She let herself enjoy this moment, the lightness of the mall, the thrill of shopping, and the distraction of good company.

Kierra went to pay for the boots, and they moved on, walking store to store, their arms filling with bags. Dionne, a self-proclaimed shopaholic, never held back when it came to spending, and Kierra matched her stride for stride. Most of the bags were filled with clothes and gifts for DJ and Demetrius, but a good portion belonged to Kierra herself.

And tucked among Dionne's own shopping haul was something special—something for Arris.

It wasn't anything extravagant, just something he had once mentioned wanting but never bought for himself. She had held onto that detail, tucking it away like a secret, waiting for the right time to surprise him.

And now she had it.

Her chest tightened at the thought of seeing him again. The last time they were together was the morning after her bachelorette party. Every moment of that day had been burned into her memory. His hands gripping her body, his lips claiming hers, the way he filled her so perfectly, like they had been made for each other.

She still felt him.

And no amount of space, no number of days apart, could erase the way her body, her heart, and her soul still *feened* for him. But the reality was, she wasn't his.

Not yet.

And as much as she wanted to give him everything, the truth still loomed over her. She had to make a choice. And no matter how much she loved Arris, no matter how much she missed him, that choice was

Feenin'

nowhere near as easy as it should have been.

As they made their way into the food court, their arms weighed down with shopping bags, the scent of fresh-baked pretzels and sizzling burgers filled the air.

"Mommy, I want pizza," DJ pleaded, tugging at Kierra's hand.

"Okay, baby. Let's find the pizza place," she said, gripping his hand tightly as they weaved through the bustling crowd.

Just as they were nearing the pizza stand, DJ suddenly gasped, his small body jerking forward in excitement.

"There go my girlfriend!" he shouted, yanking Kierra in the direction of whatever had caught his attention.

Kierra let out a chuckle, amused at the bold declaration. "Girlfriend?" she repeated, shaking her head.

Dionne followed DJ's gaze, her eyes scanning the food court until they landed on a familiar little girl dressed in a pink Adidas outfit, her two curly ponytails neatly decorated with pink and white bows.

Mia.

But it wasn't Mia who made Dionne's heart nearly stop in her chest. It was the man standing beside her.

Arris.

Her breath hitched as her eyes drank him in, scanning from his fresh lineup down to the black Essentials hoodie that clung to his frame, the loose-fitted pants hanging just right, and the black Travis Scott Dunks on his feet.

Damn, he looked good.

So good that her body reacted instantly, a slow heat creeping up her spine at the mere sight of him.

DJ's impatient voice snapped her back to reality. "Come on! I wanna say hi!" he whined, pulling harder on Kierra's arm.

Kierra finally followed her son's line of sight, her lips curving into a grin as she spotted the little girl he was running toward.

"Aww, DJ, you got a type, huh?" Kierra teased, eyeing Mia with amusement. "I see you like 'em pretty."

But Dionne barely heard their exchange. Her focus was locked on Arris, who still hadn't noticed her yet. Every step in his direction felt heavier, her heartbeat erratic, a nervous energy curling in her stomach.

As they finally reached them, DJ spoke first, puffing out his chest.

"Hey, Mia," he said, his voice dropping in an attempt to sound smooth.

Kierra and Dionne stifled their laughter, while Arris and Mia turned at the same time.

Ann

The moment Arris's gaze landed on Dionne, it was like the entire food court faded into the background.

Dionne, who had tried to keep her distance, felt her resolve weaken under his stare. The intensity in his dark eyes pulled her in, saying things that words never could.

"Hey, Demetrius," Mia responded brightly, completely unaware of the thick tension between the adults.

DJ groaned dramatically. "I told you to stop calling me that."

Arris chuckled, shaking his head at the small exchange before his gaze returned to Dionne, holding her captive.

Kierra, completely unaware of the silent war going on between them, turned to Arris with a polite smile. "Oh, I'm sorry. Didn't mean to interrupt your day, but I think your daughter and my son know each other somehow."

Arris mirrored her smile, about to respond when Mia's excited voice rang out.

"Aunt Dee!" she squealed before darting forward.

Dionne's tension melted away as Mia threw her little arms around her. She bent down, scooping Mia up effortlessly, pressing a kiss to her cheek.

"Hey, baby!" Dionne cooed, hugging her tightly like she hadn't seen her in years.

Kierra watched the interaction unfold, brows raised in confusion.

But Arris just stood there, his smile wide as he watched the two most important girls in his life embrace.

Damn, he missed her.

And as Dionne held Mia in her arms, laughing at whatever the little girl was whispering in her ear, Arris knew one thing for sure—

He was never letting her go.

Kierra crossed her arms, her gaze bouncing between Dionne and Arris as a slow smirk curled on her lips. "Okay, now I'm really confused."

Dionne let out a soft chuckle, but the moment her eyes locked with Arris's, the air between them thickened with unspoken emotions.

"Sis, this is Mia. She's one of Karmen's students," Dionne started, her tone carefully measured, "and this is her uncle, Arris." She kept her explanation short, deliberately omitting the depth of his presence in her life. "Mia and Arris, this is DJ's mom, Kierra."

Arris caught the way Dionne subtly avoided standing too close to him, her movements calculated, careful. It made him smirk, though the ache in his chest only deepened.

Feenin'

"It's nice meeting you, Kierra," Arris said smoothly, his deep voice sending an involuntary shiver down Dionne's spine. "I'm also good friends with your husband. We grew up playing in the same baseball league as kids."

Kierra's brows lifted in surprise as she shook his hand. "Small world," she remarked. But then her eyes dropped to his hand, her gaze narrowing slightly as something clicked.

The subtle tattoo on the back of his palm.

She had seen that hand before.

Her mind flashed back to the night at the tattoo shop, when Dionne, drunk and emotional, got a man's hand inked on her left breast. The same veins. The same fingers. The same tattoo.

Oh, hell no.

Kierra masked her realization with a polite smile. "Nice to meet you too, Arris. And you, Mia," she added, shifting her attention to the little girl.

Dionne, completely unaware of Kierra's discovery, finally set Mia down, only to find herself trapped under Arris's smoldering gaze again. Kierra saw it all now—the silent war between them, the way they spoke without saying a word. This wasn't casual. This wasn't friendly. This was something deeper.

"It's good seeing you, Dionne," Arris said, his voice smooth, yet laced with something unspoken.

Dionne swallowed hard. "Same here." Her words were light, forced, but Kierra wasn't fooled. She saw the way Dionne's body betrayed her, the way her breath hitched, the way her fingers fidgeted ever so slightly.

Nah.

This wasn't just a business relationship.

"So... how do you two know each other?" Kierra asked, folding her arms across her chest, her tone thick with suspicion.

Dionne's eyes snapped to her sister-in-law's face, immediately recognizing the skepticism. The way Kierra studied them, the way her lips curled just slightly—she was putting pieces together, and Dionne silently prayed she wouldn't land on the truth.

"She sold me a house," Arris answered smoothly, completely unbothered. "The best agent in town."

His words were simple, but Kierra caught the way he said it.

Like he wasn't talking about real estate.

Dionne shifted uncomfortably. "We should get back to eating before we're late for taking DJ to Demetrius for his haircut appointment." The urgency in her voice was clear—an escape before Kierra could ask any more questions.

Kierra didn't buy it, but she played along, letting her smirk widen. "Right." Her tone dripped with amusement, though her suspicion remained. "It was nice meeting you, Arris. And you too, Mia. You're so pretty."

"Thank you!" Mia beamed, flashing a toothy smile.

"Same here, Kierra," Arris replied, extending his hand again.

Kierra took it, this time holding on a second longer, pressing her fingers slightly against his palm. She needed confirmation. The shape. The feel.

Yup. That's him.

She released his hand, turning back to Dionne, whose expression was damn near panicked.

Dionne knew.

She knew Kierra was onto something, and she wasn't ready for the interrogation that was surely coming.

The only thing missing from Arris's hand compared to the tattoo inked on Dionne's skin was a wedding band. A small detail, yet one that carried a weight far heavier than its absence suggested. Kierra's eyes flickered between his hand and the faint outline of the tattoo beneath Dionne's shirt, her mind racing with possibilities.

This wasn't just some random ink. It wasn't impulsive. It wasn't meaningless.

It was a claim.

A statement.

A confession of something deeper, something Dionne had yet to fully admit.

Kierra's suspicion grew, the pieces slowly clicking into place. If Arris was the man behind that tattoo, then what did that say about everything else Dionne had kept hidden? About the engagement she was still holding onto? About the man she was still promising a future to, while her body—her skin—told an entirely different story?

Yeah. She needed answers. And soon.

Before they walked away, Mia's bubbly voice called out again. "Come on, Uncle! We have to get my matching boots with Ms. Karmen, so I can show her and daddy, when I get home!"

Arris chuckled, nodding as he took Mia's hand. But Kierra?

Kierra was already plotting.

These bitches got some explaining to do.

As they waited in line for DJ's pizza, Kierra stole glances at Dionne, who sat at the table, fidgeting with her phone, looking everywhere but at

Feenin'

her.

Oh, she nervous nervous.

Kierra smirked, taking her time grabbing napkins and condiments. She wouldn't press Dionne now.

No, she'd wait. She'd let Dionne sweat a little. Because knowing her sister-in-law, she'd fold before Kierra even had to ask.

Dionne sat stiffly at the table, her fingers flying across her phone screen as she angrily typed back to Arris. Her heart was still racing from their unexpected encounter at the mall, and Kierra's sharp eyes weren't helping the situation.

Arris: Check your account. I sent you something for what you spent today. Make sure that's enough.

Her jaw clenched as she read the message. Of course, he did. Just like him to insert himself into her life, taking care of her even when she refused to let him. She exhaled sharply before going to her account.

She stared at the $3,000 deposit in her account, her stomach twisting with frustration. Her jaw clenched as she tapped open her messages, her fingers moving swiftly across the screen.

Mama: I'm about to send it back.

A response came almost immediately, making her stomach tighten.

Arris: Do it if you want to. Your sister-in-law finding out about us is going to be the least of your worries.

Dionne's lips parted slightly, her breath catching at the veiled threat laced in his words. She could practically hear his voice, that deep, commanding tone that sent a shiver down her spine every damn time. He knew exactly how to get under her skin, how to make her pause.

Her fingers hovered over the keyboard before she typed her final message.

Mama: Bye, Arris.

She ended the conversation, locking her phone before she did something reckless like calling him just to hear his voice.

Instead, she sat back, fidgeting with her hands, trying to shake off the lingering heat that Arris always left in his wake. But no matter how hard she tried, he was still there under her skin, in her thoughts, and in the rapid beat of her heart that refused to slow down.

When Kierra returned to the table with DJ holding his pizza, Dionne kept her eyes glued to her phone, avoiding her gaze like her life depended on it. But she could feel Kierra's stare burning into the side of her face.

"You're not hungry?" Kierra asked casually, though the amusement in her voice was anything but.

Dionne finally looked up, sighing. "Lost my appetite."

Kierra smirked, leaning back in her seat. "I bet. We walked away from it."

Dionne clenched her jaw, rolling her eyes at the pettiness in Kierra's tone. She knew it. Kierra had picked up on every single thing—the tension, the stolen glances, the way her body reacted to Arris like he was gravity and she was weightless around him. She just hoped, prayed, that Kierra would drop it.

"Please, Ki. Not now." Dionne's voice was low, almost pleading. She wasn't in the mood for this. Not here. Not with DJ sitting between them, blissfully unaware of the silent war brewing at the table.

"Oh, of course." Kierra's voice was too sweet, too knowing. "Because this conversation doesn't need to be had in public or around DJ. But it will be had."

Dionne closed her eyes for a second, exhaling through her nose. There was no escaping this, not with Kierra. The weight of everything—her secrets, her lies, the exhausting act of pretending—was pressing down on her like a slow, suffocating grip. And Kierra? Kierra saw it all. Even if she wasn't outright saying it, Dionne knew she was already piecing things together.

A chuckle broke through Dionne's spiraling thoughts. She opened her eyes to see Kierra shaking her head, a smirk tugging at her lips.

"I understand though." Kierra shrugged, grabbing a fry from DJ's tray before popping it into her mouth. "He is fine."

Dionne scoffed, rolling her eyes again, but this time, her lips twitched slightly. The comment—so blunt, so Kierra—cut through the thick anxiety building in her chest, lightening it just a little.

Kierra returned to her food, engaging DJ in playful conversation while Dionne stared down at her phone, mind spinning. The pending conversation with Kierra loomed over her like a storm cloud. She wasn't ready.

Hell, she wasn't even ready to face herself.

The weight of her life, her choices, and the undeniable, overwhelming pull she still felt toward Arris swirled through her mind, leaving her drained before she could even think of a way out.

***

Dionne stepped into her home with Kierra right on her heels. The moment the door shut behind them, she started up the stairs, desperate for a moment to breathe, but Kierra's voice stopped her dead in her tracks.

"Where do you think you going, missy? We need to talk." Kierra's

Feenin'

tone held a playful sternness, like a mother catching her child trying to sneak away. The smirk tugging at her lips softened her words, but Dionne wasn't in the mood for games.

She exhaled through her nose, rolling her eyes as she turned halfway toward her sister-in-law. "I'm going to change into something more comfortable. These boots hurt," she said, keeping her voice as casual as possible.

Kierra chuckled, shaking her head. "Bitch, please. You going to change out those wet-ass panties Arris caused. Play with someone else," she shot back without hesitation.

Dionne closed her eyes briefly, sighing at the truth in her words but refusing to give her the satisfaction of a response. Kierra was relentless, and there was no escaping this conversation.

"Hurry up, because we have a lot to talk about," Kierra added, strolling toward the living room while Dionne continued up the stairs, her steps feeling heavier with every step.

Once in her bedroom, she stripped out of her clothes, her skin still buzzing from the earlier encounter with Arris. Kierra wasn't lying. The moment she saw him, her body betrayed her. He had that effect on her—always had, always would.

Dionne peeled off her soaked panties with a frustrated sigh before stepping into the shower, hoping the hot water would rinse away more than just the exhaustion of the day. She let the steam rise around her, pressing her palms against the cool tiles as the water cascaded down her body. But even as she stood under the spray, trying to clear her mind, Arris consumed her.

He was everywhere.

In the way her body still tingled from the heat of his gaze, in the ache between her thighs that refused to go away, in the way his voice played on a loop in her head, low and rich, stirring emotions she had no business feeling.

She squeezed her eyes shut, taking a deep breath. No matter how hard she tried to fight it, no matter how much she told herself to let him go—Arris had taken up permanent residence inside of her. Mind, body, and soul.

And the worst part?

She didn't want to let him go.

Dionne quickly washed up, knowing Kierra was waiting downstairs, ready to dig into the conversation she had been avoiding for far too long. But the decision Kierra wanted her to make wasn't one she could rush.

Because once she chose, there would be no turning back.

Dionne stepped out of the bathroom, letting the cool air hit her freshly moisturized skin. She slipped on a black tank top that hugged her breasts just right, the faint outline of her tattoo barely visible through the fabric since she opted against wearing a bra. Her baggy Gallery Dept sweatpants hung low on her waist, balancing out the fitted top, and she slid her feet into her black fuzzy Chanel slippers. Her curly hair, once cascading down her shoulders, was now piled into a messy bun on top of her head. Instead of putting in her contacts, she grabbed her glasses, adjusting them on her face as she took one last look in the mirror.

She took a deep breath, bracing herself for what was coming.

Kierra wasn't going to let this go.

Saying a quick prayer, Dionne walked out of her room and made her way downstairs. The sound of her slippers brushing against the hardwood floors filled the quiet space, but her heartbeat was much louder.

As she entered the living room, she found Kierra lounging on the couch, scrolling through her phone, waiting. The petty smirk she had been wearing since the food court incident was still plastered on her face. The moment Dionne sat down across from her, Kierra didn't waste a second.

"I see you showered. He got that much of an effect on you?" Kierra teased with a chuckle, her eyes dancing with amusement.

Dionne rolled her eyes, refusing to entertain her. She sat back into the couch, crossing her legs as Kierra got comfortable, tucking her feet under her. The anticipation in the air was thick.

"So..." Kierra dragged out, her eyes locked on Dionne. "Who was that man? And don't even try to play me by saying Mia's uncle or a damn client, 'cause we both know that man is way more than that." She paused for effect, tilting her head with a knowing smirk. "Especially since that nigga's hand is tattooed on your fucking boob."

Dionne exhaled deeply, feeling the weight of months of secrecy pressing down on her chest. There was no running from this conversation. Not with Kierra.

"He is the man I'm in love with."

Kierra's mouth fell open in shock. "Woah." She leaned forward, processing the confession. "But what about Malik?"

Dionne scoffed, rolling her eyes. "What about him? That love died a long time ago."

Kierra blinked, taking in Dionne's words, her confusion deepening. "Okay, sis. You're gonna have to explain all this shit, 'cause last I checked, you and Malik are about to get married in a couple of months. And now you're sitting here, telling me you're in love with another man,

Feenin'

while the man you're engaged to—you don't even love anymore?"

Her voice was laced with disbelief, but there was no judgment—just the need to understand what the hell was going on.

Dionne swallowed, feeling the knot in her throat tighten. This was it. The truth was out. But was she really ready to face what came next?

Dionne took a deep breath, bracing herself for the weight of the truth she was about to unload. Her life was tangled in complications, each thread pulling her in a different direction. "I guess I should start from the beginning," she said, her voice steady despite the storm inside her.

Kierra nodded, her expression open, ready to listen.

"Malik and I were once in love. The idea of marrying him was something I dreamed about. But as time went on, it didn't feel like love anymore. He only loved me for my looks…and me getting sick proved that."

Kierra's eyes widened, the words hitting her like a gut punch. Sick? That was something she never knew, something Dionne had never let slip—not once in all the years they'd been in each other's lives. She and Demetrius had been together since college, meaning she had known Dionne since high school. And yet, not a single hint of this had ever been revealed.

"You were sick?" Kierra's voice cracked with emotion, the realization cutting deep.

Dionne inhaled sharply, steadying herself. "Yeah. I had a blood disorder—aplastic anemia. I was born with it, but it got worse when I was in college." Her voice faltered slightly, but she forced herself to push through.

Kierra shook her head, disbelief written all over her face. "Why didn't you tell me? I would have been there for you, Dionne."

Dionne sighed, her fingers gripping the hem of her sweatpants. "It was a lot to deal with, Ki. And I couldn't put that burden on anyone else. The only people who knew were Demetrius and my parents."

Kierra's heart broke, the thought of Dionne going through something so terrifying alone made her stomach twist. "Dionne, you would never be a burden to me." She reached across the space between them, squeezing Dionne's hand. "I'm so sorry you had to go through that without me."

Dionne gave her a small, appreciative smile, but there was still so much more to say. She took another breath and continued. She told Kierra how the sickness had drained her, how it had stolen pieces of her little by little. How Malik had started treating her differently, how his warmth had faded. How she had felt like nothing more than a shell of the woman he had fallen for.

By the time she finished, Kierra sat back, shaking her head, anger flashing in her eyes.

"Now I hate that nigga."

Dionne let out a soft, bitter chuckle, but it was laced with pain. "Don't hate him. He was young, and what I was going through…it was a lot. I just had to learn the hard way that it was my beauty that drew him in. And once my health made me look…less than perfect, I saw the truth."

Kierra studied her, taking in the quiet sadness in Dionne's eyes. "So why stay?" she asked, her voice softer this time, no judgment, just a need to understand.

Dionne exhaled, her gaze drifting slightly, as if lost in thought. "Mama Glen." Her voice was barely above a whisper, but it carried the weight of every choice she had made. "She's the only thing holding this relationship together. If it weren't for her…Malik and I wouldn't have lasted this long."

Kierra leaned back, exhaling deeply. The mention of Mama Glen softened her, made her anger toward Malik momentarily fade. She was a good woman—one of the few people who could make you feel like family, even if you weren't. And now, she was fighting a battle of her own.

Kierra could see the emotions swelling in Dionne, her eyes slightly glassy as she thought about Mama Glen. And before the moment could break them both, Kierra decided to shift the conversation.

"Alright," she exhaled, adjusting in her seat. "That explains Malik. But now let's talk about *him*."

Dionne already knew who she meant.

Arris.

The name alone sent a shiver down her spine. The man who consumed her thoughts. The man whose touch still burned on her skin. The man she loved.

She sighed, rubbing her temples. "Ki…"

"Nah, don't Ki me," Kierra cut her off, crossing her arms. "You got that man's hand tattooed on your *titty*, sis. We talking about him."

"So how did Arris come about?" Kierra asked, watching the way Dionne's entire face softened, the smallest smile breaking through her turmoil.

Dionne exhaled, a quiet chuckle escaping her lips. "He started out as a client… then a business partner… then, one night, we crossed a line. I was mad at Malik for cheating, I needed an escape, and Arris was just… there."

Feenin'

Kierra's amused smirk faded instantly. "Hold the fuck up, that nigga cheated on you?" she asked, her voice sharp with anger.

"Yes, Ki," Dionne admitted, but quickly shook her head. "But I don't want to talk about that."

Kierra sat back, her jaw tight, but she nodded, letting it go—for now. "Okay, fine. At least you got your lick back. In a major way," she added with a smirk, trying to lighten the mood.

Dionne let out another small laugh, but it didn't last long. Her eyes softened, lost in memory. "What I thought was just one night of escape turned into... something more. Arris wasn't letting up, and truthfully? I didn't want him to."

Kierra watched the way Dionne's entire demeanor shifted, the way she seemed to feel his presence even though he wasn't here. "Damn," Kierra muttered, intrigued. "That deep?"

Dionne nodded, a dreamy yet conflicted look in her eyes. "Ever since I laid eyes on him, Ki, it was like he just... took over every part of me. My body reacts to him, like it has a mind of its own. It don't matter how much I fight it, how much I try to deny it—he's just there. In my head. In my skin. In my soul."

Kierra studied her for a second before shaking her head with a knowing smirk. "Like a drug," she said, watching Dionne closely.

A deep breath left Dionne's lips as she nodded. "Yes," she whispered. "A drug I *feen* for constantly. I can't even control it sometimes."

Kierra smiled at her, but there was still confusion in her eyes. "So... does he know you're engaged?" she asked, hesitant but needing to understand.

"Yeah," Dionne admitted, her voice barely above a whisper. "And he didn't give a fuck." She looked down, but Kierra saw the flicker of something in her eyes—guilt mixed with longing. "He continued to love me. Protect me. And most of all... *feen* for me in ways I've never been *feened* for."

Kierra exhaled, shaking her head. "So why the hell are you marrying Malik, when your heart, mind, body, and soul belong to Arris?" Kierra demanded, her frustration bubbling over. "Bitch, you got this man's hand tatted on you! I still can't get over that!"

Dionne let out a sad laugh, rubbing her forehead. "It's... complicated."

Kierra folded her arms, shaking her head. "Well, bitch, uncomplicated it, because it don't look that complicated to me," she said with a scoff. "This man got his hand on your damn titty! Make it make sense!"

Dionne's laughter faded, and the room grew heavy. She swallowed hard before finally speaking. "My senior year, I was dying," she confessed, her voice cracking.

Kierra's smirk dropped instantly. "What?" she whispered, eyes wide.

Dionne took a deep breath, steadying herself. "The only thing that could save me was a bone marrow transplant. When I was rushed to the hospital, I thought it was over. My parents were on their way, but I didn't have time to wait for them. I needed it immediately or I was gone."

Kierra's throat tightened as she watched tears form in Dionne's eyes.

"My parents couldn't make it in time," Dionne continued, her voice trembling. "So, Mama Glen did it."

Kierra's heart dropped. "Dionne…"

"She risked everything to save my life, Ki," Dionne whispered, her tears slipping freely now. "And now… she's dying. The doctors say she has a year, but we know it's sooner than that. And her only wish is to see her son get married to the woman she's always seen as her daughter."

Kierra blinked, trying to process it all as she watched her sister-in-law crumble in front of her.

"Me," Dionne whispered, her voice barely audible. "She wants me to be that woman."

Kierra sucked in a breath, her chest tightening. She knew Mama Glen. She knew how much she loved Dionne like her own, but damn.

"I have to do this for her, Ki," Dionne continued, her voice breaking completely. "I owe it to her. She didn't just support me in college—she saved my fucking life." Her body shook as she broke down, the weight of her reality suffocating her.

Kierra stared at her, heart aching, but something in her gut told her this wasn't right. "D…" she started softly, reaching for her hand. "Mama Glen saved you so you could live. Not so you could trap yourself in a life you don't want."

Dionne squeezed her eyes shut, but the tears kept falling.

Kierra sighed, gripping her hand tighter. "And I hate to be the one to say it, but what happens after she's gone? Because you might be doing this for her now… but what about you? What about the rest of your life?"

Dionne shook her head, her voice barely above a whisper. "Kierra, you didn't look that woman in the eyes and promise her you would marry her son." She exhaled shakily, rubbing her hands down her sweatpants as if she could smooth away the turmoil inside her. "The way Mama Glen's face lit up when I said yes… Ki, it was like I gave her another reason to hold on, to keep fighting. I can't break that promise. I can't break her heart just because mine belongs to someone else."

Feenin'

Kierra sighed, her expression tight with frustration. "But, Dee—"

"Just let it go, please." Dionne's voice cracked, her fingers wiping furiously at the fresh tears spilling down her cheeks. She was exhausted—mentally, emotionally, spiritually. Every single day felt like she was carrying the weight of an avalanche on her back, and she was barely keeping herself from getting buried alive.

Kierra didn't let up. "What about Arris, Dionne?" she pushed, her voice laced with something firm and unrelenting. "That man loves you. And I know that for sure. Not just because of what you told me, but because of the way he looked at you earlier. That was not some casual look. He feens for you just as much as you *feen* for him. And I know it's killing him, watching you stay with another man—one, who doesn't deserve you, and two, who you don't even love!"

Dionne clenched her jaw, her gaze lowering as her arms wrapped around herself. "I don't know, Ki," she admitted, her voice thick with frustration. "He's giving me the space to figure it out, but it's so much harder than he or anyone else understands."

Kierra studied her, taking in the visible weight Dionne was carrying—the exhaustion in her eyes, the stress pressing down on her shoulders, the way she looked like she hadn't truly breathed in months.

"Please don't tell anyone about this," Dionne said, looking at her with pleading eyes. "London and Karmen don't know any of it. Not my sickness, not Arris, nothing. In their minds, Malik and I are happy, and I need it to stay that way. At least until I figure everything out."

Kierra hesitated before nodding, but she couldn't ignore the pit growing in her stomach. "What about Demetrius? Or your parents?" she asked gently. "You can't do this alone, Dionne."

Dionne let out a bitter chuckle, shaking her head. "Demetrius already hates Malik enough. If he finds out that I'm trapped in a marriage I don't want? It's going to make things ten times worse. And if he finds out about Arris…" She trailed off, rubbing her forehead. "Ain't no telling what he'd do or say. I don't need that drama on top of everything else."

Kierra sighed. "And your parents?"

"They think I'm happy," Dionne said simply, the sadness in her tone so deep it made Kierra's chest tighten. "I need them to think I'm happy. I don't need them worrying about me. I don't want anyone worrying about me." She looked at Kierra, her expression raw. "So please, just keep this between us."

Kierra exhaled, her heart aching for Dionne in a way she couldn't fully explain. She hated seeing her baby sister like this—shouldering all of this pain alone, suffocating under a love she wasn't allowed to have, drowning in obligations she couldn't walk away from.

But Kierra nodded anyway. "I got you, sis," she said, squeezing Dionne's hand. "But you need to figure out what you're going to do. And fast." Her voice was softer now, but still firm. "Because what you're caught up in? It's more dangerous than just choosing between two men. And whatever you decide—make sure it's not out of obligation. Make sure it's because of love."

Dionne swallowed hard, nodding even though her heart felt like it was splitting in half.

One love.

One promise.

One had to go.

And no matter which choice she made—either way, she was going to break.

Love, she once thought, was supposed to be easy.

But it was dangerous.

Risky.

And more *addictive* than she ever realized.

"I just have one question though," Kierra said, smirking as she snapped Dionne out of her thoughts.

Dionne turned to her, already bracing herself. "What?"

Kierra's smirk widened. "How the fuck hasn't Malik seen this big ass tattoo on your boob? He gotta know that hand ain't his."

Dionne chuckled, shaking her head. "He hasn't seen it. I'm always wearing big shirts or hoodies around him."

Kierra's eyes widened in disbelief. "Damn, bitch—so the nigga ain't asking no questions? Wondering why you dressing like it's the middle of winter inside the house?"

"Nope." Dionne shrugged. "Just goes to show how much he doesn't pay attention to me. Plus, his ass is always at work to be worried about what I got on."

Kierra sucked her teeth, shaking her head. "I swear I can't wait until you give me permission to beat that nigga ass."

Dionne laughed, shaking her head. "You and my brother are wild."

"Nah, we just real. And that nigga deserves it," Kierra muttered, still irritated by everything Dionne had told her.

Dionne sighed, but for the first time in a while, she felt lighter. The weight of her secrets was still there, still pressing on her chest, but at least she wasn't carrying it completely alone anymore.

Thankfully, Kierra seemed to pick up on her shift in energy because she let the conversation move on, switching to something lighter. Soon,

Feenin'

they were watching some messy reality show, laughing and dragging the cast like they always did.

For the first time all day, Dionne felt like she could breathe.

Kierra had always been her safe space, the one who could pull her out of her own head when things got too overwhelming. And even though Arris still consumed every part of her mind—his touch, his voice, the weight of his love pressing against her chest—at least for now, Kierra was a reprieve from her chaotic life.

And right now, she needed that more than anything.

***

Two days later:

Arris drove through the stillness of the early morning, the city barely awake as he made his way to the airport. The Jeep's clock read 5:45 AM, the sky still blanketed in darkness. Fall break had arrived, Thanksgiving was just a week away, and A'Lani was finally back in town. Having his little sister around always made the world feel a little less chaotic, a little more at peace.

As he pulled into the packed airport—because even at this ungodly hour, Houston never slept—he found a parking spot and settled in to wait. His eyes drifted to the glowing screen of his phone, thumb hovering over a familiar contact.

Dionne.

His jaw tightened as he stared at her name, debating whether to call. He knew she was probably still asleep, curled up in bed, tangled in sheets he wished were his instead of that nigga's.

Fuck.

He missed her voice.

Since seeing her at the mall the other day, he'd kept his distance. That had been their last conversation, and despite Dionne's constant messages checking in on him, he had ignored every single one. Not because he didn't want to talk to her—he needed to talk to her—but because every conversation made it harder to let her go.

And he didn't know how much more of this shit he could take.

His fingers twitched over the call button, but at the last second, he locked his phone and leaned his head back against the seat with a heavy sigh.

Fuck, I need her.

The thought hit him like a gut punch, the image of her face flashing through his mind. Those soft brown eyes, the way she looked at him like he was her entire world—even though she still belonged to another man.

His chest tightened, fingers gripping the steering wheel as frustration swelled inside him. He could feel himself spiraling, going through withdrawals like she was a drug he was *addicted* to, one he couldn't quit no matter how hard he tried.

He wanted to say fuck it. Wanted to pull up on her, snatch her out of whatever bed she was in, and remind her exactly who she belonged to.

But he couldn't.

Because as much as he loved her, *feened* for her, he couldn't keep putting himself through this.

Not unless she made the choice.

His thoughts were interrupted by the buzzing of his phone, A'Lani's name flashing across the screen.

With one last deep breath, he pushed Dionne to the back of his mind—at least for now—and answered the call.

"Lani, where you at?"

"Coming out, now."

Arris leaned against the side of his Jeep, watching as A'Lani strolled out of the airport with a suitcase damn near the size of her. He shook his head with a chuckle, already knowing what was coming.

"Damn, Lani. You do know you're only staying a week, right?" he teased as he walked up to grab her bag.

A'Lani smirked, brushing a stray curl from her face. "Yeah, and? You can never have too many clothes," she quipped with a chuckle, making his chest warm. No matter how much time passed, she was still his little sister, the one person who could make him laugh without even trying.

He pulled her into a tight hug, pressing a soft kiss against her forehead.

After loading her overpacked suitcase into the trunk, they climbed into the Jeep, and Arris pulled off, merging onto the highway.

"So, did you miss me?" A'Lani asked, a wide grin stretching across her face.

Arris scoffed, keeping his eyes on the road. "Eh... a little."

A'Lani gasped in mock offense, shoving his arm. "A little?"

Arris smirked, knowing damn well he had missed her like crazy.

She gave him a knowing look before settling deeper into the seat, adjusting her hoodie like she was getting comfortable for a nap.

"So you just gonna knock out on me, huh?" he asked, glancing over at her before turning his attention back to the road.

"I'm exhausted," she mumbled, already half-asleep. "I had finals yesterday, and I couldn't sleep on the flight."

Arris nodded, understanding. "You staying with me or Ma?"

"You," she answered instantly, her tone firm despite the sleepiness in

Feenin'

it. "I can't be in the same house as him."

Her voice was calm, but the irritation was unmistakable. Arris' jaw flexed. He didn't have to ask who him was—he already knew.

When he told A'Lani about their mother and Calvin trying to work things out, she damn near lost it. Unlike Arris, who had been trying—forcing—himself to forgive their father for their mother's sake, A'Lani wasn't there yet. She didn't even pretend to be.

What Arris didn't know was that her resentment ran deeper than just abandonment.

A'Lani clutched onto a secret that changed everything for her, something she knew would shatter the progress Arris was making toward healing.

So, she stayed quiet.

For now.

Arris saw the tension brewing beneath A'Lani's exhaustion, the frustration sitting just behind her heavy eyelids. He knew better than to press her about it now. Instead, he let the silence settle, allowing her to rest while he drove, the low hum of music filling the space between them.

As he pulled into his driveway, the first streaks of sunlight stretched across the sky, bathing his house in a soft golden glow. Arris cut the engine but left the car running, not wanting to disturb A'Lani's much-needed sleep. He stepped out, retrieving her overpacked suitcase from the trunk before unlocking the front door with a quick tap on his phone's security app.

The house was still and quiet, untouched by the chaos of the day that had yet to begin. He walked to the guest room—the room A'Lani had claimed the second she laid eyes on his new place—and set her luggage down before pulling back the comforter.

Back outside, he shut off the Jeep, then moved to the passenger side, carefully scooping her up into his arms. She barely stirred, her head naturally resting against his chest as if she belonged there. The weight of her in his arms reminded him of when they were younger, back when she'd fall asleep in the backseat on late-night drives, and he'd have to carry her inside. Some things never changed.

He laid her down gently, tucking the blankets around her like he used to when they were kids. He knew she'd cuss him out later for not waking her up to change out of her "outside clothes" before getting in the bed, but he didn't care. She needed sleep more than anything right now.

Satisfied that she was settled, Arris left the room, making his way to his own. He grabbed the wooden box where he kept his stash and stepped out onto the balcony, his hands already moving on instinct, rolling up with precision.

He leaned against the railing, sparking the blunt and pulling in a slow, deep drag. The thick smoke curled into the crisp morning air, mixing with the scent of dew and fading night. The buzz hit almost immediately, but it barely scratched the surface of what he really needed.

Dionne.

She was the one high that weed couldn't replicate, the addiction he couldn't shake.

Even with the distance he tried to put between them, she was still there—lingering in his mind, pressing against his chest, making his body ache for something he was trying so hard to stay away from.

He exhaled slowly, watching the smoke drift into the sky.

He didn't know how much longer he could take it.

Without her.

Without them.

But for now, all he could do was stand there, letting the weed and the cool morning breeze do their best to calm what couldn't be soothed.

The sun had fully risen, casting a golden hue over the city as Arris remained planted on his balcony, the morning haze blending with the lingering smoke from his third blunt. His backyard stretched endlessly beneath him, a tranquil contrast to the chaos running rampant in his mind. In the distance, Houston's skyline loomed, blurred by the fog of his high, his thoughts too consumed by a certain woman to fully take in the view.

The sharp chime of his phone snapped him from his daze. He blinked sluggishly, glancing down at the screen. Mario's name flashed across it, FaceTiming him. But what caught him off guard was the time—9:30 AM.

Damn.

He'd been outside smoking for hours and hadn't even realized it.

Dragging a slow hand down his face, he answered just before the call could end.

"Wassgood?" Arris muttered, his voice smooth, lazy, and heavy from the high. His red-rimmed eyes barely stayed open, the blunt dangling between his fingers as he exhaled a slow stream of smoke.

"Aye, you mind—wait… nigga, you high?" Mario asked, immediately catching the state of his friend.

"Yeah," Arris answered simply, taking another pull from his blunt.

"Oh shit… who pissed you off?" Mario asked, his tone shifting from casual to serious in an instant. He knew Arris. Knew he didn't just

Feenin'

smoke for the hell of it. If he was up at this time of morning getting high, something—or someone—had him deep in his thoughts, or angry as fuck. And right now, it was both.

Dionne.

Always Dionne.

She consumed him, lived in every fiber of his being, but not having her? That shit made his blood boil.

"No one. Wassup?" Arris deflected smoothly, his voice even despite the storm raging inside him.

"Shi, somebody did. Yo ass smokin' this early in the morning," Mario challenged, unconvinced.

Arris wanted to spill it all—to say her name, to lay out every reason why the thought of Dionne made his chest tighten and his hands itch to pull her closer—but what was the point? Mario wouldn't get it. No one would.

Instead, he exhaled another slow drag of smoke before chuckling. "Nigga, what do you want?"

Mario let out a short laugh, knowing Arris well enough to know he wouldn't press—at least not right now. "Aight, fine. I was tryna see if you could watch Mia for a few hours. I wanna surprise Karmen with lunch today, but I see yo ass busy… or sulking."

At the mention of Mia, Arris' lips curled into a genuine smile, something rare these days. His niece was the one thing that could ease his mind when everything else felt like a damn war. "Man, you know I got you. I miss my niece anyway," he said, already looking forward to spending time with her.

He wanted a Mia of his own. A daughter. A family. But not just with anyone—with *her*.

Mario chuckled, snapping Arris from his thoughts. "Well, you need to sober yo ass up first," he joked, knowing damn well Arris would never be around Mia while high.

"I am, nigga. What time you want me to come get her?" Arris asked, already mentally preparing to push through his haze.

"11:30. Karmen's lunch is at 12."

"Wait, why Mia ain't at school?" Arris asked, his red eyes low with confusion as he leaned back in the chair.

"Lil Mama didn't want to go, so I let her stay home," Mario answered casually, shrugging like it was no big deal.

"Aight, I got you."

There was a pause before Mario's tone softened. "You sure you good, nigga?"

Arris nodded even though his insides twisted with everything he wasn't saying. "Yeah, bro. I'm straight."

Mario didn't sound convinced. "Aight... Tell yo woman to give you some pussy, you know that always cheer yo ass up. Unless she cut you off... that's why you smokin' yo pain away?" Mario teased, laughing.

Arris let out a short burst of laughter, shaking his head.

"Bye, nigga." He hung up before Mario could press him any further.

But the moment the screen went black, the laughter faded, and the silence settled back in.

Because Mario wasn't wrong.

She was the reason he was smoking his pain away.

And the longer he went without her, the worse the withdrawals got.

The sound of the balcony door sliding open pulled Arris from his thoughts. He turned to see A'Lani stepping out, now dressed in fresh clothes, looking far more energized than she had earlier that morning. She stretched her arms above her head before smirking at him.

"Damn, brother. Smoking the whole stash, ain't you?" she teased, crossing her arms as she took in the remnants of his high.

Arris chuckled, shaking his head as he stubbed out the last of his blunt. "Something like that."

A'Lani studied him for a moment, her playful expression shifting into one of quiet concern. "You good?" she asked, her voice softer now, more serious. She knew her brother too well—knew there were only two reasons he smoked like this: stress or anger.

Arris exhaled deeply, tilting his head back as he let the cool morning air touch his face. "Yeah, just needed a stress reliever," he answered honestly, though he wasn't about to unpack everything weighing him down.

A'Lani's eyes narrowed slightly. "Who the fuck stressing my brother out?" she asked, her protectiveness coming out full force.

Arris chuckled at her tone, shaking his head. "No one. Just a lot of business shit I have to handle." The lie rolled off his tongue effortlessly, but A'Lani nodded, accepting his answer—at least for now.

"Well, I'm about to head out," she announced, glancing down at her Apple Watch as a message came through.

Arris smacked his lips, feigning offense. "Damn, I thought you wanted to spend your first day back with your big brother," he said, clutching his chest in mock hurt.

A'Lani rolled her eyes. "Here you go."

"I was headed to get Mia," he continued, doubling down on the guilt trip, "figured I'd hang with my two favorite girls, but I see where I stand

Feenin'

now."

A'Lani let out a laugh. "Nigga, please. I miss my Mia boo, but I'll have to catch up with y'all later. I got a tattoo appointment with True."

Arris raised a brow at that. "Better not be getting no nigga tatted on you," he warned, only half-joking. "I will blow that bitch up, and I don't give a damn about it being True's shop."

A'Lani burst out laughing, shaking her head. "I gotta get a nigga first. And if I ever let a nigga get that close, I wish I would tat his name on me." She scoffed. "The fuck I look like? A sign-in sheet?"

Arris smirked, nodding in approval. "Long as you know."

She playfully nudged his shoulder before turning back toward the house. "I'll see you later, big bro."

Arris watched her leave before standing up himself, rolling his shoulders as he tried to shake off the weight pressing down on him. He had to get ready before heading to pick up Mia—but even as he moved, the lingering ache in his chest wouldn't let up.

No amount of weed could numb this.

Only she could.

After saying their goodbyes, Arris headed straight to the bathroom, brushed his teeth, then stepped into the shower letting the steaming water cascade down his body. He closed his eyes, hoping the heat would wash away not just the lingering high but also the emotions clawing at him. Dionne still lived in his mind rent-free, and no amount of weed, distractions, or hot showers could change that.

By the time he stepped out, his smooth dark skin glistened with moisture, and his head felt clearer—at least for now. He took his time rubbing in his shea butter, the rich scent mixing with the steam still swirling in the air. Afterward, he dressed in a black and white *Givenchy* t-shirt that fitted loosely over his muscular frame perfectly, paired with black jeans that sat just right on his waist. He slid his feet into his Jordan *Concord* 11s before adding the finishing touches—two gold chains gleaming against his skin, a gold *Van Cleef* bracelet resting on his wrist, and a pristine gold AP watch that caught the light with every movement.

The final step was his *Creed* cologne, the luxurious scent sealing everything together. He took one last glance in the mirror, adjusting his chains before nodding to himself. The signs of his earlier high were gone—visibly, at least. His body still felt the haze of relaxation from how much he smoked, but he was functional enough. And more importantly, he was about to see Mia, and there wasn't anything that could take away the joy he felt spending time with his niece.

With that, he grabbed his keys and stepped out the door, sliding into his Jeep with ease. As the engine rumbled to life, he exhaled, preparing for another eventful—and likely expensive—day with his favorite little girl.

***

Arris weaved through the city streets, glancing in the rearview mirror as Mia tapped away on her iPad. "Uncle, I'm hungry," she announced, her tiny voice filled with expectation.

"Alright, baby girl. What you in the mood for?" he asked, his gaze shifting between her and the road.

Mia's little face scrunched up in deep thought, making him chuckle. "Umm... I don't know."

Arris shook his head, amused. He already knew how this would go—Mia taking forever to decide, then settling on something she had just eaten the day before. His thoughts drifted to Dionne, and this time, he didn't fight it. He needed to see her face, even if she was going to give him hell for ignoring her texts.

"Let's see what Aunt Dee is doing," he said, pulling up her contact. "Maybe she can help you decide."

At the mention of Dionne, Mia's face lit up. "Okay!" she said, excitement lacing her voice.

Arris hit the FaceTime button, his heartbeat picking up slightly as it rang. A part of him expected her not to answer, to make him suffer a little for shutting her out. But after the third ring, her face filled the screen. Even with her scowl, she still looked fine as hell.

"You ignored me for damn near two days, and now you FaceTiming me like we cool?" she said, her eyes narrowing behind her glasses.

Arris smirked, resting back in his seat. "We ain't cool?" he teased, his voice smooth.

Dionne sucked her teeth, adjusting her glasses with a pointed glare. "Boy, what do you want?"

"Damn, Mama. You ain't happy to see me?" His smirk deepened, loving how easy it was to push her buttons.

She rolled her eyes, but he caught the slight curl at the corner of her lips. "You're annoying."

"And you love it," he countered, watching her open her mouth to argue—only to close it just as fast. He chuckled. "Where you at?"

"Working," she answered dryly, the background of her home office confirming it.

"You eat yet?" he asked, already knowing the answer.

Dionne hesitated before shaking her head. "No, not yet."

Feenin'

Arris exhaled sharply. "Woman, I told you about skipping meals."

She sighed, already knowing where this was going. "Arris, I'm fine. I was gonna grab something after I finished this contract."

"Nah, fuck that. I'll bring you something."

She blinked, caught off guard. "Wait, you serious?"

He raised an eyebrow. "Why wouldn't I be?"

She studied him for a moment, her expression softening. "You just started talking to me again, now you wanna bring me food?"

Arris shrugged like it was the simplest thing in the world. "You my woman, ain't you?"

Dionne's heart did a little flip, but she quickly masked it. "Am I?"

His playful smirk faded, his gaze turning intense. "You tell me, Mama."

The weight of his words settled between them, thick and unspoken. She wanted to say yes—God, she wanted to—but the reality of her situation loomed over her like a storm cloud. Before she could find the words, Mia's little face popped into the camera, full of excitement.

"We going to see Aunt Dionne?" she asked, her big brown eyes filled with hope.

Dionne's lips parted in surprise, but she couldn't fight the smile forming. "Hey, Mia baby!" she greeted warmly, waving through the screen.

"Hey, Aunt Dee!" Mia beamed. "Me and Uncle Arris don't know what to eat. What should we get?"

Dionne chuckled, shaking her head. "Hmm... how about tacos?"

Mia's eyes widened with delight. "Yes! Uncle Arris, we want tacos!"

Arris laughed, his gaze flickering back to Dionne. "Tacos for my girls, then."

Dionne rolled her eyes, but her heart fluttered at the way he said *my girls*.

Arris smirked. "I'll be there in a few, Mama. You better open the door."

Dionne huffed playfully, but the warmth in her voice betrayed her. "Okay, Arris. Only because you have Mia and you're bringing tacos."

He chuckled, already knowing she missed him as much as he did her. "See you soon, Mama."

Arris ended the call, letting his phone rest on the passenger seat as a rare, genuine smile played on his lips. Just hearing Dionne's voice, seeing her face—even through a screen—was enough to lift the weight he had been carrying.

For the past few days, he'd been fighting it, trying to keep his distance, trying to protect himself from the agony of wanting her while knowing she wasn't his—not fully. But all it took was one conversation, one moment of hearing her say his name in that soft, teasing tone, and he was right back where he started. Feening for her.

Mia's excited voice from the backseat pulled him from his thoughts. "Uncle Arris, we get tacos now?" she asked, her little legs swinging.

"Yeah, baby girl. We getting tacos."

"And then we go see Aunt Dee?" she added, the excitement clear in her voice.

Arris smirked as he pulled in the drive thru, his grip on the steering wheel tightening. "Yeah, we going to see Aunt Dee."

He didn't even try to hide how much he was looking forward to it. No more ignoring her calls, no more pushing her away. He was done with that. He needed her too much.

And today, he was going to remind her of that.

***

Dionne sat in her home office, scrolling through contracts and house listings, but her focus was shot. The familiar chime of her doorbell made her pause, and despite herself, she smiled. She already knew who it was. Sliding her feet into her Chanel slippers, she made her way to the door, inhaling deeply before pulling it open.

Her breath hitched the second her eyes landed on him.

Arris stood there, his presence commanding as always, dressed in black, licking his lips as he took her in. The weight of his gaze sent her heart into a frenzy, but before she could say anything, a small, excited voice interrupted the moment.

"Aunt Dee!"

Mia came running toward her, and Dionne instantly softened, bending down to scoop the little girl into her arms. "Hey, boo! I missed you," she said, squeezing Mia close as she carried her further inside, purposely ignoring Arris's heavy stare.

Arris chuckled, stepping inside and shutting the door behind him, watching as Dionne and Mia chatted like he wasn't even there. It was one of the many things he loved—how naturally Dionne fit into his life, into his family. She didn't have to try. She just belonged.

Dionne walked into the living room, finally setting Mia down on the couch.

"Mia, go to the table so you can eat," Arris instructed, moving further into the room.

"She can stay right here," Dionne countered without missing a beat.

Feenin'

Arris smirked at Mia's satisfied grin. The little girl clearly loved being treated like an adult.

"Alright, but don't waste anything," he warned, setting her food out on the coffee table before handing her the iPad. Mia nodded eagerly, already engrossed in her meal.

Dionne watched her for a moment, smiling, before she felt Arris's looming presence behind her. Slowly, she looked up, locking eyes with him.

"So Mia's the only one who gets a greeting?" Arris's voice was low, teasing, but there was something else there—something challenging.

Dionne leaned back slightly, crossing her arms. "Mia didn't ignore me for two days. Now give me my food." She reached for the bag in his hand, but before she could snatch it, he pulled it back behind his broad frame.

"Give me a kiss first," he said, smirking.

Dionne's eyes narrowed. "Arris, stop playing with me and my food."

"No kiss, no food."

She rolled her eyes, but she could feel the heat crawling up her neck. He was entirely too close, too intoxicating, too damn irresistible. His scent—his cologne mixed with something purely him—clouded her thoughts, and for a split second, she forgot about everything else.

"Fine," she muttered, grabbing his face and pulling him down to her level, pressing her lips against his.

What was supposed to be a quick peck turned into something much deeper the moment Arris tilted his head and parted her lips, slipping his tongue inside. Dionne inhaled sharply, gripping his shirt as heat coiled low in her stomach.

"Arris, stop…" she whispered breathlessly, trying to pull away, but failing miserably. "Mia is sitting right there."

"She's too into those tacos to be paying attention to us," he murmured, lips brushing against hers as he smirked.

Dionne glanced at the couch, and sure enough, Mia was completely focused on her food and iPad, oblivious to anything else.

She turned back to Arris, shaking her head with a laugh. "You're ridiculous."

"And you love it," he said, finally handing her the food.

She took it with a playful glare, but the way her heart was racing told her everything she already knew—she was never going to stop feening for this man.

Arris settled into the couch, pulling out Dionne's tacos and handing them to her before grabbing his own. They ate in comfortable silence, the weight of unspoken words hanging between them, but neither of them wanted to disturb the rare peace of just being in each other's presence again.

"How you been, Mama?" Arris finally asked, his gaze locked on her as he took a bite of his taco, admiring the way she looked in her casual homewear.

Dionne rolled her eyes, her lips curving into a slight smirk. "Oh, now you care?" she said, her tone laced with pettiness.

Arris chuckled, already knowing she wasn't going to let him slide for ignoring her for two days. He leaned back into the couch, shaking his head before repeating his question, this time with more firmness. "How you been, Mama?"

The playfulness in her expression dimmed as she sighed, lowering her gaze to her food. "I've been okay," she answered, her voice honest but distant.

Arris's jaw tensed. "Why just okay? That nigga ain't hurting you, is he?" His voice dropped, a dangerous edge creeping into his tone.

Dionne's eyes widened slightly as she flicked her gaze toward Mia, who was still lost in her iPad, oblivious to the tension brewing in the room. "Arris," she warned, keeping her voice low. "Mia is sitting right there."

"I don't give a fuck," Arris snapped, his patience running thin. The thought of Malik mistreating her, even in the slightest way, made his blood boil. He shifted forward, his entire demeanor darkening. "Is he hurting you in any way?"

Dionne reached out, lightly resting her hand on his arm, a silent plea for him to calm down. "No, Arris," she assured him softly. "He's not hurting me. I've just been tired from work."

Arris searched her face for any trace of a lie before exhaling, his muscles relaxing slightly. "Alright," he murmured, focusing back on his food, but the tension still simmered beneath the surface.

"I need your opinion on something," Arris said, his deep voice pulling Dionne's attention from her food. She swallowed, wiping her fingers before looking at him curiously.

"Wassup?" she asked, sensing the seriousness in his tone.

Arris pulled out his phone, scrolling to the digital blueprints of the Comets facility along with the business proposal Demetrius had sent him. He handed it over, watching as Dionne's brows furrowed in concentration.

"What's this?" she asked, setting her taco down as she read over the details carefully.

Feenin'

"Demetrius wants me to own part of the Comets," Arris explained, his voice steady but laced with something deeper. "They're offering him the GM position, but he won't take it unless I buy in. He doesn't trust the current owner and doesn't want to work under him.

Dionne's eyes skimmed the numbers, nodding in understanding. "This looks like a solid deal. What's making you hesitate?" she asked, glancing up at him. She could sense it—the doubt lingering in his voice, the hesitation in his posture.

Arris exhaled, running a hand over his chin. "I haven't touched baseball since college. I don't know if I want to step back into that world again." His vulnerability slipped through, raw and unfiltered.

Dionne tilted her head, her voice soft. "I thought baseball was your first love?"

Arris's jaw tightened for a moment before he leaned back. "It was. But it's also a part of my life I've been trying to leave behind."

Dionne didn't press. She could tell whatever was tied to his past with baseball ran deeper than he was willing to admit right now. Instead, she shifted the conversation.

"This is an incredible opportunity," she said, her voice laced with encouragement. "You and Demetrius could change the franchise for the better."

Arris let out a small chuckle, shaking his head as he admired how quickly she grasped the business side of things. "Yeah, I was leaning toward saying yes. I know how big of a move this is—it sets my future family up for life. Bigger than what I'm doing now."

He paused, locking eyes with her, his expression unreadable.

"But I wanted to run it by my future wife before making a decision."

Dionne's breath hitched. Her stomach tightened, her eyes widening slightly at the weight of his words. He said it so casually, yet with so much certainty. Like it was a fact. Like it was already written.

Arris smirked as he caught the soft blush she tried to hide.

Dionne forced herself to play it cool, even though his words had sent a wave of emotions through her. "I think you should do it," she said, keeping her tone as steady as possible.

"Yeah?"

"Yeah," she nodded.

"Happy wife, happy life," Arris murmured with a teasing grin, but Dionne could see the seriousness behind it.

Arris grabbed his phone and dialed Demetrius' number, his gaze flickering to Dionne as she took a bite of her taco.

"Hey D, I'm in. Wifey said yes," Arris said with a smirk, watching as

Dionne's lips curled into a smile, her heart fluttering at his words.

"Sounds good, bruh! We about to kill it!" Demetrius responded, his voice filled with excitement and pride.

"Yeah, we are. I'll hit you up later, I'm with her right now," Arris said, his eyes never leaving Dionne as she chuckled softly.

"Aight, bet. Tell Wifey thank you for convincing yo stubborn ass," Demetrius joked, making Arris chuckle. If only he knew who that 'wifey' really was.

"We'll finalize everything soon. Aye, let's work!" Demetrius continued, his energy contagious.

Arris laughed as they ended the call, slipping his phone back into his pocket. He leaned back in his seat, a satisfied smirk on his face. "Looks like your brother's staying in Houston. And he said thank you." He winked at her, fully aware of how much this meant to her. That was another reason he had agreed—he knew having Demetrius close was important to her.

Dionne let out a laugh, shaking her head at how oblivious her brother was to everything happening between her and Arris. And for now, she wanted to keep it that way. She couldn't help the warmth that spread through her at Arris' actions, the way he factored in her happiness into his decisions without hesitation. The man she truly wanted was sitting right in front of her, and every day, resisting him became harder.

She smiled, but before they could move on, she reached out, her fingers tracing lightly along the side of his face. "I hope one day, you'll open up to me about what baseball really did to you."

Arris stilled under her touch, closing his eyes briefly before nodding. "One day," he murmured.

They continued eating, the conversation shifting to lighter topics, and for a while, it felt normal. But no matter how much they tried to distract themselves, the undeniable pull between them remained, thickening the air with longing neither of them wanted to acknowledge.

Then, the door opened.

Dionne stiffened instantly at the sound of keys turning in the lock. Her heart dropped, and a cold dread washed over her as she turned toward the doorway, where Malik stood, his eyes narrowing at the scene before him.

The smell of tacos and the sound of laughter had lured him into the living room, but the moment his gaze landed on Arris, his entire expression darkened.

"The fuck is this?" Malik asked, his voice stern, suspicion dripping from every word.

Feenin'

Dionne swallowed her irritation, masking her initial shock with a neutral expression. "Malik, what are you doing here?" she asked, her tone carefully controlled.

"Forgot my lunch," he said flatly, his eyes never leaving Arris. "Didn't expect an audience."

Arris slowly turned his head, his once-relaxed posture now stiff with restrained hostility. His expression remained calm, but the shift in his energy was unmistakable—he was on edge, ready to explode at the slightest provocation.

Dionne could see it in the way his jaw clenched, his fingers tightening around his drink, and she knew she had to defuse this before it escalated.

"Malik, you remember Arris Black, right?" she said, trying to keep her voice steady.

Malik's eyes flicked between them before landing back on Arris, his skepticism evident. "Yeah," he muttered, his jaw tightening. "But no disrespect, Arris—what you doing in my house?"

Arris let out a low, humorless chuckle. "All disrespect," he corrected, his voice dripping with venom. "It's really none of your business."

Dionne stood up abruptly, stepping in between them before things could spiral out of control. Malik's posture had stiffened, and Arris had already squared his shoulders, his eyes dark with warning.

"Arris was here to discuss our partnership with his company," she said quickly. "He brought Mia because I haven't seen her in a while."

Malik's gaze lingered on Dionne, searching her face for something—guilt, maybe—but she kept her expression unreadable.

Arris, on the other hand, stood his ground, his dark eyes locked on Malik, daring him to say something out of line.

Malik scoffed, shaking his head before muttering under his breath, "I don't have time for this shit."

Dionne clenched her fists at her sides, knowing exactly what that meant—an argument was coming later.

Malik walked past them, heading to the table to grab his forgotten lunch, but before leaving, he threw one last look over his shoulder. "I should let you get back to your... playdate," he said sarcastically. "I gotta get back to work."

Arris took a step forward, closing the space between them. Even though he didn't say a word, the silent message in his stance was clear—watch your mouth.

Dionne immediately placed a hand on Arris's chest, standing between them, her touch the only thing keeping him from snapping.

Malik stared at them for a moment, his eyes flicking between Dionne's hand on Arris and Arris's unmoving glare. With one last skeptical look, he turned and left, shutting the door behind him.

A heavy silence filled the room.

Dionne exhaled deeply, turning to Arris, guilt flickering in her eyes. "I'm sorry—"

Arris cut her off, pulling her into him by her waist, his grip firm yet reassuring. "Don't apologize for that nigga," he murmured, voice thick with frustration but laced with something softer. "I'm good, Mama."

She nodded, relief washing over her as she studied his face.

Their moment was interrupted by Mia's curious voice.

"Who was that, Uncle Arris?" she asked, her big eyes blinking up at them.

Arris looked down at her, his expression flat as he deadpanned, "The help."

Dionne's laughter burst out before she could stop it. She covered her mouth, shaking her head as she leaned into Arris's chest, trying to stifle the giggles that wouldn't stop.

She knew Arris was pissed about Malik showing up, but the fact that he wasn't taking it out on her meant everything.

She looked up at him, her heart still pounding from the tension, but in this moment, standing in his arms, it felt like home.

And that scared her more than anything.

***

Mia had barely finished the last game before sleep began to weigh her down. Now, nestled in Dionne's arms, she dozed off as if she were still a newborn, her tiny hands curled into fists against Dionne's chest. After their meal, they had spent the evening playing games, laughing, and even shooting hoops on Dionne's basketball court—one she never used until Arris and Mia were there to make it worthwhile. The fun had drained Mia completely, and now she was out like a light, her soft breaths warm against Dionne's skin.

Arris cleared the table, his movements slow and deliberate as he stole glances at Dionne rocking Mia. His chest tightened at the sight. Dionne, so effortlessly nurturing, so beautiful in her element. He watched as she carefully shifted Mia in her arms, preparing to take her to the guest room.

"I can take her, Mama," Arris offered, stepping closer.

Dionne shook her head, a soft smile playing on her lips. "No, I got it, baby."

Arris didn't argue. He just watched as she carried Mia to the guest room, gently tucking her in before cracking the door slightly so they

Feenin'

could hear if she stirred. The tenderness in her movements made his stomach tighten with something he couldn't even name.

When Dionne stepped back into the living room, she barely had a second to react before Arris swept her off her feet, lifting her into his arms with one smooth motion. A startled gasp left her lips before it melted into a quiet laugh, her arms instinctively wrapping around his neck.

"Arris—"

I miss you so much," he murmured, his voice low and thick with need.

Dionne shivered at the heat in his tone, her fingers tightening around the fabric of his hoodie. The way he held her, the way his voice wrapped around her like a warm embrace, sent a familiar ache through her body. But she couldn't help the flicker of pettiness rising up in her chest, the sting of being ignored for two days still fresh.

"You miss me, but you ignored me for two days," she muttered, rolling her eyes, though her body betrayed her, instinctively pressing closer to his warmth.

Arris exhaled heavily, his grip on her tightening. "I had a lot on my mind, baby. Most of it was you," he admitted, his voice carrying the weight of everything he had been holding back. "I just didn't know how to deal with what I'm feeling. I've never felt like this with no other woman—this shit is all new." His words were raw, unfiltered, exposing a vulnerability he rarely let anyone see.

Dionne's irritation melted away, replaced by something deeper—something that made her heart race and her stomach tighten. She searched his eyes, reading every emotion swirling in the depths of them. "How do you feel?" she asked softly, her voice barely above a whisper.

Arris didn't hesitate. His dark eyes burned into hers, filled with an intensity that made her breath catch. "Let me show you," he rasped, his thumb brushing over her jaw as he leaned in, his lips hovering just above hers, waiting.

A slow exhale left her lips, her body already surrendering before her mind could catch up. "Okay," she breathed, her voice laced with anticipation.

That was all the permission he needed. Arris crashed his lips onto hers, the kiss deep and consuming, his tongue claiming hers like he was making up for every second they had been apart. His grip on her tightened, holding her against him as if he was afraid she'd slip away again.

Dionne melted into him, her body betraying every ounce of logic she tried to hold onto. His lips trailed from her mouth to her jaw, then down her neck, sending shockwaves of pleasure straight to her core. Her breath hitched, a quiet moan slipping past her lips as his teeth grazed her skin.

"Baby, we can't," she whispered, her head tilting to the side even as she tried to resist. "Mia is in the other room."

"She sleep, Mama," Arris growled against her skin, his voice thick with need. "I need you. I need you now."

His hands roamed her body, gripping her thighs as he pressed her against the wall, his kisses turning rougher, more urgent. Dionne's head swam, her pulse racing as desire pooled low in her stomach. She was fighting a losing battle—one she wasn't sure she even wanted to win.

"Arris," she moaned softly, her fingers threading through his waves, tugging him closer.

Arris carried her upstairs with purpose, his grip firm as he moved through the familiar hallways of her home, straight to her bedroom. As soon as he laid her down, his jaw tightened at the thought of her sleeping in this same bed with him. Malik. The man who didn't deserve her. The man who had the right to be here when Arris was the one she *feened* for. The one she belonged to.

Fucking her in this bed, making her scream his name within these walls, and leaving his mark all over these sheets was a raw, unapologetic way of claiming what was his. A twisted way of getting back at Malik for having the woman he loved. Every thrust, every moan ripped from her lips, was a reminder that no matter whose ring was on her finger, her body, her soul—every fucking part of her—belonged to him.

That thought alone fueled the fire burning inside him. His lips crashed onto hers as his hands worked fast, stripping her bare in one swift motion, his need for her undeniable. Dionne's breath hitched, her body already reacting to his touch before her mind could catch up. She was his drug, his most dangerous addiction, and there was no rehab in the world that could make him quit her.

His gaze dropped to her chest, landing on the tattoo of his hand permanently inked over her left breast. His lips curved into a dark smirk before he leaned down, taking her into his mouth, his tongue swirling around her nipple, teeth grazing it just enough to send a shiver down her spine. She arched into him, fingers tangling in his waves as she let out a soft, breathless moan.

Arris wasn't satisfied with just tasting her there. He needed all of her.

His mouth traveled down her stomach, his hands gripping her thighs before spreading them apart with a dominant force that had her gasping. He wasted no time, his tongue attacking her clit with precision, licking,

Feenin'

sucking, devouring her like she was his last meal.

"Damn... I missed this!" Dionne cried out, all logic, all stress, all worry vanishing the moment his tongue worked its magic. Her body trembled, overwhelmed by pleasure, but Arris wasn't done. He slipped two fingers inside her, curling them just right, hitting that spot that had her thighs quaking, her back arching off the mattress.

"Fuck... Arris!" she screamed, gripping the sheets as her orgasm threatened to crash over her.

Arris smirked darkly, his name rolling off her tongue like a melody he'd been starving to hear. He lived for this—her unraveling under his touch, her body surrendering to him completely.

But just as she was about to break, he pulled away, leaving her panting, desperate for more.

"Arris—" her voice was hoarse, filled with need, but before she could finish her sentence, he was already pushing inside her.

Deep.

Hard.

Dionne barely registered when he had stripped out of his own clothes, but now, he was fully inside her, stretching her in the way only he could, filling every inch of the void she'd been craving.

"Shit," Arris groaned, gripping her waist as he set a brutal pace, his strokes deep and unrelenting.

The room filled with the sounds of their bodies colliding, moans, gasps, the bed creaking beneath them. The worry of Mia hearing them? Gone. The weight of her reality? Forgotten. Right now, nothing existed beyond them—this moment, this connection, this undeniable need.

But what they didn't know was that True had just walked into the house.

He had come for their scheduled meeting, needing to discuss a new property investment for his next shop.

And now, he was about to walk into something he damn sure wasn't expecting.

Chapter 17

"Dee!" True called out as he stepped into the living room, glancing around for her. He knew she was working from home today—she had told him to come over, said the door would be unlocked.

Silence greeted him at first, but then a sound echoed through the house. Dionne's muffled screams.

His heart dropped. Without a second thought, he bolted up the stairs, his protective instincts kicking in. If someone was hurting her, he was ready to handle it.

True shoved open the bedroom door—only to freeze in complete shock.

His eyes went wide, his mouth parting slightly as he took in the scene before him.

Arris. Dionne. Tangled in sheets. Moving in sync.

"Fuck." True whispered, his voice barely leaving his lips.

Arris glanced back mid-thrust, locking eyes with True as if his sudden entrance was nothing more than an inconvenience. Instead of stopping, he shot his friend an irritated look and waved him off aggressively, his focus snapping right back to the woman beneath him. Dionne was right on the edge, her body trembling beneath him, and not even his friend's unexpected intrusion was about to ruin the release she needed—or the one he was desperate to witness.

True stood there, too stunned to react. He had suspected, sure. Arris was acting different. But seeing it with his own damn eyes? Watching his best friend deep inside a woman who was supposed to be someone else's fiancée?

This shit was insane.

True quickly turned on his heel and walked out, shutting the door

Feenin'

behind him. "What the fuck," he mumbled under his breath, rubbing his temples as he paced downstairs.

Meanwhile, completely oblivious to what had just gone down, Dionne had her face buried in the mattress, her body shaking from the force of Arris's relentless thrusts.

"Let go, Mama," Arris demanded, his voice dark and commanding.

On cue, Dionne's body tensed before she shattered around him, her loud moan filling the room. Arris groaned, finally pulling out, watching as she flipped over onto her back, her chest rising and falling with exhaustion.

A lazy smirk pulled at his lips. "We have a guest, Mama."

Dionne's brows furrowed as she turned her head to look at him, confused. "What?"

Arris nodded toward the door. "True walked in on us."

Dionne shot up so fast she nearly gave herself whiplash. "What?!"

She scrambled to check the time, realizing she had completely forgotten about their meeting. "Oh my God—Arris!" She grabbed at the sheets, covering herself as embarrassment flooded her. "Why are you so calm right now?"

Arris simply chuckled, standing up to put his clothes back on. "Because I'm tired of us being a secret."

"Baby, I'm engaged!" she hissed, scrambling to find her discarded clothes. "True knows that! Do you know how bad this makes me look?"

Arris caught her wrist, pulling her close. "True don't give a fuck about Malik, and neither do I. He's been suspicious about us for a while now. Honestly, it feels good that someone finally knows. I'm not hiding anymore, Mama."

Dionne let out a shaky breath, torn between the weight of her reality and the undeniable truth in Arris's eyes.

"It's just True," he reassured her, his voice softer now. "I'll make sure he keeps this between us until you're ready."

She hesitated, then gave him a slow nod. "Okay."

Arris pressed a lingering kiss to her lips before stepping back. "Now, go take a hot shower and relax. And when I get rid of True?" He winked, his smirk dripping with arrogance. "Round two."

With that, Arris walked out, making his way downstairs to deal with the very stunned, very confused True.

Dionne sank deeper into the steaming water, letting the heat soothe the aches Arris had left all over her body. The warmth wrapped around her, easing the tension in her muscles, but it did nothing to calm the turmoil in her mind.

True knew.

Her secret—the one she had been balancing so carefully between right and wrong, love and obligation—was slipping further out of her control. First Kierra, now True. Each day, the walls she had built to protect herself were slowly crumbling, exposing everything she had tried to keep hidden.

How long until everyone knew? Until Malik found out? Until there was nothing left for her to salvage?

She let out a deep sigh, tilting her head back, eyes closing as the weight of everything pressed against her chest.

Arris made her feel safe, made her feel alive, but the truth of their relationship was a ticking time bomb. She knew there would come a day when the truth would no longer be hers to control. It would all come crashing down, and she wasn't sure she was ready for the wreckage it would leave behind.

She just had to hope Arris could convince True to keep their secret—at least until she could figure it out for herself. Because once their truth was out in the open, there would be no turning back.

***

True paced the living room, running a hand down his face as he tried to process what he had just walked in on. He had suspected there was something between Arris and Dionne, but seeing it? Witnessing his best friend deep inside a woman who was supposed to be someone else's fiancée? That was something else entirely.

Before he could think too much on it, Arris strolled downstairs, calm as ever, like he didn't just get caught rearranging another man's future wife. He walked over to the bar in the corner of the room, casually pouring himself a glass of whiskey before leaning against the counter.

True scoffed. "Nigga, are you deadass right now? You not even gonna pretend to be embarrassed? Apologize? Something?"

Arris took a slow sip, his smirk unwavering. "For what?"

True blinked. "For what?! Nigga, you just fucked Malik's fiancée—in the bed they share—and you asking me for what?"

"Nigga, keep your voice down. Mia's asleep in the next room," Arris hissed, his tone sharp with warning.

True scoffed, shaking his head. "And y'all in here fucking with Mia in the house?" he shot back, his voice low but firm, laced with disbelief.

"She's asleep, bro. And don't act like your ass ain't done the same when you be watching her sometimes," Arris shot back, his tone cool and unbothered.

True chuckled despite himself, knowing damn well Arris had a

Feenin'

point. But just as quickly, his expression hardened. "True," he admitted, shaking his head before leveling Arris with a serious look. "But back to this shit—she's engaged, nigga."

Arris chuckled, placing his glass down. "She ain't his. Never was."

True let out a dry laugh, shaking his head. "Wow. So that's what we on now? Just rewriting history?"

Arris pushed off the counter, walking up to True until they were standing face to face. "History been written wrong, bro. I just put the pen back in her hands."

True studied him, searching for some hint of hesitation, some sign that Arris knew this was reckless, but there was none. He was deadass serious.

True exhaled, shaking his head. "Man, this some wild shit. You know that, right? She got a whole ass ring on her finger. What happens when Malik finds out? 'Cause let's be real, nigga—he will find out."

Arris didn't flinch. He leaned back against the counter, his expression unreadable. "Then he finds out."

True laughed dryly. "Oh, so you ready for war?"

Arris shrugged. "Been ready. I'm done pretending like she ain't mine. She is mine, and the second she stops fighting it, the whole world will know."

True stared at him for a long moment, rubbing his temples. "Bruh… Dionne ain't built like you. You all calm and collected, but she's up there probably losing her mind, freaking out about this shit."

Arris smirked slightly. "She'll be fine."

True folded his arms. "How you so sure?"

Arris took another sip of his whiskey, his gaze unwavering. "Because she feens for me just as much as I *feen* for her."

True sucked his teeth, shaking his head again. "Man, you deep in this shit. I don't even know what to say." He paused before adding, "So what you want me to do? Act like I didn't just walk in on my best friend breaking up a whole engagement with his dick?"

Arris let out a low chuckle. "Something like that."

True exhaled through his nose, his lips tightening. He wasn't mad—hell, he didn't even like Malik—but this situation was messy as fuck, and Arris was acting like he had it all figured out.

"She got that nigga hand tatted on her breast, my nigga, and you standing here telling me she *feen* for you?" True said, disbelief heavy in his tone. His brows furrowed, his stance tense, like he was trying to process the impossible.

Arris let out a low chuckle, shaking his head at his friend's blindness.

"Nigga, that's my hand." He took a slow sip of his drink, completely unbothered. "You been my best friend since we were kids, and you don't recognize my hand? I know yo ass did it."

True stood frozen, his mind racing. He had seen that hand before, had stared at it long enough to know it looked familiar, but he had been too high at the time to piece it together. Now it hit him like a brick.

True stared at him for a moment, still processing everything. The tattoo, the secrecy, the undeniable pull between them—shit was deeper than he thought. "Man…" He exhaled again, rubbing his temple. "You really got this girl inked up with your hand like you own her."

Arris smirked, taking another slow sip of his drink. "I do own her. Just like she own me—every fucking part of me." His voice dropped, low and cold. "And no nigga—not Malik, not nobody—gonna change that."

True ran a hand down his face, exhaling sharply as the weight of everything settled in. "Damn..you two really deeply in love," he muttered, shaking his head in disbelief.

Arris leaned back against the counter, his expression unreadable, but his tone sharp and unwavering. "Yes, nigga. "That's my baby—no, my wife. And nothing's gonna stop that either."

"Look, I ain't saying you wrong for loving her," True admitted. "But Dionne? She got a lot to lose, bruh. She ain't like us. We built for war. She built for peace. So unless you ready to carry her through the fire, you need to figure out what the fuck you really doing."

Arris didn't hesitate. "I been ready, True. She just needs to stop holding onto something that died a long time ago."

True studied him one last time before sighing. "Aight, man. I'll keep my mouth shut—for now. But you know Dionne, she ain't gon' be able to hide this shit forever. She gotta make a choice."

Arris finished his drink and placed the glass down. "She already made it. She just don't know it yet."

True let out a low whistle, shaking his head. "Damn, nigga. You really in deep."

Arris smirked. "The deepest."

Before True could respond, they both heard the sound of the shower shutting off upstairs. Arris stretched, rolling his shoulders like he was getting ready for round two.

"You staying or you heading out?" Arris asked casually.

True gave him an incredulous look. "Nigga, I just caught y'all, and you tryna go back for seconds?"

Arris shrugged. "You already seen what's up. Ain't no point in

Feenin'

stopping now."

True held up his hands in surrender, already heading toward the door. "Yeah, I'm out. Y'all wild." He paused at the doorway, looking over his shoulder. "But hey, when this shit blows up? Don't say I ain't warn you."

Arris smirked, watching as True left, then turned his attention back upstairs. He could hear Dionne moving around in her room, probably still trying to process everything.

He licked his lips, already imagining her body tangled with his again. Fuck a secret. She was *his*, and soon, everybody would know it.

***

Arris ended a call, a satisfied smirk still tugging at his lips as he navigated through the city's glowing skyline. He had just gotten off the phone with one of his medical contacts—an executive on the Medical Board. Thanks to his mother's long-standing reputation in the field and the extensive business connections he built across the city, pulling strings was never an issue for him.

After hearing about Malik cheating on Dionne, he couldn't sit back and do nothing. Part of it was about protecting her, but most of it was personal. Getting back at the man who had the woman he wanted more than anything in this world. He was tired of playing second to a nigga who didn't deserve her, sick of watching her wear another man's ring while knowing her heart belonged to him. Every time she had to play fiancée, it gnawed at his patience, inflaming the anger and abandonment issues he kept buried deep.

So he did what he thought was right—what he knew would show who really had power. Who really had Dionne's heart.

The vibration of his phone snapped him from his thoughts, pulling his attention down to the screen. His brows furrowed slightly when he saw the name flashing across it—his father. Since their talk, Calvin had been making an effort, reaching out more, trying to mend what was broken. Arris wasn't sure how he felt about it. He wasn't ready to fully forgive, but he was exhausted from carrying the resentment. With his mother giving Calvin another chance, he figured he could at least try.

With a deep breath, he answered. "Wassup, Calvin?"

"Aye, son. You wanna come by the bar?" Calvin's voice came through the speaker, easygoing and filled with a warmth Arris still wasn't used to. "You can help me take these niggas' money in pool."

Arris chuckled despite himself. Calvin had been doing his best, reaching out, trying to build something between them. And while it was unfamiliar—sometimes overwhelming—Arris couldn't deny that a part of him wanted this. Wanted his father in his life.

He wasn't putting his all into it yet, not ready to risk being let down again. But he was trying.

"Aight," Arris finally said, turning the wheel in the direction of the bar Calvin always went to. "I'm headed there now."

Arris stepped out of his car, pulling out his phone to send Dionne his usual daily message—letting her know he was thinking about her and hoping her day was going well. It had become routine, something small, but necessary for him. A way to keep her close even when they were apart.

Sliding his phone back into his pocket, he walked into the bar, immediately greeted by the deep thrum of old-school R&B and the hum of conversation. The air smelled of whiskey, cigars, and the faint scent of fried food from the kitchen. The crowd was older, men and women posted up at the bar nursing their drinks, others occupied with slot machines or standing around the pool tables, engaged in heavy betting.

Arris spotted Calvin in the back, holding down a table with two other men standing around him. He walked over, dapping his father up with a firm handshake.

"Now you niggas really about to lose," Calvin said with a wide grin, hyping up his friends as they chuckled, taking swigs of their beers.

"Arris, these my boys—Lucky and Frank. We ran the streets together back in the day," Calvin introduced, nodding toward the two men beside him.

Arris gave both men a firm handshake. "Wassup, I'm Arris."

Lucky eyed him up and down before smirking. "Man, Calvin, this boy your twin."

Calvin grinned proudly, but Arris clenched his jaw, his fingers subtly tightening around his pool stick. He had heard that shit all his life, and it never sat right with him. Even though they were working on their relationship, the last thing he wanted was to be compared to the man who had spent most of his life absent.

Still, he let the comment roll off, chuckling darkly before turning his attention back to the game.

The match started, Arris lining up his shot against Lucky. He aimed, the cue ball striking with precision, sinking a solid into the corner pocket. He barely took a breath before he moved to his next shot, knocking in another ball with smooth confidence.

Frank whistled low, nodding in approval. "Damn, Calvin. He might be better than you."

Calvin laughed, slapping his hand against the table. "That's my fuckin' son, what you expect?"

Feenin'

Arris's grip tightened around the cue stick, his jaw clenching again at Calvin's words. That father-son shit was getting to him, but he masked it, keeping his expression unreadable. He exhaled through his nose, pushing the irritation down as he lined up his next shot. He was here for a game of pool, nothing more.

At least, that's what he kept telling himself.

The game continued, and unsurprisingly, Arris came out on top. The night unfolded the way most nights in a bar full of old heads did—loud debates over sports, stories about women, and money exchanging hands over pool bets. The easy camaraderie almost made Arris forget the lingering tension that always seemed to exist between him and Calvin. Almost.

As the night wore on, Arris and Calvin stepped out of the bar, still laughing over their last sports argument.

"Aight, son, this shit was fun," Calvin said, pride clear in his tone.

Arris smirked, nodding. "Yeah, it was cool. Got some money off y'all old asses, though."

Calvin chuckled, shaking his head. He glanced at his watch, then cursed under his breath. "Damn, yo mama gon' kill me if I don't get my ass home."

Arris let out a low laugh. He was still wrapping his head around the fact that his parents were back together. It didn't seem real, even now.

"I still can't believe she really took your ass back," Arris said bluntly, shaking his head.

Calvin smirked, rubbing his jaw. "Man, it took a lot of fucking begging and pleading, but it worked. I was serious, Arris. I wanna make things right—not just with your mama, but with you and your sister, too." He placed a firm hand on Arris's shoulder, his gaze steady.

Arris exhaled, his chest tightening at the words. That's all he ever wanted—for his father to just be there. For their family to be whole, even if it was years too late.

"Don't fuck it up," Arris said simply, his voice low but full of meaning.

Calvin nodded, understanding the weight behind the words.

"I should be heading out, though. Got my own woman to talk to when I get home," Arris said, the thought of Dionne instantly coming to mind.

Calvin raised a brow, clearly intrigued. "Will me and your mama be meeting this woman soon?" he asked with a knowing smirk.

Arris chuckled but hesitated. The thought of Dionne meeting Angel? No problem. His mama would love her. But Calvin? That was something else entirely. How could he introduce her to the man he spent most of his life resenting?

"I don't know," Arris admitted, his voice quieter now.

Calvin picked up on his hesitation and nodded, respecting it. "I get it."

They dapped up, a silent agreement passing between them.

"See you later, A," Calvin said before heading to his car.

Arris watched him drive off, gripping the steering wheel as he sat in his own car. He took a deep breath, exhaling slowly.

This shit was crazy. Twenty years of hatred, resentment, and disappointment—and now, somehow, they were here. Building something.

He wasn't sure what it was yet, but for the first time, he didn't feel the weight of it so heavy on his chest.

***

Dionne sat curled up on the couch, her fingers lightly tracing over the screen of her phone as she reread Arris's message. He was telling her about his night with Calvin, about the effort he was making to mend old wounds. Her heart warmed at the thought—seeing him take that step toward healing, toward forgiving his father, was something she knew wasn't easy for him.

A soft smile played on her lips, her body still aching from the night before. Since Malik had worked through the night, Arris and Mia ended up lingering at her place long after True had left. They'd spent the evening wrapped up in each other, watching movies, stealing lazy kisses, and soaking in the kind of peace she only felt when she was with him.

Now, she missed him more than ever. She wanted to be in his arms, but he was busy, so seeing him wasn't an option. The ache of longing settled deep in her chest, but it wasn't just Arris on her mind. The weight of her secrets was pressing down on her—Kierra knowing, True knowing—it was all unraveling faster than she could control. Arris assured her that True wouldn't say anything, but that wasn't enough to calm her nerves. Every day, it felt like the truth was clawing its way to the surface, and she was running out of ways to bury it.

The sound of the front door opening pulled her from her thoughts. Her heart clenched, and she quickly locked her phone, tucking it beside her just as Malik stepped in. His presence filled the space, heavy and tense, his footsteps carrying a quiet storm of exhaustion and anger.

His dark eyes landed on her. "We have another unexpected guest today?" Malik asked, his voice laced with pettiness as his gaze swept around the room like he was looking for something—or someone.

Feenin'

Dionne exhaled sharply, already irritated. "Stop being an asshole, Malik," she said, her focus still on the TV, unwilling to entertain his energy.

"Just saying," Malik shrugged, his tone cool but cutting. "You inviting niggas over and shit."

Dionne's patience snapped. She turned her head, eyes narrowing. "First of all, Arris was here for business," she lied effortlessly, her voice steady.

Malik let out a humorless chuckle, shaking his head. "Yeah? What kind of business requires tacos and bringing his daughter along? And don't think I didn't see how y'all were looking at each other. How you put your hand on his chest like you really thought he were about to check me when I walked in." His voice had edged into something deeper now, laced with suspicion and irritation.

Dionne sat up straighter, meeting his hostility head-on. "First of all, nigga, if you're gonna assume shit, at least get your facts straight." Her voice was sharp, cutting through the air between them. "Mia is not his daughter. She's his niece—one of Karmen's students. I met her through Karmen. And as for Arris, he's a business partner, and our companies are in the middle of a deal. If you need to see paperwork to settle your insecure ass, I'll be happy to provide it."

Her words cut deep, and she knew it. But she didn't care. Malik had been doing whatever he wanted for years, fucking around behind her back, neglecting their relationship, treating her like an obligation instead of a woman. And now, suddenly, he wanted to play the role of a jealous fiancé?

Malik clenched his jaw, but she saw the flicker of something in his eyes. He wasn't stupid—he knew what this was. This wasn't about love. It hadn't been for a long time. They were still together because of a promise to Mama Glen, and they both knew it.

Dionne didn't flinch under his gaze. If he was finally realizing that, then good. He should've known it a long time ago.

"And lastly," Dionne continued, her voice steady but sharp, "I stopped him because, let's be real, Arris can beat your ass. If we're being honest, you should be thanking me instead of coming at me with this bullshit."

She watched as Malik's jaw tightened, his hands clenching into fists at his sides. The truth stung, and she knew it.

"Man, just tell me you fucking the nigga," Malik snapped, his anger bubbling over as he threw his stuff down. "Ain't like you want my ass anyway."

Dionne let out a bitter laugh, shaking her head. "I don't want you, Malik. And you don't want me either."

His eyes flickered with something—denial? Guilt? He opened his mouth, then hesitated.

"I do," he said finally, but even he didn't sound convinced.

Dionne scoffed, stepping closer, her words cutting through the air between them. "No, you don't. You want me because Mama Glen wants you to marry me. That's it. That's all this has ever been." Her voice wavered slightly, but her resolve held strong. "I'm tired of falling for the lies. Tired of pretending you actually love me. Tired of pretending I don't know what this really is. I'm just a fucking trophy to you, Malik, and I've accepted that. If staying in this fake-ass engagement gives the woman I love her last wish, then so be it."

Silence stretched between them, heavy and suffocating. Malik stood frozen, his lips slightly parted like he wanted to argue—but nothing came out. Because she was right.

"Dionne..." he started, his voice barely above a whisper.

"Tell me I'm wrong, Malik." She stepped even closer, staring straight into his eyes, daring him to lie to her face.

He said nothing.

"TELL ME!" she screamed, the years of frustration, heartbreak, and exhaustion breaking through all at once.

Malik's shoulders slumped, his silence saying everything she needed to hear.

Dionne exhaled slowly, her chest rising and falling as she steadied herself. "You don't have to. I already know."

Malik could feel himself losing the argument, so he reached for something he hoped would shift the blame—something that had been fueling his frustration all day. "I'm suspended from the hospital," he admitted, his voice laced with frustration.

Dionne froze for a second, genuinely caught off guard. But she quickly masked her shock with a blank stare. "What? Why?" she asked, her tone calm but distant.

Malik sighed heavily, running a hand down his face. "The news about me and Nurse Brittany messing around got out, and someone reported it to the Medical Board. I got called into a meeting, and now I'm under investigation for an inappropriate relationship with a subordinate." His voice was laced with stress, the weight of it all pressing down on him.

Dionne, however, didn't flinch. "Well, it's the truth," she said flatly, making Malik glare at her.

Feenin'

"So you don't care that my job is threatening to fire me if I can't prove this is false?!" he snapped, his anger bubbling over. He expected at least a shred of concern from her.

Dionne tilted her head, unimpressed. "Why would I care? Isn't that the same bitch you were cheating on me with, Malik?" Her voice was steady, sharp like a knife.

Malik's jaw tightened. His suspicion flared. "Did you tell the board?"

Dionne's expression darkened, her patience wearing thin. "Why the fuck would I report my own fiancé for sleeping with a nurse?" Her sarcasm was thick, anger creeping into her tone. "What the fuck do I get out of that?"

Malik didn't back down. "Well, you bring it up every chance you get—even though I've apologized a thousand times. Who's to say you didn't try to get revenge by getting me fired?"

Dionne let out a dark chuckle, shaking her head in disbelief as she clenched her fists at her sides. "First, you accuse me of cheating with a business partner. Now, I'm trying to sabotage your career?" Her voice rose with every word, the fury in her eyes making Malik shift uncomfortably. He knew how ridiculous he sounded, but he was desperate.

"How about this, Malik?" she continued, her voice sharp as a blade. "Instead of accusing me of some shit I didn't do, maybe you should stop fucking the bitches you work with. Or better yet, make sure the bitches you cheat with don't run their mouths. Or—and this is an even better idea—how about you keep your fucking dick in your pants?" She was yelling now, her patience completely snapped.

Malik exhaled, guilt flashing across his face. "I'm sorry—"

"Save that shit." Dionne cut him off, already standing and sliding her feet into her fuzzy Balenciaga slides. She didn't care about his apology. She didn't care about his job. And at this moment, she damn sure didn't care about Malik.

She turned on her heel, grabbing her purse and keys.

"Where are you going, Dee?" Malik finally spoke, his voice hoarse, almost desperate.

"Anywhere but here." She didn't even glance back as she grabbed her jacket.

Malik watched her, jaw tight, but the anger in his eyes flickered with something else—regret.

"The contract for me and Arris's business deal is on my desk if that makes you feel better," she added, her tone clipped, but there was an undeniable finality in her voice.

Ann

She reached for the doorknob, pausing just long enough to deliver one last blow. "And I really hope you figure out who outed you and your little girlfriend. Because when you do, I hope you feel like shit knowing it wasn't me."

With that, she pulled the door shut behind her, leaving Malik standing in the silence of his own guilt.

He exhaled, rubbing a hand down his face as the weight of his accusation settled. He had been so caught up in his own frustration, in his desperation to keep a grasp on something that had slipped through his fingers long ago, that he lashed out at the one person who had always been solid.

Their love was gone—he knew that. But even in the wreckage of what they used to be, Dionne wasn't that type of woman. And he knew that, too.

Yet, the question still remained.

Who was trying to set him up?

Malik didn't have the answer.

But the man who did was the same man who had already stepped into his place. The man who held Dionne's heart now. A man who would protect her with every bone in his body—even if it meant protecting her from her own fiancé.

Malik, still skeptical about her and Arris despite her words, walked into her office, his eyes immediately scanning the desk. His breath hitched slightly when he saw the business deal between Dionne and Arris, the official documents laid out in plain sight. His jaw clenched as he flipped through the pages, each one confirming what she had said.

She wasn't lying.

He exhaled deeply, rubbing his hands down his face as tension drained from his shoulders. So she wasn't cheating—at least, not in the way he thought. But something still didn't sit right. The way she looked at Arris, the way she shut him down so easily tonight... that wasn't just business. That was something deeper. Something real.

And if he didn't make things right soon, he was going to lose her.

Meanwhile, Dionne gripped the steering wheel tightly as she drove toward Karmen's house, her mind swirling with too many thoughts, too many emotions. She needed to get out of that house. Away from Malik. Away from the weight of all the secrets she was carrying, secrets that were getting heavier by the day.

Karmen had invited all the girls over for a game night, and right now, that was exactly what she needed—an escape. A few hours to pretend everything was normal, to drown herself in laughter, drinks, and

Feenin'

whatever chaos the night would bring.

But even as she pulled up to Karmen's house, parking in the driveway, she knew deep down that the peace she was looking for wouldn't last long. The truth was closing in on her. And sooner or later, she'd have no choice but to face it.

***

Day Before Thanksgiving:

Dionne stepped out of her car, locking the door behind her as she grabbed the bags of groceries her father had sent her to pick up. The crisp November air carried the scent of the approaching holiday season, and despite the chaos in her personal life, she couldn't help but feel a small spark of joy. Thanksgiving had always been her favorite time of year—a moment to pause, to be with family and friends, and now that Demetrius and Kierra had officially decided to stay in Houston, it meant even more. Having them around permanently, watching her nephew grow up close to her, and knowing she played a part in helping them settle into a new home filled her with a sense of pride she hadn't felt in a long time. And she owed a lot of that to Arris.

She smiled to herself, thinking about how involved he had been in making sure Demetrius took the deal that brought him back home. Her job was to find them the perfect house, and knowing how much it meant to them made the responsibility even more rewarding.

Like every year since she was a child, the day before Thanksgiving was dedicated to helping her father in the kitchen. It was a tradition she looked forward to, one of the few constants in her life that still held pure joy. But this year, she was especially eager for it—not just for the tradition, but because it gave her a much-needed escape from Malik.

Since his suspension, Malik had been unbearable. Hovering over her every move, constantly looking for an argument, questioning where she was, who she was with, and worst of all, embarrassing her with his nonstop calls whenever she stepped outside. His paranoia had reached a suffocating level, and though he had no real proof, she knew in his gut, he felt her slipping away. And he wasn't wrong.

But she wasn't about to let him ruin her time with her family.

The only thing missing from her holiday plans was Arris. She wanted nothing more than to be with him, to be wrapped up in his arms, even if just for a moment. But he was away on a business trip, something she had no choice but to accept. And even if he was in town, Malik's overbearing nature would have made it nearly impossible to see him.

That didn't stop her from finding small ways to stay connected. The second she had a free moment, she was on FaceTime with Arris, sending him messages about how much she missed him, counting down the days until she could see him again.

His trip had taken him to Africa for a charity event, something that only made her fall for him more. He was the type of man who didn't just make money—he gave back. He used his power and resources to help others, and that was something Malik never understood.

"Daddy!" Dionne called out as she stepped into the house, the warmth of home immediately wrapping around her. The familiar scent of seasoned meats and fresh herbs already lingered in the air, signaling that Lamar had been in his element for hours.

From the kitchen, her father appeared wearing his signature apron—of course, with no shirt on, his toned arms flexing as he moved, long black sweatpants hanging low on his hips.

Dionne shook her head, laughing at the sight. "Put a shirt on!" she teased as he grabbed the grocery bags from her hands with ease.

"Yo mama like it," he shot back with a smirk.

As they walked into the kitchen, there was Danita sitting at the island, a glass of wine in hand, watching her husband with adoration, just like she always did.

Dionne chuckled, catching the way her mother's gaze lingered on Lamar, full of admiration and love. Even after all these years, their affection for each other was unwavering. It was the kind of love Dionne had always dreamed of, the kind she once thought she had with Malik—the kind she now only felt with Arris.

"Hey, Ma," Dionne greeted, stepping over to hug her mother.

"Hey, Dooda," Danita said with a knowing smile, clearly aware her daughter had caught her staring at her husband again.

Lamar had already begun unloading the groceries, setting everything out with precision, ready to create the masterpiece he did every year. Thanksgiving at the Smith house wasn't just a meal—it was an event. His feast was legendary, requiring a full day of cooking, which is why they always prepped the night before.

The menu was set, as it always was: a perfectly roasted turkey, dressing with his famous sweet cranberry sauce made from scratch, creamy mashed potatoes, collard greens, baked mac and cheese, sweet candied yams, chitterlings, juicy honey-glazed ham, crispy fried chicken, buttery cornbread, and honey-baked rolls. And that was just dinner.

Dessert was a whole other masterpiece—his signature sweet potato pie, pecan pie, and peach cobbler, the last of which Dionne had officially claimed as her specialty. After years of perfecting the recipe, she had finally beaten her father's, a fact she loved to remind him of.

Feenin'

As the preparations began, the kitchen filled with the sounds of laughter, the clinking of pots and pans, and the occasional sip of wine as Dionne and her father cooked side by side. The lighthearted teasing between her parents, the smell of home-cooked food, the warmth of family—it was the kind of moment she cherished, the kind that reminded her, despite all the chaos in her life, this was where she truly belonged.

"Are Karmen and London coming for Thanksgiving?" Danita asked, her voice full of excitement as she glanced at Dionne.

Dionne turned around with a smile. "Of course. You know they don't miss a Smith Thanksgiving. Ever since college, they've been hooked on Daddy's cooking."

Danita chuckled, pleased that her daughter had such strong, lasting friendships. Just as Dionne turned back to help with the food, her phone vibrated loudly on the counter.

"Dionne, your phone is ringing," Danita announced, peering at the screen. "Who's Arris?"

At the sound of his name, Dionne's entire body tensed. Without thinking, she rushed forward, snatching the phone from the counter. Danita blinked in surprise at her urgency, her brows raising slightly.

"Just a client," Dionne said quickly, her voice too forced, too rehearsed. "I need to take this." Without giving her mother time to question further, she hurried into a nearby room, closing the door behind her.

The moment she was alone, she exhaled deeply, pressing the green button.

"Damn, Mama," Arris' deep, teasing voice greeted her, his smirk clear even through the screen. "What took you so long to answer the phone?"

Dionne rolled her eyes, but the warmth in her chest was undeniable. Just seeing his face, the way his lips curved up slightly, sent her heart racing again. "I'm cooking," she answered, trying to steady her breathing. The thought of her mother finding out about Arris—or worse, the depth of her love for him—made her stomach flip.

"What you cookin'?" he asked, licking his lips, his gaze slowly roaming over her face.

She blushed under his stare. "Food for tomorrow," she said softly, suddenly forgetting all about the simmering pots and the fact that she was supposed to be helping in the kitchen.

Arris let out a low chuckle. "Didn't mean to interrupt, Mama," he murmured, his voice smooth and full of affection. "I just wanted to see your beautiful face. Just got back in town, heading home now."

Ann

"How was your trip?" Dionne asked, tucking a loose curl behind her ear.

Arris smirked knowingly. He could tell she wanted to keep talking, wanted to stay on the phone just a little longer. Truth be told, so did he.

"I'll tell you about it when I see you," he said, his tone softer now. "Enjoy your time with the family, baby."

"Okay," she whispered, not wanting to hang up just yet.

There was a pause before Arris spoke again, his voice quieter but firm. "I love you, Mama."

A slow smile spread across Dionne's lips. "I love you too, baby," she said, her voice just as tender.

The call ended, but the warmth he left behind lingered. She stood there for a moment, staring at the dark screen, still feeling the way his presence wrapped around her like a comforting embrace.

Letting out another deep breath, she shook her head, trying to pull herself together before walking back out. But even as she stepped back into the kitchen, the flutter in her heart refused to settle.

Danita's curious gaze met Dionne the moment she stepped back into the kitchen. Lamar, on the other hand, stayed focused on preparing the food, wisely choosing not to interfere in women's business.

"A client calling you during the holidays?" Danita asked, a knowing smile playing on her lips, her voice laced with curiosity. She had seen the way Dionne's body reacted when she read Arris' name on the screen—the slight panic, the way her eyes lit up in something that looked a lot like love before she rushed off to answer.

Dionne playfully rolled her eyes, already seeing where this was going. "Arris Black is our new and big partner for the firm. We're handling all the commercial real estate for his business." She explained it quickly, keeping her voice even, hiding just how much Arris really meant to her.

Danita's smirk deepened. "Arris Black? I've heard that name before." Her eyes glimmered with recognition as she tried to place it.

"He's also played with Demetrius in baseball back in the day," Dionne added, hoping that tidbit would be enough to keep her mother from digging deeper.

Danita snapped her fingers as the connection finally clicked. "Oh, AB! That boy was something else back in the day!" Lamar turned around now, his interest piqued.

"He gave your brother a run for his money when they played against each other," Lamar chimed in. "Boy could pitch his ass off. He was younger, but damn near unstoppable." His voice held a note of nostalgia

Feenin'

and respect.

Dionne's smile grew as she listened, realizing how close Arris had always been to her world without her ever knowing. She had missed a lot of Demetrius' games growing up—her sickness had kept her in and out of hospitals—but hearing her father speak so highly of Arris made her feel like she was discovering another layer of him she never knew.

"It's sad what happened to him in college, though," Lamar added, shaking his head.

The smile on Dionne's face faltered. "What happened?" she asked, her tone now filled with concern.

Before Lamar could answer, the sharp vibration of her phone interrupted them. She glanced down and instantly rolled her eyes in frustration.

Malik.

Danita didn't miss the change in her daughter's expression, the way her entire mood shifted from curiosity to irritation in an instant. Her motherly instincts flared—something wasn't right.

Dionne wanted to decline the call and continue the conversation, but she knew Malik. If she didn't answer now, he would just keep calling, over and over, his possessiveness growing stronger by the minute.

"Sorry, Daddy, I have to take this," she sighed, stepping into the living room with her phone pressed against her ear.

Danita watched her go, her smile fading. Something was definitely wrong, and she intended to find out what.

"What, Malik?" Her voice was low, but the ice in her tone was unmistakable.

"It's getting late, Dionne." His voice carried a sharp edge, more demand than concern.

Dionne rolled her eyes so hard it nearly hurt. She pulled the phone away briefly, glaring at it as if Malik were standing in front of her.

"So? I'm still at my parents' house cooking." Her attitude was clear, laced with exhaustion from the same argument, the same toxic cycle.

"Did you forget you have a man at home?" His voice hardened, the possessiveness in it grating on her nerves. Then she caught it—that slight slur in his words.

Her lips curled in frustration. "Nigga, are you drunk?"

She hadn't meant to raise her voice, but the disbelief was too strong to contain. That was another thing Malik had picked up now that he wasn't working—drinking. What started as one or two glasses a night had quickly turned into four, sometimes five, and it was grating on her last nerve.

Malik exhaled into the phone, his tone shifting from anger to something meant to be seductive. Instead, it made Dionne's stomach turn. "Yeah, and I miss my woman."

Her skin crawled.

"I'll be home in the morning, Malik." Her voice was firm, no room for discussion.

She could hear his irritation building. "The morning?! I want you now, Dee. We haven't had sex in months, and I miss you." His words slurred, his tone switching from demanding to pathetic in the span of a second.

Dionne clenched her jaw, inhaling deeply, forcing herself to stay composed. She wasn't about to let this nigga ruin her night. Not here. Not in her parents' house.

"I will see you in the morning, Malik. When you're sober." Her voice was sharp but quiet, keeping her emotions in check.

A muffled "Man, aight." came through the line, followed by a loud thud—probably his phone hitting the wall, knowing his childish tantrums.

She ended the call, her fingers tightening around her phone as she fought the urge to scream. This was supposed to be her escape—time with her family, time away from the obligation, the chaos, and the heavy weight Malik kept throwing on her shoulders. At first, she had found it amusing when someone outed him for messing with Brittany, but now she wished his job would take him back just so he could leave her the hell alone.

By the time she re-entered the kitchen, she had forced a smile onto her face, pushing down the frustration clawing at her chest.

Danita caught it, though. She always did. "Everything okay, sweetie?" Her voice was gentle, but her eyes scanned Dionne's face, noticing the slight wrinkle in her forehead—a telltale sign of stress or anger.

Dionne put on her best carefree smile. "Yes, Ma. Let's just get back to this delicious-smelling food and this wine!" She lifted her glass, determined to let the alcohol drown out Malik's bullshit, if only for the night.

Danita smiled, clinking her glass against Dionne's.

But, when Dionne lifted her wine glass to her lips, Danita's eyes caught the absence of her engagement ring, making her curiosity instantly spike.

"Dee, where's your ring?" Danita asked, her tone light but probing.

Dionne froze for a split second, her gaze flickering to her bare finger

Feenin'

wrapped around the glass. She hadn't worn that ring in days.

Maybe part of her was just tired of pretending. Maybe Malik's recent actions had made the decision easier.

But she still had to keep up the act in front of her parents.

"It's getting cleaned," she said smoothly, taking a slow sip of her wine.

Danita nodded, believing her.

And just like that, the lie settled between them.

Lamar, sensing the shift, cranked up the music, and just like that, the kitchen filled with warmth and laughter again. They talked, they danced, they cooked until exhaustion finally won over. And for a few hours, Dionne let herself pretend everything was just as it should be.

***

Thanksgiving:

Arris stepped into his mother's house, immediately greeted by the sounds of laughter and conversation echoing from the living room. The familiar warmth of home wrapped around him, but he could already sense the undercurrent of tension lingering beneath the holiday cheer.

True and Mario were posted up on the couch, locked in a game of dominoes with Calvin. Arris dapped them up, offering a nod before making his way to the kitchen, where his mother and A'Lani were setting up the Thanksgiving feast.

"Hey, Ma. It smells good in here," Arris complimented, the rich aroma of spices and seafood filling his senses.

Angel turned around with a bright smile, immediately pulling him into a hug. "Hey, baby. Glad you made it."

He hugged his sister next, lowering his voice just enough for only her to hear. "You good?"

A'Lani gave a short nod, her lips pressed together. She didn't have to say much for Arris to know how she felt. Spending Thanksgiving with their father for the first time in years wasn't easy, and even though she promised to be on her best behavior for their mother's sake, the storm in her eyes told Arris just how much of a battle she was fighting.

He leaned in slightly. "I got you. Whenever you ready to go, we out."

A'Lani gave another subtle nod, focusing on the food instead of the emotions she was barely keeping in check.

"Food's ready!" Angel called out, snapping the tension just in time as the men gathered around the table.

Everyone quickly made their plates, the spread far from the traditional turkey and stuffing. Angel had put together a full seafood boil—juicy crab legs, crawfish, fried catfish, corn on the cob, sausage, potatoes, gumbo, dirty rice, and honey-baked cornbread. The rich aroma of Cajun spices and butter filled the air, making Arris' stomach tighten with hunger. He didn't waste any time digging in as the family settled around the table.

Conversation flowed easily at first, but as expected, Calvin attempted to bridge the gap that had been broken for years.

"A'Lani, how's school going?" Calvin asked, his tone careful but hopeful.

A'Lani didn't even blink in his direction. She didn't acknowledge him, didn't pause her movements, just kept eating as if he hadn't spoken at all.

Silence stretched across the table, thick and suffocating. All eyes darted from A'Lani to Calvin, but no one spoke.

Angel, ever the peacemaker, quickly stepped in to shift the mood. "Mario, where's my grandbaby? I was hoping to see her today. You know she loves seafood."

Mario's lips twitched into a small smile, clearly grateful for the change in topic. "She's spending Thanksgiving with her mom this year, but she'll be here for Christmas."

Angel nodded, though a slight frown tugged at her lips. "Is Briana acting any better?" she asked cautiously, knowing the strain between Mario and his child's mother.

Mario exhaled through his nose, shaking his head. "No, but I'm handling it."

The conversation took a lighter turn as Angel turned her attention to True, her eyes sharp with curiosity.

"So, True, who's the special woman?" she asked, making him snap his head up from his plate like a deer caught in headlights.

"Huh?" True feigned cluelessness, chewing a little slower as if that would somehow save him.

Angel rolled her eyes playfully. "Nigga, stop playing with me. You missed the last three Sunday dinners, and that's unusual as hell because you love my cooking. So, either you died, or there's a woman in your life feeding you better than I do."

Laughter broke out around the table, Mario shaking his head while A'Lani smirked, watching True scramble for a response.

True exhaled, knowing he couldn't get out of this one. "Don't nothing get past you, Ma," he admitted, setting his fork down. "Her name's London. She cool." He tried to sound casual, but the slight smirk tugging at his lips gave him away.

Angel leaned forward, her interest piqued. "Seems like more than

Feenin'

just cool, but I won't pry—for now." She paused, then turned her teasing attention elsewhere. "At least one of my sons is finding love."

Arris felt her words hit him dead on, but he kept his expression neutral, sipping his drink to avoid the conversation swinging his way.

True, always the instigator, decided he wasn't going down alone. "Mario's simp ass is in love too."

Mario sucked his teeth, but the grin breaking through his front exposed him. "Man, shut up."

"Ouu, with who?!" A'Lani perked up, fully invested now.

Mario exhaled, trying to keep his cool, but the second he said her name, his whole demeanor softened. "Her name's Karmen. She's Mia's kindergarten teacher."

His smile was damn near splitting his face in half, and Angel and A'Lani exchanged glances before matching his grin.

"Oh, I like this already." Angel clapped her hands together. "So, when am I meeting these women? I need to approve before y'all get too deep."

"It's too early, Ma," True said, shaking his head, his tone cool but his smirk telling.

Mario, on the other hand, didn't hesitate. "You'll definitely meet her soon, Ma," he said, sounding damn near whipped.

"That woman got his ass hooked," Calvin joked, chuckling along with the boys, but A'Lani didn't find any humor in it.

Arris let the conversation move past him, relieved no one had shifted the spotlight onto him. While his heart belonged to Dionne, their situation was far too complicated to bring to his family's dinner table. His mother might've been nosy, but even she wasn't ready for that truth.

"Arris, I heard you're stepping back into baseball again. The new owner of the Houston Comets—I'm proud of you," Angel said, her smile warm as she looked at her son.

Arris grinned, pride swelling in his chest. Stepping back into baseball was something he never thought he'd do again, but partnering with Demetrius was an opportunity too good to pass up. The news had broken just the other day, his name splashed across every sports network. He didn't care about the attention—he was ready to handle business, like always.

"Damn, so you own the whole franchise now?" Calvin spoke up, his eyes lighting up with something that almost looked like pride. Almost.

Arris nodded, keeping his expression neutral. "Yeah, the team's worth about $6.9 billion. Demetrius and I split ownership, so we got it at a discounted price. Came out to about $12.5 million each." He spoke casually, as if dropping that amount on a team wasn't a big deal.

"Damn," Calvin muttered, shaking his head. His tone was unreadable, but A'Lani caught it instantly.

"You should've never told him that," she muttered under her breath, her fork clinking against her plate.

Arris frowned, snapping his head toward her. "What?"

A'Lani's gaze flickered to their father, and then back to Arris, something burning behind her eyes. The room grew still, tension seeping into the air. Angel stiffened in her seat, while True and Mario exchanged wary glances, sensing the storm brewing.

"He can't tell me about his accomplishments?" Calvin asked, his voice carrying that same self-righteous tone that always rubbed A'Lani the wrong way.

Her jaw clenched. "No, because you didn't come back to make amends," she said, her voice even, but laced with something sharp. "You came back because you needed something."

Arris narrowed his eyes, confusion settling deep in his chest. His gaze bounced between A'Lani, Calvin, and Angel, trying to make sense of what the hell was happening.

"Lani, don't," Angel warned, her voice a sharp plea.

"No," A'Lani snapped, turning her fury onto their mother now. "I'm tired of the bullshit. I'm tired of everyone pretending this nigga came back out of the kindness of his heart."

Arris tensed. "What are you talking about?" His voice was low, calm—too calm.

Calvin exhaled heavily, rubbing his hands down his face. "Arris, let's talk outside. Just you and me."

Arris stared at him, his expression darkening. "Nah," he said, shaking his head slowly. "We family, right? So say that shit right here."

Calvin hesitated.

A'Lani let out a bitter laugh. "Exactly. Be honest for once in your sorry ass life," she spat.

"A'LANI, STOP!" Angel's voice boomed across the table, her usual composed demeanor cracking.

But A'Lani wasn't done. Her hands curled into fists at her sides as she took a step back. "And you're no better," she threw at their mother, shaking her head. "Taking this nigga back like he didn't fuck up our family in the first place."

Angel's face hardened, her lips pressing into a thin line, but she didn't respond.

Arris slowly stood, his entire body coiled tight. His patience was

Feenin'

wearing thin.

"What the fuck is going on?" His voice was dangerously low now, demanding answers.

A'Lani grabbed her purse and snatched Arris's keys off the table. "Let him talk to you outside," she said, her tone eerily calm now. "Gives you more space to beat his ass. I'll be waiting in the car."

She turned to True and Mario, her gaze deadly. "True, Mario—y'all might wanna go for backup. Somebody in this bitch *dying* tonight, and it ain't gonna be my brother."

The front door slammed behind her, leaving behind a room full of silence, tension, and unanswered questions.

The room was heavy with silence, thick with tension no one dared to break. Calvin shifted on his feet before finally speaking, his voice low and a little shaky.

"Arris, can we talk outside?"

Arris cut his eyes at him, then glanced at his mother. The nervous look on Angel's face, the slight tremble in her hands as she gripped the napkin in front of her, told him everything he needed to know—whatever Calvin had to say wasn't good. Without another word, he turned and walked out to the backyard, his father trailing behind.

The night air was cool, but it did nothing to ease the heat building in Arris's chest. He shoved his hands into his pockets, jaw clenched tight, his patience hanging by a thin thread.

"Wassup?" His voice was clipped, already defensive.

Calvin took a deep breath. "I really did come back to make things right with you, your mother, and Lani."

Arris stayed still, his stance rigid. He could already hear the but coming.

"But..." Calvin hesitated, and that was all Arris needed to hear.

His head tilted, eyes narrowing to slits. "But what, nigga?" His voice dropped, cold and sharp, cutting through the tension like a blade.

Calvin hesitated again before finally exhaling. "I need some money."

Arris's jaw flexed as he stepped closer, his entire body going stone cold.

Calvin saw the anger flash in his son's eyes but pushed forward. "Before I quit the game for good, I did one last drop. Thought it was gonna set me up for life. It was supposed to be one clean run, one city to the next. But somebody got word, and I was robbed."

Arris stared, his fists twitching in his pockets.

"The product that got stolen? It belonged to somebody serious, son. Nigga's high up, untouchable. He spared my life, but only under one condition—I either come up with the money for his product or pay him back in blood."

Arris inhaled slowly, trying to push down the fury clawing at his chest. His father's words echoed in his mind, but all he could hear was betrayal.

"So you suddenly decided to come back into my life," Arris said, his tone chillingly calm. "Acting like you gave a fuck, all because you needed a bailout?"

Calvin flinched, but he didn't deny it. Instead, he nodded, confirming everything Arris already knew deep down but never wanted to believe.

Arris let out a humorless chuckle, dark and void of warmth. "You played me."

He took another step forward, the abandonment, the hurt, the years of being fatherless—all of it boiling over inside him.

"I didn't play you, son," Calvin tried, his voice pleading now. "Just give me the money, and I swear we can fix this. We can be a family, for real this time."

Arris stared at him, a slow, dangerous smirk stretching across his face, but there was no humor in his eyes.

"Nigga, fuck you."

He turned on his heel and walked away, fists clenched so tight his nails dug into his palms. He had to leave before he did something he'd regret. Because right now? The rage coursing through him was dangerous.

Before Arris could take another step, Calvin's voice cut through the night air, cold and taunting.

"You just like me, son. I know you was in the streets when you was younger. If it wasn't for that baseball coach of yours, you'd still be there."

Arris stopped dead in his tracks, his entire body stiffening. His heart pounded, rage simmering under his skin. He slowly turned around, eyes burning with fury.

"The fuck you just say?" His voice was low, dangerous.

Calvin smirked slightly, sensing he hit a nerve. "Nigga, baseball got you all the shit you have. You just another hood nigga who got lucky. Could've ended up just like me."

Arris took a step forward, his fists clenching at his sides. "I'm nothing like you."

Calvin chuckled, shaking his head. "Take a look in the fucking mirror, son. You are me, through and through. And that's what eats you up inside."

Feenin'

"Shut the fuck up," Arris growled, his voice dangerously low.

"You turned to the streets when shit got tough. Same as me," Calvin continued, ignoring the warning in Arris's tone. "You stayed to yourself because you knew no one could love you the way the streets did. And that's what got you fucked up in college. You got shot on that field because you couldn't let that life go. The thrill was too much, the money too easy, the respect too addicting. And if that damn coach of yours hadn't bailed your ass out, if he hadn't pulled strings to get them charges dropped, you'd be just like me—another washed-up nigga with nothing."

That was it.

Arris saw red.

Before Calvin could get another word out, Arris's fist crashed into his face with all the force he had, sending his father stumbling back. He didn't stop. He hit him again. And again. Each punch carried years of abandonment, pain, and rage.

Calvin had the nerve to speak on shit he had no right to.

The streets had never been about drugs or quick money for Arris—it was about survival. It was about filling the void his father left when he walked out. The *love* he never got from a man who was supposed to be there was found in the streets, in the brotherhood, in the security that money and respect provided.

He had been shot during the College World Series, not because of some street shit he couldn't let go of, but because of envy—because of the legacy his father left behind. Someone wanted to take him out before he could make it further than his father ever did.

And when he survived that? When he fought through the pain and healed? The cops still came for him, dragging him out of that hospital bed on drug charges that weren't even his.

His coach saved him.

Not Calvin.

Not his so-called father.

If it weren't for his coach using his connections, Arris would've rotted in a cell, just another statistic.

And now this nigga—this man who left him, left his mother, left his sister—had the audacity to tell him they were the same?

Arris barely felt his friends yanking him back as his fists kept swinging, blind rage fueling every hit. Blood covered his knuckles, Calvin's face a mess beneath them, and still, it didn't feel like enough.

"Let me go!" Arris roared, his chest rising and falling in deep, seething breaths. True and Mario held on tighter, their grips ironclad, refusing to let him go.

Ann

"Bro, chill! You gon' kill this nigga!" Mario warned, struggling to keep Arris back as he thrashed in their hold.

Angel rushed to Calvin's side, her voice frantic. "Get him inside!" she ordered, completely focused on her bleeding husband.

And that's when Arris felt it—the sharp, gut-wrenching stab of betrayal. His mother, the woman he had always put first, the one he protected at all costs, was tending to him.

To Calvin. Not him. Not her son.

Not the boy who had grown up without his father, who had to learn to be a man by himself.

Arris's vision blurred for a different reason now, his breathing ragged, but he shoved the emotion down before it could fully take hold.

"Man, get the fuck off me!" He snapped, violently shrugging out of Mario and True's hold, his body still vibrating with rage.

"Arris, you gotta calm down," True tried, his voice steady, but Arris wasn't hearing none of that shit.

"Fuck this family," he muttered under his breath, jaw clenched so tight it ached. He turned on his heel and stalked toward the front of the house, his long strides eating up the pavement.

A'Lani was already in the passenger seat of his car, waiting, because she knew.

She knew exactly how this was about to go.

She didn't say a word as he climbed in, the car growling to life beneath his grip. The second he threw it in drive, tires screeched against the pavement, smoke billowing behind him as he peeled off without so much as a glance back.

True and Mario stood in the yard, watching in stunned silence, worry creasing their brows.

They'd never seen Arris like this before.

And that meant one thing—Calvin—Was done.

Chapter 18

Dionne struggled under the dead weight of a drunken, battered Malik, dragging him through the house with pure exhaustion laced in every muscle. The echoes of the night replayed in her mind like a bad fucking dream—except this nightmare was real.

Thanksgiving was supposed to be peaceful, filled with love, laughter, and family. And at first, it was. The vibes had been good—board games being played, the sound of football blaring on the TV, and Mama Glen having one of her better days despite her sickness. Everyone had been caught up in the warmth of the holiday, their glasses raised, their laughter ringing through the house.

Until dinner.

Until Demetrius, beaming with pride, shared the news about his new business deal—becoming the general manager of the Houston Comets and co-owning the franchise alongside his longtime baseball friend. Arris.

And that was all it took for Malik, already deep into his whiskey, to find a reason to lose his shit.

Dionne had barely reacted—maybe she had smiled a little too hard, maybe her pride in her brother and her love for Arris slipped through the cracks of her carefully constructed facade. But to Malik, it was confirmation of everything he'd been accusing her of.

He had snapped—loud and reckless, slurring accusations across the dinner table, throwing a tantrum like a man who had already lost.

"You been fucking that nigga, haven't you?" he had spat, the words dripping with drunken fury.

Dionne had kept her voice calm, controlled, trying to keep the peace in front of their family. "Malik, stop it."

But then he called her a cheating ass bitch.

And that was all it took for Demetrius to snap.

Her brother lunged before anyone could blink, sending Malik flying backward, his chair crashing against the floor. The house erupted into chaos. DJ was screaming, his tiny voice filled with fear, food and glasses flying everywhere as the men crashed into the table, fists swinging, rage crackling in the air like fire.

Dionne had jumped in, desperately trying to pull them apart, but her brother wasn't hearing it. He wasn't stopping until Malik felt what it meant to disrespect his sister.

Their father had jumped in next, the weight of his authority barely holding Demetrius back.

By the time it was over, Malik was barely standing, his face swollen, his lip busted, his pride completely shattered.

And now, here she was—dragging his useless, drunk, and beaten ass through their house, still feeling the weight of the night pressing down on her.

Dionne exhaled deeply, exhaustion wrapping around her like a suffocating weight. She had just spent the entire drive apologizing to Mama Glen for Malik's reckless behavior, knowing damn well she wasn't the one who should've been saying sorry. And now, here she was—dragging his drunk, battered ass into bed when all she really wanted to do was beat his ass again for humiliating her in front of her family.

"I'm sorry, baby," Malik slurred, his words thick with alcohol, his eyes barely open as he reached for her.

Dionne didn't respond. She didn't care.

She pushed him onto the bed with no gentleness, yanking off his shoes as he groaned, barely coherent. The moment his head hit the pillow, he was out cold, the liquor consuming him.

Dionne stared at him for a long moment, the rise and fall of his chest steady, completely unbothered by the storm he had caused tonight.

Her fingers curled into fists at her sides.

She should've left him right there on the damn floor.

Instead, she turned on her heels and walked into the bathroom, needing to scrub the night off her skin.

Hot water cascaded over her, but it did nothing to wash away the anger burning deep inside her. She replayed the night over and over, her emotions swirling into a dangerous mix of frustration and exhaustion.

She hadn't even been thinking about Arris when Demetrius brought up his accomplishments—she had been happy, genuinely proud of her brother. But Malik didn't see that. He saw a reason to project his own insecurities, to humiliate her, to try and make her feel guilty for

Feenin'

something she hadn't even done.

She was tired.

Tired of this obligation.

Tired of this promise.

Tired of taking care of a man who didn't deserve her.

She finished her shower, dried off, and moisturized her skin, slipping into one of her oversized T-shirts before walking back into the bedroom. Malik was still knocked out, his body sprawled across the bed in the same damn clothes, like he hadn't just shattered what little respect she had left for him.

Dionne stared at him, her fingers tightening around the towel she held.

She could feel it.

The weight of it all pressing down on her harder than ever.

She was reaching her breaking point.

Dionne refused to share a bed with Malik after everything that had unfolded tonight. Instead, she retreated to the guest bedroom, slipping under the covers in an attempt to escape the chaos weighing on her. Sleep took over quickly, but just as she began to drift into a deeper rest, her phone vibrated on the nightstand.

The sight of his name on the screen made her heart jump, a smile instantly forming on her lips as she answered without hesitation.

"Hey, baby," she murmured, her voice still laced with sleep, but undeniably soft, filled with warmth.

Silence.

Arris didn't say a word, but she could hear his breathing—deep, heavy, unsteady. The stillness on the other end made her sit up, sleep instantly forgotten.

"Arris?" she called out, concern tightening her chest. "Is everything okay?"

A long pause. Then, finally, his voice broke through the silence, quieter than usual.

"I didn't mean to wake you," he admitted, his tone raw, stripped of its usual confidence. "I just... needed to hear your voice."

Dionne's stomach twisted at the vulnerability in his words. She knew Arris—*really* knew him. And this wasn't like him.

"You didn't wake me," she reassured, her voice gentle but firm. "What's wrong?"

Another pause, this one heavier. When he finally spoke again, his voice cracked.

"I just need to see you. *Badly.*"

Dionne's heart clenched. That crack in his voice, the weight behind his words—it was enough to have her fully awake, wiping the last traces of sleep from her eyes.

"Arris... what's wrong?" she pressed, her concern deepening.

"Just please, come over," he said, his voice lower now, almost desperate. "I need you, Mama."

That was all she needed to hear.

"Come to your house," Arris said, his voice thick with emotion.

And Dionne knew instantly what house he meant.

"I'm on my way," she promised, urgency in her tone as she threw back the covers.

She didn't care that it was two in the morning. She didn't care that she was leaving Malik passed out in a drunken haze, completely oblivious to the fact that she was about to walk out the door. He wouldn't even notice she was gone.

All she cared about was *Arris*.

Because whatever had him sounding like this—she needed to be there for him.

Dionne quickly threw on a pair of baggy gray sweats that still shaped her ass just right, pairing them with a black Essentials hoodie. She slid her feet into her black Travis Scott Dunks before pulling her curly hair into a messy bun, a few strands slipping free. With a quick grab of her keys and an overnight bag she had packed in record time, she rushed out the door, her only focus on getting to Arris.

She sped through the quiet streets, her heart racing just as fast as the car beneath her. The anticipation, the worry—she could feel it all sitting heavy in her chest. When she arrived at the house Arris had purchased for her, she punched in the gate code, watching as the long driveway stretched before her, leading to the place that felt more like home than anywhere else.

Before she could even open her car door, Arris was already there.

Shirtless, his body illuminated by the dim porch lights, he wore only a pair of baggy gray sweats that hung low on his hips. His waves gleamed under the night sky, but it wasn't his appearance that made her pause—it was the energy rolling off of him. Even in the darkness, she could feel it. Something was weighing on him.

Without a word, he reached for her hand, his grip firm, his touch grounding. He took the overnight bag from her other hand as she stepped out, closing her car door behind her. They walked inside together, and the moment Dionne stepped through the threshold, she froze.

The house had been completely remodeled.

Feenin'

Every detail, every inch of the space was exactly how she had always envisioned her dream home to be. The color scheme was deep, warm, and intimate—rich browns and sleek blacks blended seamlessly, making the space feel luxurious yet deeply personal. The front office was pristine, and as she stepped further in, the living room exuded an elegance that was undeniable.

"Arris!" Dionne gasped, her voice filled with excitement, turning to look at him with wide eyes.

A small smile ghosted his lips, but the tension in his body didn't ease. He was still carrying something heavy.

"I'll give you a full tour tomorrow, Mama," he said, his voice lower, controlled.

That was all it took for her excitement to dim slightly. She could hear it now—whatever had him calling her at two in the morning wasn't gone. He was holding it in, but she could feel it pressing against him, like a storm waiting to break.

He led her upstairs, and as soon as they stepped into their bedroom, Dionne's breath hitched.

The space was stunning. The deep mocha and black color scheme was intimate and sultry, the king-size bed taking center stage. Large dressers lined each side of the room, everything polished, and curated to perfection. But it was the walls that made her chest tighten.

Lining the walls were framed photos—photos of them.

Snapshots from their date at the skating rink, candids from their helicopter ride, moments she hadn't even realized were captured. But what stole her breath completely was what hung above their bed.

Black-and-white photographs—intimate ones.

Pictures of them tangled in each other, caught in the rawness of their love. The depth in each shot made her stomach flip. She remembered that night well—a night Arris told her he wanted to photograph their love. The same night they made a sex tape. The pictures looked professional, every angle capturing the way they consumed each other, how they worshiped one another.

Dionne's smile stretched so wide it made her cheeks hurt.

She turned to Arris, ready to say something—anything—but the look in his eyes made her pause. His body was still rigid, his mind clearly somewhere else, and she knew, without question, that whatever happened before she got here wasn't something he could hold in much longer.

Her smile softened as she reached for him, her fingers lightly tracing the tattoos on his chest.

"Baby," she murmured, her voice gentle. "Talk to me."

Arris didn't say a word, just reached for her hands and walked backward until he sat on the edge of the bed, pulling her between his legs. Dionne's heart clenched at the sight of unshed tears glistening in his eyes, his jaw tight like he was holding everything inside.

"Talk to me," she urged, her voice soft, almost pleading.

He shook his head. He wanted to. God, he wanted to let it all out, to spill everything he was holding, but his anger sat too high, too close to the surface. He didn't want to lash out in a way he'd regret. Dionne watched the battle play out in his expression before wordlessly slipping her hands from his grip.

She peeled off her sweats and hoodie, leaving only the deep red lace of her bra and panties. Arris' eyes followed every movement, but it wasn't lust that filled them—it was something deeper. Something unspoken. Something raw.

She climbed onto the bed, leaning back against the headboard, her arms open. "Come here," she murmured.

Arris kicked off his slides and climbed in between her legs, resting his head against her stomach. His arms circled her thighs, locking her to him like she was his anchor. Dionne ran her fingers through his waves, her touch slow and deliberate, grounding him, soothing him. They sat like that in silence, the rise and fall of her breath becoming his only focus, his only calm.

Then he kissed her inner thigh before resting his head back against her. "I was shot, Mama."

Dionne's heart stopped.

She didn't say anything, just held him tighter, her hands continuing their soft, rhythmic motion in his hair. She felt his grip on her legs tighten, like he needed to hold onto something solid. Like he needed to hold onto her.

"It happened on the field. College World Series." His voice was steady, but there was something distant about it, like he wasn't just remembering—he was reliving it.

Dionne swallowed. "Why?" Her voice barely a whisper.

"I was in the streets after Calvin left us. Thirteen years old, doing whatever I could to make sure my family had what they needed. But the streets gave me more than just money—they gave me love." He let out a humorless chuckle, shaking his head against her stomach. "The love my father never gave me."

Dionne's fingers stilled for a second, then continued smoothing over his waves, letting him take his time.

"So I stayed in it," he continued. "Even when I had baseball. I

Feenin'

thought I could do both." His voice cracked slightly, and Dionne felt tears prick her own eyes. "But the streets don't let you just walk away. And right before my last game, they caught up to me."

She wanted to ask more, but she could feel the shift in his energy before he even spoke again. His voice, once heavy with pain, now turned ice-cold.

"I wasn't shot because of the streets, Mama. I was shot because of Calvin."

Dionne pressed a kiss to the top of his head, silently telling him to keep going, that she was here, that she had him.

"One of his opps didn't want another Black in the streets, making moves, building something bigger than them. So they shot me. Right there, on the fucking field." His fists clenched against her legs, his whole body taut with barely restrained rage. "I was done. I chose baseball. I wanted out. But the streets took that from me too. Almost took my life. And all because of him."

Dionne tightened her hold on him, her arms circling his broad shoulders, trying to hold him together while he was unraveling in front of her.

"I served time. And I hated him for that, for all of it. I had to come to terms with the fact that even though I despised my father, I was just like him. I let the streets take me away from my sister, from my mother. But my coach gave me another shot." His voice dropped lower, rougher. "I got out. Changed my whole life around. And now here he is again, pulling me back into his bullshit."

Dionne could feel his body shaking.

His anger was a live wire, wrapping itself around every word he spoke, every breath he took. She didn't try to stop it. She didn't tell him to calm down. She just held him, letting him feel whatever he needed to feel.

Because right now, she was the only thing keeping him from completely losing himself.

Dionne's voice was soft but steady. "What happened?"

Arris let out a deep, shuddering breath, his fists clenching against her thighs. "He played me, Mama. That nigga came back in my life for money. That's all he ever wanted. Not to fix shit. Not to make amends. He needed me to clean up his fucking mess." His voice was thick with anger, but Dionne felt the warmth of a tear hit her skin, breaking her heart.

His body tensed even more, and before she could say anything, his head buried deeper against her stomach, his grip tightening around her.

"He fucking played me! And I let him! I let that nigga play me!" Arris growled, the weight of betrayal thick in his voice.

Dionne's heart twisted at the pain radiating from him. "No, baby. No. Look at me," she urged, her hands threading through his beard, trying to pull him from the darkness clawing at him.

But Arris didn't budge.

"Arris," she said again, this time her tone firm, leaving no room for argument. "Look at me."

Slowly, he lifted his head. His eyes were bloodshot, filled with both rage and pain. Tears slipped down his cheeks, but his jaw remained clenched, his entire body vibrating with barely contained emotion.

Dionne wiped his tears away with her thumbs, cupping his face between her hands. "He didn't play you, baby. He played his fucking self," she said, her voice strong, filled with conviction. "He put you and your family through hell, and yet, you still came out a hundred times better than him." She shook her head, her gaze never leaving his. "You are not like him, Arris. You are better than him. A better man, a better son, a better brother. And one day, you're going to be a better father than he ever could be."

Arris swallowed hard, his chest rising and falling heavily as he took in her words.

"You don't owe that man shit," Dionne continued, her voice fierce with love. "You have to stop giving him the power to hurt you like this. You tried, baby. You tried to forgive him, and I know it hurts like hell knowing it wasn't real on his part, but fuck him." She ran her hands down his arms, grounding him. "Stop giving him the power to do this to you."

Arris exhaled sharply, his head hanging low, his shoulders shaking. "Do you hear me?" Dionne asked, lifting his chin to make him look at her again. "Let it go."

Arris blinked, his lips parting slightly as another tear fell freely down his cheek. He nodded, unable to speak.

"Let it all go," she whispered, leaning in, pressing her lips to his.

Arris melted into her, their kiss deep and slow, their tongues moving in a way that spoke louder than any words. She could feel the desperation in it, the way he was holding onto her, needing her to ground him, to be his safe space.

Dionne pulled back before it could go further, resting her forehead against his. "It's going to be okay, baby," she murmured.

Arris nodded again, his body still tense but slightly less rigid. "I love yo ass so much," he admitted, his voice raw, honest.

Feenin'

Dionne smiled, her heart swelling. "I love you, too. Now, let's get some sleep."

She laid back against the headboard, and Arris instantly repositioned himself between her legs, his head resting against her stomach like before. The tension in his body eased almost immediately as exhaustion weighed him down. His breathing slowed, his eyes fluttering shut.

Dionne watched him for a moment, her fingers absentmindedly running through his waves. Her eyes lifted to one of the framed black-and-white photos above the bed—one of their most intimate moments, frozen in time. She let out a small breath, closed her eyes, and silently prayed.

Prayed for peace.

Prayed for Arris' heart.

Prayed for protection over the man she loved.

Sleep pulled her under soon after, with her hands still tangled in his hair and her heart beating in sync with his.

***

Arris jolted awake, his body still nestled between Dionne's legs. He looked up, his gaze softening as he took in the way her head had tilted to the side, deep in sleep. A small smile tugged at his lips. He knew she was going to wake up with a crook in her neck if he didn't fix her position, but the fact that she slept uncomfortably just to make sure he was at ease made his chest tighten.

Damn, I love the fuck outta her.

Carefully, he eased himself out of bed, adjusting her body so she could lay properly. She stirred slightly, but remained asleep. He pressed a kiss to her forehead before grabbing his stash from the nightstand, needing something to calm the storm still brewing in his mind.

The sky was still dark outside, the clock on the dresser reading 5:15 a.m. Too early for most, but his thoughts wouldn't let him rest. He quietly stepped onto the bedroom's balcony, rolling up with ease before taking a slow drag. The thick smoke curled into the crisp morning air as he exhaled, his mind replaying the chaos of Thanksgiving.

The sharp sting of betrayal. The taste of blood on his fists. The sight of his mother choosing Calvin over him. It all still sat heavy on his chest.

He was so lost in thought that he didn't notice the soft shuffle of feet behind him until warm hands traced the muscles of his back. He turned slightly, instantly met with the sight of Dionne standing there, a small, knowing smile on her face. She had thrown on his hoodie, the oversized fabric swallowing her, but she didn't bother with pants.

"Mama, you gon' get sick. Put some pants on," he muttered, his voice low and gruff from sleep.

She chuckled but ignored him, stepping in front of him and taking the blunt from his fingers. Without hesitation, she brought it to her lips, inhaling deeply before exhaling a perfectly formed O into the air.

Arris smirked, his grip tightening on her hips. "That shit was sexy as fuck," he admitted, his voice laced with admiration.

Before she could respond, he lifted her effortlessly onto the railing, keeping his hands firm around her waist, his arms serving as a harness so she wouldn't fall back.

"You trust me?" he murmured, his voice husky as he stared into her eyes.

Dionne leaned in slightly, her lips just inches from his. "With everything," she whispered.

His grip tightened, his forehead resting against hers as she exhaled another cloud of smoke between them. The air was thick, not just with the haze of weed, but with unspoken emotions—love, longing, and the silent promise that no matter how heavy the world got, she'd always be the one to pull him back.

"How was your Thanksgiving?" Arris asked, taking the blunt from her as she passed it. Dionne rolled her eyes, already dreading the conversation. "I don't want to talk about it," she muttered, exhaling smoke before leaning back against the railing.

Arris studied her, his protective instincts kicking in at the shift in her demeanor. "You good?" His tone was firm, leaving no room for lies.

She nodded, forcing a small smile. "Yes, baby."

He wasn't convinced, but he didn't press, instead pulling her into a slow, lingering kiss. His hold on her tightened, anchoring her in his arms as they fell into a quiet rhythm—passing the blunt back and forth, letting the silence fill the space between them.

Then, Dionne spoke up.

"Arris... would you still love me the same if I didn't look like this?" Her voice was small, uncertain.

Arris frowned slightly, turning his attention fully to her. "What do you mean?"

She hesitated before speaking, her fingers fidgeting with the hem of her hoodie. "If my beauty suddenly disappeared... would you still love me? Would you still look at me the way you do now?"

Arris exhaled smoke, his brows furrowing in confusion before realization settled in.

She wasn't just asking about his love—she was asking if his love for her was conditional. If he only saw her as desirable because of what

Feenin'

she looked like. He knew where this was coming from. Malik. That nigga had done a number on her, and even though she knew Arris wasn't anything like him, the *scars* were still there.

His grip on her waist tightened as he stepped closer, his voice low but steady. "Mama, I don't just love you because of your looks. Yeah, you fine as fuck. But that's not what got me hooked." He paused, making sure she was really hearing him. "It's the way you walk into a room and own that shit without even trying. The way you care for people, the way you love hard, the way you push yourself to be great. The way you soft and strong at the same time. The way you let me see the parts of you nobody else gets to see. That's why I love you. And I fall for you more every single day because of who you are—not because of what you look like."

Dionne felt her throat tighten, warmth spreading through her chest.

Arris smirked slightly, his hands slipping lower to cup her ass. "But even when you old and saggy, I'ma still be on your ass, Mama. So don't even trip."

Dionne rolled her eyes, laughing softly as she pushed at his chest. "You just had to add that, huh?"

"Just making sure you know it's real," he said, still smirking, but there was nothing but sincerity in his eyes.

Her heart swelled, the lingering doubts dissolving into nothing. "Okay, baby," she whispered, her fingers grazing his jaw.

Arris tilted his head slightly, studying her. "Why'd you ask me that? Have I ever made you feel like I only love you for your looks?"

She hesitated. "No… umm."

He caught the flicker of hesitation, his eyes narrowing slightly. He could tell she was battling something in her mind, but she hadn't let it out yet. He didn't rush her, just continued rubbing slow circles over her ass, grounding her in his touch.

"Talk to me, Mama," he urged gently, his voice dropping to that low, soothing tone that always made her feel safe.

Dionne sighed, debating whether she wanted to let this part of herself out. But if there was anyone she could be honest with, it was him.

"I was born with a blood disorder," Dionne began, her voice shaky, eyes cast downward. "It got worse in college, and it changed the way I looked."

Arris' grip on her waist tightened, his jaw locking at the weight of her words. He could already tell where this was going, and the rage inside him was simmering, but he kept it contained—for now.

"Malik and I were together at the time. I thought we were in love, but once the sickness started affecting my appearance, he started acting different." She swallowed, the memories still cutting deep despite how much time had passed. "He became distant... cold. It was like he couldn't even look at me the same. And then, once I healed and started looking like myself again, suddenly he was back—loving, caring, the perfect boyfriend again. That's when I knew..." She paused, taking a shaky breath. "He only ever loved me for how I looked."

Arris' nostrils flared, his hands gripping her thighs tighter as he exhaled sharply. He wanted to say something, wanted to drag Malik's name through the dirt, but he let her finish.

"I just needed to make sure it wasn't the same with you," she admitted, her voice soft, hesitant.

Arris let out the blunt that was now nothing but a smoldering stub, his gaze locking onto hers with an intensity that sent a shiver through her body.

"Mama, I am nothing like that nigga. Or any other nigga who's ever seen you as a trophy," he said, his voice firm, unwavering. "This love shit? It's new for me. But one thing I know for sure— I love every fucking part of you." His fingers traced slow circles into her skin, grounding her. "The way I look at you? That ain't just because of your beauty. It's the way you make me feel when you smile. When you talk. When you're just near me. Your looks? That's just a bonus. But if I gotta remind you every damn day that I'm not here for that—that I *feen* for every part of you—I will."

Dionne felt herself melt at his words, at the conviction behind them. The depth of his love sat between them, undeniable.

"Don't ever let that nigga, or any other nigga—not even me—make you feel like you're just something pretty to be shown off. You are so much more than that, Mama," he said, his voice dipping lower, more intimate.

Dionne nodded, emotion thick in her throat.

"I love you, Mama. Every single part of you," he murmured, his tone softening, his eyes holding hers in a way that made her knees weak.

A slow, genuine smile spread across her lips. "I love you too."

Arris pulled her into a deep, lingering kiss, slow at first, but quickly turning desperate. It wasn't just a kiss—it was a promise. A reassurance. A declaration.

"Now let me show you how much I love you," he whispered against her lips before lifting her into his arms and carrying her back inside.

"If you know life can be gone in the blink of an eye," Arris murmured, his voice low but insistent, "then why the fuck are you

Feenin'

wasting yours with a man who doesn't love you? Instead of living it with *me*—a man who wants to give you everything you deserve."

His words hung between them, thick with meaning. Dionne's breath caught in her throat, her lips parting, but no words came. Because she didn't have an answer. And Arris knew that.

But he didn't need her to say it. He just needed her to feel it.

"Arris..." she breathed, barely getting his name out before he closed the distance between them.

"Let me love you the way you deserve," he whispered against her skin, his lips trailing along the sensitive spot on her neck.

A soft moan escaped her lips, betraying her resolve.

"Let me give you the life you've always craved," he continued, his tone dipping lower, more urgent, his fingers pressing into her hips as if trying to mold her to him. His lips traced a slow, heated path down her throat, his hands moving with purpose.

Dionne's moans deepened, her body surrendering to the way he touched her, the way he spoke to her. Every word was a plea, a promise, a claim.

"You're everything I *feen* for, Dionne," he growled, his voice thick with hunger. "And ain't shit stopping that."

And then he was inside her, slow and deep, stretching her, filling her in a way that made every thought in her mind dissolve into pure sensation. A sharp gasp tore from her lips before morphing into a scream, piercing through the thick night air, mixing with the darkness like music he had been aching to hear.

And with every stroke, every whispered vow, he made it clear—

This wasn't just fucking.

This was him giving her everything.

Their bodies collided in the darkness of their bedroom, the first rays of sunlight barely creeping through the windows. The world outside was waking up, but inside, there was only them—flesh against flesh, hands grasping, mouths claiming. Dionne's moans mixed with the distant chirping of birds, a melody of passion filling the space as they lost themselves in each other, showing—without a single doubt—just how much they *feened* for one another.

***

The next Morning:

Arris sat in the passenger seat, his knee bouncing slightly, glancing over at Dionne as she drove with an amused smirk on her face. He had no idea where she was taking him, and the mystery was starting to get under his skin.

"Mama, where are we going?" His voice carried a mix of impatience and curiosity.

Dionne glanced at him, laughing at his restless energy. "Just wait and see, nosy," she teased, tapping away at a message from her father before refocusing on the road.

Malik's name flashed across her screen, signaling that he was finally awake from his drunken state last night—probably wondering where she was. Without hesitation, Dionne declined the call, her focus fixed on the road—and the man she truly wanted to be with.

With a sigh, she switched her phone to Do Not Disturb, refusing to let Malik, his relentless calls, or his annoying messages ruin the time she was spending with Arris.

Ten minutes later, she pulled up to a large farm, gravel crunching under the tires as she parked. Arris looked around, his brow furrowing as he took in the scene—the wooden fencing, the open fields, the faint scent of hay in the air. Before he could question her again, Dionne stepped out of the car and walked toward a gate. The moment she unlatched it, two horses appeared from the distance, their powerful forms trotting toward her.

"Woah, shit!" Arris flinched, his eyes wide with surprise.

Dionne threw her head back laughing. "Come on, boy. They don't bite," she said between giggles, stroking the jet-black horse's nose with familiarity.

Arris eyed the massive animals with skepticism, stepping toward her with cautious hesitation. "Mama, what the hell we doing out here?"

Dionne turned to him, her hand still running through the horse's mane. "You ever rode a horse before?" she asked, her voice light but knowing the answer already.

Arris scoffed. "Hell nah. A nigga like me don't ride no damn horses." He said it in mock seriousness, his expression deadpan, making Dionne burst into laughter.

"Well, a nigga like you gone ride one today," she shot back, her tone playful but firm.

"Mama, I ain't getting on that damn horse," he said, shaking his head as he eyed the black stallion warily.

"Of course not," Dionne said smoothly, patting the horse's side. "Smoke belongs to me."

Arris barely had time to process before she motioned toward the second horse, a beautiful brown mare with a sleek coat and intelligent eyes. "You're riding Demetrius' horse. This is Dream," she said, stepping

Feenin'

closer to the animal.

Arris exhaled sharply, his stance still hesitant. "Mama," he said, his tone warning. "I'm not getting on no damn horse."

Dionne smirked, closing the distance between them, her touch featherlight as she ran her fingers slowly down his arm. "I'll give you something special later if you do," she murmured, her voice dripping with seduction, her eyes locked onto his in that way that made his resolve crumble every damn time.

Arris clenched his jaw, already folding under her persuasion.

"Come on, baby," Dionne whispered, her fingers gliding down his chest, slow and deliberate, her lips hovering just inches from his ear.

"You know I'm good at what I do," she murmured, her voice dripping with seduction as her tongue lightly grazed his ear.

She felt the way his body tensed beneath her touch, the restraint in his muscles betraying just how badly he wanted her.

Arris exhaled sharply, closing his eyes briefly before shaking his head with a smirk. "Man, you play too damn much."

Dionne grinned, knowing she had him right where she wanted. "That mean you getting on?" she asked, tilting her head innocently.

Arris huffed, looking from her to the horse, then back to her. "Damn you," he muttered, rubbing his hand down his face before stepping closer to Dream.

Dionne beamed, rubbing his back in encouragement. "Atta boy."

Arris carefully climbed onto the horse, his body tensing as he adjusted to the unfamiliar height and the gentle sway of Dream beneath him. His grip on the reins tightened instinctively.

"Relax, baby," Dionne soothed, watching him with a small smile. "She's not gonna hurt you." She reached out, rubbing Dream's neck affectionately before whispering, "Take care of my man, girl."

Arris chuckled lowly, shaking his head at her. "You really out here talking to the damn horse?"

"You're a sexy cowboy," Dionne teased, licking her lips as she took in the sight of him on horseback. The way his muscles flexed beneath his t-shirt, the way he sat tall despite his initial nerves—it was a whole new level of fine.

Arris, feeling the heat, tugged his t-shirt off in one swift motion, leaving him in just a white muscle tee that clung to him perfectly. Dionne bit her lip, feeling the flutter in her stomach as she reached behind her, grabbing one of the black cowboy hats she kept on the farm. She leaned over, placing it on his head with a smirk.

"Now you really look like a cowboy," she teased, tilting the brim

Ann

slightly to one side.

Dionne shot him a playful glare before mounting Smoke with effortless ease, her movements fluid and natural. Arris couldn't help but admire how at home she looked in the saddle, completely in her element.

Arris adjusted the hat, giving her that cocky smirk she loved. "You and D really grew up with horses?" he asked as they started a slow, steady ride along the trail.

"Yeah," Dionne nodded, her tone warm with nostalgia. "I'd always come out here when I needed to get away… or when I wasn't too sick." Her voice softened at the end, her gaze momentarily distant.

Arris glanced at her, nodding in understanding. He didn't press, but he stored that piece of her away, another layer to the woman he was falling deeper for every day.

They continued riding, the air crisp and peaceful around them. Conversation flowed easily—Arris cracking jokes, Dionne laughing at his attempts to get comfortable on the horse. In between the laughter, though, something deeper settled between them. They were learning more about each other, peeling back layers, connecting in ways that neither of them had ever experienced before.

And for the first time in a long time, Dionne felt free.

Chapter 19

A week later:

"Man, AB, you crazy as shit. I can't believe I just did this," True muttered in disbelief, wiping away the excess ink from the massive back piece he had just finished. Arris sat still, his back now completely covered in an intricate portrait of Dionne.

One of her eyes was hidden behind a large tulip, while smaller tulips framed the rest of her face, giving the piece an almost ethereal softness. True had poured everything into the details, making sure the tattoo looked exactly like the original photo Arris had given him. Dionne's face was calm, poised—her expression unreadable, yet her eyes carried that undeniable softness, like a model caught mid-pose.

It was beautiful.

But True still couldn't wrap his head around their obsession with each other—especially when Dionne was still technically engaged to Malik.

Arris, though? He didn't give a damn.

"Dionne is mine," Arris said simply as he slid his suit shirt over the fresh ink, then shrugged into his jacket, barely wincing at the sting. "It's only a matter of time before she calls off that bullshit engagement."

True shook his head, exhaling heavily. "Nigga, please. This is some next-level type shit," he muttered, still trying to process it. "Yo ass is hooked, and I ain't gone lie—I'm a little worried."

Arris turned toward him, buttoning his shirt with calm precision. "Worried for what?" His voice was smooth, but there was an edge to it, like he already knew what True was about to say.

"I get it, bro. You in love—deep in love. And I fuck with Dionne, you know that. She like a sister to me." True sighed, setting his tattoo gun down before turning to face Arris fully. "But she's still engaged to another nigga. That shit messy. Somebody bound to get hurt."

Arris nodded slowly, understanding True's concern—but he wasn't fazed. "Look, bruh. Relax. I got everything handled," he assured, adjusting his cuffs. "Dionne's heart ain't with that nigga."

"Then why is she still with him?" True shot back, his tone sharp.

Arris froze.

That was the one question he couldn't answer. He had been asking himself the same damn thing for a while now. He knew Dionne wasn't in love with Malik. He knew her heart belonged to him. So what the fuck was keeping her tied to a man she didn't want?

Still, he *trusted* her.

Whatever it was, she'd cut it off.

"She's figuring shit out, True," Arris finally said, rolling his shoulders before fixing his tie. "And I'm letting her. Stop worrying, I got this. I promise."

True sighed, running a hand down his face, still unconvinced. "I just don't want you getting hurt behind this shit, AB."

Arris gave him a knowing smirk. "You can let yourself out, bro. I gotta get to the club."

True studied him for a moment before nodding. "Aight. Be safe, nigga."

They dapped each other up, and Arris grabbed his keys before heading out. Sliding into his Aston Martin, he pulled off into the night, his destination clear.

The Vault.

Arris moved through his restaurant, his sharp eyes scanning every detail, making sure everything was running smoothly. He greeted guests with effortless charm, exchanged a few words with Martin to ensure the back-of-house operations were solid, and after confirming all was in order, he made his way upstairs to his club.

The atmosphere changed instantly. The bass from the music pulsed through the walls, the air thick with the scent of expensive liquor and expensive perfume. The dance floor was packed, bodies swaying under dim neon lights, and the VIP sections were buzzing with laughter, bottles being popped, and money flowing like water.

Arris spotted True and Mario in their section, turning up as usual. He slid in for a moment, dapping them up and exchanging a few jokes before excusing himself to handle business. But before he could make it to his office, China stepped into his path, her expression unreadable but her stance alert.

"Hey, boss," she greeted, her tone steady but laced with something

Feenin'

that instantly put Arris on edge.

"What's going on?" he asked, already pulling her to the side, making sure no one else could overhear.

She exhaled lightly, keeping her composure. "Two men at the VIP bar causing trouble," she explained. "They say they're friends of yours and won't leave unless they speak with you."

Arris's jaw tightened, his irritation growing. He didn't like disruptions in his business, and he damn sure didn't like anything that made his people feel uncomfortable—especially not China.

"I'll handle it," he said, his tone clipped. His gaze swept over the crowd, already searching for the problem.

China subtly nodded toward the bar. Arris followed her line of sight and immediately locked in on them. Two men, built like enforcers, dressed in all black, heavy diamond chains weighing down their thick necks. Their body language was arrogant—territorial even. The kind of men who walked into rooms like they owned them. The kind of men Arris had outgrown dealing with.

His nostrils flared slightly, but his expression remained unreadable.

"I got this," he said coolly. "Have Eric on standby."

China gave a curt nod as Arris rolled his shoulders back and strode toward them, his presence alone shifting the energy in the room. He wasn't about to let anybody come into his place, disrupt his club, and think they could demand his time like he owed them something.

He was about to shut that shit down.

Arris moved with intention, his presence cutting through the club like a blade as he approached the bar. The neon lights cast shifting shadows over his face, highlighting the sharp set of his jaw and the cold focus in his eyes. The two men waiting for him noticed immediately. Their bodies tensed just slightly, their postures shifting—subtle, but telling. They knew they were in the presence of someone who didn't tolerate bullshit.

Arris stopped just short of them, his stance deceptively relaxed, but his aura lethal. He let the tension hang in the air for a beat before speaking.

"You got my attention. Now, who the fuck are you, and why are you in my club causing problems?" His voice was level, calm, but lined with something dangerous.

The man with the thick Cuban link around his neck smirked, taking a slow sip of his drink before setting the glass down with deliberate ease. "We ain't here to cause no trouble, AB," he said, his voice gravelly, the weight of his words carrying something unspoken. "Just wanted to have a little chat."

Ann

Arris's eyes narrowed, his patience already wearing thin. "A chat?" He cut a glance toward China, who stood at a distance, still watching with wary eyes, before turning his gaze back to them. "The fuck do I got to talk about with y'all?"

The second man, stockier with a gold watch gleaming under the club lights, leaned forward, resting his elbows on the bar. He studied Arris with a slow, assessing look, his tone casual but laced with intent. "Word is, you been gettin' real comfortable in the city. Making moves. Expanding." He let the words settle before adding, "We respect that. But we also heard you got ties to someone who's got history with our people."

Arris's jaw tightened, but his face remained unreadable. He already knew where this was going. His father's past was like a ghost—always creeping in, always trying to pull him back into a world he'd left behind.

"Aye, Tommy, the usual," Arris said to his head bartender, his tone calm but firm.

His eyes barely lingered before snapping back to the men in front of him—cold, lethal, and unreadable.

"I don't know what the fuck you talkin' about," Arris said smoothly, his tone even but edged with warning. "And I don't appreciate motherfuckers poppin' up in my establishment like they run shit." He took a slow sip of his drink before placing the glass down with a controlled click. "So unless y'all ordering another round, get the fuck up outta here."

"This nigga got balls. His father was right." The man chuckled, exchanging looks with his partner before shifting his attention back to Arris.

"Prince," he introduced himself, extending a hand for a shake.

Arris barely glanced at it before bringing his drink to his lips, taking a slow, deliberate sip. The air between them thickened with tension. Prince smirked, pulling his hand back, realizing Arris wasn't the type to be impressed—or intimidated.

"I'm sure you don't know who I am, but your father does," Prince continued, his tone casual, but the weight behind his words was undeniable. "And that nigga owes me a lot of money."

Arris didn't flinch. He just watched Prince, his jaw tightening slightly, but his face otherwise unreadable.

"Whatever you and Calvin got going on ain't got shit to do with me," Arris finally said, draining the last of his drink before placing the empty glass down with precision. "Now, if y'all plan on enjoying the club like paying customers, cool. But if not, Eric here can show you the way out."

Feenin'

He straightened his suit jacket, ready to walk away.

Prince, bold and reckless, reached out and grabbed Arris's arm.

Before Eric could even react, Arris was already in motion—his fist connecting with Prince's nose in a sharp, bone-cracking hit. The force sent Prince stumbling back, blood instantly dripping from his nostrils.

A few heads in VIP turned at the commotion, but the music was too loud for most to catch on.

The second man, caught off guard but quick to react, pulled a gun on Arris.

Eric moved just as fast, his own weapon drawn, ready to end the situation in an instant.

Arris, however, remained still. His eyes locked onto the man's shaky hands gripping the gun. He could see it—hesitation. Uncertainty. This wasn't a man who was ready to pull the trigger.

With a single look, Arris signaled Eric to lower his weapon.

"Pull the trigger, nigga." Arris said coldly, his tone like ice, daring the man to follow through.

Now, True and Mario stood behind Arris, their own guns drawn, ready to protect their brother without hesitation. The air in the club grew suffocating, tension so thick it felt like time had frozen. All eyes were locked on the man gripping his gun, his hands shaking slightly as he weighed the consequences.

Prince, still dabbing at the blood trickling from his nose, chuckled darkly. "Got a mean left hook, I'll give you that," he muttered, amusement laced with malice. "But that shit don't spare your father's life."

Arris didn't flinch. His stare remained deadlocked on Prince, but his fists clenched at his sides, rage bubbling under his skin.

"If you don't come up with the two million that nigga owes me," Prince continued, his tone dropping to something even deadlier, "then more than just his ass is gonna die."

Arris's jaw tightened. His father's mistakes had already stolen too much from him—his childhood, his peace, his goddamn future. And now, they were threatening to take even more.

"This place?" Prince gestured around the club with a lazy smirk. "Up in flames in seconds. You got a week, my nigga."

He turned to leave, but Arris couldn't control his own anger any longer.

Fuck this.

He lunged.

The impact was instant—Arris tackled Prince, sending both men crashing into the VIP section. Tables flipped, bottles shattered, and chaos erupted as they threw vicious punches, neither willing to back down.

Prince got a hit in, but Arris was fueled by something deeper—rage, betrayal, years of unresolved pain. He landed blow after blow, his fists connecting with raw force.

The fight spiraled into a full-blown brawl, Prince's man jumping in just as True and Mario did the same. The sound of fists colliding with flesh mixed with the frantic screams of bystanders scrambling to get out of the way.

Eric, ever the enforcer, fired a single shot into the air.

The deafening blast halted everything.

Prince staggered back, breathing heavy, wiping blood from his mouth. He was about to throw another punch when the wail of sirens sliced through the air.

"Boss, we gotta go!" his man shouted, yanking him back.

Prince locked eyes with Arris one last time, a silent promise of unfinished business, before disappearing through the exit just as police stormed the club.

The crowd had already thinned out, people fleeing the scene before they could get caught up in the madness. Officers flooded the space, their flashlights bouncing off the shiny interior.

Arris wiped his mouth, exhaling heavily as he straightened his suit. He knew the drill.

He stepped forward, pulling out his ID, his voice steady despite the adrenaline still coursing through his veins. "I own this place."

The officers eyed him warily, assessing the scene—the wrecked VIP section, the overturned furniture, the lingering smell of gunpowder in the air.

"We're gonna need a statement," one of them said.

Arris rolled his shoulders, feeling the bruise forming along his jaw. His club, his restaurant—his entire fucking empire was now tangled in his father's mess.

Again.

"Yeah," he muttered, already thinking ten steps ahead. "I figured."

After talking to the police, Arris was now in his office, completely losing it. Papers, glasses, anything within reach—he sent it flying against the walls, the loud crashes doing little to drown out the rage boiling inside him. His curses filled the room, raw and unfiltered, as the weight of his father's fuck-ups suffocated him.

"Aye, Arris, calm down," Mario said, stepping closer, his voice edged with concern. But Arris was too far gone, too blinded by fury.

Feenin'

He wanted to kill his father.

Not just for the debt, not just for the past, but for this—dragging him back into the mess he'd spent years climbing out of. Now, not only was his life on the line, but so was his business. The empire he built from the ground up was in jeopardy because of a man who had never done shit for him.

"That nigga keeps taking everything from me!" Arris roared, his fist slamming into the wall so hard the drywall cracked.

True and Mario stood frozen for a second, watching their friend unravel in his own rage. They had seen him mad before, but this? This was different. This was destruction, a storm he was losing control of.

"Arris," True started, his voice calmer, trying to reel him in, but Arris wasn't hearing it. He swung again, another dent in the wall, his breaths ragged.

True had already sent all the employees home—thankfully, no one was left to witness Arris coming undone.

"Bro, what can we do?" Mario asked, his own anger stirring at the sight of his friend like this. He hated feeling helpless, hated that he couldn't fix this shit for him.

Then, as if struck by lightning, Arris stopped abruptly. His whole body stilled, his heavy breathing the only sound filling the office.

"Dionne." The name left his lips like a prayer, like the answer to the storm raging inside him.

"Take me to her," he demanded, his voice still laced with anger but suddenly determined.

Mario frowned, confused. "Arris, man, maybe we should just—"

"No, take me to her! Now!" Arris barked, his patience completely gone.

True exhaled, shaking his head. He already knew what this was. He knew Dionne was the only person who could pull Arris out of this darkness. "Man, this ain't a good idea," he warned. "You too heated. You really want her seeing you like this?"

Arris ignored him, already pulling his phone out, dialing Dionne's number. It rang. And rang. Then straight to voicemail.

His jaw clenched so hard his teeth ached. He tried again. Same thing.

"Come on, Arris, let's just get you home," Mario tried again, this time softer, trying to reason with him.

Arris jerked away. "No. Take me to her!" His voice boomed through the office, his eyes burning with an intensity neither of them had ever seen before.

True sighed, rubbing a hand down his face. "Man, this nigga not gonna calm down till he sees her. Let's just go."

Mario still looked lost, like he was missing something major between Arris and Dionne. But True didn't waste time explaining. Instead, he pulled out his phone and dialed London's number.

"Hey, baby," London answered, her voice warm but laced with curiosity.

"Hey, baby. You still with Dionne?" True asked, getting straight to the point.

"Yeah, we're about to head to Karmen's house," London replied, now sounding even more curious.

"Okay, baby. We're gonna meet you there." True didn't give her time to ask questions before he ended the call.

Arris didn't wait either. He grabbed his keys and stormed out of the office, not caring whether they followed or not.

He had one destination.

He *needed* to see Dionne.

***

Dionne sat on the plush couch of the bridal boutique, legs crossed, head tilted back against the cushion, her mind miles away as Kierra, London, and Karmen took turns trying on their bridesmaid dresses. Unlike them, she wasn't buzzing with excitement—if anything, every day that brought her closer to this wedding felt like a weight pressing down on her chest.

Her heart wasn't here.

It was with Arris.

Yet here she was, still planning a wedding she didn't want, to a man she no longer loved.

London and Karmen were beaming as they twirled in front of the mirror, admiring their emerald-green gowns. The wedding was less than two months away, and their excitement was infectious. But not to Dionne.

Kierra, however, wasn't fooled by her forced smile. She saw right through it.

Sliding onto the couch beside her, Kierra leaned in, her voice low. "Dionne, you good?"

Dionne blinked out of her daze, looking down at her phone, her thumb hovering over the screen. Arris had just sent her a message—sweet, loving, effortless in the way only he could be. The warmth of his words made the guilt hit her tenfold, so she locked her phone, shutting it out.

"I don't know what I'm doing," she admitted, her voice barely above

Feenin'

a whisper, thick with emotion.

Kierra exhaled, already knowing exactly what she meant. "Then stop this shit. Just call it off. Be with him," she urged, nodding toward the phone still clutched in Dionne's hands.

"It's not that simple, Kierra." Her tone turned sharp, not at Kierra, but at the impossible situation she was trapped in.

Before Kierra could press further, London and Karmen stepped out, their dresses hugging their curves in all the right places. "Damn, y'all look good!" Dionne said, forcing a bright smile to mask the chaos swirling inside her.

London and Karmen grinned, admiring themselves in the mirror as they twirled. Kierra, already in her dress, joined them, and together, they posed, snapping pictures for memories they'd cherish—well, they would. Dionne? She felt like she was documenting a lie.

"Our girl is really getting married!" Karmen gushed, practically vibrating with excitement.

Dionne nodded, her smile tight.

"I still wanna beat Malik's ass for Thanksgiving, but he made the best decision of his life marrying my best friend," London added proudly, adjusting the strap of her dress.

Dionne laughed—forced, hollow, but convincing enough that no one noticed.

No one except Kierra.

Her sister-in-law looked at her, her own smile masking the concern in her eyes, the silent message she was sending loud and clear: *What the hell are you doing?*

Dionne swallowed hard.

She couldn't do this anymore. Couldn't keep pretending. Couldn't keep playing both sides.

She had to end this.

And *soon*.

Dionne and the girls finally left the bridal shop, spending the rest of the day indulging in good food, massages, and a much-needed girls' day. Laughter and lighthearted conversation filled the car as the night loomed over them, but the moment they pulled up to Karmen's house, the mood shifted.

The sight of True, Mario, and Arris' cars parked outside made all of them pause in confusion—except for London.

"They said they were meeting us here," London informed them, her voice tinged with curiosity. "I don't know why, but it sounded urgent."

Dionne cut the engine, gripping the wheel for a second longer before exhaling and stepping out. It wasn't just their presence that unsettled her—it was Arris.

He was leaning against his car, his head low, his entire body coiled with tension. Even under the dim glow of the streetlights, she could see the fury rolling off him in waves. His jaw clenched, his hands flexing at his sides like he was barely keeping himself together.

Her heart thumped with every step she took toward him. Concern clouded her mind, but so did nerves. True and Mario met them halfway, their expressions tight with worry, but Arris didn't move. He stayed rooted against his car, head down, his breathing controlled but heavy.

"Baby, what's going on?" London asked True, eyes flicking between his and Mario's unreadable faces.

True sighed, rubbing the back of his head before finally speaking. "Man, some shit went down at the club." He paused, glancing at Dionne before continuing. "Dionne, Arris needs you."

All attention snapped to her.

London and Karmen exchanged confused looks, but Kierra... Kierra didn't look surprised. She just looked at Dionne with quiet concern, like she already knew.

Dionne avoided her friends' questioning gazes, ignoring the silent pressure closing in on her as she stepped forward. She didn't care about their curiosity right now.

Arris needed her.

The rest of the group took the hint and gave them space, heading inside the house. But Dionne never took her eyes off Arris.

She could feel it.

Something was really wrong.

Dionne's heart pounded as she reached for him, her eyes locked onto the bloodstains and bruises covering his knuckles. "Baby, what's wrong? What happened?" she asked, her voice laced with concern.

Arris finally lifted his head, his dark, stormy gaze burning into hers. "Why didn't you answer your phone?" His tone was sharp, edged with something raw—something dangerous.

Dionne blinked at the unexpected question. "I was with the girls, and my phone died." She started to explain, but the way his gaze dropped to her hand made her pause.

Her stomach twisted.

The engagement ring.

She hadn't worn it in weeks—at least, not around him. She thought he wouldn't notice, but clearly, he had. Seeing it back on her finger made his entire body tense, his jaw ticking as anger flashed in his eyes.

Feenin'

She quickly followed his line of sight and realized what had set him off. "I just put it on for my—"

"Go inside, Dionne."

The coldness in his voice made her breath hitch. He wasn't looking at her anymore. He had already begun to shut down, his walls slamming up as he took a step back, putting space between them.

"No, Arris. I'm here. Tell me what's wrong, please." She reached for him again, desperation coating her voice, her eyes welling with unshed tears.

Arris clenched his jaw, the shine of that ring on her finger fueling his rage. He shook his head, taking another step back, his breathing uneven. "Go inside, Dionne," he repeated, but this time his voice was more strained, like he was barely holding himself together.

"Arris, please."

His patience snapped.

"Go inside, Dionne!" His voice boomed through the quiet street, laced with so much anger that Dionne flinched.

The moment she did, his heart sank. Regret flashed across his face, but it was gone just as fast.

"No, Arris!" Dionne's voice wavered, but she stood her ground, even though she was shaking on the inside.

"Man, you chose that nigga," Arris spat, his gaze burning into the engagement ring like it had personally betrayed him.

Tears streamed down Dionne's face, her chest tightening as she desperately tried to hold on to him. "No, I didn't... baby," she choked out, her voice trembling.

But he didn't hear her. Didn't want to hear her. His rage had already taken over.

"Man, I cried in your fucking arms! I loved you with every part of me, and you still chose that nigga," Arris yelled, his voice thick with emotion, his anger barely masking the deep hurt beneath it.

Dionne shook her head furiously. "Arris, no."

"Then make your choice!" he snapped, stepping closer, his presence all-consuming. "Me or him, Dionne."

Silence.

Dionne's lips parted, but nothing came out.

How was she supposed to explain? How could she tell him that this had nothing to do with love, that it was obligation—a *promise*—that was holding her back?

Arris searched her face, begging her to say his name. To *choose* him. To prove that he wasn't losing her.

But she hesitated.

And that hesitation shattered him.

"Wow," he scoffed, taking a step back, the disbelief washing over his face like a tidal wave. Before she could react, he swung his fist into his car window, the glass shattering on impact.

Dionne was supposed to be his peace, his remedy to the storm already raging inside him from his father, but the sight of that damn ring on her finger only fueled the chaos, pushing him closer to the edge—until he finally erupted.

Dionne gasped, stumbling back as shards scattered across the pavement.

Arris barely flinched, his knuckles dripping with blood, but he didn't care. The pain in his hand was nothing compared to what he felt in his chest.

"I feel fucking numb without you, Dionne," he growled, shaking his head, his breaths ragged. "That's what you do to me. I laid my heart bare for you, and it still wasn't enough to win over your love!"

Dionne's hands trembled as she tried to reach for him. "Baby, please—"

He pushed her arms away.

"You're just like everyone else," he said, voice breaking. "You fucking leave me."

Dionne's heart broke. "No, baby. No. Just please—let me explain!"

But Arris was already gone.

"I'm done, Dionne," he muttered, his voice hollow. "I hope you and that nigga live happily ever after."

Before she could stop him, he yanked open his car door, glass crunching beneath his feet, and sped off, tires screeching into the night—taking her heart with him.

Dionne broke down as Arris sped off, leaving her standing there—heartbroken, confused, and empty.

She had been ready to explain everything, to lay it all out for him, but he was too blinded by rage to let her.

True and Mario rushed outside, their expressions tight with concern after hearing the yelling and the screech of tires.

"We got him, sis," True said gently, pulling her into a hug. "He's just blinded by rage right now."

Dionne nodded through her sobs, clutching onto True like he was the only thing keeping her standing.

Her voice cracked as she spoke, her tears falling faster. "What happened?"

Feenin'

She had never seen Arris that angry before—especially not with her.

True exhaled, rubbing a hand down his face. "He'll tell you when he calms down. I'll have him call you tomorrow." His tone was reassuring, but Dionne knew better. She knew Arris.

He wasn't going to call.

He believed she had chosen Malik.

And nothing hurt more than knowing he thought she had betrayed him.

Dionne gave a weak nod, even though deep down she felt helpless.

True and Mario left, heading straight to Arris' house to check on him, while Dionne turned toward the house, already dreading the conversation waiting for her inside.

She sighed, wiping her face.

Her friends were about to grill her.

And after tonight, she didn't even know if she had the strength to face it.

All her concern was on Arris.

She never meant to hurt him.

Seeing the pain in his eyes as he looked at that ring made her stomach twist with guilt. She had only worn it to keep up the lie with her friends, to avoid the questions she wasn't ready to answer. But in doing that, she had broken something between them.

Now, she wasn't sure if they could come back from this.

Arris had given her everything—his love, his trust, his heart. And she had shattered it with her silence.

She couldn't let this be the end.

She had to end things with Malik.

She couldn't keep hurting Arris, the only man she wanted to be with.

"Dionne!" London's sharp voice snapped her out of her thoughts, pulling her attention back to the present. Her head lifted to meet the fiery stares of her best friends, their confusion and frustration evident.

"What the fuck was that?!" London demanded, eyes darting between Dionne and the door. "Why was he so angry, and why did he need to see you?"

Dionne swallowed hard, her chest tightening. "It's nothing major," she muttered, but Karmen immediately arched an eyebrow, her expression doubtful.

"Dionne, come on," Karmen pressed, her voice softer but firm. "We've been friends for too long for you to hit us with the 'nothing major' bullshit. What happened?"

Dionne's eyes flickered to Kierra for backup, but she already knew there was no saving her this time. Kierra met her gaze with a knowing look, giving her a slight nod.

"Tell them, Dee," Kierra urged.

Taking a deep breath, Dionne reached for her engagement ring, twisting it around her finger looking down at it like it was a shackle. The silence in the room thickened as all eyes locked on her emotions.

London's mouth parted slightly, realization dawning. Karmen sat up straighter, bracing herself.

Dionne clenched her hands in her lap, her fingers fidgeting with the strap of her purse as if she could unravel her emotions along with the fabric. She exhaled, voice barely above a whisper.

"Malik cheated."

London and Karmen's sharp gasps filled the room.

"He what?" London's tone cut through the air like a blade. "That nigga cheated on you? And you stayed?"

"London!" Karmen hissed, attempting to calm her, but the fury in London's face was undeniable.

Karmen turned back to Dionne, her voice softer now. "Why, D? You don't have to stay with him. Not for any reason."

Dionne let out a shaky breath, her chest tightening under the weight of her friends' concern. "It's not about Malik," she admitted, her voice breaking. "It's about Mama Glen."

London and Karmen froze, their anger momentarily replaced with confusion.

"She's dying, Karmen," Dionne continued, her eyes glistening. "She's the only reason I'm still in this... whatever this is. I promised her I'd make it work. I can't break her heart, not when she doesn't have much time left."

London's frustration softened into something more delicate—pity. She ran a hand down her face before exhaling, shaking her head.

"Dionne, that's not fair to you," she said gently. "You can love Mama Glen and still walk away from Malik. Staying in a relationship you don't want, just to make someone else happy, is only going to destroy you."

"It's more complicated than that, but I'm figuring it out. I can't marry a man when my heart belongs to someone else." Dionne's voice was steady, but the weight of her words hung heavy in the air.

London and Karmen sat frozen, shock written all over their faces, while Kierra had a knowing smile playing at her lips.

"Arris?" Karmen asked, her mind piecing things together, realizing there was something much deeper between them than just business.

Dionne nodded without hesitation. "Yes. I love him with everything

Feenin'

in me, and he's the man I want to be with." Her conviction was unwavering, even though Arris's anger still lingered in her mind.

"What in the entire fuck?!" London blurted, completely flabbergasted.

"When did this even start?" she continued, her voice laced with curiosity and a hint of intrigue despite her initial shock.

Dionne sighed, knowing this conversation was long overdue. "When I caught Malik cheating. Months ago."

London's face twisted as she started putting the pieces together. "That's why you stayed at my house for those few days?"

Dionne nodded.

"And those sex marks that were all over you... they weren't from Malik, were they? That was Arris?"

Another nod.

"Damn." London exhaled, shaking her head in disbelief.

"So how long have you been pretending?" Karmen asked, her voice softer now, like she was bracing herself for the truth.

"For years," Dionne admitted. "Since our senior year of college."

London's brow furrowed. "Pretending? What do you mean?"

Dionne hesitated for a moment before revealing what she had kept from them for so long. "I was really sick, and—"

"Sick?!" Karmen's voice cracked, interrupting her.

Dionne exhaled slowly, then explained everything—her blood disorder, the way it had worsened in college, how Mama Glen had been the reason she was still here today.

By the time she was done, both Karmen and London had silent tears running down their faces. Dionne's heart clenched. She never wanted to make them cry, but she knew they were hurting—not just because of what she had endured, but because they had no idea it was happening.

"We're sorry," Karmen choked out, wiping her tears.

Dionne shook her head immediately. "There's nothing to apologize for. I chose not to say anything, and I'm fully healed now."

"But we're your best friends, Dee. Your sisters," London emphasized, her voice breaking. "And we didn't even notice you were sick. And now, we didn't even notice you were unhappy with a man we thought you loved. What kind of sisters does that make us?"

Dionne's chest tightened at the pain in London's voice. Without thinking, she moved between them, wrapping her arms around both of them, holding them close.

"I was good at hiding it," she admitted. "I should've trusted you two with all of this, but I was afraid."

"Afraid of what?" Karmen sniffled.

Dionne pulled back slightly, looking at them both with so much love it made their hearts ache. "Afraid that I'd lose the two people who made my life feel worth living again. I was dying, and you two were the only people who showed me the beauty of life."

London and Karmen melted into her embrace, their tears mixing with quiet laughter as they held on tighter.

"Aww," Kierra finally spoke, wiping her own tears as she watched the sisterhood in front of her. "Y'all really love each other, huh?"

All three girls burst into laughter through their emotions, but it was the kind of laughter that carried relief, love, and understanding.

Dionne finally felt lighter. Now, she just had one more thing to do—end things with Malik, for good.

"I just lost the man I love."

Dionne broke down, her sobs shaking her body as her friends instantly pulled her into their arms, holding her as she cried.

"He thinks I chose Malik," she whispered through her tears, the weight of those words suffocating her.

Kierra, always the voice of reason, glanced down at Dionne's hand—the engagement ring still sitting on her finger. "Well... did you?" she asked cautiously.

Dionne stared at the ring, her vision blurred with tears. "I love him, y'all. But I love Mama Glen, and I can't break that promise," she admitted, torn between duty and the love that consumed her every thought.

Kierra sighed, shaking her head. "Look, you need to talk to Mama Glen and tell her where your heart is. You can't keep living this lie for her sake. You're not just hurting yourself anymore, Dee—you're hurting that man that just left here mad and heartbroken." Her tone was firm, leaving no room for Dionne to argue.

Dionne sniffled, wiping her face as she nodded. "You're right."

Silence settled in the room for a brief moment before Karmen suddenly perked up.

"Damn," Karmen shook her head, a smirk creeping onto her face. "You and Arris. Bitch, I should've known! That man looks at you like you hung the damn moon."

London's eyes widened, her brain working overtime as she gasped suddenly. "Wait, hold the fuck up!" she shrieked, pointing at Dionne's chest. "Is he the hand tattooed on your titty?"

Dionne's mouth fell open, but before she could say a word, Kierra grinned and beat her to it.

Feenin'

"YES!" Kierra confirmed dramatically, making London and Karmen gasp in pure shock.

"Bitch!" Dionne turned, glaring at Kierra. "You just had to answer, huh?"

Kierra simply shrugged. "I mean… it was already obvious," she said, feigning innocence. "And I'm still not over that shit, by the way."

The room erupted into laughter, but the moment settled just as quickly as it came. Karmen's expression turned serious again.

"For real though, Dionne. It's time to talk to Mama Glen."

Dionne nodded, knowing they were right. There was no more room for hesitation. No more excuses.

They spent the rest of the night curled up under blankets, watching movies, but Dionne's mind wasn't on the screen. She kept glancing at her phone, sending message after message to Arris. He wasn't responding.

Her chest tightened with worry, but she knew she had to give him space. Still, the silence was killing her.

Her heart was with him.

Because her heart belonged to Arris—and it was time to finally fight for him.

Chapter 20

Arris sat slumped on the couch, shirtless, a glass of whiskey dangling from his fingers. His jaw clenched as his body trembled with barely contained rage. The events from last night refused to leave him, looping in his mind like a cruel, inescapable nightmare. It wasn't just that his father's old street enemies had come knocking—it was her. Dionne. The woman he wanted more than his next breath had chosen another man over him. And the worst part? He never even gave her a chance to explain.

Not that she needed to. That engagement ring on her finger told him everything he needed to know. She chose Malik.

The fury, the feeling of abandonment, burned through him like acid. He hadn't moved from this damn couch since he got home last night. Just sat there, whiskey in hand, staring at the blank TV screen, drowning in his own thoughts, his own rage. It swallowed him whole, suffocating him, making it impossible to think straight.

The distant sound of the doorbell barely registered, but his sister's voice finally cut through the storm raging in his head.

"You didn't hear the doorbell ringing?" A'Lani's voice was sharp with concern as she descended the stairs, heading toward the door. She pulled it open, revealing their mother, Angel.

A'Lani barely hesitated before calling her inside. She was scared. No—terrified. If anyone could pull Arris out of this storm, it was their mother.

But Arris didn't acknowledge either of them. Didn't flinch. Didn't move. He just lifted his glass and took another slow sip, the whiskey burning his throat but failing to numb the ache inside him.

"He's been like this since he got home last night," A'Lani whispered, eyes locked on her brother as worry seeped into every word. "Hasn't

Feenin'

said a word, hasn't moved, hasn't even looked at anything but that damn screen."

Angel inhaled deeply, her chest tightening at the sight of her son. "Hey, son," she said cautiously, stepping closer.

Nothing. No reaction.

Arris took another sip, the only movement in his entire body coming from the slight twitch in his jaw, his muscles locked tight with fury.

Angel and A'Lani exchanged a look before Angel stepped in front of him. "Arris," she tried again, voice softer now, gentle, like she was speaking to the broken boy she'd held together so many years ago.

Still, nothing.

Then, finally—his voice, cold and sharp as a blade.

"Why she in my house?"

He didn't even turn his head, didn't look at her. Just kept his dead stare on the TV screen.

"I called her here, Arris," A'Lani admitted, her voice cracking with emotion. "You been like this since True and Mario left last night. You won't talk, won't move. I was scared… I am *scared*."

Arris exhaled slowly, finally shifting just enough to rest his glass on the table. His fingers tapped against it, restless, angry, his body still radiating heat from everything boiling inside him.

"I'm good." The words came out flat, empty, but the tension in his body screamed otherwise.

"No, you're not," Angel said softly. "I know you're mad at me, son."

Arris let out a humorless huff, reaching for his whiskey again. He took another deep sip, waiting for the burn to calm him. It didn't. Nothing did.

"Your nigga check is sitting right there." His voice was low, venomous, barely above a whisper. "Two million for his bitch ass. So he can finally leave my fucking life for good, like everyone else."

His grip on the glass tightened as his vision blurred. But it wasn't from the whiskey. His eyes burned, his breath shallow as the pain clawed up his throat.

"I'm done with every fucking body," he muttered, voice hollow. "Nobody loves me unless I can do some shit for them."

The words shattered something in Angel, in A'Lani.

"That's not true, Arris," Angel said, desperation coating every syllable. "We love you."

But he didn't react.

Didn't move.

Didn't blink.

Angel swallowed hard. She had seen this before—the cold, distant, broken shell of a boy who lost his father and had to learn too damn early that love came with conditions. He was only eight years old back then. But now, as a man, his rage was so much deeper, so much darker.

And this time... she didn't know if she could pull him out of it.

"Lani loves me. True and Mario love me. But Ma, you don't."

Arris's voice cracked, betraying the depth of his pain, and Angel felt it like a dagger to the chest. A single tear slipped from her eye at his admission.

"I do, son. I promise I do," she said, voice thick with emotion. "And I apologize if I ever did things that made you feel that way."

Arris let out a bitter chuckle, the sound empty, hollow. He took another slow sip from his glass, savoring the burn like it was the only thing keeping him upright. Angel turned back to A'Lani, the concern on her face so deep it aged her in that moment.

She thought she had seen this before. Thought she understood the way her son shut down when hurt. But this? This was different. This wasn't just rage. This wasn't just abandonment.

This was heartbreak.

And someone had shattered Arris completely.

"Brother," A'Lani whispered, stepping closer, her voice gentle, hesitant.

For the first time since last night, Arris finally looked at her.

A'Lani sucked in a breath, her heart aching at the sight. She had never seen her brother like this. Ever. His eyes—red-rimmed, glossy with unshed tears—looked like they belonged to someone else. Someone lost. Someone who had given everything and got nothing in return.

Arris exhaled sharply, gaze still locked onto A'Lani as his voice turned sharp, cutting, but unwavering.

"Tell Ma to take the check and please get the fuck outta my house—respectfully."

A'Lani flinched at his words, her mouth parting to protest, to say something, anything, but before she could, Angel stood.

"I'm very sorry, Arris," Angel said softly, her voice trembling with remorse. "I really am. And I hope one day, you can find it in your heart to forgive me... and your father."

She reached for the signed two-million-dollar check on the table, fingers hesitant, but she took it anyway. That was all Arris needed to see. His mother—walking away with a check meant for the man who had failed them. The man she still chose.

Arris chuckled, dark and humorless. A'Lani's stomach twisted as

Feenin'

she scowled at their mother, watching her walk away with the check—proving Arris's fucking point.

She cared more about Calvin than the one person who had always had her back.

The sound of the door clicking shut was the final fucking straw.

Arris's fury exploded. With a raw, guttural yell, he hurled the whiskey glass at the TV, the impact shattering both the glass and cracking the screen. The sound was deafening, shards flying everywhere, a physical manifestation of everything breaking inside him.

A'Lani jumped, heart pounding, snapping her head back to her brother.

"Arris! What the fuck is wrong?!" she screamed, voice laced with panic, with fear.

His chest rose and fell rapidly, his breathing ragged, his hands clenched into fists at his sides. His entire body vibrated with barely controlled rage, with a pain so sharp he felt like he was bleeding out in real time.

"She chose him, Lani! She fucking chose him!" Arris roared, standing so suddenly the energy in the room shifted.

A'Lani blinked, still shaken. "You know how Ma is—" she started, thinking he meant their mother, trying to rationalize, trying to calm him down.

But Arris wasn't talking about their mother. He wasn't talking about Calvin.

He was talking about *her*.

"Not Ma, Dionne!" Arris shouted, his voice nearly breaking under the weight of the name.

A'Lani stilled, completely thrown off.

"Who... who is Dionne?" she asked hesitantly, the name unfamiliar, yet suddenly holding so much weight.

Arris turned away for a moment, dragging a hand down his face.

A'Lani's stomach dropped.

Her eyes widened as she took in the tattoo covering his entire back.

A portrait.

Not just any portrait—a woman.

Her hand flew to her mouth as the realization crashed into her like a tidal wave. She had seen this woman before.

The same woman she once caught Arris looking at on his phone.

The same woman who, without saying a word, had broken her brother into a million pieces.

"What. The. Fuck?" she breathed, barely above a whisper.

"I love her, Lani. I fucking loved every part of her, and she chose someone else. She broke me."

Arris's voice cracked, his anger barely masking the heartbreak tearing him apart. His chest heaved as the weight of his words settled between them.

A'Lani didn't hesitate. She moved quickly, wrapping her arms around him, grounding him in a way only a sister could. "Slow down, Arris. Talk to me," she urged gently as they sank onto the couch.

Arris dragged a hand down his face, exhaling heavily before he finally started.

And he told her everything.

From the moment he met Dionne, how their connection ignited like wildfire, how every moment with her was like a drug he could never get enough of. He didn't leave anything out—not the fact that she was engaged, not the way he ignored that ring on her finger because he knew her heart belonged to him. He even admitted to getting her fiancé suspended for cheating on her.

By the time he finished, A'Lani sat there in stunned silence.

"Damn," she muttered, still processing.

Arris leaned forward, elbows on his knees, fingers locked together as his jaw tightened. "She fucking left me for that sorry ass nigga, and I know her heart ain't with him." His fists clenched, knuckles turning white from the sheer force of his rage.

"But Arris... she was engaged," A'Lani said carefully. "You had to know there was a chance she'd choose her fiancé."

Arris snapped his head toward her, shaking it violently. "You didn't see the way her eyes light up when she looks at me. You didn't feel the way her body reacts when I touch her. That woman is my fucking drug, and I'm addicted. And I know she's addicted to me too." His nostrils flared, his voice shaking with conviction. "My fucking hand is tatted on her titty."

A'Lani's eyes nearly popped out of her head. "Damn... that's some *feenin'* shit," she breathed.

Arris sat back, his mind running in circles, his heart pounding in his chest.

"So why did she choose him?" A'Lani finally asked, hitting him with the million-dollar question. "If you're the man she's deeply in love with?"

Arris stared at the ground, jaw locked. "I don't know. None of this shit makes sense." He ran his hands down his face, frustration and pain merging into something unbearable.

Feenin'

"Then you need to talk to her," A'Lani said simply. "Ask her yourself."

Arris's head snapped up, eyes flashing with resistance. "Fuck no. She's back wearing that ring. I already know who she chose."

A'Lani exhaled, taking a different approach. "You said you talked to her last night, right? After everything went down at the club?"

Arris nodded stiffly.

A'Lani leaned in, holding his gaze. "Arris, when you get angry, you let that shit consume you so much that you don't see what's right in front of you. You just told me Dionne don't love her fiancé. Her heart is with you. But she's still walking around with that ring on her finger."

"Maybe what you saw wasn't a woman choosing her fiancé," A'Lani said slowly, letting the words sink in, "but a woman stuck between love and obligation."

Arris's brows furrowed, confusion flashing across his face. "What?"

His face still held confusion, like he was trying to fit pieces of a puzzle that didn't make sense.

"What if that engagement isn't about love but obligation?" A'Lani continued. "What if something—or someone—is keeping her tied to a man she doesn't love?"

Arris's chest tightened.

Dionne had always told him her situation was complicated. And he knew she didn't love Malik. He felt it.

"I don't know her personally," A'Lani said, "but I know you. And you don't let nobody this close to your heart—especially not a woman. She has to be a damn good one to have you this hooked." She looked him dead in the eye. "And a woman like that isn't going to stay in a marriage, break your heart, and marry a man she doesn't love unless she has no choice but to break her own heart… and the man she feens for."

Arris sat there, stunned, A'Lani's words bouncing around in his head like an echo he couldn't shake.

She was right.

Something—or someone—was forcing Dionne to marry Malik.

And he was going to find out what the fuck it was.

A'Lani stood, grabbing her keys. "Just talk to her, bro." She leaned down, pressing a soft kiss to his forehead. "I'll be back later. Call me if you need anything."

And with that, she was gone.

But Arris barely noticed.

He sat there, gripping the sides of his head, his mind racing.

This wasn't over.

Not by a fucking long shot.

***

Dionne stepped through the front door, determination in every step. She had spent the night at Karmen's, mentally preparing herself for the conversation she needed to have with Malik. It was time to end this—to finally be with the man she truly wanted.

But the sight of Mama Glen sitting on the couch stopped her cold.

Her stomach tightened.

"Mama Glen?" Dionne's voice wavered just slightly as she froze in her tracks.

She hadn't expected this. Malik, yes. But not her.

Mama Glen turned to her with that signature warm smile, the kind that could soften even the hardest hearts. "Hey, sweetie," she greeted, waving Dionne over.

Dionne swallowed her hesitation, forcing herself forward. She leaned down, hugging Mama Glen, inhaling the familiar scent of her perfume—the scent of comfort, of familiarity.

"Where's Malik?" she asked, scanning the room for the man she had come to confront.

"He told me he had a meeting with the board today—to get himself off suspension," Mama Glen answered easily.

Dionne nodded but groaned internally. Damn it. She had been ready to face him, to say what needed to be said. And now, he wasn't even here.

"Where you coming from? Malik said you didn't come home last night."

Dionne stiffened at the subtle probe in Mama Glen's soft tone. She caught herself before she could react, rolling her shoulders back, keeping her expression neutral.

"Girls' night at Karmen's," she said smoothly, shutting down any further questions.

Mama Glen nodded, but her eyes held something unreadable. Dionne ignored it, glancing down at the time on her watch. "Did Malik say when he'll be back?" she asked, her impatience creeping in.

Mama Glen shook her head. "No, he didn't. But I think we need to talk."

Dionne's heart clenched.

There it was.

That gut feeling, that instinct screaming at her to walk away. But Mama Glen's voice, her presence, was an anchor—a force Dionne had never been able to fight against.

Feenin'

So, despite every fiber of her being telling her to run, she forced a smile. "Okay."

Mama Glen's smile widened, almost relieved, as she began. "Malik tells me that counseling is actually working for you two."

Dionne's brow furrowed instantly. What?

Her confusion must've shown because Mama Glen continued before she could even react. "Thank you for forgiving him for what he did on Thanksgiving. He was under a lot of stress with the suspension and everything else."

Dionne's chest tightened painfully.

Forgiven? Counseling working?

They hadn't gone back after that one session weeks ago.

She knew counseling wasn't going to fix this—nothing could fix this.

But none of that mattered right now.

What mattered was the way Mama Glen's entire face radiated relief. Hope.

Dionne could feel it—like a noose tightening around her throat.

She loved Mama Glen. She had always loved her. And after everything she was going through, Dionne hated the thought of taking away the one thing still making her smile.

She could feel herself slipping.

Submitting.

Just like she always did.

"Did he tell you why he was suspended?" Dionne asked cautiously, her voice careful, controlled.

Mama Glen nodded, her expression unreadable. "Yeah. A nurse lied on him, saying they were sleeping together. I'm happy you didn't believe that, baby. It would shatter me if you two broke up."

Dionne felt the knife twist deeper in her chest.

Her breath caught, her stomach churned, and suddenly, the words she had been ready to say—the words that would finally free her—were choking her instead.

She had come here to end things.

She had come to tell Malik that she was done, that she had chosen herself, that she had chosen Arris.

But then there was this.

Mama Glen's soft, hopeful voice. The love in her eyes.

The guilt clawing at Dionne's ribcage.

She could feel herself slipping further and further back—back into pleasing Mama Glen.

Back into obligation.

"Yeah," Dionne murmured, her voice hollow, barely audible.

Mama Glen beamed, taking her answer as confirmation, as peace of mind.

"I can't wait for the wedding," Mama Glen continued, her smile widening, her tone filled with warmth. "Me and your mother were just talking about it the other day. It's going to be a dream come true seeing you two getting married."

Dionne's pulse pounded in her ears.

No.

No, no, no.

"I know I don't have that much time left," Mama Glen went on, her voice softer now, more reflective. "So the only memories I'll cherish on my deathbed are seeing my baby boy come into this world… and watching him happily marry the woman of his dreams."

Dionne's breath hitched.

Her heart shattered.

There it was. The line that broke her. The restraint she had been desperately trying to hold onto? Gone.

The fight in her? Gone.

Her voice was nothing more than a whisper when she said the words—words that felt like shattered glass slicing her from the inside out.

"I can't wait to give you that memory."

She wanted to vomit.

She wanted to scream.

But most of all, she wanted to run.

Instead, she sat there, watching Mama Glen beam at her, believing every single word.

And in that moment, Dionne knew—really knew—what she had to do.

She had to kiss Arris goodbye.

No matter how much she *feened* for him, no matter how deep his love had wrapped around her soul, she had made a promise.

A promise to the woman who saved her life.

The conversation shifted, moving into talks of her and Malik's future children, wedding plans, a picture-perfect life Dionne didn't even recognize as her own.

She wanted to scream. She wanted to cry. She wanted to grab her keys and drive straight to Arris. But this? This had always been her reality.

Putting Mama Glen's happiness over her own.

Feenin'

By the time Malik returned, they fell into the act seamlessly—pretending to be the perfect couple in front of Mama Glen.

Every kiss felt like a lie.

Every loving comment burned her throat.

Every mention of the wedding chipped away at the last piece of herself she had left.

She was supposed to be leaving the man she no longer loved for the one she couldn't live without.

Instead, she had to break it off with Arris for good.

And the thought of that hurt more than anything she had ever known.

***

The night settled over the city as Arris drove through the streets, his mind in chaos. No matter how hard he tried to clear it, no matter how many turns he took, every thought circled back to her.

Dionne.

After his talk with A'Lani earlier, he knew he needed to see her. Needed to talk to her. Needed to understand.

And it was as if Dionne sensed it too.

His phone buzzed, and his heart nearly stopped when he saw her name.

Mama: We need to talk. Meet at our place.

A slow smile spread across his face, fingers moving quickly over the screen.

Arris: On my way, Mama.

He didn't hesitate.

Before heading to their shared house, he made a quick stop at his favorite flower shop, handpicking a bouquet of soft white tulips—the ones she always said reminded her of peace. She deserved that. She deserved to feel how much he missed her, how sorry he was for last night.

He paid and left, heart pounding, hands gripping the bouquet like it was his lifeline.

When he pulled up to the house, his smile widened.

Her black Urus was parked in the driveway. She was here.

He barely put the car in park before stepping out, gripping the flowers tightly as he walked inside.

"Mama!" His deep voice echoed through the house, eager, hungry for her presence.

"Upstairs," she called back.

His heartbeat quickened.

Ann

Arris took the stairs two at a time, rushing toward their bedroom like a man starved for her.

The moment he stepped inside, though, his world tilted.

Dionne was sitting on the edge of the bed, her head bowed, hands locked together as if in prayer.

Something was wrong.

His brows knitted as he stepped forward, voice gentler now. "Mama?"

She whispered, Amen, before slowly lifting her head and standing.

Then he saw them.

The tears.

Tears that shattered something deep inside him.

He rushed to her instantly, guilt already eating at his insides. "Mama? I'm sorry. I should've never lashed out on you like that last night." His words tumbled out, desperate, believing he was the cause of her pain.

But then she did something that confused the fuck out of him.

She pushed him away.

Soft, hesitant. But still—a push.

Arris froze, his body stiff, confusion flickering in his eyes.

"These are for you," he started, holding out the tulips, his voice softer now, pleading.

Dionne looked at the bouquet, her lips curving into the smallest, most heartbreaking smile—before she completely broke down.

Her sobs punched the air from his lungs.

Arris's heart clenched so hard, he thought it might fucking stop.

He reached for her, instinct taking over. His hands slid around her waist, desperate to pull her close, to fix whatever was wrong, to hold her together.

But again—she stopped him.

She pressed her hands against his chest, shaking her head.

"No, Arris. Stop."

Her voice was trembling, wrecked, and it sent panic racing through his veins.

He frowned, his grip tightening, his body screaming for her. "Mama, what—?"

She swallowed thickly, willing herself to be strong. She had come here for a reason.

To end this.

To let him *go*.

She knew if she let him get too close, if she let herself drown in the warmth of his body, the strength of his arms, the addiction that was

Feenin'

him—she'd never be able to do it.

But Arris was done with this distance.

He grabbed her waist again, this time firm, unshakable, demanding. He pulled her against him, their bodies colliding, fitting together like they always did—like they were fucking meant to.

And despite the war raging inside her, her body melted into him, betraying her, responding to him naturally, uncontrollably.

Because that's what they were.

Uncontrollable.

Undeniable.

"Baby, I'm sorry," he whispered, his lips brushing against her temple, his hands pressing her tighter against him.

He thought this was about last night.

He thought she was pulling away because of how he lashed out, because of his anger, because of the words he had thrown in the heat of the moment.

He didn't know.

Didn't realize that this moment, this touch, this goodbye—was killing her.

And she wasn't sure if she was strong enough to do it.

"Arris."

Dionne tried to speak, to ground herself, to resist the magnetic pull he had on her. But her restraint was already slipping.

Before she could say another word, he lifted her effortlessly, his hands gripping her thighs, and instinct took over—her legs wrapped around him for support like second nature.

"I'm sorry for yelling at you. I'm sorry for brushing you off, Mama," he murmured, his voice low, vulnerable. "It's just... I can't control my anger sometimes."

His words were filled with regret, but Dionne's tears weren't because of that.

She had already forgiven him for last night.

Her tears were for something so much worse.

For the decision that was about to break them both.

Arris held her tighter, as if he could sense she was slipping away. His lips found the delicate curve of her neck, trailing soft, reverent kisses along her skin. His breath was warm, familiar, addictive.

Dionne's fingers curled into the back of his hoodie, gripping it like it was the only thing anchoring her.

God, she *wanted* him.

She always wanted him.

But the promise she made to Mama Glen loomed over her like a dark cloud, warning her that this moment—this man—was too dangerous.

"Arris," she whispered, voice shaky, laced with need but edged with hesitation.

"Mama," he breathed against her collarbone, his grip on her thighs tightening as he pressed her closer, erasing the space between them.

"You feel how bad I need you?"

Dionne shuddered, her resolve crumbling piece by piece.

He was her weakness. He had always been her weakness. The one thing she could never say no to, no matter how much she tried.

His presence set her on fire.

His touch was the only thing that could put it out.

Still, she tried to fight it.

"Arris, we can't..." she whispered, her voice trembling, thick with regret.

Her hands pressed lightly against his chest, a weak attempt to create space. To stop this before it spiraled beyond control.

She was supposed to be ending things with him.

She was supposed to be walking away.

But here she was, her body betraying her again, molding into him like she belonged there.

Arris pulled back just enough to look into her eyes, his gaze dark, hungry. His lips were slightly swollen, evidence of how easily she had already given in.

"Then tell me to stop."

His voice was rough, demanding, his chest rising and falling heavily.

Dionne opened her mouth.

She tried to say it.

Tried to end this, to stop this train before it crashed.

But nothing came out.

Arris smirked knowingly, leaning in, pressing his forehead against hers. His voice was a whisper of temptation.

"Exactly."

And then his lips claimed hers.

Dionne moaned before she could stop herself, her arms tightening around his neck, pulling him closer instead of pushing him away.

Arris walked them backward until her back hit the nearest wall, caging her in, making escape impossible—not that she was even trying anymore.

His hands roamed down her curves, memorizing her, like he was afraid this would be the last time. His kisses grew deeper, more urgent,

Feenin'

and she felt herself falling, slipping, drowning in the space that only he knew how to fill.

Her mind screamed at her—

No, Dionne. Stop this.

But her body?

Her body only *knew* him.

Dionne's fingers trembled as they slipped beneath the hem of his hoodie, her fingertips tracing the hard ridges of his abs. His skin was hot—burning—and the second her touch met his flesh, Arris let out a deep, guttural growl.

His grip on her tightened like he was afraid she'd slip through his fingers.

"Mama," he groaned against her lips, his forehead pressing against hers as he tried to catch his breath. His hands dug into her hips, anchoring himself to her, begging without words. "I swear, I can't keep doing this. I need you, for real."

His words hit her harder than his touch ever could.

Her breath caught. She pulled back slightly, her wide, desperate eyes searching his face. His jaw was clenched, his expression twisted with something deeper than just lust.

This was longing.

This was desperation.

This was love.

And she had to stop it.

"Arris… please stop."

Her voice wavered, almost a moan, and he felt the war raging inside her.

Arris cursed under his breath, his body stiff, his fists clenched at his sides. The air between them was thick, suffocating, filled with words neither of them had the strength to say.

Finally—he let go.

He took a step back, his breath ragged, his jaw so tight it looked like it might shatter.

Dionne swallowed hard, forcing herself to breathe. The space between them wasn't enough, but it had to be.

"We have to stop," she whispered.

But even she didn't believe it.

Arris exhaled sharply, his hands still hovering over her hips, his body still gravitating toward hers like an unbreakable force.

"Why, Dionne? What's wrong?" His voice was hoarse, thick with frustration and something even more dangerous—hope.

Dionne's mind screamed at her to run, but her heart—her heart ached for him.

Her lips parted, but the words burned on the way out.

"I *choose* him."

Arris stilled.

His entire expression shifted—confusion flashing first before anger and hurt took over.

"You what?" His voice was quiet now, dangerous.

Dionne's chest felt like it was caving in. She forced herself to say it again, to rip herself away from him for good.

"I have to choose him."

The words sliced through them both.

Arris stepped back, his nostrils flaring, his fists clenching. She could see him fighting to keep his rage in check, but it was bubbling over, his entire body vibrating with it.

"Why, Dionne? WHY?!"

His voice boomed through the room, making her jump.

But this time—he didn't care.

This time, she was breaking him again.

The only thing keeping him together were the words A'Lani had spoken earlier. That something—someone—was forcing Dionne to make this choice.

And now he needed to know who.

"Who the fuck is making you do this?"

He stepped closer, his entire body tensed, his eyes burning into hers—searching, demanding the truth.

Dionne felt her bottom lip tremble.

She wanted to tell him.

She wanted to tell him that she was doing this for the woman who saved her life.

But she knew—*knew*—he wouldn't understand.

Even if she explained it, even if she begged him to believe her, he wouldn't.

So instead, she did the only thing she could.

She lied.

"No one, Arris."

She lifted her chin, her voice small, but firm. "I love Malik."

Her voice cracked at the end, betraying her.

And Arris saw it.

He heard it.

His eyes darkened, his fists tightening at his sides.

Feenin'

"No, you don't."

His voice was low, like he was barely holding himself together.

He stepped closer, invading the space she thought she had created, refusing to let her go.

"Please, Arris." Dionne's voice broke, tears burning her eyes. "Don't make this harder than it already is. Just let me go."

Arris let out a bitter chuckle, his head tilting back as if trying to stop the fury from consuming him whole.

"Let you go?"

His voice was ragged, torn, wrecked.

And then—he *snapped*.

He reached for the hem of his hoodie and ripped it over his head, the fabric flying across the room. His chest rose and fell heavily as he stepped back, challenging her.

"Let you *go*, huh?"

He yanked his shirt off next, his muscles tense, his skin burning with frustration, with pain, with rage.

Then he turned around.

And there it was. The *tattoo*. Her face—tattooed across his back.

The breath in Dionne's lungs vanished. Her hand flew to her mouth as she stared, shook.

Dionne's breath hitched at the sight of her face covering Arris's back.

Every delicate detail, every soft curve of her features, perfectly inked into his skin. The pink tulips surrounding her portrait made her heart stutter, but it was the pink sprouting tulip—the one covering her eye—that stole the air from her lungs. It was her—his love, his pain, his fucking *addiction* to her, permanently etched onto his body.

But then he turned back around.

And when their eyes met—his burning with anger and tears—her heart shattered all over again.

Arris's voice was raw, his body tense as he faced her again.

"I can't fucking let you go."

"I fucking love you, Dionne! And you standing here telling me your heart belongs to that nigga?!" Arris's voice roared through the room, vibrating through her bones, through her soul.

Dionne flinched, more tears slipping down her cheeks.

"Arris..." She tried, but he wasn't finished.

"My fucking hand is permanently inked over your heart, Dionne!" His voice cracked, his pain bleeding through every word. "I know you don't love that nigga, so why the fuck are you marrying him? Why the fuck are you doing this to us?"

His voice was sharp as a blade, but his eyes—his eyes—were filled with so much pain it nearly killed her.

Dionne felt her back press against the wall as Arris closed in, pinning her, his presence towering over hers, leaving her nowhere to run, nowhere to hide.

Her body ached for him. But she couldn't have him.

"Arris, please... just let me go."

Her voice cracked, barely above a whisper. But her eyes—her cowardly eyes—stayed downcast. She couldn't look at him. She couldn't meet his gaze and say the words.

And that was all the confirmation Arris needed.

"You can't even fucking look me in the eyes and say that shit." His voice was hoarse now, laced with heartbreak, his fists clenched like he was holding himself together by a thread. "I know something is keeping you tied to that nigga."

Dionne squeezed her eyes shut, forcing herself to breathe.

This was it.

This was the moment she had to choose. She slowly lifted her head, forcing her teary gaze to meet his burning, desperate one.

And then she lied.

"I love Malik."

Her voice was distant, hollow, dead inside.

But she forced it.

"He's the man I'm marrying."

And just like that—she killed them.

Arris froze.

The anger in his face twisted into something darker.

Something *final*.

His breathing deepened, his jaw flexed—then, before she could react, his hand gripped her neck.

Dionne gasped, her heart racing, her body shaking from the contact.

His touch was firm but gentle.

Possessive but not cruel.

His thumb pressed against her throat, feeling her pulse race beneath his fingers. His grip wasn't to hurt—it was to remind her.

"You're lying," he whispered, his voice a low growl.

And then he kissed her.

A claiming. A punishment. A plea.

And despite everything—despite the lie she had just told—Dionne melted.

Her body betrayed her instantly, responding the way it always did.

Feenin'

Because no matter what her words said—her heart would never belong to anyone else.

Arris felt it.

Felt her need, felt her love, felt everything she was trying to bury.

But he was done playing this game.

He pulled back, his lips still brushing against hers, his voice thick with pain.

"Stay the fuck away from me."

The words hit harder than any slap.

Dionne's breath caught, her eyes wide, her heart bleeding as he unleashed her, stepping back like she was nothing.

Arris didn't look at her again.

Didn't hesitate.

He grabbed his things and walked out, his broad, inked-back disappearing through the doorway.

Then—

The front door slammed shut. And that sound—*that sound*—was the final nail in the coffin of their love.

Dionne crumbled right there, her knees hitting the floor as sobs wracked through her body.

She had lost him.

And it was all her fault.

Chapter 21

Two Months Later:

Arris sat in his large glass-walled office, overlooking the sprawling Houston Comets facility. The view stretched before him like a kingdom he was determined to rebuild. His office was a reflection of him—powerful, controlled, unforgiving. Dark tones of black and deep red surrounded him, exuding an aura of dominance and calculated elegance. Yet, no matter how much he tried to immerse himself in the world of deals, contracts, and revenue projections, his eyes kept drifting to the framed jersey on the wall.

Bob Gibson.

The autograph, the frame, the gift Dionne had given him months ago—before she shattered his heart. At the time, it had meant everything.

She had known—without him ever saying it—how much he had idolized Gibson. She had gone out of her way to find it, to make it personal, to give him something irreplaceable.

Just like her.

Now, every time he looked at it, it wasn't just a jersey. It was a reminder. Of her. Of them. Of the love that had consumed him, wrecked him, ruined him.

His jaw tightened as he exhaled sharply, forcing his attention back to the documents in front of him. He wasn't that man anymore. He couldn't be.

But no matter how much he tried to focus on business, the ghost of Dionne still lingered. It had been two months. Two months since she stood in front of him and chose Malik. Two months since she lied to his face and shattered everything they had. Two months of resentment battling the ache of missing her.

It was fucking exhausting.

Feenin'

So he buried himself in the one thing that had never failed him—money. Power. Control.

Demetrius sat across from him, scrolling through franchise revenue reports, his sharp gaze analyzing the numbers on the screen. Arris forced his focus back to work, trying to drown out the ever-present sting of betrayal. This—business—was all he had now.

Arris and Demetrius had taken on the daunting task of restoring the Houston Comets franchise, piece by piece. Their vision? To make it the greatest in baseball history. It was a slow climb, but they were making strides. Arris clenched his jaw, flipping through business endorsement contracts. He knew that the only way to silence the storm inside him was to win—not just in baseball, but in life. Demetrius snapped him out of his thoughts, tapping on the tablet in front of him.

"We need to boost the team's image and get players who can expand the franchise." His voice was all business, all focus.

Arris nodded, forcing his thoughts away from Dionne, away from his mother, away from the past. Focus on the future. He had been hesitant to step back into baseball after everything that happened—the injury, the gunshot, the way his dreams were ripped from him in a single, bloody moment.

But now?

Now, being the owner of the Houston Comets felt like the only way to heal the broken boy who never got to finish his last game. Even as Arris sat, discussing business and planning the future of the Houston Comets, he couldn't shake her from his mind.

Two months.

Two fucking months.

And still, his body craved her like an addict going through withdrawals. He felt the absence of her touch in his bones, the emptiness of his bed, the cold space in his life where she used to be. But the ache that consumed him wasn't just longing—it was resentment.

Resentment for the way she broke his heart. For the way she chose Malik. For the way she lied to his face, telling him she loved another man when he knew—knew with every fucking part of him—that her heart had never belonged to Malik.

It was his. Always his. Still, she walked away. Still, she was marrying that nigga. The thought alone made his fists clench. He exhaled sharply, glancing up at Demetrius, who was lost in a file, oblivious to the storm raging behind Arris's eyes.

"How's the family doing?" Arris asked casually, masking the real reason behind the question.

Ann

Demetrius glanced up, smiling. "They good, bro. We just moved into a new spot my sister found for us. The house is nice as hell—she did her thing finding that place."

Arris's chest tightened at the mention of Dionne. Of course she found them a new home. She always handled everything—perfectly.

"That's good," he muttered, swallowing back the lump in his throat before dropping the only question he actually gave a fuck about. "Speaking of your sister, has she left that sorry-ass nigga you was telling me about?"

His jaw locked as he said it, the words practically burning on the way out.

Demetrius caught the slight shift in Arris's tone this time—the tension that wasn't there before. His brow furrowed slightly, curiosity sparking.

"Nah," Demetrius said, his own voice dipping into frustration. "The wedding is actually tomorrow. I guess she did love him since she forgave his ass for everything he did."

Arris's entire body stiffened. Tomorrow?

Tomorrow.

His fingers curled into fists beneath the desk. His heartbeat pounded in his ears, but he forced himself to keep his expression blank. "Well, seems like she did," Arris said, forcing a nonchalant tone, but Demetrius saw right through him.

The way his jaw tightened. The way his grip on the desk hardened. Demetrius narrowed his eyes slightly. "Arris, you good? You seem real tense hearing about my sister's wedding."

Arris chuckled—a dry, bitter sound. He could feel Demetrius catching on, could see the curiosity in his eyes turning into realization.

"Yeah, I'm good," Arris said, his voice calmer now, more measured. "Just wish your sister got with a man who really loves her."

The moment the words left his mouth, Demetrius knew. He saw it. He saw the way Arris's voice dropped, the way his entire demeanor shifted into something almost painful.

And then it clicked.

Demetrius leaned back in his chair, exhaling, his lips twitching into a smirk even though his tone was dead serious.

"That man is you, ain't it?"

Arris looked up at him, feigning confusion, but Demetrius wasn't fooled.

He knew that look. Knew that feeling.

"Nigga, I see the love in your eyes. You *love* her. You the man you

Feenin'

talking about."

Arris let out another bitter chuckle, shaking his head as if it didn't matter—as if it didn't feel like a knife twisting in his chest just to admit it out loud. "Yeah, bruh."

His voice was quieter now, heavier. "My bad for not telling you, but yeah—I'm in love with your sister."

Demetrius's brows lifted, but he stayed silent, letting Arris speak.

"We were in love with each other—was—but she chose that nigga. So I gotta respect it."

The words burned, but saying them out loud made them real. Demetrius stared at him for a moment, his smirk gone now, realization sinking in just how deep this ran.

"Damn."

Arris exhaled, finally letting go of the mask he'd been wearing. "Yeah."

And then he told him everything.

From the moment they met. The *feenin'* connection that never dulled. The way she looked at him, the way she reacted to him—how she was his drug and he was hers. How Malik never fucking mattered. How her heart had always belonged to him.

And yet—

She was still marrying that nigga.

Demetrius listened, and with every word Arris spoke, he saw it—felt it. The love. The heartbreak. The anger. The confusion. And most of all—the pain in Arris's eyes, the ache in his voice, the resentment in his heart. Demetrius leaned back, running a hand down his face, exhaling sharply.

"Shit, bruh."

Arris let out a humorless laugh, shaking his head. "Yeah."

Demetrius sat quietly for a moment before speaking. "You ever think... she didn't really choose him?"

Arris's jaw clenched. "Don't, bruh."

But Demetrius just nodded, like he knew something Arris didn't yet.

"Damn. So the woman you said you had... she was my sister the entire time?"

Demetrius sat back, stunned. But the amused smirk tugging at his lips softened the shock.

He had always thought Arris was a hoe—never the type to really be in love. But sitting across from him now? Seeing the way Arris's entire demeanor shifted when it came to Dionne, the way his jaw clenched, his fists tightened, the way love and anger warred in his eyes—Demetrius couldn't deny it.

This wasn't some fling. Arris was gone over his sister. And truthfully? He was cool with it. Arris was a way better man than Malik.

"Yeah," Arris muttered, his voice bitter, thick with frustration. His eyes drifted away slightly as if looking at Demetrius too long would only piss him off more. "That was my wife."

My wife.

The words came out sharp, like he was reminding himself of what he lost—of what she threw away.

Demetrius exhaled, shaking his head. "Damn."

Then his tone shifted—more serious now, more certain.

"Look, bruh, I don't know why my sister is marrying that nigga, but I can assure you that shit is not because of love."

Arris immediately shook his head, rejecting the idea before Demetrius could even finish.

Because if that were true—if love wasn't the reason—then why? Why did she walk away from him? Why did she break him?

Demetrius saw the disbelief in his eyes and leaned forward, unwavering. "I know my sister. And based on everything you just told me about y'all? Her heart is fully with you."

Arris let out a humorless laugh, shaking his head. "Then why the fuck is she marrying that nigga, Demetrius?"

His voice was calm, but barely. There was an undercurrent of frustration, of confusion, of something darker.

Demetrius sighed. "Man, I don't have the answer for that. But don't think she didn't love you. Because she did. And I know she still does."

Arris clenched his jaw. Two months. Two months without her. Two months of trying to forget, trying to move on, trying to accept the fact that she was somebody else's woman.

Somebody else's fucking wife. And the thought of it made his blood fucking boil. Without another word, Arris flipped the conversation back to business, his tone sharp, clipped, final. Demetrius caught the shift and let it go, letting his boy bury himself in work, letting him pretend he had moved on.

But he knew the truth.

Arris wasn't over Dionne.

And from the way his anger simmered just beneath the surface?

He *never* would be.

***

Dionne's brown YSL heels clicked against the tile floor in a steady rhythm, each step exuding the poise and confidence she no longer felt. She greeted her colleagues with polite smiles as she passed by, her voice

Feenin'

smooth, composed—effortless. But beneath the mask of perfection, she was barely holding herself together.

She looked flawless—wrapped in an immaculate white Alexander McQueen pantsuit. The sharp-cut blazer framed her shoulders with power, while the flowing fabric of her pants hugged her curves just right. Her natural hair, silk and straight, cascaded down her back in a precise middle part, highlighting the delicate beauty of her features.

On the outside? She was the epitome of grace, success, control. On the inside? She was breaking.

Shattered.

Exhausted. Frustrated. Heartbroken.

Because no matter how well she played the role—no matter how much she tried to distract herself—tomorrow was still coming. The wedding of her nightmares. She wasn't supposed to be at work today. But Ms. Jean had called her in for an important meeting, and she welcomed the distraction. She needed something—anything—to take her mind off the prison she was about to lock herself in. Because if she thought about it too long, she wouldn't be able to go through with it.

She reached her office and closed the door behind her, releasing a breath she hadn't even realized she was holding. But the second she sat down?

Arris.

His name crashed into her mind like a tidal wave, drowning her. His voice. His touch. His anger. His last words haunted her every single day for the last two months. *"Stay the fuck away from me."*

The pain in his voice. The betrayal in his eyes. The way his body had tensed when she chose another man. Even though his words had shredded her, she couldn't blame him. Because she broke him. She chose Malik. And since that day, she had paid the price.

Some nights, she cried herself to sleep, drowning in the emptiness of a bed that wasn't his. Other nights, she walked around like a zombie—numb, emotionless, existing but not living. And she missed him. God, she missed him.

She craved to see him, to touch him, to hear his voice just one more time—but she knew she would never get that chance again. Her hands trembled as she dropped her head into them, fighting the sting of tears. Not now. Not here.

She had made her choice. She had to live with it. There was no turning back now.

A sudden knock at her door snapped Dionne from her thoughts.

She quickly blinked away the tears threatening to fall, swiping at her eyes before clearing her throat. "Come in." Her voice was soft but steady, trying to mask the storm raging inside her.

The door swung open, revealing Ms. Jean, her usual bright smile radiating warmth—a stark contrast to the emotions swirling inside Dionne.

"Good morning, love. It's time for the meeting. I was hoping we could walk to the conference room together."

Dionne inhaled deeply, pushing aside her feelings for the moment. She returned Jean's smile, grateful for the connection they shared. "Of course."

Grabbing her notebook to take notes, she rounded her desk and followed Jean through the office halls. Focus on work. Focus on business. Focus on anything but tomorrow.

As they neared the conference room, Jean reached for the door handle, and the second it swung open—

"CONGRATULATIONS!"

A chorus of cheers erupted, filling the large room with an energy Dionne hadn't felt in months. She jumped slightly, eyes widening as she took in the sight of her coworkers and two closest friends, London and Karmen, beaming with excitement.

"What is all of this?" she asked, breathless, glancing around in shock.

Jean stepped in front of her, glowing with pride. "Pull back that curtain," she instructed, pointing to the large white sheet covering the wall where the company's name was usually displayed. Dionne hesitated for just a moment before stepping forward. Her hands gripped the fabric, and with one pull—

There it was. The bold, elegant letters gleamed under the lights: WILLIAMS-SMITH LUXE REALTY.

Her heart stopped. For a moment, she forgot how to breathe.

"Congratulations to our new managing partner, Dionne Smith!" Jean's words echoed in the room, triggering another round of cheers and applause.

Dionne's hands flew to her mouth, her eyes instantly welling with happy tears. "Oh my God." Her voice trembled with disbelief.

It finally happened. She did it.

This was the rainbow in the middle of the storm consuming her life. This was everything she had worked for—every late night, every deal, every sacrifice. The weight of it hit her all at once, pride swelling in her chest. Her friends rushed toward her, their faces lit with excitement.

"My girl is finally partner!" London screamed, grabbing Dionne's hands as they jumped up and down.

Feenin'

"I can't believe this." Her voice cracked, happy tears slipping down her cheeks.

"Aww, you worked for this, Dee," Karmen said softly, pulling her into a hug.

Dionne melted into the embrace, letting her tears fall.

She deserved this moment. She had earned this moment. But as she stood there, surrounded by love, by celebration— A hollow ache settled in her chest. Because the one person she wanted to share this with…

The one man she needed to bask in this moment with her… Was no longer a part of her life.

The celebration continued in the conference room, laughter and chatter filling the space as Dionne basked in the moment. Her friends and coworkers toasted to her success, and every now and then, her eyes would drift to the new sign on the wall—her name permanently engraved.

She had worked tirelessly for this. She was proud of herself. And for a moment—just a moment—she let herself feel that pride. But soon, the small office party came to an end, and the real celebration with her girls was just beginning.

Dionne left work and headed straight to the store to grab wine and snacks for the night at London's house. She pulled into the parking lot, stepping out in her black Lamborghini Urus, her heels clicking against the pavement as she made her way inside.

The store was quiet, the aisles nearly empty as she grabbed everything she needed—wine, chocolates, chips, the essentials for a girls' night done right.

Dionne walked down the aisle filled with bottles of wine, scanning the shelves for her and her friends' favorites, trying to lose herself in the simplicity of the task. For one night, she wanted to pretend her world wasn't crumbling, that tomorrow wasn't the start of a nightmare she couldn't escape. As she reached for a bottle, a small voice in the distance pulled her from her search.

Her gaze shifted, landing on a little girl clutching her mother's hand, excitement bubbling in her soft voice as she pointed at a shelf full of cookies. Dionne's chest tightened at the sight, warmth flickering deep in her heart before a sharp ache settled in. She had always dreamed of having a little girl of her own, one that looked exactly like her, with big, curious eyes and thick curls. She imagined spoiling her, dressing her in the cutest outfits, watching her grow up surrounded by love, protected by the kind of husband who would move mountains for both of them.

But reality was cruel.

Ann

Because her reality was nothing like what she had envisioned.

Instead of marrying the man who made her feel alive, the one she *feened* for in every way possible, she was preparing to walk down the aisle for a promise—a promise she had made to Mama Glen, not for love, not for herself. And the man she truly wanted, the man she saw a real future with, was out of her life for good.

A familiar hollow pain settled in her chest, but before she could tear her eyes away from the mother and daughter, she saw him.

And everything stopped.

Her body went still, her pulse pounded in her ears, and her fingers instinctively clenched around the bottle in her hand.

Malik.

Her fiancé.

The man she was supposed to marry tomorrow.

Kissing a woman.

Then smiling down at her daughter.

Dionne's blood boiled.

Her vision blurred with rage as reality crashed down on her like a tidal wave, drowning her in fury, in disbelief.

She couldn't believe her fucking eyes.

Dionne didn't waste another second before making her presence known. Her heels clicked against the floor with a slow, deliberate rhythm, each step carrying the weight of controlled fury. Her head was high, her expression smooth, but inside, her blood boiled. She walked straight toward Malik and the woman beside him, the scene before her making her stomach twist with rage and disgust.

"Hey, Malik."

Her voice was calm—too calm.

Malik turned around, and the second his eyes landed on her, his entire body locked up.

Dionne saw it—the panic, the way his Adam's apple bobbed, the way his eyes darted around like he was scrambling for an exit.

And she smiled.

Not because she was happy—because she knew he was caught.

Her gaze flicked to the woman beside him, who was already staring at her, confusion flickering in her features. But Dionne recognized her instantly—Brittany.

The same woman she had once walked in on, tangled with Malik in their bed.

Brittany's eyes widened, her entire body tensing, and then—fear.

Good.

Feenin'

Dionne's smile didn't waver as she looked back at Malik. "What is this?" Her tone was polite, still laced with sweetness, but the steel behind her words was unmistakable.

Malik swallowed hard. "Umm... uhh..." He rubbed the back of his neck, his eyes darting to Brittany, then back to Dionne.

"The cat got your tongue?" Dionne's arms crossed, her nails pressing into her skin to keep herself from throwing the bottle of wine straight at his face.

Malik's jaw tensed. "Brittany, can you take Blair to get those snacks she wants? I'll meet you two in line."

Dionne didn't move, didn't blink—until she heard it.

"But Daddy, I thought you were gonna get me that toy?"

Her entire body stiffened. Her breath caught. Her fingers gripped the bottle tighter.

"Daddy?"

Her voice was quiet, but the storm raging inside her was anything but.

Malik didn't answer immediately, but the way he tensed? The way he wouldn't meet her eyes? She already knew.

"I think we need to tell her, Malik," Brittany spoke up, her voice shaky, her nerves clear in every syllable.

Dionne's jaw locked.

Her patience? Gone.

She shifted, her body turning to fully face him, her chin tilted up. "Yeah, Malik. Tell me."

Her tone left no room for him to wiggle out of this.

Malik inhaled deeply, his eyes flicking toward Brittany before settling back on Dionne. "Brittany and I... are engaged."

Dionne's heart dropped.

Her entire stomach twisted.

What?

"We've been engaged for two years... and this is our four-year-old daughter, Blair."

Dionne blinked.

Once.

Twice.

Then she looked at the little girl again, really looked at her, and her blood turned to fire.

Because now? She saw it.

The resemblance.

The spitting fucking image of Malik.

510

Her blood boiled.

Her jaw clenched so tight it ached.

"Hold up." Her voice was low—dangerous. "Let me get this straight."

She stepped closer, her eyes burning into his.

"You've been engaged to her for two years... and y'all share a child?"

Malik nodded slowly. "Yes. I wanted to tell you, but my mother was stuck on us getting married, and I didn't want to break her heart—especially since she's dying."

Dionne let out a dark, bitter laugh.

She had risked everything for this man. Her happiness. Her peace. Her love for Arris. She had sacrificed herself for a woman she adored, convinced herself that honoring her promise was more important than choosing her own future. And this motherfucker had a whole-ass family she knew nothing about?

Her lips curled in rage, her tone razor-sharp.

"All the shit you put me through."

Malik stiffened.

"The constant manipulation—telling me how much you loved me, forcing me into pre-marital counseling, arguing with me every other day, accusing me of cheating..."

Her voice rose, but she didn't care.

"Holding the promise I made to Mama Glen over my head—making me feel like shit if I even thought about leaving—when this whole fucking time, you had a whole-ass family?"

Malik and Brittany both looked terrified, standing frozen as Dionne's fury consumed her.

"Dionne, it's more complicated—" Malik started, but she snapped her attention to Brittany.

"Did you know about all of this?" Her voice was sharp, lethal. "That he was marrying me, while you two were supposed to be engaged?"

Brittany hesitated—then nodded. "Yes. I knew. And I agreed to support it."

Dionne stared at her, eyes narrowed in pure disbelief.

"So you're okay with all this shit?"

Brittany nodded again, though her nervousness never left.

"Malik told me about Mama Glen's wish," Brittany said, voice soft, hesitant. "Even though Malik is the man I want to marry, I understand the love you and Mama Glen share. If marrying you made Malik happy by giving his mother her dying wish, then... I was okay with that."

Feenin'

Dionne blinked.

Then laughed.

A low, humorless laugh that bubbled up from somewhere dark inside of her.

This shit?

This shit was fucking crazy.

She had sacrificed everything—her future, her happiness, her soul—for this bullshit.

And she wasn't about to let this slide.

"I'm done with this shit," Dionne said lowly, her voice steady, but the fire in her eyes burned hotter than ever. She was exhausted, angry, and sick of being manipulated, sick of sacrificing herself for the happiness of others while her own dreams turned to dust. Malik had the audacity to stand there with his real family—the fiancée and child he had hidden from her—and still ask her to go through with this sham of a marriage.

"Please, still marry me. For my mother," Malik spoke up, desperation laced in his tone, his eyes pleading as if he hadn't just shattered every last ounce of faith she had in him. Dionne's head snapped up, her stare cutting through him like glass. "Do you hear yourself?" Her voice was eerily calm, the kind of quiet that came before destruction. "I am looking at your family, Malik, and you have the audacity to stand here and tell me we should still get married tomorrow?" The disbelief dripped from every word, but the anger—the fury—was unmistakable.

"My mother wants it to be you, Dee. She doesn't know about Brittany or Blair, and telling her now is only going to break her heart. I can't do that to her. Not when she's in her last days," Malik begged, and Dionne sighed heavily, her chest rising and falling with the weight of the decision she already knew she had to make. She wanted to tell him to go fuck himself, wanted to walk away from this entire nightmare and never look back, but no matter how much she loathed Malik, she loved Mama Glen. And the one man who could've given her the life she truly wanted was gone, his last words still haunting her like a ghost. Stay the fuck away from me. Arris hated her. There was no fixing what she had broken, no erasing the betrayal in his eyes, no undoing the damage she had caused. And if she couldn't have him, then what was the point in walking away from Malik now? At least this way, she could still make one of the people she loved happy.

"Fine, Malik," she said, the words tasting like acid on her tongue. She watched his shoulders relax in relief, but before he could get another word out, her expression hardened. "But once we're married, we're staying in separate houses. We're together by law and appearances for

Mama Glen—nothing more. And when she passes, I want a divorce." Her voice was like ice, and when Malik nodded, agreeing without hesitation, it only made her blood boil hotter. He didn't love her. He never had. She had ruined her life for a man who was willing to let her go without a fight, and that realization made her feel more foolish than anything else ever had.

"Thank you, Dee," he said softly, but his gratitude meant nothing to her. Dionne clenched her jaw, refusing to look at him, refusing to acknowledge the betrayal clawing at her insides, refusing to let herself feel the devastation that threatened to consume her whole. She was staying in this prison, but only for Mama Glen. Without another word, she turned on her heel, walking away from him, from Brittany, from the entire mess she had been blind to for far too long. She paid for her items quickly, her hands trembling from the sheer force of the rage she was suppressing. She needed to get out of here. She needed air. She needed to go home, change, and pretend—just for one night—that her life wasn't completely unraveling at the seams. Because tomorrow, she was walking into a future she wanted no part of, and she wasn't sure if she'd ever forgive herself for it.

***

Dionne stepped out of the shower, the steam swirling around her like a suffocating cloud as she reached for her lotion, moisturizing her skin with slow, methodical movements. No matter how much she tried to focus on the warmth of the water that had just kissed her skin or the vanilla-scented cream she smoothed over her body, nothing could ease the fire still burning inside her.

Malik had a whole secret family.

It wasn't the years of cheating that made her blood simmer—she had stopped caring about that a long time ago. The love between them had died before she ever truly admitted it to herself. But what had her skin crawling, her chest tightening with rage, was the fact that she had sacrificed so much—her happiness, her life, her craving for Arris—all to honor a promise.

She had shattered the heart of the only man she had ever truly loved, forced herself to believe she was doing the right thing, suffered every day just to keep Mama Glen happy.

And for what?

For a man who had been living a lie, building a future with another woman, raising a daughter she never even knew about.

The walls of her bathroom felt like they were closing in, but she was too exhausted to keep crying over it.

Feenin'

Crying wouldn't fix it.

Crying wouldn't bring Arris back.

Because it wasn't like she could just walk away and he would be there, waiting for her with open arms.

She had destroyed them.

She had broken him, and he had told her, clear as day—stay the fuck away from him.

He wanted nothing to do with her.

So what was the point?

Dionne swallowed hard, forcing down the lump in her throat as she slipped into a black matching Essentials tracksuit, pairing it with her Black Cat Jordan 4s, deciding comfort was the only thing she could control right now. She was done dwelling on the prison that had become her life.

For just one night, she would focus on the good—as small as it felt compared to the crushing weight of her mistakes.

Tonight, she would celebrate herself.

Even if it was the only thing she had left.

Dionne styled her hair in a perfect half-up, half-down look, the soft waves cascading down her back. She swiped on a layer of lip gloss, the subtle shine enhancing her makeup-free face. Once satisfied with her appearance, she grabbed her purse and made her way downstairs, ready to head out.

She stepped out of the house, the cool evening wind brushing against her skin, but it did nothing to extinguish the rage burning inside her. The weight of her choices pressed against her chest like an unbearable weight, and as she climbed into her car, she felt like she could barely breathe.

The drive to London's house was a blur, the city lights flickering past her like ghosts of every decision she had made, every step that had led her here. No matter how much she tried to steady her thoughts, they spun violently inside her mind, unraveling her.

Sickness.

College.

Meeting Malik.

Mama Glen's sacrifice.

Meeting Arris. Falling for Arris. Loving Arris.

The memories came like a flood, each one hitting harder than the last, and regret sank its claws into her.

She had destroyed everything.

She had made the worst decisions of her life, and now she was walking straight into another one.

But falling in love with Arris? That was the one thing she would never regret. Not for a second.

His voice, his touch, the way his eyes held hers like she was the only thing in his world—it all came crashing down on her, suffocating her, breaking her. She gripped the steering wheel, her breath coming out in ragged gasps before the sobs ripped through her. Deep, gut-wrenching, uncontrollable sobs.

She had shattered the heart of the man she loved.

And nothing—no celebration, no accomplishment, no amount of pretending—could ever make her forget it.

And now?

She was about to destroy her life even further.

Marrying Malik.

The thought alone made her physically ill.

She felt like the dumbest, most foolish woman alive, but this wasn't about her. It was never about her. She was doing this for Mama Glen.

And that—that was the only thing keeping her from losing her mind completely.

But it didn't stop the withdrawals.

It didn't stop the aching, the deep, relentless craving for Arris.

She could feel him—his absence, his love still lingering in every part of her, pulling at her even as she tried to let go.

But there was nothing she could do.

She had already signed her soul away to live this lie for the woman who saved her life.

And now, she had no choice but to survive it.

Feenin'

Chapter 22

Malik & Dionne Wedding

Dionne couldn't believe what she was doing. She stood in front of the mirror in her bridal suite, staring at her reflection as if it belonged to someone else. The diamond-embellished nude wedding dress hugged her figure like a second skin, the intricate details shimmering under the soft light. She looked flawless, elegant—the perfect bride.

But inside? Inside, she was crumbling.

Even after learning that she didn't have to marry Malik anymore, even after being given an out, she had still chosen this. Because walking away meant facing a life without Arris alone, and that was a pain she wasn't ready to bear.

So, she went through with it anyway.

Her fingers trembled slightly as she adjusted the diamond veil that cascaded behind her. Her hair was pinned in an elegant messy bun, soft tendrils framing her face. She looked like the type of woman any man would be lucky to marry—the kind of bride that belonged in fairytales.

But this wasn't a fairytale. She wasn't marrying her prince. She was marrying a man she didn't even love.

A sudden knock at the door made her stiffen, forcing her emotions deep into the pit of her stomach. She turned just as the door opened, revealing her mother and her closest friends, their bright smiles filling the room. They all looked stunning in their bridesmaids' dresses, Danita wearing the dress she had picked out for the special occasion.

Dionne did what she did best—she mirrored their joy.

She smiled, even though her heart felt like it was sinking deeper into a void she would never crawl out of.

"Oh, my baby girl, you look so beautiful," Danita gushed, her eyes glistening as she took in her daughter. Without hesitation, she pulled Dionne into a warm embrace, holding her tight.

Dionne melted into her mother's arms—not out of happiness, but because she needed something to hold onto before she shattered completely.

Danita's voice softened, "Are you ready?"

Dionne's throat tightened.

She couldn't say the words, because she knew the moment she opened her mouth, the truth would slip out.

So, instead, she nodded.

Danita beamed, believing her daughter was truly happy, when in reality, Dionne had never felt more trapped.

Her eyes flickered to Kierra, London, and Karmen, standing just behind her mother, their smiles softer, hesitant. Unlike Danita, they knew the truth.

They saw the way her hands shook. They saw the way her eyes—always so full of fire—now carried nothing but a deep, suffocating sadness. And as Dionne took a slow, shaky breath, she realized something.

This wasn't just a mistake. This was the biggest mistake of her life. And the worst part?

She was still about to walk down that aisle and make it anyway.

Danita and Dionne finally pulled away, Danita's eyes shining with pride as she took in her daughter one last time. "My baby is really getting married," she whispered, her voice thick with emotion. Dionne forced another smile, letting her mother bask in a happiness that wasn't real.

"I'm going to leave you with your girls, but I just want you to know how proud I am of you, baby. I'll see you out there." Danita pulled her into a quick but tight hug before walking toward the door.

The moment it clicked shut, Dionne's smile vanished. The air in the room shifted instantly, tension filling the silence like a dark, suffocating cloud.

Kierra was the first to speak, her arms crossed over her chest, her expression tight. "So you're really about to throw your entire life away?" Her tone was sharp, cutting through the fragile control Dionne was desperately trying to hold onto.

Dionne rolled her eyes, turning her attention back to her reflection in the mirror, refusing to engage. "Ki, please just let it go." Her voice was low, clipped, a warning—but Kierra wasn't letting this go.

"She's right, Dee," London added, her voice softer, but no less stern. "You're really about to marry a man you don't love, just for his mother?"

Feenin'

Dionne's jaw clenched, her nails digging into the edge of the vanity as her patience thinned.

"Look, I'm doing this," she snapped, her tone final, her hands tightening into fists. "So please stop trying to convince me not to, or make me feel worse than I already do."

For a second, silence filled the room.

Then—

"What about Arris?"

Karmen's voice was soft, hesitant, but the second his name left her lips, Dionne's entire body stiffened.

Her heart sank, the weight of his absence crashing over her all over again.

Arris.

The only man she had ever truly loved. The only man who had ever made her feel like more. Like everything. The man she had walked away from, the man she had broken.

She sucked in a deep breath, forcing the ache down, burying it beneath the decision she had already made.

"Me and Arris are over."

The words tasted like acid.

She looked down, gripping the counter harder, her voice tight with forced acceptance. "I fucked that up, and he wants nothing to do with me. So please... it's my life, and I'm a grown-ass woman. I'm doing what I think is right."

Her friends stared at her, their eyes filled with sadness, with disappointment, with a truth she refused to face.

But they didn't push anymore. Because they knew. They could see it. Dionne wasn't making the right choice. She was making the only choice she thought she had left.

A soft knock at the door made the room fall silent, the lively chatter of Dionne's friends coming to an abrupt halt as all eyes turned toward the entrance. The door creaked open slowly, and Mama Glen stepped inside.

The room shifted instantly, an unspoken respect and admiration settling over them. Despite the storm raging inside Dionne, she couldn't help but smile. Mama Glen looked stunning, the deep hues of her dress elegant and regal, a stark contrast to the frailty Dionne knew she had been trying to hide.

"Hey, Mama Glen," Dionne said, her voice steady, though inside, her stomach twisted.

Mama Glen's lips curled into a gentle smile, but her gaze was knowing. She turned toward the girls, eyes kind but firm.

Ann

"Can we have the room for a minute?"

The request was soft, polite, but there was no mistaking the finality behind it. Kierra, London, and Karmen glanced at Dionne, hesitating, but she gave a small nod, silently urging them to go.

One by one, they filed out, casting one last lingering look before closing the door behind them.

Now, it was just them.

Mama Glen moved slowly toward the elegant white couch, every step measured, each breath slower than usual. She lowered herself down, then patted the seat beside her.

Dionne hesitated for just a second before moving toward her, the layers of her wedding gown rustling softly as she sat.

An uneasy silence stretched between them.

Mama Glen turned, her eyes sweeping over Dionne, admiration flickering in them. "You look beautiful," she murmured, voice thick with emotion.

Dionne swallowed. "Thank you," she whispered.

But the warmth of the moment didn't last. Something unspoken lingered between them. A heaviness that pressed down on Dionne's chest, making it hard to breathe.

Mama Glen finally inhaled deeply, exhaling like she was bracing herself. Then, she turned fully to Dionne, her eyes sharper now, her expression unreadable.

"Dionne, I'm going to ask you this once," she said, her voice steady, but carrying a weight that made Dionne's stomach churn. "And I need you to be honest with me."

Dionne's breath hitched.

"Are you happy?"

Her heart plummeted.

The question landed like a punch, knocking the air from her lungs. She wasn't ready for this.

Still, she did what she had trained herself to do—she smiled. The kind of smile she had perfected over the years, the one that masked the pain, the one that made it easy for people to believe her lies

"Yes, Mama Glen. I'm happy," Dionne lied smoothly, effortlessly. "I'm healthy for the first time in my life, thanks to you. I am managing partner at the firm, and in a few minutes, I'm about to get married."

She forced pride into the last part, hoping desperately it would be enough.

Mama Glen smiled back, but Dionne saw it—the way her eyes didn't quite believe her.

Feenin'

"That's wonderful, sweetie," Mama Glen said softly. But then, her face changed.

And her next words sent ice through Dionne's veins.

"But I'm talking about you and my son," she pressed, her voice calm but unwavering. "Are you happy in your relationship? Is marrying him what you really want?"

Dionne blinked.

Her heart slammed against her ribs.

Where was this coming from?

She had spent years convincing herself that she could live this lie. That her duty—to Mama Glen, to the promise she made—was bigger than her own happiness.

And yet, here was Mama Glen, seeing right through her.

Dionne scrambled to recover, rebuilding her mask in an instant.

"Yes, Mama Glen," she said, her voice smooth, practiced, though the words felt like shards of glass on her tongue. "I'm happy with Malik and our relationship."

This time, it wasn't enough.

Mama Glen shook her head.

Her expression crumbled, disbelief settling into the creases of her face.

"Dionne, why are you lying to me?"

Dionne's heart clenched.

The tears forming in Mama Glen's eyes shattered her.

"I know you're not happy," Mama Glen continued, her voice breaking. "I know you and Malik no longer love each other. And the truth is, you two haven't loved each other in a long time."

Dionne froze.

Her entire body stiffened, her breath catching in her throat.

She knew.

Mama Glen knew.

All the years of pretending, of pushing through, of convincing herself this was what she had to do—it all came crashing down in a single moment.

"Mama—" Dionne started, her voice barely above a whisper.

But Mama Glen shook her head, her shoulders trembling.

"I'm so sorry," she whispered, her voice cracking, a sob slipping through before she could stop it.

And that was all it took.

Dionne immediately pulled her into a hug, holding her tightly, protectively, fiercely—the same way Mama Glen had held her when she saved her life.

"No, Mama. Don't do this. It's not your fault," Dionne whispered, her own voice breaking.

Mama Glen just shook her head again and again, her body trembling in Dionne's embrace.

But they both knew the truth.

"I know you're marrying my son because of me," Mama Glen's voice was soft, but it cut straight through Dionne like a blade. "And I'm sorry for making you feel like you had to sacrifice your life just to give me something you thought I wanted, just because I saved your life."

Dionne's brows furrowed, her heart stalling.

"Thought?" she echoed, her voice barely above a whisper.

Mama Glen chuckled softly, wiping away the tears that had fallen onto her cheeks, but her smile was heavy—weighted with something that felt like regret.

"Sweetie, I didn't do that surgery to save your life just so you could spend the rest of it miserable, marrying a man you don't love."

The words hit so hard, Dionne almost flinched.

She had spent so long convincing herself that this was the right thing to do, that this was what Mama Glen wanted, that the pain in her chest, the hollowness in her soul, the constant ache for Arris—none of it mattered.

But now, sitting in her wedding dress, moments away from marrying a man who never truly owned her heart, she was being told that everything she thought was obligation was never what Mama Glen asked of her at all.

Mama Glen reached for her hands, gripping them gently, her warmth grounding Dionne in a way that almost hurt.

"Yes, I believed you were the perfect woman for my son," she continued, her voice softer now, yet carrying more weight than ever. "I truly thought the two of you were in love. But more than anything, all I ever wanted—for both of you—was to be happy."

Happy.

Dionne felt the word wrap around her like a noose.

Mama Glen sighed deeply. "And now, I know that happiness doesn't lie with him."

Dionne felt her entire body lock up.

Her hands gripped Mama Glen's tighter, her breath catching, her stomach churning because something about those words—those five words—felt like a breaking point.

"You're in love with someone else," Mama Glen said, her voice

Feenin'

gentle, but it sent a tremor through Dionne's entire soul.

Dionne's heart stopped.

Arris.

His face flooded her mind. His touch, his voice, the fire in his eyes, the way he loved her so deeply it terrified her. She thought of the way his hands trembled when he held her, like she was the most precious thing in the world. The way he spoke to her like he could see inside her soul. The way she felt his absence like a drug withdrawal every single day since she walked away from him.

And Mama Glen saw it.

She saw the way Dionne's expression shifted, the way her eyes brightened and darkened all at once, like just thinking of him was both relief and agony.

"You need to marry that man, Dionne," Mama Glen continued, squeezing her hands a little tighter, like she was trying to pull Dionne back from the ledge she had been teetering on for months. "Not my son. Not just to make me happy."

Dionne blinked rapidly, frozen in shock.

Her mind wasn't catching up fast enough.

They were sitting in her bridal suite. She was in her wedding dress. The wedding was starting in minutes. And Mama Glen—the one person Dionne had centered her entire sacrifice around—was telling her to walk away.

Dionne opened her mouth, but nothing came out.

Mama Glen just smiled knowingly, her voice full of nothing but love.

"My one and only wish was for both of you to be happy, whether that was together or apart. And I know my son is happy with the family he's trying to keep a secret—don't think I don't know about that, either."

Dionne gasped slightly, lips parting, her chest tightening.

Mama Glen cupped her cheek, her eyes filled with so much love it nearly crushed her.

"I want you to know that living the life you enjoy, being with the man who truly makes you happy—that's my only wish."

Dionne's chest ached, burned, screamed inside of her. Her eyes widened, heart pounding in her ears as the words broke her. She thought she had been doing this for Mama Glen. That this was the only way to repay her for saving her life. That if she couldn't be with Arris, she could at least give Mama Glen this one last thing before she left this world.

But she had it all wrong.

Mama Glen never wanted her to be miserable. She never wanted her to be trapped in a loveless marriage. She never wanted her to choose duty over love. She just wanted the two people she loved most in this world to be happy.

Together or apart.

And now, for the first time in two months, Dionne had something she thought she had lost forever—

A *choice.*

Dionne sat in silence, her entire body trembling, her mind screaming.

She had spent months believing she had no choice, that her life was set in stone, that her sacrifice was necessary.

But now?

Now she was free.

So why did she still feel trapped?

Even though she was relieved to hear she wasn't obligated to marry Malik anymore, the truth still cut deep.

Because the life she craved?

The life that had set her soul on fire?

The life she let go of?

It was already over.

She had already caused too much damage.

Already shattered the heart of the man she *feened* for. Already made choices that couldn't be undone.

Mama Glen squeezed her hand one last time.

"Just be happy, Dionne."

Dionne nodded, offering a small, forced smile, even though inside, her chest ached, her soul cracked, her breath felt like it was slipping away.

Because how was she supposed to be happy...

When she had already walked away from the only person that ever truly made her feel alive?

Mama Glen pulled her into one last embrace, the warmth of it sinking deep into Dionne's bones, grounding her for just a moment before she stepped back. Her wise eyes, filled with nothing but love, held Dionne's gaze as she whispered her final words.

"Go be with the man you truly love."

Then she turned and walked out of the room, leaving Dionne standing there with her breath caught in her throat, her heart hammering against her ribcage, her entire soul at war.

She was *free.*

So why did she still feel trapped?

A sharp knock at the door shattered the moment, making her jump. The wedding planner poked her head in, her voice soft, oblivious to the

Feenin'

storm raging inside Dionne. "Hey, it's time."

Dionne swallowed, her body locked in place.

She looked in the mirror, wondering why she didn't run, scream, do something—anything—other than what she knew would destroy her.

But Dionne just nodded.

"Let's do this," she murmured, but her voice wasn't steady.

She shook her head, exhaling sharply, as if trying to force the doubts out of her mind. But they clung to her, sinking deeper, wrapping around her lungs like a vice.

What the hell am I doing?

Everyone was outside, waiting for her to marry the man they believed was the love of her life. And now that she wasn't bound by Mama Glen's promise, she had no idea what to do.

Her body moved on autopilot. She stepped out of the bridal suite, her head held high, shoulders back—the alluring, beautiful, poised bride everyone expected to see. But inside?

She felt like she was walking toward her own execution.

Her father was waiting at the end of the hall, the man who had always been her quiet protector, her anchor even when she never let him be.

Dionne's breath hitched.

For the first time in her twenty-eight years of life, she saw emotion flicker in her father's eyes.

Lamar, the man who never let his guard down, looked at her like she was still his little girl.

Like he knew something was wrong.

"You're beautiful, baby girl," Lamar said, his voice thick, filled with so much love it nearly made her knees buckle.

Dionne forced a smile. She wanted to fall into his arms, bury herself in his embrace, and tell him everything.

She wanted to say, Daddy, I don't know what I'm doing. I don't want to do this.

But she couldn't.

Because she didn't even know what she was doing herself.

The music started.

The groomsmen and bridesmaids began their slow procession down the aisle. Dionne stood beside her father, her pulse thundering in her ears.

The grand doors of the venue shut.

A hush fell over the crowd.

Then, the first chords of "First Time" by TEEKS floated through the space, signaling that the bride was about to make her entrance.

Ann

The large black grand doors creaked open.
And there she was.
Dionne.
Every head turned. Every guest gasped.
She moved gracefully, gliding forward with a practiced elegance, every detail about her—from the delicate shimmer of her gown to the softness of her veil cascading down her back—screaming perfection.
But perfection was a lie.
She felt nothing.
Not the admiration in the eyes of her guests. Not the love in her mother's proud smile. Not the way Malik's eyes softened as he looked at her, standing at the altar in a crisp black and white suit, beaming like a man who truly believed this was the happiest day of his life.
Her body moved forward.
Her mind screamed run.
She glanced at the front row, her gaze locking onto Mama Glen.
The soft, faint smile on her face said she was proud.
But her eyes?
Her eyes said she knew the truth.
Mama Glen saw through the veil, through the gown, through the poised, perfect image Dionne had spent her entire life curating.
She knew this wasn't what Dionne wanted.
So why was she still walking?
Each step forward felt like a betrayal to herself.
Each second that passed felt like she was losing something she could never get back.
Her heart wasn't pounding with excitement.
It was breaking.
And she was seconds away from shattering completely.
Lamar handed Dionne off to Malik, her fingers slipping into his, but there was no warmth. No rush of love, no comfort, nothing but the weight of obligation pressing against her chest.
They stood at the altar, hand in hand, staring at each other—but there was no love staring back.
To the guests, it was a beautiful moment. To her friends, Demetrius, and Mama Glen, it was a performance.
The pastor began the ceremony, his voice echoing through the grand venue, but Dionne barely heard a word.
She couldn't breathe.
Malik began his vows, and she forced herself to listen, but the words blurred together—empty, rehearsed, a lie wrapped in poetic phrases.

Feenin'

"Dionne, when I first saw you in college, I knew you were the woman I wanted to spend the rest of my life with."

She subtly rolled her eyes, resisting the urge to laugh at the irony.

Her gaze drifted to the back of the venue. Brittany. Blair.

Malik's real family. The ones he hid while she sacrificed everything for him.

It was insane.

And yet, here she was.

Still playing her role. Still standing in a wedding dress beside a man she didn't love.

"I love you," Malik finished, his voice thick with fake emotion.

A lie.

Another lie.

She had heard enough.

"Dionne, it's your turn," the pastor announced, pulling her back into the moment.

Karmen handed her the small, folded piece of paper—the vows she had written, the ones meant to seal her fate.

Her fingers trembled as she unfolded it. She took a deep breath, feeling every eye in the room on her.

She started to read.

"Growing up, love was the thing I craved more than anything in the world. Watching my '90s love movies, singing love songs at the top of my lungs, seeing love with my own eyes through my parents..."

A small smile touched her lips, her first real one of the day.

"I didn't know how addicting love was until I met a man. A man who looked beyond my beauty, who touched me like I was the most precious thing in the world, and loved me like I was a drug he couldn't stop using. This man protects me, provides for me, cares for me, and feens for me in ways I never thought were possible."

Malik smiled.

So did the guests.

Everyone drank in her words, believing them, thinking she was speaking about the man standing in front of her.

She wasn't.

Her eyes flickered up, scanning the crowd. Mama Glen.

Mama Glen smiled, her expression unreadable, but Dionne knew she saw through it all.

Her throat tightened. Her chest burned.

This was it. The moment of no return.

"I thought the love my parents had was one of a kind," she continued, her voice growing stronger. More certain. "That I'd never find a love that wasn't perfect, but still beautiful—even when it looked like chaos."

She exhaled, the words pouring from her like a confession.

"I experienced what it felt like to have life sucked out of me, to have it threatened to be taken away. And I don't ever want to experience that with love."

Her fingers tightened around the paper, her pulse roaring in her ears.

Then, she lifted her head, locking eyes with Malik.

"So, I need to go find the love that I *feen* for... and it's not with you, Malik."

Gasps rippled through the venue.

Malik's smile vanished.

Dionne's chest heaved, her heart pounding violently against her ribs.

She turned to the pastor. Then to the crowd.

"I'm sorry, everyone," she said, her voice firm, unwavering. "But I can't do this."

And before anyone could stop her—before Malik could grab her hand, before her mother could call her name, before logic and obligation could drag her back into that prison—

She ran.

The guests erupted into whispers and stunned murmurs as Dionne darted from the altar, ripping off her veil, her heels clicking against the marble floors as she made her escape.

She didn't stop.

Didn't hesitate.

Didn't look back.

She tore through the grand hallway, pushing open the doors to the bridal suite, yanking off the suffocating wedding dress, stripping herself of every expectation, every lie she had forced herself to live.

She was *free*.

Her lips curled into a breathless smile, her chest rising and falling as she let the moment sink in.

She chose herself.

She chose love.

She chose *Arris*.

No matter how much he tried to fight her, no matter how much he hated her for breaking his heart—she was going to get him back.

Because he was the man she *feened* for.

And she wasn't leaving without him.

London, Kierra, and Karmen burst into the suite, their eyes widening at the sight before them—Dionne out of her wedding dress, now draped

Feenin'

in a long black trench coat and heels, ready to run.

"Damn, you really left his ass at the altar!" London cackled, shaking her head in disbelief. "That nigga was just standing there lookin' stupid."

But Dionne wasn't laughing.

She barely heard them. Her hands moved with urgency, her breath coming faster, her body wired with adrenaline.

"Where are you going, Dionne?" Karmen asked, her voice careful, like she was afraid of the answer.

Dionne didn't even glance up. Her eyes darted across the suite, scanning for the one thing she needed.

"To go get my man," she said, her voice thick with conviction, thick with certainty, thick with everything that had been buried inside of her for too damn long.

Her friends froze, the weight of her words sinking in. Then, they grinned.

"Yes, ma'am!" Kierra cheered, instantly diving into the chaos, helping her look.

"What are we looking for?" London asked, her own excitement building, her hands already flipping through the mess.

"My phone," Dionne answered, frustration creeping into her voice, lifting up pillows, yanking open drawers. Time was running out.

She needed to leave. Now.

"Found it!" Karmen called out, tossing it across the room.

Dionne caught it mid-air, clutching it tight like it held the only path to salvation.

Then, she ran.

She didn't hesitate, didn't look back, didn't stop.

Danita and Mama Glen were stepping into the hallway, their faces drawn with confusion as they watched her rush past.

"Dionne!" Danita called after her.

But Dionne didn't stop.

She couldn't.

Mama Glen, however, smiled. Her eyes glowed with something wise, something knowing, something proud.

"She's finally going to find her true happiness," she murmured to Danita, her voice soft, full of peace.

And for the first time, she could breathe.

Because Dionne—the woman she loved like a daughter—was finally choosing the life she was always meant to have.

Dionne barely caught Mama Glen's words as she shoved open the doors of the venue, the cold air hitting her like a shock to the system.

Her heart pounded.

Her chest burned.

But for the first time in forever, she felt alive.

"I'll explain later, Ma!" she yelled over her shoulder, her trench coat billowing behind her as she sprinted to the black Escalade waiting at the curb.

She yanked the door open, slid inside, and slammed it shut.

She had only one place in mind.

And she prayed to God that's where he was.

***

Arris sat at an elegant table, the soft glow of candlelight casting a romantic hue over the restaurant. The atmosphere was filled with love—couples leaning into each other, whispering sweet nothings, hands intertwined over shared plates.

It was Valentine's Day, after all.

And yet, despite the beauty of it all, Arris felt nothing.

He wasn't alone tonight—not technically.

Sitting across from him was a woman he had met a couple of weeks ago. She was beautiful, sweet, and had a way of making conversation flow effortlessly.

But she wasn't Dionne.

She could never be Dionne.

Arris forced himself to stay present, to focus on the woman in front of him, to push the ache out of his chest. Dionne wasn't coming back. She was marrying another man today, and he had to live with it.

The resentment was still there, coiled tight in his gut, battling against the craving that never fully disappeared.

Even if he saw her again, could he ever forgive her?

Could he ever let go of the rage, the heartbreak, the betrayal?

He didn't know.

So instead, he exhaled, forcing Dionne out of his mind, even if it was only for now.

Meanwhile, Dionne stepped into the restaurant, her heart pounding so hard she thought it might crack through her ribs.

She had never been more nervous in her life. The restaurant was packed, filled with couples, laughter, clinking glasses—a celebration of love. She didn't care about any of it. She cared about one thing.

Finding him.

Her eyes darted across the room, scanning every table, searching for the man she had to see. He had to be here. This was his business, and if she knew anything about Arris, it was that he never neglected business—

Feenin'

not even on a day like this.

"Hello, Ms. Smith. It's a pleasure."

She turned to see Martin, one of Arris's most trusted employees, greeting her with a warm, professional smile. Dionne forced herself to return it, even though her heart was still racing, her mind still searching. "Hey, Martin. It's a pleasure seeing you again, as well."

Martin's sharp gaze didn't miss the way her eyes kept darting around the restaurant, scanning the room, desperate for something—for someone.

"Looking for a table?" Martin asked smoothly. "We have an open one in the back by the windows."

Dionne hesitated, disappointed that she still hadn't spotted Arris, but she nodded anyway. "That sounds perfect."

Martin smiled, leading her to an empty table.

As she sat, she instinctively tightened the trench coat around her body, grounding herself, trying to still the nerves thrumming in her veins.

"I'll be back with your favorite wine," Martin said, his tone warm and knowing, as if he could sense there was more to her presence than she was letting on.

Dionne nodded, flashing a small smile, but as soon as Martin disappeared, she was back to scanning the restaurant.

Her hands twitched, the urge to call him overwhelming. But she already knew he wouldn't answer. She had tried before. And all she got was silence. Because Arris had blocked her.

But now?

Now, she was here.

And she wasn't leaving until she saw him.

Martin returned with her wine, setting the glass down gently before turning to walk away. Dionne's hand shot out instinctively, stopping him before he could go. "Umm... Martin, is Arris here?" Her voice was polite, steady on the surface, but inside, her chest tightened, heart pounding against her ribs.

Martin smiled, oblivious to the storm brewing behind her calm expression. "Yes, he is. He's a customer tonight, though, but I can call him over if you need him." He reached for his earpiece, prepared to summon Arris without hesitation.

"No!" The word left her too quickly, too forcefully. She swallowed hard, forcing her tone back to neutral. "I was just wondering if he was here tonight."

Martin studied her for a beat before nodding. "He is actually over there."

Dionne followed his gaze as he pointed toward a secluded table, elegantly set, glowing under the soft golden lights.

The second she saw him, her heart plummeted.

Arris sat across from a woman—strikingly beautiful, poised, a picture of effortless confidence. But it wasn't the woman that sent a tight, sickening knot twisting in Dionne's stomach.

It was him.

The way his mouth curved into that smile, the one she used to think belonged only to her. The way his fingers kept brushing over the woman's hand, slow, deliberate, a touch that held intent. The way his eyes softened when she spoke, as if every word leaving her lips was something worth memorizing.

This wasn't business. This wasn't casual. This was romantic. And it shattered her.

Dionne's fingers tightened around her wine glass, her nails pressing hard against the cool surface, but she couldn't move, couldn't breathe, couldn't stop looking.

"Thank you," she murmured, barely hearing her own voice as Martin nodded and walked away, leaving her alone with the wreckage of her emotions.

She lifted the glass to her lips, her hands trembling slightly as she took a slow sip, her gaze never wavering from Arris and his date.

Every touch. Every glance. Every effortless laugh they shared burned her. It should have been her. But she had broken his heart. She had pushed him away. And now, he was here, looking like a man who had finally moved on. The realization clawed at her, violent and cruel.

It was like he could sense her staring, because suddenly, he looked up.

Their eyes locked.

The air between them shifted, charged, crackling with tension so thick it made her stomach flip. Dionne froze, caught like a thief in the act, but she couldn't mask the emotion on her face.

Anger. Jealousy. Heartbreak.

She had no right to be mad.

But she was.

Arris's eyes darkened as they stayed locked on hers, his entire body going still. The woman in front of him faded into the background, as if she never existed in the first place.

For a fleeting moment, Dionne saw it.

Saw him.

The heat, the longing, the ghost of something unfinished still

Feenin'

flickering in his gaze.

But it was gone just as quickly.

Her pulse roared in her ears, her emotions threatening to consume her, and she couldn't stand it anymore.

With a slow, deliberate movement, she rose from her seat, her posture high, chin lifted, masking the unraveling happening inside her. She adjusted her trench coat, smoothing the belt with a precision that masked her shaking hands.

Arris never looked away. His gaze followed her, piercing, unreadable, dangerous.

Dionne turned, her heels clicking against the floor as she walked away, her body rigid, her breaths shallow, her heart slamming against her ribs.

She could feel him still watching. And when she disappeared up the stairs, vanishing into the club above, she knew—

This wasn't over.

But really, the date wasn't great for Arris. Even with the beautiful woman sitting across from him, even with her soft laughter and effortless conversation, his mind was consumed with one person.

Dionne.

She had taken up permanent residence in his head, haunting him like an addiction he couldn't shake. Seeing her sitting two tables over, watching him, her gaze burning into him with unspoken emotion, had only made it worse. He had noticed her the second she walked in, and from that moment, the date had turned into a game.

He wanted her jealous.

So he leaned in a little closer, let his fingers graze over his date's hand, let his lips curl into soft smiles he didn't mean. He knew every single movement was making Dionne angrier, and he fed off it, watching her barely contain her emotions.

And then she got up.

Wearing that damn black trench coat, those red-bottom heels, her natural hair sleek and flowing effortlessly down her back, she moved with purpose, but not before sending him a look.

That look said, Find me.

And he was determined to do just that.

Snapping his attention back to the woman in front of him, Arris barely gave her a second thought. She had been talking, lost in her own conversation, not realizing that she had lost him long before she even sat down at this table.

He cleared his throat, already reaching for his wallet. "I'm sorry, but an emergency at my club came up. I have to cut this short. I'll call you tonight once I get everything situated."

She blinked, slightly surprised but still smiling, nodding in understanding. If she suspected his lie, she didn't show it. Not that he cared. His focus was already somewhere else.

On Dionne.

He stood, pulling her chair back as they made their way outside. He made sure she got into her car, waited until she was gone, then turned and walked back inside. His steps were deliberate, his pace quick and urgent as he took the stairs two at a time.

The club was alive, the music pulsing, bodies moving to the rhythm, but Arris's focus was unwavering. He scanned the packed room, searching for her, but deep down, he already knew where she was.

There was only one place he hadn't checked.

His office.

His jaw clenched as he pushed the door open, the air in the room thick before he even stepped inside.

And there she was.

Sitting on the edge of his desk, one leg crossed over the other, her coat still on but slightly parted, giving him just a tease of the curves he knew too well.

His breath hitched, just for a second.

She was still the most beautiful woman he had ever laid eyes on, and it pissed him off how easily she could still unravel him.

But resentment quickly took over.

No matter how good she looked, no matter how much he *feened* for her, she had still broken him.

Arris exhaled sharply, eyes narrowing as he stepped inside and closed the door behind him.

Arris barely had time to process before Dionne spoke, her voice smooth but laced with the jealousy she was trying so hard to hide.

"How was your date?"

A dark chuckle left his lips, low and sharp, because she had the nerve to be jealous. But he didn't care. She did this. She left him. She broke him.

"What you doing here, Dionne?" he asked, his tone cold as he turned to lock the door behind him.

"I came to talk," she admitted softly, but he caught the nerves in her voice, the hesitation, the weight of guilt pressing into her.

Another bitter chuckle rumbled from his chest. She was nervous now? Where was all that conviction when she left him standing in the

Feenin'

wreckage of what they were? Dionne could see it in his eyes—the damage she caused, the pain buried beneath the ice. It twisted something in her, made her want to take it all back, but she couldn't. All she could do was fight for him.

"Talk?" he repeated, voice coated in resentment as he moved past her, headed for his desk. "I don't want nothing to do with you, Dionne. You chose that nigga, so go be with that nigga."

He ignored her presence, moving like she wasn't even standing there, but she wasn't letting him slip away this time. She jumped off the desk, stepping into his path before he could escape her again.

"Arris, please," she whispered, her hands pressing firmly against his chest, her touch familiar but now foreign in its desperation.

Arris exhaled sharply, his jaw clenching. He missed this. Missed her. But it didn't feel the same anymore, didn't soothe him the way it once did.

Slowly, he reached up, his fingers curling around her wrists, pulling her hands off of him—not rough, not forceful, just enough to let her know.

"I don't have shit to say to you, Dionne. So please, leave." His voice was firm, empty, so distant it made her chest ache.

"No, baby. Just let me explain," she pleaded, eyes flickering with the desperation of a woman who still saw the love beneath his anger. She knew it was still there. Buried. But there.

Arris tried to push past her, tried to move around her, but she blocked his path again, refusing to let him get away.

"Dionne, move," he ordered, his tone sharp, his patience running razor-thin.

"Arris—"

"Move!" he roared, making her flinch, his voice like thunder cracking through the tension already thickening the room.

Dionne was done holding back.

In one swift motion, she yanked open her trench coat, letting it fall to the floor, revealing her bare body underneath.

"I CHOOSE YOU!" she yelled, her voice breaking, her chest rising and falling rapidly as she watched his entire body go still.

Arris froze, his breath hitching, his eyes dark and unreadable, but still cold.

She had his attention now.

He stared at her, his gaze trailing over the curves he knew too well, the skin he had memorized like a map, the body that once only belonged to him.

His jaw tightened, his fists clenched at his sides, but his control was slipping.

"I choose you, Arris," she whispered, her voice trembling, her eyes begging him to believe her. "I didn't marry him."

Silence.

She felt the weight of it pressing into her chest, suffocating her.

Then, he moved.

Slow, deliberate steps, closing the space between them. Each step made her breath quicken, her heart hammer against her ribs.

He grabbed her by the throat, rough but controlled, pushing her against the wall. Her breath hitched, the cool surface of the wall sending chills down her spine, mixing with the heat of his palm against her neck. And then his fingers were inside her.

Two, deep and slow, curling with the precision that only he knew, dragging a soft moan from her lips before she could stop it.

"Ahh..." she gasped, her head falling back against the wall. She had missed this. Missed him.

But just as quickly as he gave it to her, he ripped it away.

He pulled his fingers out, leaving her trembling, her body on edge, hovering over the pleasure he refused to let her have.

"Aight," he muttered, his voice dripping with something lethal, something possessive, something cruel.

He brought his fingers to his lips, licking them slow, his eyes locked onto hers with a look so cold, so knowing, so dominant it made her legs weak.

"Just making sure that nigga ain't touch what's still mine."

Dionne's breath hitched, her lips parting, but no words came out.

Arris smirked, but it wasn't soft. There was no warmth in it. Just territorial, relentless ownership.

"I see you know better," he said, voice low and dark, but there was something missing—something she used to see in his eyes when he spoke to her like this.

The softness. The love. It wasn't there this time. But the possessiveness was.

Arris knew Dionne's body like he designed her himself. He knew her cycle, knew when she was ovulating, knew how her body reacted to only him. And more than anything, he knew—without a doubt—that no other man had touched her.

Because she wouldn't dare.

Even though she had chosen Malik, even though she had broken Arris's heart, she had never let Malik have her. Because to her, it was still

Feenin'

cheating. Because her body still belonged to Arris. And now, as she stood there, vulnerable, exposed, laid bare in every way possible, she knew—

This wasn't over.

Not even close.

Arris walked away, his posture rigid, his expression unreadable, moving like he hadn't just had his fingers buried inside her seconds ago. He settled behind his desk, his demeanor distant, controlled—so unlike the man she once knew, the man who used to love her without restraint.

Dionne pressed her back against the wall, watching him, confusion tightening in her chest. This wasn't how things were supposed to go. Arris had never acted like this toward her, never kept himself at such a distance even when he was angry. But she knew she had done this. She had shattered him, and now, she was standing in the wreckage trying to put him back together.

"Why you choose that nigga?" he finally asked, his voice sharp, his eyes lifting to meet hers, waiting—daring her to lie.

Dionne took a slow breath, her heart hammering against her ribs. "I made a promise to the woman I love, who is dying."

Arris's jaw clenched, his expression shifting from cold detachment to something else—something curious, like the puzzle pieces were finally clicking together. "Your mother?"

Dionne sighed, reaching for her trench coat, pulling it over her shoulders, but not fastening it. She caught the way Arris's eyes commanded her to keep it open, to let him look, to let him see what was still his.

"Not my biological mother," she corrected softly. "Malik's mother. Mama Glen is the woman who's sick... and she saved my life. I promised her I would give her last dying wish, which was marrying her son."

Arris's expression softened, his walls cracking just slightly, the truth settling in.

She hadn't chosen Malik out of love. It had never been about Malik at all. She had tied herself to him out of duty, out of a debt she thought she could never repay.

And even though Arris understood now, it didn't erase the damage, didn't undo the pain of watching her leave him when she was always meant to stay.

"Why you didn't tell me? Why lie?" His voice wasn't as sharp now, but it still carried the weight of hurt, of loss, of everything she had put him through.

Dionne sighed, stepping closer before finally sinking into the chair across from him, her throat thick with emotions she could barely contain. "I was scared that I was going to lose you... even though I ended up losing you anyway." She swallowed the lump forming in her throat, her voice trembling as tears welled in her eyes. "But baby, I couldn't do it. I couldn't marry him when my heart, my body, my soul... they all belong to you."

Arris didn't speak, didn't move, but the wall around his heart cracked even further.

"Come here," he said, his voice low, rough, commanding.

Dionne didn't hesitate.

She stood slowly, rounding his desk, and before she could fully settle in front of him, he pulled her onto his lap, their lips colliding in a kiss so deep, so desperate, it felt like it was meant to glue the broken pieces back together.

She straddled him, feeling the heat of his body, feeling the tension, the anger, the love, the longing—all of it swirling in the space between them.

Her fingers tangled into his waves, pulling him deeper into the kiss, and that's when she saw it—the glisten in his eyes, the unspoken emotion threatening to spill over.

Dionne's heart clenched at the sight, her voice cracking as she whispered, "I choose you, Arris. I want to marry you. I love you. I *feen* for you."

That was it.

The last straw, the final push that sent him spiraling.

A growl rumbled from his chest, raw, hungry, filled with everything he had been holding back, and in one swift motion, he lifted her, gripping her thighs as he stood, her breath hitching as he set her down on the desk with zero hesitation.

Arris still hadn't said a word, but his body spoke for him.

He reached down, unfastening his belt, yanking down his pants, his arousal springing free, thick and heavy with need.

Dionne's eyes widened, a gasp leaving her lips at the sudden urgency, the rawness of it all, but she didn't move.

Didn't stop him.

Couldn't.

And without another glance, without another second of hesitation, he slammed into her, filling her to the hilt, a loud, guttural moan escaping both of them at the connection they had craved for months.

"Fuck," Arris growled, his forehead pressing against hers, his hands gripping her hips as he thrust into her with a feverish need, a desperation

Feenin'

that made the entire office feel like it was closing in around them.

Dionne's moans filled the space, mixing with the sound of his movements, the weight of his body pressing against hers, the way he stretched her, filled her, claimed her all over again.

There were no more words.

Only this.

Only the feeling of finally having her back.

Arris watched her, watched the way her body surrendered to him, her head tilted back, her eyes squeezed shut as she took every inch of him. She was heaven and hell wrapped in one woman, and no matter how much she had hurt him, he couldn't stop *feenin'* for her.

His strokes remained deep, slow, deliberate, but his hand moved, reaching into the drawer beside him without breaking rhythm. He gripped the small velvet box, the weight of it feeling heavier than before.

"Yes!" Dionne moaned, her eyes still shut, drowning in the pleasure he was giving her, unaware of what he was about to do.

Arris stared down at the ring.

It wasn't just any ring. It was the black diamond engagement ring he had designed for her on his trip to Africa.

Every cut, every curve, every detail had been crafted specifically for her. One of one, just like she was. He had traveled for business, but he couldn't leave without creating something permanent—something that symbolized her place in his life.

He didn't know if she would ever find her way back to him, but keeping the ring had been his silent hope, his unfinished promise.

Now she was here.

And he was ready to do what he'd been **Feenin'** to do since the first moment he laid eyes on her.

His thumb brushed over the stone, the rare black diamond glistening beneath the dim office lights, before he lifted it for her to see.

"Look at me," he demanded, his voice rough, his thrusts slowing but never stopping.

Dionne's eyes fluttered open, glazed with lust, heavy with pleasure, but when she saw the tears in his eyes, her breath caught.

Her heart clenched in guilt.

Arris had never let himself cry in front of her before. But now? His walls were breaking, and so was hers.

She felt it.

The weight of what she had done.

The depth of what they still were.

Her body tensed around him, and he felt it, felt the way she clenched, felt the way she reacted to his emotions even when she didn't say a word.

"Mama, I tried to let you go," he murmured, his grip on the ring firm in one hand while his other hand stayed anchored to her waist, his movements inside her slow and devastatingly deep.

Dionne moaned softly, trying to focus on his words, but he felt too good, dragging pleasure through her in a way that made her body shake.

"I told myself to keep my distance. But here I am, drowning in you, *feenin'* for you like a fucking addict."

She let out another moan, her lips trembling as her hands clutched onto his arms, but she was listening to every word.

"Dionne, you are my drug. The purest high I've ever tasted. One hit, one look, one moment in your presence, and I was done for. You flow through my veins, cloud my thoughts, invade my every breath. You are the craving I can't shake, the addiction I don't want to fight. I tried— God knows I tried—to resist you, to convince myself this was nothing but passing interest, just another feeling I could control. But you are not something to be controlled. You are wild, uncontainable, intoxicating in a way that leaves me helpless."

His pace picked up, his strokes harder, deeper, hitting every nerve inside her that made her crumble.

"Fuck.." he groaned, feeling her tighten around him, her body responding perfectly, desperately to every word, every movement. Her eyes rolled back, lost in the high of him, the pleasure, the meaning behind it all.

"From the moment I laid eyes on you, I knew you were dangerous. The kind of dangerous that comes with beauty too sharp, confidence too effortless, a presence too damn magnetic. I walked into your office, and suddenly, the air changed. I told myself I was just watching, just admiring. But the truth? I was already hooked. Already gone."

Their bodies slapped together, the wet, rhythmic sound of their connection echoing through his office, mixing with her whimpers, her cries, the soft curses leaving his lips.

"Fuck baby, I love you," she moaned out in a scream, her nails digging into his arms as her orgasm rushed toward her.

Arris felt it, felt the way her walls started to flutter, the way her thighs shook against him, but he wasn't done.

"And it's not just how you look, though, God knows, you are breathtaking. It's your mind, sharp as a blade, cutting through bullshit like it's beneath you. It's the way you move, like the whole world is yours, like it should be. It's the fire in your eyes, the ice in your tone when you want it to be, the warmth you don't give freely but when you

Feenin'

do… it burns, Dionne. It burns so good."

His hand moved, his fingers finding the tattoo of his handprint on her breast, his thumb rubbing over it, claiming her all over again.

This was his.

She was his.

His control started slipping.

He was close, so fucking close, but he refused to stop, refused to let her go again.

"I don't want a cure for this addiction. I don't want to be free of you. I don't care if this is *dangerous*, if it wrecks me, ruins me—I'll take every last hit, every high, every low, if it means I get to have you. I *feen* for you. Desperately. Shamelessly. And if you tell me you feel even a fraction of what I do, I'll never stop chasing this high. I'll never stop chasing you. So marry me, baby. Be my addiction for forever."

And that was it.

Dionne shattered.

Her scream filled the air, her body locking up, her back arching as waves of pleasure ripped through her so violently she couldn't hold it back.

Her body gave him everything. Her release came hard and fast, soaking him, dripping down onto his desk, making a mess of everything just like their love did. Her name left his lips in a deep, ragged growl, his strokes becoming sloppy, desperate, before he finally let go, his release filling her, claiming her, owning her all over again. Their breathing was ragged, the room filled with nothing but heat and lingering tension, the ring still clenched in his hand.

Dionne's body trembled, her lips parted, her forehead resting against his as her fingers tangled into his hair, pulling him closer.

Her eyes locked on his, glassy, overwhelmed, full of love, full of surrender.

Her voice barely above a whisper, she answered.

"Yes."

Arris slid the ring onto her finger, his eyes locked on hers, their chests still heaving from the explosive, soul-binding moment they just shared. The cool metal settled against her skin, a permanent mark of possession, of love, of something unbreakable between them.

"I love you, Mama," he murmured, his forehead pressing against hers, their breaths mingling, hearts beating in perfect sync.

Dionne smiled, her fingers trailing gently down his face, memorizing the feel of the man who had always owned her. "I love you too, Husband," she whispered, her voice warm, teasing, but full of conviction.

Arris's grin stretched wide, his joy radiating from his entire being, and before she could react, he lifted her into his arms, spinning her around like he couldn't contain his excitement.

"God brought you back to me," he said, his voice thick with emotion, his tone soft, raw, cracked with the weight of everything they had been through.

Dionne let out a soft laugh, her happy tears spilling freely, melting into the love they had fought so hard for. This wasn't just her man anymore. This was her fiancé, her soon-to-be husband, the only man she had ever truly belonged to.

She gently pulled away, grabbing her trench coat and wrapping it around herself, tying it snugly at her waist. Arris watched her every move, his eyes still hungry, still addicted, still locked onto her like she was the only thing in the world that mattered.

Without another word, he took her hand, leading her toward the back exit of the club, sneaking them out into the night, just them, just love, just fate pulling them back to where they always belonged.

As they got in the car, Arris's hand never left hers, his grip firm, his thumb tracing circles on the back of her hand, brushing over the ring like he still couldn't believe she was his again.

He lifted her hand to his lips, pressing soft, reverent kisses against her knuckles, his eyes never leaving the road, but his heart fully on her.

Dionne sighed softly, letting herself fall deeper into him, into them, into everything they had fought to reclaim.

They pulled up to the house—the one Arris had bought for her, the one he had refused to sell, no matter how much he tried to convince himself to let go.

It had always been meant for them.

And tonight, it finally felt like home.

The moment they stepped inside, there were no more words needed.

Arris's hands were on her in seconds, lips crashing into hers, bodies colliding with the same fevered desperation they had never been able to shake.

They spent the rest of the night tangled in each other, losing themselves in the addiction, the love, the hunger that had never truly faded.

And when exhaustion finally pulled them under, they fell asleep wrapped in each other—connected, complete, exactly where they had always belonged.

Dionne slept peacefully, wrapped in the warmth of Arris's arms, her body finally at ease after months of unrest. The night had been

Feenin'

everything—the passion, the confession, the promise of forever—but the piercing sound of her phone shattered the dark morning silence.

She didn't move, too exhausted, too comfortable, tucked against the only man who had ever truly made her feel safe.

"Mama?" Arris's voice was low, thick with grogginess, as he shifted slightly, reaching over to shake her gently. "Baby, wake up."

Dionne stirred, but didn't wake.

"Dionne!" Arris called again, tapping her arm as the phone continued its relentless ringing.

"Baby, stop!" she whined, swatting his hand away, burrowing deeper into his chest, making him chuckle.

"Someone's calling you," he murmured, voice laced with amusement, his fingers lazily tracing circles on her bare back.

"Ignore it."

She nuzzled closer, pressing her cheek against his skin, clinging to him like she wasn't ready to face reality yet.

Arris chuckled again, low, deep, warm, but his tone grew more serious as the phone rang again. "They keep calling. It's late, it might be important."

Dionne groaned, her frustration clear as she begrudgingly sat up, snatching the phone from his hand, ready to decline the call.

But then she saw the name.

Ma.

Her breath hitched, hesitation creeping into her bones.

She considered ignoring it, knowing her mother would have a million questions about why she ran off at the altar, why she left Malik, why she had chosen Arris in front of the entire world.

But something inside her told her to pick up. She swallowed, forcing herself to answer.

"Hey, Ma?" Her voice was soft, still laced with sleep, but the second she heard Danita's tone, her entire body went rigid.

"Dooda, she gone."

Danita's voice was raw, broken, drenched in sorrow. Dionne's heart stopped. Her breath hitched. The world around her blurred. She didn't have to ask who. She already knew.

Mama Glen was gone.

The weight of the words crushed her chest, her stomach sinking so deep it felt like she was free-falling into emptiness.

The phone trembled in her hand as she and her mother exchanged a few more words, but she barely processed any of it. The only thing she could hear was the silence left behind.

When she finally hung up, she didn't move.

She sat there, frozen, numb, her hands gripping the sheets, her gaze glassy and unfocused.

Even in the darkness, Arris saw it. Saw the tears brimming in her eyes, the way her chest rose and fell unevenly, the shock that paralyzed her.

"Mama... what happened?" His voice was softer now, gentle, already knowing something was wrong.

Dionne opened her mouth, but no words came out.

Her lip quivered, her throat felt tight, and then...

"She's gone. Mama Glen is gone."

The second the words broke free, so did she.

A sob tore from her chest, raw, guttural, shaking her entire body as Arris immediately pulled her into his arms, holding her tightly, like he could somehow hold her together.

He said nothing, because there were no words that could fix this.

He just held her, letting her fall apart in his arms, his fingers tangled in her hair, his lips pressing soft kisses against her forehead, his embrace the only thing anchoring her through the pain.

Dionne clutched onto him like she was drowning, tears soaking his skin, her body shaking with every sob that wracked through her.

She had known this day would come.

They all had.

But she hadn't been ready.

She hadn't gotten to say goodbye. And that's what broke her the most.

Arris didn't let go.

Not when she cried into his chest. Not when the sobs turned into silent, painful gasps. Not even when the night stretched into morning, and exhaustion finally pulled her into a restless sleep.

Because no matter what—

He wasn't letting her go again.

***

Two Weeks Later: Mama Glen Funeral

Today was the day of Mama Glen's funeral, and the weight of it sat heavily on Dionne's chest. Even though she had known this day would come, it didn't make it any easier.

She slipped into the black Tom Ford dress, the fabric flowing elegantly to her ankles, molding to her curves in a way that spoke of quiet grace and reverence. The matching Tom Ford open-toed heels added the final touch, elevating her presence with effortless beauty, but

Feenin'

nothing could cover the grief that clung to her like a second skin.

She stood in front of the mirror, staring at her reflection, and though she saw beauty, strength, poise, her eyes told another story. They were dim, clouded with sorrow, the loss of a woman she cherished etched deep within them.

She took a deep breath, willing herself to hold it together, but before the ache could consume her, a familiar touch wrapped around her waist, grounding her.

Arris.

The moment his hands settled against her, her body relaxed, sinking into the warmth of the one person who had never let her fall. She glanced down, her lips curving into the faintest smile at the custom black diamond wedding band on his hand—the very one she had made for him.

Because Arris wasn't her fiancé anymore.

He was officially her husband.

They had eloped two days ago, unable to wait, unwilling to let anything else stand between them. The wedding was still being planned, but that didn't matter. What mattered was that he was hers, and she was his—now and forever.

Arris stood behind her, his tall, commanding presence draped in an elegant black Dior suit, his strength a silent promise that he would stand beside her through this day, through this loss, through everything.

His eyes met hers in the mirror, his voice low, soothing, steady.

"You okay, Mama?"

Dionne turned in his arms, tilting her head up until their eyes locked, letting him see her, truly see her.

Love. Security. Devotion.

It was all there, etched in the way they held each other, in the way they breathed each other in.

"Yes, baby," she whispered, and he smiled, believing her.

He didn't need to hear anything else. He just pulled her closer, held her tighter, letting his embrace say what words never could.

I *got* you.

I'll hold you up.

I'll be your ground when you feel like falling.

They kissed, slow and deep, a silent exchange of strength, of love, of the unshakable bond between them.

And as they pulled away, their foreheads resting against each other's, Dionne knew one thing for certain—

She wouldn't have to face this day alone. Not now. Not ever.

They finally pulled away, the quiet weight of the day settling between them as Dionne grabbed her purse and Arris took his keys. Without another word, they left the house, the drive to the church heavy with unspoken emotions.

As soon as they arrived, Dionne was met with the warm embraces of family and friends, their shared grief mixing with quiet smiles as she introduced Arris—not as her fiancé, but as her husband. The news was met with joy, her friends immediately lighting up, and her parents and brother embracing Arris like he had always been part of the family. Seeing their happiness only made Dionne's heart swell, because for the first time in a long time, she felt whole.

What touched her most was the way Arris instantly bonded with her family. She watched as he and her father clicked like they had known each other their entire lives, deep in conversation that carried the ease of old friends. The sight warmed her heart, offering a bittersweet comfort in a day filled with sorrow.

As the funeral began, they gathered inside the church, Arris's hand resting on the small of Dionne's back, his presence steady beside her. She sat silently, her fingers curling around his, as she listened to the service unfold. But nothing prepared her for the moment she looked up.

The sight of Mama Glen's casket, draped in pristine white, with a large framed photo beside it, made her breath catch in her throat.

The picture was beautiful. She was beautiful.

Her warm brown skin glowed, her long hair framing her face in perfect waves, and her smile—the smile that had always felt like home—lit up the room, just as it had every space she had ever walked into.

She didn't look sick.

She didn't look like the woman Dionne had spent nights worrying over, holding her hand through the pain, hoping for more time.

She looked like the Mama Glen she remembered.

Vibrant. Whole. The woman who had saved her life, given her a second chance, and never asked for anything in return.

Dionne swallowed hard, her chest tightening as her eyes blurred with tears.

Mama Glen had been her hero.

The service continued, voices blending into murmurs around her, but Dionne barely heard them. The weight of grief sat heavily on her chest, pressing down, stealing her breath. Then she heard her name being called, and she knew.

It was time.

She took a deep breath, her body trembling slightly as she rose from her seat, walking gracefully to the podium. She could feel the weight of

Feenin'

every pair of eyes on her, the church packed with people who had come to say goodbye. Mama Glen was loved—so deeply, so widely—her presence had touched so many lives.

Dionne's gaze swept over the front row, landing on Malik.

He sat stiffly, his expression unreadable, his sad eyes locked on hers. But beneath the sorrow, there was something else. Something she couldn't quite name.

Beside him sat the family he had kept secret from her. Brittany and their daughter, the life he had built behind her back.

But Dionne didn't react. She didn't glare, didn't let her emotions shift. Because this wasn't about him.

This was about Mama Glen.

Steadying herself, she exhaled slowly, then leaned into the microphone.

"Good morning, everyone," she said, her voice smooth but fragile, the pain threading through her tone impossible to hide.

A quiet wave of greetings returned to her, warm but heavy with sorrow.

"Bear with me," she murmured, a shaky breath escaping as she tried to hold herself together.

Her eyes drifted down to the white casket in front of her, the finality of it hitting her like a wave. Her chest tightened, her grip on the podium tightening with it. Tears blurred her vision as memories flooded her mind, stealing her breath, her composure. This was real.

Mama Glen was really gone.

"My sweet Mama Glen..." Dionne began, her voice instantly cracking, the weight of her emotions pressing down on her chest. She paused, taking a slow breath, willing herself to get through it, to be strong for the woman who had always been strong for her.

"I don't know how to say goodbye to you," she continued, her voice fragile but determined. "I don't know how to put into words the love I have for you, the gratitude, the ache in my heart knowing you're gone. You weren't just my saving grace—you were my second chance at life."

Her tears came silently, slipping down her cheeks as she quickly wiped them away, her fingers trembling against the paper in her hands.

"When life was literally slipping from my grasp, you yanked it back and saved me. You were my angel before you became Heavens'. You didn't just give me a second chance; you gave me the life I always dreamed of but never thought I'd get to have.

"When everyone else saw me as fragile, you saw my strength. When I was drowning in fear, you pulled me out with your love, with your faith in me. You told me I was meant for more, and because of you, I believed it. I believed in myself because you believed in me first."

The church was silent, the weight of her words settling over everyone like a warm, aching embrace. She didn't have to look up to know that every person in the room felt it.

Even Malik.

Through sad eyes, he managed a small, bittersweet smile, touched by the depth of her love for his mother.

"You were the greatest woman I've ever known—strong, kind, wise, and selfless in a way this world didn't deserve. You loved so deeply, so fully, and I am so blessed to have been one of the ones you chose to love."

A warm, tearful smile graced her lips as she looked up from her notes, her eyes searching through the crowd for the only person who could hold her together.

Arris.

His gaze found hers immediately.

The second their eyes locked, her body settled, like his presence alone was enough to ground her, to remind her that she wasn't standing up there alone.

"Losing you feels like losing a piece of myself," Dionne admitted, her voice shaking, her heart heavy with grief. "But I know you wouldn't want me to sit in my sorrow. You'd tell me to keep living, to keep loving, to keep pushing forward like I always have. So I will.

"I will honor you with every breath I take, with every choice I make, with the life you gave me.

"I love you forever.

"I'll miss you always.

Your Dee Bug,

Dionne."

The church filled with gentle applause, a quiet, tearful appreciation for her words, for the love she had poured into every syllable.

Dionne stepped away from the podium, her legs feeling weak as she made her way toward the casket.

With trembling hands, she bent down and pressed a gentle kiss against the smooth white wood, her whispered goodbye barely audible, but heavy with meaning.

She turned, walking back to her seat, and before she even sat down, Arris was reaching for her. His hand found hers, lacing their fingers together, his grip firm, reassuring, unbreakable. As she sank into her seat, his lips brushed against her ear, the warmth of his breath sending a shiver

Feenin'

down her spine.

"You did great, Mama."

Dionne exhaled, the tension in her body melting away, a soft smile tugging at her lips as she turned to him, gripping his hand even tighter.

She wasn't alone.

Not in her grief.

Not in her love.

And *never* again in this life.

The service ended, but the weight of the day still hung heavy in the air as everyone gathered outside, talking in hushed voices while Mama Glen's casket was escorted to the hearse, preparing for the burial. Dionne stood with Arris and their friends, grateful for the lightheartedness they brought in a moment that felt so heavy.

"Man, I still can't believe y'all got married!" Mario exclaimed, shaking his head, still trying to process the news. True had already filled him in, but the fact that Arris—out of all people—fell for a woman who had been engaged to someone else was wild. Still, he was happy for his brother. Arris found real love. And in a woman like Dionne? Even better.

"Yeah, this hoe just went and eloped without telling anybody," London quipped, making Dionne laugh.

"The wedding is soon," Dionne reassured them, watching their expressions shift to excitement.

"Arris, I'm still looking for that $500 you owe me." True suddenly cut in, his tone sharp but playful.

"What $500?" Dionne asked intrigued.

Arris smirked, his arms wrapping possessively around Dionne's waist.

"Nothing, baby." He brushed it off quickly, before flicking his middle finger toward True. "Fuck you, True."

Dionne gasped, playfully smacking his arm. "Baby, we on church grounds!"

"Oh damn—my bad, God... and Mama Glen." Arris quickly looked up, his expression suddenly solemn, before his lips twitched into a smirk. The group burst into laughter, the tension of the day momentarily lifted.

Then Malik approached.

Dionne felt him before she even saw him, the subtle shift in energy enough to make her body tense.

A light tap on her shoulder made her turn, her once beaming smile fading slightly the moment her eyes met his.

"Can I talk to you? Privately?" Malik asked, his voice calm, but his eyes anything but.

Ann

Before Dionne could respond, Arris's gaze was already on him, sizing Malik up. His grip on her waist tightened slightly, a silent message. She was his. Malik knew it. And Arris was making damn sure he remembered it.

Arris caught the hesitance in Dionne's body language.

She didn't want to talk to Malik.

But he knew it was still something unspoken between them.

Before she could answer, he spoke for her.

"Go ahead, Mama. We'll be over there," Arris said, his voice even, but the warning was there. He shot one last cold glance at Malik before walking off to rejoin her father and brother.

Dionne exhaled, shifting her attention back to Malik. Her patience was already thin.

She quickly glanced past his shoulder, spotting Arris walking away—but his gaze never left her.

Protecting her, even from a distance.

That alone made her smile.

"Wassup?" she asked, her tone light, but void of warmth.

"Engaged, huh?" Malik scoffed, his chuckle bitter as hell, his eyes locked onto the massive diamond glinting under the light, mocking him.

Dionne smirked, easily catching the jealousy woven through his voice.

"Actually, married. Happily." Her words were sharp, final—leaving no room for doubt. She didn't hesitate. Didn't soften the blow.

Malik's breath hitched.

Despite everything—every lie, every mistake, every reason she had to walk away—a part of him still wished it was his ring on her finger.

Still wished it was him she had chosen.

Malik studied her, his gaze lingering too long, as if trying to find something—anything—to hold onto.

"Was that all?" she asked, already tired of this conversation.

Before Malik could even respond, Arris was back.

His touch found her immediately, his presence washing over her, commanding the moment without even trying. Dionne exhaled, melting into him, her body responding to his like it always did.

And Malik saw it.

And it made him sick.

The way she softened in Arris's arms.

The way she looked at him—like he was her entire world.

The way Arris held her—like she was his.

And worst of all? She was.

Feenin'

She had been Arris's all along.

Malik had suspected it, accused her, fought with her over it, but she had always denied it. She made him feel like he was crazy.

But he wasn't.

And now, seeing her wrapped up in Arris like this? It confirmed everything.

Malik's anger burned through him, but his voice dropped lower, sharp and venomous.

"So you was cheating on me with this nigga the entire time?"

Dionne's face didn't flinch.

Arris's grip on her waist didn't loosen.

She let out a short, humorless laugh, shaking her head.

"Malik," she said, her voice calm but lethal, "you have a whole fiancée and a four-year-old daughter—which means you cheated on me long before I ever did."

Her words should've sunk in.

But they didn't.

Malik's eyes never left Arris's hand, possessively resting on Dionne's waist.

His mind was spinning. His resentment was suffocating him.

"Man, this shit is crazy." His voice rose, his fury spilling over, his pride cracking. "You was fucking this nigga the entire time?!"

People turned. Eyes shifted toward them. The air thickened.

Arris took a step closer.

His grip on Dionne's waist never wavered, but now?

Now, he was towering over Malik.

His presence was suffocating.

His patience? Gone.

"Aye, bruh," Arris's voice was calm, deadly, lethal. "You betta lower your tone when you talking to my wife."

His eyes were ice cold, his entire body coiled with quiet rage.

And for the first time, Malik felt it. Felt the shift in power. Felt the quiet, looming threat in Arris's stance. But jealousy made him reckless. His pride wouldn't let him back down.

Arris took another step forward, his voice dropping even lower.

"Now be smart for once and walk away." His tone was controlled, but the rage in his eyes burned hot.

Malik's jaw clenched, but he didn't move.

So Arris took it further.

"'Cause if you talk to my wife wrong again, or even look at her the wrong way—your mother gone meet her son early."

The air shifted.

Dionne felt the words hit, felt the weight of them settle like a final warning.

Malik froze.

His anger simmered, but he knew.

He couldn't take Arris.

Not in this battle.

Not in any battle.

His jaw clenched, his pride shattered, but finally, he turned and walked away.

And the second he was gone, Dionne turned back to Arris, placing a calming hand on his chest.

His jaw was still tight, his muscles still coiled, but the second his eyes met hers, he exhaled.

And just like always—

She was the only thing that could calm the fire in him.

Arris turned back to Dionne, who shook her head, amused yet completely captivated by the possessiveness and undeniable protectiveness he carried for her. He was hers. She was his.

"You okay?" he asked, his voice low, intimate, meant only for her.

Dionne smiled, her heart pounding, her soul settled.

"Yes, baby. I have the man I'm *feenin'* for."

Their eyes locked, a silent understanding passing between them— this was it. No more running. No more doubt. Just them. Always.

As their lips met, the world around them faded, the weight of the past dissolving into nothing but the fire between them. Dionne could feel it in the way Arris held her— firm, unwavering, absolute. She had spent so much of her life searching, sacrificing, surviving—but now, she was finally living.

This wasn't just love.

This was addiction. Obsession. ***Feenin'***.

And as Arris pulled her in closer, his lips ghosting over hers with a promise only they understood, Dionne knew—this was forever.

The End… maybe

Acknowledgments

Writing Feenin' has been a journey—one filled with late nights, endless revisions, and moments of doubt. But through it all, I've been blessed with an incredible support system that has kept me grounded and inspired.

To my family—thank you for your unwavering love and encouragement. Your belief in me, even when I questioned myself, has meant everything. I couldn't have done this without your prayers, patience, and constant reminders that I was made for this.

To my friends—you know who you are. Thank you for being my sounding board, my hype squad, and my safe space. Your laughter, late-night brainstorming sessions, and honest feedback have helped shape this book in ways I can't even begin to explain.

To every reader who picks up Feenin'—this book is for you. Thank you for taking this journey with me, for feeling these characters, and for embracing their world as your own. Your support means the world, and I hope this story stays with you long after the last page.

Lastly, to the dreamers—never stop. The world needs your stories.

With love and gratitude,

Ann

Stay Connected!

Thank you for reading Feenin'! This journey doesn't end here—I'd love for you to stay connected and be the first to know about new releases, exclusive updates, and behind-the-scenes content.

> Follow me for book updates, giveaways, and more!
> TikTok: *@Anntheauthor*
> Instagram (Author Page): *@annproductions*
> Instagram (Personal): *@semaajae*

Join the conversation, share your thoughts on Feenin', and tag me—I'd love to hear from you! Your support means everything, and I can't wait to share more stories with you.

Stay tuned, because this is just the beginning!

With love,

Ann

Made in the USA
Columbia, SC
15 April 2025